the great **SCIENCE FICTION** series

the great SCIENCE FICTION series

*stories from the best
of the series
from 1944 to 1980
by twenty all-time
favorite writers*

Edited by Frederik Pohl

Martin Harry Greenberg

and Joseph Olander

HARPER & ROW, PUBLISHERS, New York
Cambridge, Hagerstown, Philadelphia, San Francisco,
London, Mexico City, São Paulo, Sydney

1817

Through Time and Space with Ferdinand Feghoot." Copyright © 1980 by R. Bretnor.

Grateful acknowledgment is made for permission to reprint:

"Hothouse" by Brian W. Aldiss. From *The Magazine of Fantasy and Science Fiction.* Copyright © 1961 by Mercury Press, Inc. Reprinted by permission of the author and his agents, the Scott Meredith Literary Agency, Inc., 845 Third Avenue, New York, N.Y. 10022.

"A Little Knowledge" by Poul Anderson. From *Analog.* Copyright © 1971 by Condé Nast Publications, Inc. Reprinted by permission of the author and his agents, the Scott Meredith Literary Agency, Inc., 845 Third Avenue, New York, N.Y. 10022.

"The Talking Stone" by Isaac Asimov. From *The Magazine of Fantasy and Science Fiction.* Copyright © 1955 by Mercury Press, Inc. Reprinted by permission of the author.

"The Cloud-Sculptors of Coral D." by J. G. Ballard. From *The Magazine of Fantasy and Science Fiction.* Copyright © 1967 by Mercury Press, Inc. Introduction copyright © 1964 by J. G. Ballard. Reprinted by permission of the author and his agents, C & J Wolfers, Ltd.

"Bridge" by James Blish. From *Astounding.* Copyright 1952 by Condé Nast Publications, Inc. Reprinted by permission of Richard Curtis Associates, agents for the author's estate.

"Surface Tension" by James Blish. From *Galaxy.* Copyright 1952 by Galaxy Publishing Corporation. Reprinted by permission of Richard Curtis Associates, agents for the author's estate.

(continued on page 420)

THE GREAT SCIENCE FICTION SERIES. Copyright © 1980 by Frederik Pohl, Martin Harry Greenberg, and Joseph Olander. All rights reserved. Printed in the United States of America. No part of this book may be used or reproduced in any manner whatsoever without written permission except in the case of brief quotations embodied in critical articles and reviews. For information address Harper & Row, Publishers, Inc., 10 East 53rd Street, New York, N.Y. 10022. Published simultaneously in Canada by Fitzhenry & Whiteside Limited, Toronto. 9-81 B+J 1695

FIRST EDITION

Designer: Ruth Bornschlegel

Library of Congress Cataloging in Publication Data

Main entry under title:

The Great science fiction series.

Includes bibliographies.
1. Science fiction, American. 2. Science fiction, English. I. Pohl, Frederik. II. Greenberg, Martin Harry. III. Olander, Joseph D.
PZ1.G7984   [PS648.S3]   813'.0872   79–1705
ISBN 0–06–013382–1

80 81 82 83 84 10 9 8 7 6 5 4 3 2 1

Contents

INTRODUCTION Frederik Pohl / ix

THE HOTHOUSE SERIES Brian W. Aldiss / 1
   HOTHOUSE / 3

THE NICHOLAS VAN RIJN SERIES Poul Anderson / 32
   A LITTLE KNOWLEDGE / 34

THE WENDELL URTH SERIES Isaac Asimov / 52
   THE TALKING STONE / 54

THE VERMILION SANDS SERIES J. G. Ballard / 71
   THE CLOUD-SCULPTORS OF CORAL D / 72

THE CITIES IN FLIGHT SERIES James Blish / 86
       Introduction by James and Judith Blish / 86
   BRIDGE / 88

THE PANTROPY SERIES James Blish / 112
       Introduction by James and Judith Blish / 112
   SURFACE TENSION / 114

THE FEGHOOT SERIES Grendel Briarton (R. Bretnor) / 150
   THROUGH TIME AND SPACE WITH
   FERDINAND FEGHOOT / 152

THE WHITE HART SERIES Arthur C. Clarke / 154
   THE RELUCTANT ORCHID / 155

TALES FROM GAVAGAN'S BAR SERIES
L. Sprague de Camp and Fletcher Pratt / 164
Introduction by L. Sprague de Camp / 164
THE ANCESTRAL AMETHYST / 166

THE PEOPLE SERIES Zenna Henderson / 173
ARARAT / 175

THE RETIEF SERIES Keith Laumer / 194
BALLOTS AND BANDITS / 196

THE CHANGE WAR SERIES Fritz Leiber / 221
NO GREAT MAGIC / 223

THE DRAGON SERIES Anne McCaffrey / 259
THE SMALLEST DRAGONBOY / 261

THE HELVA SERIES Anne McCaffrey / 273
THE SHIP WHO SANG / 274

THE KNOWN SPACE SERIES Larry Niven / 290
A RELIC OF EMPIRE / 292

THE BERSERKER SERIES Fred Saberhagen / 308
SIGN OF THE WOLF / 309

THE SLOW GLASS SERIES Bob Shaw / 317
BURDEN OF PROOF / 318

THE AAA ACE SERIES Robert Sheckley / 331
THE LIFEBOAT MUTINY / 332

THE IN HIDING SERIES Wilmar H. Shiras / 343
OPENING DOORS / 344

THE CITY SERIES Clifford D. Simak / 373
    AESOP / 374

THE INSTRUMENTALITY SERIES Cordwainer Smith / **400**
        Introduction by john j. pierce / 400
   THE GAME OF RAT AND DRAGON / 402

NOTES ON CONTRIBUTORS / 416

INTRODUCTION

by Frederik Pohl

Say this: Because science fiction was a magazine business for the first few decades of its life in America, most science-fiction stories had to be short. And, because a short story does not give room to exploit a really large idea, the growth of the science-fiction series was inevitable.

Or say this: Because magazine editors wanted to keep the readers coming back for more, the series was a sales gimmick. Or say that an author who had found, perhaps to his astonishment, that he had hit upon something that pleased readers was loath to let it go.

Are any of these true? Why, they are all true, but not complete. The sf series phenomenon was not just a buck-hustle. It was also a delight.

And it still is.

It began well before the science-fiction magazines did, really. When Edward Elmer Smith, Ph.D., wrote *The Skylark of Space* in 1919 he had no real intention of publishing it in a science-fiction magazine. He couldn't have; there weren't any. (It wasn't for another seven years that the first of them, *Amazing Stories,* was born, and *Skylark* languished in his desk drawer all that time.) But he did even then have the itch to carry Richard Ballinger Seaton and Marc C. DuQuesne farther into space and time, and as soon as he got the chance he did. When Edgar Rice Burroughs wrote *A Princess of Mars* around the same time, he knew he had a treasure in Barsoom, with its six-limbed white apes and deliciously pink-skinned princesses. He wrote a couple more about his Virginian swordsman-hero, John Carter, John's children, and grandchildren; heaven knows where it might have ended if Burroughs hadn't.

Of course, the series concept is not a science-fiction invention. The boob tube lives off its sitcoms and sci-fis and private eyes and Westerns. (A fact which is arguably responsible for at least half of what is wrong with current American television.) Before that, the big slick magazines like the *Saturday Evening Post* (the real one, not the current pale imitation) had its Tugboat Annies and Florian Slappeys and Alexander Bottses, to give weekly evidence that the world was cute, comic and, above all, *safe.* And even before that, Arthur Conan Doyle kept pumping out further adventures of Sherlock Holmes to meet the insatiable demand—until, desperate, he killed off the Great Detective to end it once and for all.

(And then had to bring him back to life because the demand did not die with the detective.) And before *that*—well, where do you stop? With Chaucer? The Norse sagas? The Bible? Not to mention the Sam Spades and the Lord Peter Wimseys, or the Tom Sawyers and the Tom Swifts, or the Penrods and the Poppy Otts. The series concept is as hallowed as the art of fiction itself; but in science fiction it became special.

I said that for the magazine editor the series was a very useful sales gimmick, and so it was. (And is.) No one knows for sure just how much of the newsstand sale of a magazine is impulse buying, but editors know that at least some of it is, and they do everything they can to move those impulses the right way. To put an author's name on the cover, even a very good author's, does not actually guarantee sales (much less so than most authors would like to think). But if the name is coupled with the title of a well-liked series, so that the rack-shopping buyer has had a foretaste of the pleasure waiting for him inside, the process works well. (*Analog*'s circulation went up substantially when it ran the most recent of Frank Herbert's *Dune* novels.)

How do I know so much about buck-hustling aspects of sf series?

Well—confession time—I must admit I hustled a few of those bucks myself. I played some part, as agent or editor, in about a third of the series sampled in this volume. As editor, I published much or most of Keith Laumer's *Retief*, Fred Saberhagen's *Berserkers*, Cordwainer Smith's *Instrumentality* and Larry Niven's *Known Space* stories. As agent, many years ago, I was involved in the James Blish, Robert Sheckley and Cliff Simak series. It wasn't all a buck-hustle. It was also a way of getting to hear more about ideas I had come to treasure, Laumer's interstellar diplomat and Saberhagen's immense, insane fighting machines. I still want to hear more about them, and hope you will, too.

In fact, that is what this volume is all about. There is a tremendous amount of science fiction being published these days, a thousand books a year—not counting the magazines; not counting the TV and the films. Even the dyed-in-the-wool aficionados can't read it all, and can't readily tell which new offerings, out of sf's great diversity of kind and of quality, they are likely to like. So here is a way to test your tastes. Each story in this book represents anywhere from a couple to a couple of dozen other stories, on the same subjects by the same authors, that are waiting for you if you had not previously discovered them. What we are hoping, Joseph Olander and Martin Harry Greenberg and I, is that you will indeed come across something here that pleases you, and can help you form your decision next time you're browsing through the bookstore.

Personally, I don't see how you can miss!

Red Bank, New Jersey
June 1980

the great SCIENCE FICTION series

THE HOTHOUSE SERIES

by Brian W. Aldiss

At first I didn't know what I had got on to. My writing career was sailing towards the rocks almost as soon as it was launched, encumbered by the emotional shipwreck of a marriage fast sinking with all hands.

This situation influenced what went into the *Hothouse* series. But the original image, the image which lured me into writing, was one of those heaven-sent pictures which occasionally visits a writer and simplifies his complicated life. What I saw was the Earth, blue and green under its fleece of cloud, with great cobwebs trailing up from it to the Moon. A perfect metaphor for the old age of Earth.

There was the picture, unassailable. Its imprimatur ensured that the whole novel (*Hothouse*, but unfortunately retitled *The Long Afternoon of Earth* by my first American publisher) was highly pictorial. That early mental picture has never been used as a cover illustration, funnily enough, although the novel has gone through many editions and translations since it ran in separate parts in *F&SF*.

Having the grand image, I needed to justify it in scientific terms. Or rather, I needed to rationalize it. It was not desirable that the picture should be justified within the novel in scientific terms, since there was no character in the story who thought in anything remotely like such orders of logic. It was not desirable, and moreover I was not sure that it was possible. I regarded my great metaphor as striking but hardly plausible scientifically, the product of a core of creativity which cares little for any number of laws of thermodynamics.

In my previous novel, *Non-Stop* (retitled *Starship* by my American publishers), I had taken pains to get the underlying facts correct and produce some indication within the story itself of the scientific procedures I had worked through. In the case of *Hothouse,* I was taken to task by several writers for omitting to do this.

All the complaints were directed towards astronomical flaws in my scheme. My critics denied that it was possible for Earth and Moon to slow their axial rotation so that they presented always the same face towards the Sun and to each other. They could only do so if the three bodies assumed a Trojan position, which *ménage à trois* would entail Earth and Moon being much farther apart than at present.

Well, I saw the force of that argument. But I could not do much about it because I had run against a far more basic objection on my own account. Given the fact—necessary for my story—that the Sun was going nova, I was convinced that Earth's atmosphere would long since have boiled off into space, leaving not a giant forest but a desert, bereft of all possibility of life.

Come to that, I didn't believe in perambulating vegetation either; an article in *Astounding* had made it clear that chlorophyll did not make for powerful musculature.

I contemplated such impossibilities, together with the many objections to my idea of "devolution," a term which had not in the early sixties been applied to the breaking up of national states into smaller components. I saw that what I had on my hands was a fantasy, a scientific fantasy; I did not see that that necessarily made it cease to be science fiction, since I have always regarded science fiction as a special branch of fantasy. Anyone writing about the future is indulging in fantasy; anyone reading a story of the future without wondering how the manuscript reached his hands is equally indulging in fantasy. Of course there are—as Oscar Wilde wittily observed—fantasies and fantasies.

What I also saw was that I had on my hands a marvelous story in the ancient mode of a continuing journey. All I had to do was pile Pelion on Ossa.

The stories were written between May 1960 and May 1961. During that period, I was suffering almost as many vicissitudes as my central character, Gren. On more than one occasion in my life, I have been forced to leave home and venture into a strange world—for instance at the age of seventeen, when I joined the army and was despatched to the Far East; after the war, when I set forth with typewriter and suitcase to look for work; and, most traumatically, at the age of eight, when I was packed off to boarding school for what turned out to be nearly ten years (of course I got remission during the sentence for occasional holidays).

Now I was compelled to set off once more, aged thirty-five, and with only the old papier-mâché suitcase which had come in handy on a previous occasion. I hadn't even got a typewriter. That had to be left behind. What happened then, as I lodged in an ex-Chinese laundry with an alcoholic journalist, a journalistic alcoholic, and a chap who went on holiday in North Africa, met a Bedouin woman and never came back, may provide the material for a social novel some day; but something of the exciting flavor of the period is echoed in Gren's adventures among the alarms and allurements and the bleak chill slopes of my Hothouse world.

Long afternoon of Earth, indeed! That was the brief dawn of my new self!

It was cheering to receive encouragement from readers who responded to the series. Eventually, a Hugo arrived. That arrival was typical, too. The Hugo is a big hefty phallic object on an oak base. Someone—a TAFF winner, maybe, I forget—managed to lug the trophy across the Atlantic, flying or swimming, and deposited it in Ireland, where it languished for a while. But it finally got to England and materialized one fine spring morning in dubious circumstances which recall the old joke about where the parson left his bike; for that revered prize was left with the morning milk on my girl friend's doorstep. (England is the only country in the world where, throughout the land, the amount of milk you require is delivered fresh every morning, in glass bottles, on your doorstep. I'm the only person in the world to have had a Hugo delivered by the same method.)

No doubt many fans regarded it as basest ingratitude that within a year I was sitting down to work on a new novel—*Report on Probability A*. Not a bit like *Hothouse*, you may say. Right. But I have too much love of the medium to wish to repeat myself any more than I can help. Besides, a new Aldiss had arisen, eager to try anything. My belief is that, if you win a Hugo, you should then be encouraged to pull out all stops and offer your indulgent public a few surprises.

A multi-million dollar film is now being made of *Hothouse,* following many years of planning. Will it ever materialize in actuality? Well, I still keep looking on my doorstep. . . .

Hothouse

*My vegetable love should grow
Vaster than empires and more slow.*
—ANDREW MARVELL

I

The heat, the light, the humidity—these were constant and had remained constant for . . . but nobody knew how long. Nobody cared any more for the big questions that begin "How long . . . ?" or "Why . . . ?" It was no longer a place for mind. It was a place for growth, for vegetables. It was like a hothouse.

In the green light, some of the children came out to play. Alert for enemies, they ran along the branch, calling to each other in soft voices. A fast-growing berrywhisk moved upwards to one side, its sticky crimson mass of berries gleaming. Clearly it was intent on seeding and would offer the children no harm. They scuttled past it. Beyond the margin of the group strip, some nettlemoss had sprung up during their period of sleep. It stirred as the children approached.

"Kill it," Toy said simply. She was the head child of the group. She was ten. The others obeyed her. Unsheathing the sticks every child carried in imitation of every adult, they scraped at the nettlemoss. They scraped at it and hit it. Excitement grew in them as they beat down the plant, squashing its poisoned tips.

Clat fell forward in her excitement. She was only five, the youngest of the group's children. Her hands fell among the poisonous stuff. She cried aloud and rolled aside. The other children also cried, but did not venture into the nettlemoss to save her.

Struggling out of the way, little Clat cried again. Her fingers clutched at the rough bark—then she was tumbling from the branch.

The children saw her fall onto a great spreading leaf several lengths below, clutch it, and lie there quivering on the quivering green. She looked up pitifully.

"Fetch Lily-yo," Toy told Gren. Gren sped back along the branch to get Lily-yo. A tigerfly swooped out of the air at him, humming its anger deeply. He struck it aside with a hand, not pausing. He was nine, a rare man child, very brave already, and fleet and proud. Swiftly he ran to the Headwoman's hut.

Under the branch, attached to its underside, hung eighteen great home-maker nuts. Hollowed out they were, and cemented into place with the cement distilled from the acetoyle plant. Here lived the eighteen members of the group, one to each homemaker's nut—the Headwoman, her five women, their man, and the eleven surviving children.

Hearing Gren's cry, out came Lily-yo from her nuthut, climbing up a line to stand on the branch beside him.

"Clat falls!" cried Gren.

With her stick, Lily-yo rapped sharply on the bough before running on ahead of the child.

Her signal called out the other six adults, the women Flor, Daphe, Hy, Ivin, and Jury, and the man Haris. They hastened from their nuthuts, weapons ready, poised for attack or flight.

As Lily-yo ran, she whistled on a sharp split note.

Instantly to her from the thick foliage nearby came a dumbler, flying to her shoulder. The dumbler rotated, a fleecy umbrella whose separate spokes controlled its direction. It matched its flight to her movement.

Both children and adults gathered around Lily-yo when she looked down at Clat, still sprawled some way below on her leaf.

"Lie still, Clat! Do not move!" called Lily-yo. "I will come to you." Clat obeyed that voice, though she was in pain and fear.

Lily-yo climbed astride the hooked base of the dumbler, whistling softly to it. Only she of the group had fully mastered the art of commanding dumblers. These dumblers were the half-sentient spores of the whistlethis-tle. The tips of their feathered spokes carried seeds; the seeds were strangely shaped, so that a light breeze whispering in them made them into ears that listened to every advantage of the wind that would spread their propagation. Humans, after long years of practice, could use these crude ears for their own purposes and instructions, as Lily-yo did now.

The dumbler bore her down to the rescue of the helpless child. Clat lay on her back, watching them come, hoping to herself. She was still looking up when green teeth sprouted through the leaf all about her.

"Jump, Clat!" Lily-yo cried.

The child had time to scramble to her knees. Vegetable predators are not so fast as humans. Then the green teeth snapped shut about her waist.

Under the leaf, a trappersnapper had moved into position, sensing the presence of prey through the single layer of foliage. It was a horny, caselike affair, just a pair of square jaws hinged and with many long teeth. From one corner of it grew a stalk, very muscular and thicker than a human. It looked like a neck. Now it bent, carrying Clat away, down to its true mouth, which lived with the rest of the plant far below on the unseen forest Ground, slobbering in darkness and wetness and decay.

Whistling, Lily-yo directed her dumbler back up to the home bough. Nothing now could be done for Clat. It was the way.

Already the rest of the group was dispersing. To stand in a bunch was to invite trouble from the unnumbered enemies of the forest. Besides, Clat's was not the first death they had witnessed.

Lily-yo's group had once been of seven underwomen and two men. Two women and one man had fallen to the green. Among them, the eight women had borne twenty-two children to the group, four of them being man children. Deaths of children were many, always. Now that Clat was gone, over half the children had fallen to the green. Only two man children were left, Gren and Veggy.

Lily-yo walked back along the branch in the green light. The dumbler drifted from her unheeded, obeying the silent instructions of the forest air, listening for word of a seeding place. Never had there been such an overcrowding of the world. No bare places existed. The dumblers sometimes drifted through the jungles for centuries waiting to alight.

Coming to a point above one of the nuthuts, Lily-yo lowered herself into it by the creeper. This had been Clat's nuthut. The headwoman could hardly enter it, so small was the door. Humans kept their doors as narrow as possible, enlarging them as they grew. It helped to keep out unwanted visitors.

All was tidy in the nuthut. From the interior soft fiber a bed had been cut; there the five-year-old had slept when a feeling for sleep came among the unchanging forest green. On the cot lay Clat's soul. Lily-yo took it and thrust it into her belt.

She climbed out onto the creeper, took her knife, and began to slash at the place where the bark of the tree had been cut away and the nuthut was attached to the living wood. After several slashes the cement gave. Clat's nuthut hinged down, hung for a moment, then fell.

As it disappeared among huge coarse leaves, there was a flurry of foliage. Something was fighting for the privilege of devouring the huge morsel.

Lily-yo climbed back onto the branch. For a moment she paused to breathe deeply. Breathing was more trouble than it had been. She had gone on too many hunts, borne too many children, fought too many fights. With a rare and fleeting knowledge of herself, she glanced down at her bare green breasts. They were less plump than they had been when she first took the man Haris to her; they hung lower. Their shape was less beautiful.

By instinct she knew her youth was over. By instinct she knew it was time to Go Up.

The group stood near the Hollow, awaiting her. She ran to them. The Hollow was like an upturned armpit, formed where the branch joined the trunk. In the Hollow collected their water supply.

Silently, the group was watching a line of termights climb the trunk. One of the termights now and again signaled greetings to the humans. The humans waved back. As far as they had allies at all, the termights were their allies. Only five great families survived here in the all-conquering vegetable world; the tigerflies, the treebees, the plantants, and the termights were social insects, mighty and invincible. And the fifth family was man, lowly and easily killed; not organized as the insects were, but not extinct—the last animal species remaining.

Lily-yo came up to the group. She too raised her eyes to follow the moving line of termights until it disappeared into the layers of green. The termights could live on any level of the great forest, in the Tips or down on the Ground. They were the first and last of insects; as long as anything lived, the termights and tigerflies would.

Lowering her eyes, Lily-yo called to the group.

When they looked, she brought out Clat's soul, lifting it above her head to show to them.

"Clat has fallen to the green," she said. "Her soul must go to the Tips, according to the custom. Flor and I will take it at once, so that we can go with the termights. Daphe, Hy, Ivin, Jury, you guard well the man Haris and the children till we return."

The women nodded solemnly. Then they came one by one to touch Clat's soul.

The soul was roughly carved of wood into the shape of a woman. As a child was born, so with rites its male parent carved it a soul, a doll, a totem soul—for in the forest when one fell to the green there was scarcely ever a bone surviving to be buried. The soul survived for burial in the Tips.

As they touched the soul, Gren adventurously slipped from the group. He was nearly as old as Toy, as active and as strong. Not only had he power to run. He could climb. He could swim. Ignoring the cry of his friend Veggy, he scampered into the Hollow and dived into the pool.

Below the surface, opening his eyes, he saw a world of bleak clarity. A few green things like clover leaves grew at his approach, eager to wrap around his legs. Gren avoided them with a flick of his hand as he shot deeper. Then he saw the crocksock—before it saw him.

The crocksock was an aquatic plant, semiparasitic by nature. Living in hollows, it sent down its saw-toothed suckers into the trees' sap. But the upper section of it, rough and tongue-shaped like a sock, could also feed. It unfolded, wrapping around Gren's left arm, its fibers instantly locking to increase the grip.

Gren was ready for it.

With one slash of his knife, he clove the crocksock in two, leaving the lower half to thrash uselessly at him. Before he could rise to the surface, Daphe the skilled huntress was beside him, her face angered, bubbles flashing out silver like fish from between her teeth. Her knife was ready to protect him.

He grinned at her as he broke surface and climbed out onto the dry bank. Nonchalantly he shook himself as she climbed beside him.

" 'Nobody runs or swims or climbs alone,' " Daphe called to him, quoting one of the laws. "Gren, have you no fear? Your head is an empty burr!"

The other women too showed anger. Yet none of them touched Gren. He was a man child. He was tabu. He had the magic powers of carving souls and bringing babies—or would have when fully grown, which would be soon now.

"I am Gren, the man child!" he boasted to them. His eyes sought Haris's for approval. Haris merely looked away. Now that Gren was so big, Haris did not cheer as once he had, though the boy's deeds were braver than before.

Slightly deflated, Gren jumped about, waving the strip of crocksock still wrapped around his left arm. He called and boasted at the women to show how little he cared for them.

"You are a baby yet," hissed Toy. She was ten, his senior by one year. Gren fell quiet.

Scowling, Lily-yo said, "The children grow too old to manage. When Flor and I have been to the Tips to bury Clat's soul, we shall return and break up the group. Time has come for us to part. Guard yourselves!"

It was a subdued group that watched their leader go. All knew that the group had to split; none cared to think about it. Their time of happiness and safety—so it seemed to all of them—would be finished, perhaps forever. The children would enter a period of lonely hardship, fending for themselves. The adults embarked on old age, trial, and death when they Went Up into the unknown.

II

Lily-yo and Flor climbed the rough bark easily. For them it was like going up a series of more or less symmetrically placed rocks. Now and again they met some kind of vegetable enemy, a thinpin or a pluggyrug, but these were small-fry, easily dispatched into the green gloom below. Their enemies were the termights' enemies, and the moving column had already dealt with the foes in its path. Lily-yo and Flor climbed close to the termights, glad of their company.

They climbed for a long while. Once they rested on an empty branch, capturing two wandering burrs, splitting them, and eating their oily white flesh. On the way up, they had glimpsed one or two groups of humans on different branches; sometimes these groups waved shyly, sometimes not. Now they were too high for humans.

Nearer the Tips, new danger threatened. In the safer middle layers of the forest the humans lived, avoided the perils of the Tips or the Ground.

"Now we move on," Lily-yo told Flor, getting to her feet when they had rested. "Soon we will be at the Tips."

A commotion silenced the two women. They looked up, crouching against the trunk for protection. Above their heads, leaves rustled as death struck.

A leapycreeper flailed the rough bark in a frenzy of greed, attacking the termight column. The leapycreeper's roots and stems were also tongues and lashes. Whipping around the trunk, it thrust its sticky tongues into the termights.

Against this particular plant, flexible and hideous, the insects had little defense. They scattered but kept doggedly climbing up, each perhaps trusting in the blind law of averages to survive.

For the humans, the plant was less of a threat—at least when met on a branch. Encountered on a trunk, it could easily dislodge them and send them helplessly falling to the green.

"We will climb on another trunk," Lily-yo said.

She and Flor ran deftly along the branch, once jumping a bright parasitic bloom around which treebees buzzed, a forerunner of the world of color above them.

A far worse obstacle lay waiting in an innocent-looking hole in the branch. As Flor and Lily-yo approached, a tigerfly zoomed up at them. It was all but as big as they were, a terrible thing that possessed both weapons and intelligence—and malevolence. Now it attacked only through viciousness, its eyes large, its mandibles working, its transparent wings beating. Its head was a mixture of shaggy hair and armorplating, while behind its slender waist lay the great swivel-plated body, yellow and black, sheathing a lethal sting on its tail.

It dived between the women, aiming to hit them with its wings. They fell flat as it sped past. Angrily, it tumbled against the branch as it turned on them again; its golden-brown sting flicked in and out.

"I'll get it!" Flor said. A tigerfly had killed one of her babes.

Now the creature came in fast and low. Ducking, Flor reached up and seized its shaggy hair, swinging the tigerfly off balance. Quickly she raised her sword. Bringing it down in a mighty sweep, she severed that chitinous and narrow waist.

The tigerfly fell away in two parts. The two women ran on.

The branch, a main one, did not grow thinner. Instead, it ran on for another twenty yards and grew into another trunk. The tree, vastly old, the longest lived organism ever to flourish on this little world, had a myriad of trunks. Very long ago—two thousand million years past—trees had grown in many kinds, depending on soil, climate, and other conditions. As temperatures climbed, they proliferated and came into competition with each other. The banyan, thriving in the heat, using its complex system of self-rooting branches, gradually established ascendancy over the other species. Under pressure, it evolved and adapted. Each banyan spread out farther and farther, sometimes doubling back on itself for safety. Always it grew higher and crept wider, protecting its parent stem as its rivals multiplied, dropping down trunk after trunk, throwing out branch after branch, until at last it learned the trick of growing into its neighbor banyan, forming a thicket against which no other tree could strive. Their complexity became unrivaled, their immortality established.

On this great continent where the humans lived, only one banyan tree grew now. It had become first King of the forest, then it had become the forest itself. It had conquered the deserts and the mountains and the swamps. It filled the continent with its interlaced scaffolding. Only before the wider rivers or at the margins of the sea, where the deadly seaweeds could assail it, did the tree not go.

And at the terminator, where all things stopped and night began, there too the tree did not go.

The women climbed slowly now, alert as the odd tigerfly zoomed in their direction. Splashes of color grew everywhere, attached to the tree, hanging from lines, or drifting free. Lianas and fungi blossomed. Dumblers moved mournfully through the tangle. As they gained height, the air grew fresher and color rioted, azures and crimsons, yellows and mauves, all the beautifully tinted snares of nature.

A dripperlip sent its scarlet dribbles of gum down the trunk. Several thinpins, with vegetable skill, stalked the drops, pounced, and died. Lily-yo and Flor went by on the other side.

Slashweed met them. They slashed back and climbed on.

Many fantastic plant forms there were, some like birds, some like butterflies. Ever and again, whips and hands shot out.

"Look!" Flor whispered. She pointed above their heads.

The tree's bark was cracked almost invisibly. Almost invisibly, a part of it moved. Thrusting her stick out at arm's length, Flor eased herself up until stick and crack were touching. Then she prodded.

A section of the bark gaped wide, revealing a pale, deadly mouth. An oystermaw, superbly camouflaged, had dug itself into the tree. Jabbing swiftly, Flor thrust her stick into the trap. As the jaws closed, she pulled with all her might, Lily-yo steadying her. The oystermaw taken by surprise, was wrenched from its socket.

Opening its maw in shock, it sailed outward through the air. A rayplane took it without trying.

Lily-yo and Flor climbed on.

The Tips was a strange world of its own, the vegetable kingdom at its most imperial and most exotic.

If the banyan ruled the forest, *was* the forest, then the traversers ruled the Tips. The traversers had formed the typical landscape of the Tips. Theirs were the great webs trailing everywhere, theirs the nests built on the tips of the tree.

When the traversers deserted their nests, other creatures built there, other plants grew, spreading their bright colors to the sky. Debris and droppings knitted these nests into solid platforms. Here grew the burnurn plant, which Lily-yo sought for the soul of Clat.

Pushing and climbing, the two women finally emerged onto one of these platforms. They took shelter from the perils of the sky under a great leaf and rested from their exertions. Even in the shade, even for them, the heat of the Tips was formidable. Above them, paralyzing half the heaven, burned a great sun. It burned without cease, always fixed and still at one point in the sky, and so would burn until that day—now no longer impossibly distant—when it burned itself out.

Here in the Tips, relying on that sun for its strange method of defense, the burnurn ruled among stationary plants. Already its sensitive roots told it that intruders were near. On the leaf above them, Lily-yo and Flor saw a circle of light move. It wandered over the surface, paused, contracted. The leaf smoldered and burst into flames. Focusing one of its urns on them, the plant was fighting them with its terrible weapon—fire!

"Run!" Lily-yo commanded, and they dashed behind the top of a whistlethistle, hiding beneath its thorns, peering out at the burnurn plant.

It was a splendid sight.

High reared the plant, displaying perhaps half a dozen cerise flowers, each flower larger than a human. Other flowers, fertilized, had closed together, forming many-sided urns. Later stages still could be seen, where the color drained from the urns as seed swelled at the base of them. Finally, when the seed was ripe, the urn—now hollow and immensely strong—turned transparent as glass and became a heat weapon the plant could use even after its seeds were scattered.

Every vegetable and creature shrank from fire—except humans. They alone could deal with the burnurn plant and use it to advantage.

Moving cautiously, Lily-yo stole forth and cut off a big leaf which grew through the platform on which they stood. A pluggyrug launched a spine at her from underneath, but she dodged it. Seizing the leaf, so much bigger than herself, she ran straight for the burnurn, hurling herself among its foliage and shinning to the top of it in an instant, before it could bring its urn-shaped lenses up to focus on her.

"Now!" she cried to Flor.

Flor was already on the move, sprinting forward.

Lily-yo raised the leaf above the burnurn, holding it between the plant and the sun. As if realizing that this ruined its method of defense, the plant drooped in the shade as though sulking. Its flowers and its urns hung down limply.

Her knife out ready, Flor darted forward and cut off one of the great transparent urns. Together the two women dashed back for the cover of the whistlethistle while the burnurn came back to furious life, flailing its urns as they sucked in the sun again.

They reached cover just in time. A vegbird swooped out of the sky at them—and impaled itself on a thorn.

Instantly, a dozen scavengers were fighting for the body. Under cover of the confusion, Lily-yo and Flor attacked the urn they had won. Using both their knives and all their strength, they prized up one side far enough to put Clat's soul inside the urn. The side instantly snapped back into place again, an airtight join. The soul stared woodenly out at them through the transparent facets.

"May you Go Up and reach heaven," Lily-yo said.

It was her business to see the soul stood at least a sporting chance of doing so. With Flor, she carried the urn across to one of the cables spun by a traverser. The top end of the urn, where the seed had been, was enormously sticky. The urn adhered easily to the cable and hung there in the sun.

Next time a traverser climbed up the cable, the urn stood an excellent chance of sticking like a burr to one of its legs. Thus it would be carried away to heaven.

As they finished the work, a shadow fell over them. A mile-long body drifted down toward them. A traverser, a gross vegetable-equivalent of a spider, was descending to the Tips.

Hurriedly, the women burrowed their way through the platform. The last rites for Clat had been carried out: it was time to return to the group.

Before they climbed down again to the green world of middle levels, Lily-yo looked back.

The traverser was descending slowly, a great bladder with legs and jaws, fibery hair covering most of its bulk. To her it was like a god, with the powers of a god. It came down a cable, floated nimbly down the strand trailing up into the sky.

As far as could be seen, cables slanted up from the jungle, pointing like slender drooping fingers to heaven. Where the sun caught them, they glittered. They all trailed up in the same direction, toward a floating silver half-globe, remote and cool, but clearly visible even in the glare of eternal sunshine.

Unmoving, steady, the half-moon remained always in the same sector of the sky.

Through the eons, the pull of this moon had gradually slowed the axial revolution of its parent planet to a standstill, until day and night slowed, and became fixed forever, day always on one side of the planet, night on the other. At the same time, a reciprocal braking effect had checked the moon's apparent flight. Drifting farther from Earth, the moon had shed its role as Earth's satellite and rode along in Earth's orbit, an independent planet in its own right. Now the two bodies, for what was left of the afternoon of eternity, faced each other in the same relative position. They were locked face to face, and so would be, until the sands of time ceased to run, or the sun ceased to shine.

And the multitudinous strands of cable floated across the gap, uniting the worlds. Back and forth the traversers could shuttle at will, vegetable astronauts huge and insensible, with Earth and Luna both enmeshed in their indifferent net.

With surprising suitability, the old age of the Earth was snared about with cobwebs.

III

The journey back to the group was fairly uneventful. Lily-yo and Flor traveled at an easy pace, sliding down again into the middle levels of the tree. Lily-yo did not press forward as hard as usual, for she was reluctant to face the breakup of the group.

She could not express her few thoughts easily.

"Soon we must Go Up like Clat's soul," she said to Flor, as they climbed down.

"It is the way," Flor answered, and Lily-yo knew she would get no deeper word on the matter than that. Nor could she frame deeper words herself; human understandings trickled shallow these days.

The group greeted them soberly when they returned. Being weary, Lily-yo offered them a brief salutation and retired to her nuthut. Jury and Ivin soon brought her food, setting not so much as a finger inside her home, that being tabu. When she had eaten and slept, she climbed again onto the home strip of branch and summoned the others.

"Hurry!" she called, staring fixedly at Haris, who was not hurrying. Why should a difficult thing be so precious—or a precious thing so difficult?

At that moment, while her attention was diverted, a long green tongue licked out from behind the tree trunk. Uncurling, it hovered daintily for a second. It took Lily-yo around the waist, pinning her arms to her sides, lifting her off the branch. Furiously she kicked and cried.

Haris pulled a knife from his belt, leaped forward with eyes slitted, and hurled the blade. Singing, it pierced the tongue and pinned it to the rough trunk of the tree.

Haris did not pause after throwing. As he ran toward the pinioned tongue, Daphe and Jury ran behind him, while Flor scuttled the children to safety. In its agony, the tongue eased its grip on Lily-yo.

Now a terrific thrashing had set in on the other side of the tree trunk: the forest seemed full of its vibrations. Lily-yo whistled up two dumblers, fought her way out of the green coils around her, and was now safely back on the branch. The tongue, writhing in pain, flicked about meaninglessly. Weapons out, the four humans moved forward to deal with it.

The tree itself shook with the wrath of the trapped creature. Edging cautiously around the trunk, they saw it. Its great vegetable mouth distorted, a wiltmilt stared back at them with the hideous palmate pupil of its single eye. Furiously it hammered itself against the tree, foaming and mouthing. Though they had faced wiltmilts before, yet the humans trembled.

The wiltmilt was many times the girth of the tree trunk at its present extension. If necessary, it could have extended itself up almost to the Tips, stretching and becoming thinner as it did so. Like an obscene jack-in-the-box, it sprang up from the Ground in search of food, armless, brainless, gouging its slow way over the forest floor on wide and rooty legs.

"Pin it!" Lily-yo cried.

Concealed all along the branch were sharp stakes kept for such emergencies. With these they stabbed the writhing tongue that cracked like a whip about their heads. At last they had a good length of it secured, staked down to the tree. Though the wiltmilt writhed, it would never get free now.

"Now we must leave and Go Up," Lily-yo said.

No human could ever kill a wiltmilt. But already its struggles were attracting predators, the thinpins—those mindless sharks of the middle levels—rayplanes, trappersnappers, gargoyles, and smaller vegetable vermin. They would tear the wiltmilt to living pieces and continue until nothing of it remained—and if they happened on a human at the same time . . . well, it was the way.

Lily-yo was angry. She had brought on this trouble. She had not been alert. Alert, she would never have allowed the wiltmilt to catch her. Her mind had been tied with thought of her own bad leadership. For she had caused two dangerous trips to be made to the Tips where one would have done. If she had taken all the group with her when Clat's soul was disposed of, she would have saved this second ascent. What ailed her brain that she had not seen this beforehand?

She clapped her hands. Standing for shelter under a giant leaf, she made the group come about her. Sixteen pairs of eyes stared trustingly at her. She grew angry to see how they trusted her.

"We adults grow old," she told them. "We grow stupid. I grow stupid. I am not fit to lead. Not any more. The time is come for the adults to Go Up and return to the gods who made us. Then the children will be on their own. They will be the group. Toy will lead the group. By the time you are sure of your group, Gren and soon Veggy will be old enough to give you children. Take care of the man children. Let them not fall to the green, or the group dies. Better to die yourself than let the group die."

Lily-yo had never made, the others had never heard, so long a speech. Some of them did not understand it all. What of this talk about falling to the green? One did or one did not; it needed no talk. Whatever happened was the way, and talk could not touch it.

May, a girl child, said cheekily, "On our own we can enjoy many things."

Reaching out, Flor clapped her on an ear.

"First you make the hard climb to the Tips," she said.

"Yes, move," Lily-yo said. She gave the order for climbing, who should lead, who follow.

About them the forest throbbed, green creatures sped and snapped as the wiltmilt was devoured.

"The climb is hard. Begin quickly," Lily-yo said, looking restlessly about her.

"Why climb?" Gren asked rebelliously. "With dumblers we can fly easily to the Tips and suffer no pain."

It was too complicated to explain to him that a human drifting in the air was far more vulnerable than a human shielded by a trunk, with the good rough bark nodules to squeeze between in case of attack.

"While I lead, you climb," Lily-yo said. She could not hit Gren. He was a tabu man child.

They collected their souls from their nuthuts. There was no pomp about saying good-bye to their old home. Their souls went in their belts, their swords—the sharpest, hardest thorns available—went in their hands. They ran along the branch after Lily-yo, away from the disintegrating wiltmilt, away from their past.

Slowed by the younger children, the journey up to the Tips was long. Although the humans fought off the usual hazards, the tiredness growing in small limbs could not be fought. Halfway to the Tips, they found a side branch to rest on, for there grew a fuzzypuzzle, and they sheltered in it.

The fuzzypuzzle was a beautiful disorganized fungus. Although it looked like nettlemoss on a larger scale, it did not harm humans, drawing in its poisoned pistils as if with disgust when they came to it. Ambling in the eternal branches of the tree, fuzzypuzzles desired only vegetable food. So the group climbed into the middle of it and slept. Guarded among the waving viridian and yellow stalks, they were safe from nearly all forms of attack.

Flor and Lily-yo slept most deeply of the adults. They were tired by their previous journey. Haris the man was the first to awake, knowing something was wrong. As he roused, he woke up Jury by poking her with his stick. He was lazy; besides, it was his duty to keep out of danger. Jury sat up. She gave a shrill cry of alarm and jumped at once to defend the children.

Four winged things had invaded the fuzzypuzzle. They had seized

Veggy, the man child, and Bain, one of the younger girl children, gagging and tying them before the pair could wake properly.

At Jury's cry, the winged ones looked around.

They were flymen!

In some aspects they resembled humans. They had one head, two long and powerful arms, stubby legs, and strong fingers on hands and feet. But instead of smooth green skin, they were covered in a glittering horny substance, here black, here pink. And large scaly wings resembling those of a vegbird grew from their wrists to their ankles. Their faces were sharp and clever. Their eyes glittered.

When they saw the humans waking, the flymen grabbed up the two captive children. Bursting through the fuzzypuzzle, which did not harm them, they ran toward the edge of the branch to jump off.

Flymen were crafty enemies, seldom seen but much dreaded by the group. They worked by stealth. Though they did not kill unless forced to, they stole children. Catching them was hard. Flymen did not fly properly, but the crash glides they fell into carried them swiftly away through the forest, safe from human reprisal.

Jury flung herself forward with all her might, Ivin behind her. She caught an ankle, seized part of the leathery tendon of wing where it joined the foot, and clung on. One of the flymen holding Veggy staggered with her weight, turning as he did so to free himself. His companion, taking the full weight of the boy child, paused, dragging out a knife to defend himself.

Ivin flung herself at him with savagery. She had mothered Veggy: he should not be taken away. The flyman's blade came to meet her. She threw herself on it. It ripped her stomach till the brown entrails showed, and she toppled from the branch with no cry. There was a commotion in the foliage below as trappersnappers fought for her.

Deciding he had done enough, the flyman dropped the bound Veggy and left his friend still struggling with Jury. He spread his wings, taking off heavily after the two who had borne Bain away between them into the green thicket.

All the group were awake now. Lily-yo silently untied Veggy, who did not cry, for he was a man child. Meanwhile, Haris knelt by Jury and her winged opponent, who fought without words to get away. Quickly, Haris brought out a knife.

"Don't kill me. I will go!" cried the flyman. His voice was harsh, his words hardly understandable. The mere strangeness of him filled Haris with savagery, so that his lips curled back and his tongue came thickly between his bared teeth.

He thrust his knife deep between the flyman's ribs, four times over, till the blood poured over his clenched fist.

Jury stood up gasping and leaned against Haris. "I grow old," she said. "Once it was no trouble to kill a flyman."

She looked at the man Haris with gratitude. He had more than one use.

With one foot she pushed the limp body over the edge of the branch. It rolled messily, then dropped. Its old wizened wings tucked uselessly about its head, the flyman fell to the green.

IV

They lay among the sharp leaves of two whistlethistle plants, dazed by the bright sun but alert for new dangers. Their climb had been completed. Now the nine children saw the Tips for the first time—and were struck mute by it.

Once more Lily-yo and Flor lay siege to a burnurn, with Daphe helping them. As the plant slumped defenselessly in the shadow of their upheld leaves, Daphe severed six of the great transparent pods that were to be their coffins. Hy helped her carry them to safety, after which Lily-yo and Flor dropped their leaves and ran for the shelter of the whistlethistles.

A cloud of paperwings drifted by, their colors startling to eyes generally submerged in green: sky-blues and yellows and bronzes and a viridian that flashed like water.

One of the paperwings alighted fluttering on a tuft of emerald foliage near the watchers. The foliage was a dripperlip. Almost at once the paperwing turned gray as its small nourishment content was sucked out. It disintegrated like ash.

Rising cautiously, Lily-yo led the group over to the nearest cable of traverser web. Each adult carried her own urn.

The traversers, largest of all creatures, vegetable or otherwise, could never go into the forest. They spurted out their line among the upper branches, securing it with side strands.

Finding a suitable cable with no traverser in sight, Lily-yo turned, signaling for the urns to be put down. She spoke to Toy, Gren, and the seven other children.

"Now help us climb with our souls into our burnurns. See us tight in. Then carry us to the cable and stick us to it. Then good-bye. We Go Up. You are the group now."

Toy momentarily hesitated. She was a slender girl, her breasts like pearfruit.

"Do not go, Lily-yo," she said. "We still need you."

"It is the way," Lily-yo said firmly.

Prizing open one of the facets of her urn, she slid into her coffin. Helped by the children, the other adults did the same. From habit, Lily-yo glanced to see that Haris was safe.

They were all in now, and helpless. Inside the urns it was surprisingly cool.

The children carried the coffins between them, glancing nervously up at the sky meanwhile. They were afraid. They felt helpless. Only the bold man child Gren looked as if he were enjoying their new sense of independence. He more than Toy directed the others in the placing of the urns upon the traverser's cable.

Lily-yo smelled a curious smell in the urn. As it soaked through her lungs, her senses became detached. Outside, the scene which had been clear, clouded and shrank. She saw she hung suspended on a traverser cable above the treetops, with Flor, Haris, Daphe, Hy and Jury in other urns nearby, hanging helplessly. She saw the children, the new group, run to shelter. Without looking back, they dived into the muddle of foliage on the platform and disappeared.

The traverser hung ten and a half miles above the Tips, safe from its enemies. All about it, space was indigo, and the invisible rays of space bathed it and nourished it. Yet the traverser was still dependent on Earth for some food. After many hours of vegetative dreaming, it swung itself over and climbed down a cable.

Other traversers hung motionless nearby. Occasionally one would blow a globe of oxygen or hitch a leg to try and dislodge a troublesome parasite. Theirs was a leisureliness never attained before. Time was not for them; the sun was theirs, and would ever be until it became unstable, turned nova, and burned both them and itself out.

The traverser fell fast, its feet twinkling, hardly touching the cable, fell straight to the forest, plunging toward the leafy cathedrals of the forest. Here in the air lived its enemies, enemies many times smaller, many times more vicious, many times more clever. Traversers were prey to one of the last families of insect, the tigerflies.

Only tigerflies could kill traversers—kill in their own insidious, invincible way.

Over the long slow eons as the sun's radiation increased, vegetation had evolved to undisputed supremacy. The wasps had developed too, keeping pace with the new developments. They grew in numbers and size as the animal kingdom fell into eclipse and dwindled into the rising tide of green. In time they became the chief enemies of the spiderlike traversers. Attacking in packs, they could paralyze the primitive nerve centers, leaving the traversers to stagger to their own destruction. The tigerflies also laid their eggs in tunnels bored into the stuff of their enemies' bodies; when the eggs hatched, the larvae fed happily on living flesh.

This threat it was, more than anything, that had driven the traversers farther and farther into space many millennia past. In this seemingly inhospitable region, they reached their full and monstrous flowering.

Hard radiation became a necessity for them. Nature's first astronauts, they changed the face of the firmament. Long after man had rolled up his affairs and retired to the trees whence he came, the traversers reconquered that vacant pathway he had lost. Long after intelligence had died from its peak of dominance, the traversers linked indissolubly the green globe and the white—with that antique symbol of neglect, a spider's web.

The traverser scrambled down among the upper leaves, erecting the hairs on its back, where patchy green and black afforded it natural camouflage. On its way down it had collected several creatures caught fluttering in its cables. It sucked them peacefully. When the soupy noises stopped, it vegetated.

Buzzing roused it from its doze. Yellow and black stripes zoomed before its crude eyes. A pair of tigerflies had found it.

With great alacrity, the traverser moved. Its massive bulk, contracted in the atmosphere, had an overall length of over a mile, yet it moved lightly as pollen, scuttling up a cable back to the safety of vacuum.

As it retreated, its legs brushing the web, it picked up various spores, burrs, and tiny creatures that adhered there. It also picked up six burn-urns, each containing an insensible human, which swung unregarded from its shin.

Several miles up, the traverser paused. Recovering from its fright, it ejected a globe of oxygen, attaching it gently to a cable. It paused. Its palps trembled. Then it headed out toward deep space, expanding all the time as pressure dropped.

Its speed increased. Folding its legs, the traverser began to eject fresh web from the spinnerets under its abdomen. So it propelled itself, a vast vegetable almost without feeling, rotating slowly to stabilize its temperature.

Hard radiations bathed it. The traverser basked in them. It was in its element.

Daphe roused. She opened her eyes, gazing without intelligence. What she saw had no meaning. She only knew she had Gone Up. This was a new existence and she did not expect it to have meaning.

Part of the view from her urn was eclipsed by stiff yellowy wisps that might have been hair or straw. Everything else was uncertain, being washed either in blinding light or deep shadow. Light and shadow revolved.

Gradually Daphe identified other objects. Most notable was a splendid green half-ball mottled with white and blue. Was it a fruit? To it trailed cables, glinting here and there, many cables, silver or gold in the crazy light. Two traversers she recognized at some distance, traveling fast, looking mummified. Bright points of light sparkled painfully. All was confusion.

This was where gods lived.

Daphe had no feeling. A curious numbness kept her without motion or the wish to move. The smell in the urn was strange. Also the air seemed thick. Everything was like an evil dream. Daphe opened her

mouth, her jaw sticky and slow to respond. She screamed. No sound came. Pain filled her. Her sides in particular ached.

Even when her eyes closed again, her mouth hung open.

Like a great shaggy balloon, the traverser floated down to the moon.

It could hardly be said to think, being a mechanism or little more. Yet somewhere in it the notion stirred that its pleasant journey was too brief, that there might be other directions in which to sail. After all, the hated tigerflies were almost as many now, and as troublesome, on the moon as on the earth. Perhaps somewhere there might be a peaceful place, another of these half-round places with green stuff, in the middle of warm delicious rays. . . .

Perhaps some time it might be worth sailing off on a full belly and a new course. . . .

Many traversers hung above the moon. Their nets straggled untidily everywhere. This was their happy base, better liked than the earth, where the air was thick and their limbs were clumsy. This was the place they had discovered first—except for some puny creatures who had been long gone before they arrived. They were the last lords of creation. Largest and lordliest, they enjoyed their long lazy afternoon's supremacy.

The traverser slowed, spinning out no more cable. In leisurely fashion, it picked its way through a web and drifted down to the pallid vegetation of the moon. . . .

Here were conditions very unlike those on the heavy planet. The many-trunked banyans had never gained supremacy here; in the thin air and low gravity they outgrew their strength and collapsed. In their place, monstrous celeries and parsleys grew, and it was into a bed of these that the traverser settled. Hissing from its exertions, it blew off a great cloud of oxygen and relaxed.

As it settled down into the foliage, its great sack of body rubbed against the stems. Its legs too scraped into the mass of leaves. From legs and body a shower of light debris was dislodged—burrs, seeds, grit, nuts, and leaves caught up in its sticky fibers back on distant earth. Among this detritus were six seed casings from a burnurn plant. They rolled over the ground and came to a standstill.

Haris the man was the first to awaken. Groaning with an unexpected pain in his sides, he tried to sit up. Pressure on his forehead reminded him of where he was. Doubling up knees and arms, he pushed against the lid of his coffin.

Momentarily, it resisted him. Then the whole urn crumbled into pieces, sending Haris sprawling. The rigors of total vacuum had destroyed its cohesive powers.

Unable to pick himself up, Haris lay where he was. His head throbbed, his lungs were full of an unpleasant odor. Eagerly he gasped in fresh air. At first it seemed thin and chill, yet he sucked it in with gratitude.

After a while, he was well enough to look about him.

Long yellow tendrils were stretching out of a nearby thicket, working their way gingerly toward him. Alarmed, he looked about for a woman to protect him. None was there. Stiffly, his arms so stiff, he pulled his knife from his belt, rolled over on one side, and lopped the tendrils off as they reached him. This was an easy enemy!

Haris cried. He screamed. He jumped unsteadily to his feet, yelling in disgust at himself. Suddenly he had noticed he was covered in scabs. Worse, as his clothes fell in shreds from him, he saw that a mass of leathery flesh grew from his arms, his ribs, his legs. When he lifted his arms, the mass stretched out almost like wings. He was spoiled, his handsome body ruined.

A sound made him turn, and for the first time he remembered his fellows. Lily-yo was struggling from the remains of her burnurn. She raised a hand in greeting.

To his horror, Haris saw that she bore disfigurements like his own. In truth, at first he scarcely recognized her. She resembled nothing so much as one of the hated flymen. He flung himself to the ground and wept as his heart expanded in fear and loathing.

Lily-yo was not born to weep. Disregarding her own painful deformities, breathing laboriously, she cast about, seeking the other four coffins.

Flor's was the first she found, half buried though it was. A blow with a stone shattered it, Lily-yo lifted up her friend, as hideously transformed as she, and in a short while Flor roused. Inhaling the strange air raucously, she too sat up. Lily-yo left her to seek the others. Even in her dazed state, she thanked her aching limbs for feeling so light.

Daphe was dead. She lay stiff and purple in her urn. Though Lily-yo shattered it and called aloud, Daphe did not stir. Her swollen tongue stayed dreadfully protruding from her mouth. Daphe was dead, Daphe who had lived, Daphe who had been the sweet singer.

Hy also was dead, a poor shriveled thing lying in a coffin that had cracked on its arduous journey between the two worlds. When that coffin shattered under Lily-yo's blow, Hy fell away to powder. Hy was dead. Hy who had borne a man child. Hy always so fleet of foot.

Jury's urn was the last. She stirred as the headwoman reached her. A minute later, she was sitting up, eyeing her deformities with a stoical distaste, breathing the sharp air. Jury lived.

Haris staggered over to the women. In his hand he carried his soul.

"Four of us!" he exclaimed. "Have we been received by the gods or no?"

"We feel pain—so we live," Lily-yo said. "Daphe and Hy have fallen to the green."

Bitterly, Haris flung down his soul and trampled it underfoot.

"Look at us! Better be dead!" he said.

"Before we decide that, we will eat," said Lily-yo.

Painfully, they retreated into the thicket, alerting themselves once more to the idea of danger. Flor, Lily-yo, Jury, Haris, each supported the other. The idea of tabu had somehow been forgotten.

V

"No proper trees grow here," Flor protested, as they pushed among giant celeries whose crests waved high above their heads.

"Take care!" Lily-yo said. She pulled Flor back. Something rattled and snapped like a chained dog, missing Flor's leg by inches.

A trappersnapper, having missed its prey, was slowly reopening its jaws, baring its green teeth. This one was only a shadow of the terrible trappersnappers spawned on the jungle floors of earth. Its jaws were weaker, its movements far more circumscribed. Without the shelter of the giant banyans, the trappersnappers were disinherited.

Something of the same feeling overcame the humans. They and their ancestors for countless generations had lived in the high trees. Safety was arboreal. Here there were only celery and parsley trees, offering neither the rock-steadiness nor the unlimited boughs of the giant banyan.

So they journeyed, nervous, lost, in pain, knowing neither where they were nor why they were.

They were attacked by leapycreepers and sawthorns, and beat them down. They skirted a thicket of nettlemoss taller and wider than any to be met with on earth. Conditions that worked against one group of vegetation favored others. They climbed a slope and came on a pool fed by a stream. Over the pool hung berries and fruits, sweet to taste, good to eat.

"This is not so bad," Haris said. "Perhaps we can still live."

Lily-yo smiled at him. He was the most trouble, the most lazy; yet she was glad he was still here. When they bathed in the pool, she looked at him again. For all the strange scales that covered him, and the two broad sweeps of flesh that hung by his side, he was still good to look on just because he was Haris. She hoped she was also comely. With a burr she raked her hair back; only a little of it fell out.

When they had bathed, they ate. Haris worked then, collecting fresh knives from the bramblebushes. They were not as tough as the ones on earth, but they would have to do. Then they rested in the sun.

The pattern of their lives was completely broken. More by instinct than intelligence they had lived. Without the group, without the tree, without the earth, no pattern guided them. What was the way or what was not became unclear. So they lay where they were and rested.

As she lay there, Lily-yo looked about her. All was strange, so that her heart beat faintly.

Though the sun shone bright as ever, the sky was as deep blue as a vandalberry. And the half-globe in the sky was monstrous, all streaked with green and blue and white, so that Lily-yo could not know it for somewhere she had lived. Phantom silver lines pointed to it, while nearer at hand the tracery of traverser webs glittered, veining the whole sky. Traversers moved over it like clouds, their great bodies slack.

All this was their empire, their creation. On their first journeys here, many millennia ago, they had literally laid the seeds of this world. To begin with, they had withered and died by the thousand on the inhospitable ash. But even the dead had brought their little legacies of oxygen, soil, spores, and seed, some of which later sprouted on the fruitful corpses. Under the weight of dozing centuries, they gained a sort of foothold.

They grew. Stunted and ailing in the beginning, they grew. With vegetal tenacity, they grew. They exhaled. They spread. They thrived. Slowly the broken wastes of the moon's lit face turned green. In the craters creepers grew. Up the ravaged slopes the parsleys crawled. As the atmosphere deepened, so the magic of life intensified, its rhythm strengthened, its tempo increased. More thoroughly than another dominant species had once managed to do, the traversers colonized the moon.

Lily-yo could know or care little about any of this. She turned her face from the sky.

Flor had crawled over to Haris the man. She lay against him in the circle of his arms, half under the shelter of his new skin, and she stroked his hair.

Furious, Lily-yo jumped up, kicked Flor on the shin, and then flung herself upon her, using teeth and nails to pull her away. Jury ran to join in.

"This is not time for mating!" Lily-yo cried.

"Let me *go!*" cried Flor.

Haris in his startlement jumped up. He stretched his arms, waved them, and rose effortlessly into the air.

"Look!" he shouted in alarmed delight.

Over their heads he circled once, perilously. Then he lost his balance and came sprawling head first, mouth open in fright. Head first he pitched into the pool.

Three anxious, awe-struck, love-struck female humans dived after him in unison.

While they were drying themselves, they heard noises in the forest. At once they became alert, their old selves. They drew their new swords and looked to the thicket.

The wiltmilt when it appeared was not like its Earthly brothers. No longer upright like a jack-in-the-box, it groped its way along like a caterpillar.

The humans saw its distorted eye break from the celeries. Then they turned and fled.

Even when the danger was left behind, they moved rapidly, not knowing what they sought. Once they slept, ate, and then again pressed on through the unending growth, the undying daylight, until they came to where the jungle gaped.

Ahead of them, everything seemed to cease and then go on again.

Cautiously they approached. The ground underfoot had been badly uneven. Now it broke altogether into a wide crevasse. Beyond the crevasse the vegetation grew again—but how did humans pass the gulf? The four of them stood anxiously where the ferns ended, looking across at the far side.

Haris the man screwed his face in pain to show he had a troublesome idea in his head.

"What I did before—going up in the air," he began awkwardly. "If we do it again now, all of us, we go in the air across to the other side."

"No!" Lily-yo said. "When you go up you come down hard. You will fall to the green!"

"I will do better than before."

"No!" repeated Lily-yo. "You are not to go."

"Let him go," Flor said.

The two women turned to glare at each other. Taking his chance, Haris raised his arms, waved them, rose slightly from the ground, and began to use his legs too. He moved forward over the crevasse before his nerve broke.

As he fluttered down, Flor and Lily-yo, moved by instinct, dived into the gulf after him. Spreading their arms, they glided about him, shouting. Jury remained behind, crying in baffled anger down to them.

Regaining a little control, Haris landed heavily on an outcropping ledge. The two women alighted chattering and scolding beside him. They looked up. Two lips fringed with green fern sucked a narrow purple segment of sky. Jury could not be seen, though her cries still echoed down to them.

Behind the ledge on which they stood, a tunnel ran into the cliff. All the rock face was peppered with similar holes, so that it resembled a sponge. From the hole behind the ledge ran three flymen, two male and one female. They rushed out with ropes and spears.

Flor and Lily-yo were bending over Haris. Before they had time to recover, they were knocked sprawling and tied with the ropes. Helpless, Lily-yo saw other flymen launch themselves from other holes and come gliding in to help secure them. Their flight seemed more sure, more graceful, than it had on earth. Perhaps the way humans were lighter here had something to do with it.

"Bring them in!" the flymen cried to each other. Their sharp, clever faces jostled around eagerly as they hoisted up their captives and bore them into the tunnel.

In their alarm, Lily-yo, Flor, and Haris forgot about Jury, still crouching on the lip of the crevasse. They never saw her again. A pack of thinpins got her.

The tunnel sloped gently down. Finally it curved and led into another which ran level and true. This in its turn led into an immense cavern with regular sides and a regular roof. Gray daylight flooded in at one end, for the cavern stood at the bottom of the crevasse.

To the middle of this cavern the three captives were brought. Their knives were taken from them and they were released. As they huddled together uneasily, one of the flymen stood forward and spoke.

"We will not harm you unless we must," he said. "You come by traverser from the Heavy World. You are new here. When you learn our ways, you will join us."

"I am Lily-yo," Lily-yo proudly said. "Let me go. We three are humans. You are flymen."

"Yes, you are humans, we are flymen. Also we are humans, you are flymen. Now you know nothing. Soon you will know, when you have seen the Captives. They will tell you many things."

"I am Lily-yo. I know many things."

"The Captives will tell you many more things."

"If there were many more things, then I would know them."

"I am Band Appa Bondi and I say come to see the Captives. Your talk is stupid Heavy World talk, Lily-yo."

Several flymen began to look aggressive, so that Haris nudged Lily-yo and muttered, "Let us do what he asks."

Grumpily, Lily-yo let herself and her two companions be led to another chamber. This one was partially ruined, and it stank. At the far end of it, a fall of cindery rock marked where the roof had fallen in, while a shaft of the unremitting sunlight burned on the floor, sending up a curtain of golden light about itself. Near this light were the Captives.

"Do not fear to see them. They will not harm you," Band Appa Bondi said, going forward.

The encouragement was needed, for the Captives were not prepossessing.

Eight of them there were, eight Captives, kept in eight great burnurns big enough to serve them as narrow cells. The cells stood grouped in a semicircle. Band Appa Bondi led Lily-yo, Flor, and Haris into the middle of this semicircle, where they could survey and be surveyed.

The Captives were painful to look on. All had some kind of deformity. One had no legs. One had no flesh on his lower jaw. One had four gnarled dwarf arms. One had short wings of flesh connecting earlobes and thumbs, so that he lived perpetually with hands half raised to his face. One had boneless arms trailing at his side and one boneless leg. One had monstrous wings which trailed about him like carpet. One was hiding his ill-shaped form away behind a screen of his own excrement, smearing it onto the transparent walls of his cell. And one had a second head, a small, wizened thing growing from the first that fixed Lily-yo with a malevolent eye. This last Captive, who seemed to lead the others, spoke now, using the mouth of his main head.

"I am the Chief Captive. I greet you. You are of the Heavy World. We are of the True World. Now you join us because you are of us. Though your wings and your scars are new, you may join us."

"I am Lily-yo. We three are humans. You are only flymen. We will not join you."

The Captives grunted in boredom. The Chief Captive spoke again.

"Always this talk from you of the Heavy World! You *have* joined us! You are flymen, we are human. You know little, we know much."

"But we—"

"Stop your stupid talk, woman!"

"We are—"

"Be silent, woman, and listen," Band Appa Bondi said.

"We know much," repeated the Chief Captive. "Some things we will tell you. All who make the journey from the Heavy World become changed. Some die. Most live and grow wings. Between the worlds are many strong rays, not seen or felt, which change our bodies. When you come here, when you come to the True World, you become a true human. The grub of the tigerfly is not a tigerfly until it changes. So humans change."

"I cannot know what he says," Haris said stubbornly, throwing himself down. But Lily-yo and Flor were listening.

"To this True World, as you call it, we come to die," Lily-yo said, doubtingly.

The Captive with the fleshless jaw said, "The grub of the tigerfly thinks it dies when it changes into a tigerfly."

"You are still young," said the Chief Captive. "You begin newly here. Where are your souls?"

Lily-yo and Flor looked at each other. In their flight from the wiltmilt they had heedlessly thrown down their souls. Haris had trampled on his. It was unthinkable!

"You see. You needed them no more. You are still young. You may be able to have babies. Some of those babies may be born with wings."

The Captive with the boneless arms added, "Some may be born wrong, as we are. Some may be born right."

"You are too foul to live!" Haris growled. "Why are you not killed?"

"Because we know all things," the Chief Captive said. Suddenly his second head roused itself and declared, "To be a good shape is not all in life. To know is also good. Because we cannot move well we can— *think*. This tribe of the True World is good and knows these things. So it lets us rule it."

Flor and Lily-yo muttered together.

"Do you say that you poor Captives *rule* the True World?" Lily-yo asked at last.

"We do."

"Then why are you Captives?"

The flyman with earlobes and thumbs connected, making his perpetual little gesture of protest, spoke for the first time.

"To rule is to serve, woman. Those who bear power are slaves to it. Only an outcast is free. Because we are Captives, we have the time to talk and think and plan and know. Those who know command the lives of others."

"No hurt will come to you, Lily-yo," Band Appa Bondi added. "You will live among us and enjoy your life free from harm."

"No!" the Chief Captive said with both mouths. "Before she can enjoy, Lily-yo and her companion Flor—this other man creature is plainly useless—must help our great plan."

"The invasion?" Bondi asked.

"What else? Flor and Lily-yo, you arrive here at a good time. Memories of the Heavy World and its savage life are still fresh in you. We need such memories. So we ask you to go back there on a great plan we have."

"Go back?" gasped Flor.

"Yes. We plan to attack the Heavy World. You must help to lead our force."

VI

The long afternoon of eternity wore on, that long golden road of an afternoon that would somewhere lead to an everlasting night. Motion there was, but motion without event—except for those negligible events that seemed so large to the creatures participating in them.

For Lily-yo, Flor and Haris there were many events. Chief of these was that they learned to fly properly.

The pains associated with their wings soon died away as the wonderful new flesh and tendons strengthened. To sail up in the light gravity became an increasing delight—the ugly flopping movements of flymen on the Heavy World had no place here.

They learned to fly in packs, and then to hunt in packs. In time they were trained to carry out the Captives' plan.

The series of accidents that had first delivered humans to this world in burnurns had been a fortunate one, growing more fortunate as millennia tolled away. For gradually the humans adapted better to the True World. Their survival factor became greater, their power surer. And all this as on the Heavy World conditions grew more and more adverse to anything but the giant vegetables.

Lily-yo at least was quick to see how much easier life was in these new conditions. She sat with Flor and a dozen others eating pulped pluggyrug, before they did the Captives' bidding and left for the Heavy World.

It was hard to express all she felt.

"Here we are safe," she said, indicating the whole green land that sweltered under the silver network of webs.

"Except from the tigerflies," Flor agreed.

They rested on a bare peak, where the air was thin and even the giant creepers had not climbed. The turbulent green stretched away below them, almost as if they were on Earth—although here it was continually checked by the circular formations of rock.

"This world is smaller," Lily-yo said, trying again to make Flor know what was in her head. "Here we are bigger. We do not need to fight so much."

"Soon we must fight."

"Then we can come back here again. This is a good place, with nothing so savage and with not so many enemies. Here the groups could live without so much fear. Veggy and Toy and May and Gren and the other little ones would like it here."

"They would miss the trees."

"We shall soon miss the trees no longer. We have wings instead."

This idle talk took place beneath the unmoving shadow of a rock. Overhead, silver blobs against a purple sky, the traversers went, walking their networks, descending only occasionally to the celeries far below. As Lily-yo fell to watching these creatures, she thought in her mind of the grand plan the Captives had hatched. She flicked it over in a series of vivid pictures.

Yes, the Captives knew. They could see ahead as she could not. She and those about her had lived like plants, doing what came. The Captives were not plants. From their cells they saw more than those outside.

This, the Captives saw: that the few humans who reached the True World bore few children, because they were old, or because the rays that made their wings grow made their seed die; that it was good here, and would be better still with more humans; that one way to get more humans here was to bring babies and children from the Heavy World.

For countless time, this had been done. Brave flymen had traveled back to that other world and stolen children. The flymen who had once attacked Lily-yo's group on their climb to the Tips had been on that mission. They had taken Bain to bring her to the True World in burnurns—and had not been heard of since.

Many perils and mischances lay in that long double journey. Of those who set out, few returned.

Now the Captives had thought of a better and more daring scheme.

"Here comes a traverser," Band Appa Bondi said. "Let us be ready to move."

He walked before the pack of twelve flyers who had been chosen for this new attempt. He was the leader. Lily-yo, Flor, and Haris were in support of him, together with eight others, three male, five female. Only one of them, Band Appa Bondi himself, had been carried to the True World as a boy.

Slowly the pack stood up, stretching their wings. The moment for their great adventure was here. Yet they felt little fear; they could not look ahead as the Captives did, except perhaps for Band Appa Bondi and Lily-yo. She strengthened her will by saying, "It is the way." Then they all spread their arms wide and soared off to meet the traverser.

The traverser had eaten.

It had caught one of its most tasty enemies, a tigerfly, in a web, and had sucked it till only a shell was left. Now it sank down into a bed of celeries, crushing them under its great bulk. Gently, it began to bud. Afterward, it would head out for the great black gulfs, where heat and radiance called it. It had been born on this world. Being young, it had never yet made that dreaded, desired journey.

Its buds burst up from its back, hung over, popped, fell to the ground, and scurried away to bury themselves in the pulp and dirt where they might begin their ten thousand years' growth in peace.

Young though it was, the traverser was sick. It did not know this. The enemy tigerfly had been at it, but it did not know this. Its vast bulk held little sensation.

The twelve humans glided down and landed on its back, low down on the abdomen in a position hidden from the creature's cluster of eyes. They sank among the tough shoulder-high fibers that served the traverser as hair, and looked about them. A rayplane swooped overhead and disappeared. A trio of tumbleweeds skittered into the fibers and were seen no more. All was as quiet as if they lay on a small deserted hill.

At length they spread out and moved along in line, heads down, eyes searching, Band Appa Bondi at one end, Lily-yo at the other. The great body was streaked and pitted and scarred, so that progress down the slope was not easy. The fiber grew in patterns of different shades, green, yellow, black, breaking up the traverser's bulk when seen from the air, serving it as natural camouflage. In many places, tough parasitic plants had rooted themselves, drawing their nourishment entirely from their host; most of them would die when the traverser launched itself out between worlds.

The humans worked hard. Once they were thrown flat when the traverser changed position. As the slope down which they moved grew steeper, so progress became more slow.

"Here!" cried Y Coyin, one of the women.

At last they had found what they sought, what the Captives sent them to seek.

Clustering around Y Coyin with their knives out, the pack looked down. Here the fibers had been neatly champed away in swathes, leaving a bare patch as far across as a human was long. In this patch was a round scab. Lily-yo felt it. It was immensely hard.

Lo Jint put his ear to it. Silence.

They looked at each other.

No signal was needed, none given.

Together they knelt, prizing with their knives around the scab. Once the traverser moved, and they threw themselves flat. A bud rose nearby, popped, rolled down the slope and fell to the distant ground. A thinpin devoured it as it ran. The humans continued prizing.

The scab moved. They lifted it off. A dark and sticky tunnel was revealed to them.

"I go first," Band Appa Bondi said.

He lowered himself into the hole. The others followed. Dark sky showed roundly above them until the twelfth human was in the tunnel. Then the scab was drawn back into place. A soft slobber of sound came from it as it began to heal back into position again.

They crouched where they were for a long time. They crouched, their knives ready, their wings folded around them, their human hearts beating strongly.

In more than one sense they were in enemy territory. At the best of times, traversers were only allies by accident; they ate humans as readily as they devoured anything else. But this burrow was the work of that yellow and black destroyer, the tigerfly. One of the last true insects to survive, the tough and resourceful tigerflies had instinctively made the most invincible of all living things its prey.

The female tigerfly alights and bores her tunnel into the traverser. Working her way down, she at last stops and prepares a natal chamber, hollowing it from the living traverser, paralyzing the matter with her needletail to prevent its healing again. There she lays her store of eggs before climbing back to daylight. When the eggs hatch, the larvae have fresh and living stuff to nourish them.

After a while, Band Appa Bondi gave a sign and the pack moved forward, climbing awkwardly down the tunnel. A faint luminescence guided their eyes. The air lay heavy and green in their chests. They moved very slowly, very quietly, for they heard movement ahead.

Suddenly the movement was on them.

"Look out!" Band Appa Bondi cried.

From the terrible dark, something launched itself at them.

Before they realized it, the tunnel had curved and widened into the natal chamber. The tigerfly's eggs had hatched. Two hundred larvae with jaws as wide as a man's reach turned on the intruders, snapping in fury and fear.

Even as Band Appa Bondi sliced his first attacker, another had his head off. He fell, and his companions launched themselves over him. Pressing forward, they dodged those clicking jaws.

Behind their hard heads, the larvae were soft and plump. One slash of a sword and they burst, their entrails flowing out. They fought, but knew not how to fight. Savagely the humans stabbed, ducked, and stabbed. No other human died. With backs to the wall they cut and thrust, breaking jaws, ripping flimsy stomachs. They killed unceasingly with neither hate nor mercy until they stood knee deep in slush. The larvae snapped and writhed and died. Uttering a grunt of satisfaction, Haris slew the last of them.

Wearily then, eleven humans crawled back to the tunnel, there to wait until the mess drained away—and then to wait a longer while.

The traverser stirred in its bed of celeries. Vague impulses drifted through its being. Things it had done. Things it had to do. The things it had done had been done, the things it had to do were still to do. Blowing off oxygen, it heaved itself up.

Slowly at first, it swung up a cable, climbing to the network where the air thinned. Always, always before in the eternal afternoon it had stopped here. This time there seemed no reason for stopping. Air was nothing, heat was all, the heat that blistered and prodded and chafed and coaxed increasingly with height. . . .

It blew a jet of cable from a spinneret. Gaining speed, gaining intention, it rocketed its mighty vegetable self out and away from the place where the tigerflies flew. Ahead of it floated a semicircle of light, white and blue and green; it was a useful thing to look at to avoid getting lost.

For this was a lonely place for a young traverser, a terrible-wonderful bright-dark place, so full of nothing. Turn as you speed and you fry well on all sides . . . nothing to trouble you. . . .

. . . Except that deep in your core a little pack of humans use you as an ark for their own purposes. You carry them back to a world that once—so staggeringly long ago—belonged to their kind; you carry them back so that they may eventually—who knows?—fill another world with their own kind.

For remember, there is always plenty of time.

BIBLIOGRAPHY

These stories appeared in *The Magazine of Fantasy and Science Fiction:*
  "Hothouse," February 1961
  "Nomansland," April 1961
  "Undergrowth," July 1961
  "Timberline," September 1961
  "Evergreen," December 1961
Hothouse (novel), Signet Books, 1962 (abridged); Faber & Faber, 1962

THE NICHOLAS VAN RIJN SERIES

by Poul Anderson

Across a gap of more than twenty years, it is not easy to recall what went on in one's head. However, the origins of the van Rijn series look fairly clear to me. At first I had an idea for a short story; a particular kind of protagonist seemed appropriate; I visualized him, sketchily, and wrote it. That was "Margin of Profit," which appeared in 1956.

Basically, he was—well, "anti-hero" is the fashionable word nowadays, but may not quite fit. Much earlier, I'd grown tired of the perfectly fearless, perfectly moral, perfectly Anglo-Saxon paladin who dominated most science fiction in those days, and had created Dominic Flandry. He was not exactly a James Bond, because Agent 007 would not come into being for many years. Insofar as he derived from any earlier character, it was doubtless the Saint. However, he was Gallic in name and temperament, he lived in the twilight of an empire whose decadence had, he knew, touched his own soul, and as an officer of that empire he must needs make the best of a generally bad bargain.

In contrast, van Rijn was supposed to inhabit an era of exuberant, ofttimes ruthless expansion. I modeled that largely on the Renaissance and the Age of Discovery, with elements of the Hansa, and him on men of those centuries, such as King Christian IV of Denmark. His surname was filched from Rembrandt; the pronunciation is, more or less, "fan rine." As said, his character was not at all well defined in the first story. I have lately rewritten that one for a planned collection.

Meanwhile, I gave him no further thought for a couple of years. Then I got interested in doing "hard" science fiction, the kind in which Hal Clement had long excelled. As the planet Diomedes took shape in my mind, so did notions about what sorts of people might find themselves there and how they would interact with each other as well as their environment. Hm-m-m . . . another cliché, the handsome young fellow gets the girl . . . why not demolish that while we're at it? The fact is, a man's success with a woman has virtually no relation to his looks or age or any other conventionally attractive qualities, but depends on what he can *do*—at least, that's the case if she's a doer herself, intelligent enough to look past the surface. Well, here was this person I'd used before, van Rijn. Of course, he would have to be made far more real. . . .

The result was *The Man Who Counts*. That was John Campbell's title, much better than my own, for the serial version of the story. A later paperback had wished upon it a wretched *War of the Wing-Men,* and suffered mutilations at the hands of some idiot copy editor. I'm happy to report that these things will be corrected in forthcoming editions.

I went on writing an occasional shorter van Rijn story, as ideas occurred, and also revived Flandry. While drafting *A Plague of Masters,* which featured the latter, I impulsively put in a mention of van Rijn as living in folk memory like Robin Hood. From this nucleus, the two men on the same time-line, grew an entire "future history" which by now includes about forty separate stories and covers a span of several thousand years. Notes upon it fill to overflowing a big looseleaf binder.

The parallels to real-world events are deliberate. In the past few years, a voluminous and exciting though yet unpublished study of the rise and fall of civilizations, by John K. Hord, has helped me work out the underlying sociological and temporal structure in detail. Needless to say, patterns don't repeat themselves exactly. We get countless variations, most obviously—in fiction—where nonhuman races are concerned. Indeed, many of my borrowings from the Terrestrial past aren't meant to be taken literally, but only as rough equivalents of quite different future words, concepts, and practices.

Since it was not logical that van Rijn would go on having all the breakneck adventures, I provided him with a young protégé, David Falkayn. However, he got kicked back into action in *Satan's World.* That book developed out of correspondence with John Campbell, who proposed the basic speculative notion, and discussions with Chesley Bonestell, who did a superb cover painting after I'd calculated the astronomical specifications.

By then, I thought, van Rijn would be starting to feel his age a bit, and to brood upon a breakdown of society which was growing more and more evident around him. This became a motif of the novelette "Lodestar." The novel *Mirkheim* was supposed to tie up numerous loose ends in the series and, incidentally, offer a few thoughts on just where the Polesotechnic League went wrong. You can't keep a bad man down; van Rijn ended that tale in a pretty cheerful, forward-looking mood. If his own world was going under, well, no end of stars lay beyond it.

Falkayn, who had married his boss's granddaughter, would presently lead an exodus of his own, to the planet Avalon. Thence came *The People of the Wind,* partly bridging the gap between him and Flandry.

While some readers loathe him, on the whole van Rijn is the most popular character I have ever come up with, and the "history" in general has evoked considerable discussion. The stories about him were actually used once as material for a graduate seminar in management; and even sinister Aycharaych has his own fans. Thus the entire series has, over the years, evolved a certain personal and professional importance to me.

I don't know how much longer it can go on. Consistency becomes harder and harder to maintain, and occasionally fails, especially as science keeps changing our picture of the universe. True, perfect consistency is possible only to God Himself, and a close study of Scripture will show that He doesn't always make it. Yet if nothing else, eventually something like this gets too involuted—and after all, the cosmos is full of other themes. Nevertheless, it's been fun, and the old bastard will always be close to my heart.

A Little Knowledge

They found the planet during the first Grand Survey. An expedition to it was organized very soon after the report appeared; for this looked like an impossibility.

It orbited its G9 sun at an average distance of some three astronomical units, thus receiving about one eighteenth the radiation Earth gets. Under such a condition—and others, e.g., the magnetic field strength which was present—a subjovian ought to have formed; and indeed it had fifteen times the terrestrial mass. But—that mass was concentrated in a solid globe. The atmosphere was only half again as dense as on man's home, and breatheable by him.

"Where 'ave h'all the h'atoms gone?" became the standing joke of the research team. Big worlds are supposed to keep enough of their primordial hydrogen and helium to completely dominate the chemistry. Paradox, as it was unofficially christened, did retain some of the latter gas, to a total of eight percent of its air. This posed certain technical problems which had to be solved before anyone dared land. However, land the men must; the puzzle they confronted was so delightfully baffling.

A nearly circular ocean basin suggested an answer which studies of its bottom seemed to confirm. Paradox had begun existence as a fairly standard specimen, complete with four moons. But the largest of these, probably a captured asteroid, had had an eccentric orbit. At last perturbation brought it into the upper atmosphere, which at that time extended beyond Roche's limit. Shock waves, repeated each time one of those ever-deeper grazings was made, blew vast quantities of gas off into space:

especially the lighter molecules. Breakup of the moon hastened this process and made it more violent, by presenting more solid surface. Thus at the final crash, most of those meteoroids fell as one body, to form that gigantic astrobleme. Perhaps metallic atoms, thermally ripped free of their ores and splashed as an incandescent fog across half the planet, locked onto the bulk of what hydrogen was left, if any was.

Be that as it may, Paradox now had only a mixture of what had hitherto been comparatively insignificant impurities, carbon dioxide, water vapor, methane, ammonia, and other materials. In short, except for a small amount of helium, it had become rather like the young Earth. It got less heat and light, but greenhouse effect kept most of its water liquid. Life evolved, went into the photosynthesis business, and turned the air into the oxynitrogen common on terrestrials.

The helium had certain interesting biological effects. These were not studied in detail. After all, with the hyperdrive opening endless wonders to them, spacefarers tended to choose the most obviously glamorous. Paradox lay a hundred parsecs from Sol. Thousands upon thousands of worlds were more easily reached; many were more pleasant and less dangerous to walk on. The expedition departed and had no successors.

First it called briefly at a neighboring star, on one of whose planets were intelligent beings that had developed a promising set of civilizations. But, again, quite a few such lay closer to home.

The era of scientific expansion was followed by the era of commercial aggrandizement. Merchant adventurers began to appear in the sector. They ignored Paradox, which had nothing to make a profit on, but investigated the inhabited globe in the nearby system. In the language dominant there at the time, it was called something like Trillia, which thus became its name in League Latin. The speakers of that language were undergoing their equivalent of the First Industrial Evolution, and eager to leap into the modern age.

Unfortunately, they had little to offer that was in demand elsewhere. And even in the spacious terms of the Polesotechnic League, they lived at the far end of a long haul. Their charming arts and crafts made Trillia marginally worth a visit, on those rare occasions when a trader was on such a route that the detour wasn't great. Besides, it was as well to keep an eye on the natives. Lacking the means to buy the important gadgets of Technic society, they had set about developing these for themselves.

Bryce Harker pushed through flowering vines which covered an otherwise doorless entrance. They rustled back into place behind him, smelling like allspice, trapping gold-yellow sunlight in their leaves. That light also slanted through ogive windows in a curving wall, to glow off the grain of the wooden floor. Furniture was sparse: a few stools, a low table bearing an intricately faceted piece of rock crystal. By Trillian standards the ceiling was high; but Harker, who was of average human size, must stoop.

Witweet bounced from an inner room, laid down the book of poems he had been reading, and piped, "Why, be welcome, dear boy—Oo-oo-ooh!"

He looked down the muzzle of a blaster.

The man showed teeth. "Stay right where you are," he commanded. The vocalizer on his breast rendered the sounds he made into soprano cadenzas and arpeggios, the speech of Lenidel. It could do nothing about his vocabulary and grammar. His knowledge did include the fact that, by omitting all honorifics and circumlocutions without apology, he was uttering a deadly insult.

That was the effect he wanted—deadliness.

"My, my, my dear good friend from the revered Solar Commonwealth," Witweet stammered, "is this a, a jest too subtle for a mere pilot like myself to comprehend? I will gladly laugh if you wish, and then we shall enjoy tea and cakes. I have genuine Lapsang Soochong tea from Earth, and have just found the most darling recipe for sweet cakes—"

"Quiet!" Harker rapped. His glance flickered to the windows. Outside, flower colors exploded beneath reddish tree trunks; small bright wings went fluttering past; The Waterfall That Rings Like Glass Bells could be heard in the distance. Annanna was akin to most cities of Lenidel, the principal nation on Trillia, in being spread through an immensity of forest and parkscape. Nevertheless, Annanna had a couple of million population, who kept busy. Three aircraft were crossing heaven. At any moment, a pedestrian or cyclist might come along The Pathway Of The Beautiful Blossoms And The Bridge That Arches Like A Note of Music, and wonder why two humans stood tense outside number 1337.

Witweet regarded the man's skinsuit and boots, the pack on his shoulders, the tightly drawn sharp features behind the weapon. Tears blurred the blue of Witweet's great eyes. "I fear you are engaged in some desperate undertaking which distorts the natural goodness that, I feel certain, still inheres," he quavered. "May I beg the honor of being graciously let help you relieve whatever your distress may be?"

Harker squinted back at the Trillian. *How much do we really know about his breed, anyway? Damned nonhuman thing—Though I never resented his existence till now.* His pulse knocked; his skin was wet and stank, his mouth was dry and cottony-tasting.

Yet his prisoner looked altogether helpless. Witweet was an erect biped; but his tubby frame reached to barely a meter, from the padded feet to the big, scalloped ears. The two arms were broomstick thin, the four fingers on either hand suggested straws. The head was practically spherical, bearing a pug muzzle, moist black nose, tiny mouth, quivering whiskers, upward-slanting tufty brows. That, the tail, and the fluffy silver-gray fur which covered the whole skin, had made Olafsson remark that the only danger to be expected from this race was that eventually their cuteness would become unendurable.

Witweet had nothing upon him except an ornately embroidered kimono and a sash tied in a pink bow. He surely owned no weapons, and probably wouldn't know what to do with any. The Trillians were omnivores, but did not seem to have gone through a hunting stage in their evolution. They had never fought wars, and personal violence was limited to an infrequent scuffle.

Still, Harker thought, *they've shown the guts to push into deep space. I daresay even an unarmed policeman—Courtesy Monitor—could use his vehicle against us, like by ramming.*

Hurry!

"Listen," he said. "Listen carefully. You've heard that most intelligent species have members who don't mind using brute force, outright killing, for other ends than self-defense. Haven't you?"

Witweet waved his tail in assent. "Truly I am baffled by that statement, concerning as it does races whose achievements are of incomparable magnificence. However, not only my poor mind, but those of our most eminent thinkers have been engaged in fruitless endeavors to—"

"Dog your hatch!" The vocalizer made meaningless noises and Harker realized he had shouted in Anglic. He went back to Lenidellian-equivalent. "I don't propose to waste time. My partners and I did not come here to trade as we announced. We came to get a Trillian spaceship. The project is important enough that we'll kill if we must. Make trouble, and I'll blast you to greasy ash. It won't bother me. And you aren't the only possible pilot we can work through, so don't imagine you can block us by sacrificing yourself. I admit you are our best prospect. Obey, cooperate fully, and you'll live. We'll have no reason to destroy you." He paused. "We may even send you home with a good piece of money. We'll be able to afford that."

The bottling of his fur might have made Witweet impressive to another Trillian. To Harker, he became a ball of fuzz in a kimono, an agitated tail and a sound of coloratura anguish. "But this is insanity . . . if I may say that to a respected guest . . . One of *our* awkward, lumbering, fragile, unreliable prototype ships—when you came in a vessel representing centuries of advancement—? Why, why, why, in the name of multiple sacredness, why?"

"I'll tell you later," the man said. "You're due for a routine supply trip to, uh, Gwinsai Base, starting tomorrow, right? You'll board this afternoon, to make final inspection and settle in. We're coming along. You'll be leaving in about an hour's time. Your things must already be packed. I didn't cultivate your friendship for nothing, you see! Now, walk slowly ahead of me, bring your luggage back here and open it so I can make sure what you've got. Then we're on our way."

Witweet stared into the blaster. A shudder went through him. His fur collapsed. Tail dragging, he turned toward the inner rooms.

Stocky Leo Dolgorov and ash-blond Einar Olafsson gusted simultaneous oaths of relief when their leader and his prisoner came out onto the path. "What took you that time?" the first demanded. "Were you having a nap?"

"Nah, he entered one of their bowing, scraping, and unction-smearing contests." Olafsson's grin held scant mirth.

"Trouble?" Harker asked.

"N-no . . . three, four passersby stopped to talk—we told them the story and they went on," Dolgorov said. Harker nodded. He'd put a good deal of thought into that excuse for his guards' standing around— that they were about to pay a social call on Witweet but were waiting until the pilot's special friend Harker had made him a gift. A lie must be plausible, and the Trillian mind was not human.

"We sure hung on the hook, though." Olafsson started as a bicyclist came around a bend in the path and fluted a string of greetings.

Dwarfed beneath the men, Witweet made reply. No gun was pointed at him now, but one rested in each of the holsters near his brain. (Harker and companions had striven to convince everybody that the bearing of arms was a peaceful but highly symbolic custom in *their* part of Technic society, that without their weapons they would feel more indecent than a shaven Trillian.) As far as Harker's wire-taut attention registered, Witweet's answer was routine. But probably some forlornness crept into the overtones, for the neighbor stopped.

"Do you feel quite radiantly well, dear boy?" he asked.

"Indeed I do, honored Pwiddy, and thank you in my prettiest thoughts for your ever-sweet consideration," the pilot replied. "I . . . well, these good visitors from the starfaring culture of splendor have been describing some of their experiences—oh, I simply must relate them to you later, dear boy!—and naturally, since I am about to embark on another trip, I have been made pensive by this." Hands, tail, whiskers gesticulated. *Meaning what?* wondered Harker in a chill; and clamping jaws together: *Well, you knew you'd have to take risks to win a kingdom.* "Forgive me, I pray you of your overflowing generosity, that I rush off after such curt words. But I have promises to keep, and considerable distances to go before I sleep."

"Understood." Pwiddy spent a mere five minutes bidding farewell all around before he pedaled off. Meanwhile several others passed by. However, since no well-mannered person would interrupt a conversation even to make salute, they created no problem.

"Let's go." It grated in Dolgorov's throat.

Behind the little witch-hatted house was a pergola wherein rested Witweet's personal flitter. It was large and flashy—large enough for three humans to squeeze into the back—which fact had become an element in Harker's plan. The car that the men had used during their stay on Trillia, they abandoned. It was unmistakably an off-planet vehicle.

"Get started!" Dolgorov cuffed at Witweet.

Olafsson caught his arm and snapped: "Control your emotions! Want to tear his head off?"

Hunched over the dashboard, Witweet squeezed his eyes shut and shivered till Harker prodded him. "Pull out of that funk," the man said.

"I . . . I beg your pardon. The brutality so appalled me—" Witweet flinched from their laughter. His fingers gripped levers and twisted knobs. Here was no steering by gestures in a lightfield, let alone simply speaking an order to an autopilot. The overloaded flitter crawled skyward. Harker detected a flutter in its grav unit, but decided nothing was likely to fail before they reached the spaceport. And after that, nothing would matter except getting off this planet.

Not that it was a bad place, he reflected. Almost Earthlike in size, gravity, air, deliciously edible life forms—an Earth that no longer was and perhaps never had been, wide horizons and big skies, caressed by light and rain. Looking out, he saw woodlands in a thousand hues of green, meadows, river-gleam, an occasional dollhouse dwelling, grain-fields ripening tawny and the soft gaudiness of a flower ranch. Ahead lifted The Mountain Which Presides Over Moonrise In Lenidel, a snow-peak pure as Fuji's. The sun, yellower than Sol, turned it and a few clouds into gold.

A gentle world for a gentle people. Too gentle.

Too bad. For them.

Besides, after six months of it, three city-bred men were about ready to climb screaming out of their skulls. Harker drew forth a cigarette, inhaled it into lighting and filled his lungs with harshness. *I'd almost welcome a fight,* he thought savagely.

But none happened. Half a year of hard, patient study paid richly off. It helped that the Trillians were—well, you couldn't say lax about security, because the need for it had never occurred to them. Witweet radioed to the portmaster as he approached, was informed that everything looked O.K., and took his flitter straight through an open cargo lock into a hold of the ship he was to pilot.

The port was like nothing in Technic civilization, unless on the remotest, least visited of outposts. After all, the Trillians had gone in a bare fifty years from propeller-driven aircraft to interstellar spaceships. Such concentration on research and development had necessarily been at the expense of production and exploitation. What few vessels they had were still mostly experimental. The scientific bases they had established on planets of next-door stars needed no more than three or four freighters for their maintenance.

Thus a couple of buildings and a ground-control tower bounded a stretch of ferrocrete on a high, chilly plateau; and that was Trillia's spaceport. Two ships were in. One was being serviced, half its hull plates removed and furry shapes swarming over the emptiness within. The other, assigned to Witweet, stood on landing jacks at the far end of the field. Shaped like a fat torpedo, decorated in floral designs of pink and baby blue, it was as big as a Dromond-class hauler. Yet its payload was under a thousand tons. The primitive systems for drive, control, and life support took up that much room.

"I wish you a just too, too delightful voyage," said the portmaster's voice from the radio. "Would you honor me by accepting an invitation to dinner? My wife has, if I may boast, discovered remarkable culinary attributes of certain seaweeds brought back from Gwinsai; and for my part, dear boy, I would be so interested to hear your opinion of a new verse form with which I am currently experimenting."

"No . . . I thank you, no, impossible, I beg indulgence—" It was hard to tell whether the unevenness of Witweet's response came from terror or from the tobacco smoke that had kept him coughing. He almost flung his vehicle into the spaceship.

Clearance granted, *The Serenity of the Estimable Philosopher Ittypu* lifted into a dawn sky. When Trillia was a dwindling cloud-marbled sapphire among the stars, Harker let out a breath. "We can relax now."

"Where?" Olafsson grumbled. The single cabin barely allowed three humans to crowd together. They'd have to take turns sleeping in the hall that ran aft to the engine room. And their voyage was going to be long. Top pseudovelocity under the snail-powered hyperdrive of this craft would be less than one light-year per day.

"Oh, we can admire the darling murals," Dolgorov fleered. He kicked an intricately painted bulkhead.

Witweet, crouched miserable at the control board, flinched. "I beg you, dear, kind sir, do not scuff the artwork," he said.

"Why should you care?" Dolgorov asked. "You won't be keeping this junk heap."

Witweet wrung his hands. "Defacement is still very wicked. Perhaps the consignee will appreciate my patterns? I spent *such* a time on them, trying to get every teensiest detail correct."

"Is that why your freighters have a single person aboard?" Olafsson laughed. "Always seemed reckless to me, not taking a backup pilot at least. But I suppose two Trillians would get into so fierce an argument about the interior décor that they'd each stalk off in an absolute snit."

"Why, no," said Witweet, a trifle calmer. "We keep personnel down to one because more are not really needed. Piloting between stars is automatic, and the crewbeing is trained in servicing functions. Should he suffer harm en route, the ship will put itself into orbit around the destination planet and can be boarded by others. An extra would thus uselessly occupy space which is often needed for passengers. I am surprised that you, sir, who have set a powerful intellect to prolonged consideration of our astronautical practices, should not have been aware—"

"I was, I was!" Olafsson threw up his hands as far as the overhead permitted. "Ask a rhetorical question and get an oratorical answer."

"May I, in turn, humbly request enlightenment as to your reason for . . . sequestering . . . a spacecraft ludicrously inadequate by every standard of your oh, so sophisticated society?"

"You may." Harker's spirits bubbled from relief of tension. They'd pulled it off. They really had. He sat down—the deck was padded and perfumed—and started a cigarette. Through his bones beat the throb of the gravity drive: energy wasted by a clumsy system. The weight it made underfoot fluctuated slightly in a rhythm that felt wavelike.

"I suppose we may as well call ourselves criminals," he said; the Lenidellian word he must use had milder connotations. "There are people back home who wouldn't leave us alive if they knew who'd done certain things. But we never got rich off them. Now we will."

He had no need for recapitulating except the need to gloat: "You know we came to Trillia half a standard year ago, on a League ship that was paying a short visit to buy art. We had goods of our own to barter with, and announced we were going to settle down for a while and look into the possibility of establishing a permanent trading post with a regular shuttle service to some of the Technic planets. That's what the captain of the ship thought, too. He advised us against it, said it couldn't pay and we'd simply be stuck on Trillia till the next League vessel chanced by, which wouldn't likely be for more than a year. But when we insisted, and gave him passage money, he shrugged," as did Harker.

"You have told me this," Witweet said. "I thrilled to the ecstasy of what I believed was your friendship."

"Well, I did enjoy your company," Harker smiled. "You're not a bad little osco. Mainly, though, we concentrated on you because we'd learned you qualified for our uses—a regular freighter pilot, a bachelor so we needn't fuss with a family, a chatterer who could be pumped for any information we wanted. Seems we gauged well."

"We better have," Dolgorov said gloomily. "Those trade goods cost us everything we could scratch together. I took a steady job for two years, and lived like a lama, to get my share."

"And now we'll be living like fakirs," said Olafsson. "But afterward—afterward!"

"Evidently your whole aim was to acquire a Trillian ship," Witweet said. "My bemusement at this endures."

"We don't actually want the ship as such, except for demonstration purposes," Harker said. "What we want are the plans, the design. Between the vessel itself, and the service manuals aboard, we have that in effect."

Witweet's ears quivered. "Do you mean to publish the data for scientific interest? Surely, to beings whose ancestors went on to better models centuries ago—if, indeed, they ever burdened themselves with something this crude—surely the interest is nil. Unless . . . you think many will pay to see, in order to enjoy mirth at the spectacle of our fumbling efforts?" He spread his arms. "Why, you could have bought complete specifications most cheaply; or, indeed, had you requested of me, I would have been bubbly-happy to obtain a set and make you a gift." On a note of timid hope: "Thus you see, dear boy, drastic action is quite unnecessary. Let us return. I will state you remained aboard by mistake—"

Olafsson guffawed. Dolgorov said, "Not even your authorities can be that sloppy-thinking." Harker ground out his cigarette on the deck, which made the pilot wince, and explained at leisured length:

"We want this ship precisely because it's primitive. Your people weren't in the electronic era when the first human explorers contacted you. They, or some later visitors, brought you texts on physics. Then your bright lads had the theory of such things as gravity control and hyperdrive. But the engineering practice was something else again.

"You didn't have plans for a starship. When you finally got an opportunity to inquire, you found that the idealistic period of Technic civilization was over and you must deal with hardheaded entrepreneurs. And the price was set way beyond what your whole planet could hope to save in League currency. That was just the price for diagrams, not to speak of an actual vessel. I don't know if you are personally aware of the fact—it's no secret—but this is League policy. The member companies are bound by an agreement.

"They won't prevent anyone from entering space on his own. But take your case on Trillia. You had learned in a general way about, oh, transistors, for instance. But that did not set you up to manufacture them. An entire industrial complex is needed for that and for the million other necessary items. To design and build one, with the inevitable mistakes en route, would take decades at a minimum, and would involve regimenting your entire species and living in poverty because every bit of capital has to be reinvested. Well, you Trillians were too sensible to pay that price. You'd proceed more gradually. Yet at the same time, your scientists, all your more adventurous species, were burning to get out into space.

"I agree your decision about that was intelligent, too. You saw you couldn't go directly from your earliest hydrocarbon-fueled engines to a modern starship—to a completely integrated system of thermonuclear power plant, initiative-grade navigation and engineering computers, full-cycle life support, the whole works, using solid-state circuits, molecular-level and nuclear-level transitions, force fields instead of moving parts—an *organism* more energy than matter. No, you wouldn't be able to build that for generations, probably.

"But you could go ahead and develop huge, clumsy, but workable fission-power units. You could use vacuum tubes, glass rectifiers, kilometers of wire, to generate and regulate the necessary forces. You could store data on tape if not in single molecules, retrieve with a cathode-ray scanner if not with a quantum-field pulse, compute with miniaturized gas-filled units that react in microseconds if not with photon interplays that take a nanosecond.

"You're like islanders who had nothing better than canoes till someone stopped by in a nuclear-powered submarine. They couldn't copy that, but they might invent a reciprocating steam engine turning a screw—they might attach an airpipe so it could submerge—and it wouldn't impress the outsiders, but it would cross the ocean too, at its own pace; and it would overawe any neighboring tribes."

He stopped for breath.

"I see," Witweet murmured slowly. His tail switched back and forth. "You can sell our designs to sophonts in a proto-industrial stage of technological development. The idea comes from an excellent brain. But why could you not simply buy the plans for resale elsewhere?"

"The damned busybody League." Dolgorov spat.

"The fact is," Olafsson said, "spacecraft—of advanced type—have been sold to, ah, less advanced peoples in the past. Some of those weren't near industrialization, they were Iron Age barbarians, whose only thought was plundering and conquering. They could do that, given ships which are practically self-piloting, self-maintaining, self-everything. It's cost a good many lives and heavy material losses on border planets. But at least none of the barbarians have been able to duplicate the craft thus far. Hunt every pirate and warlord down, and that ends the problem. Or so the League hopes. It's banned any more such trades."

He cleared his throat. "I don't refer to races like the Trillians, who're obviously capable of reaching the stars by themselves and unlikely to be a menace when they do," he said. "You're free to buy anything you can pay for. The price of certain things is set astronomical mainly to keep you from beginning overnight to compete with the old, established outfits. They prefer a gradual phasing-in of newcomers, so they can adjust.

"But aggressive, warlike cultures, that'd not be interested in reaching a peaceful accommodation—they're something else again. There's a total prohibition on supplying their sort with anything that might help them to get off their planets in less than centuries. If League agents catch you at it, they don't fool around with rehabilitation like a regular government. They shoot you."

Harker grimaced. "I saw once on a telescreen interview," he remarked, "old Nick van Rijn said- he wouldn't shoot that kind of offenders. He'd hang them. A rope is reusable."

"And this ship *can* be copied," Witweet breathed. "A low industrial technology, lower than ours, could tool up to produce a modified design, in a comparatively short time, if guided by a few engineers from the core civilization."

"I trained as an engineer," Harker said. "Likewise Leo; and Einar spent several years on a planet where one royal family has grandiose ambitions."

"But the horror you would unleash!" wailed the Trillian. He stared into their stoniness. "You would never dare go home," he said.

"Don't want to anyway," Harker answered. "Power, wealth, yes, and everything those will buy—we'll have more than we can use up in our lifetimes, at the court of the Militants. Fun, too." He smiled. "A challenge, you know, to build a space navy from zero. I expect to enjoy my work."

"Will not the . . . the Polesotechnic League take measures?"

"That's why we must operate as we have done. They'd learn about a sale of plans, and then they wouldn't stop till they'd found and suppressed our project. But a non-Technic ship that never reported in won't interest them. Our destination is well outside their sphere of normal operations. They needn't discover any hint of what's going on—till an interstellar empire too big for them to break is there. Meanwhile, as we gain resources, we'll have been modernizing our industry and fleet."

"It's all arranged," Olafsson said. "The day we show up in the land of the Militants, bringing the ship we described to them, we'll become princes."

"Kings, later," Dolgorov added. "Behave accordingly, you xeno. We don't need you much. I'd soon as not boot you through an air lock."

Witweet spent minutes just shuddering.

The Serenity, et cetera moved on away from Trillia's golden sun. It had to reach a weaker gravitational field than a human craft would have needed, before its hyperdrive would function.

Harker spent part of that period being shown around, top to bottom and end to end. He'd toured a sister ship before, but hadn't dared ask for demonstrations as thorough as he now demanded. "I want to know this monstrosity we've got, inside out," he said while personally tearing down and rebuilding a cumbersome oxygen renewer. He could do this because most equipment was paired, against the expectation of eventual in-flight down time.

In a hold, among cases of supplies for the research team on Gwinsai, he was surprised to recognize a lean cylindroid, one hundred twenty centimeters long. "But here's a Solar-built courier!" he exclaimed.

Witweet made eager gestures of agreement. He'd been falling over himself to oblige his captors. "For messages in case of emergency, magnificent sir," he babbled. "A hyperdrive unit, an autopilot, a radio to call at journey's end till someone comes and retrieves the enclosed letter—"

"I know, I know. But why not build your own?"

"Well, if you will deign to reflect upon the matter, you will realize that anything we could build would be too slow and unreliable to afford very probable help. Especially since it is most unlikely that, at any given time, another spaceship would be ready to depart Trillia on the instant.

Therefore, this courier is set, as you can see if you wish to examine the program, to go a considerably greater distance—though nevertheless not taking long, your human constructions being superlatively fast—to the planet called, ah, Oasis . . . an Anglic word meaning a lovely, cool, refreshing haven, am I correct?"

Harker nodded impatiently. "You are right. One of the League companies does keep a small base there."

"We have arranged that they will send aid if requested. At a price, to be sure. However, for our poor economy, as ridiculous a hulk as this is still a heavy investment, worth insuring."

"I see. I didn't know you bought such gadgets—not that there'd be a pegged price on them; they don't matter any more than spices or medical equipment. Of course, I couldn't find out every detail in advance, especially not things you people take so for granted that you didn't think to mention them." On impulse, Harker patted the round head. "You know, Witweet, I guess I do like you. I will see you're rewarded for your help."

"Passage home will suffice," the Trillian said quietly, "though I do not know how I can face my kinfolk after having been the instrument of death and ruin for millions of innocents."

"Then don't go home," Harker suggested. "We can't release you for years in any case, to blab our scheme and our coordinates. But we could, however, smuggle in whatever and whoever you wanted, same as for ourselves."

The head rose beneath his palm as the slight form straightened. "Very well," Witweet declared.

That fast? jarred through Harker. *He is nonhuman, yes, but—* The wondering was dissipated by the continuing voice:

"Actually, dear boy, I must disabuse you. We did not buy our couriers, we salvaged them."

"What? Where?"

"Have you heard of a planet named, by its human discoverers, Paradox?"

Harker searched his memory. Before leaving Earth he had consulted every record he could find about this entire stellar neighborhood. Poorly known though it was to men, there had been a huge mass of data— suns, worlds . . . "I think so. Big, isn't it? With a freaky atmosphere."

"Yes." Witweet spoke rapidly. "It gave the original impetus to Technic exploration of our vicinity. But later the men departed. In recent years, when we ourselves became able to pay visits, we found their abandoned camp. A great deal of gear had been left behind, presumably because it was designed for Paradox only and would be of no use elsewhere, hence not worth hauling back. Among these machines we came upon a few couriers. I suppose they had been overlooked. Your civilization can afford profligacy, if I may use that term in due respectfulness."

He crouched, as if expecting a blow. His eyes glittered in the gloom of the hold.

"Hm-m-m." Harker frowned. "I suppose by now you've stripped the place."

"Well, no." Witweet brushed nervously at his rising fur. "Like the men, we saw no use in, for example, tractors designed for a gravity of two-point-eight terrestrial. They can operate well and cheaply on Paradox, since their fuel is crude oil, of which an abundant supply exists near the campsite. But we already had electric-celled grav motors, however archaic they are by your standards. And we do not need weapons like those we found, presumably for protection against animals. We certainly have no intention of colonizing Paradox!"

"Hm-m-m." The human waved, as if to brush off the chattering voice. He slouched off, hands in pockets, pondering.

In the time that followed, he consulted the navigator's bible. His reading knowledge of Lenidellian was fair. The entry for Paradox was as laconic as it would have been in a Technic reference; despite the limited range of their operations, the Trillians had already encountered too many worlds to allow flowery descriptions. Star type and coordinates, orbital elements, mass, density, atmospheric composition, temperature ranges, and the usual rest were listed. There was no notation about habitability, but none was needed. The original explorers hadn't been poisoned or come down with disease, and Trillian metabolism was similar to theirs.

The gravity field was not too strong for this ship to make landing and, later, ascent. Weather shouldn't pose any hazards, given reasonable care in choosing one's path; that was a weakly energized environment. Besides, the vessel was meant for planetfalls, and Witweet was a skilled pilot in his fashion . . .

Harker discussed the idea with Olafsson and Dolgorov. "It won't take but a few days," he said, "and we might pick up something really good. You know I've not been too happy about the Militants' prospects of building an ample industrial base fast enough to suit us. Well, a few machines like this, simple things they can easily copy but designed by good engineers, could make a big difference."

"They're probably rust heaps," Dolgorov snorted. "That was long ago."

"No, durable alloys were available then," Olafsson said. "I like the notion intrinsically. I don't like the thought of our xeno taking us down. He might crash us on purpose."

"That sniveling faggot?" Dolgorov gibed. He jerked his head backward at Witweet, who sat enormous-eyed in the pilot chair listening to a language he did not understand. "By accident, maybe, seeing how scared he is!"

"It's a risk we take at journey's end," Harker reminded them. "Not a real risk. The ship has some ingenious fail-safes built in. Anyhow, I intend to stand over him the whole way down. If he does a single thing wrong, I'll kill him. The controls aren't made for me, but I can get us aloft again, and afterward we can re-rig."

Olafsson nodded. "Seems worth a try," he said. "What can we lose except a little time and sweat?"

Paradox rolled enormous in the viewscreen, a darkling world, the sky-band along its sunrise horizon redder than Earth's, polar caps and winter snowfields gashed by the teeth of mountains, tropical forests and pampas a yellow-brown fading into raw deserts on one side and chopped off on another side by the furious surf of an ocean where three moons fought their tidal wars. The sun was distance-dwarfed, more dull in hue than Sol, nevertheless too bright to look near. Elsewhere, stars filled illimitable blackness.

It was very quiet aboard, save for the mutter of powerplant and ventilators, the breathing of men, their restless shuffling about in the cramped cabin. The air was blued and fouled by cigarette smoke; Witweet would have fled into the corridor, but they made him stay, clutching a perfume-dripping kerchief to his nose.

Harker straightened from the observation screen. Even at full magnification, the rudimentary electro-optical system gave little except blurriness. But he'd practiced on it, while orbiting a satellite, till he felt he could read those wavering traces.

"Campsite and machinery, all right," he said. "No details. Brush has covered everything. When were your people here last, Witweet?"

"Several years back," the Trillian wheezed. "Evidently vegetation grows apace. Do you agree on the safety of a landing?"

"Yes. We may snap a few branches, as well as flatten a lot of shrubs, but we'll back down slowly, the last hundred meters, and we'll keep the radar, sonar, and gravar sweeps going." Harker glanced at his men. "Next thing is to compute our descent pattern," he said. "But first I want to spell out again, point by point, exactly what each of us is to do under exactly what circumstances. I don't aim to take chances."

"Oh, no," Witweet squeaked. "I beg you, dear boy, I beg you the prettiest I can, please don't!"

After the tension of transit, landing was an anticlimax. All at once the engine fell silent. A wind whistled around the hull. Viewscreens showed low, thick-boled trees; fronded brownish leaves; tawny undergrowth; shadowy glimpses of metal objects beneath vines and amidst tall, whipping stalks. The sun stood at late afternoon in a sky almost purple.

Witweet checked the indicators while Harker studied them over his head. "Air breathable, of course," the pilot said, "which frees us of the handicap of having to wear smelly old spacesuits. We should bleed it in gradually, since the pressure is greater than ours at present and we don't want earaches, do we? Temperature—" He shivered delicately. "Be certain you are wrapped up snug before you venture outside."

"You're venturing first," Harker informed him.

"What? Oo-ooh, my good, sweet, darling friend, no, please, no! It is *cold* out there, scarcely above freezing. And once on the ground, no gravity generator to help, why, weight will be tripled. What could I possibly, possibly do? No, let me stay inside, keep the home fires burning— I mean keep the thermostat at a cozy temperature—and, yes, I will make you the nicest pot of tea . . ."

"If you don't stop fluttering and do what you're told, I'll tear your head off," Dolgorov said. "Guess what I'll use your skin for."

"Let's get cracking," Olafsson said. "I don't want to stay in this Helheim any longer than you."

They opened a hatch the least bit. While Paradoxian air seeped in, they dressed as warmly as might be, except for Harker. He intended to stand by the controls for the first investigatory period. The entering gases added a whine to the wind-noise. Their helium content made speech and other sounds higher-pitched, not quite natural; and this would have to be endured for the rest of the journey, since the ship had insufficient reserve tanks to flush out the new atmosphere. A breath of cold got by the heaters, and a rank smell of alien growth.

But you could get used to hearing funny, Harker thought. And the native life might stink, but it was harmless. You couldn't eat it and be nourished, but neither could its germs live off your body. If heavy weapons had been needed here, they were far more likely against large, blundering herbivores than against local tigers.

That didn't mean they couldn't be used in war.

Trembling, eyes squinched half shut, tail wrapped around his muzzle, the rest of him bundled in four layers of kimono, Witweet crept to the personnel lock. Its outer valve swung wide. The gangway went down. Harker grinned to see the dwarfish shape descend, step by step under the sudden harsh hauling of the planet.

"Sure you can move around in that pull?" he asked his companions.

"Sure," Dolgorov grunted. "An extra hundred-fifty kilos? I can backpack more than that, and then it's less well distributed."

"Stay cautious, though. Too damned easy to fall and break bones."

"I'd worry more about the cardiovascular system," Olafsson said. "One can stand three Gs for a while, but not for a very long while. Fluid begins seeping out of the cell walls, the heart feels the strain too much— and we've no gravanol along as the first expedition must have had."

"We'll only be here a few days at most," Harker said, "with plenty of chances to rest inboard."

"Right," Olafsson agreed. "Forward!"

Gripping his blaster, he shuffled onto the gangway. Dolgorov followed.

Below, Witweet huddled. Harker looked out at bleakness, felt the wind slap his face with chill, and was glad he could stay behind. Later he must take his turn outdoors, but for now he could enjoy warmth, decent weight—

The world reached up and grabbed him. Off balance, he fell to the deck. His left hand struck first, pain gushed, he saw the wrist and arm splinter. He screamed. The sound came weak as well as shrill, out of a breast laboring against thrice the heaviness it should have had. At the same time, the lights in the ship went out.

Witweet perched on a boulder. His back was straight in spite of the drag on him, which made his robes hang stiff as if carved on an idol of some minor god of justice. His tail, erect, blew jauntily in the bitter sunset wind; the colors of his garments were bold against murk that rose in the forest around the dead spacecraft.

He looked into the guns of three men, and into the terror that had taken them behind the eyes; and Witweet laughed.

"Put those toys away before you hurt yourselves," he said, using no circumlocutions or honorifics.

"You swine, you filthy treacherous xeno, I'll kill you," Dolgorov groaned. "Slowly."

"First you must catch me," Witweet answered. "By virtue of being small, I have a larger surface-to-volume ratio than you. My bones, my muscles, my veins and capillaries and cell membranes suffer less force per square centimeter than do yours. I can move faster than you, here. I can survive longer."

"You can't outrun a blaster bolt," Olafsson said.

"No. You can kill me with that—a quick, clean death which does not frighten me. Really, because we of Lenidel observe certain customs of courtesy, use certain turns of speech—because our males in particular are encouraged to develop aesthetic interests and compassion—does that mean we are cowardly or effeminate?" The Trillian clicked his tongue. "If you supposed so, you committed an elementary logical fallacy which our philosophers name the does-not-follow."

"Why shouldn't we kill you?"

"That is inadvisable. You see, your only hope is quick rescue by a League ship. The courier can operate here, being a solid-state device. It can reach Oasis and summon a vessel which, itself of similar construction, can also land on Paradox and take off again . . . in time. This would be impossible for a Trillian craft. Even if one were ready to leave, I doubt the Astronautical Senate would permit the pilot to risk descent.

"Well, rescuers will naturally ask questions. I cannot imagine any story which you three men, alone, might concoct that would stand up under the subsequent, inevitable investigation. On the other hand, I can explain to the League's agents that you were only coming along to look into trade possibilities and that we were trapped on Paradox by a faulty autopilot which threw us into a descent curve. I can do this *in detail*, which you could not if you killed me. They will return us all to Trillia, where there is no death penalty."

Witweet smoothed his wind-ruffled whiskers. "The alternative," he finished, "is to die where you are, in a most unpleasant fashion."

Harker's splinted arm gestured back the incoherent Dolgorov. He set an example by holstering his own gun. "I . . . guess we're outsmarted," he said, word by foul-tasting word. "But what happened? Why's the ship inoperable?"

"Helium in the atmosphere," Witweet explained calmly. "The monatomic helium molecule is ooh-how-small. It diffuses through almost every material. Vacuum tubes, glass rectifiers, electronic switches dependent on pure gases, any such device soon becomes poisoned. You, who were used to a technology that had long left this kind of thing behind, did not know the fact, and it did not occur to you as a possibility. We Trillians are, of course, rather acutely aware of the problem. I am the first who ever set foot on Paradox. You should have noted that my courier is a present-day model."

"I see," Olafsson mumbled.

"The sooner we get our message off, the better," Witweet said. "By the way, I assume you are not so foolish as to contemplate the piratical takeover of a vessel of the Polesotechnic League."

"Oh, no!" they said, including Dolgorov, and the other two blasters were sheathed.

"One thing, though," Harker said. A part of him wondered if the pain in him was responsible for his own abnormal self-possession. Counterirritant against dismay? Would he weep after it wore off? "You bargain for your life by promising to have ours spared. How do we know we want your terms? What'll they do to us on Trillia?"

"Entertain no fears," Witweet assured him. "We are not vindictive, as I have heard some species are; nor have we any officious concept of 'rehabilitation.' Wrongdoers are required to make amends to the fullest extent possible. You three have cost my people a valuable ship and whatever cargo cannot be salvaged. You must have technological knowledge to convey, of equal worth. The working conditions will not be intolerable. Probably you can make restitution and win release before you reach old age.

"Now, come, get busy. First we dispatch that courier, then we prepare what is necessary for our survival until rescue."

He hopped down from the rock, which none of them would have been able to do unscathed, and approached them through gathering cold twilight with the stride of a conquerer.

BIBLIOGRAPHY

(of stories about van Rijn, or directly related to him. ASF = *Astounding Science Fiction* or *Analog Science Fact—Science Fiction*)

"Margin of Profit," *ASF*, September 1956

The Man Who Counts, ASF, February–April 1958 (Ace Books, 1958, as *War of the Wing-Men;* Ace Books, 1978, as *Man*)

"Hiding Place," *ASF*, March 1961

"Territory," *ASF*, June 1963

"The Three-Cornered Wheel," *ASF*, October 1963

"The Master Key," *ASF*, July 1964

Trader to the Stars, Doubleday, 1964 (contains "Hiding Place," "Territory," and "The Master Key")

"Trader Team" (original title, "The Trouble Twisters"), *ASF*, July–August 1965

"A Sun Invisible," *ASF*, April 1966

The Troubletwisters, Doubleday, 1966 (contains "The Three-Cornered Wheel," "A Sun Invisible," and "The Trouble Twisters")

"Supernova" (original title, "Day of Burning"), *ASF*, January 1967

Satan's World, ASF, May–August 1968 (Doubleday, 1969)

"Birthright" (original title, "Esau"), *ASF*, February 1970

"A Little Knowledge," *ASF*, August 1971

"The Season of Forgiveness," *Boys' Life*, December 1971

"Lodestar," *Astounding*, ed. Harry Harrison, Random House, 1973

"How to Be Ethnic" (original title, "How to Be Ethnic in One Easy Lesson"), *Future Quest*, ed. Roger Elwood, Avon Books, 1974

Mirkheim, Berkley Books, 1977

The Earth Book of Stormgate, contains the short stories and novelettes above, less those in *Trader* and *Troubletwisters* but including *Man;* Berkley Books, 1978

THE WENDELL URTH SERIES

by Isaac Asimov

I suppose it is common for an early writer to long to get into some particular magazine. Even if he is a regular contributor to some magazine already, he may long to get into some other particular magazine.

In my early youth, for instance, when I was a contributor to *Astounding Science Fiction,* the best magazine in its field, I nevertheless longed to sell something to its fantasy sister magazine, *Unknown.* In a two-year period from mid-1939 to mid-1941, I submitted five stories to *Unknown*—and all were rejected. Then, in April 1943, I tried a sixth time and succeeded. But though my story was accepted, the magazine ceased publication before it could be printed.

Ten years later, by which time I had grown to be much better known, I had a similar desire to get into *Ellery Queen's Mystery Magazine.* I had, after all, written science fiction stories which were, in a way, mystery stories as well. I had even written and published "The Caves of Steel," which, although a science fiction novel, was a classic mystery in every way.

Why, then, should I not sell to *EQMM? EQMM* paid higher rates than the science fiction magazines did, and reached a different and larger audience. A sale to *EQMM* would afford me a visible breakthrough into a second field of fiction, and I was feeling, increasingly, the need to move beyond the beloved, but narrow, bounds of science fiction.

Naturally, it didn't occur to me to write a "straight" mystery. I was well known for my science fiction, and it seemed to me that *EQMM* would be interested in a science fiction mystery, if only for novelty's sake, and would recognize me as a specialist in the field.

I therefore decided to write a story about a murder on the Moon and to have it solved by some technique specifically applicable to the Moon. I would even call it "Murder on the Moon."

It struck me, too, that I might make the story symbolize my movement from science fiction to the classic mystery by having the first half of the story pure science fiction, and the second half pure detection.

To do that meant I would have to write an inverted detective story. The crime would be described in the first half, complete with the identity of the criminal and his method of operation. In the second half, the accent would be not on who committed the crime, or how, or why—but simply on how the investigator uncovers the details and pins the criminal.

This was not the usual method of telling a mystery story, but it was by no means new. R. Austin Freeman had pioneered it in his well-thought-of Dr. Thorndyke stories, so I knew the gimmick was an acceptable one.

Next I needed a detective.

There is a long history of eccentric, humorous or whimsical detectives in the history of mystery fiction. Sherlock Holmes himself lives on because of his many peculiar and out-of-the-way character traits. There is Sir Henry Merrivale and his egotism and raffish sense of humor; there is Nero Wolfe, among whose tissue of eccentricities is his refusal to leave his house on business; there is Hercule Poirot and his passion for symmetry and order.

So I decided on a whimsical detective.

I myself am thought to be whimsical in some respects. I won't fly in airplanes and already by 1953 I had encountered innumerable people who seemed to find it incredible that someone who wrote science fiction and who led his protagonists all over the Galaxy should himself refuse to fly.*

Why, then shouldn't I capitalize on this seeming contradiction and even strengthen it?

I would have a detective who would be involved with other worlds not by way of fiction, as I was, but by way of his serious profession. He would be an extra-terrologist, a specialist in the environments and properties of worlds other than Earth. *And* he would be a stay-at-home. He would not merely refuse to fly, as I did; he would refuse to enter any conveyance and would confine himself to his office and to places he could reach by walking—to his university campus, in other words.

Murders in space would be brought to him and he would solve them by means of arm-chair detection—another respectable ploy in mystery fiction. To symbolize this contradiction, I would name my extra-terrologist Urth (Earth). The first name, Wendell, was chosen merely because it seemed to make a euphonious combination.

Appearance? Well, if I were going to have a whimsical detective, he might as well have a whimsical appearance and whimsical behavior. At that time, I had just become acquainted with the great mathematician, Norbert Wiener, and if there were anyone whimsical in appearance and behavior, it was he—so I adopted both. When Wendell Urth talked or acted, I thought Norbert Wiener.

I was now ready, and on October 27, 1953, I began "Murder on the Moon." I finished it on November 3, and sent it in to *EQMM*.

Alas, my plan failed; it was rejected. In dejection, I then sent it on to science fiction outlets. It was rejected by *Astounding,* by *Galaxy,* and by *Argosy*. I submitted it to Ballantine for inclusion in an anthology of originals and they rejected it, too. It was not until June 30, 1954, that I finally managed to sell it to *The Magazine of Fantasy and Science Fiction (F&SF),* under the altered name of "The Singing Bell."

I was delighted with the sale and decided not to let Wendell Urth die. I therefore wrote other space mysteries involving him.

* My usual answer is, "Mystery writers don't commit murders and fantasy writers don't talk to rabbits, so why should a science fiction writer have to fly?"

And what about *EQMM?* Did my failure there endure forever?

No, a long literary lifetime has its advantages and, sixteen years later, in March 1971 (by which time I had become even better-known), I wrote a "straight" mystery short story about an organization called "The Black Widowers" which was modeled on a club to which I actually belong. That story was accepted by *EQMM* and I at once made it the first story of a series. The thirtieth story of the Black Widower series is soon (as I write this) to appear.

The Talking Stone

The asteroid belt is large and its human occupancy small. Larry Vernadsky, in the seventh month of his year-long assignment to Station Five, wondered with increasing frequency if his salary could possibly compensate for a nearly solitary confinement seventy million miles from Earth. He was a slight youth, who did not bear the look of either a spationautical engineer or an asteroid man. He had blue eyes and butter-yellow hair and an invincible air of innocence that masked a quick mind and an isolation-sharpened bump of curiosity.

Both the look of innocence and the bump of curiosity served him well on board the *Robert Q.*

When the *Robert Q.* landed on the outer platform of Station Five, Vernadsky was on board almost immediately. There was an eager delight about him which, in a dog, would have been accompanied by a vibrating tail and a happy cacophony of barks.

The fact that the captain of the *Robert Q.* met his grins with a stern sour silence that sat heavily on his thick-featured face made no difference. As far as Vernadsky was concerned the ship was yearned-for company and was welcome. It was welcome to any amount of the millions of gallons of ice or any of the tons of frozen food concentrates stacked away in the hollowed-out asteroid that served as Station Five. Vernadsky was ready with any power tool that might be necessary, any replacement that might be required for any hyperatomic motor.

Vernadsky was grinning all over his boyish face as he filled out the routine form, writing it out quickly for later conversion into computer notation for filing. He put down ship's name and serial number, engine number, field generator number, and so on, port of embarkation ("asteroids, damned lot of them, don't know which was last" and Vernadsky simply wrote "Belt" which was the usual abbreviation for "asteroid belt"); port of destination ("Earth"); reason for stopping ("stuttering hyperatomic drive").

"How many in your crew, Captain?" asked Vernadsky, as he looked over ship's papers.

The captain said, "Two. Now how about looking over the hyperatomics? We've got a shipment to make." His cheeks were blue with dark stubble, his bearing that of a hardened and lifelong asteroid miner, yet his speech was that of an educated, almost a cultured, man.

"Sure." Vernadsky lugged his diagnostic kit to the engine room, followed by the captain. He tested circuits, vacuum degree, forcefield density with easy-going efficiency.

He could not help wondering about the captain. Despite his own dislike for his surroundings he realized dimly that there were some who found fascination in the vast emptiness and freedom of space. Yet he guessed that a man like this captain was not an asteroid miner for the love of solitude alone.

He said, "Any special type of ore you handle?"

The captain frowned and said, "Chromium and manganese."

"That so? . . . I'd replace the Jenner manifold, if I were you."

"Is that what's causing the trouble?"

"No, it isn't. But it's a little beat-up. You'd be risking another failure within a million miles. As long as you've got the ship in here—"

"All right, replace it. But find the stutter, will you?"

"Doing my best, Captain."

The captain's last remark was harsh enough to abash even Vernadsky. He worked awhile in silence, then got to his feet. "You've got a gamma-fogged semireflector. Every time the positron beam circles round to its position the drive flickers out for a second. You'll have to replace it."

"How long will it take?"

"Several hours. Maybe twelve."

"What? I'm behind schedule."

"Can't help it." Vernadsky remained cheerful. "There's only so much I can do. The system has to be flushed for three hours with helium before I can get inside. And then I have to calibrate the new semireflector and that takes time. I could get it almost right in minutes, but that's only almost right. You'd break down before you reach the orbit of Mars."

The captain glowered. "Go ahead. Get started."

Vernadsky carefully maneuvered the tank of helium on board the ship. With ship's pseudo-grav generators shut off, it weighed virtually nothing, but it had its full mass and inertia. That meant careful handling if it were to make turns correctly. The maneuvers were all the more difficult since Vernadsky himself was without weight.

It was because his attention was concentrated entirely on the cylinder that he took a wrong turn in the crowded quarters and found himself momentarily in a strange and darkened room.

He had time for one startled shout and then two men were upon him, hustling his cylinder, closing the door behind him.

He said nothing, while he hooked the cylinder to the intake valve of the motor and listened to the soft, soughing noise as the helium flushed the interior, slowly washing absorbed radioactive gases into the all-accepting emptiness of space.

Then curiosity overcame prudence and he said, "You've got a silicony aboard ship, Captain. A big one."

The captain turned to face Vernadsky slowly. He said in a voice from which all expression had been removed, "Is that right?"

"I saw it. How about a better look?"

"Why?"

Vernadsky grew imploring. "Oh, look, Captain, I've been on this rock over half a year. I've read everything I could get hold of on the asteroids, which means all sorts of things about the siliconies. And I've never seen even a little one. Have a heart."

"I believe there's a job here to do."

"Just helium-flushing for hours. There's nothing else to be done till that's over. How come you carry a silicony about, anyway, Captain?"

"A pet. Some people like dogs. I like siliconies."

"Have you got it talking?"

The captain flushed. "Why do you ask?"

"Some of them have talked. Some of them read minds, even."

"What are you? An expert on these damn things?"

"I've been reading about them. I told you. Come on, Captain. Let's have a look."

Vernadsky tried not to show that he noticed that there was the captain facing him and a crewman on either side of him. Each of the three was larger than he was, each weightier, each—he felt sure—was armed.

Vernadsky said, "Well, what's wrong? I'm not going to steal the thing. I just want to see it."

It may have been the unfinished repair job that kept him alive at that moment. Even more so, perhaps, it was his look of cheerful and almost moronic innocence that stood him in good stead.

The captain said, "Well, then, come on."

And Vernadsky followed, his agile mind working and his pulse definitely quickened.

Vernadsky stared with considerable awe and just a little revulsion at the gray creature before him. It was quite true that he had never seen a silicony, but he had seen trimensional photographs and read descriptions. Yet there is something in a real presence for which neither words nor photographs are substitutes.

Its skin was of an oily smooth grayness. Its motions were slow, as became a creature who burrowed in stone and was more than half stone itself. There was no writhing of muscles beneath that skin; instead it moved in slabs as thin layers of stone slid greasily over one another.

It had a general ovoid shape, rounded above, flattened below, with two sets of appendages. Below were the "legs," set radially. They totaled six and ended in sharp flinty edges, reinforced by metal deposits. Those edges could cut through rock, breaking it into edible portions.

On the creature's flat undersurface, hidden from view unless the silicony were overturned, was the one opening into its interior. Shredded rocks entered that interior. Within, limestone and hydrated silicates reacted to form the silicones out of which the creature's tissues were built. Excess silica re-emerged from the opening as hard white pebbly excretions.

How extraterrologists had puzzled over the smooth pebbles that lay scattered in small hollows within the rocky structure of the asteroids until the siliconies were first discovered. And how they marveled at the manner in which the creatures made silicones—those silicone-oxygen polymers with hydrocarbon side chains—perform so many of the functions that proteins performed in terrestrial life.

From the highest point on the creature's back came the remaining appendages, two inverse cones hollowed in opposing directions and fitting snugly into parallel recesses running down the back, yet capable of lifting upward a short way. When the silicony burrowed through rock, the "ears" were retracted for streamlining. When it rested in a hollowed-out cavern, they could lift for better and more sensitive reception. Their vague resemblance to a rabbit's ears made the name *silicony* inevitable. The more serious extraterrologists, who referred to such creatures habitually as *Siliconeus asteroidea,* thought the "ears" might have something to do with the rudimentary telepathic powers the beasts possessed. A minority had other notions.

The silicony was flowing slowly over an oil-smeared rock. Other such rocks lay scattered in one corner of the room and represented, Vernadsky knew, the creature's food supply. Or at least it was its tissue-building supply. For sheer energy, he had read, that alone would not do.

Vernadsky marveled. "It's a monster. It's more than a foot across."

The captain grunted noncommittally.

"Where did you get it?" asked Vernadsky.

"One of the rocks."

"Well, listen, two inches is about the biggest anyone's found. You could sell this to some museum or university on Earth for a couple of thousand dollars, maybe."

The captain shrugged. "Well, you've seen it. Let's get back to the hyperatomics."

His hard grip was on Vernadsky's elbow and he was turning away, when there was an interruption in the form of a slow and slurring voice, a hollow and gritty one.

It was made by the carefully modulated friction of rock against rock and Vernadsky stared in near horror at the speaker.

It was the silicony, suddenly becoming a talking stone. It said, "The man wonders if this thing can talk."

Vernadsky whispered, "For the love of space. It does!"

"All right," said the captain impatiently, "you've seen it and heard it, too. Let's go now."

"And it reads minds," said Vernadsky.

The silicony said, "Mars rotates in two four hours three seven and one half minutes. Jupiter's density is one point two two. Uranus was discovered in the year one seven eight one. Pluto is the planet which is most far. Sun is heaviest with a mass of two zero zero zero zero zero zero . . ."

The captain pulled Vernadsky away. Vernadsky, half-walking backward, half-stumbling, listened with fascination to the fading bumbling of zeros.

He said, "Where does it pick up all that stuff, Captain?"

"There's an old astronomy book we read to him. Real old."

"From before space travel was invented," said one of the crew members in disgust. "Ain't even a fillum. Regular print."

"Shut up," said the captain.

Vernadsky checked the outflow of helium for gamma radiation and eventually it was time to end the flushing and work in the interior. It was a painstaking job, and Vernadsky interrupted it only once for coffee and a breather.

He said, with innocence beaming in his smile, "You know the way I figure it, Captain? That thing lives inside rock, inside some asteroid all its life. Hundreds of years, maybe. It's a damn big thing, and it's probably a lot smarter than the run-of-the-mill silicony. Now you pick it up and it finds out the universe isn't rock. It finds out a trillion things it never imagined. That's why it's interested in astronomy. It's this new world, all these new ideas it gets in the book and in human minds, too. Don't you think that's so?"

He wanted desperately to smoke the captain out, get something concrete he could hang his deductions on. For this reason he risked telling what must be half the truth, the lesser half, of course.

But the captain, leaning against a wall with his arms folded, said only, "When will you be through?"

It was his last comment and Vernadsky was obliged to rest content. The motor was adjusted finally to Vernadsky's satisfaction, and the captain paid the reasonable fee in cash, accepted his receipt, and left in a blaze of ship's hyper-energy.

Vernadsky watched it go with an almost unbearable excitement. He made his way quickly to his sub-etheric sender.

"I've got to be right," he muttered to himself. "I've *got* to be."

Patrolman Milt Hawkins received the call in the privacy of his home station on Patrol Station Asteroid No. 72. He was nursing a two-day stubble, a can of iced beer, and a film viewer, and the settled melancholy on his ruddy, wide-cheeked face was as much the product of loneliness as was the forced cheerfulness in Vernadsky's eyes.

Patrolman Hawkins found himself looking into those eyes and was glad. Even though it was only Vernadsky, company was company. He gave him the big hello and listened luxuriously to the sound of a voice without worrying too strenuously concerning the contents of the speech.

Then suddenly amusement was gone and both ears were on the job and he said, "Hold it. Ho—ld it. What are you talking about?"

"Haven't you been listening, you dumb cop? I'm talking my heart out to you."

"Well, deal it out in smaller pieces, will you? What's this about a silicony?"

"This guy's got one on board. He calls it a pet and feeds it greasy rocks."

"Huh? I swear, a miner on the asteroid run would make a pet out of a piece of cheese if he could get it to talk back to him."

"Not just *a* silicony. Not one of these little inch jobs. It's over a foot across. Don't you get it? Space, you'd think a guy would know something about the asteroids, living out here."

"All right. Suppose you tell me."

"Look, greasy rocks build tissues, but where does a silicony that size get its energy from?"

"I couldn't tell you."

"Directly from— Have you got anyone around you right now?"

"Right now, no. I wish there were."

"You won't in a minute. Siliconies get their energy by the direct absorption of gamma rays."

"Says who?"

"Says a guy called Wendell Urth. He's a big-shot extraterrologist. What's more, he says that's what the silicony's ears are for." Vernadsky put his two forefingers to his temples and wiggled them. "Not telepathy at all. They detect gamma radiation at levels no human instrument can detect."

"Okay. Now what?" asked Hawkins. But he was growing thoughtful.

"Now this. Urth says there isn't enough gamma radiation on any asteroid to support siliconies more than an inch or two long. Not enough radioactivity. So here we have one a foot long, a good fifteen inches."

"Well—"

"So it has to come from an asteroid just riddled with the stuff, lousy with uranium, solid with gamma rays. An asteroid with enough radioactivity to be warm to the touch and off the regular orbit patterns so that no one's come across it. Only suppose some smart boy landed on the asteroid by happenstance and noticed the warmth of the rocks and got to thinking. This captain of the *Robert Q.* is no rock-hopping ignoramus. He's a shrewd guy."

"Go on."

"Suppose he blasts off chunks for assay and comes across a giant silicony. Now he *knows* he's got the most unbelievable strike in all history. And he doesn't need assays. The silicony can lead him to the rich veins."

"Why should it?"

"Because it wants to learn about the universe. Because it's spent a thousand years, maybe, under rock, and it's just discovered the stars. It can read minds and it could learn to talk. It could make a deal. Listen, the captain would jump at it. Uranium mining is a state monopoly. Unlicensed miners aren't even allowed to carry counters. It's a perfect setup for the captain."

Hawkins said, "Maybe you're right."

"No maybe at all. You should have seen them standing around me while I watched the silicony, ready to jump me if I said one funny word. You should have seen them drag me out after two minutes."

Hawkins brushed his unshaven chin with his hand and made a mental estimate of the time it would take him to shave. He said, "How long can you keep the boy at your station?"

"Keep him! Space, he's gone!"

"What! Then what the devil is all this talk about? Why did you let him get away?"

"Three guys," said Vernadsky patiently, "each one bigger than I am, each one armed, and each one ready to kill, I'll bet. What did you want me to do?"

"All right, but what do we do now?"

"Come out and pick them up. That's simple enough. I was fixing their semireflectors and I fixed them my way. Their power will shut off completely within ten thousand miles. And I installed a tracer in the Jenner manifold."

Hawkins goggled at Vernadsky's grinning face. "Holy Toledo."

"And don't get anyone else in on this. Just you, me, and the police cruiser. They'll have no energy and we'll have a cannon or two. They'll tell us where the uranium asteroid is. We locate it, *then* get in touch with Patrol Headquarters. We will deliver unto them, three, count them, three, uranium smugglers, one giant-size silicony like nobody on Earth ever saw, and one, I repeat, one great big fat chunk of uranium ore like nobody on Earth saw, either. And you make a lieutenancy and I get promoted to a permanent Earth-side job. Right?"

Hawkins was dazed. "Right," he yelled. "I'll be right out there."

They were almost upon the ship before spotting it visually by the weak glinting of reflected sunlight.

Hawkins said, "Didn't you leave them enough power for ship's lights? You didn't throw off their emergency generator, did you?"

Vernadsky shrugged. "They're saving power, hoping they'll get picked up. Right now, they're putting everything they've got into a sub-etheric call, I'll bet."

"If they are," said Hawkins dryly, "I'm not picking it up."

"You're not?"

"Not a thing."

The police cruiser spiraled closer. Their quarry, its power off, was drifting through space at a steady ten thousand miles an hour.

The cruiser matched it, speed for speed, and drifted inward.

A sick expression crossed Hawkins' face. "Oh, *no!*"

"What's the matter?"

"The ship's been hit. A meteor. Lord knows there are enough of them in the asteroid belt."

All the verve washed out of Vernadsky's face and voice. "Hit? Are they wrecked?"

"There's a hole in it the size of a barn door. Sorry, Vernadsky, but this might not look good."

Vernadsky closed his eyes and swallowed hard. He knew what Hawkins meant. Vernadsky had deliberately misrepaired a ship, a procedure which could be judged a felony. And death as a result of a felony was murder.

He said, "Look, Hawkins, you know why I did it."

"I know what you've told me and I'll testify to that if I have to. But if this ship wasn't smuggling . . ."

He didn't finish the statement. Nor did he have to.

They entered the smashed ship in full spacesuit cover.

The *Robert Q.* was a shambles, inside and out. Without power, there was no chance of raising the feeblest screen against the rock that hit them or of detecting it in time or of avoiding it if they had detected it. It had caved in the ship's hull as though it were so much aluminum foil. It had smashed the pilot room, evacuated the ship's air, and killed the three men on board.

One of the crew had been slammed against the wall by the impact and was so much frozen meat. The captain and the other crewman lay in stiff attitudes, skins congested with frozen bloodclots where the air, boiling out of the blood, had broken the vessels.

Vernadsky, who had never seen this form of death in space, felt sick, but he fought against vomiting messily inside his spacesuit and succeeded.

He said, "Let's test the ore they're carrying. It's *got* to be alive." It's *got* to be, he told himself. It's *got* to be.

The door to the hold had been warped by the force of collision and there was a gap half an inch wide where it no longer met the frame.

Hawkins lifted the counter he held in his gauntleted hand and held its mica window to that gap.

It chattered like a million magpies.

Vernadsky said, with infinite relief, "I told you so."

His misrepair of the ship was now only the ingenious and praiseworthy fulfillment of a citizen's loyal duty and the meteor collision that had brought death to three men merely a regrettable accident.

It took two blaster bolts to break the twisted door loose, and tons of rock met their flashlights.

Hawkins lifted two chunks of moderate size and dropped them gingerly into one of the suit's pockets. "As exhibits," he said, "and for assay."

"Don't keep them near the skin too long," warned Vernadsky.

"The suit will protect me till I get it back to ship. It's not pure uranium, you know."

"Pretty near, I'll bet." Every inch of his cockiness was back.

Hawkins looked about. "Well, this tears things. We've stopped a smuggling ring, maybe, or part of one. But what next?"

"The uranium asteroid—uh, oh!"

"Right. Where is it? The only ones who know are dead."

"Space!" And again Vernadsky's spirits were dashed. Without the asteroid itself, they had only three corpses and a few tons of uranium ore. Good, but not spectacular. It would mean a citation, yes, but he wasn't after a citation. He wanted promotion to a permanent Earth-side job and that required something.

He yelled, "For the love of space, the *silicony!* It can live in a vacuum. It lives in a vacuum all the time and *it* knows where the asteroid is."

"Right!" said Hawkins, with instant enthusiasm. "Where is the thing?"

"Aft," cried Vernadsky. "This way."

The silicony glinted in the light of their flashes. It moved and was alive.

Vernadsky's heart beat madly with excitement. "We've got to move it, Hawkins."

"Why?"

"Sound won't carry in a vacuum, for the love of space. We've got to get it into the cruiser."

"All right. All right."

"We can't put a suit around it with a radio transmitter, you know."

"I said all right."

They carried it gingerly and carefully, their metal-sheathed fingers handling the greasy surface of the creature almost lovingly.

Hawkins held it while kicking off the *Robert Q.*

It lay in the control room of the cruiser now. The two men had removed their helmets and Hawkins was shucking his suit. Vernadsky could not wait.

He said, "You can read our minds?"

He held his breath until finally the gratings of rock surfaces modulated themselves into words. To Vernadsky no finer sound could, at the moment, be imagined.

The silicony said, "Yes." Then he said, "Emptiness all about. Nothing."

"What?" said Hawkins.

Vernadsky shushed him. "The trip through space just now, I guess. It must have impressed him."

He said to the silicony, shouting his words as though to make his thoughts clearer, "The men who were with you gathered uranium, special ore, radiations, energy."

"They wanted food," came the weak, gritty sound.

Of course! It was food to the silicony. It was an energy source. Vernadsky said, "You showed them where they could get it?"

"Yes."

Hawkins said, "I can hardly hear the thing."

"There's something wrong with it," said Vernadsky worriedly. He shouted again, "Are you well?"

"Not well. Air gone at once. Something wrong inside."

Vernadsky muttered. "The sudden decompression must have damaged it. Oh, Lord— Look, you know what I want. Where is your home? The place with the food?"

The two men were silent, waiting.

The silicony's ears lifted slowly, very slowly, trembled, and fell back. "There," it said. "Over there."

"Where?" screamed Vernadsky.

"There."

Hawkins said, "It's doing something. It's pointing in some way."

"Sure, only we don't know in what way."

"Well, what do you expect it to do? Give the coordinates?"

Vernadsky said at once, "Why not?" He turned again to the silicony as it lay huddled on the floor. It was motionless now and there was a dullness to its exterior that looked ominous.

Vernadsky said, "The captain knew where your eating place was. He had numbers concerning it, didn't he?" He prayed that the silicony would understand, that it would read his thoughts and not merely listen to his words.

"Yes," said the silicony in a rock-against-rock sigh.

"Three sets of numbers," said Vernadsky. There would have to be three. Three coordinates in space with dates attached, giving three positions of the asteroid in its orbit about the sun. From these data the orbit could be calculated in full and its position determined at any time. Even planetary perturbations could be accounted for, roughly.

"Yes," said the silicony, lower still.

"What were they? What were the numbers? Write them down, Hawkins. Get paper."

But the silicony said, "Do not know. Numbers not important. Eating place there."

Hawkins said, "That's plain enough. It didn't need the coordinates, so it paid no attention to them."

The silicony said, "Soon not"—a long pause, and then slowly, as though testing a new and unfamiliar word—"alive. Soon"—an even longer pause—"dead. What after death?"

"Hang on," implored Vernadsky. "Tell me, did the captain write down these figures anywhere?"

The silicony did not answer for a long minute and then, while both men bent so closely that their heads almost touched over the dying stone, it said, "What after death?"

Vernadsky shouted, "One answer. Just one. The captain must have written down the numbers. Where? Where?"

The silicony whispered, "On the asteroid."

And it never spoke again.

It was a dead rock, as dead as the rock which gave it birth, as dead as the walls of the ship, as dead as a dead human.

And Vernadsky and Hawkins rose from their knees and stared hopelessly at each other.

"It makes no sense," said Hawkins. "Why should he write the coordinates on the asteroid? That's like locking a key inside the cabinet it's meant to open."

Vernadsky shook his head. "A fortune in uranium. The biggest strike in history and we don't know where it is."

H. Seton Davenport looked about him with an odd feeling of pleasure. Even in repose, there was usually something hard about his lined face with its prominent nose. The scar on his right cheek, his black hair, startling eyebrows, and dark complexion all combined to make him look every bit the incorruptible agent of the Terrestrial Bureau of Investigation that he actually was.

Yet now something almost like a smile tugged at his lips as he looked about the large room, in which dimness made the rows of book-films appear endless, and specimens of who-knows-what from who-knows-where bulk mysteriously. The complete disorder, the air of separation, almost insulation, from the world, made the room look unreal. It made it look every bit as unreal as its owner.

That owner sat in a combination armchair-desk which was bathed in the only focus of bright light in the room. Slowly he turned the sheets of official reports he held in his hand. His hand moved otherwise only to adjust the thick spectacles which threatened at any moment to fall completely from his round and completely unimpressive nubbin of a nose. His paunch lifted and fell quietly as he read.

He was Dr. Wendell Urth, who, if the judgment of experts counted for anything, was Earth's most outstanding extraterrologist. On any subject outside Earth men came to him, though Dr. Urth had never in his adult life been more than an hour's-walk distance from his home on the University campus.

He looked up solemnly at Inspector Davenport. "A very intelligent man, this young Vernadsky," he said.

"To have deduced all he did from the presence of the silicony? Quite so," said Davenport.

"No, no. The deduction was a simple thing. Unavoidable, in fact. A noodle would have seen it. I was referring"—and his glance grew a trifle censorious—"to the fact that the youngster had read of my experiments concerning the gamma-ray sensitivity of *Siliconeus asteroidea.*"

"Ah, yes," said Davenport. Of course, Dr. Urth was the expert on siliconies. It was why Davenport had come to consult him. He had only one question for the man, a simple one, yet Dr. Urth had thrust out his full lips, shaken his ponderous head, and asked to see all the documents in the case.

Ordinarily that would have been out of the question, but Dr. Urth had recently been of considerable use to the T.B.I. in that affair of the Singing Bells of Luna and the singular non-alibi shattered by Moon gravity, and the Inspector had yielded.

Dr. Urth finished the reading, laid the sheets down on his desk, yanked his shirttail out of the tight confines of his belt with a grunt and rubbed his glasses with it. He stared through the glasses at the light to see the effects of his cleaning, replaced them precariously on his nose, and clasped his hands on his paunch, stubby fingers interlacing.

"Your question again, Inspector?"

Davenport said patiently, "Is it true, in your opinion, that a silicony of the size and type described in the report could only have developed on a world rich in uranium—"

"Radioactive material," interrupted Dr. Urth. "Thorium, perhaps, though probably uranium."

"Is your answer yes, then?"

"Yes."

"How big would the world be?"

"A mile in diameter, perhaps," said the extraterrologist thoughtfully. "Perhaps even more."

"How many tons of uranium, or radioactive material, rather?"

"In the trillions. Minimum."

"Would you be willing to put all that in the form of a signed opinion in writing?"

"Of course."

"Very well then, Dr. Urth." Davenport got to his feet, reached for his hat with one hand and the file of reports with the other. "That is all we need."

But Dr. Urth's hand moved to the reports and rested heavily upon them. "Wait. How will you find the asteroid?"

"By looking. We'll assign a volume of space to every ship made available to us and—just look."

"The expense, the time, the effort! And you'll never find it."

"One chance in a thousand. We might."

"One chance in a million. You won't."

"We can't let the uranium go without some try. Your professional opinion makes the prize high enough."

"But there is a better way to find the asteroid. *I* can find it."

Davenport fixed the extraterrologist with a sudden, sharp glance. Despite appearances Dr. Urth was anything but a fool. He had personal experience of that. There was therefore just a bit of half-hope in his voice as he said, "How can you find it?"

"First," said Dr. Urth, "my price."

"Price?"

"Or fee, if you choose. When the government reaches the asteroid, there may be another large-size silicony on it. Siliconies are very valuable. The only form of life with solid silicone for tissues and liquid silicone as a circulating fluid. The answer to the question whether the asteroids were once part of a single planetary body may rest with them. Any number of other problems . . . Do you understand?"

"You mean you want a large silicony delivered to you?"

"Alive and well. And free of charge. Yes."

Davenport nodded. "I'm sure the government will agree. Now what have you on your mind?"

Dr. Urth said quietly, as though explaining everything, "The silicony's remark."

Davenport looked bewildered. "What remark?"

"The one in the report. Just before the silicony died. Vernadsky was asking it where the captain had written down the coordinates, and it said, 'On the asteroid.' "

A look of intense disappointment crossed Davenport's face. "Great space, Doctor, we know that, and we've gone into every angle of it. Every possible angle. It means nothing."

"Nothing at all, Inspector?"

"Nothing of importance. Read the report again. The silicony wasn't even listening to Vernadsky. He was feeling life depart and he was wondering about it. Twice, it asked, 'What after death?' Then, as Vernadsky kept questioning it, it said, 'On the asteroid.' Probably it never heard Vernadsky's question. It was answering its own question. It thought that after death it would return to its own asteroid; to its home, where it would be safe once more. That's all."

Dr. Urth shook his head. "You are too much a poet, you know. You imagine too much. Come, it is an interesting problem and let us see if you can't solve it for yourself. Suppose the silicony's remark *were* an answer to Vernadsky."

"Even so," said Davenport impatiently, "how would it help? *Which* asteroid? The uranium asteroid? We can't find it, so we can't find the coordinates. Some other asteroid which the *Robert Q.* had used as a home base? We can't find that either."

"How you avoid the obvious, Inspector. Why don't you ask yourself what the phrase 'on the asteroid' means to the silicony. Not to you or to me, but to the silicony."

Davenport frowned. "Pardon me, Doctor?"

"I'm speaking plainly. What did the word *asteroid* mean to the silicony?"

"The silicony learned about space out of an astronomy text that was read to it. I suppose the book explained what an asteroid was."

"Exactly," crowed Dr. Urth, putting a finger to the side of his snub nose. "And how would the definition go? An asteroid is a small body, smaller than the planets, moving about the sun in an orbit which, generally speaking, lies between those of Mars and Jupiter. Wouldn't you agree?"

"I suppose so."

"And what is the *Robert Q.?*"

"You mean the ship?"

"That's what *you* call it," said Dr. Urth. "The *ship*. But the astronomy book was an ancient one. It made no mention of ships in space. One of the crewmen said as much. He said it dated from before space flight. Then what is the *Robert Q.?* Isn't it a small body, smaller than the planets? And while the silicony was aboard, wasn't it moving about the sun in an orbit which, generally speaking, lay between those of Mars and Jupiter?"

"You mean the silicony considered the ship as just another asteroid, and when he said 'on the asteroid,' he meant 'on the ship'?"

"Exactly. I told you I would make you solve the problem for yourself."

No expression of joy or relief lightened the gloom on the Inspector's face. "That is no solution, Doctor."

But Dr. Urth blinked slowly at him and the bland look on his round face became, if anything, blander and more childlike in its uncomplicated pleasure. "Surely it is."

"Not at all. Dr. Urth, we didn't reason it out as you did. We dismissed the silicony's remark completely. But still, don't you suppose we searched the *Robert Q.?* We took it apart piece by piece, plate by plate. We just about unwelded the thing."

"And you found nothing?"

"Nothing."

"Perhaps you did not look in the right place."

"We looked in *every* place." He stood up, as though to go. "You understand, Dr. Urth? When we got through with the ship there was no possibility of those coordinates existing anywhere on it."

"Sit down, Inspector," said Dr. Urth calmly. "You are still not considering the silicony's statement properly. Now the silicony learned English by collecting a word here and a word there. It couldn't speak idiomatic English. Some of its statements, as quoted, show that. For instance, it said, 'the planet which is most far' instead of 'the farthest planet.' You see?"

"Well?"

"Someone who cannot speak a language idiomatically either uses the idioms of his own language translated word by word or else he simply uses foreign words according to their literal meaning. The silicony had no spoken language of its own so it could only make use of the second alternative. Let's be literal, then. He said, *'on* the asteroid,' Inspector. *On* it. He didn't mean on a piece of paper, he meant on the ship, literally."

"Dr. Urth," said Davenport sadly, "when the Bureau searches, it searches. There were no mysterious inscriptions *on* the ship either."

Dr. Urth looked disappointed. "Dear me, Inspector. I keep hoping you will see the answer. Really, you have had so many hints."

Davenport drew in a slow, firm breath. It went hard, but his voice was calm and even once more. "Will you tell me what you have in mind, Doctor?"

Dr. Urth patted his comfortable abdomen with one hand and replaced his glasses. "Don't you see, Inspector, that there is one place on board a spaceship where secret numbers are perfectly safe? Where, although in plain view, they would be perfectly safe from detection? Where, though they were being stared at by a hundred eyes, they would be secure? Except from a seeker who is an astute thinker, of course."

"Where? Name the place!"

"Why, in those places where there happen to be numbers already. Perfectly normal numbers. Legal numbers. Numbers that are supposed to be there."

"What are you talking about?"

"The ship's serial number, etched directly on the hull. *On* the hull, be it noted. The engine number, the field generator number. A few others. Each etched on integral portions of the ship. *On* the ship, as the silicony said. *On* the ship."

Davenport's heavy eyebrows rose with sudden comprehension. "You may be right—and if you are, I'm hoping we find you a silicony twice the size of the *Robert Q.*'s. One that not only talks, but whistles, 'Up, Asteroids, Forever!' " He hastily reached for the dossier, thumbed rapidly through it and extracted an official T.B.I. form. "Of course, we noted down all the identification numbers we found." He spread the form out. "If three of these resemble coordinates . . ."

"We should expect some small effort at disguise," Dr. Urth observed. "There will probably be certain letters and figures added to make the series appear more legitimate."

He reached for a scratch pad and shoved another toward the Inspector. For minutes the two men were silent, jotting down serial numbers, experimenting with crossing out obviously unrelated figures.

At last Davenport let out a sigh that mingled satisfaction and frustration. "I'm stuck," he admitted. "I think you're right; the numbers on the engine and the calculator are clearly disguised coordinates and dates. They don't run anywhere near the normal series, and it's easy to strike out the fake figures. That gives us two, but I'll take my oath the rest of these are absolutely legitimate serial numbers. What are your findings, Doctor?"

Dr. Urth nodded. "I agree. We now have two coordinates and we know where the third was inscribed."

"We know, do we? And how—" The Inspector broke off and uttered a sharp exclamation. "Of course! The number on the very ship itself, which isn't entered here—because it was on the precise spot on the hull where the meteor crashed through—I'm afraid there goes your silicony, Doctor." Then his craggy face brightened. "But I'm an idiot. The number's gone, but we can get it in a flash from Interplanetary Registry."

"I fear," said Dr. Urth, "that I must dispute at least the second part of your statement. Registry will have only the ship's original legitimate number, not the disguised coordinate to which the captain must have altered it."

"The exact spot on the hull," Davenport muttered. "And because of that chance shot the asteroid may be lost forever. What use to anybody are two coordinates without the third?"

"Well," said Dr. Urth precisely, "conceivably of very great use to a two-dimensional being. But creatures of our dimensions," he patted his paunch, "do require the third—which I fortunately happen to have right here."

"In the T.B.I. dossier? But we just checked the list of numbers—"

"*Your* list, Inspector. The file also includes young Vernadsky's original report. And of course the serial number listed there for the *Robert Q.* is the carefully faked one under which she was then sailing—no point in rousing the curiosity of a repair mechanic by letting him note a discrepancy."

Davenport reached for a scratch pad and the Vernadsky list. A moment's calculation and he grinned.

Dr. Urth lifted himself out of the chair with a pleased puff and trotted to the door. "It is always pleasant to see you, Inspector Davenport. Do come again. And remember the government can have the uranium, but I want the important thing: one giant silicony, alive and in good condition."

He was smiling.

"And preferably," said Davenport, "whistling."

Which he was doing himself as he walked out.

BIBLIOGRAPHY

There have been four Wendell Urth stories altogether, and all four appeared in *The Magazine of Fantasy and Science Fiction:*

"The Singing Bell," January 1955

"The Talking Stone," October 1955

"The Dying Night," July 1956

"The Key," October 1966

In addition there was a fifth story that began its life as a Wendell Urth. It was rejected by *The Magazine of Fantasy and Science Fiction,* and then appeared in its short-lived sister magazine *Venture Science Fiction,* after a revision in which Wendell Urth was eliminated:

"The Dust of Death," January 1957

All five stories are included in my collection *Asimov's Mysteries,* which appeared as a Doubleday hardcover in 1968, as a Dell paperback in 1969 and again in 1973, and finally as a Fawcett paperback in 1977.

THE VERMILION SANDS SERIES

by J. G. Ballard *

Vermilion Sands is my guess at what the future will actually be like. It is a curious paradox that almost all science fiction, however far removed in time and space, is really about the present day. Very few attempts have been made to visualize a unique and self-contained future that offers no warnings to us. Perhaps because of this cautionary tone, so many of science fiction's notional futures are zones of unrelieved grimness. Even its heavens are like other people's hells.

By contrast, Vermilion Sands is a place where I would be happy to live. I once described this overlit desert resort as an exotic suburb of my mind, and something about the word "suburb"—which I then used pejoratively—now convinces me that I was on the right track in my pursuit of the day after tomorrow. As the countryside vanishes under a top-dressing of chemicals, and as cities provide little more than an urban context for traffic intersections, the suburbs are at last coming into their own. The skies are larger, the air more generous, the clock less urgent. Vermilion Sands has more than its full share of dreams and illusions, fears and fantasies, but the frame for them is less confining. I like to think, too, that it celebrates the neglected virtues of the glossy, lurid and bizarre.

Where is Vermilion Sands? I suppose its spiritual home lies somewhere between Arizona and Ipanema Beach, but in recent years I have been delighted to see it popping up elsewhere—above all, in sections of the 3,000-mile-long linear city that stretches from Gibraltar to Glyfada Beach along the northern shores of the Mediterranean, and where each summer Europe lies on its back in the sun. That posture, of course, is the hallmark of Vermilion Sands and, I hope, of the future—not merely that no one has to work, but that work is the ultimate play, and play the ultimate work.

The earliest of these tales, "Prima Belladonna," was the first short story I published, twenty-four years ago, and the image of this desert resort has remained remarkably constant ever since. I wait optimistically for it to take concrete shape around me.

---

* Introduction adapted from that which appeared in the British edition of *Vermilion Sands.* Copyright © by J. G. Ballard.

The Cloud-Sculptors of Coral D

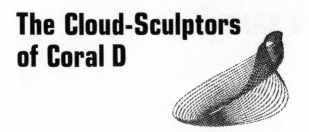

All summer the cloud-sculptors would come from Vermilion Sands and sail their painted gliders above the coral towers that rose like white pagodas beside the highway to Lagoon West. The tallest of the towers was Coral D, and here the rising air above the sand-reefs was topped by swan-like clumps of fair-weather cumulus. Lifted on the shoulders of the air above the crown of Coral D, we would carve seahorses and unicorns, the portraits of presidents and film stars, lizards and exotic birds. As the crowd watched from their cars, a cool rain would fall on to the dusty roofs, weeping from the sculptured clouds as they sailed across the desert floor towards the sun.

Of all the cloud-sculptures we were to carve, the strangest were the portraits of Leonora Chanel. As I look back to that afternoon last summer when she first came in her white limousine to watch the cloud-sculptors of Coral D, I know we barely realized how seriously this beautiful but insane woman regarded the sculptures floating above her in that calm sky. Later her portraits, carved in the whirlwind, were to weep their storm-rain upon the corpses of their sculptors.

I had arrived in Vermilion Sands three months earlier. A retired pilot, I was painfully coming to terms with a broken leg and the prospect of never flying again. Driving into the desert one day, I stopped near the coral towers on the highway to Lagoon West. As I gazed at these immense pagodas stranded on the floor of this fossil sea, I heard music coming from a sand-reef two hundred yards away. Swinging on my crutches across the sliding sand, I found a shallow basin among the dunes where sonic statues had run to seed beside a ruined studio. The owner had gone, abandoning the hangar-like building to the sand-rays and the desert, and on some half-formed impulse I began to drive out each afternoon. From the lathes and joists left behind I built my first giant kites and, later, gliders with cockpits. Tethered by their cables, they would hang above me in the afternoon air like amiable ciphers.

One evening, as I wound the gliders down on to the winch, a sudden gale rose over the crest of Coral D. While I grappled with the whirling handle, trying to anchor my crutches in the sand, two figures approached across the desert floor. One was a small hunchback with a child's over-lit eyes and a deformed jaw twisted like an anchor barb to one side. He scuttled over to the winch and wound the tattered gliders towards the ground, his powerful shoulders pushing me aside. He helped me on to my crutch and peered into the hangar. Here my most ambitious glider to date, no longer a kite but a sail-plane with elevators and control lines, was taking shape on the bench.

He spread a large hand over his chest. 'Petit Manuel—acrobat and weight-lifter. Nolan!' he bellowed. 'Look at this!' His companion was squatting by the sonic statues, twisting their helixes so that their voices became more resonant. 'Nolan's an artist,' the hunchback confided to me. 'He'll build you gliders like condors.'

The tall man was wandering among the gliders, touching their wings with a sculptor's hand. His morose eyes were set in a face like a bored boxer's. He glanced at the plaster on my leg and my faded flying-jacket, and gestured at the gliders. 'You've given cockpits to them, major.' The remark contained a complete understanding of my motives. He pointed to the coral towers rising above us into the evening sky. 'With silver iodide we could carve the clouds.'

The hunchback nodded encouragingly to me, his eyes lit by an astronomy of dreams.

So were formed the cloud-sculptors of Coral D. Although I considered myself one of them, I never flew the gliders, but taught Nolan and little Manuel to fly, and later, when he joined us, Charles Van Eyck. Nolan had found this blond-haired pirate of the café terraces in Vermilion Sands, a laconic Teuton with hard eyes and a weak mouth, and brought him out to Coral D when the season ended and the well-to-do tourists and their nubile daughters returned to Red Beach. 'Major Parker—Charles Van Eyck. He's a headhunter,' Noland commented with cold humour, '—maidenheads.' Despite their uneasy rivalry I realized that Van Eyck would give our group a useful dimension of glamour. .

From the first I suspected that the studio in the desert was Nolan's, and that we were all serving some private whim of this dark-haired solitary. At the time, however, I was more concerned with teaching them to fly—first on cable, mastering the updraughts that swept the stunted turret of Coral A, smallest of the towers, then the steeper slopes of B and C, and finally the powerful currents of Coral D. Late one afternoon, when I began to wind them in, Nolan cut away his line. The glider plummeted on to its back, diving down to impale itself on the rock spires. I flung myself to the ground as the cable whipped across my car, shattering the windshield. When I looked up, Nolan was soaring high in the tinted air above Coral D. The wind, guardian of the coral towers, carried him through the islands of cumulus that veiled the evening light.

As I ran to the winch the second cable went, and little Manuel swerved away to join Nolan. Ugly crab on the ground, in the air the hunchback became a bird with immense wings, outflying both Nolan and Van Eyck. I watched them as they circled the coral towers, and then swept down together over the desert floor, stirring the sand-rays into soot-like clouds. Petit Manuel was jubilant. He strutted around me like a pocket Napoleon, contemptuous of my broken leg, scooping up handfuls of broken glass and tossing them over his head like bouquets to the air.

Two months later, as we drove out to Coral D on the day we were to meet Leonora Chanel, something of this first feeling of exhilaration had faded. Now that the season had ended few tourists travelled to Lagoon West, and often we would perform our cloud-sculpture to the empty highway. Sometimes Nolan would remain behind in his hotel, drinking by himself on the bed, or Van Eyck would disappear for several days with some widow or divorcée, and Petit Manuel and I would go out alone.

None the less, as the four of us drove out in my car that afternoon and I saw the clouds waiting for us above the spire of Coral D, all my depression and fatigue vanished. Ten minutes later, the three cloud-gliders rose into the air and the first cars began to stop on the highway. Nolan was in the lead in his black-winged glider, climbing straight to the crown of Coral D two hundred feet above, while Van Eyck soared to and fro below, showing his blond mane to a middle-aged woman in a topaz convertible. Behind them came little Manuel, his candy-striped wings slipping and churning in the disturbed air. Shouting happy obscenities, he flew with his twisted knees, huge arms gesticulating out of the cockpit.

The three gliders, brilliant painted toys, revolved like lazing birds above Coral D, waiting for the first clouds to pass overhead. Van Eyck moved away to take a cloud. He sailed around its white pillow, spraying the sides with iodide crystals and cutting away the flock-like tissue. The steaming shards fell towards us like crumbling ice-drifts. As the drops of condensing spray fell on my face I could see Van Eyck shaping an immense horse's head. He sailed up and down the long forehead and chiselled out the eyes and ears.

As always, the people watching from their cars seemed to enjoy this piece of aerial marzipan. It sailed overhead, carried away on the wind from Coral D. Van Eyck followed it down, wings lazing around the equine head. Meanwhile Petit Manuel worked away at the next cloud. As he sprayed its sides a familiar human head appeared through the tumbling mist. The high wavy-mane, strong jaw but slipped mouth Manuel caricatured from the cloud with a series of deft passes, wingtips almost touching each other as he dived in and out of the portrait.

The glossy white head, an unmistakable parody of Van Eyck in his own worst style, crossed the highway towards Vermilion Sands. Manuel slid out of the air, stalling his glider to a landing beside my car as Van Eyck stepped from his cockpit with a forced smile.

We waited for the third display. A cloud formed over Coral D and within a few minutes had blossomed into a pristine fair-weather cumulus. As it hung there Nolan's black-winged glider plunged out of the sun. He soared around the cloud, cutting away its tissues. The soft fleece fell towards us in a cool rain.

There was a shout from one of the cars. Nolan turned from the cloud, his wings slipping as if unveiling his handiwork. Illuminated by the afternoon sun was the serene face of a three-year-old child. Its wide cheeks framed a placid mouth and plump chin. As one or two people clapped, Nolan sailed over the cloud and rippled the roof into ribbons and curls.

However, I knew that the real climax was yet to come. Cursed by some malignant virus, Nolan seemed unable to accept his own handiwork, always destroying it with the same cold humour. Petit Manuel had thrown away his cigarette, and even Van Eyck had turned his attention from the women in the cars.

Nolan soared above the child's face, following like a matador waiting for the moment of the kill. There was silence for a minute as he worked away at the cloud, and then someone slammed a car door in disgust.

Hanging above us was the white image of a skull.

The child's face, converted by a few strokes, had vanished, but in the notched teeth and gaping orbits, large enough to hold a car, we could still see an echo of its infant features. The spectre moved past us, the spectators frowning at this weeping skull whose rain fell upon their faces.

Half-heartedly I picked my old flying helmet off the back seat and began to carry it around the cars. Two of the spectators drove off before I could reach them. As I hovered about uncertainly, wondering why on earth a retired and well-to-do airforce officer should be trying to collect these few dollar bills, Van Eyck stepped behind me and took the helmet from my hand.

'Not now, major. Look at what arrives—my apocalypse . . .'

A white Rolls-Royce, driven by a chauffeur in braided cream livery, had turned off the highway. Through the tinted communication window a young woman in a secretary's day suit spoke to the chauffeur. Beside her, a gloved hand still holding the window strap, a white-haired woman with jewelled eyes gazed up at the circling wings of the cloud-glider. Her strong and elegant face seemed sealed within the dark glass of the limousine like the enigmatic madonna of some marine grotto.

Van Eyck's glider rose into the air, soaring upwards to the cloud that hung above Coral D. I walked back to my car, searching the sky for Nolan. Above, Van Eyck was producing a pastiche Mona Lisa, a picture postcard Gioconda as authentic as a plaster virgin. Its glossy finish shone in the over-bright sunlight as if enamelled together out of some cosmetic foam.

Then Nolan dived from the sun behind Van Eyck. Rolling his black-winged glider past Van Eyck's, he drove through the neck of the Gioconda, and with the flick of a wing toppled the broad-cheeked head. It fell towards the cars below. The features disintegrated into a flaccid mess, sections of the nose and jaw tumbling through the steam. Then wings brushed. Van Eyck fired his spray gun at Nolan, and there was a flurry of torn fabric. Van Eyck fell from the air, steering his glider down to a broken landing.

I ran over to him. 'Charles, do you have to play von Richthofen? For God's sake, leave each other alone!'

Von Eyck waved me away. 'Talk to Nolan, major. I'm not responsible for his air piracy.' He stood in the cockpit, gazing over the cars as the shreds of fabric fell around him.

I walked back to my car, deciding that the time had come to disband the cloud-sculptors of Coral D. Fifty yards away the young secretary in the Rolls-Royce had stepped from the car and beckoned to me. Through the open door her mistress watched me with her jewelled eyes. Her white hair lay in a coil over one shoulder like a nacreous serpent.

I carried my flying helmet down to the young woman. Above a high forehead her auburn hair was swept back in a defensive bun, as if she were deliberately concealing part of herself. She stared with puzzled eyes at the helmet held out in front of her.

'I don't want to fly—what is it?'

'A grace,' I explained. 'For the repose of Michelangelo, Ed Keinholz and the cloud-sculptors of Coral D.'

'Oh, my God. I think the chauffeur's the only one with any *money*. Look, do you perform anywhere else?'

'Perform?' I glanced from this pretty and agreeable young woman to the pale chimera with jewelled eyes in the dim compartment of the Rolls. She was watching the headless figure of the Mona Lisa as it moved across the desert floor towards Vermilion Sands. 'We're not a professional troupe, as you've probably guessed. And obviously we'd need some fair-weather cloud. Where, exactly?'

'At Lagoon West.' She took a snakeskin diary from her handbag. 'Miss Chanel is holding a series of garden parties. She wondered if you'd care to perform. Of course there would be a large fee.'

'Chanel . . . Leonora Chanel, the . . . ?'

The young woman's face again took on its defensive posture, dissociating her from whatever might follow. 'Miss Chanel is at Lagoon West for the summer. By the way, there's one condition I must point out— Miss Chanel will provide the sole subject matter. You do understand?'

Fifty yards away Van Eyck was dragging his damaged glider towards my car. Nolan had landed, a caricature of Cyrano abandoned in mid-air. Petit Manuel limped to and fro, gathering together the equipment. In the fading afternoon light they resembled a threadbare circus troupe.

'All right,' I agreed. 'I take your point. But what about the clouds, Miss—?'

'Lafferty. Beatrice Lafferty. Miss Chanel will provide the clouds.'

I walked around the cars with the helmet, then divided the money between Nolan, Van Eyck and Manuel. They stood in the gathering dusk, the few bills in their hands, watching the highway below.

Leonora Chanel stepped from the limousine and strolled into the desert. Her white-haired figure in its cobra-skin coat wandered among the dunes. Sand-rays lifted around her, disturbed by the random movements of this sauntering phantasm of the burnt afternoon. Ignoring their open stings around her legs, she was gazing up at the aerial bestiary dissolving in the sky, and at the white skull a mile away over Lagoon West that had smeared itself across the sky.

At the time I first saw her, watching the cloud-sculptors of Coral D, I had only a half-formed impression of Leonora Chanel. The daughter of one of the world's leading financiers, she was an heiress both in her own right and on the death of her husband, a shy Monacan aristocrat, Comte Louis Chanel. The mysterious circumstances of his death at Cap Ferrat on the Riviera, officially described as suicide, had placed Leonora in a spotlight of publicity and gossip. She had escaped by wandering endlessly across the globe, from her walled villa in Tangiers to an Alpine mansion in the snows above Pontresina, and from there to Palm Springs, Seville and Mykonos.

During these years of exile something of her character emerged from the magazine and newspaper photographs: moodily visiting a Spanish charity with the Duchess of Alba, or seated with Soraya and other members of café society on the terrace of Dali's villa at Port Lligat, her self-regarding face gazing out with its jewelled eyes at the diamond sea of the Costa Brava.

Inevitably her Garbo-like role seemed over-calculated, for ever undermined by the suspicions of her own hand in her husband's death. The count had been an introspective playboy who piloted his own aircraft to archaeological sites in the Peloponnese and whose mistress, a beautiful young Lebanese, was one of the world's pre-eminent keyboard interpreters of Bach. Why this reserved and pleasant man should have committed suicide was never made plain. What promised to be a significant exhibit at the coroner's inquest, a mutilated easel portrait of Leonora on which he was working, was accidentally destroyed before the hearing. Perhaps the painting revealed more of Leonora's character than she chose to see.

A week later, as I drove out to Lagoon West on the morning of the first garden party, I could well understand why Leonora Chanel had come to Vermilion Sands, to this bizarre, sandbound resort with its lethargy, beach fatigue and shifting perspectives. Sonic statues grew wild along the beach, their voices keening as I swept past along the shore road. The fused silica on the surface of the lake formed an immense rainbow mirror that reflected the deranged colours of the sand-reefs, more vivid even than the cinnabar and cyclamen wing-panels of the cloud-gliders overhead. They soared in the sky above the lake like fitful dragonflies as Nolan, Van Eyck and Petit Manuel flew them from Coral D.

We had entered an inflamed landscape. Half a mile away the angular cornices of the summer house jutted into the vivid air as if distorted by some faulty junction of time and space. Behind it, like an exhausted volcano, a broad-topped mesa rose into the glazed air, its shoulders lifting the thermal currents high off the heated lake.

Envying Nolan and little Manuel these tremendous updraughts, more powerful than any we had known at Coral D, I drove towards the villa. Then the haze cleared along the beach and I saw the clouds.

A hundred feet above the roof of the mesa, they hung like the twisted pillows of a sleepless giant. Columns of turbulent air moved within the clouds, boiling upwards to the anvil heads like liquid in a cauldron. These were not the placid, fair-weather cumulus of Coral D, but storm-nimbus, unstable masses of overheated air that could catch an aircraft and lift it a thousand feet in a few seconds. Here and there the clouds were rimmed with dark bands, their towers crossed by valleys and ravines. They moved across the villa, concealed from the lakeside heat by the haze overhead, then dissolved in a series of violent shifts in the disordered air.

As I entered the drive behind a truck filled with *son et lumière* equipment a dozen members of the staff were straightening lines of gilt chairs on the terrace and unrolling panels of a marquee.

Beatrice Lafferty stepped across the cables. 'Major Parker—there are the clouds we promised you.'

I looked up again at the dark billows hanging like shrouds above the white villa. 'Clouds, Beatrice? Those are tigers, tigers with wings. We're manicurists of the air, not dragon-tamers.'

'Don't worry, a manicure is exactly what you're expected to carry out.' With an arch glance, she added: 'Your men do understand that there's to be only one subject?'

'Miss Chanel herself? Of course.' I took her arm as we walked towards the balcony overlooking the lake. 'You know, I think you enjoy these snide asides. Let the rich choose their materials—marble, bronze, plasma or cloud. Why not? Portraiture has always been a neglected art.'

'My God, not here.' She waited until a steward passed with a tray of tablecloths. 'Carving one's portrait in the sky out of the sun and air—some people might say that smacked of vanity, or even worse sins.'

'You're very mysterious. Such as?'

She played games with her eyes. 'I'll tell you in a month's time when my contract expires. Now, when are your men coming?'

'They're here.' I pointed to the sky over the lake. The three gliders hung in the overheated air, clumps of cloud-cotton drifting past them to dissolve in the haze. They were following a sand-yacht that approached the quay, its tyres throwing up the cerise dust. Behind the helmsman sat Leonora Chanel in a trouser suit of yellow alligator skin, her white hair hidden inside a black raffia toque.

As the helmsman moored the craft Van Eyck and Petit Manuel put on an impromptu performance, shaping the fragments of cloud-cotton a hundred feet above the lake. First Van Eyck carved an orchid, then a heart and a pair of lips, while Manuel fashioned the head of a parakeet, two identical mice and the letters 'L. C.' As they dived and plunged around her, their wings sometimes touching the lake, Leonora stood on the quay, politely waving at each of these brief confections.

When they landed beside the quay, Leonora waited for Nolan to take one of the clouds, but he was sailing up and down the lake in front of her like a weary bird. Watching this strange chatelaine of Lagoon West, I noticed that she had slipped off into some private reverie, her gaze fixed on Nolan and oblivious of the people around her. Memories, caravels without sails, crossed the shadowy deserts of her burnt-out eyes.

Later that evening Beatrice Lafferty led me into the villa through the library window. There, as Leonora greeted her guests on the terrace, wearing a topless dress of sapphires and organdy, her breasts covered only by their contour jewellery, I saw the portraits that filled the villa. I counted more than twenty, from the formal society portraits in the drawing rooms, one by the President of the Royal Academy, another by Annigoni, to the bizarre psychological studies in the bar and dining room by Dali and Francis Bacon. Everywhere we moved, in the alcoves between the marble semi-columns, in gilt miniatures on the mantel shelves, even in the ascending mural that followed the staircase, we saw the same beautiful self-regarding face. This colossal narcissism seemed to have become her last refuge, the only retreat for her fugitive self in its flight from the world.

Then, in the studio on the roof, we came across a large easel portrait that had just been varnished. The artist had produced a deliberate travesty of the sentimental and powder-blue tints of a fashionable society painter, but beneath this gloss he had visualized Leonora as a dead Medea. The stretched skin below her right cheek, the sharp forehead and slipped mouth gave her the numbed and luminous appearance of a corpse.

My eyes moved to the signature. 'Nolan! My God, were you here when he painted this?'

'It was finished before I came—two months ago. She refused to have it framed.'

'No wonder.' I went over to the window and looked down at the bed-rooms hidden behind their awnings. 'Nolan was *here*. The old studio near Coral D was his.'

'But why should Leonora ask him back? They must have—'

'To paint her portrait again. I know Leonora Chanel better than you do, Beatrice. This time, though, the size of the sky.'

We left the library and walked past the cocktails and canapés to where Leonora was welcoming her guests. Nolan stood beside her, wearing a suit of white suede. Now and then he looked down at her as if playing with the possibilities this self-obsessed woman gave to his macabre humour. Leonora clutched at his elbow. With the diamonds fixed around her eyes she reminded me of some archaic priestess. Beneath the contour jewellery her breasts lay like eager snakes.

Van Eyck introduced himself with an exaggerated bow. Behind him came Petit Manuel, his twisted head ducking nervously among the tuxedos.

Leonora's mouth shut in a rictus of distaste. She glanced at the white plaster on my foot. 'Nolan, you fill your world with cripples. Your little dwarf—will he fly too?'

Petit Manuel looked at her with eyes like crushed flowers.

The performance began an hour later. The dark-rimmed clouds were lit by the sun setting behind the mesa, the air crossed by wraiths of cirrus like the gilded frames of the immense paintings to come. Van Eyck's glider rose in the spiral towards the face of the first cloud, stalling and climbing again as the turbulent updraughts threw him across the air.

As the cheekbones began to appear, as smooth and lifeless as carved foam, applause rang out from the guests seated on the terrace. Five minutes later, when Van Eyck's glider swooped down on to the lake, I could see that he had excelled himself. Lit by the searchlights, and with the overture to *Tristan* sounding from the loudspeakers on the slopes of the mesa, as if inflating this huge bauble, the portrait of Leonora moved overhead, a faint rain falling from it. By luck the cloud remained stable until it passed the shoreline, and then broke up in the evening air as if ripped from the sky by an irritated hand.

Petit Manuel began his ascent, sailing in on a dark-edged cloud like an urchin accosting a bad-tempered matron. He soared to and fro, as if unsure how to shape this unpredictable column of vapour, then began to carve it into the approximate contours of a woman's head. He seemed more nervous than I had ever seen him. As he finished a second round of applause broke out, soon followed by laughter and ironic cheers.

The cloud, sculptured into a flattering likeness of Leonora, had begun to tilt, rotating in the disturbed air. The jaw lengthened, the glazed smile became that of an idiot. Within a minute the gigantic head of Leonora Chanel hung upside down above us.

Discreetly I ordered the searchlights switched off, and the audience's attention turned to Nolan's black-winged glider as it climbed towards the next cloud. Shards of dissolving tissue fell from the darkening air, the spray concealing whatever ambiguous creation Nolan was carving. To my surprise, the portrait that emerged was wholly lifelike. There was a burst of applause, a few bars of *Tannhäuser*, and the searchlights lit up the elegant head. Standing among her guests, Leonora raised her glass to Nolan's glider.

Puzzled by Nolan's generosity, I looked more closely at the gleaming face, and then realized what he had done. The portrait, with cruel irony, was all too lifelike. The downward turn of Leonora's mouth, the chin held up to smooth her neck, the fall of flesh below her right cheek—all these were carried on the face of the cloud as they had been in his painting in the studio.

Around Leonora the guests were congratulating her on the performance. She was looking up at her portrait as it began to break up over the lake, seeing it for the first time. The veins held the blood in her face.

Then a firework display on the beach blotted out these ambiguities in its pink and blue explosions.

Shortly before dawn Beatrice Lafferty and I walked along the beach among the shells of burnt-out rockets and catherine wheels. On the deserted terrace a few lights shone through the darkness on to the scattered chairs. As we reached the steps a woman's voice cried out somewhere above us. There was the sound of smashed glass. A french window was kicked back, and a dark-haired man in a white suit ran between the tables.

As Nolan disappeared along the drive Leonora Chanel walked out into the centre of the terrace. She looked at the dark clouds surging over the mesa, and with one hand tore the jewels from her eyes. They lay winking on the tiles at her feet. Then the hunched figure of Petit Manuel leapt from his hiding place in the bandstand. He scuttled past, racing on his deformed legs.

An engine started by the gates. Leonora began to walk back to the villa, staring at her broken reflections in the glass below the window. She stopped as a tall, blond-haired man with cold and eager eyes stepped from the sonic statues outside the library. Disturbed by the noise, the statues had begun to whine. As Van Eyck moved towards Leonora they took up the slow beat of his steps.

The next day's performance was the last by the cloud-sculptors of Coral D. All afternoon, before the guests arrived, a dim light lay over the lake. Immense tiers of storm-nimbus were massing behind the mesa, and any performance at all seemed unlikely.

Van Eyck was with Leonora. As I arrived Beatrice Lafferty was watching their sand-yacht carry them unevenly across the lake, its sails whipped by the squalls.

'There's no sign of Nolan or little Manuel,' she told me. 'The party starts in three hours.'

I took her arm. 'The party's already over. When you're finished here, Bea, come and live with me at Coral D. I'll teach you to sculpt the clouds.'

Van Eyck and Leonora came ashore half an hour later. Van Eyck stared through my face as he brushed past. Leonora clung to his arm, the day-jewels around her eyes scattering their hard light across the terrace.

By eight, when the first guests began to appear, Nolan and Petit Manuel had still not arrived. On the terrace the evening was warm and lamplit, but overhead the storm-clouds sidled past each other like uneasy giants. I walked up the slope to where the gliders were tethered. Their wings shivered in the updraughts.

Barely half a minute after he rose into the darkening air, dwarfed by an immense tower of storm-nimbus, Charles Van Eyck was spinning towards the ground, his glider toppled by the crazed air. He recovered fifty feet from the villa and climbed on the updraughts from the lake, well away from the spreading chest of the cloud. He soared in again. As Leonora and her guests watched from their seats the glider was hurled back over their heads in an explosion of vapour, then fell towards the lake with a broken wing.

I walked towards Leonora. Standing by the balcony were Nolan and Petit Manuel, watching Van Eyck climb from the cockpit of his glider three hundred yards away.

To Nolan I said: 'Why bother to come? Don't tell me you're going to fly?'

Nolan leaned against the rail, hands in the pockets of his suit. 'I'm not—that's exactly why I'm here, major.'

Leonora was wearing an evening dress of peacock feathers that lay around her legs in an immense train. The hundreds of eyes gleamed in the electric air before the storm, sheathing her body in their blue flames.

'Miss Chanel, the clouds are like madmen,' I apologized. 'There's a storm on its way.'

She looked up at me with unsettled eyes. 'Don't you people expect to take risks?' She gestured at the storm-nimbus that swirled over our heads. 'For clouds like these I need a Michelangelo of the sky . . . What about Nolan? Is he too frightened as well?'

As she shouted his name Nolan stared at her, then turned his back to us. The light over Lagoon West had changed. Half the lake was covered by a dim pall.

There was a tug on my sleeve. Petit Manuel looked up at me with his crafty child's eyes. 'Major, I can go. Let me take the glider.'

'Manuel, for God's sake. You'll kill—'

He darted between the gilt chairs. Leonora frowned as he plucked her wrist.

'Miss Chanel . . .' His loose mouth formed an encouraging smile. 'I'll sculpt for you. Right now, a big storm-cloud, eh?'

She stared down at him, half-repelled by this eager hunchback ogling her beside the hundred eyes of her peacock train. Van Eyck was limping back to the beach from his wrecked glider. I guessed that in some strange way Manuel was pitting himself against Van Eyck.

Leonora grimaced, as if swallowing some poisonous phlegm. 'Major Parker, tell him to—' She glanced at the dark cloud boiling over the mesa like the effluvium of some black-hearted volcano. 'Wait! Let's see what the little cripple can do!' She turned on Manuel with an over-bright smile. 'Go on, then. Let's see you sculpt a whirlwind!'

In her face the diagram of bones formed a geometry of murder.

Nolan ran past across the terrace, his feet crushing the peacock feathers as Leonora laughed. We tried to stop Manuel, but he raced ahead up the slope. Stung by Leonora's taunt, he skipped among the rocks, disappearing from sight in the darkening air. On the terrace a small crowd gathered to watch.

The yellow and tangerine glider rose into the sky and climbed across the face of the storm-cloud. Fifty yards from the dark billows it was buffeted by the shifting air, but Manuel soared in and began to cut away at the dark face. Drops of black rain fell across the terrace at our feet.

The first outline of a woman's head appeared, satanic eyes lit by the open vents in the cloud, a sliding mouth like a dark smear as the huge billows boiled forwards. Nolan shouted in warning from the lake as he climbed into his glider. A moment later little Manuel's craft was lifted by a powerful updraught and tossed over the roof of the cloud. Fighting the insane air, Manuel plunged the glider downwards and drove into the cloud again. Then its immense face opened, and in a sudden spasm the cloud surged forward and swallowed the glider.

There was silence on the terrace as the crushed body of the craft revolved in the centre of the cloud. It moved over our heads, dismembered pieces of the wings and fuselage churned about in the dissolving face. As it reached the lake the cloud began its violent end. Pieces of the face slewed sideways, the mouth was torn off, an eye exploded. It vanished in a last brief squall.

The pieces of Petit Manuel's glider fell from the bright air.

Beatrice Lafferty and I drove across the lake to collect Manuel's body. After the spectacle of his death within the exploding replica of their hostess's face, the guests began to leave. Within minutes the drive was full of cars. Leonora watched them go, standing with Van Eyck among the deserted tables.

Beatrice said nothing as we drove out. The pieces of the shattered glider lay over the fused sand, tags of canvas and broken struts, control lines tied into knots. Ten yards from the cockpit I found Petit Manuel's body, lying in a wet ball like a drowned monkey.

I carried him back to the sand-yacht.

'Raymond!' Beatrice pointed to the shore. Storm-clouds were massed along the entire length of the lake, and the first flashes of lightning were striking in the hills behind the mesa. In the electric air the villa had lost its glitter. Half a mile away a tornado was moving along the valley floor, its trunk swaying towards the lake.

The first gust of air struck the yacht. Beatrice shouted again: 'Raymond! Nolan's there—he's flying inside it!'

Then I saw the black-winged glider circling under the umbrella of the tornado, Nolan himself riding in the whirlwind. His wings held steady in the revolving air around the funnel. Like a pilot fish he soared in, as if steering the tornado towards Leonora's villa.

Twenty seconds later, when it struck the house, I lost sight of him. An explosion of dark air overwhelmed the villa, a churning centrifuge of shattered chairs and tiles that burst over the roof. Beatrice and I ran from the yacht, and lay together in a fault in the glass surface. As the tornado moved away, fading into the storm-filled sky, a dark squall hung over the wrecked villa, now and then flicking the debris into the air. Shreds of canvas and peacock feathers fell around us.

We waited half an hour before approaching the house. Hundreds of smashed glasses and broken chairs littered the terrace. At first I could see no signs of Leonora, although her face was everywhere, the portraits with their slashed profiles strewn on the damp tiles. An eddying smile floated towards me from the disturbed air, and wrapped itself around my leg.

Leonora's body lay among the broken tables near the bandstand, half-wrapped in a bleeding canvas. Her face was as bruised now as the storm-cloud Manuel had tried to carve.

We found Van Eyck in the wreck of the marquee. He was suspended by the neck from a tangle of electric wiring, his pale face wreathed in a noose of light bulbs. The current flowed intermittently through the wiring, lighting up the coloured globes.

I leaned against the overturned Rolls, holding Beatrice's shoulders. 'There's no sign of Nolan—no pieces of his glider.'

'Poor man. Raymond, he was driving that whirlwind here. Somehow he was controlling it.'

I walked across the damp terrace to where Leonora lay. I began to cover her with the shreds of canvas, the torn faces of herself.

I took Beatrice Lafferty to live with me in Nolan's studio in the desert near Coral D. We heard no more of Nolan and never flew the gliders again. The clouds carry too many memories. Three months ago a man who saw the derelict gliders outside the studio stopped near Coral D and walked across to us. He told us he had seen a man flying a glider in the sky high above Red Beach, carving the strato-cirrus into images of jewels and children's faces. Once there was a dwarf's head.

On reflection, that sounds rather like Nolan, so perhaps he managed to get away from the tornado. In the evenings Beatrice and I sit among the sonic statues, listening to their voices as the fair-weather clouds rise above Coral D, waiting for a man in a dark-winged glider, perhaps painted like candy now, who will come in on the wind and carve for us images of seahorses and unicorns, dwarfs and jewels and children's faces.

BIBLIOGRAPHY

"Prima Belladonna," *Science Fantasy,* December 1956

"Studio 5 the Stars," *Science Fantasy,* February 1961

"The Thousand Dreams of Stellavista," *Amazing,* March 1962

"The Singing Statues," *Fantastic,* July 1962

"The Screen Game," *Fantastic,* October 1963

"Venus Smiles," *Worlds of If,* September 1967

"Cry Hope, Cry Fury," *The Magazine of Fantasy and Science Fiction,* October 1967

"The Cloud-Sculptors of Coral D," *The Magazine of Fantasy and Science Fiction,* December 1967

"Say Goodbye to the Wind," *Fantastic,* August 1970

Vermilion Sands, Berkley, 1971 (contains all of the above)

THE CITIES IN FLIGHT SERIES

by James Blish

Introduction by James and Judith Blish

The first story about the space-going cities was published in April 1950 in *Astounding Science Fiction*. Its title was "Okie." In an interview with Brian Aldiss in 1973, which was published in the fanzine *Cypher* in England, James recalled its birth:

"I came at this by an entirely roundabout route, in 1948. There was a cover on an *Astounding* of that period, for another story which I cannot identify, showing a Van Vogtian superman standing in what looked like a spaceship yard filled with towering phallic shapes. At first glance I took it to be a city, not a shipyard . . . and it occurred to me suddenly that if you have antigravity, there's no reason why there should be any limitation on the size or shape of the objects you want to lift. At that point I wondered—why would you want to do that? It was then that the concept of migrant workers came to me."

Jim then produced a version of the last two chapters of *Earthman Come Home*—not realizing that they were the last two chapters of anything. He remarked, "I set out to throw away an idea of Wagnerian proportions within the compass of ten thousand words." John W. Campbell rejected the story. He rejected it in the Campbellian manner with a four-page single-spaced letter, which Jim was to mine steadily for the next eight years, until the publication of the final volume, *The Triumph of Time* (*A Clash of Cymbals* in the U.K.) in 1958. "The main thing that Campbell contributed was this: the most valuable thing that these migrant workers could transfer in a situation involving fast interstellar travel was not gold, uranium, diamonds, the ability to drill for oil or whatever, but *information*. These cities were the pollinating agents of the Galaxy, and this idea became the central focus of the whole series. It absolutely ruled out power politics in the intergalactic-epic sense. I did use a certain amount of power politicking, since the cities are competitive with each other—political figures of varying intelligence maneuvering against one another, and a social situation on Earth in which the home planet both protects and polices the cities.

"Here I went back to the American analogy. There are two kinds of hobo—the ordinary migrant worker who goes from door to door offering to do a job for a sandwich and a glass of water—"Mow your lawn, Lady?" and who carries all his worldly possessions bound up in a bandanna on a stick over his shoulder; the other kind of tramp exists by robbing his fellows, and does no work—the bindlestiff. I set up that situation among the cities, and this seemed to me much more interesting than the then-conventional interstellar wheeling and dealing.

"As a matter of fact, by and large, I don't like wheeler-dealer characters. The ones you find in conventional interstellar intrigue turn out to be generals or dictators of the Galaxy. My people were to be workhorses involved in intrigue with each other, and never mind the wheeler-dealer—they did that within their own small compass."

Jim did like Mayor Amalfi, who was more or less modeled on Mayor Fiorello La Guardia of New York (1933–1945), and whom Jim regarded as a man who could *cope*.

"I came to realize that before the cities could have got into the sky we needed two fundamental discoveries: one of these was the faster-than-light drive, and the other was a way of achieving longevity, often mistakenly referred to as 'immortality.' My people were not immortal, they simply lived very long lives. So I wrote two stories to show how these discoveries were made. 'Bridge' is the story of the interstellar drive, and it's all done in terms of the little technicians who have to work on the bridge on Jupiter, who don't know why they are there or why they should be plunged into this hell. The other one takes place mostly on Earth, in a pharmaceutical company working on the problem of longevity. There again you have minor characters, who don't know what's going on. I then tied these stories together with a third, and made a triple sandwich of this—and had a 'prequel,' in Harlan Ellison's lovely word, *Year 2018!* (*They Shall Have Stars,* U.K. title). By that time I was working on a smaller scale, showing how it all started.

"My whole principle in writing a story, particularly if I start with a background, is to ask—*whom does it hurt?* The person whom the situation hurts most becomes my central character."

The final volume, *The Triumph of Time,* ends with a cataclysm that destroys (perhaps) the entire continuum. Jim described it as "a novel of how people, including a couple of very young people—there are some pathetic kids in that book—might react in their different ways if they knew the exact day of their deaths. This is a novel of finality, and at the end of it we revert to Amalfi, who was always the central figure; and some slight hope is given that even this apparent ultimate disaster might be survived in some way, with some fragments of one's personality left. . . . Amalfi says no. He's lived so long and seen so much, and been in charge of so much of his universe, that he knows all the nuts and bolts are coming out of it, and he's dead tired."

An admirer has posthumously applied the title *The Star-Spenglered Banter* to this series; and I am sure Jim would have enjoyed it. Certainly, the historical perspective of *Cities in Flight* as well as his other works was based in Jim's conviction that Spengler was right. (He enjoyed slotting Presidents into the system.)

Bridge

I

A screeching tornado was rocking the Bridge when the alarm sounded; it was making the whole structure shudder and sway. This was normal and Robert Helmuth barely noticed it. There was always a tornado shaking the Bridge. The whole planet was enswathed in tornadoes, and worse.

The scanner on the foreman's board had given 114 as the sector of the trouble. That was at the northwestern end of the Bridge, where it broke off, leaving nothing but the raging clouds of ammonia crystals and methane, and a sheer drop thirty miles to the invisible surface. There were no ultraphone "eyes" at that end which gave a general view of the area—in so far as any general view was possible—because both ends of the Bridge were incomplete.

With a sigh Helmuth put the beetle into motion. The little car, as flat-bottomed and thin through as a bed-bug, got slowly under way on its ball-bearing races, guided and held firmly to the surface of the Bridge by ten close-set flanged rails. Even so, the hydrogen gales made a terrific siren-like shrieking between the edge of the vehicle and the deck, and the impact of the falling drops of ammonia upon the curved roof was as heavy and deafening as a rain of cannon balls. As a matter of fact, they weighed almost as much as cannon balls here, though they were not much bigger than ordinary raindrops. Every so often, too, there was a blast, accompanied by a dull orange glare, which made the car, the deck, and the Bridge itself buck savagely.

These blasts were below, however, on the surface. While they shook the structure of the Bridge heavily, they almost never interfered with its functioning, and could not, in the very nature of things, do Helmuth any harm.

Had any real damage ever been done, it would never have been repaired. There was no one on Jupiter to repair it.

The Bridge, actually, was building itself. Massive, alone, and lifeless, it grew in the black deeps of Jupiter.

The Bridge had been well-planned. From Helmuth's point of view almost nothing could be seen of it, for the beetle tracks ran down the center of the deck, and in the darkness and perpetual storm even ultra-wave-assisted vision could not penetrate more than a few hundred yards at the most. The width of the Bridge was eleven miles; its height, thirty miles; its length, deliberately unspecified in the plans, fifty-four miles

at the moment—a squat, colossal structure, built with engineering principles, methods, materials and tools never touched before—

For the very good reason that they would have been impossible anywhere else. Most of the Bridge, for instance, was made of ice: a marvellous
structural material under a pressure of a million atmospheres, at a temperature of $-94°C$. Under such conditions, the best structural steel is a
friable, talc-like powder, and aluminum becomes a peculiar, transparent
substance that splits at a tap.

Back home, Helmuth remembered, there had been talk of starting
another Bridge on Saturn, and perhaps still later, on Uranus, too. But
that had been politicians' talk. The Bridge was almost five thousand miles
below the visible surface of Jupiter's atmosphere, and its mechanisms
were just barely manageable. The bottom of Saturn's atmosphere had
been sounded at sixteen thousand eight hundred and seventy-eight miles,
and the temperature there was below $-150°C$. There even pressure-
ice would be immovable, and could not be worked with anything except
itself. And as for Uranus . . .

As far as Helmuth was concerned, Jupiter was quite bad enough.

The beetle crept within sight of the end of the Bridge and stopped
automatically. Helmuth set the vehicle's eyes for highest penetration,
and examined the nearby beams.

The great bars were as close-set as screening. They had to be, in order
to support even their own weight, let alone the weight of the components
of the Bridge. The whole webwork was flexing and fluctuating to the
harpist-fingered gale, but it had been designed to do that. Helmuth could
never help being alarmed by the movement, but habit assured him that
he had nothing to fear from it.

He took the automatics out of the circuit and inched the beetle forward
manually. This was only Sector 113, and the Bridge's own Wheatstone-
bridge scanning system—there was no electronic device anywhere on
the Bridge, since it was impossible to maintain a vacuum on Jupiter—
said that the trouble was in Sector 114. The boundary of Sector 114
was still fully fifty feet away.

It was a bad sign. Helmuth scratched nervously in his red beard. Evidently there was really cause for alarm—real alarm, not just the deep,
grinding depression which he always felt while working on the Bridge.
Any damage serious enough to halt the beetle a full sector short of the
trouble area was bound to be major.

It might even turn out to be the disaster which he had felt lurking
ahead of him ever since he had been made foreman of the Bridge—
that disaster which the Bridge itself could not repair, sending man reeling
home from Jupiter in defeat.

The secondaries cut in and the beetle stopped again. Grimly, Helmuth
opened the switch and sent the beetle creeping across the invisible danger

line. Almost at once, the car tilted just perceptibly to the left, and the screaming of the winds between its edges and the deck shot up the scale, sirening in and out of the soundless-dogwhistle range with an eeriness that set Helmuth's teeth on edge. The beetle itself fluttered and chattered like an alarm-clock hammer between the surface of the deck and the flanges of the tracks.

Ahead there was still nothing to be seen but the horizontal driving of the clouds and the hail, roaring along the length of the Bridge, out of the blackness into the beetle's fanlights, and onward into blackness again towards the horizon no eye would ever see.

Thirty miles below, the fusillade of hydrogen explosions continued. Evidently something really wild was going on on the surface. Helmuth could not remember having heard so much activity in years.

There was a flat, especially heavy crash, and a long line of fuming orange fire came pouring down the seething atmosphere into the depths, feathering horizontally like the mane of a Lipizzan horse, directly in front of Helmuth. Instinctively, he winced and drew back from the board, although that stream of flame actually was only a little less cold than the rest of the streaming gases, far too cold to injure the Bridge.

In the momentary glare, however, he saw something—an upward twisting of shadows, patterned but obviously unfinished, fluttering in silhouette against the hydrogen cataract's lurid light.

The end of the Bridge.

Wrecked.

Helmuth grunted involuntarily and backed the beetle away. The flare dimmed; the light poured down the sky and fell away into the raging sea below. The scanner clucked with satisfaction as the beetle recrossed the line into Zone 113.

He turned the body of the vehicle 180°, presenting its back to the dying torrent. There was nothing further that he could do at the moment on the Bridge. He scanned his control board—a ghost image of which was cast across the scene on the Bridge—for the blue button marked *Garage*, punched it savagely, and tore off his helmet.

Obediently, the Bridge vanished.

II

Dillon was looking at him.

"Well?" the civil engineer said. "What's the matter, Bob? Is it bad—?"

Helmuth did not reply for a moment. The abrupt transition from the storm-ravaged deck of the Bridge to the quiet, placid air of the control shack on Jupiter V was always a shock. He had never been able to anticipate it, let alone become accustomed to it; it was worse each time, not better.

He put the helmet down carefully in front of him and got up, moving carefully upon shaky legs; feeling implicit in his own body the enormous pressures and weights his guiding intelligence had just quitted. The fact that the gravity on the foreman's deck was as weak as that of most of the habitable asteroids only made the contrast greater, and his need for caution in walking more extreme.

He went to the big porthole and looked out. The unworn, tumbled, monotonous surface of airless Jupiter V looked almost homey after the perpetual holocaust of Jupiter itself. But there was an overpowering reminder of that holocaust—for through the thick quartz the face of the giant planet stared at him, across only one hundred and twelve thousand and six hundred miles: a sphere-section occupying almost all of the sky except the near horizon. It was crawling with colour, striped and blotched with the eternal, frigid, poisonous storming of its atmosphere, spotted with the deep planet-sized shadows of farther moons.

Somewhere down there, six thousand miles below the clouds that boiled in his face, was the Bridge. The Bridge was thirty miles high and eleven miles wide and fifty-four miles long—but it was only a sliver, an intricate and fragile arrangement of ice-crystals beneath the bulging, racing tornadoes.

On Earth, even in the West, the Bridge would have been the mightiest engineering achievement of all history, could the Earth have borne its weight at all. But on Jupiter, the Bridge was as precarious and perishable as a snowflake.

"Bob?" Dillon's voice asked. "You seem more upset than usual. Is it serious?" Helmuth turned. His superior's worn young face, lantern-jawed and crowned by black hair already beginning to grey at the temples, was alight both with love for the Bridge and the consuming ardour of the responsibility he had to bear. As always, it touched Helmuth, and reminded him that the implacable universe had, after all, provided one warm corner in which human beings might huddle together.

"Serious enough," he said, forming the words with difficulty against the frozen inarticulateness Jupiter forced upon him. "But not fatal, as far as I could see. There's a lot of hydrogen vulcanism on the surface, especially at the northwest end, and it looks like there must have been a big blast under the cliffs. I saw what looked like the last of a series of fireballs."

Dillon's face relaxed while Helmuth was talking, slowly, line by engraved line. "Oh. Just a flying chunk, then."

"I'm almost sure that's what it was. The cross-draughts are heavy now. The Spot and the STD are due to pass each other some time next week, aren't they? I haven't checked, but I can feel the difference in the storms."

"So the chunk got picked up and thrown through the end of the Bridge. A big piece?"

Helmuth shrugged. "That end is all twisted away to the left, and the deck is burst to flinders. The scaffolding is all gone, too, of course. A pretty big piece, all right, Charity—two miles through at a minimum."

Dillon sighed. He, too, went to the window, and looked out. Helmuth did not need to be a mind reader to know what he was looking at. Out there, across the stony waste of Jupiter V plus one hundred and twelve thousand and six hundred miles of space, the South Tropical Disturbance was streaming towards the great Red Spot, and would soon overtake it. When the whirling funnel of the STD—more than big enough to suck three Earths into deep-freeze—passed the planetary island of sodium-tainted ice which was the Red Spot, the Spot would follow it for a few thousand miles, at the same time rising closer to the surface of the atmosphere.

Then the Spot would sink again, drifting back towards the incredible jet of stress-fluid which kept it in being—a jet fed by no one knew what forces at Jupiter's hot, rocky, twenty-two-thousand-mile core, under sixteen thousand miles of eternal ice. During the entire passage, the storms all over Jupiter became especially violent; and the Bridge had been forced to locate in anything but the calmest spot on the planet, thanks to the uneven distribution of the few permanent land-masses.

Helmuth watched Dillon with a certain compassion, tempered with mild envy. Charity Dillon's unfortunate given name betrayed him as the son of a hangover, the only male child of a Witness family which dated back to the great Witness Revival of 2003. He was one of the hundreds of government-drafted experts who had planned the Bridge, and he was as obsessed by the Bridge as Helmuth was—but for different reasons.

Helmuth moved back to the port, dropping his hand gently upon Dillon's shoulder. Together they looked at the screaming straw yellows, brick reds, pinks, oranges, browns, even blues and greens that Jupiter threw across the ruined stone of its innermost satellite. On Jupiter V, even the shadows had colour.

Dillon did not move. He said at last: "Are you pleased, Bob?"

"Pleased?" Helmuth said in astonishment. "No. It scares me white; you know that. I'm just glad that the whole Bridge didn't go."

"You're quite sure?" Dillon said quietly.

Helmuth took his hand from Dillon's shoulder and returned to his seat at the central desk. "You've no right to needle me for something I can't help," he said, his voice even lower than Dillon's. "I work on Jupiter four hours a day—not actually, because we can't keep a man alive for more than a split second down there—but my eyes and my ears and my mind are there, on the Bridge, four hours a day. Jupiter is not a nice place. I don't like it. I won't pretend I do.

"Spending four hours a day in an environment like that over a period of years—well, the human mind instinctively tries to adapt, even to the unthinkable. Sometimes I wonder how I'll behave when I'm put back in Chicago again. Sometimes I can't remember anything about Chicago except vague generalities, sometimes I can't even believe there is such a place as Earth—how could there be, when the rest of the universe is like Jupiter, or worse?"

"I know," Dillon said. "I've tried several times to show you that isn't a very reasonable frame of mind."

"I know it isn't. But I can't help how I feel. No, I don't think the Bridge will last. It can't last; it's all wrong. But I don't *want* to see it go. I've just got sense enough to know that one of these days Jupiter is going to sweep it away."

He wiped an open palm across the control boards, snapping all the toggles "Off" with a sound like the fall of a double-handful of marbles on a pane of glass. "Like that, Charity! And I work four hours a day, every day, on the Bridge. One of these days, Jupiter is going to destroy the Bridge. It'll go flying away in little flinders into the storms. My mind will be there, supervising some puny job, and my mind will go flying away along with my mechanical eyes and ears—still trying to adapt to the unthinkable, tumbling away into the winds and the flames and the rains and the darkness and the pressure and the cold."

"Bob, you're deliberately running away with yourself. Cut it out. Cut it out, I say!"

Helmuth shrugged, putting a trembling hand on the edge of the board to steady himself. "All right. I'm all right, Charity. I'm here, aren't I? Right here on Jupiter V, in no danger, in no danger at all. The Bridge is one hundred and twelve thousand and six hundred miles away from here. But when the day comes that the Bridge is swept away—

"Charity, sometimes I imagine you ferrying my body back to the cosy nook it came from, while my soul goes tumbling and tumbling through millions of cubic miles of poison. All right, Charity, I'll be good. I won't think about it out loud; but you can't expect me to forget it. It's on my mind; I can't help it, and you should know that."

"I do," Dillon said, with a kind of eagerness. "I do, Bob. I'm only trying to help, to make you see the problem as it is. The Bridge isn't really that awful, it isn't worth a single nightmare."

"Oh, it isn't the Bridge that makes me yell out when I'm sleeping," Helmuth said, smiling bitterly. "I'm not that ridden by it yet. It's while I'm awake that I'm afraid the Bridge will be swept away. What I sleep with is a fear of myself."

"That's a sane fear. You're as sane as any of us," Dillon insisted, fiercely solemn. "Look, Bob. The Bridge isn't a monster. It's a way we've developed for studying the behaviour of materials under specific conditions of temperament, pressure, and gravity. Jupiter isn't Hell, either; it's a set of conditions. The Bridge is the laboratory we set up to work with those conditions."

"It isn't going anywhere. It's a bridge to no place."

"There aren't many *places* on Jupiter," Dillon said, missing Helmuth's meaning entirely. "We put the Bridge on an island in the local sea because we needed solid ice we could sink the caissons in. Otherwise, it wouldn't have mattered where we put it. We could have floated it on the sea itself, if we hadn't wanted to fix it in order to measure storm velocities and such things."

"I know that," Helmuth said.

"But, Bob, you don't show any signs of understanding it. Why, for instance, should the Bridge *go* any place? It isn't even, properly speaking, a bridge at all. We only call it that because we used some bridge engineering principles in building it. Actually, it's much more like a travelling crane—an extremely heavy-duty overhead rail line. It isn't going anywhere because it hasn't any place interesting to go, that's all. We're extending it to cover as much territory as possible, and to increase its stability, not to span the distance between places. There's no point to reproaching it because it doesn't span a real gap—between, say, Dover and Calais. It's a bridge to knowledge, and that's far more important. Why can't you see that?"

"I can see that; that's what I was talking about," Helmuth said, trying to control his impatience. "I have as much common sense as the average child. What I was trying to point out is that meeting colossalness with colossalness—out here—is a mug's game. It's a game Jupiter will always win, without the slightest effort. What if the engineers who built the Dover-Calais bridge had been limited to broom-straws for their structural members? They could have got the bridge up somehow, sure, and made it strong enough to carry light traffic on a fair day. But what would you have had left of it after the first winter storm came down the Channel from the North Sea? The whole approach is idiotic!"

"All right," Dillon said reasonably. "You have a point. Now you're being reasonable. What better approach have you to suggest? Should we abandon Jupiter entirely because it's too big for us?"

"No," Helmuth said. "Or maybe, yes. I don't know. I don't have any easy answer. I just know that this one is no answer at all—it's just a cumbersome evasion."

Dillon smiled. "You're depressed, and no wonder. Sleep it off, Bob, if you can—you might even come up with that answer. In the meantime— well, when you stop to think about it, the surface of Jupiter isn't any more hostile, inherently, than the surface of Jupiter V, except in degree. If you stepped out of this building naked, you'd die just as fast as you would on Jupiter. Try to look at it that way."

Helmuth, looking forward into another night of dreams, said: "That's the way I look at it now."

III

There were three yellow "Critical" signals lit on the long gang board when Helmuth passed through the gang deck on the way back to duty.

All of them, as usual, were concentrated on Panel 9, where Eva Chavez worked.

Eva, despite her Latin name—such once-valid tickets no longer meant anything among Earth's uniformly mixed-race population—was a big girl, vaguely blonde, who cherished a passion for the Bridge. Unfortunately, she was apt to become enthralled by the sheer Cosmicness of it all, precisely at the moments when cold analysis and split-second decisions were most crucial.

Helmuth reached over her shoulder, cut her out of the circuit except as an observer, and donned the co-operator's helmet. The incomplete new shoals caisson sprang into being around him. Breakers of boiling hydrogen seethed seven hundred feet up along its slanted sides—breakers that never subsided, but simply were torn away into flying spray.

There was a spot of dull orange near the top of the north face of the caisson, crawling slowly towards the pediment of the nearest truss. Catalysis—

Or cancer, as Helmuth could not help but think of it. On this bitter, violent monster of a planet, even the tiny specks of calcium carbide were deadly. At these wind velocities, such specks imbedded themselves in everything; and at fifteen million pounds per square inch, pressure ice catalyzed by sodium took up ammonia and carbon dioxide, building protein-like compounds in a rapid, deadly chain of decay:

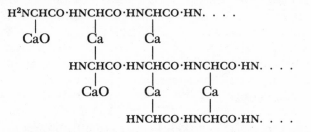

For a second, Helmuth watched it grow. It was, after all, one of the incredible possibilities the Bridge had been built to study. On Earth, such a compound, had it occurred at all, might have grown porous, bony, and quite strong. Here, under nearly eight times the gravity, the molecules were forced to assemble in strict aliphatic order, but in cross section their arrangement was hexagonal, as if the stuff would become an aromatic compound if it only could. Even here it was moderately strong in cross section—but along the long axis it smeared like graphite, the calcium atoms readily surrendering their valence hold on one carbon atom to grab hopefully for the next one in line—

No stuff to hold up the piers of humanity's greatest engineering project. Perhaps it was suitable for the ribs of some Jovian jellyfish, but in a Bridge-caisson, it was cancer.

There was a scraper mechanism working on the edge of the lesion, flaking away the shearing aminos and laying down new ice. In the meantime, the decay of the caisson-face was working deeper. The scraper could not possibly get at the core of the trouble—which was not the calcium carbide dust, with which the atmosphere was charged beyond redemption, but was instead one imbedded sodium speck which was taking no part in the reaction—fast enough to extirpate it. It could barely keep pace with the surface spread of the disease.

And laying new ice over the surface of the wound was worthless. At this rate, the whole caisson would slough away and melt like butter, within an hour, under the weight of the Bridge above it.

Helmuth sent the futile scraper aloft. Drill for it? No—too deep already, and location unknown.

Quickly he called two borers up from the shoals below, where constant blasting was taking the foundation of the caisson deeper and deeper into Jupiter's dubious "soil." He drove both blind, fire-snouted machines down into the lesion.

The bottom of that sore turned out to be forty-five metres within the immense block. Helmuth pushed the red button all the same.

The borers blew up, with a heavy, quite invisible blast, as they had been designed to do. A pit appeared on the face of the caisson.

The nearest truss bent upward in the wind. It fluttered for a moment, trying to resist. It bent farther.

Deprived of its major attachment, it tore free suddenly, and went whirling away into the blackness. A sudden flash of lightning picked it out for a moment, and Helmuth saw it dwindling like a bat with torn wings being borne away by a cyclone.

The scraper scuttled down into the pit and began to fill it with ice from the bottom. Helmuth ordered down a new truss and a squad of scaffolders. Damage of this order took time to repair. He watched the tornado tearing ragged chunks from the edges of the pit until he was sure that the catalysis had stopped. Then, suddenly, prematurely, dismally tired, he took off the helmet.

He was astounded by the white fury that masked Eva's big-boned, mildly pretty face.

"You'll blow the Bridge up yet, won't you?" she said, evenly, without preamble. "Any pretext will do!"

Baffled, Helmuth turned his head helplessly away; but that was no better. The suffused face of Jupiter peered swollenly through the picture-port, just as it did on the foreman's desk.

He and Eva and Charity and the gang and the whole of satellite V were falling forward towards Jupiter; their uneventful cooped-up lives on Jupiter V were utterly unreal compared to the four hours of each changeless day spent on Jupiter's everchanging surface. Every new day brought their minds, like ships out of control, closer and closer to that gaudy inferno.

There was no other way for a man—or a woman—on Jupiter V to look at the giant planet. It was simple experience, shared by all of them, that planets do not occupy four-fifths of the whole sky, unless the observer is himself up there in that planet's sky, falling, falling faster and faster—

"I have no intention," he said tiredly, "of blowing up the Bridge. I wish you could get it through your head that I want the Bridge to stay up—even though I'm not starry-eyed to the point of incompetence about the project. Did you think that rotten spot was going to go away by itself when you'd painted it over? Didn't you know that—"

Several helmeted, masked heads nearby turned blindly towards the sound of his voice. Helmuth shut up. Any distracting conversation or activity was taboo, down here in the gang room. He motioned Eva back to duty.

The girl donned her helmet obediently enough, but it was plain from the way her normally full lips were thinned that she thought Helmuth had ended the argument only in order to have the last word.

Helmuth strode to the thick pillar which ran down the central axis of the shack, and mounted the spiralling cleats towards his own foreman's cubicle. Already he felt in anticipation the weight of the helmet upon his own head.

Charity Dillon, however, was already wearing the helmet; he was sitting in Helmuth's chair.

Charity was characteristically oblivious of Helmuth's entrance. The Bridge operator must learn to ignore, to be utterly unconscious of anything happening around his body except the inhuman sounds of signals; must learn to heed only those senses which report something going on thousands of miles away.

Helmuth knew better than to interrupt him. Instead, he watched Dillon's white, blade-like fingers roving with blind sureness over the controls.

Dillon, evidently, was making a complete tour of the Bridge—not only from end to end, but up and down, too. The tally board showed that he had already activated nearly two-thirds of the ultraphone eyes. That meant that he had been up all night at the job; had begun it immediately after last talking to Helmuth.

Why?

With a thrill of unfocused apprehension, Helmuth looked at the foreman's jack, which allowed the operator here in the cubicle to communicate with the gang when necessary, and which kept him aware of anything said or done at gang boards.

It was plugged in.

Dillon sighed suddenly, took the helmet off, and turned.

"Hello, Bob," he said. "Funny about this job. You can't see, you can't hear, but when somebody's watching you, you feel a sort of pressure on the back of your neck. ESP, maybe. Ever felt it?"

"Pretty often, lately. Why the grand tour, Charity?"

"There's to be an inspection," Dillon said. His eyes met Helmuth's. They were frank and transparent. "A mob of Western officials, coming to see that their eight billion dollars isn't being wasted. Naturally, I'm a little anxious to see that they find everything in order."

"I see," Helmuth said. "First time in five years, isn't it?"

"Just about. What was that dust-up down below just now? Somebody— you, I'm sure, from the drastic handiwork involved—bailed Eva out of a mess, and then I heard her talk about your wanting to blow up the Bridge. I checked the area when I heard the fracas start, and it did seem as if she had let things go rather far, but— What was it all about?"

Dillon ordinarily hadn't the guile for cat-and-mouse games, and he had never looked less guileful than now. Helmuth said carefully, "Eva was upset, I suppose. On the subject of Jupiter we're all of us cracked by now, in our different ways. The way she was dealing with the catalysis didn't look to me to be suitable—a difference of opinion, resolved in my favour because I had the authority, Eva didn't. That's all."

"Kind of an expensive difference, Bob. I'm not niggling by nature, you know that. But an incident like that while the commission is here—"

"The point is," Helmuth said, "are we to spend an extra ten thousand, or whatever it costs to replace a truss and reinforce a caisson, or are we to lose the whole caisson—and as much as a third of the whole Bridge along with it?"

"Yes, you're right there, of course. That could be explained, even to a pack of senators. But—it would be difficult to have to explain it very often. Well, the board's yours, Bob. You could continue my spot-check, if you've time."

Dillon got up. Then he added suddenly, as if it were forced out of him:

"Bob, I'm trying to understand your state of mind. From what Eva said, I gather that you've made it fairly public. I . . . I don't think it's a good idea to infect your fellow workers with your own pessimism. It leads to sloppy work. I know that regardless of your own feelings you won't countenance sloppy work, but one foreman can do only so much. And you're making extra work for yourself—not for me, but for yourself— by being openly gloomy about the Bridge.

"You're the best man on the Bridge, Bob, for all your grousing about the job, and your assorted misgivings. I'd hate to see you replaced."

"A threat, Charity?" Helmuth said softly.

"*No.* I wouldn't replace you unless you actually went nuts, and I firmly believe that your fears in that respect are groundless. It's a commonplace that only sane men suspect their own sanity, isn't it?"

"It's a common misconception. Most psychopathic obsessions begin with a mild worry."

Dillon made as if to brush that subject away. "Anyhow, I'm not threatening; I'd fight to keep you here. But my say-so only covers Jupiter V; there are people higher up on Ganymede, and people higher yet back in Washington—and in this inspecting commission.

"Why don't you try to look on the bright side for a change? Obviously the Bridge isn't ever going to inspire you. But you might at least try thinking about all those dollars piling up in your account every hour you're on this job, and about the bridges and ships and who knows what-all that you'll be building, at any fee you ask, when you get back down to Earth. All under the magic words, 'One of the men who built the Bridge on Jupiter!' "

Charity was bright red with embarrassment and enthusiasm. Helmuth smiled.

"I'll try to bear it in mind, Charity," he said. "When is this gaggle of senators due to arrive?"

"They're on Ganymede now, taking a breather. They came directly from Washington without any routing. I suppose they'll make a stop at Callisto before they come here. They've something new on their ship, I'm told, that lets them flit about more freely than the usual uphill transport can."

An icy lizard suddenly was nesting in Helmuth's stomach, coiling and coiling but never settling itself. The room blurred. The persistent nightmare was suddenly almost upon him—already.

"Something . . . new?" he echoed, his voice as flat and noncommittal as he could make it. "Do you know what it is?"

"Well, yes. But I think I'd better keep quiet about it until—"

"Charity, nobody on this deserted rock-heap could possibly be a Soviet spy. The whole habit of 'security' is idiotic out here. Tell me now and save me the trouble of dealing with senators; or tell me at least that you know I know. *They have antigravity!* Isn't that it?"

One word from Dillon, and the nightmare would be real.

"Yes," Dillon said. "How did you know? Of course, it couldn't be a complete gravity screen by any means. But it seems to be a good long step towards it. We've waited a long time to see that dream come true— But you're the last man in the world to take pride in the achievement, so there's no sense exulting about it to you. I'll let you know when I get a definite arrival date. In the meantime, will you think about what I said before?"

"Yes, I will." Helmuth took the seat before the board.

"Good. With you, I have to be grateful for small victories. Good trick, Bob."

"Good trick, Charity."

IV

Instead of sleeping—for now he knew that he was really afraid—he sat up in the reading chair in his cabin. The illuminated microfilm pages of a book flipped by across the surface of the wall opposite him, timed precisely to the reading rate most comfortable for him, and he had several weeks' worry-conserved alcohol and smoke rations for ready consumption.

But Helmuth let his mix go flat, and did not notice the book, which had turned itself on, at the page where he had abandoned it last, when he had fitted himself into the chair. Instead, he listened to the radio.

There was always a great deal of ham radio activity in the Jovian system. The conditions were good for it, since there was plenty of power available, few impeding atmosphere layers, and those thin, no Heaviside layers, and few official and no commercial channels with which the hams could interfere.

And there were plenty of people scattered about the satellites who needed the sound of a voice.

". . . anybody know whether the senators are coming here? Doc Barth put in a report a while back on a fossil plant he found here, at least he thinks it was a plant. Maybe they'd like a look at it."

"They're supposed to hit the Bridge team next." A strong voice, and the impression of a strong transmitter wavering in and out; that would be Sweeney, on Ganymede. "Sorry to throw the wet blanket, boys, but I don't think the senators are interested in our rock-balls for their own lumpy selves. We could only hold them here three days."

Helmuth thought greyly: *Then they've already left Callisto.*

"Is that you, Sweeney? Where's the Bridge tonight?"

"Dillon's on duty," a very distant transmitter said. "Try to raise Helmuth, Sweeney."

"Helmuth, Helmuth, you gloomy beetle-gooser! Come in, Helmuth!"

"Sure, Bob, come in and dampen us."

Sluggishly, Helmuth reached out to take the mike, where it lay clipped to one arm of the chair. But the door to his room opened before he had completed the gesture.

Eva came in.

She said, "Bob, I want to tell you something."

"His voice is changing!" the voice of the Callisto operator said. "Ask him what he's drinking, Sweeney!"

Helmuth cut the radio out. The girl was freshly dressed—in so far as anybody dressed in anything on Jupiter V—and Helmuth wondered why she was prowling the decks at this hour, half-way between her sleep period and her trick. Her hair was hazy against the light from the corridor, and she looked less mannish than usual. She reminded him a little of the way she had looked when they first met.

"All right," he said. "I owe you a mix, I guess. Citric, sugar and the other stuff is in the locker . . . you know where it is. Shot-cans are there, too."

The girl shut the door and sat down on the bunk, with a free litheness that was almost grace, but with a determination which Helmuth knew meant that she had just decided to do something silly for all the right reasons.

"I don't need a drink," she said. "As a matter of fact, lately I've been turning my lux-R's back to the common pool. I suppose you did that for me—by showing me what a mind looked like that is hiding from itself."

"Eva, stop sounding like a tract. Obviously, you've advanced to a higher, more Jovian plane of existence, but won't you still need your metabolism? Or have you decided that vitamins are all-in-the-mind?"

"Now you're being superior. Anyhow, alcohol isn't a vitamin. And I didn't come to talk about that. I came to tell you something I think you ought to know."

"Which is?"

She said, "Bob, I mean to have a child here."

A bark of laughter, part sheer hysteria and part exasperation, jack-knifed Helmuth into a sitting position. A red arrow bloomed on the far wall, obediently marking the paragraph which, supposedly, he had reached in his reading, and the page vanished.

"*Women!*" he said, when he could get his breath back. "Really, Evita, you make me feel much better. No environment can change a human being much, after all."

"Why should it?" she said suspiciously. "I don't see the joke. Shouldn't a woman want to have a child?"

"Of course she should," he said, settling back. The flipping pages began again. "It's quite ordinary. All women want to have children. All women dream of the day they can turn a child out to play in an airless rock-garden, to pluck fossils and get quaintly star-burned. How cosy to tuck the little blue body back into its corner that night, promptly at the sound of the trick-change bell! Why, it's as natural as Jupiter-light—as Earthian as vacuum-frozen apple pie."

He turned his head casually away. "As for me, though, Eva, I'd much prefer that you take your ghostly little pretext out of here."

Eva surged to her feet in one furious motion. Her fingers grasped him by the beard and jerked his head painfully around again.

"You reedy male platitude!" she said, in a low grinding voice. "How you could see almost the whole point and make so little of it—*Women*, is it? So you think I came creeping in here, full of humbleness, to settle our technical differences."

He closed his hand on her wrist and twisted it away. "What else?" he demanded, trying to imagine how it would feel to stay reasonable for five minutes at a time with these Bridge-robots. "None of us need bother with games and excuses. We're here, we're isolated, we were all chosen because, among other things, we were judged incapable of forming permanent emotional attachments, and capable of such alliances as we found attractive without going unbalanced when the attraction diminished and the alliance came unstuck. None of us have to pretend that our living arrangements would keep us out of jail in Boston, or that they have to involve any Earth-normal excuses."

She said nothing. After a while he asked, gently, "Isn't that so?"

"Of course it's so. Also it has nothing to do with the matter."

"It doesn't? How stupid do you think I am? *I* don't care whether or not you've decided to have a child here, if you really mean what you say."

She was trembling with rage. "You really don't, too. The decision means nothing to you."

"Well, if I liked children, I'd be sorry for the child. But as it happens, I can't stand children. In short, Eva, as far as I'm concerned you can have as many as you want, and to me you'll *still* be the worst operator on the Bridge."

"I'll bear that in mind," she said. At this moment she seemed to have been cut from pressure-ice. "I'll leave you something to charge your mind with, too, Robert Helmuth. I'll leave you sprawled here under your precious book . . . what is Madame Bovary to you, anyhow, you unadventurous turtle? . . . to think about a man who believes that children must always be born into warm cradles—a man who thinks that men have to huddle on warm worlds, or they won't survive. A man with no ears, no eyes, scarcely any head. A man in terror, a man crying Mamma! *Mamma!* all the stellar days and nights long!"

"Parlour diagnosis!"

"Parlour labelling. Good trick, Bob. Draw your warm wooly blanket in tight about your brains, or some little sneeze of sense might creep in, and impair your—efficiency!"

The door closed sharply after her.

A million pounds of fatigue crashed down without warning on Helmuth's brain, and he fell back into the reading chair with a gasp. The roots of his beard ached, and Jupiters bloomed and wavered away before his closed eyes.

He struggled once, and fell asleep.

Instantly he was in the grip of the dream.

It started, as always, with commonplaces, almost realistic enough to be a documentary film-strip—except for the appalling sense of pressure, and the distorted emotional significance with which the least word, the smallest movement was invested.

It was the sinking of the first caisson of the Bridge. The actual event had been bad enough. The job demanded enough exactness of placement to require that manned ships enter Jupiter's atmosphere itself: a squadron of twenty of the most powerful ships ever built, with the five-million-ton asteroid, trimmed and shaped in space, slung beneath them in an immense cat's cradle.

Four times that squadron had disappeared beneath the clouds; four times the tense voices of pilots and engineers had muttered in Helmuth's ears; four times there were shouts and futile orders and the snapping of cables and someone screaming endlessly against the eternal howl of the Jovian sky.

It had cost, altogether, nine ships and two hundred and thirty-one men, to get one of five laboriously shaped asteroids planted in the shifting slush that was Jupiter's surface. Helmuth had helped to supervise all five operations, counting the successful one, from his desk on Jupiter V; but in the dream he was not in the control shack, but instead on shipboard, in one of the ships that was never to come back—

Then, without transition, but without any sense of discontinuity either, he was on the Bridge itself. Not *in absentia*, as the remote guiding intelligence of a beetle, but in person, in an ovular, tank-like suit the details of which would never come clear. The high brass had discovered antigravity, and had asked for volunteers to man the Bridge. Helmuth had volunteered.

Looking back on it in the dream, he did not understand why he had volunteered. It had simply seemed expected of him, and he had not been able to help it, even though he had known what it would be like. He belonged on the Bridge, though he hated it—he had been doomed to go there, from the first.

And there was . . . something wrong . . . with the antigravity. The high brass had asked for its volunteers before the scientific work had been completed. The present antigravity fields were weak, and there was some basic flaw in the theory. Generators broke down after only short periods of use, burned out, unpredictably, sometimes only moments after testing up without a flaw—like vacuum tubes in waking life.

That was what Helmuth's set was about to do. He crouched inside his personal womb, above the boiling sea, the clouds raging about him, lit by a plume of hydrogen flame, and waited to feel his weight suddenly become eight times greater than normal. He knew what would happen to him then.

It happened.

Helmuth greeted morning on Jupiter V with his customary scream.

V

The ship that landed as he was going on duty did nothing to lighten the load on his heart. In shape it was not distinguishable from any of the long-range cruisers which ran the legs of the Moon-Mars-Belt-Ganymede trip. But it grounded its huge bulk with less visible expenditures of power than one of the little intersatellary boats.

That landing told Helmuth that his dream was well on its way to coming true. If the high brass had had a real antigravity, there would have been no reason why the main jets should have been necessary at all. Obviously, what had been discovered was some sort of partial screen, which allowed a ship to operate with far less jet action than was normal, but which still left it subject to a sizeable fraction of the universal stress of space.

Nothing less than complete and completely controllable antigravity would do on Jupiter.

He worked mechanically, noting that Charity was not in evidence. Probably he was conferring with the senators, receiving what would be for him the glad news.

Helmuth realized suddenly that there was nothing left for him to do now but to cut and run.

There could certainly be no reason why he should have to re-enact the entire dream, helplessly, event for event, like an actor committed to a play. He was awake now, in full control of his own senses, and still at least partially sane. The man in the dream had volunteered—but that man would not be Robert Helmuth. Not any longer.

While the senators were here, he would turn in his resignation. Direct, over Charity's head.

"Wake up, Helmuth," a voice from the gang deck snapped suddenly. "If it hadn't been for me, you'd have run yourself off the end of the Bridge. You had all the automatic stops on that beetle cut out."

Helmuth reached guiltily and more than a little too late for the controls. Eva had already run his beetle back beyond the danger line.

"Sorry," he mumbled. "Thanks, Eva."

"Don't thank me. If you'd actually been in it, I'd have let it go. Less reading and more sleep is what I recommend for you, Helmuth."

"Keep your recommendations to yourself," he snapped.

The incident started a new and even more disturbing chain of thought. If he were to resign now, it would be nearly a year before he could get back to Chicago. Antigravity or no antigravity, the senators' ship would have no room for unexpected passengers. Shipping a man back home had to be arranged far in advance. Space had to be provided, and a cargo equivalent of the weight and space requirements he would take up on the return trip had to be deadheaded out to Jupiter.

A year of living in the station on Jupiter V without any function—as a man whose drain on the station's supplies no longer could be justified in terms of what he did. A year of living under the eyes of Eva Chavez and Charity Dillon and the other men and women who still remained Bridge operators, men and women who would not hesitate to let him know what they thought of his quitting.

A year of living as a bystander in the feverish excitement of direct, personal exploration of Jupiter. A year of watching and hearing the inevitable deaths—while he alone stood aloof, privileged and useless. A year during which Robert Helmuth would become the most hated living entity in the Jovian system.

And, when he got back to Chicago and went looking for a job—for his resignation from the Bridge gang would automatically take him out of government service—he would be asked why he left the Bridge at the moment when work on the Bridge was just reaching its culmination.

He began to understand why the man in the dream had volunteered.

When the trick-change bell rang, he was still determined to resign, but he had already concluded bitterly that there were, after all, other kinds of hells besides the one on Jupiter.

He was returning the board to neutral as Charity came up the cleats. Charity's eyes were snapping like a skyful of comets. Helmuth had known that they would be.

"Senator Wagoner wants to speak to you, if you're not too tired, Bob," he said. "Go ahead; I'll finish up there."

"He does?" Helmuth frowned. The dream surged back upon him. *NO.* They would not rush him any faster than he wanted to go. "What about, Charity? Am I suspected of un-Western activities? I suppose you've told them how I feel."

"I have," Dillon said, unruffled. "But we're agreed that you may not feel the same after you've talked to Wagoner. He's in the ship, of course. I've put out a suit for you at the lock."

Charity put the helmet over his head, effectively cutting himself off from further conversation, or from any further consciousness of Helmuth at all.

Helmuth stood looking at him a moment. Then, with a convulsive shrug, he went down the cleats.

Three minutes later, he was plodding in a spacesuit across the surface of Jupiter V, with the vivid bulk of Jupiter splashing his shoulders with colour.

A courteous Marine let him through the ship's air lock and deftly peeled him out of the suit. Despite a grim determination to be uninterested in the new antigravity and any possible consequence of it, he looked curiously about as he was conducted up towards the bow.

But the ship was like the ones that had brought him from Chicago to Jupiter V—it was like any spaceship: there was nothing in it to see but corridor walls and stairwells, until you arrived at the cabin where you were needed.

Senator Wagoner was a surprise. He was a young man, no more than sixty-five at most, not at all portly, and he had the keenest pair of blue eyes that Helmuth had ever seen. He received Helmuth alone, in his own cabin—a comfortable cabin as spaceship accommodations go, but neither roomy nor luxurious. He was hard to match up with the stories

Helmuth had been hearing about the current Senate, which had been involved in scandal after scandal of more than Roman proportions.

Helmuth looked around. "I thought there were several of you," he said.

"There are, but I didn't want to give you the idea that you were facing a panel," Wagoner said, smiling. "I've been forced to sit in on most of these endless loyalty investigations back home, but I can't see any point in exporting such religious ceremonies to deep space. Do sit down, Mr. Helmuth. There are drinks coming. We have a lot to talk about."

Stiffly, Helmuth sat down.

"Dillon tells me," Wagoner said, leaning back comfortably in his own chair, "that your usefulness to the Bridge is about at an end. In a way, I'm sorry to hear that, for you've been one of the best men we've had on any of our planetary projects. But, in another way, I'm glad. It makes you available for something much bigger, where we need you much more."

"What do you mean by that?"

"I'll explain in a moment. First, I'd like to talk a little about the Bridge. Please don't feel that I'm quizzing you, by the way. You're at perfect liberty to say that any given question is none of my business, and I'll take no offence and hold no grudge. Also, 'I hereby disavow the authenticity of any tape or other tapping of which this statement may be a part.' In short, our conversation is unofficial, highly so."

"Thank you."

"It's to my interest; I'm hoping that you'll talk freely to me. Of course my disavowal means nothing, since such formal statements can always be excised from a tape; but later on I'm going to tell you some things you're not supposed to know, and you'll be able to judge by what I say then that anything you say to me is privileged. Okay?"

A steward came in silently with the drinks, and left again. Helmuth tasted his. As far as he could tell, it was exactly like many he had mixed for himself back in the control shack, from standard space rations. The only difference was that it was cold, which Helmuth found startling, but not unpleasant after the first sip. He tried to relax. "I'll do my best," he said.

"Good enough. Now: Dillon says that you regard the Bridge as a monster. I've examined your dossier pretty closely, and I think perhaps Dillon hasn't quite the gist of your meaning. I'd like to hear it straight from you."

"I don't think the Bridge is a monster," Helmuth said slowly. "You see, Charity is on the defensive. He takes the Bridge to be conclusive evidence that no possible set of adverse conditions ever will stop man for long, and there I'm in agreement with him. But he also thinks of it as Progress, personified. He can't admit—you asked me to speak my mind, senator—that the West is a decadent and dying culture. All the other evidence that's available shows that it is. Charity likes to think of the Bridge as giving the lie to that evidence."

"The West hasn't many more years," Wagoner agreed, astonishingly. "Still and all, the West has been responsible for some really towering achievements in its time. Perhaps the Bridge could be considered as the last and the mightiest of them all."

"Not by me," Helmuth said. "The building of gigantic projects for ritual purposes—doing a thing for the sake of doing it—is the last act of an already dead culture. Look at the pyramids in Egypt for an example. Or an even more idiotic and more enormous example, bigger than anything human beings have accomplished yet, the laying out of the 'Diagram of Power' over the whole face of Mars. If the Martians had put all that energy into survival instead, they'd probably be alive yet."

"Agreed," Wagoner said.

"All right. Then maybe you'll also agree that the essence of a vital culture is its ability to defend itself. The West has beaten off the Soviets for a century now—but as far as I can see, the Bridge is the West's 'Diagram of Power,' its pyramids, or what have you. All the money and the resources that went into the Bridge are going to be badly needed, *and won't be there,* when the next Soviet attack comes."

"Which will be very shortly, I'm told," Wagoner said, with complete calm. "Furthermore, it will be successful, and in part it will be successful for the very reasons you've outlined. For a man who's been cut off from the Earth for years, Helmuth, you seem to know more about what's going on down there than most of the general populace does."

"Nothing promotes an interest in Earth like being off it," Helmuth said. "And there's plenty of time to read out here." Either the drink was stronger than he had expected, or the senator's calm concurrence in the collapse of Helmuth's entire world had given him another shove towards nothingness; his head was spinning.

Wagoner saw it. He leaned forward suddenly, catching Helmuth flat-footed. *"However,"* he said, "it's difficult for me to agree that the Bridge serves, or ever did serve, a ritual purpose. The Bridge served a huge practical purpose which is now fulfilled—the Bridge, as such, is now a defunct project."

"Defunct?" Helmuth repeated faintly.

"Quite. Of course we'll continue to operate it for a while, simply because you can't stop a process of that size on a dime, and that's just as well for people like Dillon who are emotionally tied up in it. You're the one person with any authority in the whole station who has already lost enough interest in the Bridge to make it safe for me to tell you that it's being abandoned."

"But why?"

"Because," Wagoner went on quietly, "the Bridge has now given us confirmation of a theory of stupendous importance—so important, in my opinion, that the imminent fall of the West seems like a puny event in comparison. A confirmation, incidentally, which contains in it the seeds of ultimate destruction for the Soviets, whatever they may win for themselves in the next fifty years or so."

"I suppose," Helmuth said, puzzled, "that you mean antigravity?"

For the first time, it was Wagoner's turn to be taken aback. "Man," he said at last, "do you know *everything* I want to tell you? I hope not, or my conclusions will be mighty suspicious. Surely Charity didn't tell you we had antigravity; I strictly enjoined him not to mention it."

"No, the subject's been on my mind," Helmuth said. "But I certainly don't see why it should be so world-shaking, any more than I see how the Bridge helped to bring it about. I thought it had been developed independently, for the further exploitation of the Bridge, and would step up Bridge operation, not discontinue it."

"Not at all. Of course, the Bridge has given us information in thousands of different categories, much of it very valuable indeed. But the one job that *only* the Bridge could do was that of confirming, or throwing out, the Blackett-Dirac equations."

"Which are—?"

"A relationship between magnetism and the spinning of a massive body—that much is the Dirac part of it. The Blackett Equation seemed to show that the same formula also applied to gravity. If the figures we collected on the magnetic field strength of Jupiter forced us to retire the Dirac equations, then none of the rest of the information we've gotten from the Bridge would have been worth the money we spent to get it. On the other hand, Jupiter was the only body in the solar system available to us which was big enough in all relevant respects to make it possible for us to test those equations at all. They involve quantities of enormous orders of magnitudes.

"And the figures show that Dirac was right. *They also show that Blackett was right.* Both magnetism *and* gravity are phenomena of rotation.

"I won't bother to trace the succeeding steps, because I think you can work them out for yourself. It's enough to say that there's a drive-generator on board this ship which is the complete and final justification of all the hell you people on the Bridge gang have been put through. The gadget has a long technical name, but the technies who tend it have already nicknamed it the spindizzy, because of what it does to the magnetic moment of any atom—*any* atom—within its field.

"While it's in operation, it absolutely refuses to notice any atom outside its own influence. Furthermore, it will notice no other strain or influence which holds good beyond the borders of that field. It's so snooty that it has to be stopped down to almost nothing when it's brought close to a planet, or it won't let you land. But in deep space . . . well, it's impervious to meteors and such trash, of course; it's impervious to gravity; and—it hasn't the faintest interest in any legislation about top speed limits."

"You're kidding," Helmuth said.

"Am I, now? This ship came to Ganymede directly from Earth. It did it in a little under two hours, counting manoeuvering time."

Helmuth took a defiant pull at his drink. "This thing really has no top speed at all?" he said. "How can you be sure of that?"

"Well, we can't," Wagoner admitted. "After all, one of the unfortunate things about general mathematical formulas is that they don't contain cut-off points to warn you of areas where they don't apply. Even quantum mechanics is somewhat subject to that criticism. However, we expect to know pretty soon just how fast the spindizzy can drive an object, if there is any limit. We expect you to tell us."

"I?"

"Yes, Helmuth, you. The coming débâcle on Earth makes it absolutely imperative for us—the West—to get interstellar expeditions started at once. Richardson Observatory, on the Moon, has two likely-looking systems picked out already—one at Wolf 359, another at 61 Cygni—and there are sure to be hundreds of others where Earth-like planets are highly probable. We want to scatter adventurous people, people with a thoroughly indoctrinated love of being free, all over this part of the galaxy, if it can be done.

"Once they're out there, they'll be free to flourish, with no interference from Earth. The Soviets haven't the spindizzy yet, and even after they steal it from us, they won't dare allow it to be used. It's too good and too final an escape route.

"What we want you to do . . . now I'm getting to the point, you see . . . is to direct this exodus. You've the intelligence and the cast of mind for it. Your analysis of the situation on Earth confirms that, if any more confirmation were needed. And—there's no future for you on Earth now."

"You'll have to excuse me," Helmuth said, firmly. "I'm in no condition to be reasonable now; it's been more than I could digest in a few moments. And the decision doesn't entirely rest with me, either. If I could give you an answer in . . . let me see . . . about three hours. Will that be soon enough?"

"That'll be fine," the senator said.

"And so, that's the story," Helmuth said.

Eva remained silent in her chair for a long time.

"One thing I don't understand," she said at last. "Why did you come to me? I'd have thought that you'd find the whole thing terrifying."

"Oh, it's terrifying, all right," Helmuth said, with quiet exultation. "But terror and fright are two different things, as I've just discovered. We were both wrong, Evita. I was wrong in thinking that the Bridge was a dead end. You were wrong in thinking of it as an end in itself."

"I don't understand you."

"All right, let's put it this way: The work the Bridge was doing was worth-while, as I know now—so I was wrong in being frightened of it, in calling it a bridge to nowhere.

"But you no more saw where it was going than I, and you made the Bridge the be-all and end-all of your existence.

"Now, there's a place to go to; in fact there are places—hundreds of places. They'll be Earth-like places. Since the Soviets are about to win Earth, those places will be more Earth-like than Earth itself, for the next century or so at least!"

She said, "Why are you telling me this? Just to make peace between us?"

"I'm going to take on this job, Evita, if you'll go along?"

She turned swiftly, rising out of the chair with a marvellous fluidity of motion. At the same instant, all the alarm bells in the station went off at once, filling every metal cranny with a jangle of pure horror.

"Posts!" the speaker above Eva's bed roared, in a distorted, gigantic version of Charity Dillon's voice. *"Peak storm overload! The STD is now passing the Spot. Wind velocity has already topped all previous records, and part of the land mass has begun to settle. This is an A-1 overload emergency."*

Behind Charity's bellow, the winds of Jupiter made a spectrum of continuous, insane shrieking. The Bridge was responding with monstrous groans of agony. There was another sound, too, an almost musical cacophony of sharp, percussive tones, such as a dinosaur might make pushing its way through a forest of huge steel tuning-forks. Helmuth had never heard that sound before, but he knew what it was.

The deck of the Bridge was splitting up the middle.

After a moment more, the uproar dimmed, and the speaker said, in Charity's normal voice, "Eva, you too, please. Acknowledge, please. This is it—unless everybody comes on duty at once, the Bridge may go down within the next hour."

"Let it," Eva responded quietly.

There was a brief, startled silence, and then a ghost of a human sound. The voice was Senator Wagoner's, and the sound just might have been a chuckle.

Charity's circuit clicked out.

The mighty death of the Bridge continued to resound in the little room.

After a while, the man and the woman went to the window, and looked past the discarded bulk of Jupiter at the near horizon, where there had always been visible a few stars.

BIBLIOGRAPHY

"Okie," *Astounding*, April 1950

"Bindlestiff," *Astounding*, December 1950

"Sargasso of Lost Cities," *Two Complete Science Adventure Stories*, 1952

"Earthman Come Home," *Astounding*, November 1953

Earthman Come Home (contains the above stories), Putnam, 1955

"Bridge," *Astounding*, February 1952

"At Death's End," *Astounding*, May 1954

Year 2018! (also known as *They Shall Have Stars*, expansion of the above two stories), Faber & Faber (U.K.), 1956, Avon Books (expanded from the British edition), 1957.

The Triumph of Time, Avon Books, 1958

A Life for the Stars, Analog, September–October, 1962, Putnam, 1962

Cities in Flight (contains all of the above books), Avon Books, 1970

THE PANTROPY SERIES

by James Blish

Introduction by James and Judith Blish

There's terraforming, there's giving up, and there's pantropy. You can change the planet to accommodate the colonists, or the colonists to accommodate the planet. In *The Seedling Stars,* Jim set out to speculate on the ways that man might be redesigned for other worlds. The book is a collection of five stories, of which "Surface Tension" became, mysteriously to the author, the most popular. In letters written to the British fanzines, *Cypher* and *Speculation,* in 1973, Jim discussed his puzzlement.

" 'Surface Tension' was, in fact, a commissioned sequel to 'Sunken Universe' (first published in 1942), which I incorporated as 'Cycle One' of the version which most readers know. It explored a background, fresh water microbiology, which I knew very well, and which hadn't to the best of my knowledge been explored by anybody else.

"In all other respects it struck me as being, to be blunt, a creditable piece of hack work—and the editor who commissioned it wouldn't even give it that, saying he wouldn't take it unless I cut it by one-third, which I refused to do. It took three years, and the addition of a prologue, to get 'Surface Tension' into print, by which time it was my seventy-eighth published work. 'Sunken Universe' had been my eleventh. It can be understood, I think, that when it did happen, my only emotion was relief at having finally placed an old turkey—plus a little fear (not much, because I had no emotional investment in the story by then) that readers would recognize and dismiss it as such.

"Its subsequent history astonished me, and continued to do so till 1972. I didn't *dislike* it, and still don't. But what I did dislike more and more was that it came to be, and remains, almost everyone's favorite Blish story. I couldn't see *why.* Not only had I written things I thought better on almost every count—no author's favorites ever match item for item with those of his readers and critics—but if readers were going to make a favorite of one of my scores of conventional science fiction stories, *why had they settled so overwhelmingly on this one?*

"I began to ask this question not only of fans, but of other writers who knew much about my work—and who felt the same preference without getting any further toward an answer. They mentioned the unusual backdrop, the occasionally charming little critturs, the inch-long spaceship—in short, small ingenuities of the same kind I'd used as stock-in-trade in half a hundred other conventional stories that had made no such dent.

"Once, again on commission and for a far fatter fee, I made an exhaustive analysis of the story from general structure right down to individual word choices, and then wrote another one which followed the analysis *exactly,* even including elements that I'd otherwise have tried to do better or even omit. After all, since the whole thing was a mystery still, maybe the secret was hidden in one of its mistakes! This act of critical mimicry dropped dead on publication, and I've never again tried to consciously repeat a success, let alone that minutely.

"In the meantime, in Huxley's phrase, the Absolute's tail was unsalted; and though by this time I was visibly wincing every time anyone said 'surface tension' in my hearing, it wasn't from pain or dislike of the story itself, but simply because of thirty years of mounting bafflement over what could be so compelling about it.

"In 1972 Darko Suvin was our house guest for a few days. By then I'd known him long enough, and talked to him so often to my benefit, that I made a last hopeless attempt at this question.

"He produced an answer. Though I am sure he wouldn't so describe it, to me it was like a Eucharist. It explained not only the popularity of 'Surface Tension' but of some other conventional works of mine, and why some others had quite failed to be memorable, and a good many other things too. 'Surface Tension' had shared with the other successes a unique attitude toward all the disparate backgrounds and devices that I had completely failed to detect. Hence my utter failure to imitate it." (*Speculation* 32, Spring 1973)

A year later (in *Cypher* 11, May 1974), Jim shared his revelation.

"Darko Suvin asked me to dig out of my library one of the issues of the Aldiss-Harrison *SF Horizons,* and to look at the cover picture.

" 'That,' he said, 'is the central thrill of "Surface Tension," and what most of your serious work is about.' The picture is a woodcut showing a monk" (!) "on his hands and knees, crawling out of the familiar world through a break—which he seems to have made himself—in the Aristotelian spheres, and looking amazed at the totally different universe he finds outside them.

"This insight into my central theme *includes* Damon Knight's analysis—i.e., 'getting born' (*In Search of Wonder,* Chapter 26) but isn't nearly so restrictive for me. Nor does it require any complex ingenuities of detail. . . . What could be simpler?"

Jim found this notion of Professor Suvin's profoundly satisfying; he kept pulling books from his shelf and saying, "See? See? There it is again! Darko was right!"

See for yourself.

Surface Tension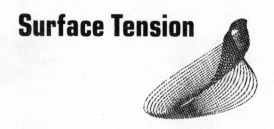

Dr. Chatvieux took a long time over the microscope, leaving la Ventura with nothing to do but look at the dead landscape of Hydrot. Waterscape, he thought, would be a better word. From space, the new world had shown only one small, triangular continent, set amid endless ocean; and even the continent was mostly swamp.

The wreck of the seed-ship lay broken squarely across the one real spur of rock which Hydrot seemed to possess, which reared a magnificent twenty-one feet above sea level. From this eminence, la Ventura could see forty miles to the horizon across a flat bed of mud. The red light of the star Tau Ceti, glinting upon thousands of small lakes, pools, ponds and puddles, made the watery plain look like a mosaic of onyx and ruby.

"If I were a religious man," the pilot said suddenly, "I'd call this a plain case of divine vengeance."

Chatvieux said: "Hmn?"

"It's as if we'd been struck down for—is it *hubris*, arrogant pride?"

"Well, is it?" Chatvieux said, looking up at last. "I don't feel exactly swollen with pride. Do you?"

"I'm not exactly proud of my piloting," la Ventura admitted. "But that isn't quite what I meant. I was thinking about why we came here in the first place. It takes a lot of arrogance to think that you can scatter men, or at least things very much like men, all over the face of the galaxy. It takes even more pride to do the job—to pack up all the equipment and move from planet to planet and actually make men, make them suitable for every place you touch."

"I suppose it does," Chatvieux said. "But we're only one of several hundred seed-ships in this limb of the galaxy, so I doubt that the gods picked us out as special sinners." He smiled dryly. "If they had, maybe they'd have left us our ultraphone, so the Colonization Council could hear about our cropper. Besides, Paul, we try to produce men adapted to Earthlike planets, nothing more than that. We've sense enough to know that we can't adapt men to a planet like Jupiter, or to a sun, like Tau Ceti."

"Anyhow, we're here," la Ventura said grimly. "And we aren't going to get off. Phil tells me that we don't even have our germ-cell bank any more, so we can't seed this place in the usual way. We've been thrown onto a dead world and dared to adapt to it. What are the pana-tropes to do with our carcasses—provide built-in waterwings?"

"No," Chatvieux said calmly. "You and I and all the rest of us are going to die, Paul. Panatropic techniques don't work on the body; that was fixed for you for life when you were conceived. To attempt to rebuild it for you would only maim you. The panatropes affect only the genes, the inheritance-carrying factors. We can't give you built-in waterwings, any more than we can give you a new set of brains. I think we'll be able to populate this world with men, but we won't live to see it."

The pilot thought about it, a lump of cold blubber collecting in his stomach. "How long do you give us?"

"Who knows? A month, perhaps."

The bulkhead leading to the wrecked section of the ship was pushed back, admitting salt, muggy air, heavy with carbon dioxide. Philip Strasvogel, the communications officer, came in, tracking mud. Like la Ventura, he was now a man without a function, and it appeared to bother him. He was not well equipped for introspection, and with his ultraphone totally smashed, unresponsive to his perpetually darting hands, he had been thrown back into his own mind, whose resources were few. Only the tasks Chatvieux had set him to had prevented him from setting like a gelling colloid into a permanent sulk.

He unbuckled from around his waist a canvas belt, into the loops of which plastic vials were stuffed like cartridges. "More samples, Doc," he said. "All alike—water, very wet. I have some quicksand in one boot, too. Find anything?"

"A good deal, Phil. Thanks. Are the others around?"

Strasvogel poked his head out and hallooed. Other voices rang out over the mudflats. Minutes later, the rest of the survivors of the crash were crowding into the panatrope deck: Saltonstall, Chatvieux' senior assistant, a perpetually sanguine, perpetually youthful technician willing to try anything once, including dying; Eunice Wagner, behind whose placid face rested the brains of the expedition's only remaining ecologist; Eleftherios Venezuelos, the always-silent delegate from the Colonization Council; and Joan Heath, a midshipman whose duties, like la Ventura's and Phil's, were now without meaning, but whose bright head and tall, deceptively indolent body shone to the pilot's eyes brighter than the home sun.

Five men and two women—to colonize a planet on which "standing room" meant treading water.

They came in quietly and found seats or resting places on the deck, on the edges of tables, in corners. Joan Heath went to stand beside la Ventura. They did not look at each other, but the warmth of her shoulder beside his was all that he needed. Nothing was as bad as it seemed.

Venezuelos said, "What's the verdict, Dr. Chatvieux?"

"This place isn't dead," Chatvieux said. "There's life in the sea and in the fresh water, both. On the animal side of the ledger, evolution seems to have stopped with the crustacea; the most advanced form I've found is a tiny crayfish, from one of the local rivulets, and it doesn't seem to be well distributed. The ponds and puddles are well-stocked with small metazoans of lower orders, right up to the rotifers—including a castle-building rotifer like Earth's *Floscularidae*. In addition, there's a wonderfully variegated protozoan population, with a dominant ciliate type much like *Paramoecium*, plus various Sarcodines, the usual spread of phytoflagellates, and even a phosphorescent species I wouldn't have expected to see anywhere but in salt water. As for the plants, they run from simple blue-green algae to quite advanced thallus-producing types—though none of them, of course, can live out of the water."

"The sea is about the same," Eunice said. "I've found some of the larger simple metazoans—jellyfish and so on—and some *Palinuridae* almost as big as lobsters. But it's normal to find salt-water species running larger than fresh-water. And there's the usual plankton and nannoplankton population."

"In short," Chatvieux said, "we'll survive if we fight."

"Wait a minute," la Ventura said. "You've just finished telling me that we wouldn't survive. And you were talking about us, the seven of us here, not about the genus Man, because we don't have our germ-cell banks any more."

"We don't have the banks. But we ourselves can contribute germ-cells, Paul. I'll get to that in a moment." Chatvieux turned to Saltonstall. "Martin, what would you think of taking to the sea? We came out of it once."

"No good," Saltonstall said immediately. "*I* like the idea, but I don't think this planet ever heard of Swinburne, or Homer either. Looking at it as a colonization problem alone, as if we weren't involved in it ourselves, I wouldn't give you an Oc dollar for *epi oinopa ponton*. The evolutionary pressure there is too high, the competition from other species is prohibitive; seeding the sea should be the last thing we attempt. The colonists wouldn't learn a thing before they'd be gobbled up."

"Why?" la Ventura said. Once more, the death in his stomach was becoming hard to placate.

"Eunice, do your sea-going Coelenterates include anything like the Portuguese man-of-war?"

The ecologist nodded.

"There's your answer, Paul," Saltonstall said. "The sea is out. It's got to be fresh water, where the competition is less formidable and there are more places to hide."

"We can't compete with a jellyfish?" la Ventura asked.

"No, Paul," Chatvieux said. "Not with one that formidable. The panatropes make adaptations, not gods. They take human germ-cells—in this case, our own, since our bank was wiped out in the crash—and modify them genetically toward those of creatures who can live in any reasonable environment. The result will be manlike, and intelligent. It usually shows the donors' personality patterns, too, since the modifications are usually made in the morphology, not mind, of the resulting individual.

"*But we can't transmit memory.* The adapted man is worse than a child in his new environment. He has no history, no techniques, no precedents, not even a language. In the usual colonization project, the seeding teams more or less take him through elementary school before they leave the planet to him, but we won't survive long enough to give such instruction. We'll have to design our colonists with plenty of built-in protections and locate them in the most favorable environment possible, so that some of them will survive learning by experience alone."

The pilot thought about it, but nothing occurred to him which did not make the disaster seem realer and more intimate with each passing second. Joan Heath moved slightly closer to him. "One of the new creatures can have my personality pattern, but it won't be able to remember being me. Is that right?"

"That's right. In the present situation we'll probably make our colonists haploid, so that some of them, perhaps many, will have a heredity traceable to you alone. There may be just the faintest of residuums of identity— panatropy's given us some data to support the old Jungian notion of ancestral memory. But we're all going to die on Hydrot, Paul, as self-conscious persons. There's no avoiding that. Somewhere we'll leave behind people who behave as we would, think and feel as we would, but who won't remember us—or the Earth."

The pilot said nothing more.

"Saltonstall, what do you recommend as a form?"

The panatropist pulled reflectively at his nose. "Webbed extremities, of course, with thumbs and big toes heavy and thornlike for defense until the creature has had a chance to learn. Smaller external ears, and the eardrum larger and closer to the outer end of the ear-canal. We're going to have to reorganize the water-conservation system, I think; the glomerular kidney is perfectly suitable for living in fresh water, but the business of living immersed in fresh water, inside and out, for a creature with a salty inside means that the osmotic pressure inside is going to be higher than outside, so that the kidneys are going to have to be pumping virtually all the time. Under the circumstances we'd best step up production of urine, and that means the antidiuretic function of the pituitary gland is going to have to be abrogated."

"What about respiration?"

"Hmm," Saltonstall said. "I suppose book-lungs, like some of the arachnids have. They can be supplied by intercostal spiracles. They're gradually adaptable to atmosphere-breathing, if our colonist ever decides to come out of the water. Just to provide for that possibility, I'd suggest retaining the nose, maintaining the nasal cavity as a part of the otological system, but cutting off the cavity from the larynx with a membrane of cells that are supplied with oxygen by direct irrigation, rather than by the respiratory system. Such a membrane wouldn't survive for many generations, once the creature took to living out of the water even for part of its life time; it'd go through two or three generations as an amphibian, and then one day it'd suddenly find itself breathing through its larynx again.

"Also, Dr. Chatvieux, I'd suggest that we have it adopt sporulation. As an aquatic animal, our colonist is going to have an indefinite life-span, but we'll have to give it a breeding cycle of about six weeks to keep up its numbers during the learning period; so there'll have to be a definite break of some duration in its active year. Otherwise it'll hit overpopulation before it's learned to cope with it."

"Also, it'd be better if our colonists could winter over inside a good, hard shell," Eunice Wagner added in agreement. "So sporulation's the obvious answer. Many other microscopic creatures have it."

"Microscopic?" Phil said incredulously.

"Certainly," Chatvieux said, amused. "We can't very well crowd a six-foot man into a two-foot puddle. But that raises a question. We'll have tough competition from the rotifers, and some of them aren't strictly microscopic; for that matter even some of the protozoa can be seen with the naked eye, just barely, with dark-field illumination. I don't think your average colonist should run much under 250 microns. Give them a chance to slug it out."

"I was thinking of making them twice that big."

"Then they'd be the biggest animals in their environment," Eunice Wagner pointed out, "and won't ever develop any skills. Besides, if you make them about rotifer size, it will give them an incentive for pushing out the castle-building rotifers, and occupying the castles."

Chatvieux nodded. "All right, let's get started. While the panatropes are being calibrated, the rest of us can put our heads together on leaving a record for these people. We'll micro-engrave the record on a set of corrosion-proof metal leaves, of a size our colonists can handle conveniently. We can tell them, very simply, what happened, and plant a few suggestions that there's more to the universe than their puddles. Some day they may puzzle it out."

"Question," Eunice Wagner said. "Are we going to tell them they're microscopic? I'm opposed to it. It may saddle their entire early history with a gods-and-demons mythology that they'd be better off without."

"Yes, we are," Chatvieux said; and la Ventura could tell by the change in the tone of his voice that he was speaking now as their senior on the expedition. "These people will be of the race of men, Eunice. We want them to win their way back into the community of men. They are not toys, to be protected from the truth forever in a fresh-water womb."

"Besides," Saltonstall observed, "they won't get the record translated at any time in their early history. They'll have to develop a written language of their own, and it will be impossible for us to leave them any sort of Rosetta Stone or other key. By the time they can decipher the truth, they should be ready for it."

"I'll make that official," Venezuelos said unexpectedly.

And then, essentially, it was all over. They contributed the cells that the panatropes would need. Privately, la Ventura and Joan Heath went to Chatvieux and asked to contribute jointly; but the scientist said that the microscopic men were to be haploid, in order to give them a minute cellular structure, with nuclei as small as Earthly rickettsiae, and therefore each person had to give germ-cells individually—there would be no use for zygotes. So even that consolation was denied them: in death they would have no children, but be instead as alone as ever.

They helped, as far as they could, in the text of the message which was to go on the metal leaves. They had their personality patterns recorded. They went through the motions. Already they were beginning to be hungry, but there was nothing on Hydrot big enough to eat.

After la Ventura had set his control board to rights—a useless gesture, but a habit he had been taught to respect, and which in an obscure way made things a little easier to bear—he was out of it. He sat by himself at the far end of the rock ledge, watching Tau Ceti go redly down.

After a while Joan Heath came silently up behind him, and sat down too. He took her hand. The glare of the red sun was almost extinguished now, and together they watched it go, with la Ventura, at least, wondering somberly which nameless puddle was to be his Lethe.

He never found out, of course. None of them did.

Old Shar set down the thick, ragged-edged metal plate at last, and gazed instead out the window of the castle, apparently resting his eyes on the glowing green-gold obscurity of the summer waters. In the soft fluorescence which played down upon him, from the Noc dozing impassively in the groined vault of the chamber, Lavon could see that he was in fact a young man. His face was so delicately formed as to suggest that it had not been many seasons since he had first emerged from his spore.

But of course there had been no real reason to have expected an old man. All the Shars had been referred to traditionally as "old" Shar. The reason, like the reasons for everything else, had been forgotten, but the custom had persisted. The adjective at least gave weight and dignity to the office—that of the center of wisdom of all the people, as each Lavon had been the center of authority.

The present Shar belonged to the generation XVI, and hence would have to be at least two seasons younger than Lavon himself. If he was old, it was only in knowledge.

"Lavon, I'm going to have to be honest with you," Shar said at last, still looking out of the tall, irregular window. "You've come to me at your maturity for the secrets on the metal plates, just as your predecessors did to mine. I can give some of them to you—but for the most part, I don't know what they mean."

"After so many generations?" Lavon asked, surprised. "Wasn't it Shar III who first found out how to read them?"

The young man turned and looked at Lavon with eyes made dark and wide by the depths into which they had been staring. "I can read what's on the plates, but most of it seems to make no sense. Worst of all, the plates are incomplete. You didn't know that? They are. One of them was lost in a battle during the final war with the Eaters, while these castles were still in their hands."

"What am I here for, then?" Lavon said. "Isn't there anything of value on the remaining plates? Do they really contain 'the wisdom of the Creators,' or is *that* myth?"

"No. No, it's true," Shar said slowly, "as far as it goes."

He paused, and both men turned and gazed at the ghostly creature which had appeared suddenly outside the window. Then Shar said gravely, "Come in, Para."

The slipper-shaped organism, nearly transparent except for the thousands of black-and-silver granules and frothy bubbles which packed its interior, glided into the chamber and hovered, with a muted whirring of cilia. For a moment it remained silent, probably speaking telepathically to the Noc floating in the vault, after the ceremonious fashion of all the protos. No human had ever intercepted one of these colloquies, but there was no doubt about their reality; humans had used protos for long-range communication for generations.

Then the Para's cilia buzzed once more. Each separate hair-like process vibrated at an independent, changing rate; the resulting sound waves spread through the water, intermodulating, reinforcing or cancelling each other. The aggregate wave-front, by the time it reached human ears, was eerie but recognizable human speech.

"We are arrived, according to the custom."

"And welcome," said Shar. "Lavon, let's leave this matter of the plates for a while, until you hear what Para has to say; that's a part of the knowledge Lavons must have as they come into their office, and it comes before the plates. I can give you some hints of what we are. First Para has to tell you something about what we aren't."

Lavon nodded, willingly enough, and watched the proto as it settled gently to the surface of the hewn table at which Shar had been sitting. There was in the entity such a perfection and economy of organization, such a grace and surety of movement, that he could hardly believe in his own new-won maturity. Para, like all the protos, made him feel unfinished.

"We know that in this universe there is logically no place for man," the gleaming, now immobile cylinder upon the table droned abruptly. "Our memory is the common property of all our races. It reaches back to a time when there were no such creatures as men here, nor any even remotely like men. It remembers also that once upon a day there were men here, suddenly, and in some numbers. Their spores littered the bottom; we found the spores only a short time after our season's Awakening, and inside them we saw the forms of men, slumbering.

"Then men shattered their spores and emerged. At first they seemed helpless, and the Eaters devoured them by scores, as in those days they devoured anything that moved. But that soon ended. Men were intelligent, active. And they were gifted with a trait, a character, possessed by no other creature in this world. Not even the savage Eaters had it. Men organized us to exterminate the Eaters, and therein lay the difference. Men had initiative. We have the word now, which you gave us, and we apply it, but we still do not know what the thing is that it labels."

"You fought beside us," Lavon said.

"Gladly. We would never have thought of that war by ourselves, but it was good and brought good. Yet we wondered. We saw that men were poor swimmers, poor walkers, poor crawlers, poor climbers. We saw that men were formed to make and use tools, a concept we still do not understand, for so wonderful a gift is largely wasted in this universe, and there is no other. What good are tool-useful members such as the hands of men? We do not know. It seems plain that so radical a thing should lead to a much greater rulership over the world than has, in fact, proven to be possible for men."

Lavon's head was spinning. "Para, I had no notion that you people were philosophers."

"The protos are old," Shar said. He had again turned to look out the window, his hands locked behind his back. "They aren't philosophers, Lavon, but they are remorseless logicians. Listen to Para."

"To this reasoning there could be but one outcome," the Para said. "Our strange ally, Man, was like nothing else in this universe. He was and is unfitted for it. He does not belong here; he has been—adopted. This drives us to think that there are other universes besides this one, but where these universes might lie, and what their properties might be, it is impossible to imagine. We have no imagination, as men know."

Was the creature being ironic? Lavon could not tell. He said slowly: "Other universes? How could that be true?"

"We do not know," the Para's uninflected voice hummed.

Shar had resumed sitting on the window sill, clasping his knees, watching the come and go of dim shapes in the lighted gulf. "It is quite true," he said. "What is written on the plates makes it plain. I'll tell you what they say.

"*We were made,* Lavon. We were made by men who were not as we are, but men who were our ancestors all the same. They were caught in some disaster, and they made us, and put us here in our universe— so that, even though they had to die, the race of men would live."

Lavon surged up from the woven spyrogyra mat upon which he had been sitting. "You must think I'm a fool!"

"No. You're our Lavon; you have a right to know the facts. Make what you like of them." Shar swung his webbed toes back into the chamber. "What I've told you may be hard to believe, but it seems to be so; what Para says backs it up. Our unfitness to live here is self-evident:

"The past four Shars discovered that we won't get any farther in our studies until we learn how to control heat. We've produced enough heat chemically to show that even the water around us changes when the temperature gets high enough. But there we're stopped."

"Why?"

"Because heat produced in open water is carried off as rapidly as it's produced. Once we tried to enclose that heat, and we blew up a whole tube of the castle and killed everything in range; the shock was terrible. We measured the pressures that were involved in that explosion, and we discovered that no substance we know could have resisted them. Theory suggests some stronger substances—*but we need heat to form them!*

"Take our chemistry. We live in water. Everything seems to dissolve in water, to some extent. How do we confine a chemical test to the crucible we put it in? How do we maintain a solution at one dilution? I don't know. Every avenue leads me to the same stone door. We're thinking creatures, Lavon, but there's something drastically wrong in the way we think about this universe we live in. It just doesn't seem to lead to results."

Lavon pushed back his floating hair futilely. "Maybe you're thinking about the wrong results. We've had no trouble with warfare, or crops, or practical things like that. If we can't create much heat, well, most of us won't miss it; we don't need any. What's the other universe supposed to be like, the one our ancestors lived in? Is it any better than this one?"

"I don't know," Shar admitted. "It was so different that it's hard to compare the two. The metal plates tell a story about men who were travelling from one place to another in a container that moved by itself. The only analogy I can think of is the shallops of diatom shells that our youngsters use to sled along the thermocline; but evidently what's meant is something much bigger.

"I picture a huge shallop, closed on all sides, big enough to hold many people—maybe twenty or thirty. It had to travel for generations through some kind of space where there wasn't any water to breathe, so that the people had to carry their own water and renew it constantly. There were no seasons; no ice formed on the sky, because there wasn't any sky in a closed shallop.

"Then the shallop was wrecked somehow. The people in it knew they were going to die. They made us, and put us here, as if we were their children. Because they had to die, they wrote their story on the plates, to tell us what had happened. I suppose we'd understand it better if we had the plate Shar III lost during the war, but we don't."

"The whole thing sounds like a parable," Lavon said, shrugging. "Or a song. I can see why you don't understand it. What I can't see is why you bother to try."

"Because of the plates," Shar said. "You've handled them yourself now, so you know that we've nothing like them. We have crude, impure metals we've hammered out, metals that last for a while and then decay. But the plates shine on, generation after generation. They don't change; our hammers and our graving tools break against them; the little heat we can generate leaves them unharmed. Those plates weren't formed in our universe—and that one fact makes every word on them important to me. Someone went to a great deal of trouble to make those plates indestructible, and to give them to us. Someone to whom the word 'stars' was important enough to be worth fourteen repetitions, despite the fact that the word doesn't seem to mean anything."

Lavon stood up once more.

"All these extra universes and huge shallops and meaningless words— I can't say that they don't exist, but I don't see what difference it makes," he said. "The Shars of a few generations ago spent their whole lives breeding better algae crops for us, and showing us how to cultivate them, instead of living haphazardly on bacteria. Farther back, the Shars devised war engines, and war plans. All that was work worth doing. The Lavons of those days evidently got along without the metal plates and their puzzles, and saw to it that the Shars did, too. Well, as far as I'm concerned, you're welcome to the plates, if you like them better than crop improvement—but I think they ought to be thrown away."

"All right," Shar said, shrugging. "If you don't want them, that ends the traditional interview. We'll go our—"

There was a rising drone from the table-top. The Para was lifting itself, waves of motion passing over its cilia, like the waves which went silently across the fruiting stalks of the fields of delicate fungi with which the bottom was planted. It had been so silent that Lavon had forgotten it; he could tell that Shar had, too.

"This is a great decision," the waves of sound washing from the creature throbbed. "Every proto has heard it, and agrees with it. We have been afraid of these metal plates for a long time, afraid that men would learn to understand them and to follow what they say to some secret place, leaving the protos. Now we are not afraid."

"There wasn't anything to be afraid of," Lavon said indulgently.

"No Lavon before you had ever said so," the Para said. "We are glad. We will throw the plates away."

With that, the shining creature swooped toward the embrasure. With it, it bore away the remaining plates, which had been resting under it on the table-top, suspended delicately in the curved tips of its supple ventral cilia. Inside its pellucid body, vacuoles swelled to increase its buoyancy and enable it to carry the heavy weight.

With a cry, Shar plunged toward the window.

"Stop, Para!"

But Para was already gone, so swiftly that it had not even heard the call. Shar twisted his body and brought up one shoulder against the tower wall. He said nothing. His face was enough. Lavon could not look into it for more than an instant.

The shadows of the two men began to move slowly along the uneven cobbled floor. The Noc descended toward them from the vault, its single thick tentacle stirring the water, its internal light flaring and fading irregularly. It, too, drifted through the window after its cousin, and sank slowly away toward the bottom. Gently its living glow dimmed, flickered in the depths, and winked out.

For many days, Lavon was able to avoid thinking much about the loss. There was already a great deal of work to be done. Maintenance of the castles, which had been built by the now-extinct Eaters rather than by human hands, was a never-ending task. The thousand dichotomously-branching wings tended to crumble with time, especially at their bases where they sprouted from one another, and no Shar had yet come forward with a mortar as good as the rotifer-spittle which had once held them together. In addition, the breaking through of windows and the construction of chambers in the early days had been haphazard and often unsound. The instinctive architecture of the Eaters, after all, had not been meant to meet the needs of human occupants.

And then there were the crops. Men no longer fed precariously upon passing bacteria snatched to the mouth; now there were the drifting mats of specific water-fungi and algae, and the mycelia on the bottom, rich and nourishing, which had been bred by five generations of Shars. These had to be tended constantly to keep the strains pure, and to keep the older and less intelligent species of the protos from grazing on them. In this latter task, to be sure, the more intricate and far-seeing proto types cooperated, but men were needed to supervise.

There had been a time, after the war with the Eaters, when it had been customary to prey upon the slow-moving and stupid diatoms, whose exquisite and fragile glass shells were so easily burst, and who were unable to learn that a friendly voice did not necessarily mean a friend. There were still people who would crack open a diatom when no one else was looking, but they were regarded as barbarians, to the puzzlement of the protos. The blurred and simple-minded speech of the gorgeously engraved plants had brought them into the category of pets—a concept which the protos were unable to grasp, especially since men admitted diatoms on the half-frustrule were delicious.

Lavon had had to agree, very early, that the distinction was tiny. After all, humans did eat the desmids, which differed from the diatoms only in three particulars: their shells were flexible, they could not move (and for that matter neither could all but a few groups of diatoms), and they did not speak. Yet to Lavon, as to most men, there did seem to be some kind of distinction, whether the protos could see it or not, and that was that. Under the circumstance he felt that it was a part of his duty, as the hereditary leader of men, to protect the diatoms from the few who poached on them, in defiance of custom, in the high levels of the sunlit sky.

Yet Lavon found it impossible to keep himself busy enough to forget that moment when the last clues to Man's origin and destination had been lifted, on authority of his own careless exaggeration, and borne away.

It might be possible to ask Para for the return of the plates, explain that a mistake had been made. The protos were creatures of implacable logic, but they respected Man, were used to illogic in Man, and might reverse their decision if pressed—

We are sorry. The plates were carried over the bar and released in the gulf. We will have the bottom there searched, but . . .

With a sick feeling he could not repress, Lavon knew that that would be the answer, or something very like it. When the protos decided something was worthless, they did not hide it in some chamber like old women. They threw it away—efficiently.

Yet despite the tormenting of his conscience, Lavon was nearly convinced that the plates were well lost. What had they ever done for Man, except to provide Shars with useless things to think about in the late seasons of their lives? What the Shars themselves had done to benefit Man, here, in the water, in the world, in the universe, had been done by direct experimentation. No bit of useful knowledge had ever come from the plates. There had never been anything in the plates but things best left unthought. The protos were right.

Lavon shifted his position on the plant frond, where he had been sitting in order to overlook the harvesting of an experimental crop of blue-green, oil-rich algae drifting in a clotted mass close to the top of the sky, and scratched his back gently against the coarse bole. The protos were seldom wrong, after all. Their lack of creativity, their inability to think an original thought, was a gift as well as a limitation. It allowed them to see and feel things at all times as they were—not as they hoped they might be, for they had no ability to hope, either.

"La-von! Laa-vah-on!"

The long halloo came floating up from the sleepy depths. Propping one hand against the top of the frond, Lavon bent and looked down. One of the harvesters was looking up at him, holding loosely the adze with which he had been splitting free from the raft the glutinous tetrads of the algae.

"I'm up here. What's the matter?"

"We have the ripened quadrant cut free. Shall we tow it away?"

"Tow it away," Lavon said, with a lazy gesture. He leaned back again. At the same instant, a brilliant reddish glory burst into being above him, and cast itself down toward the depths like mesh after mesh of the finest drawn gold. The great light which lived above the sky during the day, brightening or dimming according to some pattern no Shar ever had fathomed, was blooming again.

Few men, caught in the warm glow of that light, could resist looking up at it—especially when the top of the sky itself wrinkled and smiled just a moment's climb or swim away. Yet, as always, Lavon's bemused upward look gave him back nothing but his own distorted, bobbling reflection, and a reflection of the plant on which he rested. Here was the upper limit, the third of the three surfaces of the universe.

The first surface was the bottom, where the water ended.

The second surface was the thermocline, the invisible division between the colder waters of the bottom and the warm, light waters of the sky. During the height of the warm weather, the thermocline was so definite a division as to make for good sledding and for chilly passage. A real interface formed between the cold, denser bottom waters and the warm reaches above, and maintained itself almost for the whole of the warm season.

The third surface was the sky. One could no more pass through that surface than one could penetrate the bottom, nor was there any better reason to try. There the universe ended. The light which played over it daily, waxing and waning as it chose, seemed one of its properties.

Toward the end of the season, the water gradually became colder and more difficult to breathe, while at the same time the light grew duller and stayed for shorter periods between darknesses. Slow currents started to move. The high waters turned chill and started to fall. The bottom mud stirred and smoked away, carrying with it the spores of the fields of fungi. The thermocline tossed, became choppy, and melted away. The sky began to fog with particles of soft silt carried up from the bottom, the walls, the corners of the universe. Before very long, the whole world was cold, flocculent with dying creatures.

Then the protos encysted; the bacteria, even most of the plants—and, not long afterward, men, too—curled up in their oil-filled amber shells. The world died until the first current of warm water broke the winter silence.

"La-von!"

Just after the long call, a shining bubble rose past Lavon. He reached out and poked it, but it bounded away from his sharp thumb. The gas bubbles which rose from the bottom in late summer were almost invulnerable—and when some especially hard blow or edge did penetrate them, they broke into smaller bubbles which nothing could touch, leaving behind a remarkably bad smell.

Gas. There was no water inside a bubble. A man who got inside a bubble would have nothing to breathe.

But, of course, it was impossible to enter a bubble. The surface tension was too strong. As strong as Shar's metal plates. As strong as the top of the sky.

As strong as the top of the sky. And above that—once the bubble was broken—a world of gas instead of water? Were all worlds bubbles of water drifting in gas?

If it were so, travel between them would be out of the question, since it would be impossible to pierce the sky to begin with. Nor did the infant cosmography include any provisions for bottoms for the worlds.

And yet some of the local creatures did burrow *into* the bottom, quite deeply, seeking something in those depths which was beyond the reach of Man. Even the surface of the ooze, in high summer, crawled with tiny creatures for which mud was a natural medium. Man, too, passed freely between the two countries of water which were divided by the thermocline, though many of the creatures with which he lived could not pass that line at all, once it had established itself.

And if the new universe of which Shar had spoken existed at all, it had to exist beyond the sky, where the light was. Why could not the sky be passed, after all? The fact that bubbles could sometimes be broken showed that the surface skin that formed between water and gas wasn't completely invulnerable. Had it ever been tried?

Lavon did not suppose that one man could butt his way through the top of the sky, any more than he could burrow into the bottom, but there might be ways around the difficulty. Here at his back, for instance, was a plant which gave every appearance of continuing beyond the sky.

It had always been assumed that the plants died where they touched the sky. For the most part, they did, for frequently the dead extension could be seen, leached and yellow, the boxes of its component cells empty, floating embedded in the perfect mirror. But some were simply chopped off, like the one which sheltered him now. Perhaps that was only an illusion, and instead it soared indefinitely into some other place—some place where men might once have been born, and might still live . . .

The plates were gone. There was only one other way to find out.

Determinedly, Lavon began to climb toward the wavering mirror of the sky. His thorn-thumbed feet trampled obliviously upon the clustered sheaths of fragile stippled diatoms. The tulip-heads of Vortae, placid and murmurous cousins of Para, retracted startledly out of his way upon coiling stalks, to make silly gossip behind him.

Lavon did not hear them. He continued to climb doggedly toward the light, his fingers and toes gripping the plant-bole.

"Lavon! Where are you going? Lavon!"

He leaned out and looked down. The man with the adze, a doll-like figure, was beckoning to him from a patch of blue-green retreating over a violet abyss. Dizzily he looked away, clinging to the bole; he had never been so high before. He had, of course, nothing to fear from falling, but the fear was in his heritage. Then he began to climb again.

After a while, he touched the sky with one hand. He stopped to breathe. Curious bacteria gathered about the base of his thumb where blood from a small cut was fogging away, scattered at his gesture, and wriggled mindlessly back toward the dull red lure.

He waited until he no longer felt winded, and resumed climbing. The sky pressed down against the top of his head, against the back of his neck, against his shoulders. It seemed to give slightly, with a tough, frictionless elasticity. The water here was intensely bright, and quite colorless. He climbed another step, driving his shoulders against that enormous weight.

He might as well have tried to penetrate a cliff.

Again he had to rest. While he panted, he made a curious discovery. All around the bole of the water plant, the steel surface of the sky curved upward, making a kind of sheath. He found that he could insert his hand into it—there was almost enough space to admit his head as well. Clinging closely to the bole, he looked up into the inside of the sheath, probing it with his injured hand. The glare was blinding.

There was a kind of soundless explosion. His whole wrist was suddenly encircled in an intense, impersonal grip, as if it were being cut in two. In blind astonishment, he lunged upward.

The ring of pain travelled smoothly down his upflung arm as he rose, was suddenly around his shoulders and chest. Another lunge and his knees were being squeezed in the circular vise. Another—

Something was horribly wrong. He clung to the bole and tried to gasp, but there was—nothing to breathe.

The water came streaming out of his body, from his mouth, his nostrils, the spiracles in his sides, spurting in tangible jets. An intense and fiery itching crawled over the surface of his body. At each spasm, long knives ran into him, and from a great distance he heard more water being expelled from his book-lungs in an obscene, frothy sputtering. Inside his head, a patch of fire began to eat away at the floor of his nasal cavity.

Lavon was drowning.

With a final convulsion, he kicked himself away from the splintery bole, and fell. A hard impact shook him; and then the water, which had clung to him so tightly when he had first attempted to leave it, took him back with cold violence.

Sprawling and tumbling grotesquely, he drifted, down and down and down, toward the bottom.

For many days, Lavon lay curled insensibly in his spore, as if in the winter sleep. The shock of cold which he had felt on re-entering his native universe had been taken by his body as a sign of coming winter, as it had taken the oxygen-starvation of his brief sojourn above the sky. The spore-forming glands had at once begun to function.

Had it not been for this, Lavon would surely have died. The danger of drowning disappeared even as he fell, as the air bubbled out of his lungs and readmitted the life-giving water. But for acute desiccation and third degree sunburn, the sunken universe knew no remedy. The healing amnionic fluid generated by the spore-forming glands, after the transparent amber sphere had enclosed him, offered Lavon his only chance.

The brown sphere was spotted after some days by a prowling ameba, quiescent in the eternal winter of the bottom. Down there the temperature was always an even 4°, no matter what the season, but it was unheard of that a spore should be found there while the high epilimnion was still warm and rich in oxygen.

Within an hour, the spore was surrounded by scores of astonished protos, jostling each other to bump their blunt eyeless prows against the shell. Another hour later, a squad of worried men came plunging from the castles far above to press their own noses against the transparent wall. Then swift orders were given.

Four Para grouped themselves about the amber sphere, and there was a subdued explosion as the trichocysts which lay embedded at the bases of their cilia, just under the pellicle, burst and cast fine lines of a quickly solidifying liquid into the water. The four Paras thrummed and lifted, tugging.

Lavon's spore swayed gently in the mud and then rose slowly, entangled in the web. Nearby, a Noc cast a cold pulsating glow over the operation— not for the Paras, who did not need the light, but for the baffled knot of men. The sleeping figure of Lavon, head bowed, knees drawn up to its chest, revolved with an absurd solemnity inside the shell as it was moved.

"Take him to Shar, Para."

The young Shar justified, by minding his own business, the traditional wisdom with which his hereditary office had invested him. He observed at once that there was nothing he could do for the encysted Lavon which would not be classifiable as simple meddling.

He had the sphere deposited in a high tower room of his castle, where there was plenty of light and the water was warm, which should suggest to the estivating form that spring was again on the way. Beyond that, he simply sat and watched, and kept his speculations to himself.

Inside the spore, Lavon's body seemed rapidly to be shedding its skin, in long strips and patches. Gradually, his curious shrunkenness disappeared. His withered arms and legs and sunken abdomen filled out again.

The days went by while Shar watched. Finally he could discern no more changes, and, on a hunch, had the spore taken up to the top of the tower, into the direct daylight.

An hour later, Lavon moved in his amber prison.

He uncurled and stretched, turned blank eyes up toward the light. His expression was that of a man who had not yet awakened from a ferocious nightmare. His whole body shone with a strange pink newness.

Shar knocked gently on the wall of the spore. Lavon turned his blind face toward the sound, life coming into his eyes. He smiled tentatively and braced his hands and feet against the inner wall of the shell.

The whole sphere fell abruptly to pieces with a sharp crackling. The amnionic fluid dissipated around him and Shar, carrying away with it the suggestive odor of a bitter struggle against death.

Lavon stood among the shards and looked at Shar silently. At last he said:

"Shar—I've been above the sky."

"I know," Shar said gently.

Again Lavon was silent. Shar said, "Don't be humble, Lavon. You've done an epoch-making thing. It nearly cost you your life. You must tell me the rest—all of it."

"The rest?"

"You taught me a lot while you slept. Or are you still opposed to 'useless' knowledge?"

Lavon could say nothing. He no longer could tell what he knew from what he wanted to know. He had only one question left, but he could not utter it. He could only look dumbly into Shar's delicate face.

"You have answered me," Shar said, even more gently than before. "Come, my friend; join me at my table. We will plan our journey to the stars."

There were five of them around Shar's big table: Shar himself, Lavon, and the three assistants assigned by custom to the Shars from the families Than, Tanol and Stravol. The duties of these three men—or, sometimes, women—under many previous Shars had been simple and onerous: to put into effect in the field the genetic changes in the food crops which the Shar himself had worked out in laboratory tanks and flats. Under other Shars more interested in metal-working or in chemistry, they had been smudged men—diggers, rock-splitters, fashioners and cleaners of apparatus.

Under Shar XVI, however, the three assistants had been more envied than usual among the rest of Lavon's people, for they seemed to do very little work of any kind. They spent long hours of every day and evening talking with Shar in his chambers, poring over records, making mysterious scratch-marks on slate, or just looking at simple things about which there was no obvious mystery. Sometimes they actually worked with Shar in his laboratory, but mostly they just sat.

Shar XVI had, as a matter of fact, discovered certain rudimentary rules of inquiry which, as he explained it to Lavon, he had recognized as tools of enormous power. He had become more interested in passing these on to future workers than in the seductions of any specific experiment, the journey to the stars perhaps excepted. The Than, Tanol and Stravol of his generation were having scientific method pounded into their heads, a procedure they maintained was sometimes more painful than heaving a thousand rocks.

That they were the first of Lavon's people to be taxed with the problem of constructing a spaceship was, therefore, inevitable. The results lay on the table: three models, made of diatom-glass, strands of algae, flexible bits of cellulose, flakes of stonewort, slivers of wood, and organic glues collected from the secretions of a score of different plants and animals.

Lavon picked up the nearest one, a fragile spherical construction inside which little beads of dark-brown lava—actually bricks of rotifer-spittle painfully chipped free from the wall of an unused castle—moved freely back and forth in a kind of ball-bearing race. "Now whose is this one?" he said, turning the sphere curiously to and fro.

"That's mine," Tanol said. "Frankly I don't think it comes anywhere near meeting all the requirements. It's just the only design I could arrive at that I think we could build with the materials and knowledge we have."

"But how does it work?"

"Hand it here a moment, Lavon. This bladder you see inside at the center, with the hollow spyrogyra straws leading out from it to the skin of the ship, is a buoyancy tank. The idea is that we trap ourselves a big gas-bubble as it rises from the bottom and install it in the tank. Probably we'll have to do that piecemeal. Then the ship rises to the sky on the buoyancy of the bubble. The little paddles, here along these two bands on the outside, rotate when the crew—that's these bricks you hear shaking around inside—walks a treadmill that runs around the inside of the hull; they paddle us over to the edge of the sky. Then we pull the paddles in—they fold over into slots, like this—and, still by weight-transfer from the inside, roll ourselves up the slope until we're out in space. When we hit another world and enter the water again, we let the gas out of the tank gradually through the exhaust tubes represented by these straws, and sink down to a landing at a controlled rate."

"Very ingenious," Shar said thoughtfully. "But I can foresee some difficulties. For one thing, the design lacks stability."

"Yes, it does," Tanol agreed. "And keeping it in motion is going to require a lot of footwork. On the other hand, the biggest expenditure of energy involved in the whole trip is going to be getting the machine up to the sky in the first place, and with this design that's taken care of—as a matter of fact, once the bubble's installed, we'll have to keep the ship tied down until we're ready to go."

"How about letting the gas out?" Lavon said. "Will it go out through those little tubes when we want it to? Won't it just cling to the walls of the tank instead? The skin between water and gas is pretty difficult to deform—to that I can testify."

Tanol frowned. "That I don't know. Don't forget that the tubes will be large in the real ship, not just straws as they are in the model."

"Bigger than a man's body?" Than said.

"No, hardly. Maybe as big, though, as a man's head."

"Won't work," Than said tersely. "I tried it. You can't lead a bubble through a pipe that small. As Lavon said, it clings to the inside of the tube and won't be budged. If we build this ship, we'll just have to abandon it once we hit our new world."

"That's out of the question," Lavon said at once. "Putting aside for the moment the waste involved, we may have to use the ship again in a hurry. Who knows what the new world will be like? We're going to have to be able to leave it again if it is impossible to live in."

"Which is your model, Than?" Shar said.

"This one. With this design, we do the trip the hard way—crawl along the bottom until it meets the sky, crawl until we hit the next world, and crawl wherever we're going when we get there. No aquabatics. She's treadmill-powered, like Tanol's, but not necessarily man-powered; I've been thinking a bit about using diatoms. She steers by varying the power on one side or the other; also we can hitch a pair of thongs to opposite ends of the rear axle and swivel her that way, but that would be slower and considerably less precise."

Shar looked closely at the tube-shaped model and pushed it experimentally along the table a little way. "I like that," he said presently. "It sits still when you want it to. With Than's spherical ship, we'd be at the mercy of any stray current at home or in the new world—and for all I know there may be currents of some sort in space, too, gas currents perhaps. Lavon, what do you think?"

"How would we build it?" Lavon said. "It's round in cross-section. That's all very well for a model, but how do you make a really big tube of that shape that won't fall in on itself?"

"Look inside, through the front window," Than said. "You'll see beams that cross at the center, at right angles to the long axis. They hold the walls braced."

"That consumes a lot of space," Stravol objected. By far the quietest and most introspective of the three assistants, he had not spoken until now since the beginning of the conference. "You've pretty well got to have free passage back and forth inside the ship. How are we going to keep everything operating if we have to be crawling around beams all the time?"

"All right, come up with something better," Than said, shrugging.

"That's easy. We bend hoops."

"Hoops!" Tanol said. "On *that* scale? You'd have to soak your wood in mud for a year before it would be flexible enough, and then it wouldn't have the strength you'd need."

"No, you wouldn't," Stravol said. "I didn't build a ship-model, I just made drawings, and my ship isn't as good as Than's by a long distance. But my design for the ship is also tubular, so I did build a model of a hoop-bending machine—that's it on the table. You lock one end of your beam down in a heavy vise, like so, leaving the butt sticking out the other side. Then you tie up the other end with a heavy line, around this notch. Then you run your rope around a windlass, and five or six men wind up the windlass, like so. That pulls down the free end of the beam until the notch engages with this key-slot, which you've pre-cut at the other end. Then you unlock the vise, and there's your hoop; for safety you might drive a peg through the joint to keep the thing from springing open unexpectedly."

"Wouldn't the beam you were using break after it had bent a certain distance?" Lavon asked.

"Stock timber certainly would," Stravol said. "But for this trick you use *green* wood, not seasoned. Otherwise you'd have to soften your beam to uselessness, as Tanol says. But live wood will flex enough to make a good, strong, single-unit hoop—or if it doesn't, Shar, the little rituals with numbers that you've been teaching us don't mean anything after all!"

Shar smiled. "You can easily make a mistake in using numbers," he said.

"I checked everything."

"I'm sure of it. And I think it's well worth a trial. Anything else to offer?"

"Well," Stravol said, "I've got a kind of live ventilating system I think should be useful. Otherwise, as I said, Than's ship strikes me as the type we should build; my own's hopelessly cumbersome."

"I have to agree," Tanol said regretfully. "But I'd like to try putting together a lighter-than-water ship sometime, maybe just for local travel. If the new world is bigger than ours, it might not be possible to swim everywhere you might want to go there."

"That never occurred to me," Lavon exclaimed. "Suppose the new world *is* twice, three times, eight times as big as ours? Shar, is there any reason why that couldn't be?"

"None that I know of. The history plates certainly seem to take all kinds of enormous distances practically for granted. All right, let's make up a composite design from what we have here. Tanol, you're the best draftsman among us, suppose you draw it up. Lavon, what about labor?"

"I've a plan ready," Lavon said. "As I see it, the people who work on the ship are going to have to be on the job full-time. Building the vessel isn't going to be an overnight task, or even one that we can finish in a single season, so we can't count on using a rotating force. Besides, this is technical work; once a man learns how to do a particular task, it would be wasteful to send him back to tending fungi just because somebody else has some time on his hands.

"So I've set up a basic force involving the two or three most intelligent hand-workers from each of the various trades. Those people I can withdraw from their regular work without upsetting the way we run our usual concerns, or noticeably increasing the burden on the others in a given trade. They will do the skilled labor, and stick with the ship until it's done. Some of them will make up the crew, too. For heavy, unskilled jobs, we can call on the various seasonal pools of idle people without disrupting our ordinary life."

"Good," Shar said. He leaned forward and rested linked hands on the edge of the table—although, because of the webbing between his fingers, he could link no more than the fingertips. "We've really made remarkable progress. I didn't expect that we'd have matters advanced a tenth as far as this by the end of this meeting. But maybe I've overlooked something important. Has anybody any more suggestions, or any questions?"

"I've got one," Stravol said quietly.

"All right, let's hear it."

"*Where are we going?*"

There was quite a long silence. Finally Shar said: "Stravol, I can't answer that yet. I could say that we're going to the stars, but since we still have no idea what a star is, that answer wouldn't do you much good. We're going to make this trip because we've found that some of the fantastic things that the history plates say are really so. We know now that the sky can be passed, and that beyond the sky there's a region where there's no water to breathe, the region our ancients called 'space.' Both of these ideas always seemed to be against common sense, but nevertheless we've found that they're true.

"The history plates also say that there are other worlds than ours, and actually that's an easier idea to accept, once you've found out that the other two are so. As for the stars—well, we just don't know yet, we haven't any information at all that would allow us to read the history plates on that subject with new eyes, and there's no point in making wild guesses unless we can test the guesses. The stars are in space, and presumably, once we're out in space, we'll see them and the meaning of the word will become clear. At least we can confidently expect to see some clues—look at all the information we got from Lavon's trip of a few seconds above the sky!

"But in the meantime, there's no point in our speculating in a bubble. We think there are other worlds somewhere, and we're devising means to make the trip. The other questions, the pendant ones, just have to be put aside for now. We'll answer them eventually—there's no doubt in my mind about that. But it may take a long time."

Stravol grinned ruefully. "I expected no more. In a way, I think the whole project is crazy. But I'm in it right out to the end, all the same."

Shar and Lavon grinned back. All of them had the fever, and Lavon suspected that their whole enclosed universe would share it with them before long. He said:

"Then let's not waste a minute. There's a huge mass of detail to be worked out still, and after that, all the hard work will just have begun. Let's get moving!"

The five men arose and looked at each other. Their expressions varied, but in all their eyes there was in addition the same mixture of awe and ambition: the composite face of the shipwright and of the astronaut.

Then they went out, severally, to begin their voyages.

It was two winter sleeps after Lavon's disastrous climb beyond the sky that all work on the spaceship stopped. By then, Lavon knew that he had hardened and weathered into that temporarily ageless state a man enters after he has just reached his prime; and he knew also that there were wrinkles engraved on his brow, to stay and to deepen.

"Old" Shar, too, had changed, his features losing some of their delicacy as he came into his maturity. Though the wedge-shaped bony structure of his face would give him a withdrawn and poetic look for as long as he lived, participation in the plan had given his expression a kind of executive overlay, which at best gave it a mask-like rigidity, and at worst coarsened it somehow.

Yet despite the bleeding away of the years, the spaceship was still only a hulk. It lay upon a platform built above the tumbled boulders of the sandbar which stretched out from one wall of the world. It was an immense hull of pegged wood, broken by regularly spaced gaps through which the raw beams of the skeleton could be seen.

Work upon it had progressed fairly rapidly at first, for it was not hard to visualize what kind of vehicle would be needed to crawl through empty space without losing its water; Than and his colleagues had done that job well. It had been recognized, too, that the sheer size of the machine would enforce a long period of construction, perhaps as long as two full seasons; but neither Shar and his assistants nor Lavon had anticipated any serious snag.

For that matter, part of the vehicle's apparent incompleteness was an illusion. About a third of its fittings were to consist of living creatures, which could not be expected to install themselves in the vessel much before the actual takeoff.

Yet time and time again, work on the ship had had to be halted for long periods. Several times whole sections needed to be ripped out, as it became more and more evident that hardly a single normal, understandable concept could be applied to the problem of space travel.

The lack of the history plates, which the Para steadfastly refused to deliver up, was a double handicap. Immediately upon their loss, Shar had set himself to reproduce them from memory; but unlike the more religious of his ancestors he had never regarded them as holy writ, and hence had never set himself to memorizing them word by word. Even before the theft, he had accumulated a set of variant translations of passages presenting specific experimental problems, which were stored in his library, carved in wood. But most of these translations tended to contradict each other, and none of them related to spaceship construction, upon which the original had been vague in any case.

No duplicates of the cryptic characters of the original had ever been made, for the simple reason that there was nothing in the sunken universe capable of destroying the originals, nor of duplicating their apparently changeless permanence. Shar remarked too late that through simple caution they should have made a number of verbatim temporary records— but after generations of green-gold peace, simple caution no longer covers preparation against catastrophe. (Nor, for that matter, did a culture which had to dig each letter of its simple alphabet into pulpy water-logged wood with a flake of stonewort encourage the keeping of records in triplicate.)

As a result, Shar's imperfect memory of the contents of the history plates, plus the constant and millennial doubt as to the accuracy of the various translations, proved finally to be the worst obstacle to progress on the spaceship itself.

"Men must paddle before they can swim," Lavon observed belatedly, and Shar was forced to agree with him.

Obviously, whatever the ancients had known about spaceship construction, very little of that knowledge was usable to a people still trying to build its first spaceship from scratch. In retrospect, it was not surprising that the great hulk still rested incomplete upon its platform above the sand boulders, exuding a musty odor of wood steadily losing its strength, two generations after its flat bottom had been laid down.

The fat-faced young man who headed the strike delegation to Shar's chambers was Phil XX, a man two generations younger than Shar, four younger than Lavon. There were crow's-feet at the corners of his eyes, which made him look both like a querulous old man and like an infant spoiled in the spore.

"We're calling a halt to this crazy project," he said bluntly. "We've slaved away our youth on it, but now that we're our own masters, it's over, that's all. Over."

"Nobody's compelled you," Lavon said angrily.

"Society does; our parents do," a gaunt member of the delegation said. "But now we're going to start living in the real world. Everybody these days knows that there's no other world but this one. You oldsters can hang on to your superstitions if you like. We don't intend to."

Baffled, Lavon looked over at Shar. The scientist smiled and said, "Let them go, Lavon. We have no use for the faint-hearted."

The fat-faced young man flushed. "You can't insult us into going back to work. We're through. Build your own ship to noplace!"

"All right," Lavon said evenly. "Go on, beat it. Don't stand around here orating about it. You've made your decision and we're not interested in your self-justifications. Good-bye."

The fat-faced young man evidently still had quite a bit of heroism to dramatize which Lavon's dismissal had short-circuited. An examination of Lavon's stony face, however, seemed to convince him that he had to take his victory as he found it. He and the delegation trailed ingloriously out the archway.

"Now what?" Lavon asked when they had gone. "I must admit, Shar, that I would have tried to persuade them. We do need the workers, after all."

"Not as much as they need us," Shar said tranquilly. "I know all those young men. I think they'll be astonished at the runty crops their fields will produce next season, after they have to breed them without my advice. Now, how many volunteers have you got for the crew of the ship?"

"Hundreds. Every youngster of the generation after Phil's wants to go along. Phil's wrong about that segment of the populace, at least. The project catches the imagination of the very young."

"Did you give them any encouragement?"

"Sure," Lavon said. "I told them we'd call on them if they were chosen. But you can't take that seriously! We'd do badly to displace our picked group of specialists with youths who have enthusiasm and nothing else."

"That's not what I had in mind, Lavon. Didn't I see a Noc in these chambers somewhere? Oh, there he is, asleep in the dome. Noc!"

The creature stirred its tentacle lazily.

"Noc, I've a message," Shar called. "The protos are to tell all men that those who wish to go to the next world with the spaceship must come to the staging area right away. Say that we can't promise to take everyone, but that only those who help us to build the ship will be considered at all."

The Noc curled its tentacle again, and appeared to go back to sleep.

Lavon turned from the arrangement of speaking-tube megaphones which was his control board and looked at the Para. "One last try," he said. "Will you give us back the history plates?"

"No, Lavon. We have never denied you anything before, but this we must."

"You're going with us though, Para. Unless you give us back the knowledge we need, you'll lose your life if we lose ours."

"What is one Para?" the creature said. "We are all alike. This cell will die; but the protos need to know how you fare on this journey. We believe you should make it without the plates, for in no other way can we assess the real importance of the plates."

"Then you admit you still have them. What if you can't communicate with your fellows once we're out in space? How do you know that water isn't essential to your telepathy?"

The proto was silent. Lavon stared at it a moment, then turned deliberately back to the speaking tubes. "Everyone hang on," he said. He felt shaky. "We're about to start. Stravol, is the ship sealed?"

"As far as I can tell, Lavon."

Lavon shifted to another megaphone. He took a deep breath. Already the water seemed stifling, although the ship hadn't moved.

"Ready with one-quarter power . . . One, two, three, *go.*"

The whole ship jerked and settled back into place again. The raphe diatoms along the under hull settled into their niches, their jelly treads turning against broad endless belts of crude nematode leather. Wooden gears creaked, stepping up the slow power of the creatures, transmitting it to the sixteen axles of the ship's wheels.

The ship rocked and began to roll slowly along the sandbar. Lavon looked tensely through the mica port. The world flowed painfully past him. The ship canted and began to climb the slope. Behind him, he could feel the electric silence of Shar, Para, and the two alternate pilots, Than and Stravol, as if their gaze were stabbing directly through his body and on out the port. The world looked different, now that he was leaving it. How had he missed all this beauty before?

The slapping of the endless belts and the squeaking and groaning of the gears and axles grew louder as the slope steepened. The ship continued to climb, lurching. Around it, squadrons of men and protos dipped and wheeled, escorting it toward the sky.

Gradually the sky lowered and pressed down toward the top of the ship.

"A little more work from your diatoms, Tanol," Lavon said. "Boulder ahead." The ship swung ponderously. "All right, slow them up again. Give us a shove from your side, Tol—no, that's too much—there, that's it. Back to normal; you're still turning us! Tanol, give us one burst to line us up again. Good. All right, steady drive on all sides. It shouldn't be long now."

"How can you think in webs like that?" the Para wondered behind him.

"I just do, that's all. It's the way men think. Overseers, a little more thrust now; the grade's getting steeper."

The gears groaned. The ship nosed up. The sky brightened in Lavon's face. Despite himself, he began to be frightened. His lungs seemed to burn, and in his mind he felt his long fall through nothingness toward the chill slap of the water as if he were experiencing it for the first time. His skin itched and burned. Could he go up *there* again? Up there into the burning void, the great gasping agony where no life should go?

The sandbar began to level out and the going became a little easier.

Up here, the sky was so close that the lumbering motion of the huge ship disturbed it. Shadows of wavelets ran across the sand. Silently, the thick-barreled bands of blue-green algae drank in the light and converted it to oxygen, writhing in their slow mindless dance just under the long mica skylight which ran along the spine of the ship. In the hold, beneath the latticed corridor and cabin floors, whirring Vortae kept the ship's water in motion, fueling themselves upon drifting organic particles.

One by one, the figures wheeling about the ship outside waved arms or cilia and fell back, coasting down the slope of the sandbar toward the familiar world, dwindling and disappearing. There was at last only one single Euglena, half-plant cousin of the protos, forging along beside the spaceship into the marches of the shallows. It loved the light, but finally it, too, was driven away into deeper, cooler waters, its single whip-like tentacle undulating placidly as it went. It was not very bright, but Lavon felt deserted when it left.

Where they were going, though, none could follow.

Now the sky was nothing but a thin, resistant skin of water coating the top of the ship. The vessel slowed, and when Lavon called for more power, it began to dig itself in among the sand-grains and boulders.

"That's not going to work," Shar said tensely. "I think we'd better step down the gear-ratio, Lavon, so you can apply stress more slowly."

"All right," Lavon agreed. "Full stop, everybody. Shar, will you super-vise gear-changing, please?"

Insane brilliance of empty space looked Lavon full in the face just beyond his big mica bull's-eye. It was maddening to be forced to stop here upon the threshold of infinity; and it was dangerous, too. Lavon could feel building in him the old fear of the outside. A few moments more of inaction, he knew with a gathering coldness at the pit of his stomach, and he would be unable to go through with it.

Surely, he thought, there must be a better way to change gear-ratios than the traditional one, which involved dismantling almost the entire gear-box. Why couldn't a number of gears of different sizes be carried on the same shaft, not necessarily all in action all at once, but awaiting use simply by shoving the axle back and forth longitudinally in its sockets? It would still be clumsy, but it could be worked on orders from the bridge and would not involve shutting down the entire machine—and throwing the new pilot into a blue-green funk.

Shar came lunging up through the trap and swam himself to a stop.

"All set," he said. "The big reduction gears aren't taking the strain too well, though."

"Splintering?"

"Yes. I'd go it slow at first."

Lavon nodded mutely. Without allowing himself to stop, even for a moment, to consider the consequences of his words, he called: "Half power."

The ship hunched itself down again and began to move, very slowly indeed, but more smoothly than before. Overhead, the sky thinned to complete transparency. The great light came blasting in. Behind Lavon there was an uneasy stir. The whiteness grew at the front ports.

Again the ship slowed, straining against the blinding barrier. Lavon swallowed and called for more power. The ship groaned like something about to die. It was now almost at a standstill.

"More power," Lavon ground out.

Once more, with infinite slowness, the ship began to move. Gently, it tilted upward.

Then it lunged forward and every board and beam in it began to squall.

"Lavon! Lavon!"

Lavon started sharply at the shout. The voice was coming at him from one of the megaphones, the one marked for the port at the rear of the ship.

"Lavon!"

"What is it? Stop your damn yelling."

"I can see the top of the sky! From the *other* side, from the top side! It's like a big flat sheet of metal. We're going away from it. We're above the sky, Lavon, we're above the sky!"

Another violent start swung Lavon around toward the forward port. On the outside of the mica, the water was evaporating with shocking swiftness, taking with it strange distortions and patterns made of rainbows.

Lavon saw Space.

It was at first like a deserted and cruelly dry version of the bottom. There were enormous boulders, great cliffs, tumbled, split, riven, jagged rocks going up and away in all directions, as if scattered at random by some giant.

But it had a sky of its own—a deep blue dome so far away that he could not believe in, let alone compute, what its distance might be. And in this dome was a ball of reddish fire that seared his eyeballs.

The wilderness of rock was still a long way away from the ship, which now seemed to be resting upon a level, glistening plain. Beneath the surface-shine, the plain seemed to be made of sand, nothing but familiar sand, the same substance which had heaped up to form a bar in Lavon's own universe, the bar along which the ship had climbed. But the glassy, colorful skin over it—

Suddenly Lavon became conscious of another shout from the megaphone banks. He shook his head savagely and asked, "What is it now?"

"Lavon, this is Tol. What have you gotten us into? The belts are locked. The diatoms can't move them. They aren't faking, either; we've rapped them hard enough to make them think we were trying to break their shells, but they still can't give us more power."

"Leave them alone," Lavon snapped. "They can't fake; they haven't enough intelligence. If they say they can't give you more power, they can't."

"Well, then, you get us out of it," Tol's voice said frightenedly.

Shar came forward to Lavon's elbow. "We're on a space-water interface, where the surface tension is very high," he said softly. "This is why I insisted on our building the ship so that we could lift the wheels off the ground whenever necessary. For a long while I couldn't understand the reference of the history plates to 'retractable landing gear,' but it finally occurred to me that the tension along a space-water interface— or, to be more exact, a space-mud interface—would hold any large object pretty tightly. If you order the wheels pulled up now, I think we'll make better progress for a while on the belly-treads."

"Good enough," Lavon said. "Hello below—up landing gear. Evidently the ancients knew their business after all, Shar."

Quite a few minutes later—for shifting power to the belly treads involved another setting of the gear box—the ship was crawling along the shore toward the tumbled rock. Anxiously, Lavon scanned the jagged, threatening wall for a break. There was a sort of rivulet off toward the left which might offer a route, though a dubious one, to the next world. After some thought, Lavon ordered his ship turned toward it.

"Do you suppose that thing in the sky is a 'star'?" he asked. "But there were supposed to be lots of them. Only one is up there—and one's plenty for *my* taste."

"I don't know," Shar admitted. "But I'm beginning to get a picture of the way the universe is made, I think. Evidently our world is a sort of cup in the bottom of this huge one. This one has a sky of its own; perhaps it, too, is only a cup in the bottom of a still huger world, and so on and on without end. It's a hard concept to grasp, I'll admit. Maybe it would be more sensible to assume that all the worlds are cups in this one common surface, and that the great light shines on them all impartially."

"Then what makes it seem to go out every night, and dim even in the day during winter?" Lavon demanded.

"Perhaps it travels in circles, over first one world, then another. How could I know yet?"

"Well, if you're right, it means that all we have to do is crawl along here for a while, until we hit the top of the sky of another world," Lavon said. "Then we dive in. Somehow it seems too simple, after all our preparations."

Shar chuckled, but the sound did not suggest that he had discovered anything funny. "Simple? Have you noticed the temperature yet?"

Lavon had noticed it, just beneath the surface of awareness, but at Shar's remark he realized that he was gradually being stifled. The oxygen content of the water, luckily, had not dropped, but the temperature suggested the shallows in the last and worst part of autumn. It was like trying to breathe soup.

"Than, give us more action from the Vortae," Lavon said. "This is going to be unbearable unless we get more circulation."

There was a reply from Than, but it came to Lavon's ears only as a mumble. It was all he could do now to keep his attention on the business of steering the ship.

The cut or defile in the scattered razor-edged rocks was a little closer, but there still seemed to be many miles of rough desert to cross. After a while the ship settled into a steady, painfully slow crawling, with less pitching and jerking than before, but also with less progress. Under it, there was now a sliding, grinding sound, rasping against the hull of the ship itself, as if it were treadmilling over some coarse lubricant the particles of which were each as big as a man's head.

Finally Shar said, "Lavon, we'll have to stop again. The sand this far up is dry, and we're wasting energy using the treads."

"Are you sure we can take it?" Lavon asked, gasping for breath. "At least we are moving. If we stop to lower the wheels and change gears again, we'll boil."

"We'll boil if we don't," Shar said calmly. "Some of our algae are dead already and the rest are withering. That's a pretty good sign that we can't take much more. I don't think we'll make it into the shadows, unless we do change over and put on some speed."

There was a gulping sound from one of the mechanics. "We ought to turn back," he said raggedly. "We were never meant to be out here in the first place. We were made for the water, not for this hell."

"We'll stop," Lavon said, "but we're not turning back. That's final."

The words made a brave sound, but the man had upset Lavon more than he dared to admit, even to himself. "Shar," he said, "make it fast, will you?"

The scientist nodded and dived below.

The minutes stretched out. The great red-gold globe in the sky blazed and blazed. It had moved down the sky, far down, so that the light was pouring into the ship directly in Lavon's face, illuminating every floating particle, its rays like long milky streamers. The currents of water passing Lavon's cheek were almost hot.

How could they dare go directly forward into that inferno? The land directly under the "star" must be even hotter than it was here!

"Lavon! Look at Para!"

Lavon forced himself to turn and look at his proto ally. The great slipper had settled to the deck, where it was lying with only a feeble pulsation of its cilia. Inside, its vacuoles were beginning to swell, to become bloated, pear-shaped bubbles, crowding the granulated protoplasm, pressing upon the dark nuclei.

"Is . . . is he dying?"

"This cell is dying," Para said, as coldly as always. "But go on—go on. There is much to learn, and you may live, even though we do not. Go on."

"You're—for us now?" Lavon whispered.

"We have always been for you. Push your folly to the uttermost. We will benefit in the end, and so will Man."

The whisper died away. Lavon called the creature again, but it did not respond.

There was a wooden clashing from below, and then Shar's voice came tinnily from one of the megaphones. "Lavon, go ahead! The diatoms are dying, too, and then we'll be without power. Make it as quickly and directly as you can."

Grimly, Lavon leaned forward. "The 'star' is directly over the land we're approaching."

"It is? It may go lower still and the shadows will get longer. That's our only hope."

Lavon had not thought of that. He rasped into the banked megaphones. Once more, the ship began to move, a little faster now, but still seemingly at a crawl. The thirty-two wheels rumbled.

It got hotter.

Steadily, with a perceptible motion, the "star" sank in Lavon's face. Suddenly a new terror struck him. Suppose it should continue to go down until it was gone entirely? Blasting though it was now, it was the only source of heat. Would not space become bitter cold on the instant—and the ship an expanding, bursting block of ice?

The shadows lengthened menacingly, stretching across the desert toward the forward-rolling vessel. There was no talking in the cabin, just the sound of ragged breathing and the creaking of the machinery.

Then the jagged horizon seemed to rush upon them. Stony teeth cut into the lower rim of the ball of fire, devoured it swiftly. It was gone.

They were in the lee of the cliffs.

Lavon ordered the ship turned to parallel the rockline; it responded heavily, sluggishly. Far above, the sky deepened steadily, from blue to indigo.

Shar came silently up through the trap and stood beside Lavon, studying that deepening color and the lengthening of the shadows down the beach toward their world. He said nothing, but Lavon was sure that the same chilling thought was in his mind.

"Lavon."

Lavon jumped. Shar's voice had iron in it. "Yes?"

"We'll have to keep moving. We must make the next world, wherever it is, very shortly."

"How can we dare move when we can't see where we're going? Why not sleep it over—if the cold will let us?"

"It will let us," Shar said. "It can't get dangerously cold up here. If it did, the sky—or what we used to think of as the sky—would have frozen over every night, even in summer. But what I'm thinking about is the water. The plants will go to sleep now. In our world that wouldn't matter; the supply of oxygen there is enough to last through the night. But in this confined space, with so many creatures in it and no supply of fresh water, we will probably smother."

Shar seemed hardly to be involved at all, but spoke rather with the voice of implacable physical laws.

"Furthermore," he said, staring unseeingly out at the raw landscape, "the diatoms are plants, too. In other words, we must stay on the move for as long as we have oxygen and power—and pray that we make it."

"Shar, we had quite a few protos on board this ship once. And Para there isn't quite dead yet. If he were, the cabin would be intolerable. The ship is nearly sterile of bacteria, because all the protos have been eating them as a matter of course and there's no outside supply of them, any more than there is for oxygen. But still and all there would have been some decay."

Shar bent and tested the pellicle of the motionless Para with a probing finger. "You're right, he's still alive. What does that prove?"

"The Vortae are also alive; I can feel the water circulating. Which proves that it wasn't the heat that hurt Para. *It was the light.* Remember how badly my skin was affected after I climbed beyond the sky? Undiluted starlight is deadly. We should add that to the information from the plates."

"I still don't get the point."

"It's this. We've got three or four Noc down below. They were shielded from the light, and so must be alive. If we concentrate them in the diatom galleys, the dumb diatoms will think it's still daylight and will go on working. Or we can concentrate them up along the spine of the ship, and keep the algae putting out oxygen. So the question is: which do we need more, oxygen or power? Or can we split the difference?"

Shar actually grinned. "A brilliant piece of thinking. We may make a Shar of you yet, Lavon. No, I'd say that we can't split the difference. There's something about daylight, some quality, that the light Noc emit doesn't have. You and I can't detect it, but the green plants can, and without it they don't make oxygen. So we'll have to settle for the diatoms—for power."

"All right. Set it up that way, Shar."

Lavon brought the vessel away from the rocky lee of the cliff, out onto the smoother sand. All trace of direct light was gone now, although there was still a soft, general glow on the sky.

"Now then," Shar said thoughtfully, "I would guess that there's water over there in the canyon, if we can reach it. I'll go below again and arrange—"

Lavon gasped.

"What's the matter?"

Silently, Lavon pointed, his heart pounding.

The entire dome of indigo above them was spangled with tiny, incredibly brilliant lights. There were hundreds of them, and more and more were becoming visible as the darkness deepened. And far away, over the ultimate edge of the rocks, was a dim red globe, crescented with ghostly silver. Near the zenith was another such body, much smaller, and silvered all over . . .

Under the two moons of Hydrot, and under the eternal stars, the two-inch wooden spaceship and its microscopic cargo toiled down the slope toward the drying little rivulet.

The ship rested on the bottom of the canyon for the rest of the night. The great square doors were thrown open to admit the raw, irradiated, life-giving water from outside—and the wriggling bacteria which were fresh food.

No other creatures approached them, either with curiosity or with predatory intent, while they slept, although Lavon had posted guards at the doors. Evidently, even up here on the very floor of space, highly organized creatures were quiescent at night.

But when the first flush of light filtered through the water, trouble threatened.

First of all, there was the bug-eyed monster. The thing was green and had two snapping claws, either one of which could have broken the ship in two like a spyrogyra straw. Its eyes were black and globular, on the ends of short columns, and its long feelers were as thick through as a plant-bole. It passed in a kicking fury of motion, however, never noticing the ship at all.

"Is that—a sample of the kind of life we can expect in the next world?" Lavon whispered. Nobody answered, for the very good reason that nobody knew.

After a while, Lavon risked moving the ship forward against the current, which was slow but heavy. Enormous writhing worms, far bigger than the nematodes of home, whipped past them. One struck the hull a heavy blow, then thrashed on obliviously.

"They don't notice us," Shar said. "We're too small. Lavon, the ancients warned us of the immensity of space, but even when you see it, it's impossible to grasp. And all those stars—can they mean what I think they mean? It's beyond thought, beyond belief!"

"The bottom's sloping," Lavon said, looking ahead intently. "The walls of the canyon are retreating, and the water's becoming rather silty. Let the stars wait, Shar; we're coming toward the entrance of our new world."

Shar subsided moodily. His vision of space had disturbed him, perhaps seriously. He took little notice of the great thing that was happening, but instead huddled worriedly over his own expanding speculations. Lavon felt the old gap between their two minds widening once more.

Now the bottom was tilting upward again. Lavon had no experience with delta-formation, for no rivulets left his own world, and the phenomenon worried him. But his worries were swept away in wonder as the ship topped the rise and nosed over.

Ahead, the bottom sloped away again, indefinitely, into glimmering depths. A proper sky was over them once more, and Lavon could see small rafts of plankton floating placidly beneath it. Almost at once, too, he saw several of the smaller kinds of protos, a few of which were already approaching the ship—

Then the girl came darting out of the depths, her features blurred and distorted with distance and terror. At first she did not seem to see the ship at all. She came twisting and turning lithely through the water, obviously hoping only to throw herself over the mound of the delta and into the savage streamlet beyond.

Lavon was stunned. Not that there were men here—he had hoped for that, had even known somehow that men were everywhere in the universe—but at the girl's single-minded flight toward suicide.

"What—"

Then a dim buzzing began to grow in his ears, and he understood.

"Shar! Than! Stravol!" he bawled. "Break out crossbows and spears! Knock out all the windows!" He lifted a foot and kicked through the big bull's-eye port in front of him. Someone thrust a crossbow into his hand.

"Eh? What's happening?" Shar blurted.

"Eaters!"

The cry went through the ship like a galvanic shock. The rotifers back in Lavon's own world were virtually extinct, but everyone knew thoroughly the grim history of the long battle man and proto had waged against them.

The girl spotted the ship suddenly and paused, obviously stricken with despair at the sight of the new monster. She drifted with her own momentum, her eyes alternately fixed upon the ship and jerking back over her shoulder, toward where the buzzing snarled louder and louder in the dimness.

"Don't stop!" Lavon shouted. "This way, this way! We're friends! We'll help!"

Three great semi-transparent trumpets of smooth flesh bored over the rise, the many thick cilia of their coronas whirring greedily. Dicrans—the most predacious of the entire tribe of Eaters. They were quarreling thickly among themselves as they moved, with the few blurred, presymbolic noises which made up their "language."

Carefully, Lavon wound the crossbow, brought it to his shoulder, and fired. The bolt sang away through the water. It lost momentum rapidly, and was caught by a stray current which brought it closer to the girl than to the Eater at which Lavon had aimed.

He bit his lip, lowered the weapon, wound it up again. It did not pay to underestimate the range; he would have to wait until he could fire with effect. Another bolt, cutting through the water from a side port, made him issue orders to cease firing.

The sudden irruption of the rotifers decided the girl. The motionless

wooden monster was strange to her, but it had not yet menaced her—
and she must have known what it would be like to have three Dicrans
over her, each trying to grab away from the others the largest share.
She threw herself toward the bull's-eye port. The three Eaters screamed
with fury and greed and bored in after her.

She probably would not have made it, had not the dull vision of the
lead Dicran made out the wooden shape of the ship at the last instant.
It backed off, buzzing, and the other two sheered away to avoid colliding
with it. After that they had another argument, though they could hardly
have formulated what it was that they were fighting about. They were
incapable of saying anything much more complicated than the equivalent
of "Yaah," "Drop dead," and "You're another."

While they were still snarling at each other, Lavon pierced the nearest
one all the way through with an arbalesk bolt. It disintegrated promptly—
rotifers are delicately organized creatures despite their ferocity—and the
surviving two were at once involved in a lethal battle over the remains.

"Than, take a party out and spear me those two Eaters while they're
still fighting," Lavon ordered. "Don't forget to destroy their eggs, too.
I can see that this world needs a little taming."

The girl shot through the port and brought up against the far wall of
the cabin, flailing in terror. Lavon tried to approach her, but from somewhere she produced a flake of stonewort chipped to a nasty point. Since
she was naked, it was hard to tell where she had been hiding it, but its
purpose was plain. Lavon retreated and sat down on the stool before
his control board, waiting while she took in the cabin, Lavon, Shar, the
other pilots, the senescent Para.

At last she said: "Are—you—the gods—from beyond the sky?"

"We're from beyond the sky, all right," Lavon said. "But we're not
gods. We're human beings, just like you. Are there many humans here?"

The girl seemed to assess the situation very rapidly, savage though
she was. Lavon had the odd and impossible impression that he should
recognize her: a tall, deceptively relaxed, tawny young woman, someone
from another world, but still . . .

She tucked the knife back into her bright, matted hair—aha, Lavon
thought confusedly, that's a trick I may need to remember—and shook
her head.

"We are few. The Eaters are everywhere. Soon they will have the
last of us."

Her fatalism was so complete that she actually did not seem to care.

"And you've never co-operated against them? Or asked the protos to
help?"

"The protos?" She shrugged. "They are as helpless as we are against
the Eaters. We have no weapons which kill at a distance, like yours.
And it is too late now for such weapons to do any good. We are too
few, the Eaters too many."

Lavon shook his head emphatically. "You've had one weapon that counts, all along. Against it, numbers mean nothing. We'll show you how we've used it. You may be able to use it even better than we did, once you've given it a try."

The girl shrugged again. "We have dreamed of such a weapon now and then, but never found it. I do not think that what you say is true. What is this weapon?"

"Brains," Lavon said. "Not just one brain, but brains. Working together. Co-operation."

"Lavon speaks the truth," a weak voice said from the deck.

The Para stirred feebly. The girl watched it with wide eyes. The sound of the Para using human speech seemed to impress her more than the ship itself, or anything else it contained.

"The Eaters can be conquered," the thin, burring voice said. "The protos will help, as they helped in the world from which we came. The protos fought this flight through space, and deprived Man of his records; but Man made the trip without the records. The protos will never oppose Man again. I have already spoken to the protos of this world, and have told them that what Man can dream, Man can do, whether the protos wish it or not.

"Shar, your metal records are with you. They were hidden in the ship. My brothers will lead you to them.

"This organism dies now. It dies in confidence of knowledge, as an intelligent creature dies. Man has taught us this. There is nothing that knowledge . . . cannot do. With it, men . . . have crossed . . . have crossed space . . ."

The voice whispered away. The shining slipper did not change, but something about it was gone. Lavon looked at the girl; their eyes met. He felt an unaccountable warmth.

"We have crossed space," Lavon repeated softly.

Shar's voice came to him across a great distance. The young-old man was whispering: "But—*have* we?"

Lavon was looking at the girl. He had no answer for Shar's question. It did not seem to be important.

BIBLIOGRAPHY

"Sunken Universe," *Super Science Stories*, May 1942

"Surface Tension," *Galaxy*, August 1952

"The Thing in the Attic," *If*, July 1954

"Watershed," *If*, May 1955

"A Time to Survive," *The Magazine of Fantasy and Science Fiction*, February 1956

The Seedling Stars (contains all of the above with some modifications), Gnome Press, 1956

THE FEGHOOT SERIES

by Grendel Briarton (R. Bretnor)

Ferdinand Feghoot was born, or at least first appeared, during a Scrabble game more than twenty years ago. I was home from the hospital after virus pneumonia, a nasty variety followed by intense depression, and in the evenings my wife played Scrabble with me to cheer me up. I always arranged my letters on the rack alphabetically, and on one occasion I found myself looking at EFGHOOT. "Helen," I said, "that looks like a good name for an extraterrestrial." Then I changed the first two letters around, and there he was.

Later on, I found out that his first name was Ferdinand and that he was full of puns and spoonerisms. So I wrote the first four Feghoots—Grendel Briarton is, of course, an anagram of Reginald Bretnor—and sent them to Anthony Boucher, then editor of *Fantasy and Science Fiction.* He bought them (with minor misgivings) and the first—the one about the "furry with the syringe on top"—was published in the May 1956 issue. They soon became a regular feature, and in 1959 the magazine began to give a free subscription to any Feghoot fan who sent in an acceptable idea. (The "furry with the syringe" kept coming in as a suggestion for years, and I soon learned never to accept one without waiting a week or two—if it came in two or three or more times from different parts of the country, I knew it had been stolen from some TV show!)

Feghoot continued to appear in *F&SF* throughout Tony Boucher's tenure, and Robert P. Mills, who followed him, kept up the good work. The next editor, however, decided to drop him, perhaps because Ferdinand did not take life and literature seriously enough. In the meantime, in 1962, I had published *Through Time and Space with Ferdinand Feghoot* under my own Paradox Press imprint, having 2000 copies printed in Japan. The book was illustrated by my friend Bruce Ariss, artist and author of Monterey, and in due course I sold the edition out (not counting the copies I gave away). It contained the first forty-five Feghoots, with five more never previously published, and an odd thing about it was that its only typo, which I didn't catch in proofreading, was the heading for the first episode, which read "Efghoot I"—just as he had first materialized on the Scrabble rack.

Nineteen more Feghoots appeared in *F&SF* before the series was dropped. However, after Ed Ferman took over as editor, he picked it up again when he revived *Venture Science Fiction,* printing five more in that magazine. He also conducted a Feghoot contest in 1973, which I judged, and the first four prize winners brought Ferdinand back briefly to *F&SF*.

Finally, in 1975, Jack Chalker's Mirage Press published *The Compleat Feghoot,* containing eighty-six episodes, newly illustrated by Tim Kirk and with a wonderfully Feghootian introduction by Poul Anderson. This, of course, is presently available.

There had been one Feghoot—a Super-Feghoot, containing not one dreadful pun or spoonerism, but three—which appeared in the *Journal* of the Baker Street Irregulars. Needless to say, it was Sherlockian in nature, and Tony Boucher reprinted it in the last volume of his *Best Detective Stories* of the year. It also appeared in *Special Wonder,* the sf volume of the Boucher Memorial Anthology.

Two new Feghoots have come out since *The Compleat Feghoot* was published, both in the Autumn 1977 issue of *Isaac Asimov's Science Fiction Magazine,* and these have been anthologized in *Asimov's Choice: Astronauts and Androids.* Another, Number X in the book, was bought by Idella Purnell Stone for her Gold Medal anthology, *Never in This World.*

The Feghoot that accompanies this history is a completely new one. For me, Feghoot has been—and is, and will I hope continue to be—a lot of fun. When I published the first Feghoot collection, I launched it with a few weeks of ads in the San Francisco *Chronicle*'s personals column, then very inexpensive. *Ferdinand Feghoot, avoid London 1665. Charles madly jealous. Nell.* And, *Who is Sylvia? When is she? Ferdinand Feghoot.* And so on. One or two advertisers got in on the act and so did a couple of disk-jockeys. We also sold quite a few Feghoot sweatshirts, with Feghoot himself on the front and the Furry on the back, and I wonder how many of them are still around?

My foreword to that first Feghoot book, written for modesty's sake under my own name, ended with the following statement:

> Grendel Briarton feels—and we must admire him for it—that he himself should not boast about the hundreds of suggestions for Feghoot episodes which have reached him from a score of countries and from every continent but one, or about the many letters he has received from Feghoot's friends and even enemies, saying that they always turn to Feghoot first on opening the magazine. Fortunately, I feel no such inhibitions. Nor do I hesitate to say to Ferdinand Feghoot's unfortunate detractors, *Keep trying, lads—some day you too may be able to think one up!*

And indeed, why not? No one, to my knowledge, has yet written an impressive dissertation on the psychological intricacies of punning. No one, in any "little magazine" or academic quarterly, has yet dared to publish a Feghootian sonnet. Yet even the literary conventions of cultures other than our own open new opportunities at every turn. For instance:

> Ferdinand Feghoot,
>   Poet in German meadow,
> He calls out, "Hi, *kuh!*"

Long may he wave!

Through Time and Space with Ferdinand Feghoot

Shortly after Ferdinand Feghoot undertook the psychotherapy of Cleopatra II of Egypt in 2054, he encountered one of those desperate emergencies with which only he could successfully cope. The Queen, having restructured Egyptian society after the pattern of Aldous Huxley's *Brave New World,* had forced all her subjects to worship Henry Ford and, reverently, to make the Sign of the T. Her most sacred relic, a genuine 1913 Model T touring car, had been carefully restored, and she decided to enshrine it, with due ceremony, in the Great Pyramid. She herself, her courtiers and guards, and the whole population of Cairo accompanied the Holy Vehicle, which was driven by the Royal Chauffeur, old Mustafa.

She had issued orders that, under pain of death, no words other than Huxley's were to be uttered, so the procession was impressively silent. Then abruptly, halfway, a dreadful desert wind struck them, blasting sand in their eyes and blowing off hats and tarbooshes. It tore away one of the straps holding the Model T's top, and everyone held his breath, for the aged chauffeur had not even noticed it. They knew how terrible the Queen's rage would be if it blew off completely, but none dared cry out a warning.

They needn't have worried.

"Tie Mustafa's top!" shouted Ferdinand Feghoot.

BIBLIOGRAPHY

Through Time and Space with Ferdinand Feghoot, Paradox Press, 1962 (by "Grendel Briarton")

The Compleat Feghoot, the Many Lives and Greatest Exploits of History's Punniest Space-Time Traveller (by "Grendel Briarton"), Mirage Press, 1975, includes the following numbered episodes:

    I through XLV in *The Magazine of Fantasy and Science Fiction,* 1956–1961

    XVI through L in *Through Time and Space with Ferdinand Feghoot*

    LI through LXIX in *The Magazine of Fantasy and Science Fiction*

    LXX through LXXV in *Venture Science Fiction,* 1969–1970

    LXXVI through LXXXI in *The Compleat Feghoot,* 1975

    LXXXII through LXXXV in *The Magazine of Fantasy and Science Fiction,* 1973

    LXXXVI in *The Baker Street Journal*

Since then, additional unnumbered Feghoots have appeared in *Isaac Asimov's Science Fiction Magazine,* 1977–

THE WHITE HART SERIES

by Arthur C. Clarke *

These stories were written in spurts and spasms between 1953 and 1956 at such diverse spots on the globe as New York, Miami, Colombo, London, Sydney, and various other locations whose names now escape me. In some cases the geographical influence is obvious, though curiously enough I had never visited Australia when "What Goes Up . . ." was written.

It seems to me that there is room—one might even say a long unfelt want—for what might be called the "tall" science-fiction story. By this I mean stories that are *intentionally* unbelievable; not, as is too often the case, unintentionally so. At the same time, I should hate to say exactly where the Great Divide of plausibility comes in these tales, which range from the perfectly possible to the totally improbable.

In at least two cases, science has practically caught up with me in the few years since I wrote these stories. The technique described in "Big Game Hunt" has already been used on monkeys, so there is no reason to suppose that it could not be adapted to other creatures. For a more successful conclusion to this particular hunt—and the rest of the quotation from Herman Melville—I refer you to my novel *The Deep Range.*

It is in the field touched upon in "Patent Pending," however, that the most hair-raising discovery has been made—a discovery which should stop anyone worrying about such minor menaces as the hydrogen bomb. The first report of the work that may end our civilization will be found in James Old's article "Pleasure Centers in the Brain" (*Scientific American,* October 1956). Briefly, it has been found that an electric current flowing into a certain area in the brain of a rat can produce intense pleasure. So much so, in fact, that when the rat learns that it can stimulate itself at will by pushing a little pedal, it loses interest in anything else—even in food. I quote: "Hungry rats ran faster to reach an electric stimulator than they did to reach food. Indeed, a hungry animal often ignored available food in favor of the pleasure of stimulating itself electrically. Some rats . . . stimulated their brains more than 2,000 times per hour for 24 consecutive hours!"

The article concludes with these ominous words: "Enough of the brain-stimulating work has been repeated on monkeys . . . to indicate that our general conclusions can very likely be generalized eventually to human beings—with modifications, of course."

Of course.

For the record (written, not electroencephalographic) I believe the first writers to use the theme of "Patent Pending" were Fletcher Pratt and Laurence Manning, back in the '30s. And quite recently, in "The Big Ball of Wax," Shepherd Mead has given it a much more ribald treatment than mine. I thought his book very funny before I read Mr. Old's article. You may still do so.

Another item for which I cannot claim originality is the newspaper quotation in "Cold War." It is perfectly genuine. It may even have been true.

I must confess that, having chosen the title of this volume some years ago, I was a little disconcerted when Sprague de Camp and Fletcher Pratt brought out their "Tales from Gavagan's Bar." But as most of the odd goings-on at Mr. Cohan's establishment are concerned with the supernatural, I feel that there is plenty of room for both taverns—especially as they are separated by the width of the Atlantic.

Finally, a word to any readers of my (pause for modest cough) more serious works, who may be distressed to find me taking the universe so light-heartedly after my earlier preoccupation with such themes as the Destiny of Man and the Exploration of Space (Advt.). My only excuse is that for some years I've been irritated by critics who keep claiming that science fiction and humor are incompatible.

Now they have a chance to prove it and shut up.

The Reluctant Orchid

Though few people in the "White Hart" will concede that any of Harry Purvis' stories are actually *true*, everyone agrees that some are much more probable than others. And on any scale of probability, the affair of the Reluctant Orchid must rate very low indeed.

I don't remember what ingenious gambit Harry used to launch this narrative: maybe some orchid fancier brought his latest monstrosity into the bar, and that set him off. No matter. I do remember the story, and after all that's what counts.

The adventure did not, this time, concern any of Harry's numerous relatives, and he avoided explaining just how he managed to know so many of the sordid details. The hero—if you can call him that—of this hot-house epic was an inoffensive little clerk named Hercules Keating. And if you think *that* is the most unlikely part of the story, just stick round a while.

Hercules is not the sort of name you can carry off lightly at the best of times, and when you are four foot nine and look as if you'd have to take a physical culture course before you can even become a 97-pound weakling, it is a positive embarrassment. Perhaps it helped to explain why Hercules had very little social life, and all his real friends grew in pots in a humid conservatory at the bottom of his garden. His needs were simple and he spent very little money on himself; consequently his collection of orchids and cacti was really rather remarkable. Indeed, he had a wide reputation among the fraternity of cactophiles, and often received from remote corners of the globe, parcels smelling of mould and tropical jungles.

Hercules had only one living relative, and it would have been hard to find a greater contrast than Aunt Henrietta. She was a massive six footer, usually wore a rather loud line in Harris tweeds, drove a Jaguar with reckless skill, and chain-smoked cigars. Her parents had set their hearts on a boy, and had never been able to decide whether or not their wish had been granted. Henrietta earned a living, and quite a good one, breeding dogs of various shapes and sizes. She was seldom without a couple of her latest models, and they were not the type of portable canine which ladies like to carry in their handbags. The Keating Kennels specialized in Great Danes, Alsatians, and Saint Bernards. . . .

Henrietta, rightly despising men as the weaker sex, had never married. However, for some reason she took an avuncular (yes, that is definitely the right word) interest in Hercules, and called to see him almost every weekend. It was a curious kind of relationship: probably Henrietta found that Hercules bolstered up her feelings of superiority. If he was a good example of the male sex, then they were certainly a pretty sorry lot. Yet, if this was Henrietta's motivation, she was unconscious of it and seemed genuinely fond of her nephew. She was patronizing, but never unkind.

As might be expected, her attentions did not exactly help Hercules' own well-developed inferiority complex. At first he had tolerated his aunt; then he came to dread her regular visits, her booming voice and her bone-crushing handshake; and at last he grew to hate her. Eventually, indeed, his hate was the dominant emotion in his life, exceeding even his love for his orchids. But he was careful not to show it, realizing that if Aunt Henrietta discovered how he felt about her, she would probably break him in two and throw the pieces to her wolf pack.

There was no way, then, in which Hercules could express his pent-up feelings. He had to be polite to Aunt Henrietta even when he felt like murder. And he often did feel like murder, though he knew that there was nothing he would ever do about it. Until one day . . .

According to the dealer, the orchid came from "somewhere in the Amazon region"—a rather vague postal address. When Hercules first saw it, it was not a very prepossessing sight, even to anyone who loved orchids as much as he did. A shapeless root, about the size of a man's fist—that was all. It was redolent of decay, and there was the faintest hint of a rank, carrion smell. Hercules was not even sure that it was viable, and told the dealer as much. Perhaps that enabled him to purchase it for a trifling sum, and he carried it home without much enthusiasm.

It showed no signs of life for the first month, but that did not worry Hercules. Then, one day, a tiny green shoot appeared and started to creep up to the light. After that, progress was rapid. Soon there was a thick, fleshy stem as big as a man's forearm, and colored a positively virulent green. Near the top of the stem a series of curious bulges circled the plant: otherwise it was completely featureless. Hercules was now quite excited: he was sure that some entirely new species had swum into his ken.

The rate of growth was now really fantastic: soon the plant was taller than Hercules, not that that was saying a great deal. Moreover, the bulges seemed to be developing, and it looked as if at any moment the orchid would burst into bloom. Hercules waited anxiously, knowing how short-lived some flowers can be, and spent as much time as he possibly could in the hot-house. Despite all his watchfulness, the transformation occurred one night while he was asleep.

In the morning, the orchid was fringed by a series of eight dangling tendrils, almost reaching to the ground. They must have developed inside the plant and emerged with—for the vegetable world—explosive speed. Hercules stared at the phenomenon in amazement, and went very thoughtfully to work.

That evening, as he watered the plant and checked its soil, he noticed a still more peculiar fact. The tendrils were thickening, and they were not completely motionless. They had a slight but unmistakable tendency to vibrate, as if possessing a life of their own. Even Hercules, for all his interest and enthusiasm, found this more than a little disturbing.

A few days later, there was no doubt about it at all. When he approached the orchid, the tendrils swayed towards him in an unpleasantly suggestive fashion. The impression of hunger was so strong that Hercules began to feel very uncomfortable indeed, and something started to nag at the back of his mind. It was quite a while before he could recall what it was: then he said to himself, "Of course! How stupid of me!" and went along to the local library. Here he spent a most interesting half-hour rereading a little piece by one H. G. Wells entitled, "The Flowering of the Strange Orchid."

"My goodness!" thought Hercules, when he had finished the tale. As yet there had been no stupefying odor which might overpower the plant's intended victim, but otherwise the characteristics were all too similar. Hercules went home in a very unsettled mood indeed.

He opened the conservatory door and stood looking along the avenue of greenery towards his prize specimen. He judged the length of the tendrils—already he found himself calling them tentacles—with great care and walked to within what appeared a safe distance. The plant certainly had an impression of alertness and menace far more appropriate to the animal than the vegetable kingdom. Hercules remembered the unfortunate history of Doctor Frankenstein, and was not amused.

But, really, this was ridiculous! Such things didn't happen in real life. Well, there was one way to put matters to the test . . .

Hercules went into the house and came back a few minutes later with a broomstick, to the end of which he had attached a piece of raw meat. Feeling a considerable fool, he advanced towards the orchid as a lion-tamer might approach one of his charges at meal-time.

For a moment, nothing happened. Then two of the tendrils developed an agitated twitch. They began to sway back and forth, as if the plant was making up its mind. Abruptly, they whipped out with such speed that they practically vanished from view. They wrapped themselves round the meat, and Hercules felt a powerful tug at the end of his broomstick. Then the meat was gone: the orchid was clutching it, if one may mix metaphors slightly, to its bosom.

"Jumping Jehosophat!" yelled Hercules. It was very seldom indeed that he used such strong language.

The orchid showed no further signs of life for twenty-four hours. It was waiting for the meat to become high, and it was also developing its digestive system. By the next day, a network of what looked like short roots had covered the still visible chunk of meat. By nightfall, the meat was gone.

The plant had tasted blood.

Hercules' emotions as he watched over his prize were curiously mixed. There were times when it almost gave him nightmares, and he foresaw a whole range of horrid possibilities. The orchid was now extremely strong, and if he got within its clutches he would be done for. But, of course, there was not the slightest danger of that. He had arranged a system of pipes so that it could be watered from a safe distance, and its less orthodox food he simply tossed within range of its tentacles. It was now eating a pound of raw meat a day, and he had an uncomfortable feeling that it could cope with much larger quantities if given the opportunity.

Hercules' natural qualms were, on the whole, outweighed by his feeling of triumph that such a botanical marvel had fallen into his hands. Whenever he chose, he could become the most famous orchid-grower in the world. It was typical of his somewhat restricted view-point that it never occurred to him that other people besides orchid-fanciers might be interested in his pet.

The creature was now about six feet tall, and apparently still growing—though much more slowly than it had been. All the other plants had been moved from its end of the conservatory, not so much because Hercules feared that it might be cannibalistic as to enable him to tend them without danger. He had stretched a rope across the central aisle so that there was no risk of his accidentally walking within range of those eight dangling arms.

It was obvious that the orchid had a highly developed nervous system, and something very nearly approaching intelligence. It knew when it was going to be fed, and exhibited unmistakable signs of pleasure. Most fantastic of all—though Hercules was still not sure about this—it seemed capable of producing sounds. There were times, just before a meal, when he fancied he could hear an incredibly high-pitched whistle, skirting the edge of audibility. A new-born bat might have had such a voice: he wondered what purpose it served. Did the orchid somehow lure its prey into its clutches by sound? If so, he did not think the technique would work on him.

While Hercules was making these interesting discoveries, he continued to be fussed over by Aunt Henrietta and assaulted by her hounds, which were never as house-trained as she claimed them to be. She would usually roar up the street on a Sunday afternoon with one dog in the seat beside her and another occupying most of the baggage compartment. Then she would bound up the steps two at a time, nearly deafen Hercules with her greeting, half paralyze him with her handshake, and blow cigar smoke in his face. There had been a time when he was terrified that she would kiss him, but he had long since realized that such effeminate behaviour was foreign to her nature.

Aunt Henrietta looked upon Hercules' orchids with some scorn. Spending one's spare time in a hot-house was, she considered, a very effete recreation. When *she* wanted to let off steam, she went big-game hunting in Kenya. This did nothing to endear her to Hercules, who hated blood sports. But despite his mounting dislike for his overpowering aunt, every Sunday afternoon he dutifully prepared tea for her and they had a tête-à-tête together which, on the surface at least, seemed perfectly friendly. Henrietta never guessed that as he poured the tea Hercules often wished it was poisoned: she was, far down beneath her extensive fortifications, a fundamentally good-hearted person and the knowledge would have upset her deeply.

Hercules did not mention his vegetable octopus to Aunt Henrietta. He had occasionally shown her his most interesting specimens, but this was something he was keeping to himself. Perhaps, even before he had fully formulated his diabolical plan, his subconscious was already preparing the ground . . .

It was late one Sunday evening, when the roar of the Jaguar had died away into the night and Hercules was restoring his shattered nerves in the conservatory, that the idea first came fully-fledged into his mind. He was staring at the orchid, noting how the tendrils were now as thick around as a man's thumb, when a most pleasing fantasy suddenly flashed before his eyes. He pictured Aunt Henrietta struggling helplessly in the grip of the monster, unable to escape from its carnivorous clutches. Why, it would be the perfect crime. The distraught nephew would arrive on the scene too late to be of assistance, and when the police answered his frantic call they would see at a glance that the whole affair was a deplorable accident. True, there would be an inquest, but the coroner's censure would be toned down in view of Hercules' obvious grief . . .

The more he thought of the idea, the more he liked it. He could see no flaws, as long as the orchid co-operated. That, clearly, would be the greatest problem. He would have to plan a course of training for the creature. It already looked sufficiently diabolical; he must give it a disposition to suit its appearance.

Considering that he had no prior experience in such matters, and that there were no authorities he could consult, Hercules proceeded along very sound and business-like lines. He would use a fishing rod to dangle pieces of meat just outside the orchid's range, until the creature lashed its tentacles in a frenzy. At such times its high-pitched squeak was clearly audible, and Hercules wondered how it managed to produce the sound. He also wondered what its organs of perception were, but this was yet another mystery that could not be solved without close examination. Perhaps Aunt Henrietta, if all went well, would have a brief opportunity of discovering these interesting facts—though she would probably be too busy to report them for the benefit of posterity.

There was no doubt that the beast was quite powerful enough to deal with its intended victim. It had once wrenched a broomstick out of Hercules' grip, and although that in itself proved very little, the sickening "crack" of the wood a moment later brought a smile of satisfaction to its trainer's thin lips. He began to be much more pleasant and attentive to his aunt. In every respect, indeed, he was the model nephew.

When Hercules considered that his picador tactics had brought the orchid into the right frame of mind, he wondered if he should test it with live bait. This was a problem that worried him for some weeks, during which time he would look speculatively at every dog or cat he passed in the street, but he finally abandoned the idea, for a rather peculiar reason. He was simply too kind-hearted to put it into practice. Aunt Henrietta would have to be the first victim.

He starved the orchid for two weeks before he put his plan into action. This was as long as he dared risk—he did not wish to weaken the beast—

merely to whet its appetite that the outcome of the encounter might be more certain. And so, when he had carried the tea-cups back into the kitchen and was sitting upwind of Aunt Henrietta's cigar, he said casually: "I've got something I'd like to show you, auntie. I've been keeping it as a surprise. It'll tickle you to death."

That, he thought, was not a completely accurate description, but it gave the general idea.

Auntie took the cigar out of her mouth and looked at Hercules with frank surprise.

"Well!" she boomed. "Wonders will never cease! What *have* you been up to, you rascal?" She slapped him playfully on the back and shot all the air out of his lungs.

"You'll never believe it," gritted Hercules, when he had recovered his breath. "It's in the observatory."

"Eh?" said Auntie, obviously puzzled.

"Yes—come along and have a look. It's going to create a real sensation."

Auntie gave a snort that might have indicated disbelief, but followed Hercules without further question. The two Alsatians now busily chewing up the carpet looked at her anxiously and half rose to their feet, but she waved them away.

"All right, boys," she ordered gruffly. "I'll be back in a minute." Hercules thought this unlikely.

It was a dark evening, and the lights in the conservatory were off. As they entered, Auntie snorted, "Gad, Hercules—the place smells like a slaughter-house. Haven't met such a stink since I shot that elephant in Bulawayo and we couldn't find it for a week."

"Sorry, auntie," apologized Hercules, propelling her forward through the gloom. "It's a new fertilizer I'm using. It produces the most stunning results. Go on—another couple of yards. I want this to be a *real* surprise."

"I hope this isn't a joke," said Auntie suspiciously, as she stomped forward.

"I can promise you it's no joke," replied Hercules, standing with his hand on the light switch. He could just see the looming bulk of the orchid: Auntie was now within ten feet of it. He waited until she was well inside the danger zone, and threw the switch.

There was a frozen moment while the scene was transfixed with light. Then Aunt Henrietta ground to a halt and stood, arms akimbo, in front of the giant orchid. For a moment Hercules was afraid she would retreat before the plant could get into action: then he saw that she was calmly scrutinizing it, unable to make up her mind what the devil it was.

It was a full five seconds before the orchid moved. Then the dangling tentacles flashed into action—but not in the way that Hercules had expected. The plant clutched them tightly, protectively, *around itself*— and at the same time it gave a high-pitched scream of pure terror. In a moment of sickening disillusionment, Hercules realized the awful truth.

His orchid was an utter coward. It might be able to cope with the wild life of the Amazon jungle, but coming suddenly upon Aunt Henrietta had completely broken its nerve.

As for its proposed victim, she stood watching the creature with an astonishment which swiftly changed to another emotion. She spun around on her heels and pointed an accusing finger at her nephew.

"Hercules!" she roared. "The poor thing's scared to death. *Have you been bullying it?*"

Hercules could only stand with his head hanging low in shame and frustration.

"N-no, auntie," he quavered. "I guess it's naturally nervous."

"Well, I'm used to animals. You should have called me before. You must treat them firmly—but gently. Kindness always works, as long as you show them you're the master. There, there, did-dums—don't be frightened of auntie—she won't hurt you . . ."

It was, thought Hercules in his blank despair, a revolting sight. With surprising gentleness, Aunt Henrietta fussed over the beast, patting and stroking it until the tentacles relaxed and the shrill, whistling scream died away. After a few minutes of this pandering, it appeared to get over its fright. Hercules finally fled with a muffled sob when one of the tentacles crept forward and began to stroke Henrietta's gnarled fingers . . .

From that day, he was a broken man. What was worse, he could never escape from the consequences of his intended crime. Henrietta had acquired a new pet, and was liable to call not only at weekends but two or three times in between as well. It was obvious that she did not trust Hercules to treat the orchid properly, and still suspected him of bullying it. She would bring tasty tidbits that even her dogs had rejected, but which the orchid accepted with delight. The smell, which had so far been confined to the conservatory, began to creep into the house . . .

And there, concluded Harry Purvis, as he brought this improbable narrative to a close, the matter rests—to the satisfaction of two, at any rate, of the parties concerned. The orchid is happy, and Aunt Henrietta has something (query, someone?) else to dominate. From time to time the creature has a nervous breakdown when a mouse gets loose in the conservatory, and she rushes to console it.

As for Hercules, there is no chance that he will ever give any more trouble to either of them. He seems to have sunk into a kind of vegetable sloth: indeed, said Harry thoughtfully, every day he becomes more and more like an orchid himself.

The harmless variety, of course. . . .

BIBLIOGRAPHY

Tales from the White Hart, Ballantine, 1957. Contains the following:
    "Silence Please"
    "Big Game Hunt"
    "Patent Pending"
    "Armaments Race"
    "Critical Mass," *Space Science Fiction,* August 1957
    "The Ultimate Melody," *If,* February 1957
    "The Pacifist," *Fantastic Universe,* October 1956
    "The Next Tenants," *Satellite Science Fiction,* February 1957
    "Moving Spirit"
    "The Man Who Ploughed the Sea," *Satellite Science Fiction,* June 1957
    "The Reluctant Orchid," *Satellite Science Fiction,* December 1956
    "Cold War," *Satellite Science Fiction,* April 1957
    "What Goes Up . . . ," *The Magazine of Fantasy and Science Fiction,* January
        1956
    "Sleeping Beauty," *Infinity,* April 1957
    "The Defenestration of Ermintrude Inch"

TALES FROM GAVAGAN'S BAR SERIES

by L. Sprague de Camp and Fletcher Pratt

Introduction by L. Sprague de Camp

Fletcher Pratt (1897–1956) and I began collaborating on imaginative fiction in 1939. Pratt was then an established author of science fiction, history, biography, and military and naval books. In 1928 to 1930 he collaborated with Irvin Lester, Lawrence Manning, B. F. Ruby, and his wife Inga Stephens Pratt on stories for Hugo Gernsback's *Amazing Stories* and other early science-fiction magazines. He continued to write occasional tales in the genre through the 1930s and '40s and also, around 1930, worked for Gernsback as a translator of science-fiction stories from the French and German.

For all that the awards called "Hugos" are named for him, Gernsback was not noted for meticulous honesty in paying people what he owed them. When he failed to pay the translation fee promised to Pratt, for a novel of which the first installment had appeared but of which the latter part had not yet been translated, Pratt told Gernsback: "I'm sorry, but if you don't pay me what you owe me, I don't see how I can go on with the translation." Over a barrel, Gernsback paid.

I met Pratt through our mutual friend, Dr. John D. Clark, who was job-hunting in New York when I moved back thither from Scranton, Pennsylvania, in 1937. Clark and I were old naval buffs, and Pratt ran a monthly war game, first in his living room and later in a hired hall. He made hundreds of models of warships of balsa wood and wires, on a scale of 55' = 1". A score of players crawled around, moving these models and writing down their estimates of the range to the enemy ship. Clark and I were soon members of the war-game circle.

Pratt suggested that I collaborate with him on the stories that became the Harold Shea fantasies. Later we wrote *Land of Unreason* and *The Carnelian Cube*. The Hitlerian War interrupted our collaboration. Pratt became a military columnist and war correspondent; I joined the Naval Reserve and spent the war, with Robert A. Heinlein and Isaac Asimov, in a naval aircraft engineering laboratory at the Philadelphia Naval Base.

After the war, Pratt and I decided to develop a series of barroom tall tales, along the lines of Lord Dunsany's stories of Mr. Joseph Jorkens. I do not remember which of us first had the idea or whether we were consciously influenced by Dunsany's example. Unbeknown to us, across the sea, Arthur C. Clarke was launching a similar project with his tales of the White Hart.

The first Gavagan's Bar story was "The Better Mousetrap." This was rejected by two magazines, rewritten, rejected some more, and finally sold to the new *Magazine of Fantasy and Science Fiction* (issue of December 1950). Meanwhile we had composed several more such tales and enjoyed speedier success as we got into the swing of it.

In most of these stories, we worked out the plot in consultation. I took notes in shorthand, turned these into a synopsis, and wrote the rough draft. Pratt did the final and any intermediate drafts. We found this the most practical method.

The setting of these stories is an old-fashioned bar, in an unnamed city (not *necessarily* New York) in the northeastern United States. The time is around 1950, plus or minus a couple of years.

In those days, the dollar had several times its present value; dimes, quarters, half-dollars, and dollar coins were made of real silver. Beards were just barely beginning to appear on the general male populace, having been worn by submarine officers in the Second World War. Men wore their hair short and often in the now-rare crew cut.

Commercial television was new, with small black-and-white picture tubes only. Airliners were propeller-driven. Manhattan cocktails were popular. Women's lib, gay rights, and ethnicity were not yet burning issues. The Cold War, however, was; it did not begin to ease until after the death of the old monster, Stalin, in 1953. From 1950 to 1953, the Korean War raged. The flight of the first Sputnik (1957), the miniskirt, the sexual revolution, the fall of the "dirty word" taboo, and the student revolt of the late 1960s were still in the womb of time. "Negro" was still deemed a more polite term than "black" for a person of that race.

For six years, on and off, Pratt and I worked with these stories. The last was "The Weissenbroch Spectacles," written in 1953 and published in *Fantasy and Science Fiction* for November 1954. Of the twenty-nine tales, twelve were published in *Fantasy and Science Fiction,* three in *Weird Tales* (then in its final decline), and two in *Fantastic Universe Science Fiction.* Twenty-three appeared in a cloth-bound book, *Tales from Gavagan's Bar,* in 1953; all twenty-nine are included in a new collection of the same title published by Owlswick Press.

With the approach of the Civil War centennial, Pratt became so busy with books about that war that he had no more time for fiction before his premature death. Hence, we never got around to writing the story about the vampire who had a sweet tooth and so only attacked diabetics. It was to have drawn on Pratt's knowledge of professional boxing, he having in his youth been a fighter in the flyweight class. I have not tried to carry on the series alone, because (as often happens in collaborations) the Pratt–de Camp combination produced tales in a style decidedly different from what either of us did alone.

The Ancestral Amethyst

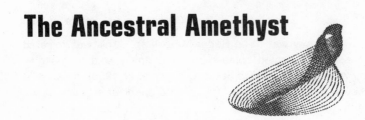

"We were very good to the Swedes when they ruled over us in Bornholm three hundred years ago," said the stocky man, downing his cherry brandy at a gulp and motioning Mr. Cohan for a refill. "We had to kill all of them one night. While it was being done, some of our people ran into the church and rang the church bells, so that the souls of all the Swedes should rise to heaven on the music. For several hours they continued to pull the ropes, although it was terribly hard work for their arms and they became very tired."

The second cherry brandy followed the first. Professor Thott contemplated the bald cranium, surrounded by a crescent of pale hair, and said thoughtfully: "I can perceive that you Danes are an extremely tender-hearted people."

"That is most true," said the stocky man. His whole face was covered by a network of tiny red lines. "But it is not always for us—how do the English say it?—'beer and skating.' I remember—"

The door opened, and he checked as into Gavagan's came a tall, thin, knobby policeman, accompanied by a small man with sharp eyes, in a neat blue serge suit. The policeman extended a hand across the bar to Mr. Cohan, who shook it fervently.

"How are you, Julius?"

"How are you, my boy?" Then he turned to face the others.

"Hello, Professor," he said to Thott. "Meet my friend, Mr. McClintock."

There was more handshaking. Thott said: "This is Captain Axel Ewaldt, of the Danish merchant marine, Officer Cohan, Mr. McClintock. Shall we have a round? He was just telling a story to illustrate how sentimental the Danes are. Make mine a Rye Highball, Mr. Cohan."

"Just a sherry," said McClintock. "A people of high moral standards. They have less crime than any nation in Europe."

Captain Ewaldt beamed; Patrolman Cohan said: "Mr. McClintock gives talks on crime. He's just been over to the Police Boys' Club doing it. He's an expert."

"I have often wondered how one became an expert on crime," said Professor Thott, meditatively.

"By personal association in my case," said McClintock. "I don't in the least mind telling you, not in the least. Until the grace of the Lord came upon me, I was engaged in criminal activity. The title of my talk is 'Crime does not pay,' and I am happy to say my efforts have been rewarding."

Patrolman Cohan said: "This was known as Dippie Louie. He was a left breech hook and could kiss the dog."

Professor Thott gazed at Dippie Louie with polite interest, but Ewaldt said: "Some schnapps, Mr. Cohan. This cherry makes one cold inside, and a man should warm himself." He addressed the officer: "Be so good to explain. I am not understanding."

"A left breech hook can lift a poke—beg pardon, take a wallet out of a man's left breeches pocket. And kissing the dog means he can do it while standing face to face."

"A highly skilled profession," said McClintock. "Ah, my friends, if the effort and training expended on criminal activity were only employed in the service of humanity, we would not—"

Thott said, rather hastily: "You were going to tell us about the Danes being kindhearted, Captain Ewaldt."

"That is correct," said the Captain. "I was yust remembering how I am in the city of Boston one St. Patrick's Day, walking down the dock and minding my own business. Along comes this big Irishman, and anybody can see he has too much to drink, and because I do not have green on for the day, he pushes me. Once is all right, but the second time, I got my little Danish up, and I pushed him in the water—with my fist. But I was really very good to him, because if I have not done this, he would be falling in the water to drown after dark when there is nobody to rescue him."

Mr. Cohan gave an inarticulate sound, but it was McClintock who said: "What makes you so certain?"

"More schnapps, please. Because this is early in the morning, and he would be drinking more all day, and everyone knows that an Irishman cannot drink all day without falling down."

Patrolman Cohan gave an inarticulate sound; Mr. Cohan put both hands on the bar, and said: "And would you be saying, now, that youse Swedes can hold your liquor better than the Irish that's brought up on it? Go on with you."

"I am not Swedish," said Ewaldt, "yust a good Danish man. And I am saying that I am brought up on the island of Bornholm, and I can drink three times as much as any Irishman."

"Would you care to bet five dollars on that, now?" said Mr. Cohan, dangerously.

"It is too little. Five dollars valuta will not even buy the schnapps I am drinking."

"Think pretty well of yourself, don't you?" said Mr. Cohan. "I can see now that you must be a real artist at drinking." Patrolman Cohan snickered at this brilliant sarcasm as Mr. Cohan went on: "Not but what everyone should have something to be proud of. But if you feel that way about it, maybe you'd be liking to have a little contest for twenty-five dollars, and the loser pays the bills?"

Wheels appeared to be revolving in Ewaldt's head. "That I will do," he said. "You are drinking with me?"

"Not me, my fine young felly," said Mr. Cohan. "I have the bar and all to take care of, and it would be worth the best part of me neck if Gavagan come in and found me trying to drink down one of the trade. But Dippie Louie here, he has more than a drop of the right blood in him, and I call to mind many's the time I've seen him lay away his share."

"It was the cause of my ruin and my descent into crime," said McClintock. "But I undeniably possess a special ability to absorb the drink. It's because my ancestors come from Galway, it is, where the wind blows so cold that if a man drinks water and then goes out of doors, he's no better than an icicle in no time at all."

"I am not wanting to ruin you again," said Ewaldt.

Patrolman Cohan spoke up: "You'll not be ruining Louie McClintock, that drank down the Bohemian champion at the truck drivers' picnic. And besides, I'm here meself to see that he gets home all right."

McClintock gravely extended his hand and took Ewaldt's. "For the honor of old Erin." he said. "Twenty-five dollars and the loser pays the bills. What shall we drink?"

"Schnapps some kind. It is no matter to me."

Mr. Cohan set a bottle of Irish whiskey on the bar, produced a couple of Scotch-and-soda glasses and filled them halfway up, adjusting the liquid level with meticulous care. "*Skaal!*" said Ewaldt, and tossed his off as though it were a pony. McClintock went more slowly, rolling the last mouthful around his tongue before he sank it, and said: "That makes you cock your tail, now! Fill them again, Mr. Cohan."

Thott said: "I think that, to be perfectly fair, a slight interval should be allowed for the—ah, dissipation of the shock effect. Mr. McClintock, if I am not too importunate, may I ask what led you to change professions?"

"Education," said McClintock. "Education and the grace of God. I took a correspondence course in writing short stories while I was in Dannemora." He reached for his glass, which Mr. Cohan had loaded again. "Ah, up Erin!" The two Cohans nodded approval, and Thott raised his own glass in salutation. Ewaldt drained his potion off without lifting an eyebrow, tapped the glass with a fingernail, and pushed it toward Mr. Cohan. The bartender reached back for another bottle of Irish and refilled the glasses for a third time.

Ewaldt beamed. "In my country," he said, "we drink not to the country, but to all the pretty girls. Now I have drunk with you to your country, and you are drinking with me to all the pretty girls in Denmark. *Skaal!*"

His third glass of Irish followed the course of the other two with the same easy, fluid motion. McClintock again took a little more time. There was a slight frown in the middle of his forehead, and he appeared to be considering something quite seriously.

"It was the prison chaplain, God bless his soul," he said. "He explained to me that the gains from the profession of crime were b'no means equal to the effort expended. He made me see, he told me that . . ." He turned halfway round and emitted a large burp.

Patrolman Cohan gazed earnestly at him, then turned toward the others and began talking rapidly: "Did I ever tell you now, about the time I found me own wife in the paddy wagon, and her mad enough to have the left leg of me, and saying it was all my fault? It was—" He laid a hand on McClintock's shoulder, but Dippie Louie shook it off.

"I'm okay," he said. "Fill them up again."

"You are not to be drinking so fast," said Ewaldt evenly. "That is how a man is—how do you say it?—be-drunken, unless he is Danish."

"I tell you I'm all right," said McClintock, "and I know how fast I can put it away. Fill them up again, Mr. Cohan."

Mr. Cohan obliged. The last drops came out of the second bottle of Irish as he was filling the glasses, and he had to open a third one.

Professor Thott said: "As a matter of fact, there's something in what the Captain says, though not quite for that reason. It's a question of liquefaction, of the body not being able to absorb any more liquid in any form. Fix me another Manhattan, will you, Mr. Cohan?"

"A Manhattan?" said Ewaldt. "I am remembering them; they are good. You will please to make me one, also." He addressed McClintock with a pleasant smile. "This is not part of the contest, but an extra for pleasure. But you are correct, Mr. Professor. I shall relieve myself."

He started toward the toilet but was detained by a cry from McClintock: "Hey, no you don't! I seen that one pulled the time I drank against the three Stranahans in Chi."

"Why don't you both go?" said Thott, "with Patrolman Cohan to see there's no foul play. After all, he represents the law and can be trusted to be impartial."

As the trio disappeared through the door, he turned to Mr. Cohan: "I hate to say it, but I think your friend Dippie Louie is beginning to come apart along the seams."

"Don't you believe it, now," said Mr. Cohan. "No more than Finn MacCool did when he met the Scotch giant and his wife baked the stove lids in the cakes. That's just the way of him. Would you like to make a side bet now, that he won't have that Swede under the bar rail before he's done?"

"A dollar," said Thott, and they shook hands across the bar, as the three emerged to find the Manhattans and glasses of Irish lined up. Ewaldt disposed of his as rapidly as before, then picked up the Manhattan and began to sip it delicately. He turned to McClintock: "You are the very good drinker for an Irishman. I salute you, as you did. Hop, Eire!"

The Manhattan followed the whiskey. There seemed to be something slightly wrong with McClintock's throat as he accepted the toast. Patrolman Cohan took on an anxious look and Mr. Cohan an inquiring one, but Ewaldt merely indicated with a gesture that he wanted a refill on both glasses. McClintock gazed at his portion of whiskey with a kind of fearful fascination, swallowed once, and then began to sip it, with his Adam's apple moving rapidly. Ewaldt slid his down as before, and picked up the Manhattan. "These I pay for," he said.

McClintock said: "It was him that gave me the office, just like I'm telling you. I was in with a couple of right gees, too, jug-heisters, but . . . mark my words, friends, *crime does not pay.*"

"I never thought I'd live to see the day," said Patrolman Cohan. "A bottle and a half apiece. Louie, you're a credit to the race."

"That is very true," said Ewaldt. "After the Danes, the Poles are the best drinkers. Now we shall change to something else, since you have been making the first choice. Mr. Cohan, you have the Russian vodka?"

"No' for me," said McClintock. "No' for me." He looked at Thott solemnly, blinked his eyes twice, and said, "You're right, perfessor. Need time for shock effec'. Think I'll sh— sit down for a minute before next round."

He took four or five long steps to one of the tables and sat down heavily, staring straight before him. Ewaldt, on whom no effect was visible beyond a slight reddening of the nose, said: "Now I have won and it is to pay me."

"Not yet," said Patrolman Cohan. "He isn't out, just resting between rounds. He'll come back." His voice seemed to lack conviction.

"It's the most marvellous thing I've ever seen," said Thott, looking at Ewaldt with an awe tinged with envy. "I wish I had your capacity, it would be useful at class reunions."

"Ah, it's not for me to speak," said Mr. Cohan, pouring the vodka, into an ordinary shot glass this time. "But the way I was brought up, it's not healthy to be mixing your liquor like that."

"Tell me, Captain," said Thott, "how do you do it? Is there a special course of training, or something?"

Ewaldt downed his vodka. "It is only because I am Danish. In my country no one is be-drunken except foolish young men who go down the Herregade and have their shoes shined on Saturday night while they make calls to the girls that pass, but I am too old for that. But some Danes are better drinkers than others. We have in Denmark a story that the best are those who have from their forefathers one of the *aedelstanar*—how do you say it?—amethysts. Observe."

His hand went to the watch chain and the end came out of his vest pocket. Instead of penknife, key ring, or other make-weight, the chain ended in a large purplish stone with an old-fashioned gold setting.

"In the olden times, six hundred years ago," Ewaldt continued, "there were many of them. They were the protection against be-drunkenhood, to place in the bottom of the winecup, and most of them belonged to bishops, from which it is easy to see that the church is very sober."

Thott peered over the top of his glasses. "Interesting. It was a regular medieval idea; the word amethyst itself means antidrunkenness, you know. Did you get yours from a bishop?"

Ewaldt tucked his pocket piece away, and gave a little laugh. "No, this one is descended to me from Tycho Brahe, that was an astronomer and supposed to be a magician. But of course, it is all superstition, like his being a magician, and I do not believe it at all."

He turned to face McClintock, who had come back to the bar and was leaning one elbow on it as he stared at the stuffed owl. "How is it now, my friend? Shall we have one more little bit?"

"Gotta make thish score or I'm a creep," mumbled the collapsing champion of old Eire.

Patrolman Cohan looked at him sharply. "Now, listen, Louie," he said. "You ain't making scores—"

He was interrupted by a kind of strangled sound from Ewaldt, and the others turned to look at the Captain, who seemed in the throes of a revolution. A fine perspiration had broken out on his forehead, and the network of lines had run together into a kind of mottling. *"Bevare!"* he uttered as they watched, and one foot came up to feel for the bar rail. He missed it, and without its support, the leg seemed to have no more stiffness than a rubber band. Captain Ewaldt took a heavy list to starboard, clutched once at the edge of the bar, missed that too, and came down hard on the floor.

As Thott and Patrolman Cohan bent to pick him up, Dippie Louie McClintock suddenly gripped the arm of the latter.

"Julius!" he wailed, and Thott saw a big tear come out on his cheek. "You should have stopped me! You know that when I drink, I just can't resist the temptation! Don't tell anyone that I did it, will you, or I'll lose my job at the fish market and won't be able to give lectures on crime any more. Here, take it, and give it back to him."

He held out the amethyst, detached from its chain, thrust it into Patrolman Cohan's hand, then in his turn swayed, missed a grab at the bar, and joined Ewaldt on the floor.

"I get a dollar," said Mr. Cohan. "The Swede is under the bar rail."

BIBLIOGRAPHY

"Elephas Frumenti," *The Magazine of Fantasy and Science Fiction*, Winter–Spring 1950

"The Gift of God," *The Magazine of Fantasy and Science Fiction*, Winter–Spring 1950

"The Better Mousetrap," *The Magazine of Fantasy and Science Fiction*, December 1950

"More Than Skin Deep," *The Magazine of Fantasy and Science Fiction*, April 1951

"Beasts of Bourbon," *The Magazine of Fantasy and Science Fiction*, October 1951

"Methought I Heard a Voice" (as "When the Night Wind Howls"), *Weird Tales*, November 1951

"The Rape of the Lock," *The Magazine of Fantasy and Science Fiction*, February 1952

"The Ancestral Amethyst," *The Magazine of Fantasy and Science Fiction*, August 1952

"Where to, Please?" *Weird Tales*, September 1952

"One Man's Meat," *The Magazine of Fantasy and Science Fiction*, September 1952

"The Black Ball," *The Magazine of Fantasy and Science Fiction*, October 1952

"The Green Thumb," *The Magazine of Fantasy and Science Fiction*, February 1953

"Caveat Emptor," *Weird Tales*, March 1953

"The Untimely Topper," *The Magazine of Fantasy and Science Fiction*, July 1953

Tales from Gavagan's Bar, Twayne Publishers, 1953, contained the following original stories: "Here Putzi!," "The Eve of St. John," "No Forwarding Address," "The Love Nest," "The Stone of the Sages," "Corpus Delectable," "The Palimpsest of St. Augustine," "My Brother's Keeper," "A Dime Brings You Success," "All That Glitters," and "Gin Comes in Bottles."

"The Weissenbroch Spectacles," *The Magazine of Fantasy and Science Fiction*, November 1954

"Oh, Say! Can You See" (as "Ward of the Argonaut"), *Fantastic Universe Science Fiction*, January 1959

"Bell, Book, and Candle," *Fantastic Universe Science Fiction*, October, 1959

Tales from Gavagan's Bar (Expanded Edition), Owlswick Press, 1978, contained the original story "There'd Be Thousands in It."

THE PEOPLE SERIES

 *by Zenna Henderson*

By profession, I am a school teacher. My avocation is writing. I have just about taught myself into retirement. Almost all my teaching has been in the first grade, though I have, at one time or another, taught all elementary grades and a little in high school.

I am a native Arizonan and have lived most of my life in this state. However, I taught for two years in France. During this time, my first book, *Pilgrimage,* was put together. And I taught a year in Connecticut, with my feet almost in Long Island Sound. In Arizona, I've taught at a Japanese relocation camp during World War II and, much later, at a military post—Fort Huachuca. I've taught at a semi-ghost mining town where the kids brought jars of water to school when the water pressure was too low to make it up to the hill-top school house, and we had to unlock the Little Houses left over from a much earlier era. That's where I taught high school typing and journalism. We had either four or five high school graduates that year.

The first story of The People, "Ararat," was published in *The Magazine of Fantasy and Science Fiction* in October 1952. It was the second science fiction story of mine that they had published and the second science fiction story I ever had published.

"Ararat" in 1952 was followed by "Gilead" in 1954 (the first time I had my name on the magazine cover), and "Pottage" in 1955. "Wilderness" was published in 1957, "Captivity" in 1958 and "Jordan" in 1959. These six stories, tied together by the narrative of Lea, were published by Doubleday as *Pilgrimage: The Book of The People,* in 1961.

The reason there was a fairly wide gap between the two books of The People is it took that long to accumulate enough stories to make another book-length narrative.

"Return" was published in 1961, "Shadow on the Moon" in 1962 and "Deluge" in 1963. These were followed by "No Different Flesh" in 1965, "Angels Unawares" in March 1966, and "Troubling of the Waters" in September 1966. These stories were tied together with the Assembling idea after being rearranged into the People chronological order, titled *The People: No Different Flesh,* and published by Doubleday in 1967.

Both of The People books were later brought out in Avon paperbacks and are still in print.

The interval between The People stories usually indicated other science fiction or fantasy stories—non-People stories—but usually only one or maybe two. The interval between the publishing of the two People books was occupied by compiling these miscellaneous stories into a short story collection, *The Anything Box.*

After the second People book, another collection of miscellaneous stories titled *Holding Wonder* was published. Both of these volumes also were brought out in Avon paperbacks and *Holding Wonder* is still in print. A second edition of *The Anything Box* is currently being arranged.

All four of the books were published in England by Gollancz and The People books in Germany also.

When I first started writing "Ararat," The People were supposed to be a weird group crossing, by magic, the Atlantic Ocean as refugees from a Transylvania-type country. However, I have difficulty writing about unpleasant people, so my characters got People-er and People-er until I discarded the original idea and developed, instead, the refugees from another world idea.

I had trouble naming the first story. I forget whether it was J. Francis McComas or Anthony Boucher—they were co-editors of the magazine at that time—who suggested "Ararat." That was the beginning of a train of thought that resulted in all the People stories. Both Boucher and McComas were very helpful and friendly. I never got a printed rejection slip from them. When I sent something that bombed completely, they let me know, firmly, but were always most encouraging to me. When the first book was just beginning to be an idea, they helped me find an agent to take care of the complicated business. They were both mid-wives to my career as a writer.

Readers not familiar with the Bible miss many nuances in the People stories. Many of my titles came from there, and most of my character names. "Deluge" was the Flood after which the ark finally came to rest on Mount Ararat. All the stories in *Pilgrimage* plus "Deluge" have themes from the Old Testament and applied to individuals or small groups: selling a birthright for a mess of "Pottage"; wandering hopeless years in the "Wilderness"; seeking healing in the balm of "Gilead"; being carried off into an alien "Captivity"; crossing the River "Jordan" into the Promised Land.

I enjoyed writing the People stories because I often started with only a first sentence and surprised and engrossed myself in the new characters that emerged, and the new Gifts, Signs and Persuasions that developed.

I think one of the appeals of The People is that they are a possible forgotten side of the coin that seems always to flip to evil, violence and cruelty.

I have received a vast—to me—amount of fan mail since I started writing about The People. Some letters were wild and far-out. One said only, "What do you do and what do you know." I was saddened by others who insisted that The People were real and that, if I wanted to, I could tell them where The People were. They *had* to know because they were one of the un-found-yet People.

In the last few years, I have begun to receive fan letters from teenagers whose parents were former teenage fans—

Well, it's nice to get fan letters, anyway.

Ararat

We've had trouble with teachers in Cougar Canyon. It's just an Accommodation school anyway, isolated and so unhandy to anything. There's really nothing to hold a teacher. But the way The People bring forth their young, in quantities and with regularity, even our small Group can usually muster the nine necessary for the County School Superintendent to arrange for the schooling for the year.

Of course I'm past school age, Canyon school age, and have been for years, but if the tally came up one short in the Fall, I'd go back for a post-graduate course again. But now I'm working on a college level because Father finished me off for my high school diploma two summers ago. He's promised me that if I do well this year I'll get to go Outside next year and get my training and degree so I can be the teacher and we won't have to go Outside for one any more. Most of the kids would just as soon skip school as not, but the Old Ones don't hold with ignorance and the Old Ones have the last say around here.

Father is the head of the school board. That's how I get in on lots of school things the other kids don't. This summer when he wrote to the County Seat that we'd have more than our nine again this fall and would they find a teacher for us, he got back a letter saying they had exhausted their supply of teachers who hadn't heard of Cougar Canyon and we'd have to dig up our own teacher this year. That "dig up" sounded like a dirty crack to me since we have the graves of four past teachers in the far corner of our cemetery. They sent us such old teachers, the homeless, the tottering, who were trying to piece out the end of their lives with a year here and a year there in jobs no one else wanted because there's no adequate pension system in the state and most teachers seem to die in harness. And their oldness and their tottering were not sufficient in the Canyon where there are apt to be shocks for Outsiders—unintentional as most of them are.

We haven't done so badly the last few years, though. The Old Ones say we're getting adjusted—though some of the nonconformists say that The Crossing thinned our blood. It might be either or both or the teachers are just getting tougher. The last two managed to last until just before the year ended. Father took them in as far as Kerry Canyon and ambulances took them on in. But they were all right after a while in the sanatorium and they're doing okay now. Before them, though, we usually had four teachers a year.

Anyway, Father wrote to a Teachers Agency on the coast and after several letters each way, he finally found a teacher.

He told us about it at the supper table.

"She's rather young," he said, reaching for a toothpick and tipping his chair back on its hind legs.

Mother gave Jethro another helping of pie and picked up her own fork again. "Youth is no crime," she said, "and it'll be a pleasant change for the children."

"Yes, though it seems a shame." Father prodded at a back tooth and Mother frowned at him. I wasn't sure if it was for picking his teeth or for what he said. I knew he meant it seemed a shame to get a place like Cougar Canyon so early in a career. It isn't that we're mean or cruel, you understand. It's only that they're Outsiders and we sometimes forget—especially the kids.

"She doesn't *have* to come," said Mother. "She could say no."

"Well, now—" Father tipped his chair forward. "Jethro, no more pie. You go on out and help 'Kiah bring in the wood. Karen, you and Lizbeth get started on the dishes. Hop to it, kids."

And we hopped, too. Kids do to fathers in the Canyon, though I understand they don't always Outside. It annoyed me because I knew Father wanted us out of the way so he could talk adult talk to Mother, so I told Lizbeth I'd clear the table and then worked as slowly as I could, and as quietly, listening hard.

"She couldn't get any other job," said Father. "The agency told me they had placed her twice in the last two years and she didn't finish the year either place."

"Well," said Mother, pinching in her mouth and frowning. "If she's that bad, why on earth did you hire her for the Canyon?"

"We have a choice?" laughed Father. Then he sobered. "No, it wasn't for incompetency. She was a good teacher. The way she tells it, they just fired her out of a clear sky. She asked for recommendations and one place wrote, 'Miss Carmody is a very competent teacher but we dare not recommend her for a teaching position.'"

"'Dare not'?" asked Mother.

"'Dare not,'" said Father. "The Agency assured me that they had investigated thoroughly and couldn't find any valid reasons for the dismissals, but she can't seem to find another job anywhere on the coast. She wrote me that she wanted to try another state."

"Do you suppose she's disfigured or deformed?" suggested Mother.

"Not from the neck up!" laughed Father. He took an envelope from his pocket. "Here's her application picture."

By this time I'd got the table cleared and I leaned over Father's shoulder.

"Gee!" I said. Father looked back at me, raising one eyebrow. I knew then that he had known all along that I was listening.

I flushed but stood my ground, knowing I was being granted admission to adult affairs, if only by the back door.

The girl in the picture was lovely. She couldn't have been many years older than I and she was twice as pretty. She had short dark hair curled all over her head and apparently that poreless creamy skin that seems to have an inner light of itself. She had a tentative look about her as though her dark eyebrows were horizontal question marks. There was a droop to the corners of her mouth—not much, just enough to make you wonder why . . . and want to comfort her.

"She'll stir the Canyon for sure," said Father.

"I don't know," Mother frowned thoughtfully. "What will the Old Ones say to a marriageable Outsider in the Canyon?"

"Adonday Veeah!" muttered Father. "That never occurred to me. None of our other teachers were ever of an age to worry about."

"What *would* happen?" I asked. "I mean if one of The Group married an Outsider?"

"Impossible," said Father, so like the Old Ones that I could see why his name was approved in Meeting last Spring.

"Why, there's even our Jemmy," worried Mother. "Already he's saying he'll have to start trying to find another Group. None of the girls here please him. Supposing this Outsider—how old is she?"

Father unfolded the application. "Twenty-three," he said. "Just three years out of college."

"Jemmy's twenty-four," said Mother, pinching her mouth together. "Father, I'm afraid you'll have to cancel the contract. If anything happened— Well, you waited over-long to become an Old One to my way of thinking and it'd be a shame to have something go wrong your first year."

"I can't cancel the contract. She's on her way here. School starts next Monday." Father ruffled his hair forward as he does when he's disturbed. "We're probably making a something of a nothing," he said hopefully.

"Well, I only hope we don't have any trouble with this Outsider."

"Or she with us," grinned Father. "Where are my cigarettes?"

"On the book case," said Mother, getting up and folding the table cloth together to hold the crumbs.

Father snapped his fingers and the cigarettes drifted in from the front room.

Mother went on out to the kitchen. The table cloth shook itself over the waste basket and then followed her.

Father drove to Kerry Canyon Sunday night to pick up our new teacher. She was supposed to have arrived Saturday afternoon, but she didn't make bus connections at the County Seat. The road ends at Kerry Canyon. I mean for Outsiders. There's not much of the look of a well-traveled road very far out our way from Kerry Canyon, which is just as well. Tourists leave us alone. Of course *we* don't have much trouble getting our cars to and fro but that's why everything dead-ends at Kerry Canyon and we have to do all our own fetching and carrying—I mean the road being in the condition it is.

All the kids at our house wanted to stay up to see the new teacher, so Mother let them, but by 7:30 the youngest ones began to drop off and by 9 there was only Jethro and 'Kiah, Lizbeth and Jemmy and me. Father should have been home long before and Mother was restless and uneasy. I knew if he didn't arrive soon, she would head for her room and the cedar box under the bed. But at 9:15 we heard the car coughing and sneezing up the draw. Mother's wide relieved smile was reflected on all our faces.

"Of course!" she cried. "I forgot. He has an Outsider in the car. He had to use the *road* and it's terrible across Jackass Flat."

I felt Miss Carmody before she came in the door. I was tingling all over from anticipation already, but all at once I felt her, so plainly that I knew with a feeling of fear and pride that I was of my Grandmother, that soon I would be bearing the burden and blessing of her Gift: the Gift that develops into free access to any mind—one of The People or Outsider—willing or not. And besides the access, the ability to council and help, to straighten tangled minds and snarled emotions.

And then Miss Carmody stood in the doorway, blinking a little against the light, muffled to the chin against the brisk fall air. A bright scarf hid her hair but her skin *was* that luminous matt-cream it had looked. She was smiling a little, but scared, too. I shut my eyes and . . . I went in—just like that. It was the first time I had ever sorted anybody. She was all fluttery with tiredness and strangeness and there was a question deep inside her that had the wornness of repetition, but I couldn't catch what it was. And under the uncertainty there was a sweetness and dearness and such a bewildered sorrow that I felt my eyes dampen. Then I looked at her again (sorting takes such a little time) as Father introduced her. I heard a gasp beside me and suddenly I went into Jemmy's mind with a stunning rush.

Jemmy and I have been close all our lives and we don't always need words to talk with one another, but this was the first time I had ever gone in like this and I knew he didn't know what had happened. I felt embarrassed and ashamed to know his emotion so starkly. I closed him out as quickly as possible, but not before I knew that now Jemmy would never hunt for another Group; Old Ones or no Old Ones, he had found his love.

All this took less time than it takes to say "How do you do?" and shake hands. Mother descended with cries and drew Miss Carmody and Father out to the kitchen for coffee and Jemmy swatted Jethro and made him carry the luggage instead of snapping it to Miss Carmody's room. After all, we didn't want to lose our teacher before she even saw the school house.

I waited until everyone was bedded down, Miss Carmody in her cold,

cold bed, the rest of us of course with our sheets set for warmth—how I pity Outsiders! Then I went to Mother.

She met me in the dark hall and we clung together as she comforted me.

"Oh Mother," I whispered. "I sorted Miss Carmody tonight. I'm afraid."

Mother held me tight again. "I wondered," she said. "It's a great responsibility. You have to be so wise and clear-thinking. Your Grandmother carried the Gift with graciousness and honor. You are of her. You can do it."

"But Mother! To be an Old One!"

Mother laughed. "You have years of training ahead of you before you'll be an Old One. Councilor to the soul is a weighty job."

"Do I have to tell?" I pleaded. "I don't want anyone to know yet. I don't want to be set apart."

"I'll tell the Oldest," she said. "No one else need know." She hugged me again and I went back, comforted, to bed.

I lay in the darkness and let my mind clear, not even knowing how I knew how to. Like the gentle reachings of quiet fingers I felt the family about me. I felt warm and comfortable as though I were cupped in the hollow palm of a loving hand. Some day I would belong to the Group as I now belonged to the family. Belong to others? With an odd feeling of panic, I shut the family out. I wanted to be alone—to belong just to me and no one else. I didn't *want* the Gift.

I slept after a while.

Miss Carmody left for the school house an hour before we did. She wanted to get things started a little before school time, her late arrival making it kind of rough on her. 'Kiah, Jethro, Lizbeth and I walked down the lane to the Armisters' to pick up their three kids. The sky was so blue you could taste it, a winey, fallish taste of harvest fields and falling leaves. We were all feeling full of bubbly enthusiasm for the beginning of school. We were light-hearted and light-footed, too, as we kicked along through the cottonwood leaves paving the lane with gold. In fact Jethro felt too light-footed and the third time I hauled him down and made him walk on the ground, I cuffed him good. He was still sniffling when we got to Armisters'.

"She's pretty!" called Lizbeth before the kids got out to the gate, all agog and eager for news of the new teacher.

"She's young," added 'Kiah, elbowing himself ahead of Lizbeth.

"She's littler'n me," sniffled Jethro and we all laughed because he's five-six already even if he isn't twelve yet.

Debra and Rachel Armister linked arms with Lizbeth and scuffled down the lane, heads together, absorbing the details of teacher's hair, dress, nail polish, luggage and night clothes, though goodness knows how Lizbeth knew anything about that.

Jethro and 'Kiah annexed Jeddy and they climbed up on the rail fence that parallels the lane and walked the top rail. Jethro took a tentative step or two above the rail, caught my eye and stepped back in a hurry. He knows as well as any child in the Canyon that a kid his age has no business lifting along a public road.

We detoured at the Mesa Road to pick up the Kroginold boys. More than once Father has sighed over the Kroginolds.

You see, when The Crossing was made, The People got separated in that last wild moment when air was screaming past and the heat was building up so alarmingly. The members of our Group left their ship just seconds before it crashed so devastatingly into the box canyon behind Old Baldy and literally splashed and drove itself into the canyon walls, starting a fire that stripped the hills bare for miles. After The People gathered themselves together from the Life Slips and founded Cougar Canyon, they found that the alloy the ship was made of was a metal much wanted here. Our Group has lived on mining the box canyon ever since, though there's something complicated about marketing the stuff. It has to be shipped out of the country and shipped in again because everyone knows that it doesn't occur in this region.

Anyway, our Group at Cougar Canyon is probably the largest of the People, but we are reasonably sure that at least one Group and maybe two survived along with us. Grandmother in her time sensed two Groups but could never locate them exactly and, since our object is to go unnoticed in this new life, no real effort has ever been made to find them. Father can remember just a little of The Crossing, but some of the Old Ones are blind and crippled from the heat and the terrible effort they put forth to save the others from burning up like falling stars.

But getting back, Father often said that of all The People who could have made up our Group, we had to get the Kroginolds. They're rebels and were even before The Crossing. It's their kids that have been so rough on our teachers. The rest of us usually behave fairly decently and remember that we have to be careful around Outsiders.

Derek and Jake Kroginold were wrestling in a pile of leaves by the front gate when we got there. They didn't even hear us coming, so I leaned over and whacked the nearest rear-end and they turned in a flurry of leaves and grinned up at me for all the world like pictures of Pan in the mythology book at home.

"What kinda old bat we got this time?" asked Derek as he scrabbled in the leaves for his lunch box.

"She's not an old bat," I retorted, madder than need be because Derek annoys me so. "She's young and beautiful."

"Yeah, I'll bet!" Jake emptied the leaves from his cap onto the trio of squealing girls.

"She is so!" retorted 'Kiah. "The nicest teacher we ever had."

"She won't teach me nothing!" yelled Derek, lifting to the top of the cottonwood tree at the turn-off.

"Well, if she won't, I will," I muttered and, reaching for a handful of sun, I platted the twishers so quickly that Derek fell like a rock. He yelled like a catamount, thinking he'd get killed for sure, but I stopped him about a foot from the ground and then let go. Well, the stopping and the thump to the ground pretty well jarred the wind out of him, but he yelled:

"I'll tell the Old Ones! You ain't supposed to platt twishers—!"

"Tell the Old Ones," I snapped, kicking on down the leafy road. "I'll be there and tell them why. And then, old smarty pants, what will be your excuse for lifting?"

And then I was ashamed. I was showing off as bad as a Kroginold—but they make me so mad!

Our last stop before school was at the Clarinades'. My heart always squeezed when I thought of the Clarinade twins. They just started school this year—two years behind the average Canyon kid. Mrs. Kroginold used to say that the two of them, Susie and Jerry, divided one brain between them before they were born. That's unkind and untrue—thoroughly a Kroginold remark—but it is true that by Canyon standards the twins were retarded. They lacked so many of the attributes of The People. Father said it might be a delayed effect of The Crossing that they would grow out of, or it might be advance notice of what our children will be like here—what is ahead for The People. It makes me shiver, wondering.

Susie and Jerry were waiting, clinging to one another's hand as they always were. They were shy and withdrawn, but both were radiant because of starting school. Jerry, who did almost all the talking for the two of them, answered our greetings with a shy "Hello."

Then Susie surprised us all by exclaiming, "We're going to school!"

"Isn't it wonderful?" I replied, gathering her cold little hand into mine. "And you're going to have the prettiest teacher we ever had."

But Susie had retired into blushing confusion and didn't say another word all the way to school.

I was worried about Jake and Derek. They were walking apart from us, whispering, looking over at us and laughing. They were cooking up some kind of mischief for Miss Carmody. And more than anything I wanted her to stay. I found right then that there *would* be years ahead of me before I became an Old One. I tried to go in to Derek and Jake to find out what was cooking, but try as I might I couldn't get past the sibilance of their snickers and the hard, flat brightness of their eyes.

We were turning off the road into the school yard when Jemmy, who should have been up at the mine long since, suddenly stepped out of the bushes in front of us, his hands behind him. He glared at Jake and Derek and then at the rest of the children.

"You kids mind your manners when you get to school," he snapped, scowling. "And you Kroginolds—just try anything funny and I'll lift you to Old Baldy and platt the twishers on you. This is one teacher we're going to keep."

Susie and Jerry clung together in speechless terror. The Kroginolds turned red and pushed out belligerent jaws. The rest of us just stared at a Jemmy who never raised his voice and never pushed his weight around.

"I mean it, Jake and Derek. You try getting out of line and the Old Ones will find a few answers they've been looking for—especially about the belfry in Kerry Canyon."

The Kroginolds exchanged looks of dismay and the girls sucked in breaths of astonishment. One of the most rigorously enforced rules of The Group concerns showing off outside the community. If Derek and Jake *had* been involved in ringing that bell all night last Fourth of July . . . well!

"Now you kids, scoot!" Jemmy jerked his head toward the schoolhouse and the terrified twins scudded down the leaf-strewn path like a pair of bright leaves themselves, followed by the rest of the children, with the Kroginolds looking sullenly back over their shoulders and muttering.

Jemmy ducked his head and scowled. "It's time they got civilized anyway. There's no sense to our losing teachers all the time."

"No," I said noncommittally.

"There's no point in scaring her to death." Jemmy was intent on the leaves he was kicking with one foot.

"No," I agreed, suppressing my smile.

Then Jemmy smiled ruefully in amusement at himself. "I should waste words with you," he said. "Here." He took his hands from behind him and thrust a bouquet of burning bright autumn leaves into my arms. "They're from you to her," he said. "Something pretty for the first day."

"Oh, Jemmy!" I cried through the scarlet and crimson and gold. "They're beautiful. You've been up on Baldy this morning."

"That's right," he said. "But she won't know where they came from." And he was gone.

I hurried to catch up with the children before they got to the door. Suddenly overcome with shyness, they were milling around the porch steps, each trying to hide behind the others.

"Oh, for goodness' sakes!" I whispered to our kids. "You ate breakfast with her this morning. She won't bite. Go on in."

But I found myself shouldered to the front and leading the subdued group into the school room. While I was giving the bouquet of leaves to Miss Carmody, the others with the ease of established habit slid into their usual seats, leaving only the twins, stricken and white, standing alone.

Miss Carmody, dropping the leaves on her desk, knelt quickly beside them, pried a hand of each gently free from their frenzied clutching and held them in hers.

"I'm so glad you came to school," she said in her warm, rich voice. "I need a first grade to make the school work out right and I have a seat that must have been built on purpose for twins."

And she led them over to the side of the room, close enough to the old pot-bellied stove for Outside comfort later and near enough to the window to see out. There, in dusted glory, stood one of the old double desks that The Group must have inherited from some ghost town out in the hills. There were two wooden boxes for footstools for small dangling feet and, spouting like a flame from the old ink well hole, a spray of vivid red leaves—matchmates to those Jemmy had given me.

The twins slid into the desk, never loosing hands, and stared up at Miss Carmody, wide-eyed. She smiled back at them and, leaning forward, poked her finger tip into the deep dimple in each round chin.

"Buried smiles," she said, and the two scared faces lighted up briefly with wavery smiles. Then Miss Carmody turned to the rest of us.

I never did hear her introductory words. I was too busy mulling over the spray of leaves, and how she came to know the identical routine, words and all, that the twins' mother used to make them smile, and how on earth she knew about the old desks in the shed. But by the time we rose to salute the flag and sing our morning song, I had it figured out. Father must have briefed her on the way home last night. The twins were an ever present concern of the whole Group and we were all especially anxious to have their first year a successful one. Also, Father knew the smile routine and where the old desks were stored. As for the spray of leaves, well, some did grow this low on the mountain and frost is tricky at leaf-turning time.

So school was launched and went along smoothly. Miss Carmody was a good teacher and even the Kroginolds found their studies interesting.

They hadn't tried any tricks since Jemmy threatened them. That is, except that silly deal with the chalk. Miss Carmody was explaining something on the board and was groping sideways for the chalk to add to the lesson. Jake was deliberately lifting the chalk every time she almost had it. I was just ready to do something about it when Miss Carmody snapped her fingers with annoyance and grasped the chalk firmly. Jake caught my eye about then and shrank about six inches in girth and height. I didn't tell Jemmy, but Jake's fear that I might kept him straight for a long time.

The twins were really blossoming. They laughed and played with the rest of the kids and Jerry even went off occasionally with the other boys at noontime, coming back as disheveled and wet as the others after a dam-building session in the creek.

Miss Carmody fitted so well into the community and was so well-liked by us kids that it began to look like we'd finally keep a teacher all year. Already she had withstood some of the shocks that had sent our other teachers screaming. For instance. . . .

The first time Susie got a robin redbreast sticker on her bookmark for reading a whole page—six lines—perfectly, she lifted all the way back to her seat, literally walking about four inches in the air. I held my breath until she sat down and was caressing the glossy sticker with one finger, then I sneaked a cautious look at Miss Carmody. She was sitting very erect, her hands clutching both ends of her desk as though in the act of rising, a look of incredulous surprise on her face. Then she relaxed, shook her head and smiled, and busied herself with some papers.

I let my breath out cautiously. The last teacher but two went into hysterics when one of the girls absent-mindedly lifted back to her seat because her sore foot hurt. I had hoped Miss Carmody was tougher—and apparently she was.

That same week, one noon hour, Jethro came pelting up to the school-house where Valancy—that's her first name and I call her by it when we are alone, after all she's only four years older than I—was helping me with that gruesome Tests and Measurements I was taking by extension from Teachers' College.

"Hey, Karen!" he yelled through the window. "Can you come out a minute?"

"Why?" I yelled back, annoyed at the interruption just when I was trying to figure what was normal about a normal grade curve.

"There's need," yelled Jethro.

I put down my book. "I'm sorry, Valancy. I'll go see what's eating him."

"Should I come too?" she asked. "If something's wrong—"

"It's probably just some silly thing," I said, edging out fast. When one of The People says "There's need," that means Group business.

"Adonday Veeah!" I muttered at Jethro as we rattled down the steep rocky path to the creek. "What are you trying to do? Get us all in trouble? What's the matter?"

"Look," said Jethro, and there were the boys standing around an alarmed but proud Jerry and above their heads, poised in the air over a half-built rock dam, was a huge boulder.

"Who lifted that?" I gasped.

"I did," volunteered Jerry, blushing crimson.

I turned on Jethro. "Well, why didn't you platt the twishers on it? You didn't have to come running—"

"On *that*?" Jethro squeaked. "You know very well we're not allowed to *lift* anything that big let alone platt it. Besides," shamefaced, "I can't remember that dern girl stuff."

"Oh, Jethro! You're so stupid sometimes!" I turned to Jerry. "How on earth did you ever lift anything that big?"

He squirmed. "I watched Daddy at the mine once."

"Does he let you lift at home?" I asked severely.

"I don't know." Jerry squashed mud with one shoe, hanging his head. "I never lifted anything before."

"Well, you know better. You kids aren't allowed to lift anything an

Outsider your age can't handle alone. And not even that if you can't platt it afterwards."

"I know it." Jerry was still torn between embarrassment and pride.

"Well, remember it," I said. And taking a handful of sun, I platted the twishers and set the boulder back on the hillside where it belonged.

Platting does come easier to the girls—sunshine platting, that is. Of course only the Old Ones do the sun-and-rain one and only the very Oldest of them all would dare the moonlight-and-dark, that can move mountains. But that was still no excuse for Jethro to forget and run the risk of having Valancy see what she mustn't see.

It wasn't until I was almost back to the schoolhouse that it dawned on me. Jerry had lifted! Kids his age usually lift play stuff almost from the time they walk. That doesn't need platting because it's just a matter of a few inches and a few seconds so gravity manages the return. But Jerry and Susie never had. They were finally beginning to catch up. Maybe it *was* just the Crossing that slowed them down—and maybe only the Clarinades. In my delight, *I* forgot and lifted to the school porch without benefit of the steps. But Valancy was putting up pictures on the high, old-fashioned moulding just below the ceiling, so no harm was done. She was flushed from her efforts and asked me to bring the step stool so she could finish them. I brought it and steadied it for her—and then nearly let her fall as I stared. How had she hung those first four pictures before I got there?

The weather was unnaturally dry all Fall. We didn't mind it much because rain with an Outsider around is awfully messy. We have to let ourselves get wet. But when November came and went and Christmas was almost upon us, and there was practically no rain and no snow at all, we all began to get worried. The creek dropped to a trickle and then to scattered puddles and then went dry. Finally the Old Ones had to spend an evening at the Group Reservoir doing something about our dwindling water supply. They wanted to get rid of Valancy for the evening, just in case, so Jemmy volunteered to take her to Kerry to the show. I was still awake when they got home long after midnight. Since I began to develop the Gift, I have long periods of restlessness when it seems I have no apartness but am of every person in the Group. The training I should start soon will help me shut out the others except when I want them. The only thing is that we don't know who is to train me. Since Grandmother died there has been no Sorter in our Group and because of the Crossing we have no books or records to help.

Anyway, I was awake and leaning on my window sill in the darkness. They stopped on the porch—Jemmy is bunking at the mine during his stint there. I didn't have to guess or use a Gift to read the pantomime before me. I closed my eyes and my mind as their shadows merged.

Under their strong emotion, I could have had free access to their minds, but I had been watching them all Fall. I knew in a special way what passed between them, and I knew that Valancy often went to bed in tears and that Jemmy spent too many lonely hours on the Crag that juts out over the canyon from high on Old Baldy, as though he were trying to make his heart as inaccessible to Outsiders as the Crag is. I knew what he felt, but oddly enough I had never been able to sort Valancy since that first night. There was something very un-Outsiderish and also very un-Groupish about her mind and I couldn't figure what.

I heard the front door open and close and Valancy's light steps fading down the hall and then I felt Jemmy calling me outside. I put my coat on over my robe and shivered down the hall. He was waiting by the porch steps, his face still and unhappy in the faint moonlight.

"She won't have me," he said flatly.

"Oh, Jemmy!" I cried. "You asked her—"

"Yes," he said. "She said no."

"I'm so sorry." I huddled down on the top step to cover my cold ankles. "But Jemmy—"

"Yes, I know!" He retorted savagely. "She's an Outsider. I have no business even to want her. Well, if she'd have me, I wouldn't hesitate a minute. This Purity-of-the-Group deal is—"

". . . is fine and right," I said softly, "as long as it doesn't touch you personally? But think for a minute, Jemmy. Would you be able to live a life as an Outsider? Just think of the million and one restraints that you would have to impose on yourself—and for the rest of your life, too, or lose her after all. Maybe it's better to accept *No* now than to try to build something and ruin it completely later. And if there should be children . . ." I paused. *"Could* there be children, Jemmy?"

I heard him draw a sharp breath.

"We don't know," I went on. "We haven't had the occasion to find out. Do you want Valancy to be part of the first experiment?"

Jemmy slapped his hat viciously down on his thigh, then he laughed.

"You have the Gift," he said, though I had never told him. "Have you any idea, sister mine, how little you will be liked when you become an Old One?"

"Grandmother was well-liked," I answered placidly. Then I cried, "Don't *you* set me apart, darn you, Jemmy. Isn't it enough to know that among a different people, *I* am different? Don't *you* desert me now!" I was almost in tears.

Jemmy dropped to the step beside me and thumped my shoulder in his old way. "Pull up your socks, Karen. We have to do what we have to do. I was just taking my mad out on you. What a world." He sighed heavily.

I huddled deeper in my coat, cold of soul.

"But the other one is gone," I whispered. "The Home."

And we sat there sharing the poignant sorrow that is a constant under-current among The People, even those of us who never actually saw The Home. Father says it's because of a sort of racial memory.

"But she didn't say no because she doesn't love me," Jemmy went on at last. "She does love me. She told me so."

"Then why not?" Sister-wise I couldn't imagine anyone turning Jemmy down.

Jemmy laughed—a short, unhappy laugh. "Because she is different."

"*She's* different?"

"That's what she said, as though it was pulled out of her. 'I can't marry,' she said. 'I'm different!' That's pretty good, isn't it, coming from an Out-sider!"

"She doesn't know we're The People," I said. "She must feel that she is different from everyone. I wonder why?"

"I don't know. There's something about her, though. A kind of shield or wall that keeps us apart. I've never met anything like it in an Outsider or in one of The People either. Sometimes it's like meshing with one of us and then *bang!* I smash the daylights out of me against that stone wall."

"Yes, I know," I said. "I've felt it, too."

We listened to the silent past-midnight world and then Jemmy stood.

"Well, g'night, Karen. Be seeing you."

I stood up, too. "Good night, Jemmy." I watched him start off in the late moonlight. He turned at the gate, his face hidden in the shadows.

"But I'm not giving up," he said quietly. "Valancy is my love."

The next day was hushed and warm—unnaturally so for December in our hills. There was a kind of ominous stillness among the trees, and, threading thinly against the milky sky, the thin smokes of little brush fires pointed out the dryness of the whole country. If you looked closely you could see piling behind Old Baldy an odd bank of clouds, so nearly the color of the sky that it was hardly discernible, but puffy and summer-thunderheady.

All of us were restless in school, the kids reacting to the weather, Valancy pale and unhappy after last night. I was bruising my mind against the blank wall in hers, trying to find some way I could help her.

Finally the thousand and one little annoyances were climaxed by Jerry and Susie scuffling until Susie was pushed out of the desk onto an open box of wet water colors that Debra for heaven only knows what reason had left on the floor by her desk. Susie shrieked and Debra sputtered and Jerry started a high silly giggle of embarrassment and delight. Valancy, without looking, reached for something to rap for order with and knocked down the old cracked vase full of drooping wildflowers and three-day-old water. The vase broke and flooded her desk with the foul-smelling deluge, ruining the monthly report she had almost ready to send in to the County School Superintendent.

For a stricken moment there wasn't a sound in the room, then Valancy burst into half-hysterical laughter and the whole room rocked with her. We all rallied around doing what we could to clean up Susie and Valancy's desk and then Valancy declared a holiday and decided that it would be the perfect time to go up-canyon to the slopes of Baldy and gather what greenery we could find to decorate our school room for the holidays.

We all take our lunches to school, so we gathered them up and took along a square tarp the boys had brought to help build the dam in the creek. Now that the creek was dry, they couldn't use it and it'd come in handy to sit on at lunch time and would serve to carry our greenery home in, too, stretcher-fashion.

Released from the school room, we were all loud and jubilant and I nearly kinked my neck trying to keep all the kids in sight at once to nip in the bud any thoughtless lifting or other Group activity. The kids were all so wild, they might forget.

We went on up-canyon past the kids' dam and climbed the bare, dry waterfalls that stair-step up to the Mesa. On the Mesa, we spread the tarp and pooled our lunches to make it more picnicky. A sudden hush from across the tarp caught my attention. Debra, Rachel and Lizbeth were staring horrified at Susie's lunch. She was calmly dumping out a half dozen *koomatka* beside her sandwiches.

Koomatka are almost the only plants that lasted through the Crossing. I think four *koomatka* survived in someone's personal effects. They were planted and cared for as tenderly as babies and now every household in the Group has a *koomatka* plant growing in some quiet spot out of casual sight. Their fruit is eaten not so much for nourishment as Earth knows nourishment, but as a last remembrance of all other similar delights that died with The Home. We always save *koomatka* for special occasions. Susie must have sneaked some out when her mother wasn't looking. And there they were—across the table from an Outsider!

Before I could snap them to me or say anything, Valancy turned, too, and caught sight of the softly glowing bluey-green pile. Her eyes widened and one hand went out. She started to say something and then she dropped her eyes quickly and drew her hand back. She clasped her hands tightly together and the girls, eyes intent on her, scrambled the *koomatka* back into the sack and Lizbeth silently comforted Susie, who had just realized what she had done. She was on the verge of tears at having betrayed The People to an Outsider.

Just then 'Kiah and Derek rolled across the picnic table fighting over a cupcake. By the time we salvaged our lunch from under them and they had scraped the last of the chocolate frosting off their T-shirts, the *koomatka* incident seemed closed. And yet, as we lay back resting a little to settle our stomachs, staring up at the smothery low-hanging clouds that had grown from the milky morning sky, I suddenly found myself trying to decide about Valancy's look when she saw the fruit. Surely it couldn't have been recognition!

At the end of our brief siesta, we carefully buried the remains of our lunch—the hill was much too dry to think of burning it—and started on again. After a while, the slope got steeper and the stubborn tangle of manzanita tore at our clothes and scratched our legs and grabbed at the rolled-up tarp until we all looked longingly at the free air above it. If Valancy hadn't been with us we could have lifted over the worst and saved all this trouble. But we blew and panted for a while and then struggled on.

After an hour or so, we worked out onto a rocky knoll that leaned against the slope of Baldy and made a tiny island in the sea of manzanita. We all stretched out gratefully on the crumbling granite outcropping, listening to our heart-beats slowing.

Then Jethro sat up and sniffed. Valancy and I alerted. A sudden puff of wind from the little side canyon brought the acrid pungency of burning brush to us. Jethro scrambled along the narrow ridge to the slope of Baldy and worked his way around out of sight into the canyon. He came scrambling back, half lifting, half running.

"Awful!" he panted. "It's awful! The whole canyon ahead is on fire and it's coming this way fast!"

Valancy gathered us together with a glance.

"Why didn't we see the smoke?" she asked tensely. "There wasn't any smoke when we left the schoolhouse."

"Can't see this slope from school," he said. "Fire could burn over a dozen slopes and we'd hardly see the smoke. This side of Baldy is a rim fencing in an awful mess of canyons."

"What'll we do?" quavered Lizbeth, hugging Susie to her.

Another gust of wind and smoke set us all to coughing and through my streaming tears, I saw a long lapping tongue of fire reach around the canyon wall.

Valancy and I looked at each other. I couldn't sort her mind, but mine was a panic, beating itself against the fire and then against the terrible tangle of manzanita all around us. Bruising against the possibility of lifting out of danger, then against the fact that none of the kids was capable of sustained progressive self-lifting for more than a minute or so and how could we leave Valancy? I hid my face in my hands to shut out the acres and acres of tinder-dry manzanita that would blaze like a torch at the first touch of fire. If only it would rain! You can't *set* fire to wet manzanita, but after these long months of drought—!

I heard the younger children scream and looked up to see Valancy staring at me with an intensity that frightened me even as I saw fire standing bright and terrible behind her at the mouth of the canyon.

Jake, yelling hoarsely, broke from the group and lifted a yard or two over the manzanita before he tangled his feet and fell helpless into the ugly, angled branches.

"Get under the tarp!" Valancy's voice was a whip-lash. "All of you get under the tarp!"

"It won't do any good," bellowed 'Kiah. "It'll burn like paper!"

"Get—under—the—tarp!" Valancy's spaced, icy words drove us to unfolding the tarp and spreading it to creep under. I lifted (hoping even at this awful moment that Valancy wouldn't see me) over to Jake and yanked him back to his feet. I couldn't lift with him so I pushed and prodded and half-carried him back through the heavy surge of black smoke to the tarp and shoved him under. Valancy was standing, back to the fire, so changed and alien that I shut my eyes against her and started to crawl in with the other kids.

And then she began to speak. The rolling, terrible thunder of her voice shook my bones and I swallowed a scream. A surge of fear swept through our huddled group and shoved me back out from under the tarp.

Till I die, I'll never forget Valancy standing there tense and taller than life against the rolling convulsive clouds of smoke, both her hands outstretched, fingers wide apart as the measured terror of her voice went on and on in words that plague me because I should have known them and didn't. As I watched, I felt an icy cold gather, a paralyzing, unearthly cold that froze the tears on my tensely upturned face.

And then lightning leaped from finger to finger of her lifted hands. And lightning answered in the clouds above her. With a toss of her hands she threw the cold, the lightning, the sullen shifting smoke upward, and the roar of the racing fire was drowned in a hissing roar of down-drenching rain.

I knelt there in the deluge, looking for an eternal second into her drained, despairing, hopeless eyes before I caught her just in time to keep her head from banging on the granite as she pitched forward, inert.

Then as I sat there cradling her head in my lap, shaking with cold and fear, with the terrified wailing of the kids behind me, I heard Father shout and saw him and Jemmy and Darcy Clarinade in the old pickup, lifting over the steaming streaming manzanita, over the trackless mountainside through the rain to us. Father lowered the truck until one of the wheels brushed a branch and spun lazily, then the three of them lifted all of us up to the dear familiarity of that beat-up old jalopy.

Jemmy received Valancy's limp body into his arms and crouched in back, huddling her in his arms, for the moment hostile to the whole world that had brought his love to such a pass.

We kids clung to Father in an ecstasy of relief. He hugged us all tight to him, then he raised my face.

"Why did it rain?" he asked sternly, every inch an Old One while the cold downpour dripped off the ends of my hair and he stood dry inside his Shield.

"I don't know," I sobbed, blinking my streaming eyes against his sternness. "Valancy did it . . . with lightning . . . it was cold . . . she talked. . . ." Then I broke down completely, plumping down on the rough floor boards and, in spite of my age, howling right along with the other kids.

It was a silent, solemn group that gathered in the schoolhouse that evening. I sat at my desk with my hands folded stiffly in front of me, half scared of my own People. This was the first official meeting of the Old Ones I'd ever attended. They all sat in desks, too, except the Oldest who sat in Valancy's chair. Valancy sat stony-faced in the twins' desk, but her nervous fingers shredded one Kleenex after another as she waited.

The Oldest rapped the side of the desk with his cane and turned his sightless eyes from one to another of us.

"We're all here," he said, "to inquire—"

"Oh, stop it!" Valancy jumped up from her seat. "Can't you fire me without all this rigmarole? I'm used to it. Just say go and I'll go!" She stood trembling.

"Sit down, Miss Carmody," said the Oldest. And Valancy sat down meekly.

"Where were you born?" asked the Oldest quietly.

"What does it matter?" flared Valancy. Then resignedly, "It's in my application. Vista Mar, California."

"And your parents?"

"I don't know."

There was a stir in the room.

"Why not?"

"Oh, this is so unnecessary!" cried Valancy. "But if you *have* to know, both my parents were foundlings. They were found wandering in the streets after a big explosion and fire in Vista Mar. An old couple who lost everything in the fire took them in. When they grew up, they married. I was born. They died. Can I go now?"

A murmur swept the room.

"Why did you leave your other jobs?" asked Father.

Before Valancy could answer, the door was flung open and Jemmy stalked defiantly in.

"Go!" said the Oldest.

"Please," said Jemmy, deflating suddenly. "Let me stay. It concerns me too."

The Oldest fingered his cane and then nodded. Jemmy half-smiled with relief and sat down in a back seat.

"Go on," said the Oldest One to Valancy.

"All right then," said Valancy. "I lost my first job because I—well—I guess you'd call it levitated—to fix a broken blind in my room. It was stuck and I just . . . went up . . . in the air until I unstuck it. The principal saw me. He couldn't believe it and it scared him so he fired me." She paused expectantly.

The Old Ones looked at one another and my silly, confused mind began to add up columns that only my lack of common sense had kept from giving totals long ago.

"And the other one?" The Oldest leaned his cheek on his doubled-up hand as he bent forward.

Valancy was taken aback and she flushed in confusion.

"Well," she said hesitantly, "I called my books to me—I mean they were on my desk. . . ."

"We know what you mean," said the Oldest.

"You know!" Valancy looked dazed.

The Oldest stood up.

"Valancy Carmody, open your mind!"

Valancy stared at him and then burst into tears.

"I can't, I can't," she sobbed. "It's been too long. I can't let anyone in. I'm different. I'm alone. Can't you understand? They all died. I'm alien!"

"You are alien no longer," said the Oldest. "You are home now, Valancy." He motioned to me. "Karen, go in to her."

So I did. At first the wall was still there; then with a soundless cry, half anguish and half joy, the wall went down and I was with Valancy. I saw all the secrets that had cankered in her since her parents died— the parents who were of The People.

They had been reared by the old couple who were not only of The People but had been the Oldest of the whole Crossing.

I tasted with her the hidden frightening things—the need for living as an Outsider, the terrible need for concealing all her differences and suppressing all the extra Gifts of The People, the ever present fear of betraying herself and the awful lostness that came when she thought she was the last of The People.

And then suddenly *she* came in to *me* and my mind was flooded with a far greater presence than I had ever before experienced.

My eyes flew open and I saw all of the Old Ones staring at Valancy. Even the Oldest had his face turned to her, wonder written as widely on his scarred face as on the others.

He bowed his head and made The Sign. "The lost persuasions and designs," he murmured. "She has them all."

And then I knew that Valancy, Valancy who had wrapped herself so tightly against the world to which any thoughtless act might betray her that she had lived with us all this time without our knowing about her or she about us, was one of us. Not only one of us but such a one as had not been since Grandmother died—and even beyond that. My incoherent thoughts cleared to one.

Now I would have someone to train me. Now I could become a sorter— but only second to her.

I turned to share my wonder with Jemmy. He was looking at Valancy as The People must have looked at The Home in the last hour. Then he turned to the door.

Before I could draw a breath, Valancy was gone from me and from the Old Ones and Jemmy was turning to her outstretched hands.

Then I bolted for the outdoors and rushed like one possessed down the lane, lifting and running until I staggered up our porch steps and collapsed against Mother, who had heard me coming.

"Oh, Mother!" I cried. "She's one of us! She's Jemmy's love! She's wonderful!" And I burst into noisy sobs in the warm comfort of Mother's arms.

So now I don't have to go Outside to become a teacher. We have a permanent one. But I'm going anyway. I want to be as much like Valancy as I can and she has her degree. Besides I can use the discipline of living Outside for a year.

I have so much to learn and so much training to go through, but Valancy will always be there with me. I won't be set apart alone because of the Gift.

Maybe I shouldn't mention it, but one reason I want to hurry my training is that we're going to try to locate the other People. None of the boys here please me.

BIBLIOGRAPHY

These stories appeared in *The Magazine of Fantasy and Science Fiction:*
    "Ararat," October 1952
    "Gilead," August 1954
    "Pottage," September 1955
    "Wilderness," January 1957
    "Captivity," June 1958
    "Jordan," March 1959
Pilgrimage: The Book of The People, Doubleday, 1961 (contains all of the above plus additional linkage material)
These stories appeared in *The Magazine of Fantasy and Science Fiction:*
    "Return," March 1961
    "Shadow on the Moon," March 1962
    "Deluge," October 1963
    "No Different Flesh," May 1965
    "Angels Unawares," March 1966
    "Troubling of the Water," September 1966
The People: No Different Flesh, Doubleday, 1967 (contains the above six stories)

THE RETIEF SERIES

by Keith Laumer

In 1956 I had the misfortune to accept appointment (tendered by and with the advice and consent of the Senate) in the United States Foreign Service, after passing a horrendous battery of written and oral examinations and a national agency check (meaning some bureaucrat comes around to delight your friends by asking questions about you, thereby giving the impression that you're in Big Trouble). I was, but not the way they thought. Our State Department, and its operative arm, the Foreign Service, is a corrupt, self-serving, cowardly, treasonous organization, which misrepresents this country with a policy based on corrupting its employees, and betrayal of the U.S. national interest for the petty advantage of its members. If, for example, a U.S. diplomat who hasn't yet gotten the word discovers and complains that the local embassy employees are engaged in a conspiracy with certain local government officials to defraud the commissary, he (the green diplomat) is violently denounced by his boss as "an isolationist," and probably is soon fired. It stinks. After resigning from this malignant organization, I wrote a novel, *Embassy,* Revealing All; the book was published with great stealth in paperback by Pyramid, and was, due to a coincidence of timing, reviewed as a "quick rewrite of *The Ugly American,* with sex."

Next I wrote a rather sardonic adventure story with a protagonist named Retief, a name that came to me after prayer and fasting, with echoes of Tenerife, Recife, etc. Jack Gaughan, the artist, later pointed out to me that H. Rider Haggard had written of "the true-hearted Retief" and his companions who were massacred by the Zulus in the late 1800s. I have deduced that he was an ancestor of our Retief. In his great genealogical work *Tarzan Alive,* Phil Farmer mentions in passing a minor fictional character named [Katrina?] Retief, doubtless a collateral relative.

Having realized that the only possible way to present the atrocities of bureaucratic stupidity and venality that are the daily routine of the State Department was as farcical satire, I wrote the second Retief story, after a lapse of some years, in that vein. The then-editor of *If* magazine liked it and encouraged me to do more. Some time later, realizing that the Retief stories were all that was keeping the sheet afloat, I undertook to supply one story for every issue, and did so for some time. At the behest of a book editor, I wrote a Retief novel (reluctantly, because the *If* editor was against it); when it was complete I sent it to the editor who had suggested it—and he casually turned it down, mentioning that his outfit didn't publish SF. The firm then was and still is one of the leading SF publishers. I wrote the next Retief novel in spite of the lack of enthusiasm of the *If* editor, who, however, agreed to publish it if I would first supply three novelets. I did so—and then he casually bounced the novel, because he "didn't think a Retief novel was a good idea." The third Retief novel was titled by me *Retief's Ransom*. I wrote a superb outline with an ingenious plot in which Retief's kidnappers at last pay handsomely to be rid of him. During the writing, this turned into another book entirely; I retitled it, so as to be able to write *Retief's Ransom* later, but the book editor retained the original title, thereby blowing it.

Altogether, there have been nineteen Retief stories, all novelets, all but three first published in *If,* all but two collected later in one of my four Retief collections. And, of course, the three novels. All, alas, are true. The stuff our State Department is pulling every day would make the antics of Mr. Magnan and Ambassador Long-spoon seem reasonable by comparison.

Incidentally, I was never able to persuade the editor of *If* that the Number Two man in an embassy is called a "Counselor" of embassy, not a "Councillor," nor that a telegram from a diplomatic post to the Department is a "despatch," not a "dispatch." Also, though I typed out and handed personally to the various book editors the information that I was a Foreign Service Officer of Class Six in the United States Foreign Service, a Vice-Consul of career in the U.S. Consular Service, and a Third Secretary of Embassy of the United States of America in the U.S. Diplomatic Service, they persisted in printing on the flap that I was a "diplomatic aide," a non-existent critter.

I had a letter from the Foreign Service Institute of the State Department inviting me to speak there (I never did) and one from a senior diplomat, admitting that he was "sort of a Magnan type."

That's about it, except that more Retief stories are on the way, including a novel.

Ballots and Bandits

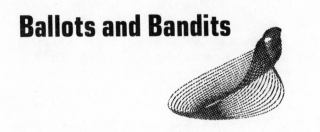

I

Second Secretary Retief of the Terran Embassy emerged from his hotel into a bunting-draped street crowded with locals: bustling, furry folk with up-raised, bushy tails, like oversized chipmunks, ranging in height from a foot to a yard. A party of placard-carrying marchers, emerging from a side street, jostled their way through the press, briskly ripping down political posters attached to shop walls and replacing them with posters of their own. Their move was immediately countered by a group of leaflet distributors who set about applying mustaches, beards and crossed eyes to the new placards. The passersby joined in cheerfully, some blacking out teeth and adding warts to the tips of button noses, others grabbing the brushes from the defacers and applying them to their former owners' faces. Fists flew; the clamor rose.

Retief felt a tug at his knee; a small Oberonian dressed in blue breeches and a spotted white apron looked up at him from wide, worried eyes.

"Prithee, fair sir," the small creature piped in a shrill voice, "come quick, ere all is lost!"

"What's the matter?" Retief inquired, noting the flour smudge on the Oberonian's cheek and the dab of pink icing on the tip of his nose. "Are the cookies burning?"

"E'en worse than that, milord—'tis the Tsuggs! The great brutes would dismantle the shop entire! But follow and observe!" The Oberonian whirled and darted away.

Retief followed along the steeply sloping cobbled alley between close-pressing houses, his head level with the second-story balconies. Through open windows he caught glimpses of doll's-houselike interiors, complete with toy tables and chairs and postage-stamp-sized TV screens. The bright-eyed inhabitants clustered at their railings, twittering like sparrows as he passed. He picked his way with care among the pedestrians crowding the way: twelve-inch Ploots and eighteen-inch Grimbles in purple and red leathers, two-foot Choobs in fringed caps and aprons, lordly three-foot-six-inch Blufs, elegant in ruffles and curled pink wigs. Ahead, he heard shrill cries, a tinkle of breaking glass, a dull thump. Rounding a sharp turn, he came on the scene of action.

Before a shop with a sign bearing a crude painting of a salami, a crowd had gathered, ringing in a group of half a dozen giant Oberonians of a type new to Retief: swaggering dandies in soiled silks, with cruelly cropped tails, scimitars slung at their waists—if creatures of the approximate shape of ten-pins can be said to have waists. One of the party held the bridles of their mounts—scaled, spike-maned brutes resembling gaily painted rhinoceroses, but for their prominent canines and long, muscular legs. Two more were busy with crowbars, levering at the lintel over the shop doorway. Another pair were briskly attacking the adjacent wall with sledge-hammers. The sixth, distinguished by a scarlet sash with a pistol thrust through it, stood with folded arms, smiling a sharp-toothed smile at the indignant mob.

"'Tis the pastry and ale shop of Binkster Druzz, my grand uncle twice removed!" Retief's diminutive guide shrilled. "A little light-hearted destruction in the course of making one's political views clear is all very well—but these pirates would reduce us to penury! Gramercy, milord, canst not impede the brutes?" He swarmed ahead, clearing a path through the onlookers. The red-sashed one, noticing Retief's approach, unfolded his arms, letting one hand linger near the butt of the pistol—a Groaci copy of a two-hundred-year-old Concordiat sliver-gun, Retief noted.

"Close enough, off-worlder," the Tsugg said in a somewhat squeaky baritone. "What would ye here? Ye'r hutch lieth in the next street yonder."

Retief smiled gently at the bear-like Oberonian, who loomed over the crowd, his eyes almost on a level with Retief's own, his bulk far greater. "I want to buy a jelly doughnut," the Terran said. "Your lads seem to be blocking the doorway."

"Aroint thee, Terry; seek refreshment elsewhere. Being somewhat fatigued with campaigning, I plan to honor this low dive with my custom; my bullies must needs enlarge the door to comport with my noble dimensions."

"That won't be convenient," Retief said smoothly. "When I want a jelly doughnut I want it now." He took a step toward the door; the pistol jumped at him. The other Tsuggs were gathering around, hefting crowbars.

"Ah-ah," Retief cautioned, raising a finger—and at the same moment swung his foot in a short arc that ended just under the gun-handler's knee-joint. The victim emitted a sharp yap and leaned forward far enough for his jaw to intersect the course of Retief's left fist. Retief palmed the gun deftly as the Tsugg staggered into the arms of his companions.

"Aroint thee, lads," the giant muttered reproachfully to his supporters, shaking his head dazedly. "We've been boon drinking chums these six Lesser Moons and this is the first time ye've give me any of the food stuff . . ."

"Spread out, lads," one of the Tsuggs ordered his companions. "We'll pound this knave into a thin paste."

"Better relax, gentlemen," Retief suggested. "This gun is messy at short range."

"An' I mistake me not," one of the crowbar wielders said, eyeing Retief sourly, "ye're one of the out-world bureaucrats, here to connive in the allocation of loot, now the Sticky-fingers have gone."

"Ambassador Clawhammer prefers to refer to his role as refereeing the elections, nothing more," Retief corrected.

"Aye," the Tsugg nodded, "that's what I said. So how is it ye're interfering with the free democratic process by coshing Dir Blash in the midst of exercising his voice in local affairs?"

"We bureaucrats are a mild lot," Retief clarified, "unless someone gets between us and our jelly doughnuts."

Red-sash was weaving on his feet, shaking his head. " 'Tis a scurvy trick," he said blurrily, "sneaking a concealed anvil into a friendly little six-to-one crowbar affray."

"Let's go," one of the others said, "ere he produces a howitzer from his sleeve." The *banditi* mounted their wild-eyed steeds amid much snorting and tossing of fanged heads.

"But we'll not forget ye're visage, off-worlder," another promised. "I wot well we'll meet again—and next time we'll be none so lenient."

A hubbub of pleased chatter broke out among the lesser Oberonians as the party passed from sight.

"Milord has saved Great-uncle Binkster's fried fat this day," the small being who had enlisted Retief's aid cried. The Terran leaned over, hands on knees, which put his face on a level only a foot or two above that of the little fellow.

"Haven't I seen you before?" he asked.

"Certes, milord—until an hour since, I eked out a few coppers as third assistant pastry cook in the inn yonder, assigned to the cupcake division, decorative icing branch." He sighed. "My specialty was rosebuds—but no need to burden your grace with my plaint."

"You lost your job?"

"Aye, that did I—but forsooth, 'tis but a trifling circumstance, in light of what I o'erheard ere the hostler bade me hie me from the premises forthwith!"

"Let's see, your name is—"

"Prinkle, milord. Ipstitch Prinkle IX, at your service." The Twilpritt turned as a slightly plumper, grayer version of himself bustled up, bobbing his head and twitching his ears in a manner expressive of effusive gratitude. "And this, milord, is Uncle Binkster, in the flesh."

"Your servant, sir," Uncle Binkster squeaked, mopping at his face with a large striped handkerchief. "Wouldst honor me by accepting a cooling draft of pringlizard milk and a lardy-tart?"

"In sooth, Uncle, he needs something stronger than whey," Prinkle objected. "And in sooth, *The Plump Sausage* offers fine ale—if your Grace can manage the approaches," he added, comparing Retief's six foot three with the doorway.

"I'll turn sideways," Retief reassured the Oberonian. He ducked through, was led across the crowded room by a bustling eighteen-inch tapman to a corner table, where he was able to squeeze himself onto a narrow bench against the wall.

"What'll it be, gents?" the landlord inquired.

"Under the circumstances, I'll stick to small beer," Retief said.

"Ale for me," Uncle Binkster said. " 'Tis vice, perhaps, to tipple ere lunchtime, but with Tsuggs roaming the Quarter and battering down walls, one'd best tipple while opportunity presents itself."

"A sound principle," Retief agreed. "Who are these Tsuggs, Uncle Binkster?"

"Lawless rogues, down from the high crags for easy pickings," the elderly baker replied with a sigh. "After you Terrans sent the Groaci packing, we thought all our troubles were over. Alas, I fear me 'tis not the case. As soon as the ruffians got the word the Five-eyes were pulling out, they came swarming down out of the hills like zing-bugs after a jam-wagon—'tis plain they mean to elect their ruffianly chief, Hoobrik the Uncouth. Bands of them roam the city, and the countryside as well, terrorizing the voters—" He broke off as the landlord placed a foaming three-inch tankard before Retief.

"Away with that thimble, Squirmkin!" he exclaimed. "Our guest requires a heartier bumper than that!"

" 'Tis an Emperor-sized mug," the landlord said, "but I allow his dimensions dwarf it. Mayhap I can knock the top out of a hogshead . . ." He hurried away.

"Pray don't mistake me, milord," Uncle Binkster resumed. "Like any patriot, I rejoiced to see the Sticky-finger go, leaving the conduct of Oberonian affairs to Oberonians. But who'd have guessed we normal-sized chaps would at once be subjected to depredations by our own over-sized kith and kin exceeding anything the invaders ever practiced!"

"A student of history might have predicted it," Retief pointed out. "But I agree: being pushed around by local hoodlums is even less satisfying than being exploited from afar."

"Indeed so," Prinkle agreed. "In the case of foreigners one can always gain a certain relief by hurling descriptive epithets, mocking their outlandish ways and blaming everything on their inherent moral leprosy—an awkward technique to use on one's relatives."

The landlord returned, beaming, with a quart-sized wooden container topped by a respectable head. Retief raised it in salute and drank deep.

"And if what my nephew o'erheard be any indication," Uncle Binkster went on, wiping foam from his whiskers, "the worst is yet to come. Hast related all to our benefactor, lad?"

"Not yet, Uncle." Prinkle turned to Retief. "I was sweeping up crumbs in the VIP breakfast room, my mind on other matters, when I heard the word 'Tsugg' bandied among the company still sitting at table. I cocked an auricle, thinking to hear the scoundrels roundly denounced, only to catch the intelligence that their chief that brawling bravo Hoobrik, representing himself to be spokesman and natural leader of all Oberon, withal, hath demanded audience of His Impressiveness, Ambassador Clawhammer! 'Twas but natural that I undertook to disabuse their Lordships of this impertinent notion, accidentally overturning a pot of chocolate in process thereof—"

"Alas, my nephew is at times too enthusiastic in his espousal of his views," Uncle Binkster put in. "Though 'tis beyond dispute, in this instance he was sorely tried."

"In sooth, so was his honor, Mr. Magnan, when the cocoa landed in his lap," Prinkle admitted. "Happily, 'twas somewhat cooled by long standing."

"A grotesque prospect," Uncle Binkster ruminated. "Those scapegrace villains, lording it over us honest folk! Perish the thought, Sir Retief! I trow I'd sooner have the Five-eyes back!"

"At least they maintained a degree of control over the ne'r-do-wells," Prinkle said, "restricting them to their hills and caves."

"As will we, lad, once the election is consummated," Uncle Binkster reminded the youth. "Naturally, we Twilpritt stand ready to assume the burden of policing the rabble, as is only right and natural, as soon as our slate is elected, by reason of our superior virtues—"

"Hark not to the old dodderer's maunderings, Giant," a tiny voice peeped from the next table. A miniature Oberonian, no more than nine inches tall, raised his one-ounce glass in salute. "We Chimberts, being nature's noblemen, are of course divinely appointed to a position of primacy among these lumbering brutes, saving your presence, milord—"

"Dost hear a dust-cricket chirping in the woodwork?" a medium-sized Oberonian with black circles resembling spectacles around his eyes inquired loudly from three tables away. " 'Twere plain e'en to an outworlder that we Choobs are the rightful inheritors of the mantle of superiority. Once in office we'll put an end to such public rantings."

"You in office?" Prinkle yelped. "O'er my corpse, varlet!" He leaped up, slopping beer as he cocked his arm to peg the mug at the offender.

"Stay, nephew!" Uncle Binkster restrained the youth. "Pay no heed to the wretch, doubtless he's in his cups—"

"Drunk, am I, you old sot!" the Choob yelled, overturning the table as he leaped up, grabbing for the hilt of his foot-long sword. "I'll ha' a strip o' thy wrinkled hide for that allegation—" His threat was cut off abruptly as a tankard, hurled from across the room, clipped him over the ear, sending him reeling into the next table, whose occupants leaped up with indignant shouts and flailing fists.

"Gentlemen, time, time!" the landlord wailed, before diving behind the bar amid a barrage of pewter. Retief finished his beer in a long swallow and rose, looming over the battle raging about his knees.

"A pleasure, gentlemen," he addressed the room at large. "I hate to leave such a friendly gathering, but Staff Meeting time is here."

"Farewell, Sir Retief," Prinkle panted from under the table, where he grappled with a pale-furred local of about his own weight. "Call around any time for a drop and a bit of friendly political chat."

"Thanks," Retief said. "If things get too slow in the front line trenches I'll remember your invitation."

II

As Retief entered the conference room—a converted packing room in the former warehouse temporarily housing the Terran Mission to the newly liberated planet Oberon—First Secretary Magnan gave him a sour look.

"Well—here you are at last. I'd begun to fear you'd lingered to roister with low companions in your usual manner."

"Not quite my usual manner," Retief corrected. "We'd barely started to roister when I remembered Staff Meeting. By the way, what do you know about a fellow called Hoobrik the Uncouth?"

Magnan looked startled. "Why, that name is known only to a handful of us in the inner security circle," he said in a lowered tone, glancing about. "Who leaked it to you, Retief?"

"A few hundred irate locals. They didn't seem to know it was a secret."

"Well, whatever you do, act surprised when the Ambassador mentions it," Magnan cautioned his junior as they took seats at the long table. "My," he went on as the shouts of the crowd outside the building rose to a thunderous level, "how elated the locals are, now they realize we've relieved them of the burdens of Groaci overlordship! Hear their merry cries!"

"Remarkable," Retief agreed. "They have a better command of invective than the Groaci themselves."

"Why, Wilbur," Magnan said as Colonel Saddlesore, the Military Attaché, slipped into the chair beside him, avoiding his glance. "However did you get that alarming discoloration under your eye?"

"Quite simple, actually." The colonel bit off his words like bullets. "I was struck by a thrown political slogan."

Magnan sniffed. "There's no need for recourse to sarcasm."

"The slogan," Saddlesore amplified, "was inscribed on the rind of a *bham-bham* fruit of the approximate size and weight of a well-hit cricket ball."

"I saw three small riots myself on the way in to the office," the Press Attaché said in a pleased tone. "Remarkable enthusiasm these locals show for universal suffrage."

"I think it's time, however," the Counselor put in ponderously, "that someone explained to them that the term 'political machine' does not necessarily refer to a medium tank."

The chatter around the long table cut off abruptly as Ambassador Claw-hammer, a small pink-faced man with an impressive paunch, entered the room, glowered at his staff as they rose, waved them to their seats as he waited for silence.

"Well, gentlemen," he looked around the table. "What progress have you to report anent the preparation of the populace for the balloting?"

A profound silence ensued.

"What about you, Chester?" Clawhammer addressed the Counselor. "I seem to recall instructing you to initiate classes in parliamentary proce-dure among these riffraff—that is to say, among the free citizens of Oberon."

"I tried, Mr. Ambassador. I tried," Chester said sadly. "They didn't seem to grasp the idea quite. They chose up sides and staged a pitched battle for possession of the chair."

"Ah—I can report a teensy bit of progress in my campaign to put across the idea of one man, one vote," a slender-necked Political Officer spoke up. "They got the basic idea, all right." He paused. "The only trouble was, they immediately deduced the corollary: one *less* man, one *less* vote." He sighed, "Luckily, they were evenly matched, so no actual votes were lost."

"You might point out the corollary to the corollary," Retief suggested, "the lighter the vote, the smaller the Post Office."

"What about your assigned task of voter registration, eh, Magnan?" the Chief of Mission barked. "Are you reporting failure too?"

"Why, no indeed, sir, not exactly failure; at least not utter failure; it's too soon to announce that—"

"Oh?" The Ambassador looked ominous. "When do you think would be an appropriate time? *After* disaster strikes?"

"I'd like to propose a rule limiting the number of political parties to P minus 1, P being the number of voters," Magnan said hastily. "Other-wise we run the risk that no one gets a majority."

"No good, Magnan," the Counselor for P R Affairs spoke up. "We don't want to risk a charge of meddling. However," he added thoughtfully, "we might just up the nomination fee to a figure sufficiently astronomical to keep the trash out—that is, to discourage the weakly motivated."

"I don't know, Irving," the Econ Officer ran his fingers through his thinning hair in a gesture of frustration. "What we really need is to prune the ranks of the voters more drastically. Now, far be it from me to propose strong-arm methods—but what if we tried out a modified Grandfather Rule?"

"Say—a touch of the traditional *might* be in order at that, Oscar," the Political Officer agreed tentatively. "Just what did you have in mind?"

"Actually I haven't worked out the details—but how about limiting the franchise to those who have grandfathers? Or possibly grandchildren? Or even both?"

"Gentlemen!" Ambassador Clawhammer cut short the debate. "We must open our sights. The election promises to degenerate into a debacle of ruinous proportions, career-wise, unless we break through with a truly fresh approach." He paused impressively. "Fortunately," he continued in the modest tones of Caesar accepting the crown, "I have evolved such an approach." He raised a hand in kindly remonstrance at the chorus of congratulations that broke out at his announcement.

"It's clear, gentlemen, that what is needed is the emergence of a political force that will weld together the strands of Oberonian political coloration into a unified party capable of seating handy majorities. A force conversant with the multitudinous benefits which would stem from a sympathetic attitude toward Terran interests in the Sector."

"Yes, Chief," an alert underling from the Admin Section took his cue. "But, gosh, who could possibly produce such a miracle from the welter of divergent political creeds here on Oberon? They're practically at swords' points with each other over each and every question of policy, both foreign and domestic."

Clawhammer nodded acknowledgment. "Your question is an acute one, Dimplick. Happily, the answer is at hand. I have made contact, through confidential channels, with a native leader of vast spiritual influence, who bids fair to fulfill the role to perfection." He paused to allow the staff to voice spontaneous expressions of admiration, then raised a palm for silence.

"While 'Golly!' and 'Wow!' are perhaps less elegant effusions than one might logically expect from an assemblage of senior career diplomats," he said sternly, but with a redeeming twinkle in his small, red-rimmed eyes, "I'll overlook the lapse this time on the basis of your obvious shock at receiving such glad tidings after your own abysmal failures to produce any discernible progress."

"Sir, may we know the name of this messiah?" Magnan chirped. "When do we get to meet him?"

"Curious that you should employ that particular term with reference to Hoobrik," Clawhammer said complacently. "At this moment, the guru is meditating in the mountains, surrounded by his chelas, or disciples, known as Tsuggs in the local patois."

"Did you say—Hoobrik?" Magnan queried uncertainly. "Goodness, what a coincidence that he should have the same name as that ruffian of a bandit chief who had the unmitigated effrontery to send one of his strong-arm men to threaten your Excellency!"

Clawhammer's pink features deepened to a dull magenta which clashed sharply with his lime-green seersucker suit.

"I fear, Magnan," he said in a tone like a tire-iron striking flesh, "that you've absorbed a number of erroneous impressions. His Truculence, Spiritual Leader Hoobrik, dispatched an emissary, it's true, to propose certain accommodations sphere-of-influence-wise; but to proceed from that circumstance to an inference that I have yielded to undue pressures is an unwarranted speculative leap!"

"Possibly I just misinterpreted his messenger's phraseology, sir," Magnan said with a tight little smile. "It didn't seem to me that 'foreign blood-suckers' and 'craven paper-pushers' sounded all that friendly."

"'IPBM's may fry our skins, but words will never hurt us,' eh, sir?" the Econ Officer piped brightly, netting himself a stab of the Ambassadorial eye.

"Still, it's rather strong language," Colonel Saddlesore spoke up to fill the conversational gap. "But I daresay you put the fellow in his place, eh, Mr. Ambassador?"

"Why, as to that, I've been pondering the precisely correct posture to adopt vis-a-vis the Tsuggs, protocol-wise. I confess for a few moments I toyed with the idea of a beefed-up 804-B: Massive Dignity, with overtones of Leashed Ire; but cooler counsels soon prevailed."

"How about a 764, sir?" the Econ Officer essayed. "Amused Contempt, with just a hint of Unpleasant Surprise in the Offing?"

"Too subtle," Colonel Saddlesore grunted. "What about the old standby, 26-A?"

"Oh, the old 'Threat to Break Off Talks' ploy, eh? Embellished with a side-issue of Table-Shape Dispute, I assume?"

"Gentlemen!" Clawhammer called the conference to heel. "You forget that the date of the elections is rushing toward us! We've no time for traditional ploys. The problem is simple: how best to arrive at a meeting of the minds with the guru."

"Why not just call him in and offer to back him in a takeover, provided he plays ball?" the PR Chief proposed bluntly.

"I assume, Irving," Clawhammer said into the shocked silence, "that what you actually meant to suggest was that we give His Truculence assurances of Corps support in his efforts to promote Oberonian welfare— in the event of his securing the confidence of the electorate, as evinced by victory at the polls, of course."

"Yeah, something like that," Irving muttered, sliding down in his chair.

"Now," Clawhammer said, "the question remains, how best to tender my compliments to His Truculence, isolated as he is in his remote fastness—"

"Why, simple enough, sir," Magnan said. "We just send a messenger along with an invitation to tea. Something impressive in a gold-embossed, I'd suggest."

"I understand this fellow Hoobrik has ten thousand blood-thirsty cutthroats—ah, that is, wisdom-hungry students—at his beck and call," the Econ Officer contributed. "They say anybody who goes up there comes back with his tail cropped."

"Small hazard, since we Terries have no tails," Magnan said.

"I've got a funny feeling they'd figure out something else to crop," Oscar retorted sharply.

"Am I to infer, Magnan, you're volunteering to convey the bid?" Clawhammer inquired blandly.

"Me, sir?" Magnan paled visibly. "Heavens, I'd love to—except that I'm under observation for possible fourth-degree cocoa burns."

"Fourth-degree burns?" Colonel Saddlesore wondered aloud. "I'd like to see that. I've heard of first, second, and third degree, but—"

"The symptoms are invisible to lay inspection," Magnan snapped. "Additionally, my asthma is aggravated by high altitudes."

"By Gad," Colonel Saddlesore whispered to his neighbor, "I'd like a chance to confront these fellows—"

"Better wear your armor, Wilbur," his confidant replied. "From all reports, they weigh in at three hundred pounds and wear six-foot cutlasses with which they lay about them freely when aroused. And they say the sight of a Terry arouses them worse than anything."

"—but, as I was about to say, my duties require that I hole up in my office for the foreseeable future," the colonel finished.

"Cutlasses, you say?" the Econ Officer pricked up his ears. "Hmm. Might be a market here for a few zillion up-to-date hand-weapons—for police use only, of course."

"Capital notion, Depew," the Political Officer nodded approvingly. "Nothing like a little firepower to bring out the natural peace-loving tendencies of the people."

"Now, gentlemen—let us avoid giving voice to any illiberal doctrines," Clawhammer said sharply. "Our only motive, let us remember, is to bring the liberated populace to terms with the political realities—in this case, the obvious need for a man on horseback—or should I say a Tsugg on Vorch-back?" The Terran envoy smiled indulgently at his whimsy.

"I have a question, Mr. Ambassador," Retief said. "Since we're here to supervise free elections, why don't we let the Oberonians work out their own political realities?"

Clawhammer looked blank.

"Just—ah—how do you mean?" the Political Officer prompted uneasily.

"Why don't we let them nominate whomever they want, vote for any candidate they like?" Retief explained.

"I suggest you forget these radical notions, young fellow," Clawhammer said sternly. "These free elections will be conducted in the way that free elections have always been conducted. And now that I've considered the matter, it occurs to me it might be valuable experience for you to pay the proposed call on His Truculence. It might serve to polish your grasp of protocol a trifle."

"But, sir," Magnan spoke up. "I need Mr. Retief to help me do the Consolidated Report of Delinquent Reports—"

"You'll have to manage alone, I fear, Magnan. And now, back to the ramparts of democracy, gentlemen! As for you, Retief—" The Ambassador fixed Retief with a sharp eye: "I suggest you comport yourself with a becoming modesty among the Tsugg. I should dislike to have to report any unfortunate incident."

"I'll do my best to see that no such report reaches you, sir," Retief said cheerfully.

III

The green morning sun of Oberon shone down warmly as Retief, mounted on a wiry Struke, a slightly smaller and more docile cousin of the fierce Vorch tamed by the Tsuggs, rode forth from the city gates. Pink and yellow borms warbled in the tree tops; the elusive sprinch darted from grass tuft to grass tuft. The rhythmic whistling of doody-bugs crying to their young supplied a somnolent backdrop to the idyl.

Retief passed through a region of small, tidy farms, where sturdy Doob peasants gaped from the furrows. The forest closed in as the path wound upward into the foothills. In mid-afternoon he tethered the Struke and lunched beside a waterfall on paté sandwiches and sparkling Bacchus Black from a coldflask. He was just finishing off his *mousse éclaire* when a two-foot steel arrow whistled past his ear to bury itself six inches in the dense blue wood of a Nunu tree behind him.

Retief rose casually, yawned, stretched, took out a vanilla dope stick and puffed it alight, at the same time scanning the underbrush. There was a quick movement behind a clump of Foon bushes; a second bolt leaped past him, almost grazing his shoulder, to rattle away in the brush. Appearing to notice nothing, Retief took a leisurely step toward the Nunu tree, slipped suddenly behind it. With a swift motion he grasped a small, limber branch growing out at waist height on his side of the two-foot bole, bent it down and pegged the tip to the shaggy, porous bark, using the match-sized dope stick to pin it in place. Then he moved quickly away, keeping the tree between himself and the unseen archer, to the concealment of a dense patch of shrubbery.

A minute passed; a twig popped. A bulky, tattooed Tsugg appeared, a vast, dumpy figure clad in dirty silks, holding a short, thick, recurved bow clamped in one boulder-like fist, a quarrel nocked, the string drawn. The dacoit tiptoed forward, jumped suddenly around the tree. Finding his quarry fled, he turned, stood with his back to the tree peering into the undergrowth.

At that moment, the bent branch, released by the burning of the dope stick, sprang outward, ramming the astounded bowman in the seat of his baggy green velveteen trousers. The arrow smacked into the dirt at his feet as he jumped, then stood rigid.

"Don't strike, sir!" he urged in a plaintive tenor. "The older lads put me up to it—"

Retief strolled from his shelter, nodded easily to the Tsugg, plucked the bow from his nerveless grip.

"Nice workmanship," he said, inspecting the weapon. "Groaci trade goods?"

"Trade goods?" the Tsugg said with a note of indignation. "Just because yer partner has a dirk at me back's no cause to make mockery of me. I plundered it from the Five-eyes all open and aboveboard, so help me."

"Sorry," Retief said. He withdrew the arrow from the loam, fitted it to the bow experimentally.

"You're not by chance a member of Hoobrik's band, are you?" he inquired off-handedly.

"Too right it's not by chance," the Tsugg said emphatically. "I went through the Ordeal, same's the other lads."

"Lucky we met," Retief said. "I'm on my way to pay a call on His Truculence. Can you lead me to him?"

The Tsugg straightened his two-hundred-and-ninety-pound bulk. "Tell yer crony to do his worst," he said with a small break in his voice. "Fim Gloob's not the Tsugg to play the treacher."

"It wasn't exactly treachery I had in mind," Retief demurred. "Just ordinary diplomacy."

"Yer threats will avail ye naught," Fim Gloob declared.

"I see what you mean," Retief said. "Still, there should be some way of working this out."

"No outsider goes to the camp of Hoobrik but as a prisoner." The Tsugg rolled his shiny black eyes at the Terran. "Ah, sir—would ye mind asking yer sidekick not to poke so hard? I fear me he'll rip me weskit, stole for me by me aged mums it were, a rare keepsake."

"Prisoner, eh, Fim? By the way, I don't have a sidekick."

"That being the way of it," Fim Gloob said carefully, after a short, thoughtful pause, "who'd be the villain holding the blade to me kip-glands?"

"As far as I know," Retief said candidly, "there's nobody here but you and me."

The Tsugg turned his head cautiously, peered behind him. With a grunt of annoyance he snapped a finger at the offending bough.

"Me and me overactive imagination," he snorted. "And now—"

He turned to Retief with a scowl.

"Remember, I still have the bow," Retief said pleasantly.

"And a mort o' good it'll do ye," Fim snarled, advancing. "Only a Tsugg born and bred has the arm to draw that stave!"

"Oh?" Retief set the arrow and with an easy motion pulled until the arrowhead rested against the bow, the latter being bent into a sharp curve. Another inch—and the stout laminated wood snapped with a sharp *twang.*

"I see what you mean," Retief said. "But then the Groaci always did produce flimsy merchandise."

"You—you broke it!" Fim Gloob said in tones of deep dismay.

"Never mind—I'll steal you a new one. We have some ladies' models in the Recreation Kits that ought not to overstrain you."

"But—I'm reckoned the stoutest bowman in the band."

"Don't give it another thought, Fim. They'll love you when you bring in a live Terry, single-handed."

"Who, me?"

"Of course. After all, I'm alone and unarmed. How could I resist?"

"Aye—but still—"

"Taking me in as a prisoner would look a lot better than having me saunter in on my own and tell Hoobrik you showed me the route."

"Wouldst do such a dirty trick?" Fim gasped.

"I wouldst—unless we start immediately," Retief assured the Tsugg.

Fim sighed. "I guess I know when I'm licked. I mean when you're licked. Let's go, prisoner. And let's hope His Truculence is in a good mood. Otherwise he'll clap ye on the rack and have the whole tale out of ye in a trice!"

IV

A few dozen heavyweights lazing about the communal cooking pot or sprawling in the shade under the striped awnings stretched between the trees looked up in mild interest as Retief appeared on Struke-back, Fim Gloob behind him astride his Vorch, glowering ferociously as he verbally prodded the lone Terran forward.

"Ho, that's far enough," he roared. "Dismount, while I seek instruction o' His Truculence whether to h'ist ye out of hand or ha' a bit o' sport wi' ye first."

"Ha, what be this, Gloob?" a bulky outlaw boomed as Retief swung down from the saddle. "An off-worlder, I trow!"

"That he's no Oberonian, is plain," another offered. "Mayhap a two-eyed variety o' Five-eyes."

Fim yelled, "Clear the way—I've fetched this Terry here to divert the great Hoobrik wi' his saucy sayings."

"Here, what passes?" a familiar baritone cut through the clamor. A large Tsugg in a red sash pushed through the mob, which gave way grudgingly, with much muttering. The newcomer halted with a jerk when his eye fell on Retief.

"Methinks," he said, "I've seen you before, sirrah."

"We've met," Retief acknowledged.

"Though all you Terries look alike to me." Dir Blash fingered his jaw gingerly. "Meseemeth 'twas in the Street of the Sweetmakers—"

"So it was."

"Aha! I've got it!" Dir Blash clapped Retief on the shoulder. "My boon companion! Ah, bullies," he addressed his fellows, "this Terry gave me a shot of something with a kick like a Vorch—though for the life of me I can't recall the precise circumstances. How wert thou yclept again, sirrah?"

"Retief; lucky you have the kind of memory you do, Dir Blash; your compatriots were just debating the best method of putting me out of my misery."

"Say you so?" Dir Blash looked around threateningly, his hand on the hilt of his cutlass. "Nobody murders my drinking buddies but me." He turned back to Retief. "Say, you wouldn't chance to have any more of the same, would you?"

"I'm saving it for a special occasion," Retief said.

"Well, what could be more special than a reprieve from being staked out on a zing-wasp hive, eh?"

"We'll celebrate later," Retief said. "Right now I'd appreciate a short interview with His Truculence."

"If I use my influence to get you in, wilt let me have another sample later?"

"If things work out as they usually do," Retief said, "I think you can be sure of it."

"Then come along, Dir Retief. I'll see what I can do."

Hoobrik the Uncouth, lounging in a hammock under a varicolored canopy, gazed indifferently at Retief as Dir Blash made the introductions. He was an immense Tsugg, above the average height of his kind, his obesity draped in voluminous beaded robes. He selected a large green berry from a dented silver bowl at his elbow, shook exotic salts over it from a heavy gold saltshaker and popped it into his mouth.

"So?" he grunted, spitting the seeds over the side. "Why disturb my meditations with trifles? Dispose of the creature in any way that amuses you, Blash—but save the head. I'll impale it on a pike and give it to the Terry chieftain—gift-wrapped, of course."

Dir Blash nodded, scratching himself under the ribs. "Well, thus doth the tart disintegrate, Retief," he said in tones of mild regret. "Let's go—"

"I don't want to be a spoilsport, your Truculence," Retief spoke up, "but Ambassador Clawhammer only allows his staff to be decapitated at Tuesday morning staff meetings."

"Staff meetings?" Hoobrik wondered aloud. "Is that anything like a barbecue?"

"Close," Retief agreed. "Quite often a diplomat or two are flayed alive and roasted over a slow fire."

"Hmm." Hoobrik looked thoughtful. "Maybe I should introduce the custom here. My wish is to keep up with the latest trends in government."

"In that connection," Retief said, offering the stiff parchment envelope containing the invitation to the reception, "His Excellency the Terrestrial

Ambassador Extraordinary and Minister Plenipotentiary presents his compliments and requests me to hand you this."

"Eh? What be this?" Hoobrik fingered the document gingerly.

"Ambassador Clawhammer requests the honor of your company at a ceremonial affair celebrating the election," Retief explained.

"Ceremonial affair?" Hoobrik shifted uneasily, causing the hammock to sway dangerously. "What kind of ceremony?"

"Just a small semi-formal gathering of kindred souls. It gives everyone a chance to show off their clothes and exchange veiled insults face to face."

"Waugh! What kind of contest is this? Give me a good hand-to-hand disemboweling any day!"

"That comes later," Retief said. "It's known as Dropping by the Residence for a Drink. After the Party."

"It hath an ominous sound," Hoobrik muttered. "Is it possible you Terries are more ferocious than I'd suspected?"

"Ha!" Dir Blash put in. "I myself dispatched half a dozen of the off-worlders only this morning when they sought to impede my entrance to a grog shop in the village."

"So?" Hoobrik yawned. "Too bad. For a moment, things were beginning to look interesting." He tore a corner off the gold-edged invitation and used it to poke at a bit of fruit rind wedged between his teeth. "Well, off with you, Blash—unless you want to play a featured role at my first staff meeting."

"Come, Terry," the red-sashed Tsugg growled, reaching for Retief's arm. "I just remembered the part of yesterday's carouse that had slipped my mind."

"I think," Retief said, evading the sub-chief's grab, "it's time for that jolt I promised you." He stepped in close and rammed a pair of pile-drive punches to Dir Blash's midriff, laced a hard right to the jaw as the giant doubled over and fell past him, out cold.

"Here!" Hoobrik yelled. "Is that any way to repay my hospitality?" He stared down at his fallen henchman. "Dir Blash, get up, thou malingerer, and avenge my honor!"

Dir Blash groaned. One foot twitched. He settled back with a snore.

"My apologies," Retief said, easing the Groaci pistol from inside his shirt. "Protocol has never been my strong suit. Having committed a *faux pas*, I'd best be on my way. Which route would be least likely to result in the demise of any of your alert sentries?"

"Stay, off-worlder. Wouldst spread tidings of this unflattering event abroad, to the detriment of my polling strength?"

"Word might leak out," Retief conceded. "Especially if any of your troops get in my way."

" 'Tis a shame not to be borne!" Hoobrik said hoarsely. "All Oberon knoweth that only a Tsugg can smite another Tsugg senseless." He looked thoughtful. "Still, if the molehill will not come to Meyer, Meyer must to the molehill, as the saying goeth. Since thou hast in sooth felled my liegeman, it follows you must be raised at once to Tsugghood, legitimizing the event after the fact, as it were."

"I'd be honored," Retief said amiably. "Provided, of course, that you authorize me to convey your gracious acceptance of His Excellency's invitation."

Hoobrik looked glum. "Well—we can always loot the Embassy afterward. Very well, Terry—Tsugg-to-be, that is. Done!" The chieftain heaved his bulk from the hammock, stirred Dir Blash with a booted toe, at which the latter groaned and sat up.

"Up, sluggard!" Hoobrik roared. "Summon a few varlets to robe me for a formal occasion! And my guest will require suitable robes, too." He glanced at Retief. "But don't don them yet, lest they be torn and muddied."

"The ceremony sounds rather strenuous," Retief commented.

"Not the ceremony," Hoobrik corrected. "That cometh later. First cometh the Ordeal. If you survive that I'll have my tailor fit you out as befits a sub-chief of the Tsugg."

The Ceremonial Site for Ordeal Number One—a clearing on a forest slope with a breath-taking view of the valley below—was crowded with Tsugg tribesmen, good-naturedly quarreling, shouting taunts, offering and accepting wagers and challenges, passing wineskins from hand to grimy hand.

"All right, everybody out of the Ring of the First Trial," Dir Blash shouted, implementing his suggestion with hearty buffets left and right. "Unless ye plan to share the novitiate's hazards."

The mountaineers gave ground, leaving an open space some fifty feet in diameter, to the center of which Retief was led.

"All right, the least ye can do is give the off-worlder breathing space." Dir Blash exhorted the bystanders to edge back another yard. "Now, Retief—this is a sore trial, 'tis true, but 'twill show you the mettle of the Tsugg, that we impose so arduous a criterion on oursel's!" He broke off at a sound of crashing in the underbrush. A pair of tribesmen on the outer fringe of the audience flew into the air as if blown up by a mine, as with ferocious snorts a wild Vorch, seven feet at the shoulder and armed with down-curving tusks, charged from the underbrush. His rush carried him through the ranks of the spectators into the inner circle, his short tail whipping, his head tossing as he sought a new target. His inflamed eye fell on Dir Blash.

"Botheration," the latter commented in mild annoyance as the beast lowered its head and charged. Leaning aside, the Tsugg raised a fist of the size and weight of a hand-axe, brought it down with a resounding *brongg!* on the carnivore's skull. The unlucky beast folded in mid-leap, skidded chin-first to fetch up against Retief's feet.

"Nice timing," he remarked.

"Ye'd think the brute did it apurpose, to plague a serious occasion," Dir Blash said disapprovingly. "Drag the silly creature away," he directed a pair of Tsugg. "He'll be broke to harness for his pains. And now," he turned to Retief, "if ye're ready—"

Retief smiled encouragingly.

"Right, then. The first trial is—take a deep breath and hold it for the count of ten." Dir Blash watched Retief's expression alertly for signs of dismay. Seeing none, he raised a finger disappointedly.

"Very well. Inhale."

Retief inhaled.

"Onetwothreefourfivesixseveneightnineten," Dir Blash said in a rush and stared curiously at the Terran, who stood relaxed before him. A few approving shouts rang out. Then came scattered hand-claps.

"Well," Dir Blash grunted. "You did pretty fair, I suppose, for an off-worlder. Hardly turned blue at all. You pass, I suppose."

"Hey," someone called from the front rank of the gallery. "He's not—"

"Not still—" someone else queried.

"Still holding his breath?" a third Tsugg then asked wonderingly.

"O' course not, lackwits!" Dir Blash bellowed. "How could he? E'en Grand Master Cutthroat Dirdir Hooch held out but to the count of twelve!" He looked closely at Retief. "Thou hast indeed resumed respiration?" he murmured.

"Of course," Retief reassured the Tsugg. "I was just grandstanding."

Dir Blash grunted. "In sooth, I've a feeling ye went a good thirteen, if truth were known," he muttered confidentially. "Hast made a specialty of suffocation?"

"Staff meetings, remember?" Retief prompted.

"To be sure." Dir Blash looked disgruntled. "Well, on to the Second Trial, Terry. Ye'll find this one e'en a straiter test of Tsugghood than the last!" He led the way upslope, Retief close behind, the crowd following. The path deteriorated into a rocky gully winding up between nearly vertical walls of rock. Pebbles rattled around the party from the crumbling cliffs above as members clambered toward choice vantage points. A medium-sized boulder came bounding down from a crag to whistle overhead and crash thunderously away among the trees below. The journey ended in a small natural amphitheater, the floor of which was thickly littered with stones of all sizes. Spectators took up positions around the periphery above as pebbles continued to clatter down around the tester and testee, who stood alone at the center of the target. A head-sized rock smashed down a yard from Retief. A chunk the size of a grand piano poised directly above him gave an ominous rumble and slid downward six inches amid a shower of gravel.

"What happens if one of those scores a bull's-eye on the candidate?" Retief inquired.

"It's considered a bad omen," Dir Blash said. "Drat the pesky motes!" he added as a small fragment bounded off the back of his neck. "These annoyances detract from the solemnity of the occasion."

"On the contrary," Retief demurred politely. "I think they add a lot of interest to the situation."

"Umm. Mayhap." Dir Blash gazed absently upward, moving his head slightly to avoid being brained by a baseball-sized missile. "Now, off-worlder," he addressed Retief, "prepare for the moment of truth. Bend over—" he paused impressively— "and touch your toes!"

"Do I get to bend my knees?" Retief temporized.

"Bend whatever you like," Dir Blash said with airy contempt. "I trow this is one feat ye've not practiced at your Ordeal of the Staff Meeting!"

"True," Retief conceded. "The closest we come is lifting ourselves by our bootstraps." He assumed a serious expression, bent over and, with a smooth motion, touched his fingertips to his toes.

"He did it in one try," someone called.

"Didn't even take a bounce!" another added.

The applause was general.

"Lacking in style," Dir Blash grumbled. "But a pass, I allow. But now you face the Third Ordeal, where ye're tricks will do ye no good. Come along." They moved off. The stone piano crunched down on the spot he and Retief had just vacated.

V

The route to the Third Site led upward through a narrow cut to emerge on a bare rock slope. Fifty feet away a flat-topped rock spire loomed up from the depths, joined to the main mass of the peak by a meandering ribbon of rock some six inches in width, except where it narrowed to a knife edge, halfway across. Dir Blash sauntered out across the narrow bridge, gazing around him at the scenery.

"A splendid prospect, eh, Retief?" he called over his shoulder. "Look on it well; it may be thy last. What comes next has broken many a strong Tsugg down into a babbling Glert."

Retief tried the footing; it held. Keeping his eyes on the platform ahead, he walked quickly across.

"Now," Dir Blash said, "you may wish to take a moment to commune with your patron devils or whatever it is you off-worlders burn incense to."

"Thanks, I'm in good shape incantation-wise," Retief reassured him. "Only last night I joined in a toast to the auditors."

"In that case—" Dir Blash pointed impressively to a flat stone that lay across two square rocks, the top of which cleared the ground by a good twelve inches.

"Leap the obstacle in a single bound."

Retief studied the hurdle from several angles before taking up his position before it.

"I see you hesitate," Dir Blash taunted. "Dost doubt thy powers at last, Terry?"

"Last year an associate of mine jumped fifty names on the promotion list," Retief said. "Can I do less?" Standing flat-footed, he hopped over the barrier. Turning, he hopped back again.

There was a moment of stunned silence.

Suddenly pandemonium broke out. Dir Blash hesitated only a moment, then joined in the glad cries.

"Congratulations, Dir Tief!" he bellowed, pounding the Terran on the shoulder. "I warrant an off-worlder of thy abilities would be an embarrassment to all hands—but in sooth thou'rt now a Tsugg of the Tsuggs, and thy attainments are an adornment to our ilk!"

"Remarkable," said Hoobrik the Uncouth as he stuffed a handful of sugar-coated green olives into his mouth. "According to Blash you went through the Ordeal like a Tsugg to the pavilion born. I may keep you on as bodyguard, Dir Tief, after I get the vote out and myself in."

"Coming from your Truculence, that's praise indeed," Retief said. "Considering your willingness to offer yourself as a candidate without a whimper."

"What's to whimper?" Hoobrik demanded. "After my lads have rounded up more voters than the opposition can muster, I'll be free to fill my pockets as best I may. 'Tis a prospect I face calmly."

"True," Retief said. "But first there are a few rituals to be gotten past. There's Whistle-stopping, Baby-kissing, Fence-sitting, and Mud-slinging, plus a considerable amount of Viewing with Alarm."

"Hmm." Hoobrik rubbed his chin thoughtfully. "Are these Ordeals the equal of our Rites of Tsugghood, Retief?"

"Possibly even worse," Retief solemnly assured the chieftain. "Especially if you wear an Indian war bonnet."

"Out upon it!" Hoobrik pounded his tankard on the table. "A Tsugg fears neither man nor beast."

"But did you ever face a quorum of Women Voters?" Retief countered quickly.

"My stout lads will ride down all opposition," Hoobrik declared with finality. "I've already made secret arrangements with certain Five-eyed off-worlders to supply me with all the write-in ballots I need to make everything legal and proper. Once in office, I can settle down to businesslike looting in an orderly manner."

"But remember," Retief cautioned, "you'll be expected to stand on your Party Platform—at least for the first few weeks."

"W-weeks?" Hoobrik faltered. "What is this platform, Retief?"

"It's a pretty shaky structure," Retief confided. "I've never known one to last past the first Legislative Rebuff."

"What, yet another Ordeal?"

"Don't worry about it, your Truculence; it seldom goes as far as Impeachment."

"Well? Don't keep me in suspense!" Hoobrik roared. "What doth this rite entail?"

"This is where your rival politicians get even with you for winning, by charging you with High Crimes and Misdemeanors—"

"Stay!" Hoobrik yelled. "Is there no end to these torments?"

"Certainly," Retief reassured the aroused leader. "After you retire, you become a Statesman and are allowed out on alternate All Fools Days to be queried as to your views on any subject sufficiently trivial to grace the pages of the Sunday Supplements."

"Arrrhh!" Hoobrik growled and drained his mug. "See here, Retief," he said. "On pondering the matter, methinks 'twould be a gracious gesture on my part to take second place on the ticket and let a younger Tsugg assume party leadership; you, for example, Blash," he addressed the sub-chief.

"Who, me?" the latter blurted. "Nay, my liege—as I've said before, I am not now and do not intend to be a candidate."

"Who, then?" Hoobrik waved his arms in agitation. "We need a Tsugg who'll appeal to a broad spectrum of voters. A good scimitarman for beating down opposition inside the party, a handy club-wielder to bring in the Independents, a cool hand with a dirk, for committee infighting—" He paused, looking suddenly thoughtful.

"Well, I'll leave you gentlemen to look over the lists," Retief said, rising. "May I tell the Ambassador to expect you at the post-election victory reception?"

"We'll be there," Hoobrik said. "And I think I have a sure-fire Tsugg standard-bearer in mind to pull in the vote—"

In the varicolored glow of lights strung in the hedges ringing the former miniature golf course pressed into service as Embassy grounds, the Terran diplomats stood in conversation clumps across the fairways and greens, glasses in hand, nervously eyeing the door through which Ambassador Clawhammer's entrance was expected momentarily.

Magnan said to Retief, glancing at his watch, "The first results will be in any moment."

"I think we need have no fear of the outcome," Saddlesore stated. "Guru Hoobrik's students have been particularly active in these final hours, zealously applying posters to the polling places."

"And applying knots to the heads of reluctant converts," the Political Officer added. "What I'm wondering is—after Hoobrik's inauguration, what's to prevent his applying the same techniques to foreign diplomats?"

"Tradition, my boy," the colonel said soothingly. "We may be shot as spies or deported as undesirables—but shaped up by wardheelers, no."

A stir crossed the lawn. Ambassador Clawhammer appeared, ornate in the burgundy cutaway and puce jodhpurs specified by CDT Regs for early evening ceremonial wear.

"Well? No word yet?" He stared challengingly at his underlings, accepting one of the four drinks simultaneously thrust at him by alert junior officers. "My private polls indicate an early lead for the Tsugg party, increasing to a commanding majority as the rural counties report."

"Commanding is right," Magnan muttered behind his hand. "One of the ruffians had the audacity to order me to hold his gluepot while he affixed a poster to the front door of the Embassy."

"What cheek," the Political Officer gasped. "You didn't do it?"

"Of course not. He held the gluepot, and I affixed the placard."

Happy shouts sounded from the direction of the gate; a party of Tsugg appeared, flamboyant in pink and yellow, handing out foot-long yellow cigars. A throng of lesser Oberonians followed, all apparently in good spirits.

"A landslide victory," one called to the assembly at large. "Break out the wassail bowl!"

"Is this official, Depew?" the Ambassador demanded of his Counselor, who arrived at that moment at a trot, waving a sheaf of papers.

"I'm afraid so—that is, I'm delighted to confirm the people's choice," he panted. "It's amazing—the Tsugg candidate polled an absolute majority, even in the oppositions' strongholds. It looks like every voter on the rolls voted the straight Tsugg ticket."

"Certes, Terry," a Grimble confirmed jovially, grabbing two glasses from a passing tray. "We know a compromise candidate when we see one."

" 'Tis a clear mandate from the people," a Tsugg declaimed. "Hoobrik will be along in a trice to help with sorting out the spoils. As for myself, I'm not greedy; a minor Cabinet post will do nicely."

"Out upon thee!" a jovial voice boomed as the Tsugg chieftain swept through the gate, flanked by an honor guard of grinning scimitar-bearers. "No undignified rooting at the trough, lads—there's plenty to go around."

"Congratulations, your Truculence," Ambassador Clawhammer cried, advancing with outstretched hand. "I'm sure that at this moment you're feeling both proud and humble as you point with pride—"

"Humble?" Hoobrik roared. "That's for losers, Terry."

"To be sure." Clawhammer conceded the point. "Now, your Truculence, I don't want to delay the victory celebration—but why don't we first just sign this little Treaty of Eternal Peace and Friendship, set up to run for five years with a renewal option—"

"You'll have to speak to the new Planetary President about that, Terry," the chieftain waved the proffered document away. "As for myself, I have some important drinking to catch up on."

"But—I was informed by a usually reliable source—" Clawhammer turned to glare at the Counselor—"that the Tsugg party had carried off all honors."

"True enough. By the way, where is he?"

"Where is who?"

"Our new Chief Executive, of course—" Hoobrik broke off, pushed past Clawhammer, rushed forward with outstretched arms, narrowly missing a small water hazard, to embrace Retief, who had just appeared on the scene.

"Stand aside, Retief," Clawhammer snapped. "I'm in the midst of a delicate negotiation—"

"Employ a more respectful tone, Terry," Hoobrik admonished the Ambassador sternly. "Consider to whom you're speaking."

"To whom I'm speaking?" Clawhammer said in bewilderment. "Whom *am* I speaking to?"

"Meet Planetary President Dir Tief," Hoobrik said proudly, waving a hand at Retief. "The winner—and new champion."

"Good lord, Retief." Magnan was the first to recover his speech. "When? How?"

"What's the meaning of this?" Clawhammer burst out. "Am I being made sport of?"

"Apparently not, Mr. Ambassador," Retief said. "It seems they put me on the ballot as a dark horse—"

"You'll be a horse of a darker color before I'm through with you—" Clawhammer went rigid as twin scimitars flashed, ended with their points pressed against his neck.

"But how can a Terran be elected as head of the Tsugg party?" the Political Officer asked.

"President Tief is no Terry," Hoobrik corrected. "He's a Tsugg after my own heart!"

"But—doesn't the president have to be a natural-born citizen?"

"Art suggesting our President is unnatural-born?" Hoobrik grated.

"Why, no—"

" 'Tis well. In that case, best you present your credentials at once and we can get down to business."

Clawhammer hesitated. A prod of the blade at his jugular assisted him in finding his tongue.

"Why, ah, Mr. President—will your Excellency kindly tell your thugs to put those horrible-looking knives away?"

"Certainly, Mr. Ambassador," Retief said easily. "Just as soon as we've cleared up a few points in the treaty. I think it would be a good idea if the new planetary government has a solemn CDT guarantee of noninterference in elections from now on—"

"Retief—you wouldn't dare—I mean, of course, my boy, whatever you say."

"Also, it would be a good idea to strike out those paragraphs dealing with CDT military advisors, technical experts and fifty-credit-a-day economists. We Oberonians would prefer to work out our own fate."

218 / THE RETIEF SERIES

"Yes—yes—of course, Mr. President. And now—"

"And as to the matter of the one-sided trade agreement—why don't we just scrap that whole section and substitute a free commerce clause?"

"Why—if I agree to that they'll have my scalp, back in the Department!"

"That's better than having it tied to a pole outside my tent," Hoobrik pointed out succinctly.

"On the other hand," Retief said, "I think we Tsuggs can see our way clear to supply a modest security force to ensure that nothing violent happens to foreign diplomats among us as long as they stick to diplomacy and leave all ordinary crime to us Oberonians."

"Agreed," Clawhammer squawked. "Where's the pen?"

It took a quarter of an hour to delete the offending paragraphs, substitute new wording and affix signatures to the imposing document establishing formal relations between the *Corps Diplomatique Terrestrienne* and the Republic of Oberon. When the last length of red tape had been affixed and the last blob of sealing wax applied, Retief called for attention.

"Now that Terran-Oberonian relations are off on a sound footing," he said, "I feel it's only appropriate that I step down, leaving the field clear for a new election. Accordingly, gentlemen, I hereby resign the office of President in favor of my vice president, Hoobrik."

Amid the clamor that broke out, Clawhammer made his way to confront Retief.

"You blundered at last, sir," he murmured in a voice aquiver with rage. "You should have clung to your spurious position long enough to have gotten a head start for the Galactic periphery! I'll see you thrown into a dungeon so deep that your food will have to be lowered to you in pressurized containers! I'll—"

"You'll be on hand to dedicate the statue to our first Ex-President, I ween?" President Hoobrik addressed the Terran envoy. "I think a hundred-foot monument will be appropriate to express the esteem in which we hold our Tsugg emeritus, Dir Tief, eh?"

"Why, ah—"

"We'll appreciate your accrediting him as permanent Political Advisor to Oberon," Hoobrik continued. "We'll need him handy to pose."

"To be sure," Clawhammer gulped.

"Now I think it's time we betook ourselves off to more private surroundings, Dir Tief," the President said. "We need to plot party strategy for the by-election."

"You're all invited to sample the hospitality of *The Plump Sausage*," Binkster Druzz spoke up. "Provided I have your promises there'd be no breeching of walls."

"Done!" Hoobrik cried heartily. "And by the way, Dir Druzz—What wouldst think of the idea of a coalition, eh?"

"Hmm—Twilpritt sagacity linked with Tsugg bulk might indeed present a formidable ticket," Binkster concurred.

"Well, Retief," Magnan said as the party streamed toward the gate, "yours was surely the shortest administration in the annals of representational government. Tell me confidentially—how in the world did you induce that band of thugs to accept you as their nominee?"

"I'm afraid that will have to remain a secret for now," Retief said. "But just wait until I write my memoirs."

BIBLIOGRAPHY

Envoy to New Worlds, Ace Books, 1963, includes the following stories which appeared in *If:*
    "Palace Revolution" ("Gambler's World"), November 1961
    "Protocol" ("The Yllian Way"), January 1962
    "Policy" ("The Madman from Earth"), March 1962
    "Sealed Orders" ("Retief of the Red-Tape Mountain"), May 1962
    "Aide Memoire," July 1962
    "Cultural Exchange," September 1962*
Galactic Diplomat, Doubleday, 1965, includes the following stories which appeared in *If:*
    "Courier" ("The Frozen Planet"), September 1961
    "Protest Note" ("The Desert and the Stars"), November 1962
    "Saline Solution," March 1963*
    "Ultimatum" ("Mightiest Qorn"), July 1963
    "Native Intelligence" ("The Governor of Glave"), November 1963
    "Wicker Wonderland" ("The City That Grew in the Sea"), March 1964*
    "The Prince and the Pirate," August 1964
    "The Castle of Light," October 1964*
    "The Brass God" ("Retief, God Speaker"), January 1965*
Retief's War, Doubleday, 1966
Retief and the Warlords, Doubleday, 1968
Retief: Ambassador to Space, Doubleday, 1969, includes the following stories which appeared in *If:*
    "Trick or Treaty," August 1965
    "Giant Killer," September 1965
    "Dam Nuisance," March 1966*
    "Truce or Consequences," November 1966
    "The Forest in the Sky," February 1967
    "The Forbidden City" ("Retief, War Criminal"), April 1967*
    "Grime and Punishment" ("Clear As Mud"), August 1967*
Retief's Ransom, Putnam, 1971

Retief of the C.D.T., Doubleday, 1971, includes the following stories which appeared in *If:*

    "Mechanical Advantage" ("Retief, the Long-Awaited Master"), April 1969*

    "The Piecemakers," May 1970*

    "Ballots and Bandits," September 1970*

    "Pime Doesn't Cray," January 1971*

    "Internal Affair" ("Retief, Insider"), March 1971

Retief: Emissary to the Stars, Dell Books, 1975, contains the following:

    "The Garbage Invasion," *The Magazine of Fantasy and Science Fiction*, December 1972

    "The Negotiators," *Analog*, February 1975

    "The Hoob Melon Crisis," (original in this book)

    "The Troubleshooter," (original in this book)

Retief at Large, Ace Books, 1978 (collection, contains above stories marked *)

THE CHANGE WAR SERIES

 *by Fritz Leiber*

I should imagine that of all science fiction series that have somehow become memo-rable, my Change War is the least in total wordage and the one most at the mercy of events beyond the author's control. A bibliography (see page 258) of first magazine publication of all the series stories helps substantiate the first of these claims, for they altogether total only about 80,000 words, enough for one fair-sized book.

During the early 1950s I developed a severe alcohol problem, so that my writing, then a part-time occupation, suffered, and I published only one short story during 1954, 1955, and 1956—the ominously named "The Silence Game." During the first half of 1956 I tried to quit drinking several times. Once, after three seemingly sleepless nights and days without a drink, I fell into a strange waking dream which had this peculiarity: Whenever I opened my eyes I was lying abed, very much in my right waking mind, listening to the night sounds of Chicago; whenever I closed them I was back in the dream of being on a steadily moving, rather gentle roller coaster that could, by stages, visit every point in space and time I wanted it to. I pleasantly went with the dream for what seemed a couple of hours, visiting a 1920s nightclub where they were singing the blues and a last-century camp meeting where the same song became a salvation spiritual, sampling Restoration England, ancient Rome, and a couple of antediluvian kingdoms, and regularly opening my eyes to check that the waking-mind feature was still operating. But then I became more and more oppressed—by the question of how, if this went on, I was ever going to get any sleep. Gradually the dream heavied up, and during a particularly scaly episode in a Cuban roadhouse with a curious spiral-staircased clock tower, it merged into total and very welcome oblivion.

In August 1956 I quit drinking successfully. By December I felt ready to stop tinkering with short shorts and revisions and do some real writing. Partly because of that dream (or persistent vision on the edge of slumber) the topic of time travel attracted me.

I had always been drawn by the idea (pioneered by Edmund Hamilton) of time-traveling warring powers which recruit soldiers from all ages. There was something irresistibly romantic to me in the notion of bringing together, say, a Roman Legionary, a Musketeer, a Swiss Guard, and a Doughboy, more for the mood and emotional effect (listening to them talk, watching them react to each other) than to see them fight.

The object of the war would be to alter the outcome of history in a way favorable to your side by going back and changing crucial events in the past (hence Change War)—a series of raids or commando operations to intervene decisively in the so-called decisive battles, assassinate or kidnap key figures, etc. In fact, they'd operate secretly, rather like history's Assassins or Hashisheen.

Many time-travel stories assume that if you could go back and alter one small key event in the past, the entire future would automatically be changed beyond all recognition, almost as if a new universe had been born. This offended my sense of proportion and realism, my conviction that there were no achievements without hard work. It made things too easy. Reality was a tougher fabric than that, I told myself, and more resistant to alteration, so that any single change you made in it would tend to damp out as its consequences tried to move toward the future. This meant that many little alterations and re-alterations would have to be made before any big general change was achieved. This concept would give me the sort of hard, long (in fact, unending) war that I wanted to write about, creating a fatalistic and melancholy mood.

I wanted my story to be one of mood and emotions, of personalities in conflict rather than of ideas. I'd make my characters unimportant people, only hazily conscious of the allover picture (they'd be enveloped in the fog of battle, as it were) but intensely aware of their own personal predicaments. Just a few ordinary soldiers, say, of diverse historical backgrounds and—for variety, for novelty—the entertainers and other personnel of a very small time-traveling rest and recuperation station. There'd be a mutiny or near-mutiny, a choosing up of sides, a momentary thrill of freedom, and then, without too much bloodshed but hopefully with a lot of self-insight, the original situation would be restored with a feeling of "Whatever it is, we're in it for better or worse."

Finally, to concentrate the story, I made it comply with the unities of classical drama: all the action interrelated and occurring in one place (the time-traveling R&R station) in a couple of hours.

The result was *The Big Time*. I wrote it in one hundred days from first notes to finished manuscript, it being one story I final-typed entirely by myself. I got so involved in it, so wrapped up in its characters, that two-thirds of the way through I got the chilly feeling (this occurred to me while sitting alone at the back of a movie house watching a French film) that they were my only friends in the world, that all the real people I knew were ghosts by comparison—even the real people those characters were based on, including my wife and son. It got me started writing again after a long sterile period and—truly to my complete surprise—it won me my first award, the Hugo for Best Novel of 1958.

Most of the other stories were spin-offs from that first one. In "Damnation Morning" I described the original waking nightmare that inspired me. I wrote "Try and Change the Past" to further explain my concept of the resistance of the universe to change, describing it as the Law of the Conservation of Reality, on the analogy of Einstein's conservation of mass-energy.

The exception was "No Great Magic." Five years had passed. I was struggling unsuccessfully to write a play about a girl with agoraphobia who literally lives backstage, the pet and patient of a group of actors, afraid to venture away from the theater or onto the stage itself—my working title was "In the Dressing Room."

Then on a trip to New York I ran into Fred Pohl, who was editing *Galaxy* magazine at the time. He told me in dead seriousness what I now believe to be a pure fairy tale he made up on the spur of the moment: that he had a wonderful atmospheric cover painting he didn't know how to use of a beautiful moody woman with haunted eyes and in a black evening dress standing beside a great clock face whose hands pointed at midnight. Why didn't I write a Change War novelette for it to illustrate?

I think I must have fallen in love with that pictured woman then and there. It occurred to me that my time-traveling soldier-entertainers could very well use the disguise of a theatrical company. I could bring most of the characters of *The Big Time* back again; one of them would be my agoraphobic girl. I'd make it a Shakespearean company like my own father's, so as to make use of my own stage experience. And once more I'd use the classical unities: I'd have the story take place backstage during a performance of *Macbeth*.

So I did, after all, manage to write "In the Dressing Room"—only Fred Pohl found a far better title in the lines of poetry I quoted at the head of my first chapter.

But the cover of the issue of *Galaxy* in which it ran depicted a peculiarly ugly alien by Emsh with four eyes and a beet-red complexion and a top-knot like a vegetable, illustrating "The Star Kings" by Jack Vance. I'm still waiting for the beautiful lady beside the midnight clock.

No Great Magic

To bring the dead to life
Is no great magic.
Few are wholly dead:
Blow on a dead man's embers
And a live flame will start.
—GRAVES

I

I dipped through the filmy curtain into the boys' half of the dressing room and there was Sid sitting at the star's dressing table in his threadbare yellowed undershirt, the lucky one, not making up yet but staring sternly at himself in the bulb-framed mirror and experimentally working his features a little, as actors will, and kneading the stubble on his fat chin.

I said to him quietly, "Siddy, what are we putting on tonight? Maxwell Anderson's *Elizabeth the Queen* or Shakespeare's *Macbeth*? It says

Macbeth on the callboard, but Miss Nefer's getting ready for Elizabeth. She just had me go and fetch the red wig."

He tried out a few eyebrow rears—right, left, both together—then turned to me, sucking in his big gut a little, as he always does when a gal heaves into hailing distance, and said, "Your pardon, sweetling, what sayest thou?"

Sid always uses that kook antique patter backstage, until I sometimes wonder whether I'm in Central Park, New York City, nineteen hundred and three quarters, or somewhere in Southwark, Merry England, fifteen hundred and same. The truth is that although he loves every last fat part in Shakespeare and will play the skinniest one with loyal and inspired affection, he thinks Willy S. penned Falstaff with nobody else in mind but Sidney J. Lessingham. (And no accent on the ham, please.)

I closed my eyes and counted to eight, then repeated my question.

He replied, "Why, the Bard's tragical history of the bloody Scot, certes." He waved his hand toward the portrait of Shakespeare that always sits beside his mirror on top of his reserve makeup box. At first that particular picture of the Bard looked too nancy to me—a sort of peeping-tom school-teacher—but I've grown used to it over the months and even palsy-feeling.

He didn't ask me why I hadn't asked Miss Nefer my question. Everybody in the company knows she spends the hour before curtain-time getting into character, never parting her lips except for that purpose—or to bite your head off if you try to make the most necessary conversation.

"Aye, 'tiz *Macbeth* tonight," Sid confirmed, returning to his frowning-practice: left eyebrow up, right down, reverse, repeat, rest. "And I must play the ill-starred Thane of Glamis."

I said, "That's fine, Siddy, but where does it leave us with Miss Nefer? She's already thinned her eyebrows and beaked out the top of her nose for Queen Liz, though that's as far as she's got. A beautiful job, the nose. Anybody else would think it was plastic surgery instead of putty. But it's going to look kind of funny on the Thaness of Glamis."

Sid hesitated a half second longer than he usually would—I thought, *his timing's off tonight*—and then he harrumphed and said, "Why, Iris Nefer, decked out as Good Queen Bess, will speak a prologue to the play—a prologue which I have myself but last week writ." He owled his eyes. " 'Tis an experiment in the new theater."

I said, "Siddy, prologues were nothing new to Shakespeare. He had them on half his other plays. Besides, it doesn't make sense to use Queen Elizabeth. She was dead by the time he whipped up *Macbeth*, which is all about witchcraft and directed at King James."

He growled a little at me and demanded, "Prithee, how comes it your peewit-brain bears such a ballast of fusty book-knowledge, chit?"

I said softly, "Siddy, you don't camp in a Shakespearean dressing room for a year, tete-a-teting with some of the wisest actors ever, without learning a little. Sure I'm a mental case, a poor little A & A existing on your sweet charity, and don't think I don't appreciate it, but—"

"A-*and*-A, thou sayest?" he frowned. "Methinks the gladsome new forswearers of sack and ale call themselves AA."

"Agoraphobe and Amnesiac," I told him. "But look, Siddy, I was going to sayest that I do know the plays. Having Queen Elizabeth speak a prologue to *Macbeth* is as much an anachronism as if you put her on the gantry of the British moonship, busting a bottle of champagne over its schnozzle."

"Ha!" he cried as if he'd caught me out. "And saying there's a new Elizabeth, wouldn't that be the bravest advertisement ever for the Empire?—perchance rechristening the pilot, copilot and astrogator Drake, Hawkins and Raleigh? And the ship *The Golden Hind?* Tilly fally, lady!"

He went on, "My prologue an anachronism, quotha! The groundlings will never mark it. Think'st thou wisdom came to mankind with the stenchful rocket and the sundered atomy? More, the Bard himself was topfull of anachronism. He put spectacles on King Lear, had clocks tolling the hour in Caesar's Rome, buried that Roman 'stead o' burning him and gave Czechoslovakia a seacoast. Go to, doll."

"Czechoslovakia, Siddy?"

"Bohemia, then, what skills it? Leave me now, sweet poppet. Go thy ways. I have matters of import to ponder. There's more to running a repertory company than reading the footnotes to Furness."

Martin had just slouched by calling the Half Hour and looking in his solemnity, sneakers, Levi's and dirty T-shirt more like an underage refugee from Skid Row than Sid's newest recruit, assistant stage manager and hardest-worked juvenile—though for once he'd remembered to shave. I was about to ask Sid who was going to play Lady Mack if Miss Nefer wasn't, or, if she were going to double the roles, shouldn't I help her with the change? She's a slow dresser and the Elizabeth costumes are pretty realistically stayed. And she would have trouble getting off that nose, I was sure. But then I saw that Siddy was already slapping on the Alboline to keep the grease paint from getting into his pores.

Greta, you ask too many questions, I told myself. *You get everybody riled up and you rack your own poor rickety little mind;* and I hied myself off to the costumery to settle my nerves.

The costumery, which occupies the back end of the dressing room, is exactly the right place to settle the nerves and warm the fancies of any child, including an unraveled adult who's saving what's left of her sanity by pretending to be one. To begin with there are the regular costumes for Shakespeare's plays, all jeweled and spangled and brocaded, stage armor, great Roman togas with weights in the borders to make them drape right, velvets of every color to rest your cheek against and dream, and the fantastic costumes for the other plays we favor: Ibsen's *Peer*

Gynt, Shaw's *Back to Methuselah* and Hilliard's adaptation of Heinlein's *Children of Methuselah,* the Čapek brothers' *Insect People,* O'Neill's *The Fountain,* Flecker's *Hassan, Camino Real, Children of the Moon, The Beggar's Opera, Mary of Scotland, Berkeley Square, The Road to Rome.*

There are also the costumes for all the special and variety performances we give of the plays: *Hamlet* in modern dress, *Julius Caesar* set in a dictatorship of the 1920's, *The Taming of the Shrew* in caveman furs and leopard skins, where Petruchio comes in riding a dinosaur, *The Tempest* set on another planet with a spaceship wreck to start it off *Karrumph!*—which means a half dozen spacesuits, featherweight but looking ever so practical, and the weirdest sort of extraterrestrial-beast outfits for Ariel and Caliban and the other monsters.

Oh, I tell you the stuff in the costumery ranges over such a sweep of space and time that you sometimes get frightened you'll be whirled up and spun off just anywhere, so that you have to clutch at something very real to you to keep it from happening and to remind you where you *really* are—as I did now at the subway token on the thin gold chain around my neck (Siddy's first gift to me that I can remember) and chanted very softly to myself, like a charm or a prayer, closing my eyes and squeezing the holes in the token: "Columbus Circle, Times Square, Penn Station, Christopher Street . . ."

But you don't ever get *really* frightened in the costumery. Not exactly, though your goosehairs get wonderfully realistically tingled and your tummy chilled from time to time—because you know it's all make-believe, a lifesize doll world, a children's dress-up world. It gets you thinking of far-off times and scenes as *pleasant* places and not as black hungry mouths that might gobble you up and keep you forever. It's always safe, always *just in the theatre, just on the stage,* no matter how far it seems to plunge and roam . . . and the best sort of therapy for a pot-holed mind like mine, with as many gray ruts and curves and gaps as its cerebrum, that can't remember one single thing before this last year in the dressing room and that can't ever push its shaking body out of that same motherly fatherly room, except to stand in the wings for a scene or two and watch the play until the fear gets too great and the urge to take just one peek at *the audience* gets too strong . . . and I remember what happened the two times I *did* peek, and I have to come scuttling back.

The costumery's good occupational therapy for me, too, as my pricked and calloused fingertips testify. I think I must have stitched up or darned half the costumes in it this last twelve-month, though there are so many of them that I swear the drawers have accordion pleats and the racks extend into the fourth dimension—not to mention the boxes of props and the shelves of scripts and prompt-copies and other books, including a couple of encyclopedias and the many thick volumes of Furness's *Variorum Shakespeare,* which as Sid had guessed I'd been boning up on. Oh,

and I've sponged and pressed enough costumes, too, and even refitted
them to newcomers like Martin, ripping up and resewing seams, which
can be a punishing job with heavy materials.

In a less sloppily organized company I'd be called wardrobe mistress,
I guess. Except that to anyone in show business that suggests a crotchety
old dame with lots of authority and scissors hanging around her neck
on a string. Although I've got my crochets, all right, I'm not that old.
Kind of childish, in fact. As for authority, everybody outranks me, even
Martin.

Of course to somebody *outside* show business, wardrobe mistress might
suggest a yummy gal who spends her time dressing up as Nell Gwyn
or Anitra or Mrs. Pinchwife or Cleopatra or even Eve (we got a legal
costume for it) and inspiring the boys. I've tried that once or twice. But
Siddy frowns on it, and if Miss Nefer ever caught me at it I think she'd
whang me.

And in a normaler company it would be the wardrobe room, too, but
costumery is my infantile name for it and the actors go along with my
little whims.

I don't mean to suggest our company is completely crackers. To get
as close to Broadway even as Central Park you got to have something.
But in spite of Sid's whip-cracking there is a comforting looseness about
its efficiency—people trade around the parts they play without fuss, the
bill may be changed a half hour before curtain without anybody getting
hysterics, nobody gets fired for eating garlic and breathing it in the leading
lady's face. In short, we're a team. Which is funny when you come to
think of it, as Sid and Miss Nefer and Bruce and Maudie are British
(Miss Nefer with a touch of Eurasian blood, I romance); Martin and Beau
and me are American (at least I *think* I am) while the rest come from
just everywhere.

Besides my costumery work, I fetch things and run inside errands and
help the actresses dress and the actors too. The dressing room's very
coeducational in a halfway respectable way. And every once in a while
Martin and I police up the whole place, me skittering about with dustcloth
and wastebasket, he wielding the scrub-brush and mop with such silent
grim efficiency that it always makes me nervous to get through and duck
back into the costumery to collect myself.

Yes, the costumery's a great place to quiet your nerves or improve
your mind or even dream your life away. But this time I couldn't have
been there eight minutes when Miss Nefer's Elizabeth-angry voice came
skirling, "Girl! Girl! Greta, where is my ruff with silver trim?" I laid
my hands on it in a flash and loped it to her, because Old Queen Liz
was known to slap even her Maids of Honor around a bit now and then
and Miss Nefer is a bear on getting into character—a real Paul Muni.

She was all made up now, I was happy to note, at least as far as her face went—I hate to see that spooky eight-spoked faint tattoo on her forehead (I've sometimes wondered if she got it acting in India or Egypt maybe).

Yes, she was already all made up. This time she'd been going extra heavy on the burrowing-into-character bit, I could tell right away, even if it was only for a hacked-out anachronistic prologue. She signed to me to help her dress without even looking at me, but as I got busy I looked at *her* eyes. They were so cold and sad and lonely (maybe because they were so far away from her eyebrows and temples and small tight mouth, and so shut away from each other by that ridge of nose) that I got the creeps. Then she began to murmur and sigh, very softly at first, then loudly enough so I got the sense of it.

"Cold, so cold," she said, still seeing things far away though her hands were working smoothly with mine. "Even a gallop hardly fires my blood. Never was such a Januarius, though there's no snow. Snow will not come, or tears. Yet my brain burns with the thought of Mary's death-warrant unsigned. There's my particular hell!—to doom, perchance, all future queens, or leave a hole for the Spaniard and the Pope to creep like old worms back into the sweet apple of England. Philip's tall black crooked ships massing like sea-going fortresses southaway—cragged castles set to march into the waves. Parma in the Lowlands! And all the while my bright young idiot gentlemen spurting out my treasure as if it were so much water, as if gold pieces were a glut of summer posies. Oh, alacka-night!"

And I thought, *Cry Iced!—that's sure going to be one tyrannosaur of a prologue. And how you'll ever shift back to being Lady Mack beats me. Greta, if this is what it takes to do just a bit part, you'd better give up your secret ambition of playing walk-ons some day when your nerves heal.*

She was really getting to me, you see, with that characterization. It was as if I'd managed to go out and take a walk and sat down in the park outside and heard the President talking to himself about the chances of war with Russia and realized he'd sat down on a bench with its back to mine and only a bush between. You see, here we were, two females undignifiedly twisted together, at the moment getting her into that crazy crouch-deep bodice that's like a big ice cream cone, and yet here at the same time was Queen Elizabeth the First of England, three hundred and umpty-ump years dead, coming back to life in a Central Park dressing room. It shook me.

She looked so much the part, you see—even without the red wig yet, just powdered pale makeup going back to a quarter of an inch from her own short dark bang combed and netted back tight. The age too. Miss Nefer can't be a day over forty—well, forty-two at most—but now she looked and talked and felt to my hands dressing her, well, at least a dozen older. I guess when Miss Nefer gets into character she does it with each molecule.

That age point fascinated me so much that I risked asking her a question. Probably I was figuring that she couldn't do me much damage because of the positions we happened to be in at the moment. You see, I'd started to lace her up and to do it right I had my knee against the tail of her spine.

"How old, I mean how young might your majesty be?" I asked her, innocently wonderingly like some dumb serving wench.

For a wonder she didn't somehow swing around and clout me, but only settled into character a little more deeply.

"Fifty-four winters," she replied dismally. " 'Tiz Januarius of Our Lord's year One Thousand and Five Hundred and Eighty and Seven. I sit cold in Greenwich, staring at the table where Mary's death warrant waits only my sign manual. If I send her to the block, I open the doors to future, less official regicides. But if I doom her not, Philip's armada will come inching up the Channel in a season, puffing smoke and shot, and my English Catholics, thinking only of Mary Regina, will rise and i' the end the Spaniard will have all. All history would alter. That must not be, even if I'm damned for it! And yet . . . and yet . . ."

A bright blue fly came buzzing along (the dressing room has *some* insect life) and slowly circled her head rather close, but she didn't even flicker her eyelids.

"I sit cold in Greenwich, going mad. Each afternoon I ride, praying for some mischance, some prodigy, to wash from my mind away the bloody question for some little space. It skills not what: a fire, a tree a-falling, Davison or e'en Eyes Leicester tumbled with his horse, an assassin's ball clipping the cold twigs by my ear, a maid crying rape, a wild boar charging with dipping tusks, news of the Spaniard at Thames' mouth or, more happily, a band of strolling actors setting forth some new comedy to charm the fancy or some great unheard-of tragedy to tear the heart—though that were somewhat much to hope for at this season and place, even if Southwark be close by."

The lacing was done. I stood back from her, and really she looked so much like Elizabeth painted by Gheeraerts or on the Great Seal of Ireland or something—though the ash-colored plush dress trimmed in silver and the little silver-edge ruff and the black-silver tinsel-cloth cloak lined with white plush hanging behind her looked most like a winter riding costume—and her face was such a pale frozen mask of Elizabeth's inward tortures, that I told myself, *Oh, I got to talk to Siddy again, he's made some big mistake, the lardy old lackwit, Miss Nefer just can't be figuring on playing in* Macbeth *tonight.*

As a matter of fact I was nerving myself to ask *her* all about it direct, though it was going to take some real nerve and maybe be risking broken bones or at least a flayed cheek to break the ice of that characterization, when who should come by calling the Fifteen Minutes but Martin. He looked so downright goofy that it took my mind off Nefer-in-character for all of eight seconds.

His Levi'd bottom half still looked like *The Lower Depths*. Martin is Village Stanislavsky rather than Ye Olde English Stage Traditions. But above that . . . well, all it really amounted to was that he was stripped to the waist and had shaved off the small high tuft of chest hair and was wearing a black wig that hung down in front of his shoulders in two big braids heavy with silver hoops and pins. But just the same those simple things, along with his tarpaper-solarium tan and habitual poker expression, made him look so like an American Indian that I thought, *Hey Zeus!—he's all set to play Hiawatha, or if he'd just cover up that straight-line chest, a frowny Pocahontas.* And I quick ran through what plays with Indian parts we do and could only come up with *The Fountain*.

I mutely goggled my question at him, wiggling my hands like guppy fins, but he brushed me off with a solemn mysterious smile and backed through the curtain. I thought, *nobody can explain this but Siddy*, and I followed Martin.

> *History does not move in one current,*
> *like the wind across bare seas,*
> *but in a thousand streams and eddies,*
> *like the wind over a broken landscape.*
> —CARY

II

The boys' half of the dressing room (two-thirds really) was bustling. There was the smell of spirit gum and Max Factor and just plain men. Several guys were getting dressed or un-, and Bruce was cussing Bloody-something because he'd just burnt his fingers unwinding from the neck of a hot electric bulb some crepe hair he'd wound there to dry after wetting and stretching it to turn it from crinkly to straight for his Banquo beard. Bruce is always getting to the theater late and trying shortcuts.

But I had eyes only for Sid. So help me, as soon as I saw him they bugged again. *Greta*, I told myself, *you're going to have to send Martin out to the drugstore for some anti-bug powder. "For the roaches, boy?" "No, for the eyes."*

Sid was made up and had his long mustaches and elf-locked Macbeth wig on—and his corset too. I could tell by the way his waist was sucked in before he saw me. But instead of dark kilts and that bronze-studded sweat-stained leather battle harness that lets him show off his beefy shoulders and the top half of his heavily furred chest—and which really does look great on Macbeth in the first act when he comes in straight from battle—but instead of that he was wearing, so help me, red tights cross-gartered with strips of gold-blue tinsel-cloth, a green doublet gold-trimmed and to top it a ruff, and he was trying to fit onto his front a bright silvered cuirass that would have looked just dandy maybe on one of the Pope's Swiss Guards.

I thought, *Siddy, Willy S. ought to reach out of his portrait there and bop you one on the koko for contemplating such a crazy-quilt desecration of just about his greatest and certainly his most atmospheric play.*

Just then he noticed me and hissed accusingly, "There thou art, slothy minx! Spring to and help stuff me into this monstrous chest-kettle."

"Siddy, what *is* all this?" I demanded as my hands automatically obeyed. "Are you going to play *Macbeth* for laughs, except maybe leaving the Porter a serious character? You think you're Red Skelton?"

"What monstrous brabble is this, you mad bitch?" he retorted, grunting as I bear-hugged his waist, shouldering the cuirass to squeeze it home.

"The clown costumes on all you men," I told him, for now I'd noticed that the others were in rainbow hues, Bruce a real eye-buster in yellow tights and violet doublet as he furiously bushed out and clipped crosswise sections of beard and slapped them on his chin gleaming brown with spirit gum. "I haven't seen any eight-inch polka-dots yet but I'm sure I will."

Suddenly a big grin split Siddy's face and he laughed out loud at me, though the laugh changed to a gasp as I strapped in the cuirass three notches too tight. When we'd got that adjusted he said, "I' faith thou slayest me, pretty witling. Did I not tell you this production is an experiment, a novelty? We shall but show *Macbeth* as it might have been costumed at the court of King James. In the clothes of the day, but gaudier, as was then the stage fashion. Hold, dove, I've somewhat for thee." He fumbled his grouch bag from under his doublet and dipped finger and thumb in it, and put in my palm a silver model of the Empire State Building, charm bracelet size, and one of the new Kennedy dimes.

As I squeezed those two and gloated my eyes on them, feeling securer and happier and friendlier for them though I didn't at the moment want to, I thought, *Well, Siddy's right about that, at least I've read they used to costume the plays that way, though I don't see how Shakespeare stood it. But it was dirty of them all not to tell me beforehand.*

But that's the way it is. Sometimes I'm the butt as well as the pet of the dressing room, and considering all the breaks I get I shouldn't mind. I smiled at Sid and went on tiptoes and necked out my head and kissed him on a powdery cheek just above an aromatic mustache. Then I wiped the smile off my face and said, "Okay, Siddy, play Macbeth as Little Lord Fauntleroy or Baby Snooks if you want to. I'll never squeak again. But the Elizabeth prologue's still an anachronism. And—this is the thing I came to tell you, Siddy—Miss Nefer's not getting ready for any measly prologue. She's set to play Queen Elizabeth all night and tomorrow morning too. Whatever you think, *she* doesn't know we're doing *Macbeth*. But who'll do Lady Mack if she doesn't? And Martin's not dressing for Malcolm, but for the Son of the Last of the Mohicans, I'd say. What's more—"

You know, something I said must have annoyed Sid, for he changed his mood again in a flash. "Shut your jaw, you crook-brained cat, and begone!" he snarled at me. "Here's curtain time close upon us, and you come like a wittol scattering your mad questions like the crazed Ophelia her flowers. Begone, I say!"

"Yessir," I whipped out softly. I skittered off toward the door to the stage, because that was the easiest direction. I figured I could do with a breath of less grease-painty air. Then, "Oh, Greta," I heard Martin call nicely.

He'd changed his Levi's for black tights, and was stepping into and pulling up around him a very familiar dress, dark green and embroidered with silver and stage-rubies. He'd safety-pinned a folded towel around his chest—to make a bosom of sorts, I realized.

He armed into the sleeves and turned his back to me. "Hook me up, would you?" he entreated.

Then it hit me. They had no actresses in Shakespeare's day, they used boys. And the dark green dress was so familiar to me because—

"Martin," I said, halfway up the hooks and working fast—Miss Nefer's costume fitted him fine. "You're going to play—?"

"Lady Macbeth, yes," he finished for me. "Wish me courage, will you, Greta? Nobody else seems to think I need it."

I punched him half-heartedly in the rear. Then, as I fastened the last hooks, my eyes topped his shoulder and I looked at our faces side by side in the mirror of his dressing table. His, in spite of the female edging and him being at least eight years younger than me, I think, looked wise, poised, infinitely resourceful with power in reserve, very very real, while mine looked like that of a bewildered and characterless child ghost about to scatter into air—and the edges of my charcoal sweater and skirt, contrasting with his strong colors, didn't dispel that last illusion.

"Oh, by the way, Greta," he said, "I picked up a copy of *The Village Times* for you. There's a thumbnail review of our *Measure for Measure*, though it mentions no names, darn it. It's around here somewhere . . ."

But I was already hurrying on. Oh, it was logical enough to have Martin playing Mrs. Macbeth in a production styled to Shakespeare's own times (though pedantically over-authentic, I'd have thought) and it really did answer all my questions, even why Miss Nefer could sink herself wholly in Elizabeth tonight if she wanted to. But it meant that I must be missing so much of what was going on right around me, in spite of spending 24 hours a day in the dressing room, or at most in the small adjoining john or in the wings of the stage just outside the dressing room door, that it scared me. Siddy telling everybody, *"Macbeth* tonight in Elizabethan costume, boys and girls," sure, that I could have missed—though you'd have thought he'd have asked my help on the costumes.

But Martin getting up in Mrs. Mack. Why, someone must have held the part on him twenty-eight times, cueing him, while he got the lines. And there must have been at least a couple of run-through rehearsals to make sure he had all the business and stage movements down pat, and Sid and Martin would have been doing their big scenes every backstage minute they could spare with Sid yelling, "Witling! Think'st *that's* a wifely buss?" and Martin would have been droning his lines last time he scrubbed and mopped . . .

Greta, they're hiding things from you, I told myself.

Maybe there was a 25th hour nobody had told me about yet when they did all the things they didn't tell me about.

Maybe they were things they didn't dare tell me because of my top-story weakness.

I felt a cold draft and shivered and I realized I was at the door to the stage.

I should explain that our stage is rather an unusual one, in that it can face two ways, with the drops and set pieces and lighting all capable of being switched around completely. To your left, as you look out the dressing-room door, is an open-air theater, or rather an open-air place for the audience—a large upward-sloping glade walled by thick tall trees and with benches for over two thousand people. On that side the stage kind of merges into the grass and can be made to look part of it by a green groundcloth.

To your right is a big roofed auditorium with the same number of seats.

The whole thing grew out of the free summer Shakespeare performances in Central Park that they started back in the 1950's.

The Janus-stage idea is that in nice weather you can have the audience outdoors, but if it rains or there's a cold snap, or if you want to play all winter without a single break, as we've been doing, then you can put your audience in the auditorium. In that case, a big accordion-pleated wall shuts off the out of doors and keeps the wind from blowing your backdrop, which is on that side, of course, when the auditorium's in use.

Tonight the stage was set up to face the outdoors, although that draft felt mighty chilly.

I hesitated, as I always do at the door to the stage—though it wasn't the actual stage lying just ahead of me, but only backstage, the wings. You see, I always have to fight the feeling that if I go out the dressing room door, go out just eight steps, the world will change while I'm out there and I'll never be able to get back. It won't be New York City any more, but Chicago or Mars or Algiers or Atlanta, Georgia, or Atlantis

or Hell and I'll never be able to get back to that lovely warm womb
with all the jolly boys and girls and all the costumes smelling like autumn
leaves.

Or, especially when there's a cold breeze blowing, I'm afraid that *I'll*
change, that I'll grow wrinkled and old in eight footsteps, or shrink down
to the witless blob of a baby, or forget altogether who I am—

—or, it occurred to me for the first time now, *remember* who I am.
Which might be even worse.

Maybe that's what I'm afraid of.

I took a step back. I noticed something new just beside the door: a
high-legged, short-keyboard piano. Then I saw that the legs were those
of a table. The piano was just a box with yellowed keys. Spinet? Harpsi-
chord?

"Five minutes, everybody," Martin quietly called out behind me.

I took hold of myself. *Greta*, I told myself—also for the first time—
*you know that some day you're really going to have to face this thing,
and not just for a quick dip out and back either. Better get in some
practice.*

I stepped through the door.

Beau and Doc were already out there, made up and in costume for
Ross and King Duncan. They were discreetly peering past the wings at
the gathering audience. Or at the place where the audience ought to
be gathering, at any rate—sometimes the movies and girlie shows and
brain-heavy beatnik brouhahas outdraw us altogether. Their costumes
were the same kooky colorful ones as the others'. Doc had a mock-ermine
robe and a huge gilt papier-mâché crown. Beau was carrying a ragged
black robe and hood over his left arm—he doubles the First Witch.

As I came up behind them, making no noise in my black sneakers, I
heard Beau say, "I see some rude fellows from the City approaching. I
was hoping we wouldn't get any of those. How should they scent us
out?"

Brother, I thought, *where do you expect them to come from if not
the City? Central Park is bounded on three sides by Manhattan Island
and on the fourth by the Eighth Avenue Subway. And Brooklyn and
Bronx boys have got pretty sharp scenters. And what's it get you insulting
the woiking and non-woiking people of the woild's greatest metropolis?
Be grateful for any audience you get, boy.*

But I suppose Beau Lassiter considers anybody from north of Vicksburg
a "rude fellow" and is always waiting for the day when the entire audience
will arrive in carriage and democrat wagons.

Doc replied, holding down his white beard and heavy on the mongrel
Russo-German accent he miraculously manages to suppress on stage: "Vot
does it matter? Ve don't convinze zem, ve don't convinze nobody. *Ni-
chevo.*"

Maybe, I thought, *Doc shares my doubts about making Macbeth plausible in rainbow pants.*

Still unobserved by them, I looked between their shoulders and got the first of my shocks.

It wasn't night at all, but afternoon. A dark cold lowering afternoon, admittedly. But afternoon all the same.

Sure, between shows I sometimes forget whether it's day or night, living inside like I do. But getting matinees and evening performances mixed is something else again.

It also seemed to me, although Beau was leaning in now and I couldn't see so well, that the glade was smaller than it should be, the trees closer to us and more irregular, and I couldn't see the benches. That was Shock Two.

Beau said anxiously, glancing at his wrist, "I wonder what's holding up the Queen?"

Although I was busy keeping up nerve-pressure against the shocks, I managed to think, *So he knows about Siddy's stupid Queen Elizabeth prologue too. But of course he would. It's only me they keep in the dark. If he's so smart he ought to remember that Miss Nefer is always the last person on stage, even when she opens the play.*

And then I thought I heard, through the trees, the distant drumming of horses' hoofs and the sound of a horn.

Now they do have horseback riding in Central Park and you can hear auto horns there, but the hoofbeats don't drum that wild way. And there aren't so many riding together. And no auto horn I ever heard gave out with that sweet yet imperious *ta-ta-ta-TA*.

I must have squeaked or something, because Beau and Doc turned around quickly, blocking my view, their expressions half angry, half anxious.

I turned too and ran for the dressing room, for I could feel one of my mind-wavery fits coming on. At the last second it had seemed to me that the scenery was getting skimpier, hardly more than thin trees and bushes itself, and underfoot feeling more like ground than a ground cloth, and overhead not theater roof but gray sky. *Shock Three and you're out, Gerta,* my umpire was calling.

I made it through the dressing room door and nothing there was wavering or dissolving, praised be Pan. Just Martin standing with his back to me, alert, alive, poised like a cat inside that green dress, the prompt book in his right hand with a finger in it, and from his left hand long black tatters swinging—telling me he'd still be doubling Second Witch. And he was hissing, "Places, please, everybody. On stage!"

With a sweep of silver and ash-colored plush, Miss Nefer came past him, for once leading the last-minute hurry to the stage. She had on the dark red wig now. For me that crowned her characterization. It made me remember her saying, "My brain burns." I ducked aside as if she were majesty incarnate.

And then she didn't break her own precedent. She stopped at the new thing beside the door and poised her long white skinny fingers over the yellowed keys, and suddenly I remembered what it was called: a virginals.

She stared down at it fiercely, evilly, like a witch planning an enchantment. Her face got the secret fiendish look that, I told myself, the real Elizabeth would have had ordering the deaths of Ballard and Babington, or plotting with Drake (for all they say she didn't) one of his raids, that long long forefinger tracing crooked courses through a crabbedly drawn map of the Indies and she smiling at the dots of cities that would burn.

Then all her eight fingers came flickering down and the strings inside the virginals began to twang and hum with a high-pitched rendering of Grieg's "In the Hall of the Mountain King."

Then as Sid and Bruce and Martin rushed past me, along with a black swooping that was Maud already robed and hooded for Third Witch, I beat it for my sleeping closet like Peer Gynt himself dashing across the mountainside away from the cave of the Troll King, who only wanted to make tiny slits in his eyeballs so that forever afterwards he'd see reality just a little differently. And as I ran, the master-anachronism of that menacing mad march music was shrilling in my ears.

> *Sound a dumbe shew. Enter*
> *the three fatall sisters,*
> *with a rocke, a threed,*
> *and a pair of sheeres.*
>
> —OLD PLAY

III

My sleeping closet is just a cot at the back end of the girls' third of the dressing room, with a three-panel screen to make it private.

When I sleep I hang my outside clothes on the screen, which is pasted and thumbtacked all over with the New York City stuff that gives me security: theater programs and restaurant menus, clippings from the *Times* and the *Mirror,* a torn-out picture of the United Nations building with a hundred tiny gay paper flags pasted around it, and hanging in an old hairnet a home-run baseball autographed by Willie Mays. Things like that.

Right now I was jumping my eyes over that stuff, asking it to keep me located and make me safe, as I lay on my cot in my clothes with my knees drawn up and my fingers over my ears so the louder lines from the play wouldn't be able to come nosing back around the trunks and tables and bright-lit mirrors and find me. Generally I like to listen to them, even if they're sort of sepulchral and drained of overtones by their crooked trip. But they're always tense-making. And tonight (I mean this afternoon)—no!

It's funny I should find security in mementos of a city I daren't go out into—no, not even for a stroll through Central Park, though I know it from the Pond to Harlem Meer—the Met Museum, the Menagerie, the Ramble, the Great Lawn, Cleopatra's Needle and all the rest. But that's the way it is. Maybe I'm like Jonah in the whale, reluctant to go outside because the whale's a terrible monster that's awful scary to look in the face and might really damage you gulping you a second time, yet reassured to know you're living in the stomach of that particular monster and not a seventeen tentacled one from the fifth planet of Aldebaran.

It's really true, you see, about me actually living in the dressing room. The boys bring me meals: coffee in cardboard cylinders and doughnuts in little brown grease-spotted paper sacks and malts and hamburgers and apples and little pizzas, and Maud brings me raw vegetables—carrots and parsnips and little onions and such, and watches to make sure I exercise my molars grinding them and get my vitamins. I take spit-baths in the little john. Architects don't seem to think actors ever take baths, even when they're browned themselves all over playing Pindarus the Parthian in *Julius Caesar.* And all my shut-eye is caught on this little cot in the twilight of my NYC screen.

You'd think I'd be terrified being alone in the dressing room during the wee and morning hours, let alone trying to sleep then, but that isn't the way it works out. For one thing, there's apt to be someone sleeping in too. Maudie especially. And it's my favorite time too for costume-mending and reading the *Variorum* and other books, and for just plain way-out dreaming. You see, the dressing room is the one place I really do feel safe. Whatever is out there in New York that terrorizes me, I'm pretty confident that it can never get in here.

Besides that, there's a great big bolt on the inside of the dressing room door that I throw whenever I'm all alone after the show. Next day they buzz for me to open it.

It worried me a bit at first and I had asked Sid, "But what if I'm so deep asleep I don't hear and you have to get in fast?" and he had replied, "Sweetling, a word in your ear: our own Beauregard Lassiter is the prettiest picklock unjailed since Jimmy Valentine and Jimmy Dale. I'll not ask where he learned his trade, but 'tis sober truth, upon my honor."

And Beau had confirmed this with a courtly bow, murmuring, "At your service, Miss Greta."

"How do you jigger a big iron bolt through a three-inch door that fits like Maudie's tights?" I wanted to know.

"He carries lodestones of great power and divers subtle tools," Sid had explained for him.

I don't know how they work it so that some Traverse-Three cop or park official doesn't find out about me and raise a stink. Maybe Sid just throws a little more of the temperament he uses to keep most outsiders out of the dressing room. We sure don't get any janitors or scrubwomen, as Martin and I know only too well. More likely he squares someone. I do get the impression all the company's gone a little way out on a limb letting me stay here—that the directors of our theater wouldn't like it if they found out about me.

In fact, the actors are all so good about helping me and putting up with my antics (though they have their own, Danu digs!) that I sometimes think I must be related to one of them—a distant cousin or sister-in-law (or wife, my God!), because I've checked our faces side by side in the mirrors often enough and I can't find any striking family resemblances. Or maybe I was even an actress in the company. The least important one. Playing the tiniest roles like Lucius in *Caesar* and Bianca in *Othello* and one of the little princes in *Dick the Three Eyes* and Fleance and the Gentlewoman in *Macbeth*, though me doing even that much acting strikes me to laugh.

But whatever I am in that direction—if I'm anything—not one of the actors has told me a word about it or dropped the least hint. Not even when I beg them to tell me or try to trick them into it, presumably because it might revive the shock that gave me agoraphobia and amnesia in the first place, and maybe this time knock out my entire mind or at least smash the new mouse-in-a-hole consciousness I've made for myself.

I guess they must have got by themselves a year ago and talked me over and decided my best chance for cure or for just bumping along half happily was staying in the dressing room rather than being sent home (funny, could I have another?) or to a mental hospital. And then they must have been cocky enough about their amateur psychiatry and interested enough in me (the White Horse knows why) to go ahead with a program almost any psychiatrist would be bound to yike at.

I got so worried about the setup once and about the risks they might be running that, gritting down my dread of the idea, I said to Sid, "Siddy, shouldn't I see a doctor?"

He looked at me solemnly for a couple of seconds and then said, "Sure, why not? Go talk to Doc right now," tipping a thumb toward Doc Pyeskov, who was just sneaking back into the bottom of his makeup box what looked like a half pint from the flash I got. I did, incidentally. Doc explained to me Kraepelin's classification of the psychoses, muttering, as he absentmindedly fondled my wrist, that in a year or two he'd be a good illustration of Korsakov's Syndrome.

They've all been pretty darn good to me in their kooky ways, the actors have. Not one of them has tried to take advantage of my situation to extort anything out of me, beyond asking me to sew on a button or polish some boots or at worst clean the wash bowl. Not one of the boys has made a pass I didn't at least seem to invite. And when my crush on Sid was at its worst he shouldered me off by getting polite—something he only is to strangers. On the rebound I hit Beau, who treated me like a real Southern gentleman.

All this for a stupid little waif, whom anyone but a gang of sentimental actors would have sent to Bellevue without a second thought or feeling. For, to get disgustingly realistic, my most plausible theory of me is that I'm a stage-struck girl from Iowa who saw her twenties slipping away and her sanity too, and made the dash to Greenwich Village, and went so ape on Shakespeare after seeing her first performance in Central Park that she kept going back there night after night (Christopher Street, Penn Station, Times Square, Columbus Circle—see?) and hung around the stage door, so mousy but open-mouthed that the actors made a pet of her.

And then something very nasty happened to her, either down at the Village or in a dark corner of the Park. Something so nasty that it blew the top of her head right off. And she ran to the only people and place where she felt she could ever again feel safe. And she showed them the top of her head with its singed hair and its jagged ring of skull and they took pity.

My least plausible theory of me, but the one I like the most, is that I was born in the dressing room, cradled in the top of a flat theatrical trunk with my ears full of Shakespeare's lines before I ever said "Mama," let alone lamped a TV; hush-walked when I cried by whoever was off stage, old props my first toys, trying to eat crepe hair my first indiscretion, sticks of grease-paint my first crayons. You know, I really wouldn't be bothered by crazy fears about New York changing and the dressing room shifting around in space and time, if I could be sure I'd always be able to stay in it and that the same sweet guys and gals would always be with me and that the shows would always go on.

This show was sure going on, it suddenly hit me, for I'd let my fingers slip off my ears as I sentimentalized and wish-dreamed and I heard, muted by the length and stuff of the dressing room, the slow beat of a drum and then a drum note in Maudie's voice taking up that beat as she warned the other two witches, "A drum, a drum! Macbeth doth come."

Why, I'd not only missed Sid's history-making and -breaking Queen Elizabeth prologue (kicking myself that I had, now it was over), I'd also missed the short witch scene with its famous "Fair is foul and foul is fair," the Bloody Sergeant scene where Duncan hears about Macbeth's victory, and we were well into the second witch scene, the one on the blasted heath where Macbeth gets it predicted to him he'll be king after Duncan and is tempted to speculate about hurrying up the process.

I sat up. I did hesitate a minute then, my fingers going back toward my ears, because *Macbeth* is specially tense-making and when I've had one of my mind-wavery fits I feel weak for a while and things are blurry and uncertain. Maybe I'd better take a couple of the barbiturate sleeping pills Maudie manages to get for me and—but *No, Greta,* I told myself, *you want to watch this show, you want to see how they do in those crazy costumes. You especially want to see how Martin makes out. He'd never forgive you if you didn't.*

So I walked to the other end of the empty dressing room, moving quite slowly and touching the edges here and there, the words of the play getting louder all the time. By the time I got to the door Bruce-Banquo was saying to the witches, "If you can look into the seeds of time, And say which grain will grow and which will not"—those lines that stir anyone's imagination with their veiled vision of the universe.

The overall lighting was a little dim (afternoon fading already?—a *late* matinee?) and the stage lights flickery and the scenery still a little spectral-flimsy. Oh, my mind-wavery fits can be. lulus! But I concentrated on the actors, watching them through the entrance-gaps in the wings. They were solid enough.

Giving a solid performance, too, as I decided after watching that scene through and the one after it where Duncan congratulates Macbeth, with never a pause between the two scenes in true Elizabethan style. Nobody was laughing at the colorful costumes. After a while I began to accept them myself.

Oh, it was a different *Macbeth* than our company usually does. Louder and faster, with shorter pauses between speeches, the blank verse at times approaching a chant. But it had a lot of real guts and everybody was just throwing themselves into it, Sid especially.

The first Lady Macbeth scene came. Without exactly realizing it I moved forward to where I'd been when I got my three shocks. Martin is so intent on his career and making good that he has me the same way about it.

The Thaness started off, as she always does, toward the opposite side of the stage and facing a little away from me. Then she moved a step and looked down at the stage-parchment letter in her hands and began to read it, though there was nothing on it but scribble, and my heart sank because the voice I heard was Miss Nefer's. I thought (and almost said out loud) *Oh, dammit, he funked out, or Sid decided at the last minute he couldn't trust him with the part. Whoever got Miss Nefer out of the ice cream cone in time?*

Then she swung around and I saw that no, my God, it *was* Martin, no mistaking. He'd been using her voice. When a person first does a part, especially getting up in it without much rehearsing, he's bound to copy the actor he's been hearing doing it. And as I listened on, I realized it was fundamentally Martin's own voice pitched a trifle high, only some of the intonations and rhythms were Miss Nefer's. He was showing a lot of feeling and intensity too and real Martin-type poise. *You're off to a great start, kid,* I cheered inwardly. *Keep it up!*

Just then I looked toward the audience. Once again I almost squeaked out loud. For out there, close to the stage, in the very middle of the reserve section, was a carpet spread out. And sitting in the middle of it on some sort of little chair, with what looked like two charcoal braziers smoking to either side of her, was Miss Nefer with a string of extras in Elizabethan hats with cloaks pulled around them.

For a second it really threw me because it reminded me of the things I'd seen or thought I'd seen the couple of times I'd sneaked a peek through the curtain-hole at the audience in the indoor auditorium.

It hardly threw me for more than a second, though, because I remembered that the characters who speak Shakespeare's prologues often stay on stage and sometimes kind of join the audience and even comment on the play from time to time—Christopher Sly and attendant lords in *The Shrew*, for one. Sid had just copied and in his usual style laid it on thick.

Well, bully for you, Siddy, I thought, *I'm sure the witless New York groundlings will be thrilled to their cold little toes knowing they're sitting in the same audience as Good Queen Liz and attendant courtiers. And as for you, Miss Nefer,* I added a shade invidiously, *you just keep on sitting cold in Central Park, warmed by dry-ice smoke from braziers, and keep your mouth shut and everything'll be fine. I'm sincerely glad you'll be able to be Queen Elizabeth all night long. Just so long as you don't try to steal the scene from Martin and the rest of the cast, and the real play.*

I suppose that camp chair will get a little uncomfortable by the time the Fifth Act comes tramping along to that drumbeat, but I'm sure you're so much in character you'll never feel it.

One thing though: just don't scare me again pretending to work witchcraft—with a virginals or any other way.

Okay?

Swell.

Me, now, I'm going to watch the play.

> *. . . to dream of new dimensions,*
> *Cheating checkmate*
> *by painting the king's robe*
> *So that he slides like a queen;*
> *—GRAVES*

IV

I swung back to the play just at the moment Lady Mack soliloquizes, "Come to my woman's breasts. And take my milk for gall, you murdering ministers." Although I knew it was just folded towel Martin was touching with his fingertips as he lifted them to the top half of his green bodice, I got carried away, he made it so real. I decided boys can play girls better than people think. Maybe they should do it a little more often, and girls play boys too.

Then Sid-Macbeth came back to his wife from the wars, looking triumphant but scared because the murder-idea's started to smoulder in him,
and she got busy fanning the blaze like any other good little *hausfrau*
intent on her husband rising in the company and knowing that she's
the power behind him and that when there are promotions someone's
always got to get the axe. Sid and Martin made this charming little domestic scene so natural yet gutsy too that I wanted to shout hooray. Even
Sid clutching Martin to that ridiculous pot-chested cuirass didn't have
one note of horseplay in it. Their bodies spoke. It was the McCoy.

After that, the play began to get real good, the fast tempo and exaggerated facial expressions actually helping it. By the time the Dagger Scene
came along I was digging my fingernails into my sweaty palms. Which
was a good thing—my eating up the play, I mean—because it kept me
from looking at the audience again, even taking a fast peek. As you've
gathered, audiences bug me. All those people out there in the shadows,
watching the actors in the light, all those silent voyeurs as Bruce calls
them. Why, they might be anything. And sometimes (to my mind-wavery
sorrow) I think they are. Maybe crouching in the dark out there, hiding
among the others, is the one who did the nasty thing to me that tore
off the top of my head.

Anyhow, if I so much as glance at the audience, I begin to get ideas
about it—and sometimes even if I don't, as just at this moment I thought
I heard horses restlessly pawing hard ground and one whinny, though
that was shut off fast. *Krishna kressed us!* I thought. *Skiddy can't have
hired horses for Nefer-Elizabeth much as he's a circus man at heart.
We don't have that kind of money. Besides—*
But just then Sid-Macbeth gasped as if he were sucking in a bucket
of air. He'd shed the cuirass, fortunately. He said, "Is this a dagger which
I see before me, The handle toward my hand?" and the play hooked
me again, and I had no time to think about or listen for anything else.
Most of the offstage actors were on the other side of the stage, as that's
where they make their exits and entrances at this point in the Second
Act. I stood alone in the wings, watching the play like a bug, frightened
only of the horrors Shakespeare had in mind when he wrote it.

Yes, the play was going great. The Dagger Scene was terrif where
Duncan gets murdered offstage, and so was the part afterwards where
hysteria mounts as the crime's discovered.

But just at this point I began to catch notes I didn't like. Twice someone
was late on entrance and came on as if shot from a cannon. And three
times at least Sid had to throw someone a line when they blew up—in
the clutches Sid's better than any prompt book. It began to look as if
the play were getting out of control, maybe because the new tempo
was so hot.

But they got through the Murder Scene okay. As they came trooping
off, yelling "Well contented," most of them on my side for a change, I

went for Sid with a towel. He always sweats like a pig in the Murder Scene. I mopped his neck and shoved the towel up under his doublet to catch the dripping armpits.

Meanwhile he was fumbling around on a narrow table where they lay props and costumes for quick changes. Suddenly he dug his fingers into my shoulder, enough to catch my attention at this point, meaning I'd show bruises tomorrow, and yelled at me under his breath, "An you love me, our crowns and robes. Presto!"

I was off like a flash to the costumery. There were Mr. and Mrs. Mack's king-and-queen robes and stuff hanging and sitting just where I knew they'd have to be.

I snatched them up, thinking, *Boy, they made a mistake when they didn't tell about this special performance,* and I started back like Flash Two.

As I shot out the dressing room door the theater was very quiet. There's a short low-pitched scene on stage then, to give the audience a breather. I heard Miss Nefer say loudly (it had to be loud to get to me from even the front of the audience): " 'Tis a good bloody play, Eyes," and some voice I didn't recognize reply a bit grudgingly, "There's meat in it and some poetry too, though rough-wrought." She went on, still as loudly as if she owned the theater, " 'Twill make Master Kyd bite his nails with jealousy—ha, ha!"

Ha, ha yourself, you scene-stealing witch, I thought, as I helped Sid and then Martin on with their royal outer duds. But at the same time I knew Sid must have written those lines himself to go along with his prologue. They had the unmistakable rough-wrought Lessingham touch. Did he really expect the audience to make anything of that reference to Shakespeare's predecessor Thomas Kyd of *The Spanish Tragedy* and the lost *Hamlet?* And if they knew enough to spot that, wouldn't they be bound to realize the whole Elizabeth-Macbeth tie-up was anachronistic? But when Sid gets an inspiration he can be very bull-headed.

Just then, while Bruce-Banquo was speaking his broody low soliloquy on stage, Miss Nefer cut in again loudly with, "Aye, Eyes, a good bloody play. Yet somehow, methinks—I know not how—I've heard it before." Whereupon Sid grabbed Martin by the wrist and hissed, "Did'st hear? Oh, I like not that," and I thought, *Oh-ho, so now she's beginning to ad-lib.*

Well, right away they all went on stage with a flourish, Sid and Martin crowned and hand in hand. The play got going strong again. But there were still those edge-of-control undercurrents and I began to be more uneasy than caught up, and I had to stare consciously at the actors to keep off a wavery-fit.

Other things began to bother me too, such as all the doubling.

Macbeth's a great play for doubling. For instance, anyone except Macbeth or Banquo can double one of the Three Witches—or one of the Three Murderers for that matter. Normally we double at least one or two of the Witches and Murderers, but this performance there'd been more multiple-parting than I'd ever seen. Doc had whipped off his Duncan beard and thrown on a brown smock and hood to play the Porter with his normal bottle-roughened accents. Well, a drunk impersonating a drunk, pretty appropriate. But Bruce was doing the next-door-to-impossible double of Banquo and Macduff, using a ringing tenor voice for the latter and wearing in the murder scene a helmet with dropped visor to hid his Banquo beard. He'd be able to tear it off, of course, after the Murderers got Banquo and he'd made his brief appearance as a bloodied-up ghost in the Banquet Scene. I asked myself, *My God, has Siddy got all the other actors out in front playing courtiers to Elizabeth-Nefer? Wasting them that way? The whore-son rogue's gone nuts!*

But really it was plain frightening, all that frantic doubling and tripling with its suggestion that the play (and the company too, Freya forfend) was becoming a rickety patchwork illusion with everybody racing around faster and faster to hide the holes. And the scenery-wavery stuff and the warped Park-sounds were scary too. I was actually shivering by the time Sid got to: "Light thickens; and the crow Makes wing to the rooky wood: Good things of day begin to droop and drowse; Whiles night's black agents to their preys do rouse." Those graveyard lines didn't help my nerves any, of course. Nor did thinking I heard Nefer-Elizabeth say from the audience, rather softly for her this time, "Eyes, I have heard that speech, I know not where. Think you 'tiz stolen?"

Greta, I told myself, *you need a Miltown before the crow makes wing through your kooky head.*

I turned to go and fetch me one from my closet. And stopped dead.

Just behind me, pacing back and forth like an ash-colored tiger in the gloomy wings, looking daggers at the audience every time she turned at that end of her invisible cage, but ignoring me completely, was Miss Nefer in the Elizabeth wig and rig.

Well, I suppose I should have said to myself, *Greta, you imagined that last loud whisper from the audience. Miss Nefer's simply unkinked herself, waved a hand to the real audience and come backstage. Maybe Sid just had her out there for the first half of the play. Or maybe she just couldn't stand watching Martin give such a bang-up performance in her part of Lady Mack.*

Yes, maybe I should have told myself something like that, but somehow all I could think then—and I thought it with a steady mounting shiver—was, *We got two Elizabeths. This one is our witch Nefer. I know. I dressed her. And I know that devil-look from the virginals. But if this is our Elizabeth, the company Elizabeth, the stage Elizabeth . . . who's the other?*

And because I didn't dare to let myself think of the answer to that question, I dodged around the invisible cage that the ash-colored skirt seemed to ripple against as the Tiger Queen turned and I ran into the dressing room, my only thought to get behind my New York City Screen.

> *Even little things are turning out to be great things*
> *and becoming intensely interesting.*
> *Have you ever thought about the properties of numbers?*
> —THE MAIDEN

V

Lying on my cot, my eyes crosswise to the printing, I looked from a pink Algonquin menu to a pale green New Amsterdam program, with a tiny doll of Father Knickerbocker dangling between them on a yellow thread. Really they weren't covering up much of anything. A ghostly hole an inch and a half across seemed to char itself in the program. As if my eye were right up against it, I saw in vivid memory what I'd seen the two times I'd dared a peek through the hole in the curtain: a bevy of ladies in masks and Nell Gwyn dresses and men in King Charles knee-breeches and long curled hair, and the second time a bunch of people and creatures just wild: all sorts and colors of clothes, humans with hoofs for feet and antennae springing from their foreheads, furry and feathery things that had more arms than two and in one case that many heads— as if they were dressed up in our *Tempest, Peer Gynt* and *Insect People* costumes and some more besides.

Naturally I'd had mind-wavery fits both times. Afterwards Sid had wagged a finger at me and explained that on those two nights we'd been giving performances for people who'd arranged a costume theater-party and been going to attend a masquerade ball, and 'zounds, when would I learn to guard my half-patched pate?

I don't know, I guess never, I answered now, quick looking at a Giants pennant, a Korvette ad, a map of Central Park, my Willie Mays baseball and a Radio City tour ticket. That was eight items I'd looked at this trip without feeling any inward improvement. They weren't reassuring me at all.

The blue fly came slowly buzzing down over my screen and I asked it, "What are *you* looking for? A spider?" when what should I hear coming back through the dressing room straight toward my sleeping closet but Miss Nefer's footsteps. No one else walks that way.

She's going to do something to you, Greta, I thought. *She's the maniac in the company. She's the one who terrorized you with the boning knife in the shrubbery, or sicked the giant tarantula on you at the dark end of the subway platform, or whatever it was, and the others are covering up for. She's going to smile the devil-smile and weave those white twig-fingers at you, all eight of them. And Birnam Wood'll come to Dunsinane and you'll be burnt at the stake by men in armor or drawn and quartered by eight-legged monkeys that talk or torn apart by wild centaurs or whirled through the roof to the moon without being dressed for it or sent burrowing into the past to stifle in Iowa 1948 or Egypt 4,008 B.C. The screen won't keep her out.*

Then a head of hair pushed over the screen. But it was black-bound-with-silver, Brahma bless us, and a moment later Martin was giving me one of his rare smiles.

I said, "Marty, do something for me. Don't ever use Miss Nefer's footsteps again. Her voice, okay, if you have to. But not the footsteps. Don't ask me why, just don't."

Martin came around and sat on the foot of my cot. My legs were already doubled up. He straightened out his blue-and-gold skirt and rested a hand on my black sneakers.

"Feeling a little wonky, Greta?" he asked. "Don't worry about me. Banquo's dead and so's his ghost. We've finished the Banquet Scene. I've got lots of time."

I just looked at him, queerly I guess. Then without lifting my head I asked him, "Martin, tell me the truth. Does the dressing room move around?"

I was talking so low that he hitched a little closer, not touching me anywhere else though.

"The Earth's whipping around the sun at 20 miles a second," he replied, "and the dressing room goes with it."

I shook my head, my cheek scrubbing the pillow. "I mean . . . shifting," I said. "By itself."

"How?" he asked.

"Well," I told him, "I've had this idea—it's just a sort of fancy, remember—that if you wanted to time-travel and, well, do things, you could hardly pick a more practical machine than a dressing room and sort of stage and half-theater attached, with actors to man it. Actors can fit in anywhere. They're used to learning new parts and wearing strange costumes. Heck, they're even used to traveling a lot. And if an actor's a bit strange nobody thinks anything of it—he's almost expected to be foreign, it's an asset to him.

"And a theater, well, a theater can spring up almost anywhere and nobody ask questions, except the zoning authorities and such and they can always be squared. Theaters come and go. It happens all the time. They're transitory. Yet theaters are crossroads, anonymous meeting places, anybody with a few bucks or sometimes nothing at all can go. And theaters attract important people, the sort of people you might want to do something to. Caesar was stabbed in a theater. Lincoln was shot in one. And . . ."

My voice trailed off. "A cute idea," he commented.

I reached down to his hand on my shoe and took hold of his middle finger as a baby might.

"Yeah," I said, "But, Martin, is it true?"

He asked me gravely, "What do you think?"

I didn't say anything.

"How would you like to work in a company like that?" he asked speculatively.

"I don't really know," I said.

He sat up straighter and his voice got brisk. "Well, all fantasy aside, how'd you like to work in this company?" he asked, lightly slapping my ankle. "On the stage, I mean. Sid thinks you're ready for some of the smaller parts. In fact, he asked me to put it to you. He thinks you never take him seriously."

"Pardon me while I gasp and glow," I said. Then, "Oh Marty, I can't really imagine myself doing the tiniest part."

"Me neither, eight months ago," he said. "Now, look. Lady Macbeth."

"But, Marty," I said, reaching for his finger again, "you haven't answered my question. About whether it's true."

"Oh that!" he said with a laugh, switching his hand to the other side. "Ask me something else."

"Okay," I said, "why am I bugged on the number eight? Because I'm permanently behind a private eight-ball?"

"Eight's a number with many properties," he said, suddenly as intently serious as he usually is. "The corners of a cube."

"You mean I'm a square?" I said. "Or just a brick? You know. 'She's a brick.' "

"But eight's most curious property," he continued with a frown, "is that lying on its side it signifies infinity. So eight erect is really—" and suddenly his made-up, naturally solemn face got a great glow of inspiration and devotion—"Infinity Arisen!"

Well, I don't know. You meet quite a few people in the theater who are bats on numerology, they use it to pick stage-names. But I'd never have guessed it of Martin. He always struck me as the skeptical, cynical type.

"I had another idea about eight," I said hesitatingly. "Spiders. That eight-legged asterisk on Miss Nefer's forehead—" I suppressed a shudder.

"You don't like her, do you?" he stated.

"I'm afraid of her," I said.

"You shouldn't be. She's a very great woman and tonight she's playing an infinitely more difficult part than I am. No, Greta," he went on as I started to protest, "believe me, you don't understand anything about it at this moment. Just as you don't understand about spiders, fearing them. They're the first to climb the rigging and to climb ashore too. They're the web-weavers, the line-throwers, the connectors, Siva and Kali united in love. They're the double mandala, the beginning and the end, infinity mustered and on the march—"

"They're also on my New York screen!" I squeaked, shrinking back across the cot a little and pointing at a tiny glinting silver-and-black thing mounting below my Willie-ball.

Martin gently caught its line on his finger and lifted it very close to his face. "Eight eyes too," he told me. Then, "Poor little god," he said and put it back.

"Marty? Marty?" Sid's desperate stage-whisper rasped the length of the dressing room.

Martin stood up. "Yes, Sid?"

Sid's voice stayed a whisper but went from desperate to ferocious. "You villainous elf-skin! Know you not the Cauldron Scene's been playing a hundred heartbeats? 'Tis 'most my entrance and we still mustering only two witches out of three! Oh, you knot-pated starveling!"

Before Sid had got much more than half of that out, Martin had slipped around the screen, raced the length of the dressing room, and I'd heard a lusty thwack as he went out the door. I couldn't help grinning, though with Martin racked by anxieties and reliefs over his first time as Lady Mack, it was easy to understand it slipping his mind that he was still doubling Second Witch.

> *I will vault credit and affect high pleasures*
> *Beyond death.*
>
> —FERDINAND

VI

I sat down where Martin had been, first pushing the screen far enough to the side for me to see the length of the dressing room and notice anyone coming through the door and any blurs moving behind the thin white curtain shutting off the boys' two-thirds.

I'd been going to think. But instead I just sat there, experiencing my body and the room around it, steadying myself or maybe readying myself. I couldn't tell which, but it was nothing to think about, only to feel. My heartbeat became a very faint, slow, solid throb. My spine straightened.

No one came in or went out. Distantly I heard Macbeth and the witches and the apparitions talk.

Once I looked at the New York Screen, but all the stuff there had grown stale. No protection, no nothing.

I reached down to my suitcase and from where I'd been going to get a Miltown I took a Dexedrine and popped it in my mouth. Then I started out, beginning to shake.

When I got to the end of the curtain I went around it to Sid's dressing table and asked Shakespeare, "Am I doing the right thing, Pop?" But he didn't answer me out of his portrait. He just looked sneaky-innocent like he knew a lot but wouldn't tell, and I found myself thinking of a little silver-framed photo Sid had used to keep there too of a cocky German-looking young actor with "Erich" autographed across it in white ink. At least I supposed he was an actor. He looked a little like Erich von Stroheim, but nicer yet somehow nastier too. The photo had used to upset me, I don't know why. Sid must have noticed it, for one day it was gone.

I thought of the tiny black-and-silver spider crawling across the remembered silver frame, and for some reason it gave me the cold creeps.

Well, this wasn't doing me any good, just making me feel dismal again, so I quick went out. In the door I had to slip around the actors coming back from the Cauldron Scene and the big bolt nicked my hip.

Outside Maud was peeling off her Third Witch stuff to reveal Lady Macduff beneath. She twitched me a grin.

"How's it going?" I asked.

"Okay, I guess," she shrugged. "What an audience! Noisy as highschool kids."

"How come Sid didn't have a boy do your part?" I asked.

"He goofed, I guess. But I've battened down my bosoms and I'm playing Mrs. Macduff as a boy."

"How does a girl do that in a dress?" I asked.

"She sits stiff and thinks pants," she said, handing me her witch robe. " 'Scuse me now. I got to find my children and go get murdered."

I'd moved a few steps nearer the stage when I felt the gentlest tug at my hip. I looked down and saw that a taut black thread from the bottom of my sweater connected me with the dressing room. It must have snagged on the big bolt and unraveled. I moved my body an inch or so, tugging it delicately to see what it felt like and I got the answers: Theseus's clew, a spider's line, an umbilicus.

I reached down close to my side and snapped it with my fingernails. The black thread leaped away. But the dressing room door didn't vanish, or the wings change, or the world end, and I didn't fall down.

After that I just stood there for quite a while, feeling my new freedom and steadiness, letting my body get used to it. I didn't do any thinking. I hardly bothered to study anything around me, though I did notice that there were more bushes and trees than set pieces, and that the flickery lightning was simply torches and that Queen Elizabeth was in (or back in) the audience. Sometimes letting your body get used to something is all you should do, or maybe can do.

And I did smell horse dung.

When the Lady Macduff Scene was over and the Chicken Scene well begun, I went back to the dressing room. Actors call it the Chicken Scene because Macduff weeps in it about "all my pretty chickens and their dam," meaning his kids and wife, being murdered "at one fell swoop" on orders of that chickenyard-raiding "hell-kite" Macbeth.

Inside the dressing room I steered down the boys' side. Doc was putting on an improbable-looking dark makeup for Macbeth's last faithful servant Seyton. He didn't seem as boozy-woozy as usual for Fourth Act, but just the same I stopped to help him get into a chain-mail shirt made of thick cord woven and silvered.

In the third chair beyond, Sid was sitting back with his corset loosened and critically surveying Martin, who'd now changed to a white wool nightgown that clung and draped beautifully, but not particularly enticingly, on him and his folded towel, which had slipped a bit.

From beside Sid's mirror, Shakespeare smiled out of his portrait at them like an intelligent big-headed bug.

Martin stood tall, spread his arms rather like a high priest, and intoned, *"Amici! Romani! Populares!"*

I nudged Doc. "What goes on now?" I whispered.

He turned a bleary eye on them. "I think they are rehearsing *Julius Caesar* in Latin." He shrugged. "It begins the oration of Antony."

"But why?" I asked. Sid does like to put every moment to use when the performance-fire is in people, but this project seemed pretty far afield—hyper-pedantic. Yet at the same time I felt my scalp shivering as if my mind were jumping with speculations just below the surface.

Doc shook his head and shrugged again.

Sid shoved a palm at Martin and roared softly, " 'Sdeath, boy, thou'rt not playing a Roman *statua* but a Roman! Loosen your knees and try again."

Then he saw me. Signing Martin to stop, he called, "Come hither, sweetling." I obeyed quickly. He gave me a fiendish grin and said, "Thou'st heard our proposal from Martin. What sayest thou, wench?"

This time the shiver was in my back. It felt good. I realized I was grinning back at him, and I knew what I'd been getting ready for the last twenty minutes.

"I'm on," I said. "Count me in the company."

Sid jumped up and grabbed me by the shoulders and hair and bussed me on both cheeks. It was a little like being bombed.

"Prodigious!" he cried. "Thou'lt play the Gentlewoman in the Sleep-walking Scene tonight. Martin, her costume! Now sweet wench, mark me well." His voice grew grave and old. "When was it she last walked?"

The new courage went out of me like water down a chute. "But Siddy, I can't start *tonight*," I protested, half pleading, half outraged.

"Tonight or never! 'Tis an emergency—we're short-handed." Again his voice changed. "When was it she last walked?"

"But Siddy, I don't *know* the part."

"You must. You've heard the play twenty times this year past. When was it she last walked?"

Martin was back and yanking down a blonde wig on my head and shoving my arms into a light gray robe.

"I've never studied *the lines,*" I squeaked at Sidney.

"Liar! I've watched your lips move a dozen nights when you watched the scene from the wings. Close your eyes, girl! Martin, unhand her. Close your eyes, girl, empty your mind, and listen, listen only. When was it she last walked?"

In the blackness I heard myself replying to that cue, first in a whisper, then more loudly, then full-throated but grave, "Since his majesty went into the field, I have seen her rise from her bed, throw her nightgown upon her, unlock her closet, take forth—"

"Bravissimo!" Siddy cried and bombed me again. Martin hugged his arm around my shoulders too, then quickly stooped to start hooking up my robe from the bottom.

"But that's only the first lines, Siddy," I protested.

"They're enough!"

"But Siddy, what if I blow up?" I asked.

"Keep your mind empty. You won't. Further, I'll be at your side, doubling the Doctor, to prompt you if you pause."

That ought to take care of two of me, I thought. Then something else struck me. "But Siddy," I quavered, "how do I play the Gentlewoman as a boy?"

"Boy?" he demanded wonderingly. "Play her without falling down flat on your face and I'll be past measure happy!" And he smacked me hard on the fanny.

Martin's fingers were darting at the next to the last hook. I stopped him and shoved my hand down the neck of my sweater and got hold of the subway token and the chain it was on and yanked. It burned my neck but the gold links parted. I started to throw it across the room, but instead I smiled at Siddy and dropped it in his palm.

"The Sleepwalking Scene!" Maud hissed insistently to us from the door.

> *I know death hath*
> *ten thousand several doors*
> *For men to take their exits,*
> *and 'tis found*
> *They go on such strange*
> *geometrical hinges,*
> *You may open them both*
> *ways.*
> —THE DUCHESS

VII

There is this about an actor on stage: he can *see* the audience but he can't *look* at them, unless he's a narrator or some sort of comic. I wasn't the first (Grendel groks!) and only scared to death of becoming the second as Siddy walked me out of the wings onto the stage, over the groundcloth that felt so much like ground, with a sort of interweaving policeman-grip on my left arm.

Sid was in a dark gray robe looking like some dismal kind of monk, his head so hooded for the Doctor that you couldn't see his face at all.

My skull was pulse-buzzing. My throat was squeezed dry. My heart was pounding. Below that my body was empty, squirmy, electricity-stung, yet with the feeling of wearing ice cold iron pants.

I heard as if from two million miles, "When was it she last walked?" and then an iron bell somewhere tolling the reply—I guess it had to be my voice coming up through my body from my iron pants: "Since his majesty went into the field—" and so on, until Martin had come on stage, stary-eyed, a white scarf tossed over the back of his long black wig and a flaring candle two inches thick gripped in his right hand and dripping wax on his wrist, and started to do Lady Mack's sleepwalking half-hinted confessions of the murders of Duncan and Banquo and Lady Macduff.

So here is what I saw then without looking, like a vivid scene that floats out in front of your mind in a reverie, hovering against a background of dark blur, and sort of flashes on and off as you think, or in my case act. All the time, remember, with Sid's hand hard on my wrist and me now and then tolling Shakespearean language out of some lightless store-house of memory I'd never known was there to belong to me.

There was a medium-size glade in a forest. Through the half-naked black branches shone a dark cold sky, like ashes of silver, early evening.

The glade had two horns, as it were, narrowing back to either side and going off through the forest. A chilly breeze was blowing out of them, almost enough to put out the candle. Its flame rippled.

Rather far back in the horn to my left, but not very far, were clumped two dozen or so men in dark cloaks they huddled around themselves. They wore brimmed tallish hats and pale stuff showing at their necks. Somehow I assumed that these men must be the "rude fellows from the City" I remembered Beau mentioning a million or so years ago. Although I couldn't see them very well, and didn't spend much time on them, there was one of them who had his hat off or excitedly pushed way back, showing a big pale forehead. Although that was all the conscious impression I had of his face, he seemed frighteningly familiar.

In the horn to my right, which was wider, were lined up about a dozen horses, with grooms holding tight every two of them, but throwing their heads back now and then as they strained against the reins, and stamping their front hooves restlessly. Oh, they frightened me, I tell you, that line of two-foot-long glossy-haired faces, writhing back their upper lips from teeth wide as piano keys, every horse of them looking as wild-eyed and evil as Fuseli's steed sticking its head through the drapes in his picture "The Nightmare."

To the center the trees came close to the stage. Just in front of them was Queen Elizabeth sitting on the chair on the spread carpet, just as I'd seen her out there before; only now I could see that the braziers were glowing and redly high-lighting her pale cheeks and dark red hair and the silver in her dress and cloak. She was looking at Martin—Lady Mack—most intently, her mouth grimaced tight, twisting her fingers together.

Standing rather close around her were a half dozen men with fancier hats and ruffs and wide-flaring riding gauntlets.

Then, through the trees and tall leafless bushes just behind Elizabeth, I saw an identical Elizabeth-face floating, only this one was smiling a demonic smile. The eyes were open very wide. Now and then the pupils darted rapid glances from side to side.

There was a sharp pain in my left wrist and Sid whisper-snarling at me, "Accustomed action!" out of the corner of his shadowed mouth.

I tolled on obediently, "It is an accustomed action with her, to seem thus washing her hands: I have known her continue in this a quarter of an hour."

Martin had set down the candle, which still flared and guttered, on a little high table so firm its thin legs must have been stabbed into the ground. And he was rubbing his hands together slowly, continually, tormentedly, trying to get rid of Duncan's blood which Mrs. Mack knows in her sleep is still there. And all the while as he did it, the agitation of the seated Elizabeth grew, the eyes flicking from side to side, hands writhing.

He got to the lines, "Here's the smell of blood still: all the perfumes of Arabia will not sweeten this little hand. Oh, oh, oh!"

As he wrung out those soft, tortured sighs, Elizabeth stood up from her chair and took a step forward. The courtiers moved toward her quickly, but not touching her, and she said loudly, " 'Tis the blood of Mary Stuart whereof she speaks—the pails of blood that will gush from her chopped neck. Oh, I cannot endure it!" And as she said that last, she suddenly turned about and strode back toward the trees, kicking out her ash-colored skirt. One of the courtiers turned with her and stooped toward her closely, whispering something. But although she paused a moment, all she said was, "Nay, Eyes, stop not the play, but follow me not! Nay, I say leave me, Leicester!" And she walked into the trees, he looking after her.

Then Sid was kicking my ankle and I was reciting something and Martin was taking up his candle again without looking at it saying with a drugged agitation, "To bed; to bed; there's knocking at the gate."

Elizabeth came walking out of the trees again, her head bowed. She couldn't have been in them ten seconds. Leicester hurried toward her, hand anxiously outstretched.

Martin moved offstage, torturedly yet softly wailing, "What's done cannot be undone."

Just then Elizabeth flicked aside Leicester's hand with playful contempt and looked up and she was smiling the devil-smile. A horse whinnied like a trumpeted snicker.

As Sid and I started our last few lines together I intoned mechanically, letting words freefall from my mind to my tongue. All this time I had been answering Lady Mack in my thoughts, *That's what you think, sister.*

> *God cannot effect that*
> *anything which is past*
> *should not have been.*
> *It is more impossible than*
> *rising the dead.*
> —SUMMA THEOLOGICA

VIII

The moment I was out of sight of the audience I broke away from Sid and ran to the dressing room. I flopped down on the first chair I saw, my head and arms trailed over its back, and I almost passed out. It wasn't a mind-wavery fit. Just normal faint.

I couldn't have been there long—well, not very long, though the battle-rattle and alarums of the last scene were echoing tinnily from the stage— when Bruce and Beau and Mark (who was playing Malcolm, Martin's usual main part) came in wearing their last-act stage-armor and carrying between them Queen Elizabeth flaccid as a sack. Martin came after them, stripping off his white wool nightgown so fast that buttons flew. I thought automatically, *I'll have to sew those.*

They laid her down on three chairs set side by side and hurried out. Unpinning the folded towel, which had fallen around his waist, Martin walked over and looked down at her. He yanked off his wig by a braid and tossed it at me.

I let it hit me and fall on the floor. I was looking at that white queenly face, eyes open and staring sightless at the ceiling, mouth open a little too with a thread of foam trailing from the corner, and at that ice-cream-cone bodice that never stirred. The blue fly came buzzing over my head and circled down toward her face.

"Martin," I said with difficulty, "I don't think I'm going to like what we're doing."

He turned on me, his short hair elfed, his fists planted high on his hips at the edge of his black tights, which now were all his clothes.

"You knew!" he said impatiently. "You knew you were signing up for more than acting when you said, 'Count me in the company.' "

Like a legged sapphire the blue fly walked across her upper lip and stopped by the thread of foam.

"But Martin . . . changing the past . . . dipping back and killing the real queen . . . replacing her with a double—"

His dark brows shot up. "The real—You think this is the real Queen Elizabeth?" He grabbed a bottle of rubbing alcohol from the nearest table, gushed some on a towel stained with grease-paint and, holding the dead head by its red hair (no, wig—the real one wore a wig too), scrubbed the forehead.

The white cosmetic came away, showing sallow skin and on it a faint tattoo in the form of an "S" styled like a yin-yang symbol left a little open.

"Snake!" he hissed. "Destroyer! The arch-enemy, the eternal opponent! God knows how many times people like Queen Elizabeth have been dug out of the past, first by Snakes, then by Spiders, and kidnaped or killed and replaced in the course of our war. This is the first big operation I've been on, Greta. But I know that much."

My head began to ache. I asked, "If she's an enemy double, why didn't she know a performance of Macbeth in her lifetime was an anachronism?"

"Foxholed in the past, only trying to hold a position, they get dulled. They turn half zombie. Even the Snakes. Even our people. Besides, she almost did catch on, twice when she spoke to Leicester."

"Martin," I said dully, "if there've been all these replacements, first by them, then by us, what's happened to the *real* Elizabeth?"

He shrugged. "God knows."

I asked softly, "But does He, Martin? Can He?"

He hugged his shoulders in, as if to contain a shudder. "Look, Greta," he said, "it's the Snakes who are the warpers and destroyers. We're restoring the past. The Spiders are trying to keep things as first created. We only kill when we must."

I shuddered then, for bursting out of my memory came the glittering, knife-flashing, night-shrouded, bloody image of my lover, the Spider soldier-of-change Erich von Hohenwald, dying in the grip of a giant silver spider, or spider-shaped entity large as he, as they rolled in a tangled ball down a flight of rocks in Central Park.

But the memory-burst didn't blow up my mind, as it had done a year ago, no more than snapping the black thread from my sweater had ended the world. I asked Martin, "Is that what the Snakes say?"

"Of course not! They make the same claims we do. But somewhere, Greta, you have to *trust.*" He put out the middle finger of his hand.

I didn't take hold of it. He whirled it away, snapping it against his thumb.

"You're still grieving for that carrion there!" he accused me. He jerked down a section of white curtain and whirled it over the stiffening body. "If you must grieve, grieve for Miss Nefer! Exiled, imprisoned, locked forever in the past, her mind pulsing faintly in the black hole of the dead and gone, yearning for Nirvana yet nursing one lone painful patch of consciousness. And only to hold a fort! Only to make sure Mary Stuart is executed, the Armada licked, and that all the other consequences flow on. The Snakes' Elizabeth let Mary live . . . and England die . . . and the Spaniard hold North America to the Great Lakes and New Scandinavia."

Once more he put out his middle finger.

"All right, all right," I said, barely touching it. "You've convinced me."

"Great!" he said. " 'By for now, Greta. I got to help strike the set."

"That's good," I said. He loped out.

I could hear the skirling sword-clashes of the final fight to the death of the two Macks, Duff and Beth. But I only sat there in the empty dressing room pretending to grieve for a devil-smiling snow tiger locked in a time-cage and for a cute sardonic German killed for insubordination that *I* had reported . . . but really grieving for a girl who for a year had been a rootless child of the theater with a whole company of mothers and fathers, afraid of nothing more than subway bogies and Park and Village monsters.

As I sat there pitying myself beside a shrouded queen, a shadow fell across my knees. I saw stealing through the dressing room a young man in worn dark clothes. He couldn't have been more than twenty-three. He was a frail sort of guy with a weak chin and big forehead and eyes that saw everything. I knew at once he was the one who had seemed familiar to me in the knot of City fellows.

He looked at me and I looked from him to the picture sitting on the reserve makeup box by Siddy's mirror. And I began to tremble.

He looked at it too, of course, as fast as I did. And then he began to tremble too, though it was a finer-grained tremor than mine.

The sword-fight had ended seconds back and now I heard the witches faintly wailing, "Fair is foul, and foul is fair—" Sid has them echo that line offstage at the end to give a feeling of prophecy fulfilled.

Then Sid came pounding up. He's the first finished, since the fight ends offstage so Macduff can carry back a red-necked papier-mâché head of him and show it to the audience. Sid stopped dead in the door.

Then the stranger turned around. His shoulders jerked as he saw Sid. He moved toward him just two or three steps at a time, speaking at the same time in breathy little rushes.

Sid stood there and watched him. When the other actors came boiling up behind him, he put his hands on the doorframe to either side so none of them could get past. Their faces peered around him.

And all this while the stranger was saying, "What may this mean?

Can such things be? Are all the seeds of time . . . wetted by some hell-trickle . . . sprouted at once in their granary? Speak . . . speak! You played me a play . . . that I am writing in my secretest heart. Have you disjointed the frame of things . . . to steal my unborn thoughts? Fair is foul indeed. Is all the world a stage? Speak, I say! Are you not my friend Sidney James Lessingham of King's Lynn . . . singed by time's fiery wand . . . sifted over with the ashes of thirty years? Speak, are you not he? Oh, there are more things in heaven and earth . . . aye, and perchance hell too . . . Speak, I charge you!"

And with that he put his hands on Sid's shoulders, half to shake him, I think, but half to keep from falling over. And for the one time I ever saw it, glib old Siddy had nothing to say.

He worked his lips. He opened his mouth twice and twice shut it. Then, with a kind of desperation in his face, he motioned the actors out of the way behind him with one big arm and swung the other around the stranger's narrow shoulders and swept him out of the dressing room, himself following.

The actors came pouring in then, Bruce tossing Macbeth's head to Martin like a football while he tugged off his horned helmet, Mark dumping a stack of shields in the corner, Maudie pausing as she skittered past me to say, "Hi, Gret, great you're back," and patting my temple to show what part of me she meant. Beau went straight to Sid's dressing table and set the portrait aside and lifted out Sid's reserve makeup box.

"The lights, Martin!" he called.

Then Sid came back in, slamming and bolting the door behind him and standing for a moment with his back against it, panting.

I rushed to him. Something was boiling up inside me, but before it could get to my brain I opened my mouth and it came out as, "Siddy, you can't fool me, that was no dirty S-or-S. I don't care how much he shakes and purrs, or shakes a spear, or just plain shakes—Siddy, that was Shakespeare!"

"Aye, girl, I think so," he told me, holding my wrists together. "They can't find dolls to double men like that—or such is my main hope." A big sickly grin came on his face. "Oh, gods," he demanded, "with what words do you talk to a man whose speech you've stolen all your life?"

I asked him, "Sid, were we *ever* in Central Park?"

He answered, "Once—twelve months back. A one-night stand. *They* came for Erich. You flipped."

He swung me aside and moved behind Beau. All the lights went out.

Then I saw, dimly at first, the great dull-gleaming jewel, covered with dials and green-glowing windows, that Beau had lifted from Sid's reserve makeup box. The strongest green glow showed his intent face, still framed by the long glistening locks of the Ross wig, as he kneeled before the thing—Major Maintainer, I remembered it was called.

"When now? Where?" Beau tossed impatiently to Sid over his shoulder.

"The forty-fourth year before our Lord's birth!" Sid answered instantly. "Rome!"

Beau's fingers danced over the dials like a musician's, or a safecracker's. The green glow flared and faded flickeringly.

"There's a storm in that vector of the Void."

"Circle it," Sid ordered.

"There are dark mists every way."

"Then pick the likeliest dark path!"

I called through the dark, "Fair is foul, and foul is fair, eh, Siddy?"

"Aye, chick," he answered me. " 'Tis all the rule we have!"

BIBLIOGRAPHY

"The Big Time," *Galaxy*, March, April 1958; Ace, 1961; Gregg Press, 1976

"Try and Change the Past," *Astounding*, March 1958

"Damnation Morning, *Fantastic*, August 1959

"The Oldest Soldier," *The Magazine of Fantasy and Science Fiction*, May 1960

"No Great Magic," *Galaxy*, December 1963

"Knight's Move," *Broadside*, December 1965

THE DRAGON SERIES

by Anne McCaffrey

It takes me two hours, talking as fast as I can, to explain the psychological, social and emotional origins of the Dragonriders of Pern. I'd rather not go into such detail, especially since every reader seems to find his own special significance in the Dragon yarns, and that's how it should be. That two-hour speech is very much after the basic fact that the stories were written first, delved second.

Believe it or not, in May 1966, I cast about in my mind for the basis of a short story about nice dragons, useful, friendly dragons. I got about halfway through said short story and stopped, undecided about its viability. My estimable agent, Virginia Kidd, read that half and, with an encouraging shine in her eyes and a wistful tone in her voice, politely asked me to finish it. I did. To my immense surprise, John Campbell bought "Weyr Search" immediately. And summoned me to lunch, at which we discussed the future of my telepathic, teleporting dragons. (Aerodynamically, they can't fly any more than hummingbirds. However, they "think" they can; ergo they do, and very nicely, thank you.) Much flattered by John's interest, I went back to my trusty typewriter and wrote 20,000 words called "Dragonflight" which I thought to be the natural progression of events. John said that the story was a good bridger for a novel, but told him nothing new about Pern or dragons. Please, would I have them fighting Thread? I sat down and wrote "Dust Fall." He sent this back, quite crushing me, but accompanied by one of his marvelous editorial letters. One of his suggestions dealt with time travel. I didn't like his notion as it didn't fit in the parameters I had set myself for Pern. But the suggestion did nudge my faltering imagination toward a solution. "The Cold Between" was written within a week of receiving "Dust Fall" and John's editorial comments; quite the easiest 20,000 words of all the dragons yarns. Those four sections comprised a novel, *Dragonflight*. And that novel is now translated into Swedish, Japanese, French, Italian, German, Spanish, Dutch and Danish. Not a bad track record for an idea that was only to be a short story.

Rather high on such success, I started *Dragonquest* and wrote at fever pitch, convinced I was writing the Great American S-F novel. Virginia read the draft and suggested in her quiet way, in her most apologetic voice, that I consign this attempt to the purifying flames. I took her advice. Nor did I start the second dragon novel until the fall of 1969. I had written 379 pages and could NOT push the story line further, which, to me, indicates a massive flaw in story logic. Betty Ballantine kindly invited me to discuss the problem with her and Ian at Woodstock over New Year's

Eve weekend. We went over what I had written, page by page, which is editorial devotion above and beyond the call of duty. Halfway through the session, Betty said mildly that she rather thought this was F'nor's story, not Lessa's and F'lar's. Her astute diagnosis answered the problem, and suddenly I knew where the story started and where it was going. By the time we had completed our discussions that weekend, it was patent that a third book was needed to answer the new questions posed, like what would happen to Jaxom and his white dragon, Ruth. With this in mind, I finished F'nor's story in roughly a month.

In August 1970 I removed myself and my mother and my children to Ireland where Roger Elwood followed me with a request for a short story about the Dragon world for a juvenile anthology he was doing. "The Smallest Dragonboy" is the result. The fringe benefit was artwork by Rod Ruth of the most lovable, delightful, whimsically appealing, pathetic, damp and lurching dragonet you will ever see. A framed copy of Heth, eyes whirling dolefully, scales limp, graces my study wall to encourage me in blue moments.

Inhibited by memory of the faulty start to *Dragonquest,* I had great trouble contemplating *White Dragon.* By this time, the Dragons of Pern, and Lessa, F'lar, F'nor and Robinton, had acquired many friends and the pressure on me, as author, to maintain a high standard made a coward of me. I evaded, avoided and did everything to put off the inevitable.

Two events brought an end to this inhibition: Boskone XII* asked me to be guest of honor in Boston in 1975 and wanted to signalize my appearance by publishing a limited edition of stories by me; Dragon stories, please? Taking a dragon by the headknobs, I started Jaxom's further adventures with Ruth. I recall completing "A Time When" in a raging fever, with almost no money in the bank, scrounging from friends enough paper to make a clear copy. Bonnie Dalzell created beautiful illustrations of dragons and fire-lizards. Wendy Glasser and Drew Whyte, out of sheer love and dedication, put together a most useful glossary of dragonic terms, called a "Dragondex"—far more valuable to me, the author, than to any confused reader.

The second event was a suggestion to write a juvenile book about Pern, implemented by Beth Blish, daughter of my estimable agent and James Blish, and Jean Karl of Atheneum Publishers.

I had actually written a half-dozen pages about a girl of a sea hold for Roger Elwood's commission, but the story had died. I reviewed it now and, after about nine first chapter drafts, found Menolly's story, and *Dragonsong.* I submitted the finished manuscript to Jean Karl in March 1975 while I was in the States for Boskone XII. During my flight back to Ireland, I found myself wondering what was going to happen to Menolly when she reached the Harper Hall. Jean Karl appeared to have much the same interest in my harper girl's future so I began what I called "A Harper

* Boskone XII was the 1975 event of the annual science fiction convention held in Boston, generally at the Sheraton Hotel, by the New England Science Fiction Association. It is the custom of such events to ask a well-known science fiction author to be the guest of honor, give an address and generally be available to meet readers in a face-to-face confrontation. Certainly a rewarding experience for an author.

of Pern." This story required exacting writing. To set just the right scene, I had to rewrite the first chapter of *Dragonsinger* some fourteen times in second draft before I got it *right*. (Damon Knight maintains that the first chapter, or first paragraph, is the hardest part of any story.)

All this thinking about Pern primed the pump for a resumption of *White Dragon*. In January 1977 I expanded the situation I had created in "A Time When." Though I was traveling in the States in February and March, I continued working wherever I could acquire a typewriter. The draft was finished in May. More revisions were needed and Judy-Lynn del Rey and Betty Ballantine were enormously helpful. While waiting for editorial comment, I started on the third book for Jean Karl and Atheneum because a young imp of a rascal, named Piemur, had emerged at the Harper Hall, as Menolly's friend, and I sort of want to know what happens to Piemur when he loses his boyish soprano.

That's the history of the writing of the Dragon stories—so far. I totaled up about 468,000 words on a theme which originally began as a short story. I don't believe any writer can *know* when an idea of his will touch the right chords in readers' minds to make a series viable. I count myself extraordinarily lucky in this past Decade of the Dragons. Could it be that dragons are grateful?

The Smallest Dragonboy

Although Keevan lengthened his walking stride as far as his legs would stretch, he couldn't quite keep up with the other candidates. He knew he would be teased again.

Just as he knew many other things that his foster mother told him he ought not to know, Keevan knew that Beterli, the most senior of the boys, set that spanking pace just to embarrass him, the smallest dragonboy. Keevan would arrive, tail fork-end of the group, breathless, chest heaving, and maybe get a stern look from the instructing wing-second.

Dragonriders, even if they were still only hopeful candidates for the glowing eggs which were hardening on the hot sands of the Hatching Ground cavern, were expected to be punctual and prepared. Sloth was not tolerated by the Weyrleader of Benden Weyr. A good record was especially important now. It was very near hatching time, when the baby dragons would crack their mottled shells, and stagger forth to choose their lifetime companions. The very thought of that glorious moment made Keevan's breath catch in his throat. To be chosen—to be a dragonrider! To sit astride the neck of a winged beast with jeweled eyes: to be his friend, in telepathic communion with him for life; to be his companion in good times and fighting extremes; to fly effortlessly over the lands of Pern! Or, thrillingly, *between* to any point anywhere on the world! Flying *between* was done on dragonback or not at all, and it was dangerous.

Keevan glanced upward, past the black mouths of the weyr caves in which grown dragons and their chosen riders lived, toward the Star Stones that crowned the ridge of the old volcano that was Benden Weyr. On the height, the blue watch dragon, his rider mounted on his neck, stretched the great transparent pinions that carried him on the winds of Pern to fight the evil Thread that fell at certain times from the skies. The many-faceted rainbow jewels of his eyes glistened fleetingly in the greeny sun. He folded his great wings to his back, and the watch pair resumed their statuelike pose of alertness.

Then the enticing view was obscured as Keevan passed into the Hatching Ground cavern. The sands underfoot were hot, even through heavy wher-hide boots. How the bootmaker had protested having to sew so small! Keeven was forced to wonder why being small was reprehensible. People were always calling him "babe" and shooing him away as being "too small" or "too young" for this or that. Keevan was constantly working, twice as hard as any other boy his age, to prove himself capable. What if his muscles weren't as big as Beterli's? They were just as hard. And if he couldn't overpower anyone in a wrestling match, he could outdistance everyone in a footrace.

"Maybe if you run fast enough," Beterli had jeered on the occasion when Keevan had been goaded to boast of his swiftness, "you could catch a dragon. That's the only way you'll make a dragonrider!"

"You just wait and see, Beterli, you just wait," Keevan had replied. He would have liked to wipe the contemptuous smile from Beterli's face, but the guy didn't fight fair even when a wingsecond was watching. "No one knows what Impresses a dragon!"

"They've got to be able to *find* you first, babe!"

Yes, being the smallest candidate was not an enviable position. It was therefore imperative that Keevan Impress a dragon in his first hatching. That would wipe the smile off every face in the cavern, and accord him the respect due any dragonrider, even the smallest one.

Besides, no one knew exactly what Impressed the baby dragons as they struggled from their shells in search of their lifetime partners.

"I like to believe that dragons see into a man's heart," Keevan's foster mother, Mende, told him. "If they find goodness, honesty, a flexible mind, patience, courage—and you've got that in quantity, dear Keevan—that's what dragons look for. I've seen many a well-grown lad left standing on the sands, Hatching Day, in favor of someone not so strong or tall or handsome. And if my memory serves me"—which it usually did: Mende knew every word of every Harper's tale worth telling, although Keevan did not interrupt her to say so—"I don't believe that F'lar, our Weyrleader, was all that tall when bronze Mnementh chose him. And Mnementh was the only bronze dragon of that hatching."

Dreams of Impressing a bronze were beyond Keevan's boldest reflections, although that goal dominated the thoughts of every other hopeful candidate. Green dragons were small and fast and more numerous. There was more prestige to Impressing a blue or brown than a green. Being practical, Keevan seldom dreamed as high as a big fighting brown, like Canth, F'nor's fine fellow, the biggest brown on all Pern. But to fly a bronze? Bronzes were almost as big as the queen, and only they took the air when a queen flew at mating time. A bronze rider could aspire to become Weyrleader! Well, Keevan would console himself, brown riders could aspire to become wingseconds, and that wasn't bad. He'd even settle for a green dragon: they were small, but so was he. No matter! He simply had to Impress a dragon his first time in the Hatching Ground. Then no one in the Weyr would taunt him anymore for being so small.

Shells, Keevan thought now, but the sands are hot!

"Impression time is imminent, candidates," the wingsecond was saying as everyone crowded respectfully close to him. "See the extent of the striations on this promising egg." The stretch marks *were* larger than yesterday.

Everyone leaned forward and nodded thoughtfully. That particular egg was the one Beterli had marked as his own, and no other candidate dared, on pain of being beaten by Beterli at his first opportunity, to approach it. The egg was marked by a large yellowish splotch in the shape of a dragon backwinging to land, talons outstretched to grasp rock. Everyone knew that bronze eggs bore distinctive markings. And naturally, Beterli, who'd been presented at eight Impressions already and was the biggest of the candidates, had chosen it.

"I'd say that the great opening day is almost upon us," the wingsecond went on, and then his face assumed a grave expression. "As we well know, there are only forty eggs and seventy-two candidates. Some of you may be disappointed on the great day. That doesn't necessarily mean you aren't dragonrider material, just that *the* dragon for you hasn't been shelled. You'll have other hatchings, and it's no disgrace to be left behind an Impression or two. Or more."

Keevan was positive that the wingsecond's eyes rested on Beterli, who'd been stood off at so many Impressions already. Keevan tried to squinch down so the wingsecond wouldn't notice him. Keevan had been reminded too often that he was eligible to be a candidate by one day only. He, of

all the hopefuls, was most likely to be left standing on the great day.
One more reason why he simply had to Impress at his first hatching.

"Now move about among the eggs," the wingsecond said. "Touch them.
We don't know that it does any good, but it certainly doesn't do any
harm."

Some of the boys laughed nervously, but everyone immediately began
to circulate among the eggs. Beterli stepped up officiously to "his" egg,
daring anyone to come near it. Keevan smiled, because he had already
touched it—every inspection day, when the others were leaving the
Hatching Ground and no one could see him crouch to stroke it.

Keevan had an egg he concentrated on, too, one drawn slightly to
the far side of the others. The shell had a soft greenish-blue tinge with
a faint creamy swirl design. The consensus was that this egg contained
a mere green, so Keevan was rarely bothered by rivals. He was somewhat
perturbed then to see Beterli wandering over to him.

"I don't know why you're allowed in this Impression, Keevan. There
are enough of us without a babe," Beterli said, shaking his head.

"I'm of age." Keevan kept his voice level, telling himself not to be
bothered by mere words.

"Yah!" Beterli made a show of standing on his toetips. "You can't even
see over an egg; Hatching Day, you better get in front or the dragons
won't see you at all. 'Course, you could get run down that way in the
mad scramble. Oh, I forget, you can run fast, can't you?"

"You'd better make sure a dragon sees *you*, this time, Beterli," Keevan
replied. "You're almost overage, aren't you?"

Beterli flushed and took a step forward, hand half-raised. Keevan stood
his ground, but if Beterli advanced one more step, he would call the
wingsecond. No one fought on the Hatching Ground. Surely Beterli knew
that much.

Fortunately, at that moment, the wingsecond called the boys together
and led them from the Hatching Ground to start on evening chores.
There were "glows" to be replenished in the main kitchen caverns and
sleeping cubicles, the major hallways, and the queen's apartment. Firestone sacks had to be filled against Thread attack, and black rock brought
to the kitchen hearths. The boys fell to their chores, tantalized by the
odors of roasting meat. The population of the Weyr began to assemble
for the evening meal, and the dragonriders came in from the Feeding
Ground on their sweep checks.

It was the time of day Keevan liked best: once the chores were done
but before dinner was served, a fellow could often get close enough to
the dragonriders to hear their talk. Tonight, Keevan's father, K'last, was
at the main dragonrider table. It puzzled Keevan how his father, a brown
rider and a tall man, could *be* his father—because he, Keevan, was so
small. It obviously puzzled K'last, too, when he deigned to notice his

small son: "In a few more Turns, you'll be as tall as I am—or taller!"

K'last was pouring Benden wine all around the table. The dragonriders were relaxing. There'd be no Thread attack for three more days, and they'd be in the mood to tell tall tales, better than Harper yarns, about impossible maneuvers they'd done a-dragonback. When Thread attack was closer, their talk would change to a discussion of tactics of evasion, of going *between,* how long to suspend there until the burning but fragile Thread would freeze and crack and fall harmlessly off dragon and man. They would dispute the exact moment to feed firestone to the dragon so he'd have the best flame ready to sear Thread midair and render it harmless to ground—and man—below. There was such a lot to know and understand about being a dragonrider that sometimes Keevan was overwhelmed. How would he ever be able to remember everything he ought to know at the right moment? He couldn't dare ask such a question; this would only have given additional weight to the notion that he was too young yet to be a dragonrider.

"Having older candidates makes good sense," L'vel was saying, as Keevan settled down near the table. "Why waste four to five years of a dragon's fighting prime until his rider grows up enough to stand the rigors?" L'vel had Impressed a blue of Ramoth's first clutch. Most of the candidates thought L'vel was marvelous because he spoke up in front of the older riders, who awed them. "That was well enough in the Interval when you didn't need to mount the full Weyr complement to fight Thread. But not now. Not with more eligible candidates than ever. Let the babes wait."

"Any boy who is over twelve Turns has the right to stand in the Hatching Ground," K'last replied, a slight smile on his face. He never argued or got angry. Keevan wished he were more like his father. And oh, how he wished he were a brown rider! "Only a dragon—each particular dragon—knows what he wants in a rider. We certainly can't tell. Time and again the theorists," K'last's smile deepened as his eyes swept those at the table, "are surprised by dragon choice. *They* never seem to make mistakes, however."

"Now, K'last, just look at the roster this Impression. Seventy-two boys and only forty eggs. Drop off the twelve youngest, and there's still a good field for the hatchlings to choose from. Shells! There are a couple of weyrlings unable to see over a wher egg much less a dragon! And years before they can ride Thread."

"True enough, but the Weyr is scarcely under fighting strength, and if the youngest Impress, they'll be old enough to fight when the oldest of our current dragons go *between* from senility."

"Half the Weyr-bred lads have already been through several Impressions," one of the bronze riders said then. "I'd say drop some of *them* off this time. Give the untried a chance."

"There's nothing wrong in presenting a clutch with as wide a choice as possible," said the Weyrleader, who had joined the table with Lessa, the Weyrwoman.

"Has there ever been a case," she said, smiling in her odd way at the riders, "where a hatchling didn't choose?"

Her suggestion was almost heretical and drew astonished gasps from everyone, including the boys.

F'lar laughed. "You say the most outrageous things, Lessa."

"Well, *has* there ever been a case where a dragon didn't choose?"

"Can't say as I recall one," K'last replied.

"Then we continue in this tradition," Lessa said firmly, as if that ended the matter.

But it didn't. The argument ranged from one table to the other all through dinner, with some favoring a weeding out of the candidates to the most likely, lopping off those who were very young or who had had multiple opportunities to Impress. All the candidates were in a swivet, though such a departure from tradition would be to the advantage of many. As the evening progressed, more riders were favoring eliminating the youngest and those who'd passed four or more Impressions unchosen. Keevan felt he could bear such a dictum only if Beterli were also eliminated. But this seemed less likely than that Keevan would be turfed out, since the Weyr's need was for fighting dragons and riders.

By the time the evening meal was over, no decision had been reached, although the Weyrleader had promised to give the matter due consideration.

He might have slept on the problem, but few of the candidates did. Tempers were uncertain in the sleeping caverns next morning as the boys were routed out of their beds to carry water and black rock and cover the "glows." Twice Mende had to call Keevan to order for clumsiness.

"Whatever is the matter with you, boy?" she demanded in exasperation when he tipped blackrock short of the bin and sooted up the hearth.

"They're going to keep me from this Impression."

"What?" Mende stared at him. "Who?"

"You heard them talking at dinner last night. They're going to turf the babes from the hatching."

Mende regarded him a moment longer before touching his arm gently. "There's lots of talk around a supper table, Keevan. And it cools as soon as the supper. I've heard the same nonsense before every hatching, but nothing is ever changed."

"There's always a first time," Keevan answered, copying one of her own phrases.

"That'll be enough of that, Keevan. Finish your job. If the clutch does hatch today, we'll need full rock bins for the feast, and you won't be around to do the filling. All my fosterlings make dragonriders."

"The first time?" Keevan was bold enough to ask as he scooted off with the rockbarrow.

Perhaps, Keevan thought later, if he hadn't been on that chore just when Beterli was also fetching black rock, things might have turned out differently. But he had dutifully trundled the barrow to the outdoor bunker for another load just as Beterli arrived on a similar errand.

"Heard the news, babe?" Beterli asked. He was grinning from ear to ear, and he put an unnecessary emphasis on the final insulting word.

"The eggs are cracking?" Keevan all but dropped the loaded shovel. Several anxieties flicked through his mind then: he was black with rock dust—would he have time to wash before donning the white tunic of candidacy? And if the eggs were hatching, why hadn't the candidates been recalled by the wingsecond?

"Naw! Guess again!" Beterli was much too pleased with himself.

With a sinking heart, Keevan knew what the news must be, and he could only stare with intense desolation at the older boy.

"C'mon! Guess, babe!"

"I've no time for guessing games," Keevan managed to say with indifference. He began to shovel black rock into the barrow as fast as he could.

"I said, guess." Beterli grabbed the shovel.

"And I said I have no time for guessing games."

Beterli wrenched the shovel from Keevan's hands. "Guess!"

"I'll have that shovel back, Beterli." Keevan straightened up, but he didn't come to Beterli's bulky shoulder. From somewhere, other boys appeared, some with barrows, some mysteriously alerted to the prospect of a confrontation among their number.

"Babes don't give orders to candidates around here, babe!"

Someone sniggered and Keevan, incredulous, knew that he must've been dropped from the candidacy.

He yanked the shovel from Beterli's loosened grasp. Snarling, the older boy tried to regain possession, but Keevan clung with all his strength to the handle, dragged back and forth as the stronger boy jerked the shovel about.

With a sudden, unexpected movement, Beterli rammed the handle into Keevan's chest, knocking him over the barrow handles. Keevan felt a sharp, painful jab behind his left ear, an unbearable pain in his left shin, and then a painless nothingness.

Mende's angry voice roused him, and startled, he tried to throw back the covers, thinking he'd overslept. But he couldn't move, so firmly was he tucked into his bed. And then the constriction of a bandage on his head and the dull sickishness in his leg brought back recent occurrences.

"Hatching?" he cried.

"No, lovey," Mende said in a kind voice. Her hand was cool and gentle on his forehead. "Though there's some as won't be at any hatching again." Her voice took on a stern edge.

Keevan looked beyond her to see the Weyrwoman, who was frowning with irritation.

"Keevan, will you tell me what occurred at the black-rock bunker?" asked Lessa in an even voice.

He remembered Beterli now and the quarrel over the shovel and . . . what had Mende said about some not being at any hatching? Much as he hated Beterli, he couldn't bring himself to tattle on Beterli and force him out of candidacy.

"Come, lad," and a note of impatience crept into the Weyrwoman's voice. "I merely want to know what happened from you, too. Mende said she sent you for black rock. Beterli—and every Weyrling in the cavern—seems to have been on the same errand. What happened?"

"Beterli took my shovel. I hadn't finished with it."

"There's more than one shovel. What did he *say* to you?"

"He'd heard the news."

"What news?" The Weyrwoman was suddenly amused.

"That . . . that . . . there'd been changes."

"Is that what he said?"

"Not exactly."

"What did he say? C'mon, lad, I've heard from everyone else, you know."

"He said for me to guess the news."

"And you fell for that old gag?" The Weyrwoman's irritation returned.

"Consider all the talk last night at supper, Lessa," Mende said. "Of course the boy would think he'd been eliminated."

"In effect, he is, with a broken skull and leg." Lessa touched his arm in a rare gesture of sympathy. "Be that as it may, Keevan, you'll have other Impressions. Beterli will not. There are certain rules that must be observed by all candidates, and his conduct proves him unacceptable to the Weyr."

She smiled at Mende and then left.

"I'm still a candidate?" Keevan asked urgently.

"Well, you are and you aren't, lovey," his foster mother said. "Is the numbweed working?" she asked, and when he nodded, she said, "You just rest. I'll bring you some nice broth."

At any other time in his life, Keevan would have relished such cosseting, but now he just lay there worrying. Beterli had been dismissed. Would the others think it was his fault? But everyone was there! Beterli provoked that fight. His worry increased, because although he heard excited comings and goings in the passageway, no one tweaked back the curtain across the sleeping alcove he shared with five other boys. Surely one of them would have to come in sometime. No, they were all avoiding him. And something else was wrong. Only he didn't know what.

Mende returned with broth and beachberry bread.

"Why doesn't anyone come see me, Mende? I haven't done anything wrong, have I? I didn't ask to have Beterli turfed out."

Mende soothed him, saying everyone was busy with noontime chores and no one was angry with him. They were giving him a chance to rest in quiet. The numbweed made him drowsy, and her words were fair enough. He permitted his fears to dissipate. Until he heard a hum. Actually, he felt it first, in the broken shin bone and his sore head. The hum began to grow. Two things registered suddenly in Keevan's groggy mind: the only white candidate's robe still on the pegs in the chamber was his; and the dragons hummed when a clutch was being laid or being hatched. Impression! And he was flat abed.

Bitter, bitter disappointment turned the warm broth sour in his belly. Even the small voice telling him that he'd have other opportunities failed to alleviate his crushing depression. *This* was the Impression that mattered! This was his chance to show *everyone*, from Mende to K'last to L'vel and even the Weyrleader that he, Keevan, was worthy of being a dragonrider.

He twisted in bed, fighting against the tears that threatened to choke him. Dragonmen don't cry! Dragonmen learn to live with pain.

Pain? The leg didn't actually pain him as he rolled about on his bedding. His head felt sort of stiff from the tightness of the bandage. He sat up, an effort in itself since the numbweed made exertion difficult. He touched the splinted leg; the knee was unhampered. He had no feeling in his bone, really. He swung himself carefully to the side of his bed and stood slowly. The room wanted to swim about him. He closed his eyes, which made the dizziness worse, and he had to clutch the wall.

Gingerly, he took a step. The broken leg dragged. It hurt in spite of the numbweed, but what was pain to a dragonman?

No one had said he couldn't go to the Impression. "You are and you aren't," were Mende's exact words.

Clinging to the wall, he jerked off his bedshirt. Stretching his arm to the utmost, he jerked his white candidate's tunic from the peg. Jamming first one arm and then the other into the holes, he pulled it over his head. Too bad about the belt. He couldn't wait. He hobbled to the door, hung on to the curtain to steady himself. The weight on his leg was unwieldy. He wouldn't get very far without something to lean on. Down by the bathing pool was one of the long crook-necked poles used to retrieve clothes from the hot washing troughs. But it was down there, and he was on the level above. And there was no one nearby to come to his aid: everyone would be in the Hatching Ground right now, eagerly waiting for the first egg to crack.

The humming increased in volume and tempo, an urgency to which Keevan responded, knowing that his time was all too limited if he was to join the ranks of the hopeful boys standing around the cracking eggs. But if he hurried down the ramp, he'd fall flat on his face.

He could, of course, go flat on his rear end, the way crawling children did. He sat down, sending a jarring stab of pain through his leg and up to the wound on the back of his head. Gritting his teeth and blinking away tears, Keevan scrabbled down the ramp. He had to wait a moment at the bottom to catch his breath. He got to one knee, the injured leg straight out in front of him. Somehow, he managed to push himself erect, though the room seemed about to tip over his ears. It wasn't far to the crooked stick, but it seemed an age before he had it in his hand.

Then the humming stopped!

Keevan cried out and began to hobble frantically across the cavern, out to the bowl of the Weyr. Never had the distance between living caverns and the Hatching Ground seemed so great. Never had the Weyr been so breathlessly silent. It was as if the multitude of people and dragons watching the hatching held every breath in suspense. Not even the wind muttered down the steep sides of the bowl. The only sounds to break the stillness were Keevan's ragged gasps and the thump-thud of his stick on the hard-packed ground. Sometimes he had to hop twice on his good leg to maintain his balance. Twice he fell into the sand and had to pull himself up on the stick, his white tunic no longer spotless. Once he jarred himself so badly he couldn't get up immediately.

Then he heard the first exhalation of the crowd, the oohs, the muted cheer, the susurrus of excited whispers. An egg had cracked, and the dragon had chosen his rider. Desperation increased Keevan's hobble. Would he never reach the arching mouth of the Hatching Ground?

Another cheer and an excited spate of applause spurred Keevan to greater effort. If he didn't get there in moments, there'd be no unpaired hatchling left. Then he was actually staggering into the Hatching Ground, the sands hot on his bare feet.

No one noticed his entrance or his halting progress. And Keevan could see nothing but the backs of the white-robed candidates, seventy of them ringing the area around the eggs. Then one side would surge forward or back and there'd be a cheer. Another dragon had been Impressed. Suddenly a large gap appeared in the white human wall, and Keevan had his first sight of the eggs. There didn't seem to be *any* left uncracked, and he could see the lucky boys standing beside wobble-legged dragons. He could hear the unmistakable plaintive crooning of hatchlings and their squawks of protest as they'd fall awkwardly in the sand.

Suddenly he wished that he hadn't left his bed, that he'd stayed away from the Hatching Ground. Now everyone would see his ignominious failure. So he scrambled as desperately to reach the shadowy walls of the Hatching Ground as he had struggled to cross the bowl. He mustn't be seen.

He didn't notice, therefore, that the shifting group of boys remaining had begun to drift in his direction. The hard pace he had set himself and his cruel disappointment took their double toll of Keevan. He tripped and collapsed sobbing to the warm sands. He didn't see the consternation in the watching Weyrfolk above the Hatching Ground, nor did he hear the excited whispers of speculation. He didn't know that the Weyrleader and Weyrwoman had dropped to the arena and were making their way toward the knot of boys slowly moving in the direction of the entrance.

"Never seen anything like it," the Weyrleader was saying. "Only thirty-nine riders chosen. And the bronze trying to leave the Hatching Ground without making Impression."

"A case in point of what I said last night," the Weyrwoman replied, "where a hatchling makes no choice because the right boy isn't there."

"There's only Beterli and K'last's young one missing. And there's a full wing of likely boys to choose from . . ."

"None acceptable, apparently. Where is the creature going? He's not heading for the entrance after all. Oh, what have we there, in the shadows?"

Keevan heard with dismay the sound of voices nearing him. He tried to burrow into the sand. The mere thought of how he would be teased and taunted now was unbearable.

Don't worry! Please don't worry! The thought was urgent, but not his own.

Someone kicked sand over Keevan and butted roughly against him.

"Go away. Leave me alone!" he cried.

Why? was the injured-sounding question inserted into his mind. There was no voice, no tone, but the question was there, perfectly clear, in his head.

Incredulous, Keevan lifted his head and stared into the glowing jeweled eyes of a small bronze dragon. His wings were wet, the tips drooping in the sand. And he sagged in the middle on his unsteady legs, although he was making a great effort to keep erect.

Keevan dragged himself to his knees, oblivious of the pain in his leg. He wasn't even aware that he was ringed by the boys passed over, while thirty-one pairs of resentful eyes watched him Impress the dragon. The Weyrmen looked on, amused, and surprised at the draconic choice, which could not be forced. Could not be questioned. Could not be changed.

Why? asked the dragon again. *Don't you like me?* His eyes whirled with anxiety, and his tone was so piteous that Keevan staggered forward and threw his arms around the dragon's neck, stroking his eye ridges, patting the damp, soft hide, opening the fragile-looking wings to dry them, and wordlessly assuring the hatchling over and over again that he was the most perfect, most beautiful, most beloved dragon in the Weyr, in all the Weyrs of Pern.

"What's his name, K'van?" asked Lessa, smiling warmly at the new dragonrider. K'van stared up at her for a long moment. Lessa would know as soon as he did. Lessa was the only person who could "receive" from all dragons, not only her own Ramoth. Then he gave her a radiant smile, recognizing the traditional shortening of his name that raised him forever to the rank of dragonrider.

My name is Heth, the dragon thought mildly, then hiccuped in sudden urgency. *I'm hungry.*

"Dragons are born hungry," said Lessa, laughing. "F'lar, give the boy a hand. He can barely manage his own legs, much less a dragon's."

K'van remembered his stick and drew himself up. "We'll be just fine, thank you."

"You may be the smallest dragonrider ever, young K'van," F'lar said, "but you're one of the bravest!"

And Heth agreed! Pride and joy so leaped in both chests that K'van wondered if his heart would burst right out of his body. He looped an arm around Heth's neck and the pair, the smallest dragonboy and the hatchling who wouldn't choose anybody else, walked out of the Hatching Ground together forever.

BIBLIOGRAPHY

"Weyr Search," *Analog,* October 1967

"Dragonrider," *Analog,* December 1968 and January 1969

Dragonflight, Ballantine Books and Walker & Company, 1968

Dragonquest, Ballantine Books, 1971

"The Smallest Dragonboy," *Science Fiction Tales,* 1973

"A Time When," NESFA Press, 1975

Dragonsong, Atheneum, 1976

Dragonsinger, Atheneum, 1977

The White Dragon, Del Rey Books, 1978

Dragondrums, Atheneum, 1979

THE HELVA SERIES

by Anne McCaffrey

I do not set about writing stories with an exact outline of why or what elements will come into them. Initially, I am telling a story to myself as well as any reader, drawing on what's been stored in my agile brain from observation and experience to make it a good yarn. Sometimes I'm downright startled at what the critical reader discovers. Consequently, I honestly didn't realize that I was writing "The Ship Who Sang" in an effort to rationalize the grief I felt at my father's death. But that's what comes through, loud and clear!

Without false modesty, I can say that the story, "Ship Who Sang," established my name as a new writer of science fiction though it was only my third published yarn. The story had, and still has, an emotional impact on the reader. In 1961, when *Fantasy and Science Fiction* published "Ship," emotion in science fiction was in short supply.

The point from which I originally started the story in 1958 had nothing to do with my father's death. Furthermore, the notion of complex machinery controlled by a "brain" is not new, nor original with me. I had been much struck by a pulp story, author unremembered, in which a young mother tries to find the space shuttle in which the brain of her child had been used as the guiding force. A repulsive concept and she succeeds in giving her child's brain the coup de grace. At that point in my life, I had two children of my own. I also had a friend with a spastic child and her tragedy, an intelligent mind handicapped by a short circuit in her body mechanics, suggested another variation on that gruesome pulp story. So, Helva was born . . . a thing . . . and became a fully realized human being.

Let me hammer/stamp/shout one point exceedingly clear! Despite all erroneous blurb copy to the contrary, Helva's BODY is there! It isn't just her brain in that titanium shell behind the central panel of the 834—it is ALL of Helva. True, her brain is attached to the controlling circuits, but she's all there! That is the whole point of Helva as a personality: she's at the mercy, and assistance, of her endocrinal system, gonads and hormones. That is what makes her so human. And the pathos of "Ship Who Sang" is that she cannot cry her grief at Jennan's death as I, the girl child, could not properly honor the death of my soldier father!

I had not meant to continue Helva: she insisted. Curiously enough, I seemed to write Helva yarns when my marriage hit periods of stress, not that Helva's problems in any way echoed my marital ones. She continued to be my escape valve.

Be that as it may, the Helva stories are special to me. Hey, Dad, this one's for you—and the echo of taps played across a grave in January!

The Ship Who Sang

She was born a thing and as such would be condemned if she failed to pass the encephalograph test required of all newborn babies. There was always the possibility that though the limbs were twisted, the mind was not, that though the ears would hear only dimly, the eyes see vaguely, the mind behind them was receptive and alert.

The electro-encephalogram was entirely favorable, unexpectedly so, and the news was brought to the waiting, grieving parents. There was the final, harsh decision: to give their child euthanasia or permit it to become an encapsulated "brain," a guiding mechanism in any one of a number of curious professions. As such, their offspring would suffer no pain, live a comfortable existence in a metal shell for several centuries, performing unusual service to Central Worlds.

She lived and was given a name, Helva. For her first 3 vegetable months she waved her crabbed claws, kicked weakly with her clubbed feet and enjoyed the usual routine of the infant. She was not alone, for there were three other such children in the big city's special nursery. Soon they all were removed to Central Laboratory School, where their delicate transformation began.

One of the babies died in the initial transferral, but of Helva's "class," 17 thrived in the metal shells. Instead of kicking feet, Helva's neural responses started her wheels; instead of grabbing with hands, she manipulated mechanical extensions. As she matured, more and more neural synapses would be adjusted to operate other mechanisms that went into the maintenance and running of a space ship. For Helva was destined to be the "brain" half of a scout ship, partnered with a man or a woman, whichever she chose, as the mobile half. She would be among the elite of her kind. Her initial intelligence tests registered above normal and her adaptation index was unusually high. As long as her development within her shell lived up to expectations, and there were no side-effects from the pituitary tinkering, Helva would live a rewarding, rich and unusual life, a far cry from what she would have faced as an ordinary, "normal" being.

However, no diagram of her brain patterns, no early I.Q. tests recorded certain essential facts about Helva that Central must eventually learn. They would have to bide their official time and see, trusting that the massive doses of shell psychology would suffice her, too, as the necessary bulwark against her unusual confinement and the pressures of her profession. A ship run by a human brain could not run rogue or insane with the power and resources Central had to build into their scout ships. Brain ships were, of course, long past the experimental stages. Most babies survived the perfected techniques of pituitary manipulation that kept their bodies small, eliminating the necessity of transfers from smaller to larger shells. And very, very few were lost when the final connection was made to the control panels of ship or industrial combine. Shell-people resembled mature dwarfs in size whatever their natal deformities were, but the well-oriented brain would not have changed places with the most perfect body in the Universe.

So, for happy years, Helva scooted around in her shell with her classmates, playing such games as Stall, Power-Seek, studying her lessons in trajectory, propulsion techniques, computation, logistics, mental hygiene, basic alien psychology, philology, space history, law, traffic, codes: all the et ceteras that eventually became compounded into a reasoning, logical, informed citizen. Not so obvious to her, but of more importance to her teachers, Helva ingested the precepts of her conditioning as easily as she absorbed her nutrient fluid. She would one day be grateful to the patient drone of the subconscious-level instruction.

Helva's civilization was not without busy, do-good associations, exploring possible inhumanities to terrestrial as well as extraterrestrial citizens. One such group—Society for the Preservation of the Rights of Intelligent Minorities——got all incensed over shelled "children" when Helva was just turning 14. When they were forced to, Central Worlds shrugged its shoulders, arranged a tour of the Laboratory Schools and set the tour off to a big start by showing the members case histories, complete with photographs. Very few committees ever looked past the first few photos. Most of their original objections about "shells" were overriden by the relief that these hideous (to them) bodies *were* mercifully concealed.

Helva's class was doing fine arts, a selective subject in her crowded program. She had activated one of her microscopic tools which she would later use for minute repairs to various parts of her control panel. Her subject was large—a copy of "The Last Supper"—and her canvas, small— the head of a tiny screw. She had tuned her sight to the proper degree. As she worked she absentmindedly crooned, producing a curious sound. Shell-people used their own vocal cords and diaphragms, but sound issued through microphones rather than mouths. Helva's hum, then, had a curious vibrancy, a warm, dulcet quality even in its aimless chromatic wanderings.

"Why, what a lovely voice you have," said one of the female visitors.

Helva "looked" up and caught a fascinating panorama of regular, dirty craters on a flaky pink surface. Her hum became a gurgle of surprise. She instinctively regulated her "sight" until the skin lost its cratered look and the pores assumed normal proportions.

"Yes, we have quite a few years of voice training, madam," remarked

Helva calmly. "Vocal peculiarities often become excessively irritating during prolonged intrastellar distances and must be eliminated. I enjoyed my lessons."

Although this was the first time that Helva had seen unshelled people, she took this experience calmly. Any other reaction would have been reported instantly.

"I meant that you have a nice singing voice . . . dear," the lady said.

"Thank you. Would you like to see my work?" Helva asked, politely. She instinctively sheered away from personal discussions, but she filed the comment away for further meditation.

"Work?" asked the lady.

"I am currently reproducing the 'Last Supper' on the head of a screw."

"Oh, I say," the lady twittered.

Helva turned her vision back to magnification and surveyed her copy critically.

"Of course, some of my color values do not match the Old Master's and the perspective is faulty, but I believe it to be a fair copy."

The lady's eyes, unmagnified, bugged out.

"Oh, I forget," and Helva's voice was really contrite. If she could have blushed, she would have. "You people don't have adjustable vision."

The monitor of this discourse grinned with pride and amusement as Helva's tone indicated pity for the unfortunate.

"Here, this will help," said Helva, substituting a magnifying device in one extension and holding it over the picture.

In a kind of shock, the ladies and gentlemen of the committee bent to observe the incredibly copied and brilliantly executed "Last Supper" on the head of a screw.

"Well," remarked one gentleman who had been forced to accompany his wife, "the good Lord can eat where angels fear to tread."

"Are you referring, sir," asked Helva politely, "to the Dark Age discussions of the number of angels who could stand on the head of a pin?"

"I had that in mind."

"If you substitute 'atom' for 'angel,' the problem is not insoluble, given the metallic content of the pin in question."

"Which you are programmed to compute?"

"Of course."

"Did they remember to program a sense of humor, as well, young lady?"

"We are directed to develop a sense of proportion, sir, which contributes the same effect."

The good man chortled appreciatively and decided the trip was worth his time.

If the investigation committee spent months digesting the thoughtful food served them at the Laboratory School, they left Helva with a morsel as well.

"Singing" as applicable to herself required research. She had, of course, been exposed to and enjoyed a music appreciation course that had included the better known classical works such as "Tristan und Isolde," "Candide," "Oklahoma," and "Le Nozze di Figaro," along with the atomic age singers, Birgit Nilsson, Bob Dylan, and Geraldine Todd, as well as the curious rhythmic progressions of the Venusians, Capellan visual chromatics, the sonic concerti of the Altairians and Reticulan croons. But "singing" for any shell-person posed considerable technical difficulties. Shell-people were schooled to examine every aspect of a problem or situation before making a prognosis. Balanced properly between optimism and practicality, the nondefeatist attitude of the shell-people led them to extricate themselves, their ships, and personnel from bizarre situations. Therefore, to Helva, the problem that she couldn't open her mouth to sing, among other restrictions, did not bother her. She would work out a method, bypassing her limitations, whereby she could sing.

She approached the problem by investigating the methods of sound reproduction through the centuries, human and instrumental. Her own sound production equipment was essentially more instrumental than vocal. Breath control and the proper enunciation of vowel sounds within the oral cavity appeared to require the most development and practice. Shell-people did not, strictly speaking, breathe. For their purposes, oxygen and other gases were not drawn from the surrounding atmosphere through the medium of lungs but sustained artificially by solution in their shells. After experimentation, Helva discovered that she could manipulate her diaphragmic unit to sustain tone. By relaxing the throat muscles and expanding the oral cavity well into the frontal sinuses, she could direct the vowel sounds into the most felicitous position for proper reproduction through her throat microphone. She compared the results with tape recordings of modern singers and was not unpleased, although her own tapes had a peculiar quality about them, not at all unharmonious, merely unique. Acquiring a repertoire from the Laboratory library was no problem to one trained to perfect recall. She found herself able to sing any role and any song which struck her fancy. It would not have occurred to her that it was curious for a female to sing bass, baritone, tenor, mezzo, soprano, and coloratura as she pleased. It was, to Helva, only a matter of the correct reproduction and diaphragmic control required by the music attempted.

If the authorities remarked on her curious avocation, they did so among themselves. Shell-people were encouraged to develop a hobby so long as they maintained proficiency in their technical work.

On the anniversary of her 16th year, Helva was unconditionally graduated and installed in her ship, the XH-834. Her permanent titanium shell was recessed behind an even more indestructible barrier in the central shaft of the scout ship. The neural, audio, visual, and sensory connections were made and sealed. Her extendibles were diverted, connected or augmented and the final, delicate-beyond-description brain taps were completed while Helva remained anesthetically unaware of the proceedings. When she woke, she *was* the ship. Her brain and intelligence controlled every function from navigation to such loading as a scout ship of her class needed. She could take care of herself, and her ambulatory half, in any situation already recorded in the annals of Central Worlds and any situation its most fertile minds could imagine.

Her first actual flight, for she and her kind had made mock flights on dummy panels since they were 8, showed her to be a complete master of the techniques of her profession. She was ready for her great adventures and the arrival of her mobile partner.

There were nine qualified scouts sitting around collecting base pay the day Helva reported for active duty. There were several missions that demanded instant attention, but Helva had been of interest to several department heads in Central for some time and each bureau chief was determined to have her assigned to *his* section. No one had remembered to introduce Helva to the prospective partners. The ship always chose its own partner. Had there been another brain ship at the base at the moment, Helva would have been guided to make the first move. As it was, while Central wrangled among itself, Robert Tanner sneaked out of the pilots' barracks, out to the field and over to Helva's slim metal hull.

"Hello, anyone at home?" Tanner said.

"Of course," replied Helva, activating her outside scanners. "Are you my partner?" she asked hopefully, as she recognized the Scout Service uniform.

"All you have to do is ask," he retorted in a wistful tone.

"No one has come. I thought perhaps there were no partners available and I've had no directives from Central."

Even to herself Helva sounded a little self-pitying, but the truth was she was lonely, sitting on the darkened field. She had always had the company of other shells and, more recently, technicians by the score. The sudden solitude had lost its momentary charm and become oppressive.

"No directives from Central is scarcely a cause for regret, but there happen to be eight other guys biting their fingernails to the quick just waiting for an invitation to board you, you beautiful thing."

Tanner was inside the central cabin as he said this, running appreciative fingers over her panel, the scout's gravity-chair, poking his head into the cabins, the galley, the head, the pressured-storage compartments.

"Now, if you want to goose Central and do *us* a favor all in one, call up the barracks and let's have a ship-warming partner-picking party. Hmmmm?"

Helva chuckled to herself. He was so completely different from the occasional visitors or the various Laboratory technicians she had encountered. He was so gay, so assured, and she was delighted by his suggestion of a partner-picking party. Certainly it was not against anything in her understanding of regulations.

"Cencom, this is XH-834. Connect me with Pilot Barracks."

"Visual?"

"Please."

A picture of lounging men in various attitudes of boredom came on her screen.

"This is XH-834. Would the unassigned scouts do me the favor of coming aboard?"

Eight figures galvanized into action, grabbing pieces of wearing apparel, disengaging tape mechanisms, disentangling themselves from bedsheets and towels.

Helva dissolved the connection while Tanner chuckled gleefully and settled down to await their arrival.

Helva was engulfed in an unshell-like flurry of anticipation. No actress on her opening night could have been more apprehensive, fearful or breathless. Unlike the actress, she could throw no hysterics, china objets d'art or grease-paint to relieve her tension. She could, of course, check her stores for edibles and drinks, which she did, serving Tanner from the virgin selection of her commissary.

Scouts were colloquially known as "brawns" as opposed to their ship "brains." They had to pass as rigorous a training program as the brains and only the top 1 percent of each contributory world's highest scholars were admitted to Central Worlds Scout Training Program. Consequently the eight young men who came pounding up the gantry into Helva's hospitable lock were unusually fine-looking, intelligent, well-coordinated and adjusted young men, looking forward to a slightly drunken evening, Helva permitting, and all quite willing to do each other dirt to get possession of her.

Such a human invasion left Helva mentally breathless, a luxury she thoroughly enjoyed for the brief time she felt she should permit it.

She sorted out the young men. Tanner's opportunism amused but did not specifically attract her; the blond Nordsen seemed too simple; dark-haired Al-atpay had a kind of obstinacy with which she felt no compassion; Mir-Ahnin's bitterness hinted an inner darkness she did not wish to lighten, although he made the biggest outward play for her attention. Hers was a curious courtship—this would be only the first of several marriages for her, for brawns retired after 75 years of service, or earlier if they were unlucky. Brains, their bodies safe from any deterioration, were indestructible. In theory, once a shell-person had paid off the massive debt of early care, surgical adaptation and maintenance charges, he or she was free to seek employment elsewhere. In practice, shell-people remained in the service until they chose to self-destruct or died in line of duty. Helva had actually spoken to one shell-person 322 years old.

She had been so awed by the contact she hadn't presumed to ask the personal questions she had wanted to.

Her choice of a brawn did not stand out from the others until Tanner started to sing a scout ditty, recounting the misadventures of the bold, dense, painfully inept Billy Brawn. An attempt at harmony resulted in cacophony and Tanner wagged his arms wildly for silence.

"What we need is a roaring good lead tenor. Jennan, besides palming aces, what do you sing?"

"Sharp," Jennan replied with easy good humor.

"If a tenor is absolutely necessary, I'll attempt it," Helva volunteered.

"My good *woman,*" Tanner protested.

"Sound your 'A,' " laughed Jennan.

Into the stunned silence that followed the rich, clear, high 'A,' Jennan remarked quietly, "Such an A Caruso would have given the rest of his notes to sing."

It did not take them long to discover her full range.

"All Tanner asked for was one roaring good lead tenor," Jennan said jokingly, "and our sweet mistress supplied us an entire repertory company. The boy who gets this ship will go far, far, far."

"To the Horsehead Nebula?" asked Nordsen, quoting an old Central saw.

"To the Horsehead Nebula and back, we shall make beautiful music," said Helva, chuckling.

"Together," Jennan said. "Only you'd better make the music and, with my voice, I'd better listen."

"I rather imagined it would be I who listened," suggested Helva.

Jennan executed a stately bow with an intricate flourish of his crush-brimmed hat. He directed his bow toward the central control pillar where Helva *was.* Her own personal preference crystallized at that precise moment and for that particular reason: Jennan, alone of the men, had addressed his remarks directly at her physical presence, regardless of the fact that he knew she could pick up his image wherever he was in the ship and regardless of the fact that her body was behind massive metal walls. Throughout their partnership, Jennan never failed to turn his head in her direction no matter where he was in relation to her. In response to this personalization, Helva at that moment and from then on always spoke to Jennan only through her central mike, even though that was not always the most efficient method.

Helva didn't know that she fell in love with Jennan that evening. As she had never been exposed to love or affection, only the drier cousins, respect and admiration, she could scarcely have recognized her reaction to the warmth of his personality and thoughtfulness. As a shell-person, she considered herself remote from emotions largely connected with physical desires.

"Well, Helva, it's been swell meeting you," said Tanner suddenly as she and Jennan were arguing about the baroque quality of "Come All Ye Sons of Art." "See you in space some time, you lucky dog, Jennan. Thanks for the party, Helva."

"You don't have to go so soon?" asked Helva, realizing belatedly that she and Jennan had been excluding the others from this discussion.

"Best man won," Tanner said, wryly. "Guess I'd better go get a tape on love ditties. Might need 'em for the next ship, if there're any more at home like you."

Helva and Jennan watched them leave, both a little confused.

"Perhaps Tanner's jumping to conclusions?" Jennan asked.

Helva regarded him as he slouched against the console, facing her shell directly. His arms were crossed on his chest and the glass he held had been empty for some time. He was handsome, they all were; but his watchful eyes were unwary, his mouth assumed a smile easily, his voice (to which Helva was particularly drawn) was resonant, deep, and without unpleasant overtones or accent.

"Sleep on it, at any rate, Helva. Call me in the morning if it's your opt."

She called him at breakfast, after she had checked her choice through Central. Jennan moved his things aboard, received their joint commission, had his personality and experience file locked into her reviewer, gave her the coordinates of their first mission. The XH-834 officially became the JH-834.

Their first mission was a dull but necessary crash priority (Medical got Helva), rushing a vaccine to a distant system plagued with a virulent spore disease. They had only to get to Spica as fast as possible.

After the initial, thrilling forward surge at her maximum speed, Helva realized her muscles were to be given less of a workout than her brawn on this tedious mission. But they did have plenty of time for exploring each other's personalities. Jennan, of course, knew what Helva was capable of as a ship and partner, just as she knew what she could expect from him. But these were only facts and Helva looked forward eagerly to learning that human side of her partner which could not be reduced to a series of symbols. Nor could the give and take of two personalities be learned from a book. It had to be experienced.

"My father was a scout, too, or is that programmed?" began Jennan their third day out.

"Naturally."

"Unfair, you know. You've got all my family history and I don't know one blamed thing about yours."

"I've never known either," Helva said. "Until I read yours, it hadn't occurred to me I must have one, too, someplace in Central's files."

Jennan snorted. "Shell psychology!"

Helva laughed. "Yes, and I'm even programmed against curiosity about it. You'd better be, too."

Jennan ordered a drink, slouched into the gravity couch opposite her, put his feet on the bumpers, turning himself idly from side to side on the gimbals.

"Helva—a made-up name . . ."

"With a Scandinavian sound."

"You aren't blonde," Jennan said positively.

"Well, then, there're dark Swedes."

"And blonde Turks and this one's harem is limited to one."

"Your woman in purdah, yes, but you can comb the pleasure houses—" Helva found herself aghast at the edge to her carefully trained voice.

"You know," Jennan interrupted her, deep in some thought of his own, "my father gave me the impression he was a lot more married to his ship, the Silvia, than to my mother. I know I used to think Silvia was my grandmother. She was a low number so she must have been a great-great-grandmother at least. I used to talk to her for hours."

"Her registry?" asked Helva, unwittingly jealous of everyone and anyone who had shared his hours.

"422. I think she's TS now. I ran into Tom Burgess once."

Jennan's father had died of a planetary disease, the vaccine for which his ship had used up in curing the local citizens.

"Tom said she'd got mighty tough and salty. You lose your sweetness and I'll come back and haunt you, girl," Jennan threatened.

Helva laughed. He startled her by stamping up to the column panel, touching it with light, tender fingers.

"I *wonder* what you look like," he said softly, wistfully.

Helva had been briefed about this natural curiosity of scouts. She didn't know anything about herself and none of them ever would or could.

"Pick any form, shape, and shade and I'll be yours obliging," she countered, as training suggested.

"Iron Maiden, I fancy blondes with long tresses," and Jennan panto-mined Lady Godiva-like tresses. "Since you're immolated in titanium, I'll call you Brunhilde, my dear," and he made his bow.

With a chortle, Helva launched into the appropriate aria just as Spica made contact.

"What'n'ell's that yelling about? Who are you? And unless you're Central Worlds Medical go away. We've got a plague. No visiting privileges."

"My ship is singing, we're the JH-834 of Worlds and we've got your vaccine. What are our landing coordinates?"

"Your *ship* is singing?"

"The greatest S.A.T.B. in organized space. Any request?"

The JH-834 delivered the vaccine but no more arias and received immediate orders to proceed to Leviticus IV. By the time they got there,

Jennan found a reputation awaiting him and was forced to defend the 834's virgin honor.

"I'll stop singing," murmured Helva contritely as she ordered up poultices for this third black eye in a week.

"You will not," Jennan said through gritted teeth. "If I have to black eyes from here to the Horsehead to keep the snicker out of the title, we'll be the ship who sings."

After the "ship who sings" tangled with a minor but vicious narcotic ring in the Lesser Magellanics, the title became definitely respectful. Central was aware of each episode and punched out a "special interest" key on JH-834's file. A first-rate team was shaking down well.

Jennan and Helva considered themselves a first-rate team, too, after their tidy arrest.

"Of all the vices in the universe, I *hate* drug addiction," Jennan remarked as they headed back to Central Base. "People can go to hell quick enough without that kind of help."

"Is that why you volunteered for Scout Service? To redirect traffic?"

"I'll bet my official answer's on your review."

"In far too flowery wording. 'Carrying on the traditions of my family, which has been proud of four generations in Service,' if I may quote you your own words."

Jennan groaned. "I was *very* young when I wrote that. I certainly hadn't been through Final Training. And once I was in Final Training, my pride wouldn't let me fail. . . .

"As I mentioned, I used to visit Dad on board the Silvia and I've a very good idea she might have had her eye on me as a replacement for my father because I had had massive doses of scout-oriented propaganda. It took. From the time I was 7, I was going to be a scout or else." He shrugged as if deprecating a youthful determination that had taken a great deal of mature application to bring to fruition.

"Ah, so? Scout Sahir Silan on the JS-44 penetrating into the Horsehead Nebulae?"

Jennan chose to ignore her sarcasm.

"With *you*, I may even get that far. But even with Silvia's nudging *I* never day-dreamed myself *that* kind of glory in my wildest flights of fancy. I'll leave the whoppers to your agile brain henceforth. I have in mind a smaller contribution to space history."

"So modest?"

"No. Practical. We also serve, et cetera." He placed a dramatic hand on his heart.

"Glory hound!" scoffed Helva.

"Look who's talking, my Nebula-bound friend. At least I'm not greedy. There'll only be one hero like my dad at Parsaea, but I *would* like to be remembered for some kudo. Everyone does. Why else do or die?"

"Your father died on his way back from Parsaea, if I may point out a few cogent facts. So he could never have known he was a hero for dam-ming the flood with his ship. Which kept Parsaean colony from being abandoned. Which gave them a chance to discover the antiparalytic quali-ties of Parsaea. Which *he* never knew."

"I know," said Jennan softly.

Helva was immediately sorry for the tone of her rebuttal. She knew very well how deep Jennan's attachment to his father had been. On his review a note was made that he had rationalized his father's loss with the unexpected and welcome outcome of the Affair at Parsaea.

"Facts are not human, Helva. My father was and so am I. And *basically,* so are you. Check over your dial, 834. Amid all the wires attached to you is a heart, an underdeveloped human heart. Obviously!"

"I apologize, Jennan," she said.

Jennan hesitated a moment, threw out his hands in acceptance and then tapped her shell affectionately.

"If they ever take us off the milkruns, we'll make a stab at the Nebula, huh?"

As so frequently happened in the Scout Service, within the next hour they had orders to change course, not to the Nebula, but to a recently colonized system with two habitable planets, one tropical, one glacial. The sun, named Ravel, had become unstable; the spectrum was that of a rapidly expanding shell, with absorption lines rapidly displacing toward violet. The augmented heat of the primary had already forced evacuation of the nearer world, Daphnis. The pattern of spectral emissions gave indication that the sun would sear Chloe as well. All ships in the immediate spatial vicinity were to report to Disaster Headquarters on Chloe to effect removal of the remaining colonists.

The JH-834 obediently presented itself and was sent to outlying areas on Chloe to pick up scattered settlers, who did not appear to appreciate the urgency of the situation. Chloe, indeed, was enjoying the first tem-peratures above freezing since it had been flung out of its parent. Since many of the colonists were religious fanatics who had settled on rigorous Chloe to fit themselves for a life of pious reflection, Chloe's abrupt thaw was attributed to sources other than a rampaging sun.

Jennan had to spend so much time countering specious arguments that he and Helva were behind schedule on their way to the fourth and last settlement.

Helva jumped over the high range of jagged peaks that surrounded and sheltered the valley from the former raging snows as well as the present heat. The violent sun with its flaring corona was just beginning to brighten the deep valley as Helva dropped down to a landing.

"They'd better grab their toothbrushes and hop aboard," Helva said. "HQ says speed it up."

"All women," remarked Jennan in surprise as he walked down to meet them. "Unless the men on Chloe wear furred skirts."

"Charm 'em but pare the routine to the bare essentials. And turn on your two-way private."

Jennan advanced smiling, but his explanation of his mission was met with absolute incredulity and considerable doubt as to his authenticity. He groaned inwardly as the matriarch paraphrased previous explanations of the warming sun.

"Revered mother, there's been an overload on that prayer circuit and the sun is blowing itself up in one obliging burst. I'm here to take you to the spaceport at Rosary—"

"That Sodom?" The worthy woman glowered and shuddered disdainfully at his suggestion. "We thank you for your warning but we have no wish to leave our cloister for the rude world. We must go about our morning meditation which has been interrupted—"

"It'll be permanently interrupted when that sun starts broiling you. You must come now," Jennan said firmly.

"Madame," said Helva, realizing that perhaps a female voice might carry more weight in this instance than Jennan's very masculine charm.

"Who spoke?" cried the nun, startled by the bodiless voice.

"I, Helva, the ship. Under my protection you and your sisters-in-faith may enter safely and be unprofaned by association with a male. I will guard you and take you safely to a place prepared for you."

The matriarch peered cautiously into the ship's open port.

"Since only Central Worlds is permitted the use of such ships, I acknowledge that you are not trifling with us, young man. However, we are in no danger here."

"The temperature at Rosary is now 99°," said Helva. "As soon as the sun's rays penetrate directly into this valley, it will also be 99°, and it is due to climb to approximately 180° today. I notice your buildings are made of wood with moss chinking. Dry moss. It should fire around noontime."

The sunlight was beginning to slant into the valley through the peaks and the fierce rays warmed the restless group behind the matriarch. Several opened the throats of their furry parkas.

"Jennan," said Helva privately to him, "our time is very short."

"I can't leave them, Helva. Some of those girls are barely out of their teens."

"Pretty, too. No wonder the matriarch doesn't want to get in."

"Helva."

"It will be the Lord's will," said the matriarch stoutly and turned her back squarely on rescue.

"To burn to death?" shouted Jennan as she threaded her way through her murmuring disciples.

"They want to be martyrs? Their opt, Jennan," said Helva dispassionately. "We must leave and that is no longer a matter of option."

"How can I leave, Helva?"

"Parsaea?" Helva asked tauntingly as he stepped forward to grab one of the women. "You can't drag them *all* aboard and we don't have time to fight it out. Get on board, Jennan, or I'll have you on report."

"They'll die," muttered Jennan dejectedly as he reluctantly turned to climb on board.

"You can risk only so much," Helva said sympathetically. "As it is we'll just have time to make a rendezvous. Lab reports a critical speedup in spectral evolution."

Jennan was already in the airlock when one of the younger women, screaming, rushed to squeeze in the closing port. Her action set off the others. They stampeded through the narrow opening. Even crammed back to breast, there was not enough room inside for all the women. Jennan broke out spacesuits to the three who would have to remain with him in the airlock. He wasted valuable time explaining to the matriarch that she must put on the suit because the airlock had no independent oxygen or cooling units.

"We'll be caught," said Helva in a grim tone to Jennan on their private connection. "We've lost 18 minutes in this last-minute rush. I am now overloaded for maximum speed and I must attain maximum speed to outrun the heat wave."

"Can you lift? We're suited."

"Lift? Yes," she said, doing so. "Run? I stagger."

Jennan, bracing himself and the women, could feel her sluggishness as she blasted upward. Heartlessly, Helva applied thrust as long as she could, despite the fact that the gravitational force mashed her cabin passengers brutally and crushed two fatally. It was a question of saving as many as possible. The only one for whom she had any concern was Jennan and she was in desperate terror about his safety. Airless and uncooled, protected by only one layer of metal, not three, the airlock was not going to be safe for the four trapped there, despite their spacesuits. These were only the standard models, not built to withstand the excessive heat to which the ship would be subjected.

Helva ran as fast as she could but the incredible wave of heat from the explosive sun caught them halfway to cold safety.

She paid no heed to the cries, moans, pleas, and prayers in her cabin. She listened only to Jennan's tortured breathing, to the missing throb in his suit's purifying system and the sucking of the overloaded cooling unit. Helpless, she heard the hysterical screams of his three companions as they writhed in the awful heat. Vainly, Jennan tried to calm them, tried to explain they would soon be safe and cool if they could be still and endure the heat. Undisciplined by their terror and torment, they tried to strike out at him despite the close quarters. One flailing arm became entangled in the leads to his power pack and the damage was quickly done. A connection, weakened by heat and the dead weight of the arm, broke.

For all the power at her disposal, Helva was helpless. She watched as Jennan fought for his breath, as he turned his head beseechingly toward *her*, and died.

Only the iron conditioning of her training prevented Helva from swinging around and plunging back into the cleansing heart of the exploding sun. Numbly she made rendezvous with the refugee convoy. She obediently transferred her burned, heat-prostrated passengers to the assigned transport.

"I will retain the body of my scout and proceed to the nearest base for burial," she informed Central dully.

"You will be provided escort," was the reply.

"I have no need of escort."

"Escort is provided, XH-834," she was told curtly. The shock of hearing Jennan's initial severed from her call number cut off her half-formed protest. Stunned, she waited by the transport until her screens showed the arrival of two other slim brain ships. The cortege proceeded homeward at unfunereal speeds.

"834? The ship who sings?"

"I have no more songs."

"Your scout was Jennan."

"I do not wish to communicate."

"I'm 422."

"Silvia?"

"Silvia died a long time ago. I'm 422. Currently MS," the ship rejoined curtly. "AH-640 is our other friend, but Henry's not listening in. Just as well—he wouldn't understand it if you wanted to turn rogue. But I'd stop *him* if he tried to deter you."

"Rogue?" The term snapped Helva out of her apathy.

"Sure. You're young. You've got power for years. Skip. Others have done it. 732 went rogue 20 years ago after she lost her scout on a mission to that white dwarf. Hasn't been seen since."

"I never heard about rogues."

"As it's exactly the thing we're conditioned against, you sure wouldn't hear about it in school, my dear," 422 said.

"Break conditioning?" cried Helva, anguished, thinking longingly of the white, white furious hot heart of the sun she had just left.

"For you I don't think it would be hard at the moment," 422 said quietly, her voice devoid of her earlier cynicism. "The stars are out there, winking."

"Alone?" cried Helva from her heart.

"Alone!" 422 confirmed bleakly.

Alone with all of space and time. Even the Horsehead Nebula would not be far enough away to daunt her. Alone with a hundred years to live with her memories and nothing . . . nothing more.

"Was Parsaea worth it?" she asked 422 softly.

"Parsaea?" 422 repeated, surprised. "With his father? Yes. We were

there, at Parsaea, when we were needed. Just as you . . . and his son
. . . were at Chloe. When you were needed. The crime is not knowing
where need is and not being there."

"But *I* need *him*. Who will supply my need?" said Helva bitterly. . . .

"834," said 422 after a day's silent speeding, "Central wishes your report. A replacement awaits your opt at Regulus Base. Change course
accordingly."

"A replacement?" That was certainly not what she needed . . . a reminder inadequately filling the void Jennan left. Why, her hull was barely
cool of Chloe's heat. Atavistically, Helva wanted time to mourn Jennan.

"Oh, none of them are impossible if *you're* a good ship," 422 remarked
philosophically. "And it is just what you need. The sooner the better."

"You told them I wouldn't go rogue, didn't you?" Helva said.

"The moment passed you even as it passed me after Parsaea, and before
that, after Glen Arhur, and Betelgeuse."

"We're conditioned to go on, aren't we? We *can't* go rogue. You were
testing."

"Had to. Orders. Not even Psych knows why a rogue occurs. Central's
very worried, and so, daughter, are your sister ships. I asked to be your
escort. I . . . don't want to lose you both."

In her emotional nadir, Helva could feel a flood of gratitude for Silvia's
rough sympathy.

"We've all known this grief, Helva. It's no consolation, but if we couldn't
feel with our scouts, we'd only be machines wired for sound."

Helva looked at Jennan's still form stretched before her in its shroud
and heard the echo of his rich voice in the quiet cabin.

"Silvia! I *couldn't* help him," she cried from her soul.

"Yes, dear, I know," 422 murmured gently and then was quiet.

The three ships sped on, wordless, to the great Central Worlds base
at Regulus. Helva broke silence to acknowledge landing instructions and
the officially tendered regrets.

The three ships set down simultaneously at the wooded edge where
Regulus' gigantic blue trees stood sentinel over the sleeping dead in
the small Service cemetery. The entire Base complement approached
with measured step and formed an aisle from Helva to the burial ground.
The honor detail, out of step, walked slowly into her cabin. Reverently
they placed the body of her dead love on the wheeled bier, covered it
honorably with the deep blue, star-splashed flag of the Service. She
watched as it was driven slowly down the living aisle which closed in
behind the bier in last escort.

Then, as the simple words of interment were spoken, as the atmosphere
planes dipped in tribute over the open grave, Helva found voice for
her lonely farewell.

Softly, barely audible at first, the strains of the ancient song of evening
and requiem swelled to the final poignant measure until black space
itself echoed back the sound of the song the ship sang.

BIBLIOGRAPHY

"The Ship Who Sang," *The Magazine of Fantasy and Science Fiction*, April 1961

"The Ship Who Mourned," *Analog*, March 1966

"The Ship Who Killed," *Galaxy*, October 1966

"The Ship Who Dissembled" (as "The Ship Who Disappeared"), *If*, March 1969

"Dramatic Mission," *Analog*, June 1969

"The Partnered Ship," *The Ship Who Sang*, Walker and Company, 1969 (also contains all of the above)

THE KNOWN SPACE SERIES

by Larry Niven

The first future history—the first set of science fiction stories with interlocked assumptions and background events—was and is Robert Heinlein's. The most extensive is Olaf Stapleton's; it reaches all the way to the heat death of the universe. The densest, Poul Anderson's, includes dozens of novels and novellas. I mention these because they were part of my background before ever I sold a story. I knew them better than I knew college-taught history. (It's been only six or seven years since Jerry Pournelle taught me that history can be fun.)

I didn't have to decide to write a future history. I never decided not to.

After all, creating a background for a story can be a hell of a lot of work. It's only sensible to use a good, detailed background again if it fits the story I want to tell. If it doesn't, I have to create a new one, of course. The same remarks apply to a well-drawn character.

Any serious attempt to predict *the* future—a game we all play, and we score ourselves heavily when some prediction comes true—must include more than one story. How else can we show our own concept of history-shaping processes at work?

Picture me at age 27, then, as a man who had sold enough stories to be developing some confidence. I was trying to make one sale a month, and being lenient with myself. Selling a story twice counted twice; a serial was three, plus one for the book sale. A few of my stories had individual backgrounds; a couple were outright fantasies; but in general I stuck to two eras:

In the time of Lucas Garner and the ARMS, the solar system was being industrialized. Humanity was polarizing into Belters and flatlanders (asteroid belt and United Nations). Slower-than-light craft were colonizing nearby stars. Cetaceans had sued certain nations for damages in the UN courts. A true alien had turned up, preserved in stasis, a relic of the Slaver Empire of a billion and a half years earlier.

Five hundred years later was the time of Beowulf Shaeffer. Faster-than-light travel was common. A dozen alien species were known and involved in interlocked trading empires throughout the region called *known space*. *Human space* was the smaller region of worlds colonized by men. The galactic core was known to have exploded, gone the Seyfert galaxy route, ten thousand years earlier, with the wave of deadly radiation still twenty thousand years away.

Understand: the two eras were not mutually exclusive. They just didn't connect. But I wanted to write a story around a certain scene. You'll recognize it in "A

Relic of Empire." It's the bonfire scene. The story I built around it involved a gentleman from one of the worlds of human space, plus a gene-tailored plant from the Slaver Empire.

Thus were two eras linked into one future history.

It's twelve years later. What has *known space* done for me?

Quite a lot. Two of the five Beowulf Shaeffer stories won Hugo awards, nine years apart. *Ringworld,* set two hundred years later, won three awards. I've written stories in five of the eras of known space, ranging in length from 1,000 to 120,000 words, plus the supplementary material in *Tales of Known Space.* In the same time I've written stories and novels outside the series, some with backgrounds in common: cheap teleportation, or magic, or interstellar empires formed with slower-than-light travel.

And I've been threatening to give up the series for seven years or so.

Isaac Asimov described the problems well enough in an article, "Ya Gotta Have a Good Foundation." A series is good for one's career, and one can have endless fun elaborating the assumptions. Wireheading and organlegging in the Lucas Garner era; the puppeteers' selective breeding experiments on humans and kzinti; details of the Man-Kzin Wars . . . But eventually the complexity catches up with one.

Isaac had to reread *everything* whenever he wanted to write another Foundation story, and it *still* didn't work. Fans sent him gloating letters pointing out inconsistencies. *Known space* has a looser background, with more room for the author to move around. But I still get gloating letters. For the sake of an individual story I make one or two assumptions; for all stories set later, they return to haunt me.

In *known space,* Mercury shows only one face to the sun.

A stasis field, properly used, can do almost anything. It follows that in any story where a stasis field wasn't used to solve a problem, I have to explain why.

I got the dates too compressed in the middle period of *known space.* Too much is happening simultaneously. True, it's a big region, isolated by the speed of light; but I should have been more careful.

And I should have made faster-than-light travel impossible in *Ringworld.* With space travel that easy, the Ringworlders should not have needed to build that structure. Yet I've got a damn good explanation . . .

The fact is that I've been writing *known space* stories for all of the time that I've been threatening to stop. The backgrounds fascinate me. I'm running a science fiction/detective series in the Early Period, with a beautiful locked-room mystery on the Moon just waiting to be written. I'm working on *The Ringworld Engineers,* in which a good many mysteries of that structure's history will be cleared up, including why the Outsiders never tried to sell the hyperdrive to the Engineers, and why the Engineers risked building that unstable structure in the first place. I never dealt with the problem of refugees fleeing the Core explosion . . . or with the Man-Kzin Wars themselves . . . or with the rather sticky Grog problem, which does turn out to have a solution, though an expensive one . . . and maybe I won't quit after all.

A Relic of Empire

When the ship arrived, Dr. Richard Schultz-Mann was out among the plants, flying over and around them on a lift belt. He hovered over one, inspecting with proprietary interest an anomalous patch in its yellow foliage. This one would soon be ripe.

The nature-lover was a breadstick of a man, very tall and very thin, with an aristocratic head sporting a close-cropped growth of coppery hair and an asymmetric beard. A white streak ran above his right ear, and there was a patch of white on each side of the chin, one coinciding with the waxed spike. As his head moved in the double sunlight, the patches changed color instantly.

He took a tissue sample from the grayish patch, stored it, and started to move on. . . .

The ship came down like a daylight meteor, streaking blue-white across the vague red glare of Big Mira. It slowed and circled high overhead, weaving drunkenly across the sky, then settled toward the plain near Mann's *Explorer*. Mann watched it land, then gave up his bumblebee activities and went to welcome the newcomers. He was amazed at the coincidence. As far as he knew, his had been the first ship ever to land here. The company would be good . . . but what could anyone possibly want here?

Little Mira set while he was skimming back. A flash of white at the far edge of the sea, and the tiny blue-white dwarf was gone. The shadows changed abruptly, turning the world red. Mann took off his pink-tinged goggles. Big Mira was still high, sixty degrees above the horizon and two hours from second sunset.

The newcomer was huge, a thick blunt-nosed cylinder twenty times the size of the *Explorer*. It looked old: not damaged, not even weathered, but indefinably old. Its nose was still closed tight, the living bubble retracted, if indeed it had a living bubble. Nothing moved nearby. They must be waiting for his welcome before they debarked.

Mann dropped toward the newcomer.

The stunner took him a few hundred feet up. Without pain and without sound, suddenly all Mann's muscles turned to loose jelly. Fully conscious and completely helpless, he continued to dive toward the ground.

Three figures swarmed up at him from the newcomer's oversized airlock. They caught him before he hit. Tossing humorous remarks at each other in a language Mann did not know, they towed him down to the plain.

The man behind the desk wore a captain's hat and a cheerful smile. "Our supply of Verinol is limited," he said in the trade language. "If I have to use it, I will, but I'd rather save it. You may have heard that it has unpleasant side effects."

"I understand perfectly," said Mann. "You'll use it the moment you think you've caught me in a lie." Since he had not yet been injected with the stuff, he decided it was a bluff. The man had no Verinol, if indeed there was such an animal as Verinol.

But he was still in a bad hole. The ancient, renovated ship held more than a dozen men, whereas Mann seriously doubted if he could have stood up. The sonic had not entirely worn off.

His captor nodded approvingly. He was huge and square, almost a cartoon of a heavy-planet man, with muscularity as smooth and solid as an elephant's. A Jinxian, for anyone's money. His size made the tiny shipboard office seem little more than a coffin. Among the crew his captain's hat would not be needed to enforce orders. He looked like he could kick holes in hullmetal, or teach tact to an armed Kzin.

"You're quick," he said. "That's good. I'll be asking questions about you and about this planet. You'll give truthful, complete answers. If some of my questions get too personal, say so; but remember, I'll use the Verinol if I'm not satisfied. How old are you?"

"One hundred and fifty-four."

"You look much older."

"I was off boosterspice for a couple of decades."

"Tough luck. Planet of origin?"

"Wunderland."

"Thought so, with that stick-figure build. Name?"

"Doctor Richard Harvey Schultz-Mann."

"Rich Mann, hah? Are you?"

Trust a Jinxian to spot a pun. "No. After I make my reputation, I'll write a book on the Slaver Empire. Then I'll be rich."

"If you say so. Married?"

"Several times. Not at the moment."

"Rich Mann, I can't give you my real name, but you can call me Captain Kidd. What kind of beard is that?"

"You've never seen an asymmetric beard?"

"No, thank the Mist Demons. It looks like you've shaved off all your hair below the part, and everything on your face left of what looks like a one-tuft goatee. Is that the way it's supposed to go?"

"Exactly so."

"You did it on purpose then."

"Don't mock me, Captain Kidd."

"Point taken. Are they popular on Wunderland?"

Dr. Mann unconsciously sat a little straighter. "Only among those willing to take the time and trouble to keep it neat." He twisted the single waxed spike of beard at the right of his chin with unconscious complacence. This was the only straight hair on his face—the rest of the beard being close-cropped and curly—and it sprouted from one of the white patches. Mann was proud of his beard.

"Hardly seems worth it," said the Jinxian. "I assume it's to show you're one of the leisure classes. What are you doing on Mira Ceti-T?"

"I'm investigating one aspect of the Slaver Empire."

"You're a geologist, then?"

"No, a xenobiologist."

"I don't understand."

"What do you know about the Slavers?"

"A little. They used to live all through this part of the galaxy. One day the slave races decided they'd had enough, and there was a war. When it was over, everyone was dead."

"You know quite a bit. Well, Captain, a billion and a half years is a long time. The Slavers left only two kinds of evidence of their existence. There are the stasis boxes and their contents, mostly weaponry, but records have been found too. And there are the plants and animals developed for the Slavers' convenience by their tnuctip slaves, who were biological engineers."

"I know about those. We have bandersnatchi on Jinx, on both sides of the ocean."

"The bandersnatchi food animals are a special case. They can't mutate; their chromosomes are as thick as your finger, too large to be influenced by radiation. All other relics of tnuctipun engineering have mutated almost beyond recognition. Almost. For the past twelve years I've been searching out and identifying the surviving species."

"It doesn't sound like a fun way to spend a life, Rich Mann. Are there Slaver animals on this planet?"

"Not animals, but plants. Have you been outside yet?"

"Not yet."

"Then come out. I'll show you."

The ship was very large. It did not seem to be furnished with a living bubble, hence the entire lifesystem must be enclosed within the metal walls. Mann walked ahead of the Jinxian down a long unpainted corridor to the airlock, waited inside while the pressure dropped slightly, then rode the escalator to the ground. He would not try to escape yet, though the sonic had worn off. The Jinxian was affable but alert, he carried a flashlight-laser dangling from his belt, his men were all around them, and Mann's lift belt had been removed. Richard Mann was not quixotic.

It was a red, red world. They stood on a dusty plain sparsely scattered with strange yellow-headed bushes. A breeze blew things like tumble-weeds across the plain, things which on second glance were the dried heads of former bushes. No other life-forms were visible. Big Mira sat on the horizon, a vague, fiery semicircular cloud, just dim enough to look at without squinting. Outlined in sharp black silhouette against the red giant's bloody disk were three slender, improbably tall spires, unnaturally straight and regular, each with a vivid patch of yellow vegetation surrounding its base. Members of the Jinxian's crew ran, walked, or floated outside, some playing an improvised variant of baseball, others at work, still others merely enjoying themselves. None were Jinxian, and none had Mann's light-planet build. Mann noticed that a few were using the thin wire blades of variable-knives to cut down some of the straight bushes.

"Those," he said.

"The bushes?"

"Yes. They used to be tnuctip stage trees. We don't know what they looked like originally, but the old records say the Slavers stopped using them some decades before the rebellion. May I ask what those men are doing in my ship?"

Expanded from its clamshell nose, the *Explorer's* living bubble was bigger than the *Explorer*. Held taut by air pressure, isolated from the surrounding environment, proof against any atmospheric chemistry found in nature, the clear fabric hemisphere was a standard feature of all camper-model spacecraft. Mann could see biped shadows moving purposefully about inside and going between the clamshell doors into the ship proper.

"They're not stealing anything, Rich Mann. I sent them in to remove a few components from the drives and the comm systems."

"One hopes they won't damage what they remove."

"They won't. They have their orders."

"I assume you don't want me to call someone," said Mann. He noticed that the men were preparing a bonfire, using stage bushes. The bushes were like miniature trees, four to six feet tall, slender and straight, and the brilliant yellow foliage at the top was flattened like the head of a dandelion. From the low, rounded eastern mountains to the western sea, the red land was sprinkled with the yellow dots of their heads. Men were cutting off the heads and roots, then dragging the logs away to pile them in conical formation over a stack of death-dry tumbleweed heads.

"We don't want you to call the Wunderland police, who happen to be somewhere out there looking for us."

"I hate to pry—"

"No, no, you're entitled to your curiosity. We're pirates."

"Surely you jest. Captain Kidd, if you've figured out a way to make piracy pay off, you must be bright enough to make ten times the money on the stock market."

"Why?"

By the tone of his voice, by his gleeful smile, the Jinxian was baiting him. Fine; it would keep his mind off stage trees. Mann said, "Because you can't *catch* a ship in hyperspace. The only way you can match courses with a ship is to wait until it's in an inhabited system. Then the police come calling."

"I know an inhabited system where there aren't any police."

"The hell you do."

They had walked more or less aimlessly to the *Explorer*'s airlock. Now the Jinxian turned and gazed out over the red plain, toward the dwindling crescent of Big Mira, which now looked like a bad forest fire. "I'm curious about those spires."

"Fine, keep your little secret. I've wondered about them myself, but I haven't had a chance to look at them yet."

"I'd think they'd interest you. They look definitely artificial to me."

"But they're a billion years too young to be Slaver artifacts."

"Rich Mann, are those bushes the only life on this planet?"

"I haven't seen anything else," Mann lied.

"Then it couldn't have been a native race that put those spires up. I never heard of a space-traveling race that builds such big things for mere monuments."

"Neither did I. Shall we look at them tomorrow?"

"Yes." Captain Kidd stepped into the *Explorer*'s airlock, wrapped a vast hand gently around Mann's thin wrist and pulled his captive in beside him. The airlock cycled and Mann followed the Jinxian into the living bubble with an impression that the Jinxian did not quite trust him.

Fine.

It was dark inside the bubble. Mann hesitated before turning on the light. Outside he could see the last red sliver of Big Mira shrinking with visible haste. He saw more. A man was kneeling before the conical bonfire, and a flickering light was growing in the dried bush-head kindling.

Mann turned on the lights, obliterating the outside view. "Go on about piracy," he said.

"Oh, yes." The Jinxian dropped into a chair, frowning. "Piracy was only the end product. It started a year ago, when I found the puppeteer system."

"The—"

"Yes. The puppeteers' home system."

Richard Mann's ears went straight up. He was from Wunderland, remember?

Puppeteers are highly intelligent, herbivorous, and very old as a species. Their corner on interstellar business is as old as the human Bronze Age. And they are cowards.

A courageous puppeteer is not regarded as insane only by other puppeteers. It *is* insane, and usually shows disastrous secondary symptoms: depression, homicidal tendencies, and the like. These poor, warped minds are easy to spot. No sane puppeteer will cross a vehicular roadway or travel in any but the safest available fashion or resist a thief, even an unarmed thief. No sane puppeteer will leave his home system, wherever that may be, without his painless method of suicide, nor will it walk an alien world without guards—nonpuppeteer guards.

The location of the puppeteer system is one of the puppeteer's most closely guarded secrets. Another is the painless suicide gimmick. It may be a mere trick of preconditioning. Whatever it is, it works. Puppeteers cannot be tortured into revealing anything about their home world, though they hate pain. It must be a world with reasonably earthlike atmosphere and temperature, but beyond that nothing is known . . . or was known.

Suddenly Mann wished that they hadn't lit the bonfire so soon. He didn't know how long it would burn before the logs caught, and he wanted to hear more about this.

"I found it just a year ago," the Jinxian repeated. "It's best I don't tell you what I was doing up to then. The less you know about who I am, the better. But when I'd got safely out of the system, I came straight home. I wanted time to think."

"And you picked piracy? Why not blackmail?"

"I thought of that—"

"I should hope so! Can you imagine what the puppeteers would pay to keep that secret?"

"Yes. That's what stopped me. Rich Mann, how much would you have asked for in one lump sum?"

"A round billion stars and immunity from prosecution."

"Okay. Now look at it from the puppeteer point of view. That billion wouldn't buy them complete safety, because you might still talk. But if they spent a tenth of that on detectives, weapons, hit men, et cetera, they could shut your mouth for keeps and also find and hit anyone you might have talked to. I couldn't figure any way to make myself safe and still collect, not with that much potential power against me.

"So I thought of piracy.

"Eight of us had gone in, but I was the only one who'd guessed just what we'd stumbled into. I let the others in on it. Some had friends they could trust, and that raised our number to fourteen. We bought a ship, a very old one, and renovated it. She's an old slowboat's ground-to-orbit auxiliary fitted out with a new hyperdrive; maybe you noticed?"

"No. I saw how old she was."

"We figured even if the puppeteers recognized her, they'd never trace her. We took her back to the puppeteer system and waited."

A flickering light glimmered outside the bubble wall. Any second now the logs would catch . . . Mann tried to relax.

"Pretty soon a ship came in. We waited till it was too deep in the system's gravity well to jump back into hyperspace. Then we matched courses. Naturally they surrendered right away. We went in in suits so they couldn't describe us even if they could tell humans apart. Would you believe they had six hundred million stars in currency?"

"That's pretty good pay. What went wrong?"

"My idiot crew wouldn't leave. We'd figured most of the ships coming into the puppeteer system would be carrying money. They're misers, you know. Part of being a coward is wanting security. And they do most of their mining and manufacturing on other worlds, where they can get labor. So we waited for two more ships, because we had room for lots more money. The puppeteers wouldn't dare attack us inside their own system." Captain Kidd made a sound of disgust. "I can't really blame the men. In a sense they were right. One ship with a fusion drive can do a hell of a lot of damage just by hovering over a city. So we stayed.

"Meanwhile the puppeteers registered a formal complaint with Earth.

"Earth hates people who foul up interstellar trade. We'd offered physical harm to a puppeteer. A thing like that could cause a stock-market crash. So Earth offered the services of every police force in human space. Hardly seems fair, does it?"

"They ganged up on you. But they still couldn't come after you, could they? The puppeteers would have to tell the police how to find their system. They'd hardly do that; not when some human descendant might attack them a thousand years from now."

The Jinxian dialed himself a frozen daiquiri. "They had to wait till we left. I still don't know how they tracked us. Maybe they've got something that can track a gravity warp moving faster than light. I wouldn't put it past them to build it just for us. Anyway, when we angled toward Jinx, we heard them telling the police of We Made It just where we were."

"Ouch."

"We headed for the nearest double star. Not my idea; Hermie Preston's. He thought we could hide in the dust clouds in the trojan points. Whatever the puppeteers were using probably couldn't find us in normal space." Two thirsty gulps had finished his daiquiri. He crumpled the cup, watched it evaporate, dialed another. "The nearest double star was Mira Ceti. We hardly expected to find a planet in the trailing trojan point, but as long as it was there, we decided to use it."

"And here you are."

"Yeah."

"You'll be better off when you've found a way to hide that ship."

"We had to find out about you first, Rich Mann. Tomorrow we'll sink the *Puppet Master* in the ocean. Already we've shut off the fusion drive. The lifters work by battery, and the cops can't detect that."

"Fine. Now for the billion-dollar—"

"No, no, Rich Mann. I will not tell you where to find the puppeteer planet. Give up the whole idea. Shall we join the campfire group?"

Mann came joltingly alert. *How* had the stage trees lasted this long? Thinking fast, he said, "Is your autokitchen as good as mine?"

"Probably not. Why?"

"Let me treat your group to dinner, Captain Kidd."

Captain Kidd shook his head, smiling. "No offense, Rich Mann, but I can't read your kitchen controls, and there's no point in tempting you. You might rashly put someth—"

WHAM!

The living bubble bulged inward, snapped back. Captain Kidd swore and ran for the airlock. Mann stayed seated, motionless, hoping against hope that the Jinxian had forgotten him.

WHAM! WHAM! Flares of light from the region of the campfire. Captain Kidd frantically punched the cycle button, and the opaque inner door closed on him. Mann came to his feet, running.

WHAM! The concussion hurt his ears and set the bubble rippling. Burning logs must be flying in all directions. The airlock recycled, empty. No telling where the Jinxian was; the outer door was opaque too. Well, that worked both ways.

WHAM!

Mann searched through the airlock locker, pushing sections of spacesuit aside to find the lift belt. It wasn't there. He'd been wearing it; they'd taken it off him after they shot him down.

He moaned: a tormented, uncouth sound to come from a cultured Wunderlander. He *had* to have a lift belt.

WHAMWHAMWHAM. Someone was screaming far away.

Mann snatched up the suit's chest-and-shoulder section and locked it around him. It was rigid vacuum armor, with a lift motor built into the back. He took an extra moment to screw down the helmet, then hit the cycle button.

No use searching for weapons. They'd have taken even a variable-knife.

The Jinxian could be just outside waiting. He might have realized the truth by now.

The door opened. . . . Captain Kidd was easy to find, a running misshapen shadow and a frantic booming voice. "Flatten out, you yeastheads! It's an attack!" He hadn't guessed. But he must know that the We Made It police would use stunners.

Mann twisted his lift control to full power.

The surge of pressure took him under the armpits. Two standard gees sent blood rushing to his feet, pushed him upward with four times Wunderland's gravity. A last stage log exploded under him, rocked him back and forth, and then all was dark and quiet.

He adjusted the attitude setting to slant him almost straight forward.

The dark ground sped beneath him. He moved northeast. Nobody was following him—yet.

Captain Kidd's men would have been killed, hurt, or at least stunned when the campfire exploded in their faces. He'd expected Captain Kidd to chase him, but the Jinxian couldn't have caught him. Lift motors are all alike, and Mann wasn't as heavy as the Jinxian.

He flew northeast, flying very low, knowing that the only landmarks big enough to smash him were the spires to the west. When he could no longer see the ships' lights, he turned south, still very low. Still nobody followed him. He was glad he'd taken the helmet; it protected his eyes from the wind.

In the blue dawn he came awake. The sky was darker than navy blue, and the light around him was dim, like blue moonlight. Little Mira was a hurtingly bright pinpoint between two mountain peaks, bright enough to sear holes in a man's retinae. Mann unscrewed his helmet, adjusted the pink goggles over his eyes. Now it was even darker.

He poked his nose above the yellow moss. The plain and sky were empty of men. The pirates must be out looking for him, but they hadn't gotten here yet. So far so good.

Far out across the plain there was fire. A stage tree rose rapidly into the black sky, minus its roots and flowers, the wooden flanges at its base holding it in precarious aerodynamic stability. A white rope of smoke followed it up. When the smoke cut off, the tree became invisible . . . until, much higher, there was a puff of white cloud like a flak burst. Now the seeds would be spreading across the sky.

Richard Mann smiled. Wonderful, how the stage trees had adapted to the loss of their masters. The Slavers had raised them on wide plantations, using the solid-fuel rocket cores inside the living bark to lift their ships from places where a fusion drive would have done damage. But the trees used the rockets for reproduction, to scatter their seeds farther than any plant before them.

Ah, well . . . Richard Mann snuggled deeper into the yellow woolly stuff around him and began to consider his next move. He was a hero now in the eyes of humanity-at-large. He had badly damaged the pirate crew. When the police landed, he could count on a reward from the puppeteers. Should he settle for that or go on to bigger stakes?

The *Puppet Master*'s cargo was bigger stakes, certainly. But even if he could take it, which seemed unlikely, how could he fit it into his ship? How escape the police of We Made It?

No. Mann had another stake in mind, one just as valuable and infinitely easier to hide.

What Captain Kidd apparently hadn't realized was that blackmail is not immoral to a puppeteer. There are well-established rules of conduct that make blackmail perfectly safe both for blackmailer and victim. Two are that the blackmailer must submit to having certain portions of his memory erased, and must turn over all evidence against the victim. Mann was prepared to do this if he could force Captain Kidd to tell him where to find the puppeteer system.

But how?

Well, he knew one thing the Jinxian didn't. . . .

Little Mira rose fast, arc blue, a hole into hell. Mann remained where he was, an insignificant mote in the yellow vegetation below one of the spires Captain Kidd had remarked on last night. The spire was a good half mile high. An artifact that size would seem impossibly huge to any but an Earthman. The way it loomed over him made Mann uncomfortable. In shape it was a slender cone with a base three hundred feet across. The surface near the base was gray and smooth to touch, like polished granite.

The yellow vegetation was a thick, rolling carpet. It spread out around the spire in an uneven circle half a mile in diameter and dozens of feet deep. It rose about the base in a thick turtleneck collar. Close up, the stuff wasn't even discrete plants. It looked like a cross between moss and wool, dyed flagrant yellow.

It made a good hiding place. Not perfect, of course; a heat sensor would pick him out in a flash. He hadn't thought of that last night, and now it worried him. Should he get out, try to reach the sea?

The ship would certainly carry a heat sensor, but not a portable one. A portable heat sensor would be a weapon, a nighttime gunsight, and weapons of war had been illegal for some time in human space.

But the *Puppet Master* could have stopped elsewhere to get such implements. Kzinti, for example.

Nonsense. Why would Captain Kidd have needed portable weapons with night gunsights? He certainly hadn't expected puppeteers to fight hand-to-hand! The stunners were mercy weapons; even a pirate would not dare kill a puppeteer, and Captain Kidd was no ordinary pirate.

All right. Radar? He need only burrow into the moss/wool. Sight search? Same answer. Radio? Mental note: Do not transmit anything.

Mental note? There was a dictaphone in his helmet. He used it after pulling the helmet out of the moss/wool around him.

Flying figures. Mann watched them for a long moment, trying to spot the Jinxian. There were only four, and he wasn't among them. The four were flying northwest of him, moving south. Mann ducked into the moss.

"Hello, Rich Mann."

The voice was low, contorted with fury. Mann felt the shock race through him, contracting every muscle with the fear of death. It came from behind him!

From his helmet.

"Hello, Rich Mann. Guess where I am?"

He couldn't turn it off. Spacesuit helmet radios weren't built to be turned off: a standard safety factor. If one were fool enough to ignore safety, one could insert an "off" switch; but Mann had never felt the need.

"I'm in your ship, using your ship-to-suit radio circuit. That was a good trick you played last night. I didn't even know what a stage tree was till I looked it up in your library."

He'd just have to endure it. A pity he couldn't answer back.

"You killed four of my men and put five more in the autodoc tanks. Why'd you do it, Rich Mann? You must have known we weren't going to kill you. Why should we? There's no blood on *our* hands."

You lie, Mann thought at the radio. *People die in a market crash. And the ones who live are the ones who suffer. Do you know what it's like to be suddenly poor and not know how to live poor?*

"I'll assume you want something, Rich Mann. All right. What? The money in my hold? That's ridiculous. You'd never get in. You want to turn us in for a reward? Fat chance. You've got no weapons. If we find you now, we'll kill you."

The four searchers passed far to the west, their headlamps spreading yellow light across the blue dusk. They were no danger to him now. A pity they and their fellows should have been involved in what amounted to a vendetta.

"The puppeteer planet, of course. The modern El Dorado. But you don't know where it is, do you? I wonder if I ought to give you a hint. Of course you'd never know whether I was telling the truth. . . ."

Did the Jinxian know how to live poor? Mann shuddered. The old memories came back only rarely; but when they came, they hurt.

You have to learn not to buy luxuries before you've bought necessities. You can starve learning which is which. Necessities are food and a place to sleep, shoes and pants. Luxuries are tobacco, restaurants, fine shirts, throwing away a ruined meal while you're learning to cook, quitting a job you don't like. A union is a necessity. Boosterspice is a luxury.

The Jinxian wouldn't know about that. He'd had the money to buy his own ship.

"Ask me politely, Rich Mann. Would you like to know where I found the puppeteer system?"

Mann had leased the *Explorer* on a college grant. It had been the latest step in a long climb upward. Before that . . .

He was half his lifetime old when the crash came. Until then boosterspice had kept him as young as the ageless idle ones who were his friends and relatives. Overnight he was one of the hungry. A number of his partners in disaster had ridden their lift belts straight up into eternity; Richard Schultz-Mann had sold his for his final dose of boosterspice. Before he could afford boosterspice again, there were wrinkles in his forehead, the texture of his skin had changed, his sex urge had decreased,

*strange white patches had appeared in his hair, there were twinges in
his back. He still got them.*

*Yet always he had maintained his beard. With the white spike and
the white streak it looked better than ever. After the boosterspice restored
color to his hair, he dyed the patches back in again.*

"Answer me, Rich Mann!"

Go ride a bandersnatch.

It was a draw. Captain Kidd couldn't entice him into answering, and
Mann would never know the pirate's secret. If Kidd dropped his ship
in the sea, Mann could show it to the police. At least that would be
something.

Luckily Kidd couldn't move the *Explorer.* Otherwise he could take
both ships half around the planet, leaving Mann stranded.

The four pirates were far to the south. Captain Kidd had apparently
given up on the radio. There were water and food syrup in his helmet;
Mann would not starve.

Where in blazes were the police? On the other side of the planet?

Stalemate.

Big Mira came as a timorous peeping Tom, poking its rim over the
mountains like red smoke. The land brightened, taking on tinges of lavender against long, long navy blue shadows. The shadows shortened and
became vague.

The morality of his position was beginning to bother Dr. Richard Mann.

In attacking the pirates, he had done his duty as a citizen. The pirates
had sullied humanity's hard-won reputation for honesty. Mann had struck
back.

But his motive? Fear had been two parts of that motive. First, the
fear that Captain Kidd might decide to shut his mouth. Second, the fear
of being poor.

That fear had been with him for some time.

Write a book and make a fortune! It looked good on paper. The thirty-
light-year sphere of human space contained nearly fifty billion readers.
Persuade one percent of them to shell out half a star each for a disposable
tape, and your four-percent royalties became twenty million stars. But
most books nowadays were flops. You had to scream very loud nowadays
to get the attention of even ten billion readers. Others were trying to
drown you out.

Before Captain Kidd, that had been Richard Schultz-Mann's sole hope
of success.

He'd behaved within the law. Captain Kidd couldn't make that claim;
but Captain Kidd hadn't killed anybody.

Mann sighed. He'd had no choice. His major motive was honor, and
that motive still held.

He moved restlessly in his nest of damp moss/wool. The day was heating up, and his suit's temperature control would not work with half a suit.

What was that?

It was the *Puppet Master,* moving effortlessly toward him on its lifters. The Jinxian must have decided to get it under water before the human law arrived.

. . . Or had he?

Mann adjusted his lift motor until he was just short of weightless, then moved cautiously around the spire. He saw the four pirates moving to intersect the *Puppet Master.* They'd see him if he left the spire. But if he stayed, those infrared detectors . . .

He'd have to chance it.

The suit's padded shoulders gouged his armpits as he streaked toward the second spire. He stopped in midair over the moss and dropped, burrowed in it. The pirates didn't swerve.

Now he'd see.

The ship slowed to a stop over the spire he'd just left.

"Can you hear me, Rich Mann?"

Mann nodded gloomily to himself. Definitely, that was it.

"I should have tried this before. Since you're nowhere in sight, you've either left the vicinity altogether or you're hiding in the thick bushes around those towers."

Should he try to keep dodging from spire to spire? Or could he outfly them?

At least one was bound to be faster. The armor increased his weight.

"I hope you took the opportunity to examine this tower. It's fascinating. Very smooth, stony surface, except at the top. A perfect cone, also except at the top. You listening? The tip of this thing swells from an eight-foot neck into an egg-shaped knob fifteen feet across. The knob isn't polished as smooth as the rest of it. Vaguely reminiscent of an asparagus spear, wouldn't you say?"

Richard Schultz-Mann cocked his head, tasting an idea.

He unscrewed his helmet, ripped out and pocketed the radio. In frantic haste he began ripping out double handfuls of the yellow moss/wool, stuffed them into a wad in the helmet, and turned his lighter on it. At first the vegetation merely smoldered, while Mann muttered through clenched teeth. Then it caught with a weak blue smokeless flame. Mann placed his helmet in a mossy nest, setting it so it would not tip over and spill its burning contents.

"I'd have said a phallic symbol, myself. What do you think, Rich Mann? If these are phallic symbols, they're pretty well distorted. Humanoid but not human, you might say."

The pirates had joined their ship. They hovered around its floating silver bulk, ready to drop on him when the *Puppet Master*'s infrared detectors found him.

Mann streaked away to the west on full acceleration, staying as low as he dared. The spire would shield him for a minute or so, and then . . .

"This vegetation isn't stage trees, Rich Mann. It looks like some sort of grass from here. Must need something in the rock they made these erections out of. Mph. No hot spots. You're not down there after all. Well, we try the next one."

Behind him, in the moments when he dared look back, Mann saw the *Puppet Master* move to cover the second spire, the one he'd left a moment ago, the one with a gray streak in the moss at its base. Four humanoid dots clustered loosely above the ship.

"Peekaboo," came the Jinxian's voice. "And good-bye, killer."

The *Puppet Master*'s fusion drive went on. Fusion flame lashed out in a blue-white spear, played down the side of the pillar and into the moss/wool below. Mann faced forward and concentrated on flying. He felt neither elation nor pity, but only disgust. The Jinxian was a fool after all. He'd seen no life on Mira Ceti-T but for the stage trees. He had Mann's word that there was none. Couldn't he reach the obvious conclusion? Perhaps the moss/wool had fooled him. It certainly did look like yellow moss, clustering around the spires as if it needed some chemical element in the stone.

A glance back told him that the pirate ship was still spraying white flame over the spire and the foliage below. He'd have been a cinder by now. The Jinxian must want him extremely dead. Well—

The spire went all at once. It sat on the lavender plain in a hemisphere of multicolored fire, engulfing the other spires and the Jinxian ship; and then it began to expand and rise. Mann adjusted his attitude to vertical to get away from the ground. A moment later the shock wave slammed into him and blew him tumbling over the desert.

Two white ropes of smoke rose straight up through the dimming explosion cloud. The other spires were taking off while still green! Fire must have reached the foliage at their bases.

Mann watched them go with his head thrown back and his body curiously loose in the vacuum armor. His expression was strangely contented. At these times he could forget himself and his ambitions in the contemplation of immortality.

Two knots formed simultaneously in the rising smoke trails. Second stage on. They rose very fast now.

"Rich Mann."

Mann flicked his transmitter on. "You'd live through anything."

"Not I. I can't feel anything below my shoulders. Listen, Rich Mann, I'll trade secrets with you. What happened?"

"The big towers are stage trees."

"Uh?" Half question, half an expression of agony.

"A stage tree has two life cycles. One is the bush, the other is the big multistage form." Mann talked fast, fearful of losing his audience.

"The forms alternate. A stage tree seed lands on a planet and grows into a bush. Later there are lots of bushes. When a seed hits a particularly fertile spot, it grows into a multistage form. You still there?"

"Yuh."

"In the big form the living part is the tap root and the photosynthetic organs around the base. That way the rocket section doesn't have to carry so much weight. It grows straight up out of the living part, but it's as dead as the center of an oak except for the seed at the top. When it's ripe, the rocket takes off. Usually it'll reach terminal velocity for the system it's in. Kidd, I can't see your ship; I'll have to wait till the smoke—"

"Just keep talking."

"I'd like to help."

"Too late. Keep talking."

"I've tracked the stage trees across twenty light-years of space. God knows where they started. They're all through the systems around here. The seed pods spend hundreds of thousands of years in space; and when they enter a system, they explode. If there's a habitable world, one seed is bound to hit it. If there isn't, there's lots more pods where that one came from. It's immortality, Captain Kidd. This one plant has traveled farther than mankind, and it's much older. A billion and a—"

"Mann."

"Yah."

"Twenty-three point six, seventy point one, six point nil. I don't know its name on the star charts. Shall I repeat that?"

Mann forgot the stage trees. "Better repeat it."

"Twenty-three point six, seventy point one, six point nothing. Hunt in that area till you find it. It's a red giant, undersized. Planet is small, dense, no moon."

"Got it."

"You're stupid if you use it. You'll have the same luck I did. That's why I told you."

"I'll use blackmail."

"They'll kill you. Otherwise I wouldn't have said. Why'd you kill me, Rich Mann?"

"I didn't like your remarks about my beard. Never insult a Wunderlander's asymmetric beard, Captain Kidd."

"I won't do it again."

"I'd like to help." Mann peered into the billowing smoke. Now it was a black pillar tinged at the edges by the twin sunlight. "Still can't see your ship."

"You will in a moment."

The pirate moaned . . . and Mann saw the ship. He managed to turn his head in time to save his eyes.

BIBLIOGRAPHY

World of Ptavvs, Ballantine Books, 1966
A Gift from Earth, Ballantine Books, 1968
Neutron Star, Ballantine Books, 1968, contains the following:
  "Neutron Star," *If*, October 1966
  "At the Core," *If*, November 1966
  "A Relic of Empire," *If*, December 1966
  "The Soft Weapon," *If*, February 1967
  "Flatlander," *If*, March 1967
  "The Ethics of Madness," *If*, April 1967
  "The Handicapped" ("Handicap"), *Galaxy*, December 1967
  "Grendel" (original in this book)
Ringworld, Ballantine Books, 1970
Protector, Ballantine Books, 1973
Tales of Known Space, Ballantine Books, 1975, contains the following:
  "The Coldest Place," *If*, December 1964
  "Becalmed in Hell," *The Magazine of Fantasy and Science Fiction*, July 1965
  "The Warriors," *If*, February 1966
  "Eye of an Octopus," *Galaxy*, February 1966
  "How the Heroes Die," *Galaxy*, October 1966
  "At the Bottom of a Hole," *Galaxy*, December 1966
  "The Jigsaw Man," *Dangerous Visions*, 1967
  "Safe at Any Speed," *The Magazine of Fantasy and Science Fiction*, May 1967
  "Wait It Out," *The Future Unbound Program Book*, 1968
  "Intent to Deceive" ("The Deceivers"), *Galaxy*, April 1968
  "There Is a Tide," *Galaxy*, July 1968
  "Cloak of Anarchy," *Analog*, March 1972
  "The Borderland of Sol," *Analog*, January 1975
The Long Arm of Gil Hamilton, Ballantine Books, 1976, contains the following:
  "Death by Ecstasy" ("The Organleggers"), *Galaxy*, January 1969
  "The Defenseless Dead," *Ten Tomorrows*, 1973
  "Arm," *Epoch*, 1975
Ringworld Engineers, Holt, Rinehart & Winston, 1980
Other *known space* stories include:
  "One Face," *Galaxy*, June 1965
  "Bordered in Black," *The Magazine of Fantasy and Science Fiction*, April 1966

THE BERSERKER SERIES

 *by Fred Saberhagen*

It seems to me sometimes that writing the first story in a series may be just a little bit like dying, or being born—the person doing it has, at the time, no idea of just what he or she is getting into ultimately.

The first Berserker story began not with a Berserker at all. There was simply an idea about a clever way of constructing a game-playing computer. This idea, when I began to write it, clothed itself (for no particular reason that I was conscious of at the time) in the form of deep-space adventure. Only when plot and setting were ripe for it did the villainous machine, as if it were the secret designer of the whole event, come bursting out of concealment in my subconscious and race through my fingers to assemble itself upon the typed-out page. I sat there regarding its description with a mixture of satisfaction and bewilderment. In one sense, I had never imagined such a thing as a Berserker machine until that moment. And in another, equally valid sense, it seemed that I had always known of its existence; it seemed not so much an invention as a recognition.

Of course I am neither the first writer nor the last to use the basic idea: an automated killer machine, almost indestructible itself, going on with its programmed task long after its living creators have been destroyed. Whether I have done better or worse with the idea than other writers have, Berserkers have come to be identified with me and I with them, though they actually represent less than half of my published science fiction. Part of the blame or credit for this state of affairs ought to go to Fred Pohl, who bought the first Berserkers for *Worlds of If* and *Worlds of Tomorrow* back in the early 1960s, and urged me to write more, with the argument that a series of stories would have a much greater impact on the public than an equal number of equally good but unconnected tales.

Fred was perfectly right. During this year—1977, and the year's not over as I write—that first Berserker story has earned several times, in reprint fees, what I received for its first magazine appearance; my evil robots have established footholds in the realm of board- and computer-games; and new stories in the series are still in demand and still being written.

I have begun to suspect that if the histories of science fiction written fifty years from now take note of me for anything, it will be for the Berserkers. I think I can now begin to understand in a small way the mixed feelings that Conan Doyle developed for Sherlock Holmes.

Sign of the Wolf

The dark shape, big as a man, came between the two smallest of the three watchfires, moving in silence like that of sleep. Out of habit, Duncan had been watching that downwind direction, though his mind was heavy with tiredness and with the thoughts of life that came with sixteen summers' age.

Duncan raised his spear and howled, and charged the wolf. For a moment the fire-eyes looked steadily at him, appearing to be a full hand apart. Then the wolf turned away; it made one deep questioning sound, and was gone into the darkness out beyond the firelight.

Duncan stopped, drawing a gasping breath of relief. The wolf would probably have killed him if it had faced his charge, but it did not yet dare to face him in the firelight.

The sheeps' eyes were on Duncan, a hundred glowing spots in the huddled mass of the flock. One or two of the animals bleated softly.

He paced around the flock, sleepiness and introspection jarred from his mind. Legends said that men in the old Earthland had animals called dogs that guarded sheep. If that were true, some might think that men were fools for ever leaving Earthland.

But such thoughts were irreverent, and Duncan's situation called for prayer. Every night now the wolf came, and all too often it killed a sheep.

Duncan raised his eyes to the night sky. "Send me a sign, sky-gods," he prayed, routinely. But the heavens were quiet. Only the stately fireflies of the dawn zone traced their steady random paths, vanishing halfway up the eastern sky. The stars themselves agreed that three fourths of the night was gone. The legends said that Earthland was among the stars, but the younger priests admitted such a statement could only be taken symbolically.

The heavy thoughts came back, in spite of the nearby wolf. For two years now Duncan had prayed and hoped for his mystical experience, the sign from a god that came to mark the future life of every youth. From what other young men whispered now and then, he knew that many faked their signs. That was all right for lowly herdsmen, or even for hunters. But how could a man without genuine vision ever be much more than a tender of animals? To be a priest, to study the things brought from old Earthland and saved—Duncan hungered for learning, for greatness, for things he could not name.

He looked up again, and gasped, for he saw a great sign in the sky, almost directly overhead. A point of dazzling light, and then a bright little cloud remaining among the stars. Duncan gripped his spear, watching, for a moment even forgetting the sheep. The tiny cloud swelled and faded very slowly.

Not long before, a berserker machine had come sliding out of the interstellar intervals toward Duncan's planet, drawn from afar by the Sol-type light of Duncan's sun. This sun and this planet promised life, but the machine knew that some planets were well defended, and it bent and slowed its hurtling approach into a long cautious curve.

There were no warships in nearby space, but the berserker's telescopes picked out the bright dots of defensive satellites, vanishing into the planet's shadow and reappearing. To probe for more data, the berserker computers loosed a spy missile.

The missile looped the planet, and then shot in, testing the defensive net. Low over nightside, it turned suddenly into a bright little cloud.

Still, defensive satellites formed no real obstacle to a berserker. It could gobble them up almost at leisure if it moved in close to them, though they would stop long-range missiles fired at the planet. It was the other things the planet might have, the buried things, that held the berserker back from a killing rush.

It was very strange that this defended planet had no cities to make sparks of light on its nightside, and also that no radio signals came from it into space.

With mechanical caution the berserker moved in, toward the area scouted by the spy missile.

In the morning, Duncan counted his flock—and then recounted, scowling. Then he searched until he found the slaughtered lamb. The wolf had not gone hungry, after all. That made four sheep lost, now, in ten days.

Duncan tried to tell himself that dead sheep no longer mattered so much to him, that with a sign such as he had been granted last night his life was going to be filled with great deeds and noble causes. But the sheep still did matter, and not only because their owners would be angry.

Looking up sullenly from the eaten lamb, he saw a brown-robed priest, alone, mounted on a donkey, climbing the long grassy slope of the grazing valley from the direction of the Temple Village. He would be going to pray in one of the caves in the foot of the mountain at the head of the valley.

At Duncan's beckoning wave—he could not leave the flock to walk far toward the priest—the man on the donkey changed course. Duncan walked a little way to meet him.

"Blessings of Earthland," said the priest shortly, when he came close. He was a stout man who seemed glad to dismount and stretch, arching his back and grunting.

He smiled as he saw Duncan's hesitation. "Are you much alone here, my son?"

"Yes, Holy One. But—last night I had a sign. For two years I've wanted one, and just last night it came."

"Indeed? That is good news." The priest's eyes strayed to the mountain, and to the sun, as if he calculated how much time he could spare. But he said, with no sound of impatience: "Tell me about it, if you wish."

When he heard that the flash in the sky was Duncan's sign, the priest frowned. Then he seemed to keep himself from smiling. "My son, that light was seen by many. Today the elders of a dozen villages, of most of the Tribe, have come to the Temple Village. Everyone has seen something different in the sky flash, and I am now going to pray in a cave, because of it."

The priest remounted, but when he had looked at Duncan again, he waited to say: "Still, I was not one of those chosen to see the sky-gods' sign; and you were. It may be a sign for you as well as for others, so do not be disappointed if it is not only for you. Be faithful in your duties, and signs will come." He turned the donkey away.

Feeling small, Duncan walked slowly back to his flock. How could he have thought that a light seen over half the world was meant for one shepherd? Now his sign was gone, but his wolf remained.

In the afternoon, another figure came into sight, walking straight across the valley toward the flock from the direction of Colleen's village. Duncan tightened the belt on his woolen tunic, and combed grass from his hair with his fingers. He felt his chin, and wished his beard would really begin to grow.

He was sure the visitor was Colleen when she was still half a mile away. He kept his movements calm and made himself appear to first notice her when she came in sight on a hilltop within hailing distance. The wind moved her brown hair and her garments.

"Hello, Colleen."

"Hello, Duncan the Herdsman. My father sent me to ask about his sheep."

He ran an anxious eye over the flock, picking out individuals. Praise be to gods of land and sky. "Your father's sheep are well."

She walked closer to him. "Here are some cakes. The other sheep are not well?"

Ah, she was beautiful. But no mere herdsman would ever have her.

"Last night the wolf killed again." Duncan gestured with empty hands. "I watch, I light fires. I have a spear and a club, and I rush at him when he comes, and I drive him away. But sooner or later he comes on the wrong side of the flock, or a sheep strays."

"Another man should come from the village," she said. "Even a boy would help. With a big clever wolf, any herdsman may need help."

He nodded, faintly pleased at her implying he was a man. But his troubles were too big to be soothed away. "Did you see the sky flash, last night?" he asked, remembering with bitterness his joy when he had thought the sign was his.

"No, but all the village is talking about it. I will tell them about the wolf, but probably no man will come to help you for a day or two. They are all dancing and talking, thinking of nothing but the sky flash." She raised puzzled eyes beyond Duncan. "Look."

It was the priest, rushing past half a mile from them on his way down-valley from the caves, doing his best to make his donkey gallop toward the Temple Village.

"He may have met your wolf," Colleen suggested.

"He doesn't look behind him. Maybe in the caves he received an important sign from the earth-gods."

They talked a while longer, sitting on the grass, while he ate the cakes she had brought him.

"I must go!" She sprang up. The sun was lowering and neither of them had realized it.

"Yes, hurry! At night the wolf may be anywhere on the plain."

Watching her hurry away, Duncan felt the wolf in his own blood. Perhaps she knew it, for she looked back at him strangely from the hilltop. Then she was gone.

On a hillside, gathering dried brush for the night's watchfires, Duncan paused for a moment, looking at the sunset.

"Sky-gods, help me," he prayed. "And earth-gods, the dark wolf should be under your dominion. If you will not grant me a sign, at least help me deal with the wolf." He bent routinely and laid his ear to a rock. Every day he asked some god for a sign, but never—

He heard a voice. He crouched there, listening to the rock, unable to believe. Surely it was a waterfall he heard, or running cattle somewhere near. But no, it was a real voice, booming and shouting in some buried distance. He could not make out the words, but it was a real god-voice from under the earth.

He straightened up, tears in his eyes, even the sheep for a moment forgotten. This wonderful sign was not for half the world, it was for him! And he had doubted that it would ever come.

To hear what it said was all-important. He bent again and listened. The muffled voice went on unceasingly, but he could not understand it. He ran a few steps up the hill, and put his ear against another exposed earth-bone of rock. Yes, the voice was plainer here; sometimes he could distinguish a word. "Give," said the voice. Mumble, mumble. "Defend," he thought it said. Even the words he recognized were spoken in strange accents.

He realized that darkness was falling, and stood up, in fearful indecision. The sheep were still his responsibility, and he had to light watchfires, he *had* to, for the sheep would be slaughtered without them. And at the same time he had to listen to this voice.

A form moved toward him through the twilight, and he grabbed up his club—then he realized it was Colleen.

She looked frightened. She whispered: "The sun went down, and I feared the dark. It was a shorter way back to you than on to the village."

The berserker moved in toward the nightside of the planet, quickly now, but still with caution. It had searched its memory of thousands of years of war against a thousand kinds of life, and it had remembered one other planet like this, with defensive satellites but no cities or radios. The fortifiers of that planet had fought among themselves, weakening themselves until they could no longer operate their defenses, had even forgotten what their planet-weapons were.

The life here might be shamming, trying to lure the berserker within range of the planet-weapons. Therefore the berserker sent its mechanical scouts ahead, to break through the satellite net and range over the land surface, killing, until they provoked the planet's maximum response.

The fires were built, and Colleen held the spear and watched the sheep. Wolf or not, Duncan had to follow his sign. He made his way up the dark hillside, listening at rock after rock. And ever the earth-god voice grew stronger.

In the back of his mind Duncan realized that Colleen had arranged to be trapped with him for the night, to help him defend the sheep, and he felt limitless gratitude and love. But even that was now in the back of his mind. The voice now was everything.

He held his breath, listening. Now he could hear the voice while he stood erect. There, ahead, at the foot of a cliff, were slabs of rock tumbled down by snowslides. Among them might be a cave.

He reached the slabs, and heard the voice rumble up between them. "Attack in progress. Request human response. Order one requested. This is defense control. Attack in progress—"

On and on it went. Duncan understood some of it. Attack, request, human. Order one requested—that must mean one wish was to be granted, as in the legends. Never again would Duncan laugh at legends, thinking himself wise. This was no prank of the other young men; no one could hide in a cave and shout on and on in such a voice.

No one but a priest should enter a cave, but probably not even the priests knew of this one. It was Duncan's, for his sign had led him here. He had been granted a tremendous sign.

More awed than fearful, he slid between slabs of rock, finding the way down, rock and earth and then metal under his feet. He dropped into a low metal cave, which was as he had heard the god-caves described, very long, smooth, round and regular, except here where it was bent and torn under the fallen rocks. In the cave's curving sides were glowing places, like huge animal eyes, giving light enough to see.

And here the shouting was very loud. Duncan moved toward it.

We have reached the surface, the scouts radioed back to the berserker, in their passionless computer-symbol language. *Here intelligent life of the earth-type lives in villages. So far we have killed eight hundred and thirty-nine units. We have met no response from dangerous weapons.*

A little while longer the berserker waited, letting the toll of life-units mount. When the chance of this planet's being a trap had dropped in computer-estimation to the vanishing point, the berserker moved in to close range, and began to mop the remaining defensive satellites out of its way.

"Here I am." Duncan fell on his knees before the metal thing that bellowed. In front of the god-shape lay woven twigs and eggshells, very old. Once priests had sacrificed here, and then they had forgotten this god.

"Here I am," said Duncan again, in a louder voice.

The god heeded him, for the deafening shouting stopped.

"Response acknowledged, from defense control alternate 9,864," said the god. "Planetary defenses now under control of post 9,864."

How could you ask a god to speak more plainly?

After a very short time of silence, the god said: "Request order one."

That seemed understandable, but to make sure, Duncan asked: "You will grant me one wish, mighty one?"

"Will obey your order. Emergency. Satellite sphere ninety percent destroyed. Planet-weapon responses fully programmed, activation command requested."

Duncan, still kneeling, closed his eyes. One wish would be granted him. The rest of the words he took as a warning to choose his wish with care. If he wished, the god would make him the wisest of chiefs or the bravest of warriors. The god would give him a hundred years of life or a dozen young wives.

Or Colleen.

But Colleen was out in the darkness, now, facing the wolf. Even now the wolf might be prowling near, just beyond the circle of firelight, watching the sheep, and watching the tender girl. Even now Colleen might be screaming—

Duncan's heart sank utterly, for he knew the wolf had beaten him, had destroyed this moment on which the rest of his life depended. He was still a herdsman. And if he could make himself forget the sheep, he would not want to forget Colleen.

"Destroy the wolf! Kill it!" he choked out.

"Term wolf questioned."

"The killer! To destroy the killer! That is the only wish I can make!" He could stand the presence of the god no longer, and ran away through the cave, weeping for his ruined life. He ran to find Colleen.

Recall, shouted the electronic voice of the berserker. *Trap. Recall.*

Hearing, its scattered brood of scout machines rose at top acceleration from their planet work, curving and climbing toward their great metal mother. Too slow. They blurred into streaks, into fireworks of incandescent gas.

The berserker was not waiting for them. It was diving for deep-space, knowing the planet-weapons reached out for it. It wasted no circuits now trying to compute why so much life had been sacrificed to trap it. Then it saw new force fields thrown up ahead of it, walling it in. No escape.

The whole sky was in flames, the bones of the hills shuddered underfoot, and at the head of the valley the top of the mountain was torn away and an enormous shaft of something almost invisible poured from it infinitely up into the sky.

Duncan saw Colleen huddling on the open ground, shouting to him, but the buried thunder drowned her voice. The sheep were running and leaping, crying under the terrible sky. Duncan saw the dark wolf among them, running with them in circles, too frightened to be a wolf. He picked up his club and ran, staggering with the shaking earth, after the beast.

He caught the wolf, for he ran toward it, while it ran in circles without regard for him. He saw the sky reflected in its eyes, facing him, and he swung his club just as it crouched to leap.

He won. And then he struck again and again, making sure.

All at once there was a blue-white, moving sun in the sky, a marvelous sun that in a minute turned red, and spread itself out to vanish in the general glow. Then the earth was still at last.

Duncan walked in a daze, until he saw Colleen trying to round up the sheep. Then he waved to her, and trotted after her to help. The wolf was dead, and he had a wonderful sign to tell. The gods had not killed him. Beneath his running feet, the steadiness of the ground seemed permanent.

BIBLIOGRAPHY

"Fortress Ship" ("Without a Thought"), *If*, January 1963
"Goodlife," *Worlds of Tomorrow*, December 1963
"The Life Hater ("The Peacemaker"), *If*, August 1964
"Stone Place," *If*, March 1965
"What 'T' and I Did," *If*, April 1965
"Sign of the Wolf," *If*, May 1965
"Patron of the Arts," *If*, August 1965
"Masque of the Red Shift," *If*, November 1965
"Mr. Jester," *If*, January 1966
"In the Temple of Mars," *If*, April 1966
"The Face of the Deep," *If*, September 1966
Berserker, Ballantine Books, 1967, contains all of the above stories
"The Stone Man," *Worlds of Tomorrow*, May 1967*
"Berserker's Prey" ("Pressure"), *If*, June 1967
"The Winged Helmet," *If*, August 1967*
"Brother Berserker," *If*, November 1967*
"Starsong," *If*, January 1968
Brother Assassin, Ballantine Books, 1969, contains stories marked * above
"Wings Out of Shadow," *If*, April 1974
"Inhuman Error," *Analog*, October 1974
"The Annihilation of Angkor Apeiron," *Galaxy*, February 1975
Berserker's Planet (*If*, June, August 1974), DAW Books, 1975
"The Game," *Flying Buffalo's Favorite Magazine*, May–June 1977
"The Smile," *Algol*, Summer 1978
"Smasher," *The Magazine of Fantasy and Science Fiction*, August 1978
Berserker Man, Ace Books, 1979
"Some Events at the Templar Radiant," *Destinies*, July 1979
The Ultimate Enemy, Ace Books, 1979
"The Metal Murderer," *Omni*, January 1980

THE SLOW GLASS SERIES

by Bob Shaw

My stories featuring the fictional substance known as "slow glass" are significant to me in a number of respects. I had begun writing and selling science fiction in the mid-1950s, suddenly realized how unsatisfactory those early stories were and—as a matter of deliberate policy—took a ten-year break from writing in order to gain more experience of life in general. In a way this was an act of faith in science fiction, because many people have an idea that you don't need to know much about the inhabitants of Sol III to write about the inhabitants of Sol IV. I, however, believed that human values were as important in science fiction as in other branches of literature—and to back up this belief I sold my typewriter!

Returning to the field a decade later, I felt *ready*—and almost the first thing I wrote was a short story called "Light of Other Days," which John W. Campbell accepted for *Analog*. Not only was that story, in a way, a vindication of my long-term strategy, but it brought me into contact with the illustrious Campbell brand of editing. It also served as a perfect illustration of the way in which a simple scientific fact can be developed into a viable idea, and—perhaps even more important to the practicing writer—of how a single idea can be used to generate a number of different stories.

The underlying idea for the slow glass stories could hardly be more simple. Everybody who has a smattering of physics knows that light passes through glass more slowly than through a less dense medium, which means that all glass is slightly "slow." When you view an event through a window you see it imperceptibly later than you would have done had the pane been removed. From there it is a short imaginative step to extrapolating glass which slows light down by years, so that when you look through it you see what was happening that number of years earlier. The production of a series with that kind of genesis illustrates my thesis that the hard thing about writing is not the finding of ideas, but appreciating and developing their story potential.

Equipped with the basic concept, I dreamed up about five stories—all of which would have sold—and set them aside for later use because none of them exploited slow glass in the intensely *human* way my instinct told me the idea demanded for its first appearance in print. That was a period of extremely hard work, but finally came the story idea I felt to be right—one in which a man uses the stored slow glass images of his wife and child, who were killed in an accident years earlier, to help him believe they are still alive. "Light of Other Days" was accepted immediately by John Campbell, though it was hardly in the classical *Analog* tradition (perhaps he accepted it in his persona of Don A. Stuart), and it was launched on an international career of anthology sales which I have lost track of and which continues to the present day.

The next event was that Campbell sent me one of his famous long letters in which he challenged me to write a story about the moral dilemma which could arise if a piece of ten-years-thick slow glass was the sole witness to a murder. The truth will come to light, as Shakespeare said, but it will take ten years—and can any legal system wait that long? Coincidentally, or perhaps not, that was the very idea I had already reserved for the next story in the series—because it too dealt with the human situation—and it eventually appeared in *Analog* as "Burden of Proof." The title, incidentally, is the neatest and most apposite I have ever conceived.

Although I kept the slow glass series short, only using those ideas I felt presented a genuinely fresh aspect of the central concept, it had a major impact on my career. The popularity of the idea—it has been used on radio, discussed in learned journals of science, and was even used as a continuity device in a run of Stan Lee SF comics—brought my name to the attention of the reading public exactly when I needed the boost, after my ten-year break from writing. It is probably not overstating the matter to say that slow glass—the corner stone of a single science fiction series—was also the stepping stone which, a few years later, enabled me to become a full-time author.

Burden of Proof

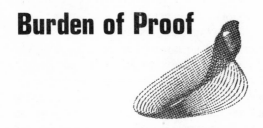

Harpur peered uncertainly through the streaming windows of his car. There had been no parking space close to the police headquarters, and now the building seemed separated from him by miles of puddled concrete and parading curtains of rain. The sky sagged darkly and heavily between the buildings around the square.

Suddenly aware of his age, he stared for a long moment at the old police block and its cascading gutters, before levering himself stiffly out of the driving seat. It was difficult to believe the sun was shining warmly in a basement room under the west wing. Yet he knew it was, because he had phoned and asked about it before leaving home.

"It's real nice down here today, Judge," the guard had said, speaking with the respectful familiarity he had developed over the years. "Not so good outside, of course, but down here it's real nice."

"Have any reporters shown up yet?"

"Just a few so far, Judge. You coming over?"

"I expect so," Harpur had replied. "Save a seat for me, Sam."

"Yes, *sir!*"

Harpur moved as quickly as he dared, feeling the cool rain penetrate to the backs of his hands in his shower-proof's pockets. The lining clung round the knuckles when he moved his fingers. As he climbed the steps to the front entrance a preliminary flutter in the left side of his chest told him he had hurried too much, pushed things too far.

The officer at the door saluted smartly.

Harpur nodded to him. "Hard to believe this is June, isn't it, Ben?"

"Sure is, sir. I hear it's nice down below, though."

Harpur waved to the guard, and was moving along the corridor when the pain closed with him. It was very clean, very pure. As though someone had carefully chosen a sterile needle, fitted it into an antiseptic handle, heated it to whiteness and—with the swiftness of compassion—run it into his side. He stopped for a moment and leaned on the tiled wall, trying not to be conspicuous, while perspiration pricked out on his fore-head. *I can't give up now,* he thought, *not when there's only another couple of weeks to go . . . But, supposing this is it? Right now!*

Harpur fought the panic, until the entity that was his pain withdrew a short distance. He drew a shuddering breath of relief and began to walk again, slowly, aware that his enemy was watching and following. But he reached the sunshine without any further attacks.

Sam Macnamara, the guard at the inner door, started to give his usual grin and then, seeing the strain on Harpur's face, ushered him quickly into the room. Macnamara was a tall Irishman whose only ambition seemed to be to drink two cups of coffee every hour on the hour, but they had developed a friendship which Harpur found strangely comfort-ing. He shook out a fold-up chair at the back of the room and held it steady while Harpur sat down.

"Thank you, Sam," Harpur said gratefully, glancing around at the unfa-miliar crowd, none of whom had noticed his arrival. They were all staring towards the sunlight.

The smell of the rain-damp clothing worn by the reporters seemed strangely out of place in the dusty, underground room. It was part of the oldest wing of the police headquarters and, until ten years before, had been used to store obsolete records. Since then, except on special press days, its bare concrete walls had housed nothing but a bank of monitoring equipment, two very bored guards, and a pane of glass mounted in a frame at one end of the room.

The glass was of the very special variety through which light took many years to pass. It was the sort people used to capture scenes of exceptional beauty for their homes.

To Harpur's eyes, the view through this piece of slow glass had no particular beauty. It showed a reasonably pretty bay on the Atlantic coast, but the water was cluttered with sports boats, and a garishly-painted service station obtruded in the foreground. A connoisseur of slow glass would have thrown a rock through it, but Emile Bennett, the original owner, had brought it to the city simply because it contained the view from his childhood home. Having it available, he had explained, saved him a two-hundred-mile drive any time he felt homesick.

The sheet of glass Bennett had used was ten years thick, which meant that it had had to stand for ten years at his parents' home before the view from there came through. It continued, of course, to transmit the same view for ten years after being brought back to the city, regardless of the fact that it had been confiscated from Bennett by impatient police officers who had a profound disinterest in his parental home. It would report, without fail, everything it ever saw—but only in its own good time.

Slumped tiredly in his seat, Harpur was reminded of the last time he had been to a movie. The only light in the room was that coming from the oblong pane of glass, and the reporters sat fidgeting in orderly rows like a movie audience. Harpur found their presence distracting. It prevented him from slipping into the past as easily as usual.

The shifting waters of the bay scattered sunlight through the otherwise dismal room, the little boats crossed and recrossed, and silent cars occasionally slid into the service station. An attractive girl in the extremely abbreviated dress of a decade ago walked across a garden in the foreground, and Harpur saw several of the reporters jot some personal angle material in their notebooks.

One of the more inquisitive left his seat and walked round behind the pane of glass to see the view from the other side, but came back looking disappointed. Harpur knew a sheet of metal had been welded into the frame at the back, completely covering the glass. The county had ruled that it would have been an invasion of the senior Bennetts' privacy to put on public view all their domestic activities during the time the glass was being charged.

As the minutes began to drag out in the choking atmosphere of the room, the reporters grew noticeably restless, and began loudly swapping yarns. Somewhere near the front, one of them began sneezing monotonously and swearing in between. No smoking was permitted near the monitoring equipment which, on behalf of the state, hungrily scanned the glass, so relays of three and four began to drift out into the corridor to light cigarettes. Harpur heard them complaining about the long wait and he smiled. He had been waiting for ten years, and it seemed even longer.

Today, June 7th, was one of the key days for which he and the rest of the country had been standing by, but it had been impossible to let the press know in advance the exact moment at which they would get their story. The trouble was that Emile Bennett had never been able to remember just what time, on that hot Sunday, he had driven to his parents' home to collect his sheet of slow glass. During the subsequent trial it had not been possible to pin it down to anything more definite than "about three in the afternoon."

One of the reporters finally noticed Harpur sitting near the door and came over to him. He was sharply dressed, fair-haired and impossibly young looking.

"Pardon me, sir. Aren't you Judge Harpur?"

Harpur nodded. The boy's eyes widened briefly then narrowed as he assessed the older man's present news value.

"Weren't you the presiding judge in the . . . Raddall case?" He had been going to say the Glass Eye case, but immediately changed his mind.

Harpur nodded again. "Yes, that's correct. But I no longer give interviews to the press. I'm sorry."

"That's all right, sir. I understand." He went on out to the corridor, walking with quicker, springier steps. Harpur guessed the young man had just decided on his angle for today's story. He could have written the copy himself:

Today Judge Kenneth Harpur—the man who ten years ago presided in the controversial "Glass Eye" case, in which twenty-one-year-old Ewan Raddall was charged with a double slaying—sat on a chair in one of the underground rooms at police headquarters. An old man now, the Iron Judge has nothing at all to say. He only watches, waits and wonders . . .

Harpur smiled wryly. He no longer felt any bitterness over the newspaper attacks. The only reason he had stopped speaking to journalists was that he had become very, very bored with that aspect of his life. He had reached the age at which a man discards the unimportant stuff and concentrates on essentials. In another two weeks he would be free to sit in the sun and note *exactly* how many shades of blue and green there were in the sea, and just how much time elapsed between the appearance of the first evening star and the second. If his physician allowed it, he would have a little good whiskey, and if his physician refused it, he would still have the whiskey. He would read a few books, and perhaps even write one . . .

As it turned out, the estimated time given by Bennett at the trial had been pretty accurate.

At eight minutes past three Harpur and the waiting newsmen saw Bennett approach the glass from the far side with a screwdriver in his hand. He was wearing the sheepish look people often have when they get in range of slow glass. He worked at the sides for a moment, then the sky flashed crazily into view, showing the glass had been tilted out of its frame. A moment later the room went dark as the image of a brown, army-type blanket unfolded across the glass, blotting out the laggard light.

The monitors at the back of the room produced several faint clicking noises which were drowned out by the sound of the reporters hurrying to telephones.

Harpur got to his feet and slowly walked out behind the reporters. There was no need to hurry now. Police records showed that the glass would remain blanked out for two days, because that was how long it had lain in the trunk of Bennett's car before he had got round to installing it in a window frame at the back of his city home. For a further two weeks after that it would show the casual day-to-day events which took place ten years before in the children's public playground at the rear of the Bennett house.

Those events were of no particular interest to anyone; but the records also showed that in the same playground, on the night of June 21, 1981, a twenty-year-old typist, Joan Calderisi, had been raped and murdered. Her boy friend, a twenty-three-year-old auto mechanic named Edward Jerome Hattie, had also been killed, presumably for trying to defend the girl.

Unknown to the murderer, there had been one witness to the double killing—and now it was getting ready to give its perfect and incontrovertible evidence.

The problem had not been difficult to foresee.

Right from the day slow glass first appeared in a few very expensive stores, people had wondered what would happen if a crime were to be committed in its view. What would be the legal position if there were, say, three suspects and it was known that, five or ten years later, a piece of glass would identify the murderer beyond all doubt? Obviously, the law could not risk punishing the wrong person; but, equally obviously, the guilty one could not be allowed to go free all that time.

This was how tabloid feature writers had summed it up, although to Judge Kenneth Harpur there had been no problem at all. When he read the speculations it took him less than five seconds to make up his mind—and he had been impressively unruffled when the test case came his way.

That part had been a coincidence. Erskine County had no more homicides and no more slow glass than any other comparable area. In fact,

Harpur had no recollection of ever seeing the stuff until Holt City's electrical street-lighting system was suddenly replaced by alternating panels of eight-hour glass and sixteen-hour glass slung in continuous lines above the thoroughfares. That was several years after techniques had been developed for the mass production of slow glass, or—as it was officially known—retardite.

It had taken some time for a retardite capable of producing delays measured in years to evolve from the first sheets which held light back by roughly half a second. The original material was developed by a glass manufacturer trying to produce a transparency which was both shatterproof and a really efficient insulator. Its unique properties might never have been noticed but for the fact that it was first used—unfortunately for a number of people—in automobile windscreens.

The auto manufacturer concerned spent upwards of half a million dollars trying to find out why one batch of one model had been involved in a statistically improbable number of accidents involving right-hand turns. Expensive as the investigation was, it paid off because retardite became a major industry in a matter of months.

"Scene-stealing" was one of the prime applications, and slow-glass farms sprang up at beauty spots all over the world. A large part of the commercial success of slow glass lay in the fact that there was absolutely no difference, emotionally, between owning a "scenedow" and owning the land which had charged it with light. The occupant of the most airless, glove-tight duplex in a city could look out on pine-clad valleys—and in every important respect they were *his*.

It was also discovered that, for many applications, cameras had become obsolete. All planetary expeditions, manned or robotic, carried practically weightless retardite slivers of appropriate periods. In any cinematic field, from industrial recording to bird-watching, where large footages had normally been wasted while waiting for an unpredictable key event, short-period slow glass was used instead. The cameras were turned on it—with comfortable hindsight—at the right moment. Spy cameras became tiny flecks of glass which operatives had been known to push into their pores, like blackheads.

But no matter how varied the purpose, all slow-glass applications had one thing in common. The user had to be absolutely certain of the time delay he wanted—because there was no way of speeding the process up. Had retardite been a "glass" in the true sense of the word, it might have been possible to plane a piece down to a different thickness and get the information sooner; but, in reality, it was an extremely opaque material. Opaque in the sense that light never actually got *into* it.

Radiations with wavelengths on the order of that of light were absorbed on the face of a retardite panel and their information converted to stress patterns within the material. The piezoluctic effect by which the information worked its way through to the opposite face involved the whole crystalline structure, and anything which disturbed that structure instantaneously randomized the stress patterns.

Infuriating as the discovery was to certain researchers, it had been an important factor in the commercial success of retardite. People would have been reluctant to install scenedows in their homes, knowing that everything they had done behind them was being stored for other eyes to see years later. So the burgeoning piezoluctics industry had been quick to invent an inexpensive "tickler" by which any piece of slow glass could be cleaned off for reuse, like a cluttered computer program.

This was also the reason why, for ten years, two guards had been on a round-the-clock watch of the scenedow which held the evidence in the Raddall case. There was always the chance that one of Raddall's relatives, or some publicity-seeking screwball, would sneak in and wipe the slate clean before its time came to resolve all doubts.

There had been moments during the ten years when Harpur had been too ill and tired to care very much, times when it would have been a relief to have the perfect witness silenced forever. But usually the existence of the slow glass did not bother him.

He had made his ruling in the Raddall case, and it had been a decision he would have expected any other judge to make. The subsequent controversy, the enmity of sections of the press, the public, and even some of his colleagues, had hurt at first, but he had got over that.

The Law, Harpur had said in his summing up, existed solely because people believed in it. Let that belief be shaken—even once—and the Law would suffer irreparable harm.

As near as could be determined, the killings had taken place about an hour before midnight.

Keeping that in mind, Harpur ate dinner early then showered and shaved for the second time that day. The effort represented a sizable proportion of his quota for the day, but it had been hot and sticky in the courtroom. His current case was involved and, at the same time, boring. More and more cases were like that lately, he realized. It was a sign he was ready to retire, but there was one more duty to perform—he owed that much to the profession.

Harpur put on a lightweight jacket and stood with his back to the valet-mirror which his wife had bought a few months earlier. It was faced with a sheet of fifteen-second retardite which allowed him, after a slight pause, to turn around and check his appearance from the back. He surveyed his frail, but upright, figure dispassionately, then walked away before the stranger in the glass could turn to look out.

He disliked valet-mirrors almost as much as the equally popular truviewers, which were merely pieces of short-term retardite pivotal on a vertical axis. They served roughly the same function as ordinary mirrors, except that there was no reversal effect. For the first time ever, the makers boasted, you could really see yourself as others saw you. Harpur objected to the idea on grounds he hoped were vaguely philosophical, but which he could not really explain, even to himself.

"You don't look well, Kenneth," Eva said as he adjusted his tie minutely. "You haven't *got* to go down there, have you?"

"No, I haven't *got* to go—that's why I've got to go. That's the whole point."

"Then I'll drive you."

"You won't. You're going to bed. I'm not going to let you drive around the city in the middle of the night." He put an arm round her shoulders. At fifty-eight, Eva Harpur was on a seemingly endless plateau of indomitable good health, but they maintained a fiction that it was he who looked after her.

He drove himself into the city, but progress through the traffic was unusually slow and, on impulse, he stopped several blocks from the police headquarters and began to walk. Live dangerously, he thought, but walk slowly—just in case. It was a bright warm evening and, with the long daylight hours of June, only the sixteen-hour panels slung above the thoroughfare were black. The alternating eight-hour panels were needlessly blazing with light they had absorbed in the afternoon. The system was a compromise with seasonal variations in daylight hours, but it worked reasonably well and, above all, the light was practically free.

An additional advantage was that it provided the law enforcement authorities with perfect evidence about events like road accidents and traffic violations. In fact, it had been the then brand-new slow-glass lighting panels in Fifty-third Avenue which had provided a large part of the evidence in the case against Ewan Raddall.

Evidence on which Harpur had sent Raddall to the electric chair.

The salient facts of the case had not been exactly as in the classic situation proposed by the tabloids, but they had been near enough to arouse public interest. There had been no other known suspect apart from Raddall, but the evidence against him had been largely circumstantial. The bodies had not been found until the next morning, by which time Raddall had been able to get home, clean himself up and have a night's sleep. When he was picked up he was fresh, composed and plausible—and the forensic teams had been able to prove almost nothing.

The case against Raddall was that he had been seen going towards the public playground at the right time, leaving it at the right time, and that he had bruises and scratches consistent with the crime. Also, between midnight and 9:30 in the morning, when he was taken in for questioning, he had "lost" the plasticord jacket he had worn on the previous evening, and it was never found.

At the end of Raddall's trial the jury had taken less than an hour to arrive at a verdict of guilty—but during a subsequent appeal his defense claimed the jury was influenced by the knowledge that the crime was recorded in Emile Bennett's rear window. The defense attorney, demanding a retrial, put forward the view that the jury had dismissed their "reasonable doubt" in the expectation that Harpur would, at the most, impose a life sentence.

But, in Harpur's eyes, the revised legal code drafted in 1977, mainly to give judges greater power in their own courts, made no provision for wait-and-see legislation, especially in cases of first-degree murder. In January 1982, Raddall was duly sentenced to be executed.

Harpur's straightforward contention, which had earned him the name "Iron Judge," was that a decision reached in a court of law always had been, and still was, sacrosanct. The superhuman entity which was the Law must not be humbled before a fragment of glass. Reduced to its crudest terms, his argument was that if wait-and-see legislation were introduced, criminals would carry pieces of fifty-year retardite with them as standard equipment.

Within two years the slow-grinding mills of the Supreme Court had ratified Harpur's decision and the sentence was carried out. The same thing, on a microscopic scale, had occurred many times before in the world of sport; and the only possible, the only workable solution, was that the umpire was always right—no matter what cameras or slow glass might say afterwards.

In spite of his vindication, or perhaps because of it, the tabloids never warmed to Harpur. He began making a point of being indifferent to all that anybody wrote or said. All he had needed during the ten years was the knowledge that he had made a good decision, as distinct from a wrong one—now he was to discover if he had made a good decision, as distinct from a bad one.

Although this night had been looming on his horizon for a decade, Harpur found it difficult to realize that, in a matter of minutes, they would *know* if Raddall was guilty. The thought caused a crescendo of uncomfortable jolts in his chest and he stopped for a moment to snatch air. After all, what difference did it really make? He had not made the law, so why feel personally involved?

The answer came quickly.

He was involved because he was part of the law. The reason he had gone on working, against medical advice, was that it was he, not some abstract embodiment of Webster's "great interest of man on earth," who had passed sentence on Ewan Raddall. And he was going to be there, personally, to face the music if he had made a mistake.

The realization was strangely comforting to Harpur as he moved on through the crowded streets. Something in the atmosphere of the late evening struck him as being odd, then he noticed the city center was jammed tight with out-of-town automobiles. Men and women thronged the sidewalks, and he knew they were strangers by the way their eyes occasionally took in the upper parts of buildings. The smell of grilling hamburger meat drifted on the thick, downy air.

Harpur wondered what the occasion might be, then he noticed the general drift towards the police headquarters. So that was it. People had not changed since the days they were drawn towards arenas, guillotines and gallows. There would be nothing for them to see, but to be close at hand would be sufficient to let them taste the ancient joy of continuing to breathe in the knowledge that someone else has just ceased. The fact that they were ten years out of date, too, made no difference at all.

Even Harpur, had he wanted to, could not have got into the underground room. Apart from the monitors, there would be only six chairs and six pairs of special binoculars with low magnifications and huge, light-hungry objective lenses. They were reserved for the state-appointed observers.

Harper had no interest in viewing the crime with his own eyes—he simply wanted to hear the result; then have a long, long rest. It occurred to him he was being completely irrational in going down to the police building, with all the exertion and lethal tension the trip meant for him, but somehow nothing else would do. *I'm guilty*, he thought suddenly, *guilty as . . .*

He reached the plaza in which the building was situated and worked his way through the pliant, strength-draining barriers of people. By the time he was halfway across sweat had bound his clothes so tightly he could hardly raise his feet. At an indeterminate point in the long journey he became aware of another presence following close behind—the sorrowful friend with the white-hot needle.

Reaching the untidy ranks of automobiles belonging to the press, Harpur realized he could not go in too early, and there was at least half an hour left. He turned and began forcing his way back to the opposite side of the plaza. The needle point caught up with him—one precise thrust—and he lurched forward clawing for support.

"What the . . . !" A startled voice boomed over his head. "Take it easy, old-timer." Its owner was a burly giant in a pale blue one-piece, who had been watching a 3-D television broadcast when Harpur fell against him. He snatched off the receiver spectacles, the tiny left and right pictures glowing with movement like distant bonfires. A wisp of music escaped from the earpiece.

"I'm sorry," Harpur said. "I tripped. I'm sorry."

"That's all right. Say! Aren't you Judge . . ."

Harpur pushed on by as the big man tugged excitedly on the arm of a woman who was with him. *I mustn't be recognized,* he thought in a panic. He burrowed into the crowd, now beginning to lose his sense of direction. Six more desperate paces and the needle caught him again—right up to its antiseptic hilt this time. He moaned as the plaza tilted ponderously away. Not here, he pleaded, not here, *please.*

Somehow, he saved himself from falling and moved on. Near at hand, but a million miles away, an unseen woman gave a beautiful, carefree laugh. At the edge of the square the pain returned, even more decisively than before—once, twice, three times. Harpur screamed as he felt the life-muscle implode in cramp.

He began to go down, then felt himself gripped by firm hands. Harpur looked up at the swarthy young man who was holding him. The handsome, worry-creased face looming through reddish mists looked strangely familiar. Harpur struggled to speak.

"You . . . you're Ewan Raddall, aren't you?"

The black eyebrows met in puzzlement. "Raddall? No. Never heard of him. I think we'd better call an ambulance for you."

Harpur thought hard. "That's right. You couldn't be Raddall. I killed him ten years ago." Then he spoke louder. "But, if you never heard of Raddall, why are you here?"

"I was on my way home from a bowling match when I saw the crowd."

The boy began getting Harpur out of the crowd, holding him up with one arm, fending uncomprehending bodies away with the other. Harpur tried to help, but was aware of his feet trailing helplessly on the concrete.

"Do you live right here in Holt?"

The boy nodded emphatically.

"Do you know who I am?"

"All I know about you, sir, is you should be in the hospital. I'll call an ambulance on the liquor store phone."

Harpur felt vaguely that there was some tremendous significance in what they had been saying, but had no time to pursue the matter.

"Listen," he said, forcing himself to stand upright for a moment, "I don't want an ambulance. I'll be fine if I can just get home. Can you help me get a cab?"

The boy looked uncertain, then he shrugged. "It's your funeral."

Harpur opened his door carefully and entered the friendly darkness of the big old house. During the ride out of town his sweat-soaked clothes had become clammy cold, and he shivered uncontrollably as he felt for the light switch.

With the light on, he sat down beside the telephone and looked at his watch. Almost midnight—by this time there would be no mystery, no doubt, about exactly what had happened in the Fifty-third Avenue playground ten years earlier. He picked up the handset, and at the same moment heard his wife begin to move around upstairs. There were several numbers he could ring to ask what the slow glass had revealed, but the thought of talking to any police executive or someone in City Hall was too much. He would call Sam Macnamara.

As a guard, Sam would not know the result officially, but he would have the answer just the same. Harpur tried to punch out the number of the direct line to the guard kiosk but his finger joints kept buckling on impact with the buttons, and he gave up.

Eva Harpur came down the stairs in her dressing gown and approached him apprehensively.

"Oh, Kenneth!" Her hand went to her mouth. "What have you done? You look . . . I'll have to call Dr. Sherman."

Harpur smiled weakly. *I do a lot of smiling these days,* he thought irrelevantly. *It's the only response an old man can make to so many situations.*

"All I want you to do is make me some coffee and help me up to my bed; but first of all get me a number on this contraption." Eva opened her mouth to protest, then closed it as their eyes met.

When Sam came to the phone Harpur worked to keep his own voice level.

"Hello, Sam. Judge Harpur here. Is the fun all over yet?"

"Yes, sir. There was a press conference afterwards and that's over, too. I guess you heard the result on the radio."

"As a matter of fact, I haven't, Sam. I was . . . out until a little while ago. Decided to ring someone about it before I went to bed, and your number just came into my head."

Sam laughed uncertainly. "Well, they were able to make a positive identification. It was Raddall, all right—but I guess you knew that all along."

"I guess I did, Sam." Harpur felt his eyes grow hot with tears.

"It'll be a load off your mind all the same, Judge."

Harpur nodded tiredly, but into the phone he said, "Well, naturally I'm glad there was no miscarriage of justice—but judges don't make the laws, Sam. They don't even decide who's guilty and who isn't. As far as I'm concerned, the presence of a peculiar piece of glass makes very little difference, one way or the other."

It was a good speech for the Iron Judge.

There was a long silence on the line, then, with a note of something like desperation in his voice, Sam persisted, "I know all that, Judge . . . but, all the same, it must have been a big load off your mind."

Harpur realized, with a warm surprise, that the big Irishman was pleading with him. *It doesn't matter any more,* he thought. *In the morning I'm going to retire and rejoin the human race.*

"All right, Sam," he said finally. "Let's put it this way—I'll sleep well tonight. All right?"

"Thank you, Judge. Good night."

Harpur set the phone down and with his eyes tight-closed, waited for peace.

BIBLIOGRAPHY

"Light of Other Days," *Analog*, August 1966
"Burden of Proof," *Analog*, May 1967
"A Dome of Many-Colored Glass," *Fantastic*, April 1972
Other Days, Other Eyes, Ace, 1972

THE AAA ACE SERIES

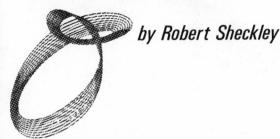

by Robert Sheckley

I suspect that the AAA Ace stories derived a measure of unconscious inspiration from certain beloved movies of the 1940s. The sort of movie I'm referring to typically starred Clark Gable and Spencer Tracy. There were these two pals, see, and they started a crazy business together, and the movie would be about the crazy, funny things that happened to them.

I was not aware of this influence at the time. I simply liked the situation of two men with a weirdo job to do who have to solve one or more bizarre problems along the way. I had used that basic situation in "One Man's Poison." My next use of it was in "Ghost V," the first of the AAA Ace stories, though I knew it not at the time.

The story was popular with readers, and Horace Gold, then editor of *Galaxy,* suggested that I try a few more. Something about the characters and the basic absurdity of their situation must have appealed to me: I wrote six more, and I'm not a writer who tends to work in series.

These stories exemplified my early ideas of what plotting was all about: I was very much into problem stories, told with economy, and ending with a twist or reversal—Aristotle by way of O. Henry. What was unusual for me was that some of the AAA Ace endings involved a shift in levels and an abrupt change of emotionality. This is especially true of "Lifeboat Mutiny."

The stories were always popular with readers, less so with my colleagues. At the time I wrote them, in the mid-fifties, science fiction was going through one of its serious, heavy, literary phases, and the beau ideal was long stories about people going crazy under ambiguous circumstances, or tone poems to changelings on gossamer worlds. My AAA Ace stories were dismissed by various critics as being "facile," "slick," and much too well plotted. These critics acted as if that were an easy way to write, when quite the opposite is true: the easiest thing in the world is to write any number of thousands of words from the viewpoint of a man going insane in a literary manner on an alien planet. (Well, even that isn't easy if you take it seriously, as I was to do some years later.)

I no longer own a copy of the last story in the series, "Skag Castle." It has been many years since I last read it. (I do have one copy of it, but it is in Italian.) I remember it as being more ambitious and less successful than the others—perhaps marking the beginning of my change out of the "well-wrought story" and into other approaches—people going crazy on alien planets, etc.

The Lifeboat Mutiny

"Tell me the truth. Did you ever see sweeter engines?" Joe, the Interstellar Junkman, asked. "And look at those servos!"

"Hmm," Gregor said judiciously.

"That hull," Joe said softly. "I bet it's five hundred years old, and not a spot of corrosion on it." He patted the burnished side of the boat affectionately. What luck, the pat seemed to say, that this paragon among vessels should be here just when AAA Ace needs a lifeboat.

"She certainly does seem rather nice," Arnold said, with the studied air of a man who has fallen in love and is trying hard not to show it. "What do you think, Dick?"

Richard Gregor didn't answer. The boat was handsome, and she looked perfect for ocean survey work on Trident. But you had to be careful about Joe's merchandise.

"They just don't build 'em this way any more," Joe sighed. "Look at the propulsion unit. Couldn't dent it with a trip-hammer. Note the capacity of the cooling system. Examine—"

"It *looks* good," Gregor said slowly. The AAA Ace Interplanetary Decontamination Service had dealt with Joe in the past, and had learned caution. Not that Joe was dishonest; far from it. The flotsam he collected from anywhere in the inhabited Universe worked. But the ancient machines often had their own ideas of how a job should be done. They tended to grow peevish when forced into another routine.

"I don't care if it's beautiful, fast, durable, or even comfortable," Gregor said defiantly. "I just want to be absolutely sure it's safe."

Joe nodded. "That's the important thing, of course. Step inside."

They entered the cabin of the boat. Joe stepped up to the instrument panel, smiled mysteriously, and pressed a button.

Immediately Gregor heard a voice which seemed to originate in his head, saying, "I am Lifeboat 324-A. My purpose—"

"Telepathy?" Gregor interrupted.

"Direct sense recording," Joe said, smiling proudly. "No language barriers that way. I told you, they just don't build 'em this way any more."

"I am Lifeboat 324-A," the boat esped again. "My primary purpose is to preserve those within me from peril, and to maintain them in good health. At present, I am only partially activated."

"Could anything be safer?" Joe cried. "This is no senseless hunk of metal. This boat will look after you. This boat *cares!*"

Gregor was impressed, even though the idea of an emotional boat was somehow distasteful. But then, paternalistic gadgets had always irritated him.

Arnold had no such feelings. "We'll take it!"

"You won't be sorry," Joe said, in the frank and open tones that had helped make him a millionaire several times over.

Gregor hoped not.

The next day, Lifeboat 324-A was loaded aboard their spaceship and they blasted off for Trident.

This planet, in the heart of the East Star Valley, had recently been bought by a real-estate speculator. He'd found her nearly perfect for colonization. Trident was the size of Mars, but with a far better climate. There was no indigenous native population to contend with, no poisonous plants, no germ-borne diseases. And, unlike so many worlds, Trident had no predatory animals. Indeed, she had no animals at all. Apart from one small island and a polar cap, the entire planet was covered with water.

There was no real shortage of land; you could wade across several of Trident's seas. The land just wasn't heaped high enough.

AAA Ace had been commissioned to correct this minor flaw.

After landing on Trident's single island, they launched the boat. The rest of the day was spent checking and loading the special survey equipment on board. Early the next morning, Gregor prepared sandwiches and filled a canteen with water. They were ready to begin work.

As soon as the mooring lines were cast off, Gregor joined Arnold in the cabin. With a small flourish, Arnold pressed the first button.

"I am Lifeboat 324-A," the boat esped. "My primary purpose is to preserve those within me from peril, and to maintain them in good health. At present, I am only partially activated. For full activation, press button two."

Gregor pressed the second button.

There was a muffled buzzing deep in the bowels of the boat. Nothing else happened.

"That's odd," Gregor said. He pressed the button again. The muffled buzz was repeated.

"Sounds like a short circuit," Arnold said.

Glancing out the forward porthole, Gregor saw the shoreline of the island slowly drifting away. He felt a touch of panic. There was so much water here, and so little land. To make matters worse, nothing on the instrument panel resembled a wheel or tiller, nothing looked like a throttle or clutch. How did you operate a partially activated lifeboat?

"She must control telepathically," Gregor said hopefully. In a stern voice he said, "Go ahead slowly."

The little boat forged ahead.

"Now right a little."

The boat responded perfectly to Gregor's clear, although unnautical command. The partners exchanged smiles.

"Straighten out," Gregor said, "and full speed ahead!"

The lifeboat charged forward into the shining, empty sea.

Arnold disappeared into the bilge with a flashlight and a circuit tester. The surveying was easy enough for Gregor to handle alone. The machines did all the work, tracing the major faults in the ocean bottom, locating the most promising volcanoes, running the flow and buildup charts. When the survey was complete, the next stage would be turned over to a subcontractor. He would wire the volcanoes, seed the faults, retreat to a safe distance and touch the whole thing off.

Then Trident would be, for a while, a spectacularly noisy place. And when things had quieted down, there would be enough dry land to satisfy even a real-estate speculator.

By mid-afternoon Gregor felt that they had done enough surveying for one day. He and Arnold ate their sandwiches and drank from the canteen. Later they took a short swim in Trident's clear green water.

"I think I've found the trouble," Arnold said. "The leads to the primary activators have been removed. And the power cable's been cut."

"Why would anyone do that?" Gregor asked.

Arnold shrugged. "Might have been part of the decommissioning. I'll have it right in a little while."

He crawled back into the bilge. Gregor turned in the direction of the island, steering telepathically and watching the green water foam merrily past the bow. At moments like this, contrary to all his previous experience, the Universe seemed a fine and friendly place.

In half an hour Arnold emerged, grease-stained but triumphant. "Try that button now," he said.

"But we're almost back."

"So what? Might as well have this thing working right."

Gregor nodded, and pushed the second button.

They could hear the faint click-click of circuits opening. Half a dozen small engines purred into life. A light flashed red, then winked off as the generators took up the load.

"That's more like it," Arnold said.

"I am Lifeboat 324-A," the boat stated telepathically. "I am now fully activated, and able to protect my occupants from danger. Have faith in me. My action-response tapes, both psychological and physical, have been prepared by the best scientific minds in all Drome."

"Gives you quite a feeling of confidence, doesn't it?" Arnold said.

"I suppose so," Gregor said. "But where is Drome?"

"Gentlemen," the lifeboat continued, "try to think of me, not as an unfeeling mechanism, but as your friend and comrade-in-arms. I understand how you feel. You have seen your ship go down, cruelly riddled by the implacable H'gen. You have—"

"What ship?" Gregor asked. "What's it talking about?"

"—crawled aboard me, dazed, gasping from the poisonous fumes of water; half-dead—"

"You mean that swim we took?" Arnold asked. "You've got it all wrong. We were just surveying—"

"—shocked, wounded, morale low," the lifeboat finished. "You are a little frightened, perhaps," it said in a softer mental tone. "And well you might be, separated from the Drome fleet and adrift upon an inclement alien planet. A little fear is nothing to be ashamed of, gentlemen. But this is war, and war is a cruel business. We have no alternative but to drive the barbaric H'gen back across space."

"There must be a reasonable explanation for all this," Gregor said. "Probably an old television script got mixed up in its response bank."

"We'd better give it a complete overhaul," Arnold said. "Can't listen to that stuff all day."

They were approaching the island. The lifeboat was still babbling about home and hearth, evasive action, tactical maneuvers, and the need for calm in emergencies like this. Suddenly it slowed.

"What's the matter?" Gregor asked.

"I am scanning the island," the lifeboat answered.

Gregor and Arnold glanced at each other. "Better humor it," Arnold whispered. To the lifeboat he said. "That island's okay. We checked it personally."

"Perhaps you did," the lifeboat answered. "But in modern, lightning-quick warfare, Drome senses cannot be trusted. They are too limited, too prone to interpret what they wish. Electronic senses, on the other hand, are emotionless, eternally vigilant, and infallible within their limits."

"But there isn't anything there!" Gregor shouted.

"I perceive a foreign spaceship," the lifeboat answered. "It has no Drome markings."

"It hasn't any enemy markings, either," Arnold answered confidently, since he had painted the ancient hull himself.

"No, it hasn't. But in war, we must assume that what is not ours is the enemy's. I understand your desire to set foot on land again. But I take into account factors that a Drome, motivated by his emotions, would overlook. Consider the apparent emptiness of this strategic bit of land; the unmarked spaceship put temptingly out for bait; the fact that our fleet is no longer in this vicinity; the—"

"All right, that's enough," Gregor was sick of arguing with a verbose and egoistic machine. "Go directly to that island. That's an order."

"I cannot obey that order," the boat said. "You are unbalanced from your harrowing escape from death—"

Arnold reached for the cutout switch, and withdrew his hand with a howl of pain.

"Come to your senses, gentlemen," the boat said sternly. "Only the decommissioning officer is empowered to turn me off. For your own safety, I must warn you not to touch any of my controls. You are mentally unbalanced. Later, when our position is safer, I will administer to you. Now my full energies must be devoted toward detection and escape from the enemy."

The boat picked up speed and moved away from the island in an intricate evasive pattern.

"Where are we going?" Gregor asked.

"To rejoin the Drome fleet!" the lifeboat cried so confidently that the partners stared nervously over the vast, deserted waters of Trident.

"As soon as I can find it, that is," the lifeboat amended.

It was late at night. Gregor and Arnold sat in a corner of the cabin, hungrily sharing their last sandwich. The lifeboat was still rushing madly over the waves, its every electronic sense alert, searching for a fleet that had existed five hundred years ago, upon an entirely different planet.

"Did you ever hear of these Dromes?" Gregor asked.

Arnold searched through his vast store of minutiae. "They were non-human, lizard-evolved creatures," he said. "Lived on the sixth planet of some little system near Capella. The race died out over a century ago."

"And the H'gen?"

"Also lizards. Same story." Arnold found a crumb and popped it into his mouth. "It wasn't a very important war. All the combatants are gone. Except this lifeboat, apparently."

"And us," Gregor reminded him. "We've been drafted as Drome soldiery." He sighed wearily. "Do you think we can reason with this tub?"

Arnold shook his head. "I don't see how. As far as this boat is concerned, the war is still on. It can only interpret data in terms of that premise."

"It's probably listening in on us now," Gregor said.

"I don't think so. It's not really a mind-reader. Its perception centers are geared only to thoughts aimed specifically at it."

"Yes siree," Gregor said bitterly, "they just don't build 'em this way any more." He wished he could get his hands on Joe, the Interstellar Junkman.

"It's actually a very interesting situation," Arnold said. "I may do an article on it for *Popular Cybernetics*. Here is a machine with nearly infallible apparatus for the perception of external stimuli. The percepts it receives are translated logically into action. The only trouble is, the logic is based upon no longer existent conditions. Therefore, you could say that the machine is the victim of a systematized delusional system."

Gregor yawned. "You mean the lifeboat is just plain nuts," he said bluntly.

"Nutty as a fruitcake. I believe paranoia would be the proper designation. But it'll end pretty soon."

"Why?" Gregor asked.

"It's obvious," Arnold said. "The boat's prime directive is to keep us alive. So he has to feed us. Our sandwiches are gone, and the only other food is on the island. I figure he'll have to take a chance and go back."

In a few minutes they could feel the lifeboat swinging, changing direction. It esped, "At present I am unable to locate the Drome fleet. Therefore, I am turning back to scan the island once again. Fortunately, there are no enemy in this immediate area. Now I can devote myself to your care with all the power of my full attention."

"You see?" Arnold said, nudging Gregor. "Just as I said. Now we'll reinforce the concept." He said to the lifeboat, "About time you got around to us. We're hungry."

"Yeah, feed us," Gregor demanded.

"Of course," the lifeboat said. A tray slid out of the wall. It was heaped high with something that looked like clay, but smelled like machine oil.

"What's that supposed to be?" Gregor asked.

"That is geezel," the lifeboat said. "It is the staple diet of the Drome peoples. I can prepare it in sixteen different ways."

Gregor cautiously sampled it. It tasted just like clay coated with machine oil.

"We can't eat that!" he objected.

"Of course you can," the boat said soothingly. "An adult Drome consumes five point three pounds of geezel a day, and cries for more."

The tray slid toward them. They backed away from it.

"Now listen," Arnold told the boat. "We are *not* Dromes. We're humans, an entirely different species. The war you think you're fighting ended five hundred years ago. We can't eat geezel. Our food is on that island."

"Try to grasp the situation. Your delusion is a common one among fighting men. It is an escape fantasy, a retreat from an intolerable situation. Gentlemen, I beg you, face reality!"

"*You* face reality!" Gregor screamed. "Or I'll have you dismantled bolt by bolt."

"Threats do not disturb me," the lifeboat esped serenely. "I know what you've been through. Possibly you have suffered some brain damage from your exposure to poisonous water."

"Poison?" Gregor gulped.

"By Drome standards," Arnold reminded him.

"If absolutely necessary," the lifeboat continued, "I am also equipped to perform physical brain therapy. It is a drastic measure, but there can be no coddling in time of war." A panel slid open, and the partners glimpsed shining surgical edges.

"We're feeling better already," Gregor said hastily. "Fine looking batch of geezel, eh, Arnold?"

"Delicious," Arnold said, wincing.

"I won a nationwide contest in geezel preparation," the lifeboat esped, with pardonable pride. "Nothing is too good for our boys in uniform. Do try a little."

Gregor lifted a handful, smacked his lips, and set it down on the floor. "Wonderful," he said, hoping that the boat's internal scanners weren't as efficient as the external ones seemed to be.

Apparently they were not. "Good," the lifeboat said. "I am moving toward the island now. And, I promise you, in a little while you will be more comfortable."

"Why?" Arnold asked.

"The temperature here is unbearably hot. It's amazing that you haven't gone into coma. Any other Drome would have. Try to bear it a little longer. Soon, I'll have it down to the Drome norm of twenty degrees below zero. And now, to assist your morale, I will play our national Anthem."

A hideous rhythmic screeching filled the air. Waves slapped against the sides of the hurrying lifeboat. In a few moments, the air was perceptibly cooler.

Gregor closed his eyes wearily, trying to ignore the chill that was spreading through his limbs. He was becoming sleepy. Just his luck, he thought, to be frozen to death inside an insane lifeboat. It was what came of buying paternalistic gadgets, high-strung, humanistic calculators, oversensitive, emotional machines.

Dreamily he wondered where it was all leading to. He pictured a gigantic machine hospital. Two robot doctors were wheeling a lawnmower down a long white corridor. The Chief Robot Doctor was saying, "What's wrong with this lad?" And the assistant answered, "Completely out of his mind. Thinks he's a helicopter." "Aha!" the Chief said knowingly. "Flying fantasies! Pity. Nice looking chap." The assistant nodded. "Overwork did it. Broke his heart on crab grass." The lawnmower stirred. "Now I'm an eggbeater!" he giggled.

"Wake up," Arnold said, shaking Gregor, his teeth chattering. "We have to do something."

"Ask him to turn on the heat," Gregor said groggily.

"Not a chance. Dromes live at twenty below. We are Dromes. Twenty below for us, and no back talk."

Frost was piled deep on the coolant tubes that traversed the boat. The walls had begun to turn white, and the portholes were frosted over.

"I've got an idea," Arnold said cautiously. He glanced at the control board, then whispered quickly in Gregor's ear.

"We'll try it," Gregor said. They stood up. Gregor picked up the canteen and walked stiffly to the far side of the cabin.

"What are you doing?" the lifeboat asked sharply.

"Going to get a little exercise," Gregor said. "Drome soldiers must stay fit, you know."

"That's true," the lifeboat said dubiously.

Gregor threw the canteen to Arnold.

Arnold chuckled synthetically and threw the canteen back to Gregor.

"Be careful with that receptacle," the lifeboat warned. "It is filled with a deadly poison."

"We'll be careful," Gregor said. "We're taking it back to headquarters." He threw the canteen to Arnold.

"Headquarters may spray it on the H'gen," Arnold said, throwing the canteen back.

"Really?" the lifeboat asked. "That's interesting. A new application of—"

Suddenly Gregor swung the canteen against the coolant tube. The tube broke and liquid poured over the floor.

"Bad shot, old man," Arnold said.

"How careless of me," Gregor cried.

"I should have taken precautions against internal accidents," the lifeboat esped gloomily. "It won't happen again. But the situation is very serious. I cannot repair the tube myself. I am unable to properly cool the boat."

"If you just drop us on the island—" Arnold began.

"Impossible!" the lifeboat said. "My first duty is to preserve your lives, and you could not live long in the climate of this planet. But I am going to take the necessary measures to ensure your safety."

"What are you going to do?" Gregor asked, with a sinking feeling in the pit of his stomach.

"There is no time to waste. I will scan the island once more. If our Drome forces are not present, we will go to the one place on this planet that can sustain Drome life."

"What place?"

"The southern polar cap," the lifeboat said. "The climate there is almost ideal—thirty below zero, I estimate."

The engines roared. Apologetically the boat added. "And, of course, I must guard against any further internal accidents."

As the lifeboat charged forward they could hear the click of the locks, sealing their cabin.

"Think!" Arnold said.

"I am thinking," Gregor answered. "But nothing's coming out."

"We must get off when he reaches the island. It'll be our last chance."

"You don't think we could jump overboard?" Gregor asked.

"Never. He's watching now. If you hadn't smashed the coolant tube, we'd still have a chance."

"I know," Gregor said bitterly. "You and your ideas."

"My ideas! I distinctly remember you suggesting it. You said—"

"It doesn't matter whose idea it was." Gregor thought deeply. "Look, we know his internal scanning isn't very good. When we reach the island, maybe we could cut his power cable."

"You wouldn't get within five feet of it," Arnold said, remembering the shock he had received from the instrument panel.

"Hmm." Gregor locked both hands around his head. An idea was beginning to form in the back of his mind. It was pretty tenuous, but under the circumstances . . .

"I am now scanning the island," the lifeboat announced.

Looking out the forward porthole, Gregor and Arnold could see the island, no more than a hundred yards away. The first flush of dawn was in the sky, and outlined against it was the scarred, beloved snout of their spaceship.

"Place looks fine to me," Arnold said.

"It sure does," Gregor agreed. "I'll bet our forces are dug in underground."

"They are not," the lifeboat said. "I scanned to a depth of a hundred feet."

"Well," Arnold said, "under the circumstances, I think we should examine a little more closely. I'd better go ashore and look around."

"It is deserted," the lifeboat said. "Believe me, my senses are infinitely more acute than yours. I cannot let you endanger your lives by going ashore. Drome needs her soldiers—especially sturdy, heat-resistant types like you."

"We like this climate," Arnold said.

"Spoken like a patriot!" the lifeboat said heartily. "I know how you must be suffering. But now I am going to the south pole, to give you veterans the rest you deserve."

Gregor decided it was time for his plan, no matter how vague it was. "That won't be necessary," he said.

"What?"

"We are operating under special orders," Gregor said. "We weren't supposed to disclose them to any vessel below the rank of super-dreadnaught. But under the circumstances—"

"Yes, under the circumstances," Arnold chimed in eagerly, "we will tell you."

"We are a suicide squad," Gregor said.

"Especially trained for hot climate work."

"Our orders," Gregor said, "are to land and secure that island for the Drome forces."

"I didn't know that," the boat said.

"You weren't supposed to," Arnold told it. "After all, you're only a lifeboat."

"Land us at once," Gregor said. "There's no time to lose."

"You should have told me sooner," the boat said. "I couldn't guess, you know." It began to move toward the island.

Gregor could hardly breathe. It didn't seem possible that the simple trick would work. But then, why not? The lifeboat was built to accept the word of its operators as the truth. As long as the "truth" was consistent with the boat's operational premises, it would be carried out.

The beach was only fifty yards away now, gleaming white in the cold light of dawn.

Then the boat reversed its engines and stopped. "No," it said.

"No what?"

"I cannot do it."

"What do you mean?" Arnold shouted. "This is war! Orders—"

"I know," the lifeboat said sadly. "I am sorry. A different type of vessel should have been chosen for this mission. Any other type. But not a *life*boat."

"You must," Gregor begged. "Think of our country, think of the barbaric H'gen—"

"It is physically impossible for me to carry out your orders," the lifeboat told them. "My prime directive is to protect my occupants from harm. That order is stamped on my every tape, giving priority over all others. I cannot let you go to your certain death."

The boat began to move away from the island.

"You'll be court-martialed for this!" Arnold screamed hysterically. "They'll decommission you."

"I must operate within my limitations," the boat said sadly. "If we find the fleet, I will transfer you to a killerboat. But in the meantime, I must take you to the safety of the south pole."

The lifeboat picked up speed, and the island receded behind them. Arnold rushed at the controls and was thrown flat. Gregor picked up the canteen and poised it, to hurl ineffectually at the sealed hatch. He stopped himself in mid-swing, struck by a sudden wild thought.

"Please don't attempt any more destruction," the boat pleaded. "I know how you feel, but—"

It was damned risky, Gregor thought, but the south pole was certain death anyhow.

He uncapped the canteen. "Since we cannot accomplish our mission," he said, "we can never again face our comrades. Suicide is the only alternative." He took a gulp of water and handed the canteen to Arnold.

"No! Don't!" the lifeboat shrieked. "That's *water!* It's a deadly poison—"

An electrical bolt leaped from the instrument panel, knocking the canteen from Arnold's hand.

Arnold grabbed the canteen. Before the boat could knock it again from his hand, he had taken a drink.

"We die for glorious Drome!" Gregor dropped to the floor. He motioned Arnold to lie still.

"There is no known antidote," the boat moaned. "If only I could contact a hospital ship . . ." Its engines idled indecisively. "Speak to me," the boat pleaded. "Are you still alive?"

Gregor and Arnold lay perfectly still, not breathing.

"Answer me!" the lifeboat begged. "Perhaps if you ate some geezel
. . ." It thrust out two trays. The partners didn't stir.

"Dead," the lifeboat said. *"Dead.* I will read the burial service."

There was a pause. Then the lifeboat intoned, "Great Spirit of the
Universe, take into your custody the souls of these, your servants. Although they died by their own hand, still it was in the service of their
country, fighting for home and hearth. Judge them not harshly for their
impious deed. Rather blame the spirit of war that inflames and destroys
all Drome."

The hatch swung open. Gregor could feel a rush of cool morning air.

"And now, by the authority vested in me by the Drome Fleet, and
with all reverence, I commend their bodies to the deep."

Gregor felt himself being lifted through the hatch to the deck. Then
he was in the air, falling, and in another moment he was in the water,
with Arnold beside him.

"Float quietly," he whispered.

The island was nearby. But the lifeboat was still hovering close to them,
nervously roaring its engines.

"What do you think it's up to now?" Arnold whispered.

"I don't know," Gregor said, hoping that the Drome peoples didn't
believe in converting their bodies to ashes.

The lifeboat came closer. Its bow was only a few feet away. They tensed.
And then they heard it. The roaring screech of the Drome National
Anthem.

In a moment it was finished. The lifeboat murmured, "Rest in peace,"
turned, and roared away.

As they swam slowly to the island, Gregor saw that the lifeboat was
heading south, due south, to the pole, to wait for the Drome fleet.

BIBLIOGRAPHY

"Ghost V," *Galaxy*, October 1954

"The Laxian Key," *Galaxy*, November 1954

"Milk Run," *Galaxy*, September 1954

"Squirrel Cage," *Galaxy*, January 1955

"The Lifeboat Mutiny," *Galaxy*, April 1955

"The Necessary Things," *Galaxy*, June 1955

"The Skag Castle," *Fantastic Universe*, March 1956

THE IN HIDING SERIES

by Wilmar H. Shiras

The In Hiding series had its origin in a question I asked myself: If a child of very high intelligence had the best possible environment from infancy on, would he or she still have problems? I was a bright child and in grade school was two years younger than my classmates but I had many problems both with children and with adults, problems I was not bright enough to solve. I made my Wonder Children much brighter, but they had problems—the major problem in the first story was Tim's essential loneliness. In *Children of the Atom* the other children and their problems as individuals and as a group were explored.

The impact of the book on my career was to kill it off. Whatever else I wrote came back with a note asking for another "In Hiding." Stories I wrote to amuse myself and my family simply didn't measure up. As Randall Garrett put it, *Children of the Atom* was my *Gone with the Wind*—I put into it all that I had to say.

Opening Doors

Timothy Paul, age fourteen-next-Wednesday, and Dr. Peter Welles, psychologist-psychiatrist, were on their way to the post office.

Tim was bursting with excitement, but he said never a word. Welles, watching him silently, knew why. One word from either of them and the floods of talk which would be loosed would never do in public. For they were going to get the first replies to the advertisement which they had placed in newspapers and magazines covering the nation.

The advertisement had been drafted by Tim himself, and he was very proud of it. He was in a fever of impatience to find the other children who were like him—if they existed, as there was reason to hope. Welles had intended to use other means, and within a week expected his first report from the detective agency which was tracing the children of all the parents who had died after the atomic explosion of 1958.

"Orphans, b c 59, i q three star plus," read the advertisement.

"We'll get all sorts of crazy replies," Tim had said, "but I want it to be plain enough so they can't miss it."

"We can weed them out," Welles had answered. "We can sell the writers neckties by mail, or something of the sort. We can explain it all by saying that I, as a psychologist, wanted to see what answers a cryptic nonsense ad would get."

"The b stands for born, and the c for circa," Tim had explained, pointing. "And the 59 is the year; they must all have been born in 1959 or very close to it. The rest is plain enough; they'll all be orphans, and it makes a catchy first word."

"Yes," Welles had replied patiently.

"I didn't mean to explain," apologized Tim, abashed. "Excuse me, Peter. It's only that I'm so used to having people never figure anything out by themselves."

"This seems almost too plain," said the psychologist. "But we'll see."

Well, at the worst, they'd get replies about bright children, and it would not do any harm for Tim to get in touch with bright children, even if they were only in the IQ 150–200 class.

Peter Welles unlocked the post-office box, and without a word began to divide the seven letters it contained, one for Tim and one for himself, one for Tim and one for himself, so that the odd one fell to the boy. Peter marched quickly out of the post office, and when Tim—who went slowly, examining the outsides of the envelopes—reached the street, he found that the doctor had flagged a taxi.

"Speed is the need of the moment," remarked Welles.

Tim smiled with his lips closed. The psychologist saw that the boy did not dare part his lips, lest indiscreet speech burst out. It was always hard to remember that this child, whose intelligence surpassed that of superior adults, was still emotionally only about thirteen years old.

"Hold everything, pal," said Welles encouragingly. "It won't be long now."

When they reached the doctor's office, which was also his home, Tim leaped from the cab and tore inside. By the time Peter got there, the first letter had been opened and read.

"This one thinks we're looking for child stars for the radio or the movies," said the boy. "But she doesn't know why orphans, she says, unless there is something wrong with our proposition."

"What shall we answer?" asked Peter, ripping open an envelope.

"Tell her we don't want the child's parents to get any of the child's salary," said Tim. "That'll settle her, all right. What's your first grab?"

"Thinks it must be some sex stuff, because it's cryptic," said Welles, tossing the letter into the fireplace.

Tim paid no attention; he was deep in the second letter which had fallen to him.

"This looks possible!" cried the boy. "It's obscure . . . but—"

"This one," interrupted Welles, "asks whether we are offering orphans for adoption or whether we want to adopt one. That's no good. But we must answer." He ripped open another, and cried, "Hello! This is in code!"

They read it together and laid it aside for the moment, with the other letter which had seemed possible but obscure.

"This one collects strange ads, so he says," Tim reported after a glance over his third letter. "Might be a possibility, but I don't think so. We can follow it up cautiously. And the last of all . . . hey! this is interesting, at any rate!"

He read the letter aloud:

"Dear Sir,

Your advertisement seems to deserve a wider audience, so I am broadcasting it over my short-wave set on the hour every hour this week. May I say that I take a personal interest in this matter? I would appreciate hearing from you further.

Jay Worthington."

"I think he's one," cried Tim. "That is, if there really are any more like me."

"Could be. We must figure out a reply to him; but it must be less plain than the ad, Tim. In fact, we'd better make some sort of reply to all the letters, just to be on the safe side."

"All but the one you threw into the fire," said Tim. "Let's see the code letter again."

They bent over it.

"Door-head tooth-head hand hook-tooth house-head-fish fish ox-serpent-fist-serpent—"

Tim began to giggle. In many ways he was a very normal small boy.

"—mouth-head-fish-sign-tooth door fish-prop ox-sign-water hand-back of the head goad-camel goad-fish-goad-hand."

"Anything else?"

"Not a word except the name and address on the envelope. Marie Heath—a girl!"

"There would be girls too, no doubt," said Tim, with elaborate carelessness which might have fooled the casual observer. "But why did she use this paper? It's folded like a greeting card. Open it all the way out flat, Peter."

Welles opened the paper to its fullest extent.

"Here's a bit of a scribble in pencil. A doodle. No, let me have a good look . . . Tim, it's Hebrew!"

"I don't know Hebrew. Do you? Then I'll stop in the main library before I go home, and transliterate it. Now for the obscure one."

Timothy read it aloud slowly:

"Dear Box Number:
It leaps to the eye that this is my cue. But perhaps you are as much in the dark as I am and it is probably better so.

B. Burke."

"Sounds promising," said Welles.

Tim muttered a moment and then exclaimed. "Better in the dark!" and fled from the room. By the time Peter Welles had got to his feet there was a shout from Tim, summoning Welles to his own bedroom, and there was Tim beckoning from the clothes closet. They shut themselves in the closet and in the dark they could make out words dimly luminous between the lines of typing:

"If there was a mental Boomfood in my bottle when I was a baby it might explain a great deal. Were others fed the same food? I must take this risk, I must find out. Beth Burke."

"Another girl," exclaimed Tim in triumph. "Look, we've found two already and I can't wait to see about this code. If we turn the Hebrew word into English letters it may help us; otherwise we'll have to ask somebody who knows the language."

"Run along, then, and give me a buzz when you have anything to report."

"Not over the phone," said Tim cautiously. "I'll get in touch, though."

"Don't you spring any codes on me, young fellow. If this keeps up, we'll have plenty of puzzles on our hands. Scamper! You need a good run."

"And how!" agreed Tim. He dashed off.

He was ringing Welles' doorbell frantically a little later.

"I've got it! When I opened the encyclopedia to transliterate the Hebrew letters, it gave the meaning of each character. Look—door is daleth, that's d, and head is resh, that's r—"

He had written it on a separate piece of paper.

"Dr sr y was brn n—and the next must be figures. The letters have a numerical value too—1–9–50–9. It makes a good code, for there are no vowels. This means, 'Dear sir, I was born in 1959.' And then it goes on, prnts d ns—I don't know what that means—atm y q lg lnly. That's all."

"Parents dead, and I don't get the ns either; maybe the writer got a little mixed. The number values would be 50–60. But atm is atom, of course, and the next is, IQ large. What's lnly?"

"Lonely," said Tim confidently.

"Seems to me these are almost too easy," worried Welles. "But I suppose they wouldn't give much away to anyone who doesn't know about the Wonder Children." He caught his breath, but it was too late. Tim merely grinned.

"So that's what you call us?"

"Not you, Tim. The rest of them . . . well, I had to call them something."

"Yes? I call them 'mine,' I think. I say to myself, 'Can we find any more of mine?' But that's silly, too. Now we can fit names to some of them; but we ought to think up a proper name for the group, and use it, Peter. That is, if we ever get a group, really."

"Timothy, it's almost your supper time," said Welles, as the clock struck six. "Run!"

"May I write answers to them?"

"Yes, but don't send them until I see them," conceded the doctor.

Writing answers was the most delightful game that Tim had ever played. Boys and girls of thirteen and fourteen have very little privacy about their incoming mail; all letters must be carefully coded and "tailored to fit" the letter they were answering, besides. Tim worked in references to Shaw's "Back to Methuselah" and Wells' "Country of the Blind."

The first list from the detective agency came two days later, and Welles dismissed a patient hurriedly and went with long strides to the school where Timothy spent his days. Miss Page raised an eyebrow when Welles beckoned to Timothy from the doorway, but nodded permission for the boy to go.

Welles hustled the boy into the middle of the empty corridor where they could not be overheard, and spoke softly.

"I have the list—nineteen names on it, this first batch. One of them, a girl, is in an insane asylum. She's probably perfectly sane. I must go to her at once."

"She must have given herself away and nobody believed her." Tim was shocked and grieved. "You can get her out, can't you, Peter?"

"I don't know. She may be insane. And I have no right to interfere. But I'll do what I can."

"Can I do anything? Or did you just want me to know you are going away?"

"You can pray hard, Tim. And here's the list I got. Make out a letter we can send to all of them, if you want to. But hold it until I come back."

Tim glanced at the list and grinned.

"Here's one of my pen pals, Gerard Chase. I thought some of my pen pals might belong. I'll write to him, all right. Look, can I send all my pen pals a copy of the ad, and just say I saw it and isn't it odd?"

"Sure. Go right ahead on that. And get the mail, too, if you like. Here's the key to the box."

Timothy pocketed the key and went back to his eighth-grade class.

Poor kid, thought Welles as he hastened to the airport. Somehow he must meet all those other kids, before too long. But not this trip.

The asylum was a small private hospital, three hours away by plane. It had pleasant grounds, flowers, trees. Dr. Mark Foxwell was in charge. Could Dr. Foxwell see Dr. Welles? Certainly, sir; this way, please.

"Elsie Lambeth is a patient here, yes," said Foxwell. He was a big man, heavier than Peter by fifty pounds at least; perhaps fifteen years older. He looked as dependable as a rock, thought Peter. And kind; he looked kind and patient. Good!

"The fact is," said Welles, "I have been asked by a friend of—well, one might say, a friend of Elsie's parents—I'll explain it all later, Dr. Foxwell. Shall we say that I have a friendly interest in the little girl, although I did not know of her existence until this morning. My credentials—"

Foxwell glanced over Welles' professional credentials and nodded.

"Heard of you," he murmured. "What do you want to know? Or do you want to see the child?"

"If possible, I want to hear all about her," said Peter. "And I want to see her, later, if I may. In exchange, I can tell you of a very interesting case, doctor—a boy about the same age. I have reason to think the cases may be related."

"Fine!" said the big doctor heartily. "Elsie's case is puzzling, and that's a fact. Nothing I'd like better than some light on her case. The whole

town knows all about it; you might as well be told frankly all I know.
Her uncle is her guardian; the child's parents died when she was a baby.
She was brought to us when she was not quite six years old—completely
unmanageable, that was the complaint."

"Dangerous?"

"Not particularly; but violent. Tantrums, alternating with fits of depression and sullen spells. Abusive language—said everyone was stupid.
Wouldn't play with other children at all. In fact, that was where the
real trouble started. She wouldn't go to school. Before she reached the
age of five, the chief problem was that she was always running away.
But always to the same place. Where would you guess a child of three
would always run to?"

"The library, in this case," said Peter.

"Humph! You must know something I don't." Dr. Foxwell, genuinely
startled, rubbed his chin thoughtfully. "You never heard of Elsie until
today? Who told you that?"

"Nobody," said Peter. "I told you I knew a case that might be similar."

"Well—the library. Yes. She'd take a book at random, open it anywhere,
hold it upside-down as like as not, and look at it by the hour. Turning
pages faster than any adult can read, but more slowly than an idle child
would flutter the pages. The librarians would call her aunt, and down
would come auntie in a rush. But that was no go. Elsie all but tore the
place apart."

"Did she damage the books?"

"No, never. Smash a chair to pieces—push a table over—scream and
rage and kick—but never damage a book. No, I take that back; she did
once. Tore a book to shreds. She said it told lies. Child of three!"

"Did it?"

"I don't know. Before my time. But the librarian was used to children,
and she told Elsie if she ever did such a thing again she couldn't come
to the library at all. And then she suggested that, since the child was
perfectly quiet while she was looking at books, that she be allowed to
stay there if she liked. After that, when she showed up, somebody would
phone her aunt, and on his way home from work her uncle would look
in every night and see if she was there, and take her home to supper."

"Would she go quietly then?"

"Usually. Sometimes not."

"Depending on what she was reading, I suppose," said Welles. "And
what happened when she was five?"

"She wouldn't go to kindergarten. Something like the old joke about
the little boy who told his mother, 'All right, if you want me to grow
up to be a bead-stringer, I'll go.' But Elsie wouldn't go. She might start
off to school, but she seldom ended up there. She'd land at the library,
or at the Junior College. The students used to smuggle her in, and she'd
sit in back where the instructor could not see her. The students thought

that was funny, to have her sit there and appear to take everything in. Trouble was, after the first week or so, she wouldn't be quiet. She'd shout out, 'Oh, you don't know what you're talking about,' or other little compliments of the same sort. She'd call the students stupid and silly when they tried to recite. One professor stopped his lecture to say that she'd better come up and teach the class if she knew so much, and Elsie said, 'I could do it as well as you, but would I get paid for it?' "

Welles chuckled. "Didn't he offer to pay her?"

"He didn't, but a few days later another instructor did. And Elsie said, 'It's no use; these stupid people don't want to learn anything anyway.' "

"Sweet child," murmured Welles. "Let me ask a question now. Did Elsie actually know anything herself? Did she ever prove that she did?"

"Not a thing we could ever prove. Sometimes she'd say, 'It's all in the book; can't you read?' or 'You've heard that often enough; any fool should know it by now.' But the child actually could read by that time, I'm sure. I didn't come on the scene until later. Well, the long and short of it is that Elsie became a public nuisance. Even the librarians got out of patience sometimes. Elsie was usually quiet at the library, but one day when people were getting out books she walked up and said, 'What do you want that junk for?' and on another day, when a man chanced to say to a librarian that only four people had ever read the Encyclopedia Britannica through, Elsie popped up at his elbow and said, 'I'm the fifth and sixth, then. I've read it through twice.' "

Foxwell stopped to light a cigarette.

"You can laugh," he commented rather acidly, "but this isn't a joke. The child is here in this asylum because people didn't think it funny very long. Her aunt and uncle had no control over her, and finally they brought her here. She had been here a year or so when I came and took charge of this hospital."

"Didn't she run away?"

"They kept the child locked up. Had to. But when I came I took another line. Elsie, I said, you want to go to the library? Well, if you'll be a good girl, you don't have to be locked up. No running away, no tantrums, no naughty talk, and I'll let you go to the library and get books out every week. Then you can read them here, in your room or out in the nice big yard. Just so you stay on the grounds, Elsie, I said, and be a good girl. It worked pretty well. We had to lock her up a couple of times, until she saw I meant it."

"What does she do besides read?"

"She writes," said Foxwell. "A scribble nobody can make out. Looks like some kind of shorthand. She keeps it locked in a drawer in her room and wears the key on a ribbon around her neck. I allow it, but once in a while she has to let somebody glance through it—make sure nothing out of the way is there, you know—matches or other contraband. She knows if she doesn't behave she can't keep it locked. Once in a while she goes through it and burns up a lot of stuff. That is, of course, somebody else burns it; she stands by and sees that it is done. She has a radio; likes it low, so we have no trouble about that."

"What's the diagnosis?"

"Who can say? We call it something for the books."

"What is her IQ?"

"We'll never know. She won't answer. Superior intelligence, no doubt, but not co-operative. She and I get along fine now, though. I know what she won't do and what she will do, and we get along fine. She won't talk, she won't answer questions, she won't take tests or play games. But she cleans up her room and makes her bed and all that, she has learned several kinds of handwork, sews nicely—makes some of her own clothes—she helps with the gardening, and she knows how to talk politely now. 'Elsie,' I said, 'no saucy speeches here; you've got to be nice to people, if you want us to be nice to you. Never mind what you think, you keep still if you can't talk like a lady.' And she makes polite small talk when her aunt and uncle come to see her, just as nice as anyone could wish. I told her she must answer when she is spoken to, be nice, and not be naughty and stubborn. There are no other children here, but Elsie doesn't mind that; she hates children. She doesn't mix much with the other patients, yet she seems to take a sort of interest in them. I started to tell her a little about the other cases, so she wouldn't be frightened at their odd ways, and she would listen as solemnly as a judge. It can't be coincidence, either, the little ways she helps with them. We have one wide-eyed old gal who always wants to run the power mower. Drives the gardener nuts, but Elsie will drop everything and get over there and do something to distract the old gal. The gardener swears that once when Elsie lured the old gal off, the child turned and winked at him."

"You think she is crazy?"

"She isn't normal. She doesn't behave normally. What do you mean, crazy?"

"Could she behave in a sane manner if she wished to?"

"Most likely she could. Where does that get you? Elsie doesn't wish to. She says she likes it here."

Foxwell went to the window and pointed.

"There she is, over there under the tree. Reading, as usual. Want to go over and speak to her? I don't promise she will make an answer, not one worth hearing."

"Small talk, such as she has been taught, eh?" mused Welles. "Does it ever sound like a caricature?"

"It usually does," admitted Foxwell. "I thought she was trying hard to please us. Maybe you're right—there was something a bit sarcastic about it, always. Or as if she is having a game with us. Humph! Want to hear about that case of yours! Well, come on."

The two men walked out into the grounds and advanced towards Elsie. She was absorbed in her book, and did not heed their approach.

"Good afternoon, Elsie," said Dr. Foxwell.

The child looked up, rose to her feet, and answered: "Good afternoon, doctor," in a sweet childish voice. She was a wiry little girl with black curls; she was dressed like any other child of her age.

"Dr. Welles, may I present Elsie Lambeth?"

"How do you do, Elsie?"

"How do you do?" The girl kept her finger in her book to mark the place. She was perfectly polite, completely disinterested.

Peter raised his eyebrows at Foxwell, who nodded, understanding the request.

"I have come here to see you, Elsie," said Peter. "I know a boy whose case is something like yours. So I came here to see if you are ready to leave this place. Dr. Foxwell says that you won't answer his questions or take the tests he wants to give you. Perhaps when you have heard my story you will think differently about things."

Elsie stared at him. She lowered her eyes after a moment, and the color rushed to her face.

"It's all right, Elsie," he went on. "I am going to tell Dr. Foxwell my story, and then we can send for you and tell you about it."

"You're going pretty fast," said Foxwell, nudging Welles. "She may not be ready to leave us. She may not want to live outside."

"There are problems about living outside, aren't there, Elsie? But perhaps we can solve them. The boy I am going to tell you about has solved them. But then he is a very bright boy."

The look Elsie shot at Dr. Welles made him smile as he nodded back at her.

"He had the breaks. But now things are going to break right for some other girls and boys. You'll listen to my story, won't you, Elsie?"

"I want to hear it first," said Foxwell, a little roughly. "Got to be sure it's worth telling her. Maybe she won't be much interested."

Welles winked at the child and turned to go.

The doctors walked off together in high satisfaction.

"Got her interested," remarked Foxwell. "But it's nothing to the way you've got me interested, Welles! Hints, hints! You must be very sure of yourself."

"We must not be overheard. Tim's case is secret."

"My office is completely soundproofed."

"I'm sure you have already taken the hints?"

"Wouldn't be surprised if I have. You think Elsie is too bright and didn't have a fair chance to get adjusted. By the time I came on the scene, she had been here a year, and I couldn't do much with her."

"Do you think she is sane?"

"I couldn't prove it. Now, what's your case, Dr. Welles?"

They went into Foxwell's office and locked the door; and then Peter Welles told the story of Timothy Paul.

Foxwell listened, agape.

"You think Elsie is shamming?"

"Hiding. She hasn't chosen the best way to do it, and by now it would tax a better brain than hers to find a way out. Her willfulness and her quick temper got her into trouble before she was old enough to devise a wiser way to manage her life; and now what can she do?"

"What have you to offer, Dr. Welles?"

"If she can prove herself sane, she can be taken out of here and into a different environment. You have taught her self-control and good manners; she could easily make a new start where her record is not known. That would be my suggestion. But she is under your care."

Foxwell waved an expansive arm.

"She is under your care now if you can do anything for her. You think your Timothy could help her adjust?"

"Possibly," said Welles. "It would be worth trying. He wants to be a psychiatrist himself. And it would do him a world of good to meet some of the other children."

"I'd like to meet your Tim."

"Certainly you must meet him. And if we could take Elsie there and let them meet . . . but perhaps he should meet some of the others first."

Dr. Foxwell said slowly: "It might be best if he meets Elsie first of all."

Welles nodded. "I see. Yes, you are right."

"If she is sane, it will still take time for her to adjust," said Foxwell. "You must help me with it."

"I had hoped you would say that. And I hope you will be able to help me with the other children if I find them. It is too big a job for one man to handle; and not many would be qualified to do it. It must be kept top secret for a while."

There was a tap at the door; a nurse reminded Dr. Foxwell that dinner time was at hand. The men ate quickly and absentmindedly, saying little. After dinner, Elsie was sent for.

The child was in her own room, nervously pacing about.

"Dr. Foxwell wants to see you now," said the nurse. "His friend is with him."

Elsie nodded obediently.

"I do hope you'll be good, Elsie," said the nurse pleadingly. "You've been such a good child lately. If you'd only talk to the doctor and answer his questions—"

"They are waiting," said Elsie sharply. "Why don't we go at once?"

"Well," cried the nurse, a little indignantly. "At least you're willing to go. Come on."

The nurse went with Elsie to the office and then was dismissed.

"Sit down, my dear, and let Dr. Welles tell you about the boy whose case is like yours," said Foxwell.

"No case is like mine," said Elsie.

"I think Tim is a little more intelligent than you are," said Welles thoughtfully. "He had all the breaks, and he made the most of them. Now things are breaking right for you."

"You said that before," said the child.

"I may say it again before I am through. But now for the story," and without further preamble, Peter plunged into the story of Timothy Paul.

Elsie listened with concentrated attention.

"Now, I know you are the child of parents who were also exposed to the same radiation," he concluded, "and who died of its effects not long after your birth. I think, and Dr. Foxwell thinks, that you are also sane and of greatly superior intelligence. If you are sane, you can leave this asylum and, under our direction, lead the kind of life such a brilliant girl should lead. But, if you are sane, you must prove it."

"Of course I am sane," said the child calmly. "I could have proved it any time these past five years."

"Why didn't you?"

"I didn't see what good it would do. I would have had to go back to school with a lot of stupid babies, and act like a little girl, and live with my stupid aunt and uncle. I can't be myself here, but I have more freedom than I would have outside. I was always unhappy until I came here."

"I am glad to see that you will answer my questions," said Peter, smiling at the child until she smiled back. "Weren't your aunt and uncle good to you?"

"They spoiled me rotten," said Elsie frankly. "Is that good? They didn't teach me to control my temper, or to be polite to people, or anything."

"They tried, didn't they?"

"Not very hard. My aunt always said she couldn't do anything with me. I was an awful brat. But grown people ought to have more control over a baby, even a bright baby. They didn't try to tell me things. I could have understood if they had told me. Dr. Foxwell did it right away. Why didn't they talk sense to me, the way he did? First they laughed and laughed and thought I was funny, and then they got mad with me. Stupids!"

"I don't think you behaved very wisely yourself, Elsie."

"Dr. Foxwell talked to me, and then I read more books, about how to bring up children, and about psychology. Then I knew how foolish I had been to be so naughty. But I couldn't think what to do, except to stay here."

"What is all this writing that you do?" asked Welles curiously.

"Poetry and stories and my diary and things. I am going to publish a lot of things when I get out of here. I meant to get out as soon as I was grown up, of course."

"What do you mean to do now?" asked Dr. Foxwell.

"I mean to get out of here and publish things now," said Elsie in some surprise. "Didn't you both say I could? Timothy Paul does."

"You'll have to behave as well as he does, and be accepted as a sane member of society," said Foxwell.

"Well, if I have pretended to be crazy for all these years," said Elsie tartly, "I can pretend to be normal if I like."

"What do you mean? Pretended to be crazy?"

"As soon as I saw where being uncontrolled got me, of course I knew how I ought to behave. But I had to keep on throwing tantrums and being sulky and not talking, so I could stay here in peace."

"You made the wrong adjustment, my dear," said Peter gently.

"I know that. I've known it for a long time. But I'm still only a little girl, and I couldn't stand living with my aunt and uncle and other children. They are all so stupid!"

"Elsie," said Dr. Foxwell, "I am glad to hear you talking so much; but you must erase that word 'stupid' from your vocabulary. It may be apt and it may not; but let's leave it out."

"Yes, sir," said the child obediently.

"Now about that writing," said Welles. "Can you write so people can read it?"

"Yes; but I had to have a secret writing for my private papers, or everyone would know I am sane. I'll copy everything out for you any time you want me to."

"You are sure the writings are sane?"

Elsie mused a moment.

"Yes, I am sure. Shall I tell you a little about them? A little is all I have time for tonight, I suppose." She was plainly eager to tell, and the doctors urged her to go on talking.

"There's one drawer full of things I found wrong in books and papers I read, and the things people said; answers to magazine articles and book reviews and things that were wrong. I couldn't correct people out loud any more, so I wrote it all down. That got it off my mind. But no magazines would print it; most of it is out of date by now. Some books say the craziest things. And teachers, too. Some of those teachers at the Junior College—one of them said we couldn't know anything! He said there was no such thing as truth, and if there was, we couldn't know it, or ever know we knew it. Such crazy people, to try to teach! and—"

"Elsie," said Dr. Foxwell, "you must not call people crazy. That is not nice, either. Cut it out."

"A privilege reserved for you," said Elsie, with an impish grin which quite took the doctor's breath away. And then she added briskly: "You see you must not call me crazy either. I can even make jokes."

"You took the words right out of my mind," Welles joked back. "Go on. What else did you write?"

"I can't say the poems off by heart, and any other way would spoil them. But the play is nice. You'll like the play I have just finished. Do you like Shakespeare, Dr. Welles?"

"Er . . . yes."

"So do I—in some ways. But sometimes he is cr . . . I mean, I don't always like him as well as I do sometimes," said the girl sedately, her eyes twinkling. "I thought he missed a good chance to write about Cataline—"

"Cataline?" said Dr. Foxwell weakly.

"Yes, and Cicero, you know. So I thought I'd write a play like 'Julius Caesar,' about the conspiracy of Catiline, and put some of Cicero's grand speeches into blank verse, and—I thought it would be an amusing hoax if I could pretend it was really by Shakespeare, undiscovered until now, but a hoax would be dishonest, so I decided against trying it. It is my first play," she added modestly, "but I like it. It was such fun. I'm so glad that you can read it, both of you. The really hard part has been keeping everything a secret. If I can be free like Tim—my aunt and uncle were snoopy. His grandparents must be wonderful. They trust him, don't they? Would you trust me?"

"That shouldn't be necessary," said Welles. "You can confide in us, you know. Now, it's getting late, and we must send you to bed. If Dr. Foxwell gives you the tests tomorrow, will you take them properly?"

"Yes, doctor."

"And answer everything we ask you?"

"Yes, doctor."

"And then what shall we do with you?"

The little girl chewed her thumbnail and screwed up her forehead.

"You could tell everybody that Dr. Welles came to town with a new treatment," she said triumphantly. "He could talk to me and pretty soon you could both say the new treatment had worked. There are always new kinds of psychotherapy being tried."

"Elsie, do you practice saying these big words when you are alone?" groaned Dr. Foxwell.

"Of course. I had to learn how to talk, didn't I?" was the cool response. "Well—could I go and live near Tim somewhere? Would his grandmother help me? But no, you said she doesn't care for children, except her grandson. And I couldn't live with you, of course, Dr. Welles, because I'm a girl."

"She thinks of everything," marveled Foxwell.

"Of course I do," Elsie flashed back. "I may be crazy but I am not stupid. I . . . oh, doctor, please excuse me, I forgot!"

"Excused," laughed the big doctor. "Welles? Have you a solution to these difficulties?"

"There must be some woman with whom she could board," said Peter, "and I have one in mind. But there is no need to tell anyone about Elsie. She must copy Tim, and present a normal face to the world. We can explain that she has not been well, had a nervous breakdown or something, that she is spoiled and needs training, and that she must be allowed to amuse herself in any proper way like other girls. When Dr. Foxwell releases you, Elsie, we think you should be away from here, and go somewhere away from all your past."

"That was one reason why I didn't see any point in being cured," said Elsie. "This whole town would think everything I did was cra . . . was odd, no matter what I did."

"Will her guardians agree to let her leave town?"

"Her uncle will gladly pay her board and care anywhere. They are eager to do their best for the child, although they do not understand her—and I can't blame them, now I see that I didn't understand her very well myself."

"I must have been a very difficult child," said the girl.

"Yes, I think you were," said Dr. Foxwell.

"Bring on your tests," said Elsie, waving her hands. "But if I'm not sane, then I want to stay here. I don't want to pretend I'm sane if I'm not. How many other boys and girls are there? Can we all live together?"

"That's my dream," admitted Welles, "but it may not be possible. You are all children, and nothing can be done without the consent of your guardians. I'll see your uncle and aunt the first thing after the tests are finished tomorrow."

"They'll agree," said Elsie. Her eyes suddenly filled with tears. "They're dreadfully stu . . . slow, poor things. But they do mean well. And they'll be so happy to think I'm going to be all right. It's been hard on them, too."

She ran out of the room, banging the door behind her.

The rest was easy. The next morning Dr. Foxwell gave Elsie the tests, and, as Timothy Paul had done, so also did Elsie. She went through the top of the IQ and C. M. tests, and on the Rorschach tests she gave normal, obviously unrehearsed answers which often made her examiners smile. Her uncle and aunt, when they were told as much as was good for them to know, were unfeignedly glad to know that Elsie could be "cured" and gave ready consent that she should move to be near Dr. Welles and under his care, as Dr. Foxwell recommended, and to board with any woman Dr. Welles suggested, to complete her adjustment to normal life.

Peter took the afternoon plane back, and reached his home city just in time to catch Tim leaving school.

"It's all right," he said. "It's all right. Come to my office after supper."

The boys were shouting to Tim to come and play ball.

"Yes, I'm coming," Tim shouted back. "May I go now, sir? Thank you, doctor," and he bounded away.

Welles watched him admiringly. The years of rigid self-control had wrought wonders. Nobody would ever have guessed that Peter had said anything of significance, anything to interest a boy whose schoolmates wanted him for a game.

The psychologist went into the school building and sat on Miss Page's desk. That brisk lady batted her eyes mischievously at him and asked concerning his health.

"I'm fine. And you, Miss Page?"

"Oh, fine, but getting no younger. Thirty-odd years of teaching age a gal before her time."

"I wondered . . . that is, have you any special plans for the summer?"

"No," said the teacher, stacking papers efficiently. "Nothing special. Can I do anything for you?"

"That depends. You see, there's a little girl . . . do you like bright children, Pagey?"

"That's hard to say. One meets so few of them."

"I'm serious for once. Many adults resent a bright child, and I need to find a woman who likes them."

"I have had one or two in my time," admitted Miss Page, "and I know what you mean. But I like them. There was one in particular—" her voice trailed off into silence.

"So you have found out that Timothy is brighter than most people think?" said Welles, gratified.

"I always thought he was. He wasn't the boy I had in mind. That one grew up to be a psychologist—but I'm beginning to think he isn't so bright after all."

Scarlet, Peter found himself laughing.

"Pagey, my love, my head is so full of a number of things that it has no room for me in it at all! Now, listen! Could you take this girl, a new patient of mine from out of the city, as a boarder for the summer? A girl of thirteen."

"A bright girl? Yes, I can, and gladly. How bright?"

"Too bright," said Welles. "A bit of a problem."

"You'll take care of the problem, no doubt. School is out in four weeks. When is she to come? Does she go to school?"

"She has not gone to school. Er . . . privately taught. She is not used to other children. That is one thing wrong with her."

"Bring her along, Peter. If she comes early, she can spend some time in my class if you like. It might do her good to visit school for a short time before vacation."

"It would, I think. But you'd rather wait until school is out, wouldn't you?"

"If the child needs your care, Peter, why not begin?"

"Pagey, you're a gem!"

When Timothy came to the psychologist's house that evening, he had three letters in his hand.

"I figured that ns out," he said, beginning to talk almost before the door was opened to him. "The letters shouldn't be together. The two should be separated. The n stands for *in* and the s is the date—60. Parents died in 1960, that's what it means."

Peter Welles, who had forgotten all about the code letter, stared in amazement for a few seconds. Then he got what the boy was talking about, and in the next second realized what desperate excitement must lie beneath this prepared talk of other things. He shut the door behind Tim and spoke quickly.

"The girl is all right," he said. "Everything is all right. We'll have to help her a little; but she is coming here to live with Miss Page for the summer. I've been telephoning to her doctor just now. Next Sunday he is going to bring her up here. Now, do you want to hear all the details?"

The boy hesitated.

"Would it be all right? I don't want to pry. Does she know about me?"

"Yes, she knows nearly all that I know about you—as much as I had time to tell. So does her doctor. I had to tell them, you see."

"Then tell me all about her."

An hour later, they remembered the three letters.

"This one is promising. A boy says he feels like Gulliver—he's always much bigger or much smaller than the people he is with, but he says he leaves it to us to guess which is mental and which is physical. That's Robin Welch. And this girl says she was aptly named Alice—her last name is Chase—that she is out of communication with everything, even her own feet, and what was in that bottle labeled 'Drink Me' that she does not even recall having drunk. I think she belongs, too. The third is no good; it advertised a boarding school with special attention to orphans. Well, Peter, I have to start home; you know grandma's rules. When . . . when can I see Elsie?"

"Sunday evening at seven. We'll have to take her to Miss Page's first, and let her unpack and get located a bit. Dr. Foxwell and I will have her here for supper, I think, and you can come over right after supper."

They filled up the intervening days as best they could, with their separate daily routines, and with the writing of letters. Welles had explained to Tim that he intended to spend his vacation, in August, getting to see as many of the boys and girls as he could, but that for the present he could only pave the way by writing letters. Tim prepared a card index of possible names, and kept a file of information gathered.

Sunday evening! Timothy, scrubbed until he shone, presented himself with the punctuality of one who had been waiting outside for the exact moment, and he was introduced formally to Dr. Foxwell and to a shy, eager Elsie.

"Elsie has brought some of her writings to show you," said Dr. Foxwell, "and she hopes you can help her decide which to offer for publication."

"Take them into my study, you two kids," suggested Peter. "Have a drink, Foxwell?"

"Thanks, I will. Good idea, Welles," he added, as the children disappeared, "but I'm dying to hear what goes on."

"There would be nothing to hear if we sat and stared at them. Give them ten minutes. How is she doing lately?"

"Fine! Just fine! She spent every minute of her spare time working over this stuff she is showing him now. Amazing stuff, Pete! By the way— I've had an offer for the hospital. I've been thinking, maybe I could sell out and come up here. Join in the work, you know." The big doctor was talking very rapidly, and he accepted his drink without looking up. "Don't want to poach. But there's Elsie—"

"That's all agreed," said Welles. "Any time you can manage it. Elsie is your patient. But I think the two children ought to be kept together, and others with them if it can be managed. But how can we arrange things? Can we get the other children here? And how can we live, if we take too much time over the children?"

They discussed the matter briefly, but without coming to any conclusion. Their minds were not on the subject; and as soon as the ten minutes had elapsed, Peter got a pitcher of fruit juice and a plate of cookies from the kitchen, and led the way quietly to the study. The men paused by the open door and listened to the chatter of the children.

"This is great," Timothy was saying. "These poems—but they're almost too good, Elsie! 'The slow sweet curve of light'—that's grand! But I don't know if it would sell."

"I know poetry doesn't sell. I wanted you to see it, that's all. I'm typing out everything."

"That whole poem about infinity and creation, honestly, it's grand. This other stuff is good, and I think this novel will sell, too. There was a novel, 'The Snake Pit' and it made a big hit when it first came out, away back thirty years or so ago, or something like that. Yours, from the synopsis and first pages, is . . . oh, hello, Peter! and Dr. Foxwell."

"We thought you might like a little refreshment," said Welles, advancing with the tray.

"Sure—thanks," said Tim, pushing papers out of the way politely. "Say, do you know what Elsie has done? She has read all the books about all the sciences she could, and then turned them into poetry!"

"Is that good?" asked Foxwell, selecting a cookie.

"Is that good! Say, it's great! She tells you what things *mean*, you know! Not just the mechanism and the equations and all that, but what it's all about. She makes you see it. And she has three novels done, she says, and some are sure to sell. She showed me the synopses of them tonight, and a sample chapter. We'll have to think up a whole raft of pen names, Elsie."

"How many do you have, Timothy?"

"Oh, I don't know—I keep a card index of them. Couple of dozen, I guess. Have some punch?" Tim filled the glasses.

"You haven't typed out all the novels, have you?" asked Dr. Foxwell.

"No, not yet," said Elsie. "The rest of this here is articles and short stories and a lot of poems. I wanted to get the short stuff typed up first. May I have a cookie?"

When it was time to take Elsie home, Dr. Foxwell lingered in the hall a moment.

"Keep notes," he begged Welles in a whisper. "I've got to take the night plane back and miss all of this. But keep notes, son!"

"We'll never know the whole of it," Welles answered. "But what we have heard tonight . . . this past hour—"

"I'll run up next Sunday . . . no, Saturday," promised Foxwell.

Monday, Elsie sat quietly in class. Tim scarcely spoke to her all day, and she replied in monosyllables when he did. He went home without a glance her way; but he was at Miss Page's house ten minutes later.

Miss Page admitted him and left the children alone together.

"Listen," said Tim, "you've got to make friends with the other girls."

"I don't like them. They're silly."

"They can do a lot of things better than you can. Play games and things. Now, listen—you've got to, that's all, Elsie. You know what the doctors told you."

"I want to be with you, that's all," said Elsie frankly. "The others have no sense. And you didn't even walk home with me."

"Gosh, no! Do you want all the kids to say you're my girl?"

Elsie stared at him in horror.

"Of course not! That's stupid!"

"Well, you have to make friends. Miss Page made it easy. She told the kids last week that a new girl was coming—"

"They don't like me. Nobody spoke to me, except 'Hello.' "

"Miss Page told them you were shy, that's why. She said you hadn't been to school, and that you weren't used to being with other girls and boys, because you had been sick, see? They think you used to have heart trouble or something, and you're just getting over it. They smiled at you, I saw them. They're trying to be polite, and not rush you too much the first day. Now, listen! you've got to practice playing with them, and getting along nice—or I won't help you get things published."

"You don't have to," said Elsie, turning her face away. "There are other boys and girls like us. They may be nice to me."

"Isn't anybody going to be nice unless you are nice, too. You might as well begin," said Tim ruthlessly. "You think fine, and you write fine, but what else can you do?"

"I never had a fair chance," Elsie flashed at him.

"You're having it now," said the boy grimly.

They glared at one another for a minute defiantly, and then both began to laugh.

"All right," said Elsie. "I know I'm maladjusted, and I have to get right. You had a head start on me, but I can catch up with you. Just give me a little time."

"We'll practice basketball for a while," said Timothy. "Come over to my place. I have a basket there to practice, myself. And then I'll show you my cats, if you like."

Peter Welles, who had reserved the last hour before supper for Elsie, was obliged to seek her out. He found the children at Timothy's, bent over the cat cages, admiring some kittens. But what were they saying?

"Are we dominants or recessives?" Elsie was asking earnestly. "Both my parents got the radiations, and both of yours."

"Yes, and so it can be recessive. We'll have to find out," Tim replied. "But we can find out if any others had only one parent exposed to it. If it's a recessive, you and I and some of the others will carry it double, but—"

"But if we marry outside the group, what then? No, we've got to know. And that is another reason for getting the whole group together."

"Statistics," gloated Tim, his eyes alight. "Bales and bales of statistics, graphs, charts, tests—too bad we can't experiment. Hello, here's Peter. I was showing Elsie the kittens. Look, I mated a silver Persian tom to one of these Siamese, and see what I got! Silver tabby!"

"They're the most beautiful of all," crooned Elsie. "I like short-haired cats best, anyway."

"You can have a couple of these," offered Tim.

"But Miss Page might not want me to have cats," the little girl objected.

"She won't mind. Peter can tell her you need pets," replied Timothy with assurance. "What did you tell her, Peter?"

"I told her that Elsie was very bright, very much maladjusted, and that she needed to live near me so I could treat her," replied Welles. "And I'd rather you two went easy when Miss Page can overhear you, but we may have to take her into our confidence before very long, if we take any steps toward having more of you children here. I still can't see how we are going to manage that."

"We'll think of a way," said Tim.

"Meanwhile, Elsie was due at my place half an hour ago."

The two children flushed.

"Oh, I'm sorry," she cried. "I didn't know it was so late. We've been playing ball, and then—"

Timothy also was trying to apologize, but Welles waved his hand and said he would forgive them this once. They finished off Elsie's scheduled hour in Tim's workshop, and he gave her some of his published writings to take away and read. The kittens, he said, would be ready to leave their mother in about a week, and Elsie could get Miss Page's consent meanwhile.

Peter did not see Tim for several days, but he knew the two children were together much of the time, discussing manuscripts, playing games, chattering constantly, and becoming well acquainted. On Friday he sought Tim out, and began to ask questions.

"Well, Timothy? Do you like her?"

"Oh, yes! I hope all the others are as good," said Tim happily. "It's wonderful to be able to talk to another person my own age and have them get everything I say, snap! just like that! no matter what I talk about. I can say anything I want to, just the way I can to you. She doesn't know exactly the same things I do, of course, but she understands everything."

"I wonder which of you is the more intelligent," hinted Peter Welles.

Timothy thought it over.

"I have been wondering that, too," he said, "and trying to judge; but it is hard to judge, being one of the two myself. I'd say we aren't exactly alike, so we can't be measured like that. She looks at things in a different way, you know. She wants to know what things mean, and I want to know what to do about things. We both have a lot to teach each other. Her memory and mine work differently, too. Of course we both read so much that we can't remember everything, or even a very big part of what we read; we remember the way we understood things, what they mean to us. She remembers sciences as if they were poems or pictures, and thinks about the significance of these things; but I remember the way things work, and think about inventions and social service and things like that, things she doesn't care about. I think of what practical use things are, and the theory of them. And yet in some ways she is much more practical than I am. She thinks about the philosophy of things and how they fit into the whole concept of everything. You can't measure any two people with the same yardstick, can you, Peter?"

"I guess not," laughed the psychologist. "Have you found out about her, some things I have been wondering? Can you tell me, perhaps, where she got that off shorthand of hers?"

"She told me," Tim answered. "When she was little she saw that people did not print when they wrote; the letters were different from printed ones. But no two handwritings were alike, and she heard her uncle say he couldn't read somebody else's writing; so when she was real little she thought everybody made up an arbitrary penmanship of his own. So she did, too. And then she found it so useful that she kept it up."

"Could it be broken as a simple substitution code, then?"

"I don't know; I haven't seen enough of it. Perhaps it could; at any rate, she never let people examine it carefully, you know, while she was in the hospital. She had some special signs for common words and frequent-letter-combinations, but mostly she spells things correctly; it is not a phonetic alphabet."

"And why did she hold books upside down so often? Was that part of her pose?"

"I didn't ask her that, but probably she could read as easily one way as another. I can; can't you? I usually don't, because it looks odd; she may have done it on purpose to look odd. But everybody does it more or less."

"And why would she always tell people they were wrong, but never tell them what was right?" asked the doctor. "She refused to instruct them. Why was that?"

Tim laughed. "She didn't say; but I think I know. She wanted to be right all the time. She despised others because they were stupid, but she couldn't stand the thought that she might make a mistake. I guess she read stories about demi-gods and magic princesses and stuff like that, when she was real little. Maybe she even got some idea that if she did make a mistake she wouldn't be so wonderful any more; sort of break the spell, or spoil the magic, or something like that. Anyway, I'm pretty sure that is what was wrong—she couldn't spoil this idea she had of herself as somebody who knew a million times as much as everybody else. Then as she grew older, and read more, and found out things, she must have found out how silly that was, and also she learned that other people she met—Dr. Foxwell for one—were much smarter than she had thought other people could be. So she wouldn't tell on herself. She's all right with me—she doesn't mind telling me that there are things she does not know, or can't do, or can't remember."

"I think she is all right, Tim. She must have been completely sane for some years, if not always. Perhaps she was a little queer for a while there, but I don't think it ever could have been called insane. Still, if you notice anything that I ought to know—we'll call Elsie your first patient, Tim—call me into consultation."

Timothy grinned. "I wouldn't keep anything from you, Peter. You're the doctor. She's making friends with the other girls at school. When is Dr. Foxwell coming back up here, Peter?"

"Tomorrow, I think."

"My grandmother wants to see both of you, while he is here," said Tim. "Can you come over tomorrow night?"

"Why, yes, I guess so. What's up?"

"Oh, she wants to talk to both of you," said Tim carelessly. "Grandfather is out of town this week end, or he would be there, too."

"We'll be over," said Peter.

The June days were long, and the doctors found Elsie skipping in at the gate as they neared Timothy's house. Her face fell when she saw them.

"Tim said I could get my kittens tonight," she said, "and Miss Page said I could come. Did you want me?"

"Not right now. We came to see Mrs. Davis," said Dr. Welles.

"I'll run ahead and ring the bell for you," said Elsie, suiting the action to the word.

"Big place," remarked Foxwell, looking about the grounds.

"Yes; Tim's grandparents are very well off, and he has a private work-room out back here, which used to be the garage. I'll take you out to see the workshop if there is time after we see Mrs. Davis," said Welles. "She probably wants to know who Elsie is, since the two kids have been spending so much time together. She lets Tim do about as he likes in some ways, but she is very strict about the company he keeps."

"How did he ever get away with so much? You say she has no idea he is anything out of the ordinary."

"She takes pains to see that he is a good boy and that he gets into no mischief. His writing and model-building and all that, she takes for ordinary schoolwork and boyish play, I suppose; she has never seen any of it. He convinced her that his cat-breeding experiments were the result of random curiosity. One can scarcely blame her for not suspecting anything like the truth."

Tim had opened the door, and was waiting for the doctors. They hastened their steps, and were taken into the house and presented to Mrs. Davis.

"And now you and your little friend may go outside and play," said that lady to her grandson, when she had received her guests. "Do sit down, Dr. Foxwell, and Dr. Welles. I have a little plan—a proposal which I dare to think may interest you. And since your time is valuable, and I know that you have little of it to spare on this visit, Dr. Foxwell, I intend to come to the point at once. My husband is not in the city at present, but he is aware of the proposal I am to make, and approves of it. Timothy, my grandson, has told me that you two men wish to start an experimental school for children who are a little above the average in intelligence. There are a few schools in this country, I understand, which take children whose intelligence quotient—I believe that is the correct term?—is above 150. I do not know what figure you had in mind, my dear Dr. Welles; perhaps something less extreme; but children above the average, Timothy tells me. I understand also that your plans and methods are as yet untried, something rather new in education. But we have every confidence in you, Dr. Welles, and since Timothy has hinted that he might, because of your interest in him, perhaps be considered as a pupil in such a school under your management—" Mrs. Davis paused, and raised her eyebrows.

The astounded doctors exchanged glances.

"Yes," said Peter feebly, "Timothy would certainly be . . . er . . . considered."

"And he tells me that you know a great architect, Paul T. Lawrence," continued the good lady, after referring to a slip of paper on which the name was apparently written. "Do you think he could be persuaded to design the buildings?"

"Er . . . yes, I think he could."

"For many years, we have had it in mind, my husband and I, to build a memorial to my daughter and to her husband. But nothing suitable has suggested itself until now. Timothy's references to this plan of yours have interested us deeply, and we have actually . . . ah . . . pumped him; I believe that is the expression. Well, Dr. Welles, if you and Dr. Foxwell are agreeable, we propose to let you have the use of a large tract of land which my husband owns, just beyond the edge of town, and we propose to erect suitable buildings for the school, whatever you may require. Estimates, of course, and such business details, we must settle later. About how many pupils did you have in mind?"

"Not very many," said Peter, trying to keep his voice steady. "Perhaps not more than ten, to start with; perhaps as many as forty or fifty. I really must explain that it is all a dream of mine. I have made no effort to contact possible pupils for such a school. I—"

Mrs. Davis bowed graciously.

"I understand all that, Dr. Welles. We thought perhaps you would care to inquire as to possible students this summer, the building could be started in the fall, and the school opened the following fall, when Timothy would be ready to enter High School. I do not expect you to tell me immediately whether you will accept this offer of ours; I realize that you have made no definite plans, and that there must be an enormous amount of figuring to be done. Let me say, briefly, what it is I propose. The use of the land; proper buildings; but, for we must be businesslike, all to remain in my husband's name, leased to you at a dollar a year for a period of, perhaps, five years, with privilege of renewal at the same figure. Your salaries, and those of a suitable number of assistants, to be guaranteed for the same length of time; and expenses also guaranteed. You will perhaps wish to put some of your own capital into the venture, and in that case we can work out some arrangement of sharing the expenses and the profits; but to my mind this is not a money-making venture, but an experiment in education."

The doctors hastened to agree with Mrs. Davis.

"It is true, Mrs. Davis, that if any such school is opened, there may be no profit at all, but heavy losses," Dr. Foxwell said earnestly.

"I am aware of that," said the lady serenely, "but the land will remain, and the buildings; and when we have lost all we can afford to lose, we shall simply close the school. Meanwhile, Timothy and the other children will have had the benefit of your guidance. You are to be in full charge, Dr. Welles, subject to whatever state laws exist; I contract not to interfere with your management of the school in any way, provided of course that the state authorities have no objections to raise. You understand, Dr. Foxwell, that I address myself largely to Dr. Welles, and put him in charge, because he is Timothy's friend and we know him well; but I wanted you to be present when the offer was made, and to share in it, since Timothy told me the idea is partly yours and that his new little friend, Elsie, would be one of the pupils. She is really a very bright little thing, isn't she? And such nice manners. And now, shall I tell my husband on his return that you are giving the matter your most serious consideration?"

Somehow the men stammered their thanks, and promised to spend the summer in trying to carry out her plans. Then Mrs. Davis dismissed them, saying that she knew it must be nearly little Elsie's bedtime—a statement which carried a definite hint that it was certainly nearing her grandson's bedtime.

"The children will be out with the cats," said Peter Welles. "We can find our way."

As soon as they were out of the house, the older man turned to Peter and demanded, "Does she mean it?"

"Certainly she does. The point is, do *we* mean it?"

"But how did she know?" marveled Foxwell. "She knows more than we do ourselves about our dream for the group! And yet she still hasn't the faintest idea what it is all about!"

"Don't let Tim hear you talking like this. It's as plain as ABC to him, and he expected us to get it in a flash. That's why he didn't even trouble to warn us."

"Oh! It's all his doing? But he is only a child. And Mrs. Davis seemed to think it would surprise him."

"He knows how to manage her, all right."

"But, confound it all! Are we to be managed, too, by a kid like—"

"By a kid like Tim, Foxwell, it's an honor. Don't worry; everything will be done right."

"I'll be darned if I'll be shoved around by a kid that size," protested the big doctor. "Why, we don't even know what he's doing!"

"It'll be your own fault if you don't. *Shh!* Here they are."

The children ran up to the men, and Elsie asked eagerly:

"Doctor, what do you think caused us? I read that people never use more than a very small part of their brains. Do you think the radiation stepped up our brains so we could use more of them? Tim doesn't think that's it."

"Well, it's an idea," said Tim slowly. "I don't know much about it. Maybe we can rig up some tests to tell us more about it. Or it could be something about our glands, for all I know."

"I haven't the least idea," said Peter, "and I'd rather leave it for later. Tim, did you know what your grandmother wanted to tell us?"

Tim's eyes danced.

"I wouldn't be surprised. But she probably thinks I would. Well? Will you do it?"

"I sure will," said Welles, "and Foxwell probably will, when he calms down enough to believe it."

"It'll cost a fortune," objected Foxwell. "Your grandmother doesn't realize . . . why, the architect's fee alone will be— Who is the fellow she spoke of, anyway?"

"Me," said Tim. "She doesn't know that. I'm not famous, but she thinks so. Anyway, I can do the buildings, and one of you men can represent me and oversee the workmen and the contractor. Now listen—I've got to go in soon. But I'll be drawing up the plans. Units of ten, I think, so we can build one or two, and more later on as we need them; it's better than starting with one huge building that would never be just the right size. A private workshop for each student, with a sink and a hood and some tables and chairs and shelves and cabinets—and the windows high, so nobody can peep in from outside—and glass in the doors like a regular school—the walls ought to be soundproofed, and—"

"Just a minute! How about classrooms?"

"We'll only have one grade. Sort of ungraded, rather. A high school, let's see—we'll have an auditorium, so we can put on plays and things, and we can have lectures and big classes there, and perhaps some small classes could meet in one of the workrooms, or outside, or somewhere."

"All you need is a log with a student on one end and a teacher on the other," muttered Foxwell.

"Well, sure. What we must have is lab facilities and quiet places to study and think, and a place where we can be together. Television equipment—we can listen in on lectures at the big universities all over the world. And a dormitory for the girls and women on this side—" Tim was sketching rapidly on a pad.

"Women!" shouted Dr. Foxwell.

"Miss Page, and whoever else we get," said Tim. "And the boys and men on this side . . . I suppose you'll both live there?"

"Us?" gasped the big doctor.

"Well, Peter, then, if you aren't coming."

"I am coming!" roared Foxwell. "Everybody said I could! Try and keep me out! But you go too fast for me, my boy."

"Gymnasium," Tim was scribbling rapidly, "and a swimming pool; maybe. We might build that ourselves."

"What are you going to use for money?" demanded Dr. Foxwell.

"Aren't you going to buy in?" asked Tim, surprised. "I am, and I thought you'd all want to, and the other boys and girls surely will, too."

"I can't," wailed Elsie, her face suddenly crumpled in grief.

"Of course you can!" cried Tim. "Wait until you start selling, that's all. You—"

"Timothy, there are laws regulating schools," said Peter Welles.

"Oh, you can get away with anything around here if you call it an experimental school," said Tim carelessly. "Give it out as a high IQ school, and it won't matter what we do. All they ask is whether you can pass Subject A and have gym every semester. And enough bathrooms for everybody. I made it a high IQ school because then we won't have to hide so much, either. It gives us a lot more freedom. But we must be careful not to make a show of it."

"Suppose others try to get in? People who aren't of the group?"

"If they test high enough, we might let them in, if we have room. They'll give us a norm to copy in public, higher than we ever had before, so that will be a big help. And it will do them good. You know a person with an IQ of 152 is as far from the average as a person with an IQ of 48. And most schools don't do a thing for the kids above 120."

"Please tell me exactly what you plan to do," said Peter Welles, "and all about it. Skip the buildings."

"I don't know that I can," said Timothy. "I haven't verbalized it yet. It's all new in my mind, you see. I only began to think of it this week, because of Elsie. We've got to set them all free, you understand. We've got to set them all free right away. I thought I was in hiding and in bondage, but when I heard about Elsie then I knew we have to do something about the others right away. This school is the best way, because we won't have to hide so much—we can pretend to be about 150 instead of 100—and we can all be together, and you two doctors can look after us and straighten out anybody that needs it. If any of the others aren't free or aren't adjusted, it's a million times worse for them than it was for me, don't you see? And a school seems so natural. If we don't advertise it, I don't think we have to let in anyone who asks, and in any case we can have tests and say we have our quota full or that applicants don't quite make it. And don't worry about the money—it'll come in fast enough. I am sure that several of them have money already, like me, and once we are free we can all earn ever so much more. And don't you see, we've got to learn how to work together and help each other, all of us children? We can't wait much longer, or we'll all be set in habits of solitude and secrecy, so we'll never be right. We can be together, and be free and independent, and have friends, and be helped, and help each other, and all work toward the same things, and—"

Tim had been talking so fast that he ran out of breath at last and had to stop and gasp.

"Toward what things?"

Tim waved his arms.

"Toward whatever we have to do. For everybody."

"The things God meant us to do," agreed Elsie, who had been standing rapt, her hands clasped, taking it all in.

"Some of them may not believe in God," said Welles. "Many people don't."

Elsie turned on him swiftly and snapped: "I don't know how to talk about people like that if I can't say either 'stupid' or 'crazy.' "

"Well, don't bite me; I'm a Thomist," replied Welles mildly.

"What's that?"

"I'll lend you the Summa tomorrow and you can read it through before lunch," replied Welles.

A bell rang violently in the workshop.

"My alarm clock," said Tim. "I've got to go in. I'll do the plans, and we'll get together pretty soon on all this."

"What do I have to do?" Peter Welles inquired. "It sounds to me as if you plan to do it all yourselves."

"Oh, no, Peter!" Tim cried in alarm. "It all depends on you. You've got to front for us, and find the others, and be the teachers too probably."

"Teachers!" roared Dr. Foxwell.

"That's just it. We need Peter and you especially to teach us how to be what we ought to be, to keep us on the right track, to help us work together right; you can see what Elsie needed! Others too must need help dreadfully. And we are only children after all. Nothing takes the place of experience. You can weld all these individuals into one group where each can help all and yet nobody's individuality will be sacrificed—"

"Timothy! Timothy!" came the call from the house.

"Yes, grandma!" Tim shouted back. "I'm coming!"

"Good night, Tim," said Welles, pushing the others toward the gate.

"My kittens!" Elsie remembered, and Tim hastily selected two and thrust them into her arms.

The men took her to Miss Page's door in a silence broken only by the child's crooning endearments to the struggling, crying kittens.

"Good night," said Mark Foxwell to the child.

She looked up at him.

"Tim forgot to mention it," she said, "but the school will have to have a dining hall and a kitchen. We can use the dining hall for a classroom, sometimes. And we'll need a cook."

"Yes."

"My aunt is a wonderful cook," said Elsie. "My uncle can sell his grocery store and buy one up here. He can give us a rate on all the things we'll need to buy. And my aunt can do the cooking."

"Do you mean you want them to come up here and live near you?" asked Foxwell.

Elsie wriggled.

"I think they'd like to," she said. "And . . . I feel different now, about them. One can feel sorry for a hen trying to bring up a duckling—ugly or not!"

She ran into the house with her kittens.

The doctors went on to Welles' home without a word, except that Dr. Foxwell shook his head and muttered to himself occasionally.

"Well?" said Mark Foxwell, when his pipe was alight. "You've chosen, yourself, to go into this thing, if it can be done?"

"There is no choice," said Welles. "I have found my life work. These kids, barely into their teens, need all kinds of help and they need it the worst way. Somehow or other, within the next few years, they have to come out of hiding and get into the adult world. I'm going to do what I can to see that they have the chance to do it right. And Tim has given us the opportunity—laid the chance of a lifetime in our laps."

Foxwell shook his head slowly.

"That's true. Most kids with IQ's of over 160 have to adjust on a lower level in order to live in this world at all. It always seemed to me a great waste. And these—what will they be like when they grow up?"

"That's more or less up to us, now," said Peter Welles. "They need each other, they need us. Tim's right—Elsie shows us."

"You mean the others may be warped in all kinds of ways!" cried the big doctor.

"They may be. Some of them must be. The bright child has all too often grown up to be a queer, maladjusted, unhappy adult. Or else he has thrown away half of his intelligence in order to adjust and be happy and get along as a social being. These children are bright beyond anything the world has ever known—if Tim is at all a fair sample, and Elsie is fully as well endowed. Think of such intelligence combined with a lust for power, a selfish greed, or an overwhelming sense of superiority so that all other people, of average intelligence or a little more, would seem as worthless as . . . as Yahoos."

"Elsie—" began Dr. Foxwell in horror.

"Elsie is all right. She adores you, she obeys you and she follows the advice that you and I and Tim give her. She only needed to be set free. But the others—"

"It's an awful responsibility," said Foxwell. "And did you hear those kids talking about heredity, last week?"

"Yes," said Peter.

"They'll be so far above us when they are adult," moaned Dr. Foxwell, "I swear I'm afraid to think of it."

"Timothy Paul has the answer, I think. A school, where they can work together under our direction, and have as much freedom as they can stand, combined with the psychotherapy that you and I can give them where it is needed. They are much like normal children in many ways, I think—looking to adults for help, emotionally still children. But Tim has solved his own problems fairly well up to now, and I think he can help us with the school. I don't doubt that he has all his plans made, as to how the school is to be run, but he looks to us for the adult supervision and for the psychological guidance that the young people must have."

Foxwell rubbed his chin and shook his head, puffed at his pipe, found it had gone out, and relighted it.

"I'm beginning to believe all this at last," he said.

"It does take time to grasp the possibilities."

"Lectures by television," mused Mark Foxwell. "A private laboratory for each child. The students contribute to the upkeep of the place—invest their own money in it, money they earned in competition with the whole adult world, and . . . Pete, tell me, do you honestly think you can find enough of these kids to make a school?"

"You have met two of them. Timothy and I are in correspondence with at least half a dozen more, and Mrs. Davis gives us the school and guarantees all expenses."

"Where's your phone?"

"In the hall."

The big doctor lumbered out of the room. He returned in a few minutes and held a match to his pipe again.

Welles waited.

"I phoned the fellow that wants my hospital," Foxwell said. "It's sold. I can leave it in a month or so. Come on now, Pete, and let's do some practical planning! The kid is miles ahead of us already. Most likely he always will be, but I'd like to pretend we're the bosses for a few months yet."

BIBLIOGRAPHY

"In Hiding," *Astounding,* November 1948

"Opening Doors," *Astounding,* November 1949

"New Foundations," *Astounding,* March 1950

Children of the Atom, Gnome, 1953

"Backward, Turn Backward," *New Worlds of Fantasy #2,* 1970

"Shadow-Led," *Fantastic,* October 1971

"Reality," *Fantastic,* February 1972

"Bird-Song," *Fantastic,* April 1973

THE CITY SERIES

by Clifford D. Simak

From the vantage point of thirty years, I now realize that the City series, from which "Aesop" is taken, stands as a watershed between my early apprentice writing and the body of work I have created since. Which does not mean that all I wrote before City is bad nor that all I wrote after City is good; writing never falls into so neat a pattern. What it does mean is that the writing of the City tales gave me a perspective and a sense of direction I had lacked before. One of the things that happened, I think, is that I wrote City from my heart while previously I had simply written stories I hoped some editor would like well enough to buy.

Another thing that City may have done for me was to demonstrate the wider scope that a novel afforded. While it is true that my *Cosmic Engineers,* written prior to City, had been serialized in *Astounding* and later became a book, it was not truly a book-length novel—I had to write several chapters to be inserted at the midpoint of the story to flesh it out to book-length. Ever since the publication of *City* I have been, in general, much more concerned with the novel than with shorter stories.

When Gnome Press proposed putting the City tales into a book, I was worried by the fact that the group of tales, simply standing by themselves, did not give the work good continuity. By themselves, they seemed to rattle around. So, in an effort to gain some continuity and to tie the stories more closely together, I wrote the story notes, which did have the effect of making the tales more of a piece. I am certain that it was the story notes that played a great part in gaining the book the acceptance it was accorded.

City was written out of a disillusion brought about by war. I was saddened and aghast at the inhumanity of a global conflict in which millions died and which brought untold misery to many other millions. I'm certain that I did not realize it at the time, but I am fairly certain now that in writing the tales I was trying to create a fantasy world that might serve as a retreat from the horror of that time—a horror that, on a somewhat smaller scale, has been continuing ever since.

Given the occasion to think the entire matter through when I was called upon recently to write an author's foreword to a new edition of the book, I came to the conclusion that I still stand upon much the same philosophical ground as when the tales were written. I still believe the concept of the city is an anachronism we would be better off without, that the western world has sold its soul to technology, that war is no solution to any problem whatsoever but the greatest evil that we face.

A few years ago Harry Harrison edited a book in which a number of the regular writers for the old *Astounding* magazine wrote stories as a memorial to John Campbell. Harry wrote me to say he thought it would be appropriate if I wrote another City story. I shied away from the idea. So far as I was concerned, the City series had been completed. I had never intended to write another. But I knew that if I were to write a final story for John (and I wanted very much to do that) it would have to be a City story.

In an attempt to reacquaint myself with the style and spirit in which the series had been written, I read through the entire book for the first time since the tales had been collected. Time and again I winced at certain passages, knowing full well that if they were written now I could do a better job. I ached to do a rewrite, but realized that if I tried to I would destroy what I had done those thirty years ago. For while, since that time, I had gained in craftsmanship and a better understanding of the storyteller's art, I also had lost something. I'd like to know what it is, but I cannot put a finger on it. It is the old story of trade-offs. You make some gains, but in the process you pay a certain price.

So *City* stands, with no regrets. It is an honest piece of work by a younger writer. Still writing as honestly as I can, I hope that some day, as an older writer, I may be able to write something that will gain as much acceptance.

Aesop

The gray shadow slid along the rocky ledge, heading for the den, mewing to itself in frustration and bitter disappointment—for the Words had failed.

The slanting sun of early afternoon picked out a face and head and body, indistinct and murky, like a haze of morning mist rising from a gully.

Suddenly the ledge pinched off and the shadow stopped, bewildered, crouched against the rocky wall—for there was no den. The ledge pinched off before it reached the den!

It whirled around like a snapping whip, stared back across the valley. And the river was all wrong. It flowed closer to the bluffs than it had flowed before. There was a swallow's nest on the rocky wall and there'd never been a swallow's nest before.

The shadow stiffened and the tufted tentacles upon its ears came up and searched the air.

There was life! The scent of it lay faint upon the air, the feel of it vibrated across the empty notches of the marching hills.

The shadow stirred, came out of its crouch, flowed along the ledge.

There was no den and the river was different and there was a swallow's nest plastered on the cliff.

The shadow quivered, drooling mentally.

The Words had been right. They had not failed. This was a different world.

A different world—different in more ways than one. A world so full of life that it hummed in the very air. Life, perhaps, that could not run so fast nor hide so well.

The wolf and bear met beneath the great oak tree and stopped to pass the time of day.

"I hear," said Lupus, "there's been killing going on."

Bruin grunted. "A funny kind of killing, brother. Dead, but not eaten."

"Symbolic killing," said the wolf.

Bruin shook his head. "You can't tell me there's such a thing as symbolic killing. This new psychology the Dogs are teaching us is going just a bit too far. When there's killing going on, it's for either hate or hunger. You wouldn't catch me killing something that I didn't eat."

He hurried to put matters straight. "Not that I'm doing any killing, brother. You know that."

"Of course not," said the wolf.

Bruin closed his small eyes lazily, opened them and blinked. "Not, you understand, that I don't turn over a rock once in a while and lap up an ant or two."

"I don't believe the Dogs would consider that killing," Lupus told him, gravely. "Insects are a little different than animals and birds. No one has ever told us we can't kill insect life."

"That's where you're wrong," said Bruin. "The Canons say so very distinctly. You must not destroy life. You must not take another's life."

"Yes, I guess they do," the wolf admitted sanctimoniously. "I guess you're right, at that, brother. But even the Dogs aren't too fussy about a thing like insects. Why, you know, they're trying all the time to make a better flea powder. And what's flea powder for, I ask you? Why, to kill fleas. That's what it's for. And fleas are life. Fleas are living things."

Bruin slapped viciously at a small green fly buzzing past his nose.

"I'm going down to the feeding station," said the wolf. "Maybe you would like to join me."

"I don't feel hungry," said the bear. "And, besides, you're a bit too early. Ain't time for feeding yet."

Lupus ran his tongue around his muzzle. "Sometimes I just drift in, casual like, you know, and the webster that's in charge gives me something extra."

"Want to watch out," said Bruin. "He isn't giving you something extra for nothing. He's got something up his sleeve. I don't trust them websters."

"This one's all right," the wolf declared. "He runs the feeding station and he doesn't have to. Any robot could do it. But he went and asked for the job. Got tired of lolling around in them foxed-up houses, with nothing to do but play. And he sits around and laughs and talks, just like he was one of us. That Peter is a good Joe."

The bear rumbled in his throat. "One of the Dogs was telling me that Jenkins claims webster ain't their name at all. Says they aren't websters. Says that they are men—"

"What's men?" asked Lupus.

"Why, I was just telling you. It's what Jenkins says—"

"Jenkins," declared Lupus, "is getting so old he's all twisted up. Too much to remember. Must be all of a thousand years."

"Seven thousand," said the bear. "The Dogs are figuring on having a big birthday party for him. They're fixing up a new body for him for a gift. The old one he's got is wearing out—in the repair shop every month or two."

The bear wagged his head sagely. "All in all, Lupus, the Dogs have done a lot for us. Setting up feeding stations and sending out medical robots and everything. Why, only last year I had a raging toothache—"

The wolf interrupted. "But those feeding stations might be better. They claim that yeast is just the same as meat, has the same food value and everything. But it don't taste like meat—"

"How do you know?" asked Bruin.

The wolf's stutter lasted one split second. "Why . . . why, from what my granddad told me. Regular old hellion, my granddad. He had him some venison every now and then. Told me how red meat tasted. But then they didn't have so many wardens as they have nowadays."

Bruin closed his eyes, opened them again. "I been wondering how fish taste," he said. "There's a bunch of trout down in Pine Tree Creek. Been watching them. Easy to reach down with my paw and scoop me out a couple."

He added hastily. "Of course, I never have."

"Of course not," said the wolf.

One world and then another, running like a chain. One world treading on the heels of another world that plodded just ahead. One world's tomorrow, another world's today. And yesterday is tomorrow and tomorrow is the past.

Except, there wasn't any past. No past, that was, except the figment of remembrance that flitted like a night-winged thing in the shadow of one's mind. No past that one could reach. No pictures painted on the wall of time. No film that one could run backward and see what-once-had-been.

Joshua got up and shook himself, sat down and scratched a flea. Ichabod sat stiffly at the table, metal fingers tapping.

"It checks," the robot said. "There's nothing we can do about it. The factors check. We can't travel in the past."

"No," said Joshua.

"But," said Ichabod, "we know where the cobblies are."

"Yes," said Joshua, "we know where the cobblies are. And maybe we can reach them. Now we know the road to take."

One road was open, but another road was closed. Not closed, of course, for it had never been. For there wasn't any past, there never had been any, there wasn't room for one. Where there should have been a past there was another world.

Like two dogs walking in one another's tracks. One dog steps out and another dog steps in. Like a long, endless row of ball bearings running down a groove, almost touching, but not quite. Like the links of an endless chain running on a wheel with a billion billion sprockets.

"We're late," said Ichabod, glancing at the clock. "We should be getting ready to go to Jenkins' party."

Joshua shook himself again. "Yes, I suppose we should. It's a great day for Jenkins, Ichabod. Think of it . . . seven thousand years."

"I'm all fixed up," Ichabod said, proudly. "I shined myself this morning, but you need a combing. You've got all tangled up."

"Seven thousand years," said Joshua. "I wouldn't want to live that long."

Seven thousand years and seven thousand worlds stepping in one another's tracks. Although it would be more than that. A world a day. Three hundred sixty-five times seven thousand. Or maybe a world a minute. Or maybe even one world every second. A second was a thick thing—thick enough to separate two worlds, large enough to hold two worlds. Three hundred sixty-five times seven thousand times twenty-four times sixty times sixty—

A thick thing and a final thing. For there was no past. There was no going back. No going back to find out about the things that Jenkins talked about—the things that might be truth or twisted memory warped by seven thousand years. No going back to check up on the cloudy legends that told about a house and a family of websters and a closed dome of nothingness that squatted in the mountains far across the sea.

Ichabod advanced upon him with a comb and brush and Joshua winced away.

"Ah, shucks," said Ichabod, "I won't hurt you any."

"Last time," said Joshua, "you damn near skinned me alive. Go easy on those snags."

The wolf had come in, hoping for a between-meals snack, but it hadn't been forthcoming and he was too polite to ask. So now he sat, bushy tail tucked neatly around his feet, watching Peter work with the knife upon the slender wand.

Fatso, the squirrel, dropped from the limb of an overhanging tree, lit on Peter's shoulder.

"What you got?" he asked.

"A throwing stick," said Peter.

"You can throw any stick you want to," said the wolf. "You don't need a fancy one to throw. You can pick up just any stick and throw it."

"This is something new," said Peter. "Something I thought up. Something that I made. But I don't know what it is."

"It hasn't got a name?" asked Fatso.

"Not yet," said Peter. "I'll have to think one up."

"But," persisted the wolf, "you can throw a stick. You can throw any stick you want to."

"Not as far," said Peter. "Not as hard."

Peter twirled the wand between his fingers, feeling the smooth roundness of it, lifted it and sighted along it to make sure that it was straight.

"I don't throw it with my arm," said Peter. "I throw it with another stick and a cord."

He reached out and picked up the thing that leaned against the tree trunk.

"What I can't figure out," said Fatso, "is what you want to throw a stick for."

"I don't know," said Peter. "It is kind of fun."

"You websters," said the wolf, severely, "are funny animals. Sometimes I wonder if you have good sense."

"You can hit any place you aim at," said Peter, "if your throwing stick is straight and your cord is good. You can't just pick up any piece of wood. You have to look and look—"

"Show me," said Fatso.

"Like this," said Peter, lifting up the shaft of hickory. "It's tough, you see. Springy. Bend it and it snaps back into shape again. I tied the two ends together with a cord and I put the throwing stick like this, one end against the string, and then pull back—"

"You said you could hit anything you wanted to," said the wolf. "Go ahead and show us."

"What shall I hit?" asked Peter. "You pick it out and—"

Fatso pointed excitedly. "That robin, sitting in the tree."

Swiftly Peter lifted his hands, the cord came back and the shaft to which the cord was tied bent into an arc. The throwing stick whistled in the air. The robin toppled from the branch in a shower of flying feathers. He hit the ground with a soft, dull thud and lay there on his back—tiny, helpless, clenched claws pointing at the treetops. Blood ran out of his beak to stain the leaf beneath his head.

Fatso stiffened on Peter's shoulders and the wolf was on his feet. And there was a quietness, the quietness of unstirring leaf, of floating clouds against the blue of noon.

Horror slurred Fatso's words. "You killed him! He's dead! You killed him!"

Peter protested, numb with dread. "I didn't know. I never tried to hit anything alive before. I just threw the stick at marks—"

"But you killed him. And you should never kill."

"I know," said Peter. "I know you never should. But you told me to hit him. You showed him to me. You—"

"I never meant for you to kill him," Fatso screamed. "I just thought you'd touch him up. Scare him. He was so fat and sassy—"

"I told you the stick went hard."

The webster stood rooted to the ground.

Far and hard, he thought. *Far and hard—and fast.*

"Take it easy, pal," said the wolf's soft voice. "We know you didn't mean to. It's just among us three. We'll never say a word."

Fatso leaped from Peter's shoulder, screamed at them from the branch above. "I will," he shrieked. "I'm going to tell Jenkins."

The wolf snarled at him with a sudden, red-eyed rage. "You dirty little squealer. You lousy tattletale."

"I will so," yelled Fatso. "You just wait and see. I'm going to tell Jenkins."

He flickered up the tree and ran along a branch, leaped to another tree.

The wolf moved swiftly.

"Wait," said Peter, sharply.

"He can't go in the trees all the way," the wolf said, swiftly. "He'll have to come down to the ground to get across the meadow. You don't need to worry."

"No," said Peter. "No more killings. One killing is enough."

"He will tell, you know."

Peter nodded. "Yes, I'm sure he will."

"I could stop him telling."

"Someone would see you and tell on you," said Peter. "No, Lupus, I won't let you do it."

"Then you better take it on the lam," said Lupus. "I know a place where you could hide. They'd never find you, not in a thousand years."

"I couldn't get away with it," said Peter. "There are eyes watching in the woods. Too many eyes. They'd tell where I had gone. The day is gone when anyone can hide."

"I guess you're right," the wolf said slowly. "Yes, I guess you're right."

He wheeled around and stared at the fallen robin.

"What you say we get rid of the evidence?" he asked.

"The evidence—"

"Why, sure—" The wolf paced forward swiftly, lowered his head. There was a crunching sound. Lupus licked his chops and sat down, wrapped his tail around his feet.

"You and I could get along," he said. "Yes, sir, I have the feeling we could get along. We're so very much alike."

A telltale feather fluttered on his nose.

The body was a lulu.

A sledge hammer couldn't dent it and it would never rust. And it had more gadgets than you could shake a stick at.

It was Jenkins' birthday gift. The line of engraving on the chest said so very neatly:

TO JENKINS FROM THE DOGS

But I'll never wear it, Jenkins told himself. It's too fancy for me, too fancy for a robot that's as old as I am. I'd feel out of place in a gaudy thing like that.

He rocked slowly back and forth in the rocking chair, listening to the whimper of the wind in the eaves.

They meant well. And I wouldn't hurt them for the world. I'll have to wear it once in a while just for the looks of things. Just to please the Dogs. Wouldn't be right for me not to wear it when they went to so much trouble to get it made for me. But not for every day—just for my very best.

Maybe to the Webster picnic. Would want to look my very best when I go to the picnic. It's a great affair. A time when all the Websters in the world, all the Websters left alive, get together. And they want me with them. Ah, yes, they always want me with them. For I am a Webster robot. Yes, sir, always was and always will be.

He let his head sink and mumbled words that whispered in the room. Words that he and the room remembered. Words from long ago.

A rocker squeaked and the sound was one with the time-stained room. One with the wind along the eaves and the mumble of the chimney's throat.

Fire, thought Jenkins. It's been a long time since we've had a fire. Men used to like a fire. They used to like to sit in front of it and look into it and build pictures in the flames. And dream—

But the dreams of men, said Jenkins, talking to himself—the dreams of men are gone. They've gone to Jupiter and they're buried at Geneva and they sprout again, very feebly, in the Websters of today.

The past, he said. The past is too much with me. And the past has made me useless. I have too much to remember—so much to remember that it becomes more important than the things there are to do. I'm living in the past and that is no way to live.

For Joshua says there is no past and Joshua should know. Of all the Dogs, he's the one to know. For he tried hard enough to find a past to travel in, to travel back in time and check up on the things I told him. He thinks my mind is failing and that I spin old robot tales, half-truth, half-fantasy, touched up for the telling.

He wouldn't admit it for the world, but that's what the rascal thinks. He doesn't think I know it, but I do.

He can't fool me, said Jenkins, chuckling to himself. None of them can fool me. I know them from the ground up—I know what makes them tick. I helped Bruce Webster with the first of them. I heard the first word that any of them said. And if they've forgotten, I haven't—not a look or word or gesture.

Maybe it's only natural that they should forget. They have done great things. I have let them do them with little interference, and that was for the best. That was the way Jon Webster told me it should be, on that night of long ago. That was why Jon Webster did whatever he had to do to close off the city of Geneva. For it was Jon Webster. It had to be he. It could be no one else.

He thought he was sealing off the human race to leave the earth clear for the dogs. But he forgot one thing. Oh, yes, said Jenkins, he forgot one thing. He forgot his own son and the little band of bow and arrow faddists who had gone out that morning to play at being cavemen—and cavewomen, too.

And what they played, thought Jenkins, became a bitter fact. A fact for almost a thousand years. A fact until we found them and brought them home again. Back to the Webster House, back to where the whole thing started.

Jenkins folded his hands in his lap and bent his head and rocked slowly to and fro. The rocker creaked and the wind raced in the eaves and a window rattled. The fireplace talked with its sooty throat, talked of other days and other folks, of other winds that blew from out the west.

The past, thought Jenkins. It is a footless thing. A foolish thing when there is so much to do. So many problems that the Dogs have yet to meet.

Overpopulation, for example. That's the thing we've thought about and talked about too long. Too many rabbits because no wolf or fox may kill them. Too many deer because the mountain lions and the wolves must eat no venison. Too many skunks, too many mice, too many wildcats. Too many squirrels, too many porcupines, too many bear.

Forbid the one great check of killing and you have too many lives. Control disease and succor injury with quick-moving robot medical technicians and another check is gone.

Man took care of that, said Jenkins. Yes, men took care of that. Men killed anything that stood within their path—other men as well as animals.

Man never thought of one great animal society, never dreamed of skunk and coon and bear going down the road of life together, planning with one another, helping one another—setting aside all natural differences.

But the Dogs had. And the Dogs had done it.

Like a Br'er Rabbit story, thought Jenkins. Like the childhood fantasy of a long gone age. Like the story in the Good Book about the Lion and the Lamb lying down together. Like a Walt Disney cartoon except that the cartoon never had rung true, for it was based on the philosophy of mankind.

The door creaked open and feet were on the floor. Jenkins shifted in his chair.

"Hello, Joshua," he said. "Hello, Ichabod. Won't you please come in? I was just sitting here and thinking."

"We were passing by," said Joshua, "and we saw a light."

"I was thinking about the lights," said Jenkins, nodding soberly. "I was thinking about the night five thousand years ago. Jon Webster had come out from Geneva, the first man to come here for many hundred years. And he was upstairs in bed and all the Dogs were sleeping and I stood there by the window looking out across the river. And there were no lights. No lights at all. Just one great sweep of darkness. And I stood there, remembering the day when there had been lights and wondering if there ever would be lights again."

"There are lights now," said Joshua, speaking very softly. "There are lights all over the world tonight. Even in the caves and dens."

"Yes, I know," said Jenkins. "It's even better than it was before."

Ichabod clumped across the floor to the shining robot body standing in the corner, reached out one hand and stroked the metal hide, almost tenderly.

"It was very nice of the Dogs," said Jenkins, "to give me the body. But they shouldn't have. With a little patching here and there, the old one's good enough."

"It was because we love you," Joshua told him. "It was the smallest thing the Dogs could do. We have tried to do other things for you, but you'd never let us do them. We wish that you would let us build you a new house, brand new, with all the latest things."

Jenkins shook his head. "It wouldn't be any use, because I couldn't live there. You see, this place is home. It has always been my home. Keep it patched up like my body and I'll be happy in it."

"But you're all alone."

"No, I'm not," said Jenkins. "The house is simply crowded."

"Crowded?" asked Joshua.

"People that I used to know," said Jenkins.

"Gosh," said Ichabod, "what a body! I wish I could try it on."

"Ichabod!" yelled Joshua. "You come back here. Keep your hands off that body—"

"Let the youngster go," said Jenkins. "If he comes over here some time when I'm not busy—"

"No," said Joshua.

A branch scraped against the eave and tapped with tiny fingers along the windowpane. A shingle rattled and the wind marched across the roof with tripping, dancing feet.

"I'm glad you stopped by," said Jenkins. "I want to talk to you."

He rocked back and forth and one of the rockers creaked.

"I won't last forever," Jenkins said. "Seven thousand years is longer than I had a right to expect to hang together."

"With the new body," said Joshua, "you'll be good for three times seven thousand more."

Jenkins shook his head. "It's not the body I'm thinking of. It's the brain. It's mechanical, you see. It was made well, made to last a long time, but not to last forever. Sometime something will go wrong and the brain will quit."

The rocker creaked in the silent room.

"That will be death," said Jenkins. "That will be the end of me.

"And that's all right. That's the way it should be. For I'm no longer any use. Once there was a time when I was needed."

"We will always need you," Joshua said softly. "We couldn't get along without you."

But Jenkins went on, as if he had not heard him.

"I want to tell you about the Websters. I want to talk about them. I want you to understand."

"I will try to understand," said Joshua.

"You Dogs call them websters and that's all right," said Jenkins. "It doesn't matter what you call them, just so you know what they are."

"Sometimes," said Joshua, "you call them men and sometimes you call them websters. I don't understand."

"They were men," said Jenkins, "and they ruled the earth. There was one family of them that went by the name of Webster. And they were the ones who did this great thing for you."

"What great thing?"

Jenkins hitched the chair around and held it steady.

"I am forgetful," he mumbled. "I forget so easily. And I get mixed up."

"You were talking about a great thing the websters did for us."

"Eh," said Jenkins. "Oh, so I was. So I was. You must watch them.

You must care for them and watch them. Especially you must watch them."

He rocked slowly to and fro and thoughts ran in his brain, thoughts spaced off by the squeaking of the rocker.

You almost did it then, he told himself. You almost spoiled the dream.

But I remembered in time. Yes. Jon Webster, I caught myself in time. I kept faith, Jon Webster.

I did not tell Joshua that the Dogs once were pets of men, that men raised them to the place they hold today. For they must never know. They must hold up their heads. They must carry on their work. The old fireside tales are gone and they must stay gone forever.

Although I'd like to tell them. Lord knows, I'd like to tell them. Warn them against the thing they must guard against. Tell them how we rooted out the old ideas from the cavemen we brought back from Europe. How we untaught them the many things they knew. How we left their minds blank of weapons, how we taught them love and peace.

And how we must watch against the day when they'll pick up those trends again—the old human way of thought.

"But, you said . . ." persisted Joshua.

Jenkins waved his hand. "It was nothing, Joshua. Just an old robot's mumbling. At times my brain gets fuzzy and I say things that I don't mean. I think so much about the past—and you say there isn't any past."

Ichabod squatted on his haunches on the floor and looked up at Jenkins.

"There sure ain't none," he said. "We checked her, forty ways from Sunday, and all the factors check. They all add up. There isn't any past."

"There isn't any room," said Joshua. "You travel back along the line of time and you don't find the past, but another world, another bracket of consciousness. The earth would be the same, you see, or almost the same. Same trees, same rivers, same hills, but it wouldn't be the world we know. Because it has lived a different life, it has developed differently. The second back of us is not the second back of us at all, but another second, a totally separate sector of time. We live in the same second all the time. We move along within the bracket of that second, that tiny bit of time that has been allotted to our particular world."

"The way we keep time was to blame," said Ichabod. "It was the thing that kept us from thinking of it in the way it really was. For we thought all the time that we were passing through time when we really weren't, when we never have. We've just been moving along with time. We said, there's another second gone, there's another minute and another hour and another day, when, as a matter of fact, the second or the minute or the hour was never gone. It was the same one all the time. It had just moved along and we had moved with it."

Jenkins nodded. "I see. Like driftwood on the river. Chips moving with the river. And the scene changes along the river bank, but the water is the same."

"That's roughly it," said Joshua. "Except that time is a rigid stream and the different worlds are more firmly fixed in place than the driftwood on the river."

"And the cobblies live in those other worlds?"

Joshua nodded. "I'm sure they must."

"And now," said Jenkins, "I suppose you are figuring out a way to travel to those other worlds."

Joshua scratched softly at a flea.

"Sure he is," said Ichabod. "We need the space."

"But the cobblies—"

"The cobblies might not be on all the worlds," said Joshua. "There might be some empty worlds. If we can find them, we need those empty worlds. If we don't find space, we are up against it. Population pressure will bring on a wave of killing. And a wave of killing will set us back to where we started out."

"There's already killing," Jenkins told him quietly.

Joshua wrinkled his brow and laid back his ears. "Funny killing. Dead, but not eaten. No blood. As if they just fell over. It has our medical technicians half crazy. Nothing wrong. No reason that they should have died."

"But they did," said Ichabod.

Joshua hunched himself closer, lowered his voice. "I'm afraid, Jenkins. I'm afraid that—"

"There's nothing to be afraid of."

"But there is. Angus told me. Angus is afraid that one of the cobblies . . . that one of the cobblies got through."

A gust of wind sucked at the fireplace throat and gamboled in the eaves. Another gust hooted in some near, dark corner. And fear came out and marched across the roof, marched with thumping, deadened footsteps up and down the shingles.

Jenkins shivered and held himself tight and rigid against another shiver. His voice grated when he spoke.

"No one has seen a cobbly."

"You might not see a cobbly."

"No," said Jenkins. "No. You might not see one."

And that is what Man had said before. You did not see a ghost and you did not see a haunt—but you sensed that one was there. For the water tap kept dripping when you had shut it tight and there were fingers scratching at the pane and the dogs would howl at something in the night and there'd be no tracks in the snow.

And there were fingers scratching on the pane.

Joshua came to his feet and stiffened, a statue of a dog, one paw lifted, lips curled back in the beginning of a snarl. Ichabod crouched, toes dug into the floor—listening, waiting.

The scratching came again.

"Open the door," Jenkins said to Ichabod. "There is something out there wanting to get in."

Ichabod moved through the hushed silence of the room. The door creaked beneath his hand. As he opened it, the squirrel came bounding in, a gray streak that leaped for Jenkins and landed in his lap.

"Why, Fatso," Jenkins said.

Joshua sat down again and his lip uncurled, slid down to hide his fangs. Ichabod wore a silly metal grin.

"I saw him do it," screamed Fatso. "I saw him kill the robin. He did it with a throwing stick. And the feathers flew. And there was blood upon the leaf."

"Quiet," said Jenkins, gently. "Take your time and tell me. You are too excited. You saw someone kill a robin."

Fatso sucked in a breath and his teeth were chattering.

"It was Peter," he said.

"Peter?"

"Peter, the webster."

"You said he threw a stick?"

"He threw it with another stick. He had the two ends tied together with a cord and he pulled on the cord and the stick bent—"

"I know," said Jenkins. "I know."

"You know! You know all about it?"

"Yes," said Jenkins, "I know all about it. It was a bow and arrow."

And there was something in the way he said it that held the other three to silence, made the room seem big and empty and the tapping of the branch against the pane a sound from far away, a hollow, ticking voice that kept on complaining without the hope of aid.

"A bow and arrow?" Joshua finally asked. "What is a bow and arrow?"

And what was it, thought Jenkins.

What is a bow and arrow?

It is the beginning of the end. It is the winding path that grows to the roaring road of war.

It is a plaything and a weapon and a triumph in human engineering.

It is the first faint stirring of an atom bomb.

It is a symbol of a way of life.

And it's a line in a nursery rhyme.

Who killed Cock Robin?
I, said the sparrow.
With my bow and arrow,
I killed Cock Robin.

And it was a thing forgotten. And a thing relearned.

It is the thing that I've been afraid of.

He straightened in his chair, came slowly to his feet.

"Ichabod," he said, "I will need your help."

"Sure," said Ichabod. "Anything you like."

"The body," said Jenkins. "I want to wear my new body. You'll have to unseat my brain case—"

Ichabod nodded. "I know how to do it, Jenkins."

Joshua's voice had a sudden edge of fear. "What is it, Jenkins? What are you going to do?"

"I'm going to the Mutants," Jenkins said, speaking very slowly. "After all these years, I'm going to ask their help."

The shadow slithered down the hill, skirting the places where the moonlight flooded through forest openings. He glimmered in the moonlight— and he must not be seen. He must not spoil the hunting of the others that came after.

There would be others. Not in a flood, of course, but carefully controlled. A few at a time and well spread out so that the life of this wondrous world would not take alarm.

Once it did take alarm, the end would be in sight.

The shadow crouched in the darkness, low against the ground, and tested the night with twitching, high-strung nerves. He separated out the impulses that he knew, cataloguing them in his knife-sharp brain, filing them neatly away as a check against his knowledge.

And some he knew and some were mystery and others he could guess at. But there was one that held a hint of horror.

He pressed himself close against the ground and held his ugly head out straight and flat and closed his perceptions against the throbbing of the night, concentrating on the thing that was coming up the hill.

There were two of them and the two were different. A snarl rose in his mind and bubbled in his throat and his tenuous body tensed into something that was half slavering expectancy and half cringing outland terror.

He rose from the ground, still crouched, and flowed down the hill, angling to cut the path of the two who were coming up.

Jenkins was young again, young and strong and swift—swift of brain and body. Swift to stride along the wind-swept, moon-drenched hills. Swift to hear the talking of the leaves and the sleepy chirp of birds— and more than that.

Yes, much more than that, he admitted to himself.

The body was a lulu. A sledge hammer couldn't dent it and it would never rust. But that wasn't all.

Never figured a body'd make this much difference to me. Never knew how ramshackle and worn out the old one really was. A poor job from the first, although it was the best that could be done in the days when it was made. Machinery sure is wonderful, the tricks they can make it do.

It was the robots, of course. The wild robots. The Dogs had fixed it up with them to make the body. Not very often the Dogs had much truck with the robots. Got along all right and all of that—but they got along because they let one another be, because they didn't interfere, because neither one was nosey.

There was a rabbit stirring in his den—and Jenkins knew it. A raccoon was out on a midnight prowl and Jenkins knew that, too—knew the cunning, sleek curiosity that went on within the brain behind the little eyes that stared at him from the clump of hazel brush. And off to the left, curled up beneath a tree, a bear was sleeping and dreaming as he slept— a glutton's dream of wild honey and fish scooped out of a creek, with ants licked from the underside of an upturned rock as relish for the feast.

And it was startling—but natural. As natural as lifting one's feet to walk, as natural as normal hearing was. But it wasn't hearing and it wasn't seeing. Nor yet imagining. For Jenkins knew with a cool, sure certainty about the rabbit in the den and the coon in the hazel brush and the bear who dreamed in his sleep beneath the tree.

And this, he thought, is the kind of bodies the wild robots have—for certainly if they could make one for me, they'd make them for themselves.

They have come a long ways, too, in seven thousand years, even as the Dogs have traveled far since the exodus of humans. But we paid no attention to them, for that was the way it had to be. The robots went their way and the Dogs went theirs and they did not question what one another did, had no curiosity about what one another did. While the robots were building spaceships and shooting for the stars, while they built bodies, while they worked with mathematics and mechanics, the Dogs had worked with animals, had forged a brotherhood of the things that had been wild and hunted in the days of Man—had listened to the cobblies and tried to probe the depths of time to find there was no time.

And certainly if the Dogs and robots have gone as far as this, the Mutants had gone farther still. And they will listen to me, Jenkins said, they will have to listen, for I'm bringing them a problem that falls right into their laps. Because the Mutants are men—despite their ways, they are the sons of Man. They can bear no rancor now, for the name of Man is a dust that is blowing with the wind, the sound of leaves on a summer day—and nothing more.

Besides, I haven't bothered them for seven thousand years—not that I ever bothered them. Joe was a friend of mine, or as close to a friend as a Mutant ever had. He'd talk with me when he wouldn't talk with men. They will listen to me—they will tell me what to do. And they will not laugh.

Because it's not a laughing matter. It's just a bow and arrow, but it's not a laughing matter. It might have been at one time, but history takes the laugh out of many things. If the arrow is a joke, so is the atom bomb, so is the sweep of disease-laden dust that wipes out whole cities, so is the screaming rocket that arcs and falls ten thousand miles away and kills a million people.

Although now there are no million people. A few hundred, more or less, living in the houses that the Dogs built for them because then the Dogs still knew what human beings were, still knew the connection that existed between them and looked on men as gods. Looked on men as gods and told the old tales before the fire of a winter evening and built against the day when Man might return and pat their heads and say, "Well done, thou good and faithful servant."

And that wasn't right, said Jenkins, striding down the hill, that wasn't right at all. For men did not deserve that worship, did not deserve the godhood. Lord knows I loved them well enough, myself. Still love them, for that matter—but not because they are men, but because of the memory of a few of the many men.

It wasn't right that the Dogs should build for Man. For they were doing better than Man had ever done. So I wiped the memory out and a long, slow work it was. Over the long years I took away the legends and misted the memory and now they call men websters and think that's what they are.

I wondered if I had done right. I felt like a traitor and I spent bitter nights when the world was asleep and dark and I sat in the rocking chair and listened to the wind moaning in the eaves. For it was a thing I might not have the right to do. It was a thing the Websters might not have liked. For that was the hold they had on me, that they still have on me, that over the stretch of many thousand years I might do a thing and worry that they might not like it.

But now I know I'm right. The bow and arrow is the proof of that. Once I thought that Man might have got started on the wrong road, that somewhere in the dim, dark savagery that was his cradle and his toddling place, he might have got off on the wrong foot, might have taken the wrong turning. But I see that I was wrong. There's one road and one road alone that Man may travel—the bow and arrow road.

I tried hard enough, Lord knows I really tried.

When we rounded up the stragglers and brought them home to Webster House, I took away their weapons, not only from their hands but from their minds. I re-edited the literature that could be re-edited and I burned the rest. I taught them to read again and sing again and think again. And the books had no trace of war or weapons, no trace of hate or history, for history is hate—no battles or heroics, no trumpets.

But it was wasted time, Jenkins said to himself. I know now that it was wasted time. For a man will invent a bow and arrow, no matter what you do.

He had come down the long hill and crossed the creek that tumbled toward the river and now he was climbing again, climbing against the dark, hard uplift of the cliff-crowned hill.

There were tiny rustlings and his new body told his mind that it was mice, mice scurrying in the tunnels they had fashioned in the grass. And for a moment he caught the little happiness that went with the running, playful mice, the little, unformed, uncoagulated thoughts of happy mice.

A weasel crouched for a moment on the bole of a fallen tree and his mind was evil, evil with the thought of mice, evil with remembrance of the old days when weasels made a meal of mice. Blood hunger and fear, fear of what the Dogs might do if he killed a mouse, fear of the hundred eyes that watched against the killing that once had stalked the world.

But a man had killed. A weasel dare not kill, and a man had killed. Without intent, perhaps, without maliciousness. But he had killed. And the Canons said one must not take a life.

In the years gone by others had killed and they had been punished. And the man must be punished, too. But punishment was not enough. Punishment, alone, would not find the answer. The answer must deal not with one man alone, but with all men, with the entire race. For what one of them had done, the rest were apt to do. Not only apt to do, but bound to do—for they were men, and men had killed before and would kill again.

The Mutant castle reared black against the sky, so black that it shimmered in the moonlight. No light came from it and that was not strange at all, for no light had come from it ever. Nor, so far as anyone could know, had the door ever opened into the outside world. The Mutants had built the castles, all over the world, and had gone into them and that had been the end. The Mutants had meddled in the affairs of men, had fought a sort of chuckling war with men and when the men were gone, the Mutants had gone, too.

Jenkins came to the foot of the broad stone steps that led up to the door and halted. Head thrown back, he stared at the building that reared its height above him.

I suppose Joe is dead, he told himself. Joe was long-lived, but he was not immortal. He would not live forever. And it will seem strange to meet another Mutant and know it isn't Joe.

He started the climb, going very slowly, every nerve alert, waiting for the first sign of chuckling humor that would descend upon him.

But nothing happened.

He climbed the steps and stood before the door and looked for something to let the Mutants know that he had arrived.

But there was no bell. No buzzer. No knocker. The door was plain, with a simple latch. And that was all.

Hesitantly, he lifted his fist and knocked and knocked again, then waited. There was no answer. The door was mute and motionless.

He knocked again, louder this time. Still there was no answer.

Slowly, cautiously, he put out a hand and seized the latch, pressed down with his thumb. The latch gave and the door swung open and Jenkins stepped inside.

"You're cracked in the brain," said Lupus. "I'd make them come and find me. I'd give them a run they would remember. I'd make it tough for them."

Peter shook his head. "Maybe that's the way you'd do it, Lupus, and maybe it would be right for you. But it would be wrong for me. Websters never run away."

"How do you know?" the wolf asked pitilessly. "You're just talking through your hair. No webster had to run away before and if no webster had to run away before, how do you know they never—"

"Oh, shut up," said Peter.

They traveled in silence up the rocky path, breasting the hill.

"There's something trailing us," said Lupus.

"You're just imagining," said Peter. "What would be trailing us?"

"I don't know, but—"

"Do you smell anything?"

"Well, no."

"Did you hear anything or see anything?"

"No, I didn't, but—"

"Then nothing's following us," Peter declared, positively. "Nothing ever trails anything any more."

The moonlight filtered through the treetops, making the forest a mottled black and silver. From the river valley came the muffled sound of ducks in midnight argument. A soft breeze came blowing up the hillside, carrying with it a touch of river fog.

Peter's bowstring caught in a piece of brush and he stopped to untangle it. He dropped some of the arrows he was carrying and stooped to pick them up.

"You better figure out some other way to carry them things," Lupus growled at him. "You're all the time getting tangled up and dropping them and—"

"I've been thinking about it," Peter told him, quietly. "Maybe a bag of some sort to hang around my shoulder."

They went on up the hill.

"What are you going to do when you get to Webster House?" asked Lupus.

"I'm going to see Jenkins," Peter said. "I'm going to tell him what I've done."

"Fatso's already told him."

"But maybe he told him wrong. Maybe he didn't tell it right. Fatso was excited."

"Lame-brained, too," said Lupus.

They crossed a patch of moonlight and plunged on up the darkling path.

"I'm getting nervous," Lupus said. "I'm going to go back. This is a crazy thing you're doing. I've come part way with you, but—"

"Go back, then," said Peter, bitterly. "I'm not nervous. I'm—"

He whirled around, hair rising on his scalp.

For there was something wrong—something in the air he breathed, something in his mind—an eerie, disturbing sense of danger and, much more than danger, a loathsome feeling that clawed at his shoulder blades and crawled along his back with a million prickly feet.

"Lupus!" he cried. "Lupus!"

A bush stirred violently down the trail and Peter was running, pounding down the trail. He ducked around a bush and skidded to a halt. His bow came up and with one motion he picked an arrow from his left hand, nocked it to the cord.

Lupus was stretched upon the ground, half in shade and half in moonlight. His lip was drawn back to show his fangs. One paw still faintly clawed.

Above him crouched a shape. A shape—and nothing else. A shape that spat and snarled, a stream of angry sound that screamed in Peter's brain. A tree branch moved in the wind and the moon showed through and Peter saw the outline of the face—a faint outline, like the half erased chalk lines upon a dusty board. A skull-like face with mewling mouth and slitted eyes and ears that were tufted with tentacles.

The bow cord hummed and the arrow splashed into the face—splashed into it and passed through and fell upon the ground. And the face was there, still snarling.

Another arrow nocked against the cord and back, far back, almost to the ear. An arrow driven by the snapping strength of well-seasoned straight-grained hickory—by the hate and fear and loathing of the man who pulled the cord.

The arrow spat against the chalky outlines of the face, slowed and shivered, then fell free.

Another arrow and back with the cord. Farther yet this time. Farther for more power to kill the thing that would not die when an arrow struck it. A thing that only slowed an arrow and made it shiver and then let it pass on through.

Back and back—and back. And then it happened.

The bow string broke.

For an instant, Peter stood there with the useless weapon dangling in one hand, the useless arrow hanging from the other. Stood and stared across the little space that separated him from the shadow horror that crouched across the wolf's gray body.

And he knew no fear. No fear, even though the weapon was no more. But only flaming anger that shook him and a voice that hammered in his brain with one screaming word:

KILL—KILL—KILL

He threw away the bow and stepped forward, hands hooked at his sides, hooked into puny claws.

The shadow backed away—backed away in a sudden pool of fear that lapped against its brain—fear and horror at the flaming hatred that beat at it from the thing that walked toward it. Hatred that seized and twisted it. Fear and horror it had known before—fear and horror and disquieting resignation—but this was something new. This was a whiplash of torture that seared across its nerves, that burned across its brain.

This was hatred.

The shadow whimpered to itself—whimpered and mewed and backed away and sought with frantic fingers of thought within its muddled brain for the symbols of escape.

The room was empty—empty and old and hollow. A room that caught up the sound of the creaking door and flung it into muffled distances, then hurled it back again. A room heavy with the dust of forgetfulness, filled with the brooding silence of aimless centuries.

Jenkins stood with the door pull in his hand, stood and flung all the sharp alertness of the new machinery that was his body into the corners and the darkened alcoves. There was nothing. Nothing but the silence and the dust and darkness. Nor anything to indicate that for many years there had been anything but silence, dust and darkness. No faintest tremor of a residuary thought, no footprints on the floor, no fingermarks scrawled across the table.

An old song, an incredibly old song—a song that had been old when he had first been forged, crept out of some forgotten corner of his brain. And he was surprised that it still was there, surprised that he had ever known it—and knowing it, dismayed at the swirl of centuries that it conjured up, dismayed at the remembrance of the neat white houses that had stood upon a million hills, dismayed at the thought of men who had loved their acres and walked them with the calm and quiet assurance of their ownership.

Annie doesn't live here any more.

Silly, said Jenkins to himself. Silly that some absurdity of an all-but-vanished race should rise to haunt me now. Silly.

Annie doesn't live here any more.

Who killed Cock Robin? I, said the sparrow—

He closed the door behind him and walked across the room.

Dust-covered furniture stood waiting for the man who had not returned. Dust-covered tools and gadgets lay on the table tops. Dust covered the titles of the rows of books that filled the massive bookcase.

They are gone, said Jenkins, talking to himself. And no one knew the hour or the reason of their going. Nor even where they went. They slipped off in the night and told no one they were leaving. And sometimes, no doubt, they think back and chuckle—chuckle at the thought of our thinking that they still are here, chuckle at the watch we keep against their coming out.

There were other doors and Jenkins strode to one. With his hand upon the latch he told himself the futility of opening it, the futility of searching any further. If this one room was old and empty, so would be all the other rooms.

His thumb came down and the door came open and there was a blast of heat, but there was no room. There was desert—a gold and yellow desert stretching to a horizon that was dim and burnished in the heat of a great blue sun.

A green and purple thing that might have been a lizard, but wasn't, skittered like a flash across the sand, its tiny feet making the sound of eerie whistling.

Jenkins slammed the door shut, stood numbed in mind and body.

A desert. A desert and a thing that skittered. Not another room, not a hall, nor yet a porch—but a desert.

And the sun was blue—blue and blazing hot.

Slowly, cautiously, he opened the door again, at first a crack and then a little wider.

The desert still was there.

Jenkins slammed the door and leaned with his back against it, as if he needed the strength of his metal body to hold out the desert, to hold out the implication of the door and desert.

They were smart, he told himself. Smart and fast on their mental feet. Too fast and too smart for ordinary men. We never knew just how smart they were. But now I know they were smarter than we thought.

This room is just an anteroom to many other worlds, a key that reaches across unguessable space to other planets that swing around unknown suns. A way to leave this earth without ever leaving it—a way to cross the void by stepping through a door.

There were other doors and Jenkins stared at them, stared and shook his head.

Slowly he walked across the room to the entrance door. Quietly, unwilling to break the hush of the dust-filled room, he lifted the latch and let himself out and the familiar world was there. The world of moon and stars, of river fog drifting up between the hills, of treetops talking to one another across the notches of the hills.

The mice still ran along their grassy burrows with happy mouse thoughts that were scarcely thoughts. An owl sat brooding in the tree and his thoughts were murder.

So close, thought Jenkins. So close to the surface still, the old blood-hunger, the old bone-hate. But we're giving them a better start than Man had—although probably it would have made no difference what kind of a start mankind might have had.

And here it is again, the old blood-lust of Man, the craving to be different and to be stronger, to impose his will by things of his devising—things that make his arm stronger than any other arm or paw, to make his teeth sink deeper than any natural fang, to reach and hurt across distances that are beyond his own arm's reach.

I thought I could get help. That is why I came here. And there is no help.

No help at all. For the Mutants were the only ones who might have helped and they have gone away.

It's up to you, Jenkins told himself, walking down the stairs. Mankind's up to you. You've got to stop them somehow. You've got to change them somehow. You can't let them mess up the thing the Dogs are doing. You can't let them turn the world again into a bow and arrow world.

He walked through the leafy darkness of the hollow and knew the scent of moldy leaves from the autumn's harvest beneath the new green of growing things and that was something, he told himself, he'd never known before.

His old body had no sense of smell.

Smell and better vision and a sense of knowing, of knowing what a thing was thinking, to read the thoughts of raccoons, to guess the thoughts of mice, to know the murder in the brains of owls and weasels.

And something more—a faint and wind-blown hatred, an alien scream of terror.

It flicked across his brain and stopped him in his tracks, then sent him running, plunging up the hillside, not as a man might run in darkness, but as a robot runs, seeing in the dark and with the strength of metal that has no gasping lungs or panting breath.

Hatred—and there could be one hatred only that could be like that.

The sense grew deeper and sharper as he went up the path in leaping strides and his mind moaned with the fear that sat upon it—the fear of what he'd find.

He plunged around a clump of bushes and skidded to a halt.

The man was walking forward, with his hands clenched at his sides, and on the grass lay the broken bow. The wolf's gray body lay half in the moonlight, half in shadow, and backing away from it was a shadowy thing that was half-light, half-shadow, almost seen but never surely, like a phantom creature that moves within one's dream.

"Peter!" cried Jenkins, but the words were soundless in his mouth.

For he sensed the frenzy in the brain of the half-seen creature, a frenzy of cowering terror that cut through the hatred of the man who walked forward toward the drooling, spitting blob of shadow. Cowering terror and frantic necessity—a necessity of finding, of remembering.

The man was almost on it, walking straight and upright—a man with puny body and ridiculous fists—and courage. Courage, thought Jenkins, courage to take on hell itself. Courage to go down into the pit and rip up the quaking flagstones and shout a lurid, obscene jest at the keeper of the damned.

Then the creature had it—had the thing it had been groping for, knew the thing to do. Jenkins sensed the flood of relief that flashed across its being, heard the thing, part word, part symbol, part thought, that it performed. Like a piece of mumbo-jumbo, like a spoken charm, like an incantation, but not entirely that. A mental exercise, a thought that took command of the body—that must be nearer to the truth.

For it worked.

The creature vanished. Vanished and was gone—gone out of the world. There was no sign of it, no single vibration of its being. As if it had never been.

And the thing it had said, the thing that it had thought? It went like this. Like this—

Jenkins jerked himself up short. It was printed on his brain and he knew it, knew the word and thought and the right inflection—but he must not use it, he must forget about it, he must keep it hidden.

For it had worked on the cobbly. And it would work on him. He knew that it would work.

The man had swung around and now he stood limp, hands dangling at his sides, staring at Jenkins.

His lips moved in the white blur of his face. "You . . . you—"

"I am Jenkins," Jenkins told him. "This is my new body."

"There was something here," said Peter.

"It was a cobbly," said Jenkins. "Joshua told me one had gotten through."

"It killed Lupus," said Peter.

Jenkins nodded. "Yes, it killed Lupus. And it killed many others. It was the thing that has been killing."

"And I killed it," said Peter. "I killed it . . . or drove it away . . . or something."

"You frightened it away," said Jenkins. "You were stronger than it was. It was afraid of you. You frightened it back to the world it came from."

"I could have killed it," Peter boasted, "but the cord broke—"

"Next time," said Jenkins, quietly, "you must make stronger cords. I will show you how it's done. And a steel tip for your arrow—"

"For my what?"

"For your arrow. The throwing stick is an arrow. The stick and cord you throw it with is called a bow. All together, it's called a bow and arrow."

Peter's shoulders sagged. "It was done before, then. I was not the first?"

Jenkins shook his head. "No, you were not the first."

Jenkins walked across the grass and laid his hand upon Peter's shoulder. "Come home with me, Peter."

Peter shook his head. "No. I'll sit here with Lupus until the morning comes. And then I'll call in his friends and we will bury him."

He lifted his head to look into Jenkins' face. "Lupus was a friend of mine. A great friend, Jenkins."

"I know he must have been," said Jenkins. "But I'll be seeing you?"

"Oh, yes," said Peter. "I'm coming to the picnic. The Webster picnic. It's in a week or so."

"So it is," said Jenkins, speaking very slowly, thinking as he spoke. "So it is. And I will see you then."

He turned around and walked slowly up the hill.

Peter sat down beside the dead wolf, waiting for the dawn. Once or twice, he lifted his hand to brush at his cheeks.

They sat in a semicircle facing Jenkins and listened to him closely.

"Now, you must pay attention," Jenkins said. "That is most important. You must pay attention and you must think real hard and you must hang very tightly to the things you have—to the lunch baskets and the bows and arrows and the other things."

One of the girls giggled. "Is this a new game, Jenkins?"

"Yes," said Jenkins, "sort of. I guess that is what it is—a new game. And an exciting one. A most exciting one."

Someone said: "Jenkins always thinks up a new game for the Webster picnic."

"And now," said Jenkins, "you must pay attention. You must look at me and try to figure out the thing I'm thinking—"

"It's a guessing game," shrieked the giggling girl. "I love guessing games."

Jenkins made his mouth into a smile. "You're right," he said. "That's exactly what it is—a guessing game. And now if you will pay attention and look at me—"

"I want to try out these bows and arrows," said one of the men. "After this is over, we can try them out, can't we, Jenkins?"

"Yes," said Jenkins patiently, "after this is over you can try them out."

He closed his eyes and made his brain reach out for each of them, ticking them off individually, sensing the thrilled expectancy of the minds that yearned toward his, felt the little probing fingers of thought that were dabbing at his brain.

"Harder," Jenkins thought. "Harder! Harder!"

A quiver went across his mind and he brushed it away. Not hypnotism—nor yet telepathy, but the best that he could do. A drawing together, a huddling together of minds—and it was all a game.

Slowly, carefully, he brought out the hidden symbol—the words, the thought and the inflection. Easily he slid them into his brain, one by one, like one would speak to a child, trying to teach it the exact tone, the way to hold its lips, the way to move its tongue.

He let them lie there for a moment, felt the other minds touching them, felt the fingers dabbing at them. And then he thought them aloud— thought them as the cobbly had thought them.

And nothing happened. Absolutely nothing. No click within his brain. No feeling of falling. No vertigo. No sensation at all.

So he had failed. So it was over. So the game was done.

He opened his eyes and the hillside was the same. The sun still shone and the sky was robin's egg.

He sat stiffly, silently, and felt them looking at him.

Everything was the same as it had been before.

Except—

There was a daisy where the clump of Oswego tea had bloomed redly before. There was a pasture rose beside him and there had been none when he had closed his eyes.

"Is that all there's to it?" asked the giggly girl, plainly disappointed.

"That is all," said Jenkins.

"Now we can try out the bows and arrows?" asked one of the youths.

"Yes," said Jenkins, "but be careful. Don't point them at one another. They are dangerous. Peter will show you how."

"We'll unpack the lunch," said one of the women. "Did you bring a basket, Jenkins?"

"Yes," said Jenkins. "Esther has it. She held it when we played the game."

"That's nice," said the woman. "You surprise us every year with the things you bring."

And you'll be surprised this year, Jenkins told himself. You'll be surprised at packages of seeds, all very neatly labeled.

For we'll need seeds, he thought to himself. Seeds to plant new gardens and to start new fields—to raise food once again. And we'll need bows and arrows to bring in some meat. And spears and hooks for fish.

Now other little things that were different began to show themselves. The way a tree leaned at the edge of the meadow. And a new kink in the river far below.

Jenkins sat quietly in the sun, listening to the shouts of the men and boys, trying out the bows and arrows, hearing the chatter of the women as they spread the cloth and unpacked the lunches.

I'll have to tell them soon, he told himself. I'll have to warn them to go easy on the food—not to gobble it up all at one sitting. For we will need that food to tide us over the first day or two, until we can find roots to dig and fish to catch and fruit to pick.

Yes, pretty soon I'll have to call them in and break the news to them.

Tell them they're on their own. Tell them why. Tell them to go ahead and do anything they want to. For this is a brand-new world.

Warn them about the cobblies.

Although that's the least important. Man has a way with him—a very vicious way. A way of dealing with anything that stands in his path.

Jenkins sighed.

Lord help the cobblies, he said.

BIBLIOGRAPHY

"City," *Astounding*, May 1944

"Huddling Place," *Astounding*, July 1944

"Census," *Astounding*, September 1944

"Desertion," *Astounding*, November 1944

"Paradise," *Astounding*, June 1946

"Hobbies," *Astounding*, November 1946

"Aesop," *Astounding*, December 1947

"The Simple Way" (as "The Trouble with Ants"), *Fantastic*, January 1951

"Epilog," *Astounding: The John W. Campbell Memorial Anthology*, 1973

City, Gnome Press, 1952

THE INSTRUMENTALITY SERIES

by Cordwainer Smith

Introduction by john j. pierce

"The Game of Rat and Dragon" was Cordwainer Smith's second coming to science fiction . . . well, maybe his third.

It was written in a single afternoon in 1954, published a year later, and followed by about twenty other Cordwainer Smith stories that appeared at frequent intervals until 1966—the year Dr. Paul Myron Anthony Linebarger died, and his secret literary identity was revealed to the world at large.

Cordwainer Smith is no doubt destined to be one of those writers who are researched to death, and made the subjects of innumerable term papers, dissertations and the like. The undersigned pleads guilty to having helped begin this process, if only for a fanzine and (later) introductions to paperback editions of Smith's works. So, first, a cautionary note:

Creative artists are more important than the reviewers or critics who write about them. And the individual experience of reading fiction is *far* more important than anything to be gleaned from learned (or not so learned) treatises. Because this anthology may be read by students of science fiction, this warning is all the more important: enjoy science fiction for its own sake first; *then* discuss it and theorize about it.

One of the greatest pleasures of reading science fiction is the experience of created worlds and created universes. This experience is sometimes lost on those who, while quite properly studying literature in terms of style and "language," forget that these are a means to an end. As C. S. Lewis once pointed out, style is a lens—it is something we look *through*, not *at*.

In science fiction, to be effective, the writer must use every element at his command to make the reader part of the world he is creating. It is very well to speak of sf and other fiction as metaphorical, and sometimes they are; but even then, they can succeed only to the extent that both the characters and events therein are *real*. If nothing in the story matters to the characters supposedly involved in it, if images and symbols do not grow out of events and relationships within the story, then that story just won't *work*.

If "The Game of Rat and Dragon" is your first exposure to Cordwainer Smith, you already know that Smith's fiction works. Everything we know about the experience of the pinlighters and their partners is what Underhill knows. Everything we feel about them is what Underhill feels. Seen dispassionately, his emotional involvement with the partners is—in our experience—absurd, even disquieting. But the whole point, of course, is *not* to see things merely as we see them.

It was this quality that marked the fiction of Cordwainer Smith from his first published appearance—"Scanners Live in Vain" in 1950 (using his real name, Linebarger had ventured into sf with "War No. 81-Q" in a high school paper a few weeks before his fifteenth birthday in 1928). But it was only gradually that his larger universe, of which "Scanners" and "Game" were parts, began to emerge.

Science fiction has had its future histories before—often (as in the case of Robert A. Heinlein) with dates, events and characters all carefully plotted out on the authors' own charts. Smith's future had something in common with those, and there were private notebooks to keep it straight (though the published charts are *not* his creation, and are based partly on guesswork). But it went beyond them in its essential spirit.

Exposition is always a difficult task in science fiction: an author must somehow orient the reader in an unfamiliar future without resorting to such artificial devices as lectures or dialogue that is clearly aimed at the reader rather than from one character to another. Smith is more successful at this than almost any other science fiction writer.

Anyone reading Smith for the first time quickly comes across references to the all-powerful Lords of the Instrumentality, to pinlighting, underpeople, sailships, manshonyaggers, the Vomact family, Norstrilia, stroon, the Rediscovery of Man, scanners and many other people, places and things. Yet in no single story are all these things explained; they come up only in the context of each story, and only as they relate to the characters and events in that story. The characters in "Scanners Live in Vain" already knew what a manshonyagger was, so no explanation was given— it wasn't until seven years later, in another story, that readers could learn what a manshonyagger *was*.

Smith's future history—beginning with the Ancient Wars and the Dark Age, and leading successively through the emergence of the Instrumentality, the second Age of Space, the materialistic utopia and the spiritual Rediscovery of Man—is something that is never set forth as such, but can only be pieced together from references and cross-references among the stories. A casual remark in one story will often clear up a loose end, or offer a completely new insight, into another. And because Smith did not live to finish all his intended stories, there are still mysterious allusions that may *never* be cleared up but somehow make the extant stories more convincing (after all, *real* history still holds its unsolved, and unsolvable, mysteries).

Familiar with a number of languages, cultures and storytelling traditions (thanks to his upbringing in China, Japan, France and Germany), Smith adopted a variety of literary styles and techniques for his science fiction, Oriental as well as Occidental. He was fascinated with myth and legend, and once called himself a pre-Cervantean author in the tradition of those who wrote the medieval romances like the *Chanson de Roland*. His later stories, such as "Under Old Earth" and "The Dead Lady of Clown Town," increasingly take the form of legends or "explanations" of legends, and several of them form an interconnected cycle centering on the Rediscovery of Man, the Holy Insurgency of the Underpeople, and what led up to them.

There are many other things to be said of Smith. Although not evident here, the borrowing of names and terms from many languages is common in most of his stories, and at least one concordance has been worked up (but alas, not printed) to explain the meanings of An Fang, spieltier, panc ashash, jonasoidal and other such borrowings. There was his experience in psychological warfare as a colonel in the U.S. Army. There was his deeply felt Christian faith, playing against the hard-headed realism of his involvement with soulless politics and social science. Above all, there was the synthesis he seemed to be trying to create—a philosophy of the nature and destiny of man—out of his diverse impressions and experiences and beliefs.

Any introduction of this length can only be superficial; but then perhaps all introductions are superficial. It is the experience of the fiction itself that counts—and if some of you are puzzled by some of the references in this introduction, there's only one cure: go read the rest of Cordwainer Smith.

The Game of Rat and Dragon

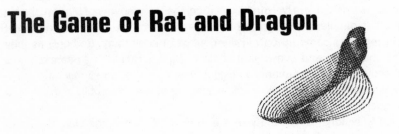

I THE TABLE

Pinlighting is a hell of a way to earn a living. Underhill was furious as he closed the door behind himself. It didn't make much sense to wear a uniform and look like a soldier if people didn't appreciate what you did.

He sat down in his chair, laid his head back in the headrest, and pulled the helmet down over his forehead.

As he waited for the pin-set to warm up, he remembered the girl in the outer corridor. She had looked at it, then looked at him scornfully.

"Meow." That was all she had said. Yet it had cut him like a knife.

What did she think he was—a fool, a loafer, a uniformed nonentity? Didn't she know that for every half-hour of pinlighting, he got a minimum of two months' recuperation in the hospital?

By now the set was warm. He felt the squares of space around him, sensed himself at the middle of an immense grid, a cubic grid, full of nothing. Out in that nothingness, he could sense the hollow aching horror of space itself and could feel the terrible anxiety which his mind encountered whenever it met the faintest trace of inert dust.

As he relaxed, the comforting solidity of the Sun, the clockwork of the familiar planets and the moon rang in on him. Our own solar system was as charming and as simple as an ancient cuckoo clock filled with familiar ticking and with reassuring noises. The odd little moons of Mars swung around their planet like frantic mice, yet their regularity was itself an assurance that all was well. Far above the plane of the ecliptic, he could feel half a ton of dust more or less drifting outside the lanes of human travel.

Here there was nothing to fight, nothing to challenge the mind, to tear the living soul out of a body with its roots dripping in effluvium as tangible as blood.

Nothing ever moved in on the solar system. He could wear the pin-set forever and be nothing more than a sort of telepathic astronomer, a man who could feel the hot, warm protection of the sun throbbing and burning against his living mind.

Woodley came in.

"Same old ticking world," said Underhill. "Nothing to report. No wonder they didn't develop the pin-set until they began to planoform. Down here with the hot sun around us, it feels so good and so quiet. You can feel everything spinning and turning. It's nice and sharp and compact. It's sort of like sitting around home."

Woodley grunted. He was not much given to flights of fantasy.

Undeterred, Underhill went on, "It must have been pretty good to have been an ancient man. I wonder why they burned up their world with war. They didn't have to planoform. They didn't have to go out to earn their livings among the stars. They didn't have to dodge the rats or play the game. They couldn't have invented pinlighting because they didn't have any need of it, did they, Woodley?"

Woodley grunted, "Uh-huh." Woodley was twenty-six years old and due to retire in one more year. He already had a farm picked out. He had gotten through ten years of hard work pinlighting with the best of them. He had kept his sanity by not thinking very much about his job, meeting the strains of the task whenever he had to meet them and thinking nothing more about his duties until the next emergency arose.

Woodley never made a point of getting popular among the partners. None of the partners liked him very much. Some of them even resented him. He was suspected of thinking ugly thoughts of the partners on occasion, but since none of the partners ever thought a complaint in articulate form, the other pinlighters and the chiefs of the Instrumentality left him alone.

Underhill was still full of the wonder of their job. Happily he babbled on, "What does happen to us when we planoform? Do you think it's sort of like dying? Did you ever see anybody who had his soul pulled out?"

"Pulling souls is just a way of talking about it," said Woodley. "After all these years, nobody knows whether we have souls or not."

"But I saw one once. I saw what Dogwood looked like when he came apart. There was something funny. It looked wet and sort of sticky as if it were bleeding and it went out of him—and you know what they did to Dogwood? They took him away, up in that part of the hospital where you and I never go—way up at the top part where the others are, where the others always have to go if they are alive after the rats of the up-and-out have gotten them."

Woodley sat down and lit an ancient pipe. He was burning something called tobacco in it. It was a dirty sort of habit, but it made him look very dashing and adventurous.

"Look here, youngster. You don't have to worry about that stuff. Pinlighting is getting better all the time. The partners are getting better. I've seen them pinlight two rats forty-six million miles apart in one and a half milliseconds. As long as people had to try to work the pin-sets themselves, there was always the chance that with a minimum of four hundred milliseconds for the human mind to set a pinlight, we wouldn't light the rats up fast enough to protect our planoforming ships. The partners have changed all that. Once they get going, they're faster than rats. And they always will be. I know it's not easy, letting a partner share your mind—"

"It's not easy for them, either," said Underhill.

"Don't worry about them. They're not human. Let them take care of themselves. I've seen more pinlighters go crazy from monkeying around with partners than I have ever seen caught by the rats. How many of them do you actually know of that got grabbed by rats?"

Underhill looked down at his fingers, which shone green and purple in the vivid light thrown by the tuned-in pin-set, and counted ships. The thumb for the *Andromeda*, lost with crew and passengers, the index finger and the middle finger for *Release Ships 43* and *56*, found with their pin-sets burned out and every man, woman, and child on board dead or insane. The ring finger, the little finger, and the thumb of the other hand were the first three battleships to be lost to the rats—lost as people realized that there was something out there *underneath space itself* which was alive, capricious, and malevolent.

Planoforming was sort of funny. It felt like—

Like nothing much.

Like the twinge of a mild electric shock.

Like the ache of a sore tooth bitten on for the first time.

Like a slightly painful flash of light against the eyes.

Yet in that time, a forty-thousand-ton ship lifting free above Earth disappeared somehow or other into two dimensions and appeared half a light-year or fifty light-years off.

At one moment, he would be sitting in the Fighting Room, the pin-set ready and the familiar solar system ticking around inside his head. For a second or a year (he could never tell how long it really was, subjectively), the funny little flash went through him and then he was loose in the up-and-out, the terrible open spaces between the stars, where the stars themselves felt like pimples on his telepathic mind and the planets were too far away to be sensed or read.

Somewhere in this outer space, a gruesome death awaited, death and horror of a kind which man had never encountered until he reached out for interstellar space itself. Apparently the light of the suns kept the dragons away.

Dragons. That was what people called them. To ordinary people, there was nothing, nothing except the shiver of planoforming and the hammer blow of sudden death or the dark spastic note of lunacy descending into their minds.

But to the telepaths, they were dragons.

In the fraction of a second between the telepaths' awareness of a hostile something out in the black, hollow nothingness of space and the impact of a ferocious, ruinous psychic blow against all living things within the ship, the telepaths had sensed entities something like the dragons of ancient human lore, beasts more clever than beasts, demons more tangible than demons, hungry vortices of aliveness and hate compounded by unknown means out of the thin, tenuous matter between the stars.

It took a surviving ship to bring back the news—a ship in which, by sheer chance, a telepath had a light-beam ready, turning it out at the innocent dust so that, within the panorama of his mind, the dragon dissolved into nothing at all and the other passengers, themselves nontelepathic, went about their way not realizing that their own immediate deaths had been averted.

From then on, it was easy—almost.

Planoforming ships always carried telepaths. Telepaths had their sensitiveness enlarged to an immense range by the pin-sets, which were telepathic amplifiers adapted to the mammal mind. The pin-sets in turn were electronically geared into small dirigible light bombs. Light did it.

Light broke up the dragons, allowed the ships to reform three-dimensionally, skip, skip, skip, as they moved from star to star.

The odds suddenly moved down from a hundred to one against mankind to sixty to forty in mankind's favor.

This was not enough. The telepaths were trained to become ultrasensitive, trained to become aware of the dragons in less than a millisecond.

But it was found that the dragons could move a million miles in just under two milliseconds and that this was not enough for the human mind to activate the light beams.

Attempts had been made to sheath the ships in light at all times.

This defense wore out.

As mankind learned about the dragons, so too, apparently, the dragons learned about mankind. Somehow they flattened their own bulk and came in on extremely flat trajectories very quickly.

Intense light was needed, light of sunlike intensity. This could be provided only by light bombs. Pinlighting came into existence.

Pinlighting consisted of the detonation of ultra-vivid miniature photonuclear bombs, which converted a few ounces of a magnesium isotope into pure visible radiance.

The odds kept coming down in mankind's favor, yet ships were being lost.

It became so bad that people didn't even want to find the ships because the rescuers knew what they would see. It was sad to bring back to Earth three hundred bodies ready for burial and two hundred or three hundred lunatics, damaged beyond repair, to be wakened, and fed, and cleaned, and put to sleep, wakened and fed again until their lives were ended.

Telepaths tried to reach into the minds of the psychotics who had been damaged by the dragons, but they found nothing there beyond vivid spouting columns of fiery terror bursting from the primordial id itself, the volcanic source of life.

Then came the partners.

Man and partner could do together what man could not do alone. Men had the intellect. Partners had the speed.

The partners rode their tiny craft, no larger than footballs, outside the spaceships. They planoformed with the ships. They rode beside them in their six-pound craft ready to attack.

The tiny ships of the partners were swift. Each carried a dozen pinlights, bombs no bigger than thimbles.

The pinlighters threw the partners—quite literally threw—by means of mind-to-firing relays directly at the dragons.

What seemed to be dragons to the human mind appeared in the form of gigantic rats in the minds of the partners.

Out in the pitiless nothingness of space, the partners' minds responded to an instinct as old as life. The partners attacked, striking with a speed faster than man's, going from attack to attack until the rats or themselves were destroyed. Almost all the time it was the partners who won.

With the safety of the interstellar skip, skip, skip of the ships, commerce increased immensely, the population of all the colonies went up, and the demand for trained partners increased.

Underhill and Woodley were a part of the third generation of pinlighters and yet, to them, it seemed as though their craft had endured forever.

Gearing space into minds by means of the pin-set, adding the partners to those minds, keying up the minds for the tension of a fight on which all depended—this was more than human synapses could stand for long. Underhill needed his two months' rest after half an hour of fighting.

Woodley needed his retirement after ten years of service. They were young. They were good. But they had limitations.

So much depended on the choice of partners, so much on the sheer luck of who drew whom.

II THE SHUFFLE

Father Moontree and the little girl named West entered the room. They were the other two pinlighters. The human complement of the Fighting Room was now complete.

Father Moontree was a red-faced man of forty-five who had lived the peaceful life of a farmer until he reached his fortieth year. Only then, belatedly, did the authorities find he was telepathic and agree to let him late in life enter upon the career of pinlighter. He did well at it, but he was fantastically old for this kind of business.

Father Moontree looked at the glum Woodley and the musing Underhill. "How're the youngsters today? Ready for a good fight?"

"Father always wants a fight," giggled the little girl named West. She was such a little little girl. Her giggle was high and childish. She looked like the last person in the world one would expect to find in the rough, sharp dueling of pinlighting.

Underhill had been amused one time when he found one of the most sluggish of the partners coming away happy from contact with the mind of the girl named West.

Usually the partners didn't care much about the human minds with which they were paired for the journey. The partners seemed to take the attitude that human minds were complex and fouled up beyond belief, anyhow. No partner ever questioned the superiority of the human mind, though very few of the partners were much impressed by that superiority.

The partners liked people. They were willing to fight with them. They were even willing to die for them. But when a partner liked an individual the way, for example, that Captain Wow or the Lady May liked Underhill, the liking had nothing to do with intellect. It was a matter of temperament, of feel.

Underhill knew perfectly well that Captain Wow regarded his, Underhill's, brains as silly. What Captain Wow liked was Underhill's friendly emotional structure, the cheerfulness and glint of wicked amusement that shot through Underhill's unconscious thought patterns, and the gaiety with which Underhill faced danger. The words, the history books, the ideas, the science—Underhill could sense all that in his own mind, reflected back from Captain Wow's mind, as so much rubbish.

Miss West looked at Underhill. "I bet you've put stickum on the stones."

"I did not!"

Underhill felt his ears grow red with embarrassment. During his novitiate, he had tried to cheat in the lottery because he got particularly fond of a special partner, a lovely young mother named Murr. It was so much easier to operate with Murr and she was so affectionate toward him that he forgot pinlighting was hard work and that he was not instructed to have a good time with his partner. They were both designed and prepared to go into deadly battle together.

One cheating had been enough. They had found him out and he had been laughed at for years.

Father Moontree picked up the imitation-leather cup and shook the stone dice which assigned them their partners for the trip. By senior rights he took first draw.

He grimaced. He had drawn a greedy old character, a tough old male whose mind was full of slobbering thoughts of food, veritable oceans full of half-spoiled fish. Father Moontree had once said that he burped cod liver oil for weeks after drawing that particular glutton, so strongly had the telepathic image of fish impressed itself upon his mind. Yet the glutton was a glutton for danger as well as for fish. He had killed sixty-three dragons, more than any other partner in the service, and was quite literally worth his weight in gold.

The little girl West came next. She drew Captain Wow. When she saw who it was, she smiled.

"I *like* him," she said. "He's such fun to fight with. He feels so nice and cuddly in my mind."

"Cuddly, hell," said Woodley. "I've been in his mind, too. It's the most leering mind in this ship, bar none."

"Nasty man," said the little girl. She said it declaratively, without reproach.

Underhill, looking at her, shivered.

He didn't see how she could take Captain Wow so calmly. Captain Wow's mind *did* leer. When Captain Wow got excited in the middle of a battle, confused images of dragons, deadly rats, luscious beds, the smell of fish, and the shock of space all scrambled together in his mind and he and Captain Wow, their consciousnesses linked together through the pin-set, became a fantastic composite of human being and Persian cat.

That's the trouble with working with cats, thought Underhill. It's a pity that nothing else anywhere will serve as partner. Cats were all right once you got in touch with them telepathically. They were smart enough to meet the needs of the fight, but their motives and desires were certainly different from those of humans.

They were companionable enough as long as you thought tangible images at them, but their minds just closed up and went to sleep when you recited Shakespeare or Colegrove, or if you tried to tell them what space was.

It was sort of funny realizing that the partners who were so grim and mature out here in space were the same cute little animals that people had used as pets for thousands of years back on Earth. He had embarrassed himself more than once while on the ground saluting perfectly ordinary non-telepathic cats because he had forgotten for the moment that they were not partners.

He picked up the cup and shook out his stone dice.

He was lucky—he drew the Lady May.

The Lady May was the most thoughtful partner he had ever met. In her, the finely bred pedigree mind of a Persian cat had reached one of its highest peaks of development. She was more complex than any human woman, but the complexity was all one of emotions, memory, hope, and discriminated experience—experience sorted through without benefit of words.

When he had first come into contact with her mind, he was astonished at its clarity. With her he remembered her kittenhood. He remembered every mating experience she had ever had. He saw in a half-recognizable gallery all the other pinlighters with whom she had been paired for the fight. And he saw himself radiant, cheerful, and desirable.

He even thought he caught the edge of a longing—

A very flattering and yearning thought: *What a pity he is not a cat.*

Woodley picked up the last stone. He drew what he deserved—a sullen, scarred old tomcat with none of the verve of Captain Wow. Woodley's partner was the most animal of all the cats on the ship, a low, brutish type with a dull mind. Even telepathy had not refined his character. His ears were half chewed off from the first fights in which he had engaged. He was a serviceable fighter, nothing more.

Woodley grunted.

Underhill glanced at him oddly. Didn't Woodley ever do anything but grunt?

Father Moontree looked at the other three. "You might as well get your partners now. I'll let the scanner know we're ready to go into the up-and-out."

III THE DEAL

Underhill spun the combination lock on the Lady May's cage. He woke her gently and took her into his arms. She humped her back luxuriously, stretched her claws, started to purr, thought better of it, and licked him on the wrist instead. He did not have the pin-set on, so their minds were closed to each other, but in the angle of her mustache and in the movement of her ears, he caught some sense of the gratification she experienced in finding him as her partner.

He talked to her in human speech, even though speech meant nothing to a cat when the pin-set was not on.

"It's a damn shame, sending a sweet little thing like you whirling around in the coldness of nothing to hunt for rats that are bigger and deadlier than all of us put together. You didn't ask for this kind of fight, did you?"

For answer, she licked his hand, purred, tickled his cheek with her long fluffy tail, turned around and faced him, golden eyes shining.

For a moment, they stared at each other, man squatting, cat standing erect on her hind legs, front claws digging into his knee. Human eyes and cat eyes looked across an immensity which no words could meet, but which affection spanned in a single glance.

"Time to get in," he said.

She walked docilely to her spheroid carrier. She climbed in. He saw to it that her miniature pin-set rested firmly and comfortably against the base of her brain. He made sure that her claws were padded so that she could not tear herself in the excitement of battle.

Softly he said to her, "Ready?"

For answer, she preened her back as much as her harness would permit and purred softly within the confines of the frame that held her.

He slapped down the lid and watched the sealant ooze around the seam. For a few hours, she was welded into her projectile until a workman with a short cutting arc would remove her after she had done her duty.

He picked up the entire projectile and slipped it into the ejection tube. He closed the door of the tube, spun the lock, seated himself in his chair, and put his own pin-set on.

Once again he flung the switch.

He sat in a small room, *small, small, warm, warm,* the bodies of the other three people moving close around him, the tangible lights in the ceiling bright and heavy against his closed eyelids.

As the pin-set warmed, the room fell away. The other people ceased to be people and became small glowing heaps of fire, embers, dark red fire, with the consciousness of life burning like old red coals in a country fireplace.

As the pin-set warmed a little more, he felt Earth just below him, felt the ship slipping away, felt the turning Moon as it swung on the far side of the world, felt the planets and the hot, clear goodness of the sun which kept the dragons so far from mankind's native ground.

Finally, he reached complete awareness.

He was telepathically alive to a range of millions of miles. He felt the dust which he had noticed earlier high above the ecliptic. With a thrill of warmth and tenderness, he felt the consciousness of the Lady May pouring over into his own. Her consciousness was as gentle and clear and yet sharp to the taste of his mind as if it were scented oil. It felt relaxing and reassuring. He could sense her welcome of him. It was scarcely a thought, just a raw emotion of greeting.

At last they were one again.

In a tiny remote corner of his mind, as tiny as the smallest toy he had ever seen in his childhood, he was still aware of the room and the ship, and of Father Moontree picking up a telephone and speaking to a Go-captain in charge of the ship.

His telepathic mind caught the idea long before his ears could frame the words. The actual sound followed the idea the way that thunder on an ocean beach follows the lightning inward from far out over the seas.

"The Fighting Room is ready. Clear to planoform, sir."

IV THE PLAY

Underhill was always a little exasperated the way that Lady May experienced things before he did.

He was braced for the quick vinegar thrill of planoforming, but he caught her report of it before his own nerves could register what happened.

Earth had fallen so far away that he groped for several milliseconds before he found the Sun in the upper rear right-hand corner of his telepathic mind.

That was a good jump, he thought. *This way we'll get there in four or five skips.*

A few hundred miles outside the ship, the Lady May thought back at him, "O warm, O generous, O gigantic man! O brave, O friendly, O tender and huge partner! O wonderful with you, with you so good, good, good, warm, warm, now to fight, now to go, good with you . . ."

He knew that she was not thinking words, that his mind took the clear amiable babble of her cat intellect and translated it into images which his own thinking could record and understand.

Neither one of them was absorbed in the game of mutual greetings. He reached out far beyond her range of perception to see if there was anything near the ship. It was funny how it was possible to do two things at once. He could scan space with his pin-set mind and yet at the same time catch a vagrant thought of hers, a lovely, affectionate thought about a son who had had a golden face and a chest covered with soft, incredibly downy white fur.

While he was still searching, he caught the warning from her.

We jump again!

And so they had. The ship had moved to a second planoform. The stars were different. The sun was immeasurably far behind. Even the nearest stars were barely in contact. This was good dragon country, this open, nasty, hollow kind of space. He reached farther, faster, sensing and looking for danger, ready to fling the Lady May at danger wherever he found it.

Terror blazed up in his mind, so sharp, so clear, that it came through as a physical wrench.

The little girl named West had found something—something immense, long, black, sharp, greedy, horrific. She flung Captain Wow at it.

Underhill tried to keep his own mind clear. "Watch out!" he shouted telepathically at the others, trying to move the Lady May around.

At one corner of the battle, he felt the lustful rage of Captain Wow as the big Persian tomcat detonated lights while he approached the streak of dust which threatened the ship and the people within.

The lights scored near misses.

The dust flattened itself, changing from the shape of a sting ray into the shape of a spear.

Not three milliseconds had elapsed.

Father Moontree was talking human words and was saying in a voice that moved like cold molasses out of a heavy jar, "C-a-p-t-a-i-n." Underhill knew that the sentence was going to be "Captain, move fast!"

The battle would be fought and finished before Father Moontree got through talking.

Now, fractions of a millisecond later, the Lady May was directly in line.

Here was where the skill and speed of the partners came in. She could react faster than he. She could see the threat as an immense rat coming directly at her.

She could fire the light-bombs with a discrimination which he might miss.

He was connected with her mind, but he could not follow it.

His consciousness absorbed the tearing wound inflicted by the alien enemy. It was like no wound on Earth—raw, crazy pain which started like a burn at his navel. He began to writhe in his chair.

Actually he had not yet had time to move a muscle when the Lady May struck back at their enemy.

Five evenly spaced photonuclear bombs blazed out across a hundred thousand miles.

The pain in his mind and body vanished.

He felt a moment of fierce, terrible, feral elation running through the mind of the Lady May as she finished her kill. It was always disappointing to the cats to find out that their enemies disappeared at the moment of destruction.

Then he felt her hurt, the pain and the fear that swept over both of them as the battle, quicker than the movement of an eyelid, had come and gone. In the same instant there came the sharp and acid twinge of planoform.

Once more the ship went skip.

He could hear Woodley thinking at him. "You don't have to bother much. This old son-of-a-gun and I will take over for a while."

Twice again the twinge, the skip.

He had no idea where he was until the lights of the Caledonia space port shone below.

With a weariness that lay almost beyond the limits of thought, he threw his mind back into rapport with the pin-set, fixing the Lady May's projectile gently and neatly in its launching tube.

She was half dead with fatigue, but he could feel the beat of her heart, could listen to her panting, and he grasped the grateful edge of a "Thanks" reaching from her mind to his.

V THE SCORE

They put him in the hospital at Caledonia.

The doctor was friendly but firm. "You actually got touched by that dragon. That's as close a shave as I've ever seen. It's all so quick that it'll be a long time before we know what happened scientifically, but I suppose you'd be ready for the insane asylum now if the contact had lasted several tenths of a millisecond longer. What kind of cat did you have out in front of you?"

Underhill felt the words coming out of him slowly. Words were such a lot of trouble compared with the speed and the joy of thinking, fast and sharp and clear, mind to mind! But words were all that could reach ordinary people like this doctor.

His mouth moved heavily as he articulated words. "Don't call our partners cats. The right thing to call them is partners. They fight for us in a team. You ought to know we call them partners, not cats. How is mine?"

"I don't know," said the doctor contritely. "We'll find out for you. Meanwhile, old man, you take it easy. There's nothing but rest that can help you. Can you make yourself sleep, or would you like us to give you some kind of sedative?"

"I can sleep," said Underhill. "I just want to know about the Lady May."

The nurse joined in. She was a little antagonistic. "Don't you want to know about the other people?"

"They're okay," said Underhill. "I knew that before I came in here."

He stretched his arms and sighed and grinned at them. He could see they were relaxing and were beginning to treat him as a person instead of a patient.

"I'm all right," he said. "Just let me know when I can go see my partner."

A new thought struck him. He looked wildly at the doctor. "They didn't send her off with the ship, did they?"

"I'll find out right away," said the doctor. He gave Underhill a reassuring squeeze of the shoulder and left the room.

The nurse took a napkin off a goblet of chilled fruit juice.

Underhill tried to smile at her. There seemed to be something wrong with the girl. He wished she would go away. First she had started to be friendly and now she was distant again. *It's a nuisance being telepathic,* he thought. *You keep trying to reach even when you are not making contact.*

Suddenly she swung around on him.

"You pinlighters! You and your damn cats!"

Just as she stamped out, he burst into her mind. He saw himself a radiant hero, clad in his smooth suede uniform, the pin-set crown shining like ancient royal jewels around his head. He saw his own face, handsome and masculine, shining out of her mind. He saw himself very far away and he saw himself as she hated him.

She hated him in the secrecy of her own mind. She hated him because he was—she thought—proud and strange and rich, better and more beautiful than people like her.

He cut off the sight of her mind and, as he buried his face in the pillow, he caught an image of the Lady May.

"She *is* a cat," he thought. "That's all she is—a *cat!*"

But that was not how his mind saw her—quick beyond all dreams of speed, sharp, clever, unbelievably graceful, beautiful, wordless and undemanding.

Where would he ever find a woman who could compare with her?

BIBLIOGRAPHY

The Planet Buyer, Pyramid Books, 1964 ("The Boy Who Bought Old Earth," *Galaxy,* April 1964)
Space Lords, Pyramid Books, 1965, includes:
> "Mother Hitton's Littul Kittons," *Galaxy,* June 1961
> "A Planet Named Shayol," *Galaxy,* October 1961
> "The Ballard of Lost C'Mell," *Galaxy,* October 1962
> "Drunkboat," *Amazing,* October 1963
> "The Dead Lady of Clown Town," *Galaxy,* August 1964
The Underpeople, Pyramid Books, 1968
Norstrilia, Ballantine Books, 1975
> Other Instrumentality stories include:
> "The Game of Rat and Dragon," *Galaxy,* October 1955
> "The Burning of the Brain," *If,* November 1958
> "The Lady Who Sailed the *Soul,*" *Galaxy,* April 1960
> "Alpha Ralpha Boulevard," *The Magazine of Fantasy and Science Fiction,* June 1961
> "The Store of Heart's Desire," *If,* May 1964
The Instrumentality of Mankind, Ballantine Books, 1979, contains the following Instrumentality stories:
> "No, No, Not Rogov," *If,* February 1959
> "Mark Elf," *Saturn,* May 1957

"The Queen of the Afternoon," *Galaxy*, April 1958
"When the People Fell," *Galaxy*, 1959
"Think Blue, Count Two," *Galaxy*, February 1963
"From Gustible's Planet," *If*, July 1962
"Drunkboat," *Amazing*, October 1963

NOTES ON CONTRIBUTORS

BRIAN W. ALDISS was born in England in 1925. One of the most erudite members of the science fiction world, he is a former literary editor of the *Oxford Mail*. He has been producing outstanding speculative fiction for almost thirty years, including such important books as *Barefoot in the Head*, *The Dark Light Years*, *Frankenstein Unbound*, *The Malacia Tapestry*, and *Report on Probability A*. He was the Guest of Honor at the 1965 World Science Fiction Convention. An astute observer and critic of the sf scene, he is the editor of the excellent *Science Fiction Art* (1975).

POUL ANDERSON was born in Bristol, Pennsylvania in 1926 and graduated with a degree in physics from the University of Minnesota. A substantial portion of his work constitutes a "Future History" scenario, but he is best known for his series characters (including the Dominic Flandry stories) and for outstanding novels like *Brain Wave*, *The Byworlder*, *The High Crusade*, *Tau Zero* and *The Avatar*. He is a former President of the Science Fiction Writers of America. He is also a talented mystery writer and historical novelist.

ISAAC ASIMOV is one of the two or three best-known science fiction writers. Born in the Soviet Union in 1920, but a resident of New York since the age of three, he holds a Ph.D. from Columbia University in biochemistry and is as well known as a science writer as he is for his sf. His most famous books include *The Foundation "Trilogy,"* *I Robot*, *The Caves of Steel*, *The Naked Sun*, and *The Gods Themselves*. Almost all his short fiction is available in his numerous collections, which include *The Bicentennial Man*, *The Early Asimov*, and *Nightfall and Other Stories*. He published his autobiography in two volumes, 1979 and 1980.

J. G. BALLARD was born in Shanghai in 1930. His beautifully crafted stories and novels have attracted a wide following, especially *The Burning World*, *The Drowned World*, *The Crystal World*, and *The Wind from Nowhere*. His best short fiction can be found in *Chronopolis and Other Stories*. Recently he has turned to graphic and surrealistic portraits of possible near futures characterized by violence and urban decay like *Crash* and *High Rise*. He was squarely in the center of the movement in Great Britain that became the "New Wave."

The late JAMES BLISH (1921–1975) was a noted science fiction author and critic who wrote one of the most significant novels using sf to treat religious concerns, *A Case of Conscience*. In addition, he wrote many other notable works like *Jack of Eagles*, *Vor*, and *The Warriors of Day*. As a critic he has left us two fine collections, *The Issue at Hand* and *More Issues at Hand* (both written as "William Atheling, Jr."). He lived in England for the last decade of his too-short life.

REGINALD C. BRETNOR was born in Russia in 1911. He has edited three important collections of original essays on sf, *Modern Science Fiction* (1953, a pioneering symposium), *Science Fiction Today and Tomorrow,* and *The Craft of Science Fiction.* Primarily a short story writer within the field, one of his best known stories is "The Man on Top" originally published in *Esquire.* Mr. Bretnor lives in Medford, Oregon.

ARTHUR C. CLARKE was born in Minehead, England in 1917. One of the premier figures in modern science fiction, his major novels like *The City and the Stars, Childhood's End,* and *Rendezvous with Rama* are milestones in the development of the field. His screenplay for *2001: A Space Odyssey* was developed from his short story "The Sentinel" and the film is a watershed in the history of sf movies. His most recent collection is *The Wind from the Sun.* Mr. Clarke now resides in Sri Lanka.

L. SPRAGUE DE CAMP has had a long and distinguished career in science fiction. Born in 1907, he is a graduate of the California Institute of Technology and of Stevens Institute of Technology. His science fiction has featured a number of popular series in addition to the one represented in this book, including the "Johnny Black" stories and the "Harold Shea" and "Viagens" tales. His novels include *Rogue Queen* and *Lest Darkness Fall,* and his short fiction can be found in *A Gun for Dinosaur* and *The Best of L. Sprague de Camp.* His *Science Fiction Handbook* (1953, revised 1976) is a useful guide to the field. He is a resident of Villanova, Pennsylvania.

ZENNA HENDERSON was born in Tucson, Arizona in 1917 and has lived in the surrounding area most of her life. A schoolteacher by profession, she has used this setting and her knowledge of youngsters as background for her famous "People" series, which constitutes much of her published science fiction. Some non-"People" stories can be found in her collection *The Anything Box.*

KEITH LAUMER was born in Syracuse, New York in 1925 but has lived all over the world. He presently resides in Florida. During the 1960s he was one of the most popular writers in the sf magazines. He was also one of the most prolific authors during that period, with such books as *Greylorn, The Long Twilight, The Monitors,* and *A Trace of Memory.* More recent works include *The Glory Game* and *The Ultimax Man.* He is a model airplane enthusiast.

FRITZ LEIBER has won a number of science fiction's highest awards, including the Hugo for *The Big Time* (1958), and the Hugo and Nebula for "Gonna Roll the Bones" in 1968. Other notable novels include *Conjure Wife, Gather Darkness, The Wanderer,* and *The Silver Eggheads.* He was born in 1910, the son of the noted actor of the same name. Equally talented as a fantasy writer, his tales of "Fafhrd and the Gray Mouser" have delighted readers since "Two Sought Adventure" (1939), his first published story. The pick of his short fiction has been collected as *The Best of Fritz Leiber*.

ANNE McCAFFREY is one of the small number of American science fiction authors now living in Ireland. She was born in 1926 and first appeared in the sf magazines in 1953, although she really emerged as a major figure in the 1960s. In addition to the "Helga" and "Dragon" series, she has written *Decision at Doona*, *Dinosaur Planet* and *Restoree*. Her most recent Dragon novel is *Dragondrums* (1979).

LARRY NIVEN (b. 1933) has been a professional writer since 1964. He has a reputation for "hard science fiction," but there is usually some interesting sociology and psychology in his work. His novels include the justly famous *Ringworld*, *World of Ptavvs*, *A Gift from Earth* and *A World Out of Time*. Recently, he has collaborated with Jerry Pournelle on three very successful books, *The Mote in God's Eye*, *Inferno*, and the best-selling *Lucifer's Hammer*. He has developed one of the most interesting detective characters in science fiction, Gil Hamilton, whose exploits can be found in *The Long Arm of Gil Hamilton*.

JOHN J. PIERCE edited *Galaxy Science Fiction* in the late 1970s and is a noted authority on Cordwainer Smith. He edited and wrote the introduction to *The Best of Cordwainer Smith* (1975).

FRED SABERHAGEN sold his first science fiction story in 1961, and has been writing steadily since. Best known for the series which he discusses in this book, his other fiction includes the novels *Changing Earth* and *Specimens* and the collection which contains the best of his shorter sf, *The Book of Fred Saberhagen*. A long-time resident of the midwest, he now resides in New Mexico.

BOB SHAW is an Ulster-born (1931) writer now living in England. A former newspaper columnist, he was a prominent figure in fan circles in Great Britain. A generally underrated writer, his novels include *Ground Zero Man*, *One Million Tomorrows*, *The Palace of Eternity*, and *Orbitsville*. His short fiction has also been of high quality and can be found in *Tomorrow Lies in Ambush* and *Cosmic Kaleidoscope*.

ROBERT SHECKLEY was born in New York City in 1928 and presently resides in that city after many years in Europe. During the 1950s and early 1960s his brilliantly crafted short stories were a feature in *Galaxy Science Fiction*. A prolific writer, his stories can be found in a number of collections including *Can You Feel Anything When I Do This?*, *Pilgrim-*

age to Earth, Store of Infinity, and *Untouched by Human Hands.* His novels include *The 10th Victim, Journey Beyond Tomorrow,* and *Crompton Divided,* as well as several non-sf efforts.

WILMAR H. SHIRAS was born in Boston in 1908. Primarily known in the science fiction field for the series represented in this book (which was published as *Children of the Atom* in 1953), she has also published non-fiction under the name "Jane Howes." She is a resident of California.

CLIFFORD D. SIMAK has been producing entertaining and often brilliant science fiction since the publication of his first story, "World of the Red Sun" in *Wonder Stories* in 1931. A native of Millville, Wisconsin, he has been a newspaperman in Minneapolis for most of his life. He was the winner of the International Fantasy Award in 1953 for *City* and of the Hugo Award in 1964 for the novel *Way Station.* He has managed to maintain a high level of productivity and quality for over forty-five years, and along with Jack Williamson, is the "Dean" of science fiction. He was honored by the SFWA with its Grandmaster Award for his life's contribution to the field.

CORDWAINER SMITH was a pseudonym for Paul M. Linebarger, although this was not known during most of his lifetime (1913–1966)— indeed, the identity of "Smith" was the subject of considerable controversy. Dr. Linebarger was born in Milwaukee, Wisconsin and was a Professor of Asiatic History at (among others) Johns Hopkins University. The majority of his work uses the setting and creatures discussed in this volume.